FOREIGN ENEMIES
and traitors

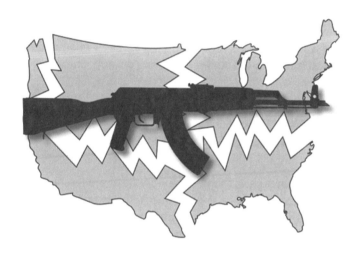

MATTHEW BRACKEN

Steelcutter Publishing
Orange Park, Florida

5th Printing 2013

ISBN 0-9728310-3-7

Library of Congress Control Number
2009903357

Printed in the United States of America

www.EnemiesForeignAndDomestic.com

To Ellie, Brendan and Lauren, who are my world.

Acknowledgements:

Thank you to my brother, Joe Bracken, Jefferson Adams, Matt Bastian, Kasey Beltz, Dave Brown, Charlie Byrd, Beth Gunn, H.J. Halterman, Rob Henry, Arthur Hines, Kevin Knox, Jim Kononoff, Frank Parker, Robert Patty, Caylen Perry, Rita Samols, Joe Smith, Mark Spungin, Tim Ziegler and my sister Clare Strange for creating all of my cover art.

Also by Matt Bracken:

Enemies Foreign And Domestic
A novel about the true meaning of loyalty and the high cost of freedom in the age of terror. (2003)

Domestic Enemies: The Reconquista
A novel about the deconstruction of the American national identity and the loss of the Southwest. (2006)

Castigo Cay
The adventures of Dan Kilmer, a former Marine sniper trying to live as a free man in an unfree world. (2011)

Over 100 pages of each book may be read at
www.EnemiesForeignAndDomestic.com

Turning and turning in the widening gyre
The falcon cannot hear the falconer:
Things fall apart; the centre cannot hold;
Mere anarchy is loosed upon the world,
The blood-dimmed tide is loosed, and everywhere
The ceremony of innocence is drowned;
The best lack all conviction, while the worst
Are full of passionate intensity.

The Second Coming, by William Butler Yeats

Treason doth never prosper: what's the reason?
Why if it prosper, none dare call it treason.
Sir John Harrington, 1607

Quis custodiet ipsos custodies?
Who shall guard the guards?

1

The sailor cranked the wheel from side to side, swerving the fifty-foot catamaran in time to match the waves. Lightning lit the ocean every few seconds. In between flashes, his world was a black void, with mountainous swells rushing at him unseen. The trick was to surf the waves at an angle, riding the biggest ones for as long as possible. The problem was he couldn't see them in the dark. He'd surfed hundreds of waves in the last day and night, and had developed a finely tuned feel for the rhythm of their lift and rush, but in the end, his steering was intuition and guesswork.

The greatest danger was stuffing the boat's two knifelike bows into the bottom of a trough, then being lifted from behind by the next wave, flipping the boat stern over bow. Once over, she would be permanently capsized, her mast aiming at the sea floor, her cockpit submerged under salt water.

The boat was running northward without a scrap of sail up, but even the bare mast and rigging presented too much resistance to the storm winds. His backlit digital speedometer was reading in the twenties, as it had been for more than a day. Since before Paulo had been lost overboard. Since before the autopilot had burned out and he'd been forced to hand-steer the big catamaran.

Phil Carson was sailing in a nameless December hurricane, lost somewhere in the northern Gulf of Mexico. The Gulf was wide enough to produce storm waves twenty feet and higher, and shallow enough to make their onrushing faces stand up vertically. Unlike in the open Atlantic, there was not enough sea room to sail out of danger before running into the land lurking over the unseen horizon. He had no idea how much Gulf he had left in front of him. GPS was a memory, a fondly recalled dream. Either the old global positioning satellites were down, or their information was encoded and unreadable by civilians. It didn't matter which. GPS was finished as far as Phil Carson was concerned.

In this ugly weather, old-fashioned celestial navigation was just as useless. He had not glimpsed the sun through the cloud cover in the two days since rounding Cuba, so he had no idea of his location. After three days of "dead reckoning" in storm winds, navigation was a wild-ass guess, give or take hundreds of miles in any direction. Now he was too fatigued to dedicate any mental energy to refining his guesswork. He was somewhere between Texas and Florida. He'd know where the land was only when he hit it—if he didn't capsize and drown first.

Since dawn, he'd been alone. At the 0600 change of watch he'd come up from the boat's Spartan galley with a thermos of coffee, only to find no trace of his crewman. The boat was still running fast on the electric autopilot, leaving twin wakes of churning white water astern. Paulo wouldn't wear a safety harness. Safety lines violated his fatalistic sense of Latin machismo. Well, too bad for him—there was no way possible to bring the cat around and sail back against the storm winds. By now Paulo was dead, drowned fighting the monster seas. After sixty-four years, Phil Carson had seen enough death to know that there were worse ways to check out. He was too numb from exhaustion to grieve for his crew.

He'd picked up the young Brazilian as last-minute crew in Recife, when the Dutch kid and his Martiniquen girlfriend had jumped ship. He didn't even know Paulo's last name—or for that matter if Paulo was even his real name. He had no papers that Carson had seen, and smugglers weren't much on sharing biographies—especially across a language divide. Only sailing skill, stamina and guts mattered for a smuggling voyage. Now with Paulo gone and the autopilot dead, he was unable to take his hands off the leather-covered stainless steel wheel, lest the catamaran swerve out of control and capsize amidst the wild waves.

Lightning strikes crashed down to port and starboard like artillery, and his bare mast was a sixty-foot aluminum finger scratching the clouds. Then, without warning, green balls of light were rolling up and down his mast's wire rigging—Saint Elmo's fire. Phil Carson was out of adrenaline and incapable of greater fear or new amazement. When the crackling glow disappeared with a final upward flash, so did the comforting backlights of his speedometer, his depth sounder and his magnetic compass. His last remaining electronics had been fried. Now the only light came from the strobe-like flashes of lightning, illuminating the saltwater canyons.

The catamaran climbed again, over the next wave, fifteen, twenty feet up and over. At the crest, a brighter flash far ahead left the flat line of the horizon clearly frozen for an instant. On the horizon, still printed on his rods and cones after the flaring millisecond view, was a line of ships. On the next wave top the ships became a row of buildings, which meant land dead ahead. They were no more than a mile away if they were small structures, maybe a few miles off if they were large towers.

At over twenty knots of boat speed, he knew that it wouldn't take long to get there. His teeth and his hands were clenched as salt spray hit his face like warm hailstones flying sideways. Another instantaneous view atop another lightning-lit crest, and the buildings were much closer. Beyond astonishment or fear, Phil Carson hung onto the wheel as the catamaran's twin hulls flew between concrete towers. With the last of his energy, he braced for impact but none came. Past the line of buildings, the waves diminished to less than ten feet in height for the first time in days.

These mere ripples were no impediment to the catamaran. He thought he'd probably surfed right over a narrow barrier island, a coastal strip drowned under the storm surge, and into a bay.

Then as swiftly as he'd passed between the condominium towers, the catamaran was sailing into a debris field. Lightning bolts strobe-lit a mad wilderness of trees, roofs, boats and cars. The yacht flew over and through the storm-driven trash.

Then came the impact—and nothing after that.

The wind awakened her. Not the wind per se, but the sound of trees blown about and jostled by the wind. Her newly constructed home was in a clearing surrounded on three sides by ponderosa pines as tall as a clipper ship's mast. It took a strong breeze to start the Wyoming giants to groaning and creaking like this. Ranya's bedroom was on the second floor, and with no close neighbors there was no need to shut the curtains. As the big pines swayed, between them she caught glimpses of the moon above the rim of Mount Baldy. That wasn't the mountain's real name, but the one that her eight-year-old son, Brian, had given it.

Their home was surrounded by miles of pine forest, but its exterior was not built of wood. She had insisted on this. Instead, they had it custom built from granite stones, trucked up from a quarry near the Wind River and cemented together. The steeply pitched metal roof was guaranteed to be fireproof, also at her insistence. The gray rock home was their fortress and their refuge.

The bedroom door slowly creaked open, and she sensed small feet padding across the floor. A warm wraith slid under the down comforter and nestled against her back. Ranya turned, wrapped Brian in her arms, and pulled him tightly to her.

"I'll protect you, Mommy," he murmured sleepily, as she smiled and pressed his little face to her flannel pajama top.

"I know you will," she whispered back. Outside, the trees continued to growl and snap as the wind hissed and moaned through a million branches.

"When is daddy coming home?"

"Friday."

"Two weeks is a *long* time."

"I know," she agreed. "Two weeks is a very long time."

Alex was in Spokane, Washington, training for the Wyoming State Militia. He was learning how to fire the new Korean shoulder-launched anti-aircraft missiles. When his course was finished, he'd be qualified as an instructor. This meant that for two weeks, Ranya and Brian were alone on their two hundred acre estate, but she wasn't worried. Ranya Bardiwell could take care of herself, and neighbors could be reached on the emergency radio net by day or night.

Her neighbors (the closest were a half mile away), didn't know her as Ranya Bardiwell. She was now Robin Douglas, thirty years old, the wife of Alan Douglas and the mother of Brian. This had been her identity for two years, and she had grown into it. She had *become* Robin Douglas, even if she could not forget her old life.

Alex—Alan—had suggested their new last name. Garabanda and Bardiwell were far too unusual, glowing beacons for any identity-tracking program. A last name that was also a common first name was just the opposite: database camouflage. Alex became Alan, so that if anyone from his previous life as an FBI Special Agent recognized him in public and called out his old first name, it was similar enough to his alias, that the alias would not be betrayed to anyone in earshot. Brian kept his own first name. It was ordinary enough, and the child had been through too many wrenching changes already.

Ranya chose Robin. This was not a common first name, but she had insisted. Robin was a nom de guerre from her old life, and she was comfortable with it. It was a private link to her secret past, a name given to her by Phil Carson during their month of high adventure and eventual tragedy in Virginia. She briefly thought of Carson and wondered where he was now, and if he was well. Years ago, he had said that she was the closest thing to family that he had in the world. Despite their thirty-year age difference and lack of blood connection, they were sibling orphans because of their shared experiences and losses.

The last time she had seen Phil was when she left Colombia, to fly home to America. She had returned so that Brian could be born in the USA as an American citizen, instead of being raised on false papers as the child of an overseas fugitive. No good deed going unpunished, she had been arrested in Phoenix Sky Harbor International Airport upon her arrival in the States. Brian was born while she was in prison. Ranya lost the first five years of his life before escaping from the detention camp in Oklahoma. It seemed like a dream now, rediscovering Brian in New Mexico, then kidnapping him in San Diego with Alex's help, and flying to Wyoming to begin new lives.

And so, the freshly minted Douglas family had settled into the foothills of the Rockies after their escape from California. Their arrival had drawn no attention—they were one family among many thousands making a similar trek to freedom. The source of their wealth was never challenged, gold and silver coins being universally accepted in the American West. With gold coins offered in payment, signatures and identification were never an issue. Gold required no official stamp of government approval, no bureaucrat's printed form nor any banker's countersigned validation.

Gold coins carried no history or baggage, but only unquestioned value based on their weight and purity, and nothing else. In the free states there were no more dollars and cents, only grams and ounces of gold and silver.

Alex called it "God's money," because unlike paper dollars, only He could create gold. Ranya thought of their golden treasure as a measure of God's mercy, after what she had endured before arriving in Wyoming with Brian and Alex.

He sensed light, but his eyes were stuck closed. Phil Carson was lying on his back on a hard surface. His head ached, and it took a long time to regain full consciousness. His first memories were of the storm, and sailing between condominium towers. His fingertips touched the floor beside him and fanned out from his sides, and after a period of uncertainty, he determined that he was down below in one of the catamaran's twin hulls. The boat was still. Perfectly still. It was the stillness of dry land, a foreign sensation after weeks of ceaseless motion. He was not sure if he was in the port or starboard hull. He felt around himself with a weak right hand and found the seat of his navigation station, and with grim determination he pulled himself up to a sitting position. The navigation station meant that he was in the starboard hull, and the head, the toilet compartment, was behind him.

He made it up to a crouch and felt his way through the narrow bathroom door to the sink, found a tap and turned it, but no water came out. There was not even the sound of the electric pump. He was puzzled until he remembered the ball lightning, and the electronics going out. Probably his entire electrical system was shot. There was also a manual lever-operated backup water pump. He found the hand towel by feel, still hanging from its ring. He leaned against the sink, wet the towel with a dozen quick strokes of the hand pump, and gently swabbed his eyes. After a while, whatever dried gunk had stuck them together released its grip, and he tentatively opened them one at a time.

Well Phil, you've looked better, he thought. The face staring back at him from the mirror was a mess. Both eyes were encircled by raccoon rings, and his skin was encrusted with dried blood. His nose was cut and broken again. Worse, he had a horizontal gash at the top of his forehead, just below his hairline. The wound was as long and wide as a finger, still oozing blood. His pale blue eyes were bloodshot, and his stubble of gray hair was matted with more dried blood. The hair on his head was only a bit longer than his beard. He'd gotten a boot camp crewcut in Recife, Brazil, before the voyage, and had not shaved since. He slowly turned his head, studying his grizzled face, now bloody and bruised. He filled a plastic cup with water from the hand pump, and drank it down. At least the freshwater tank hadn't been breached, even if the electrical system was ruined.

He left the tiny bathroom. He had to walk hunched over; the head-room inside the hulls was an inch under his five foot eleven. Forward of the navigation station and his narrow berth, the hull was still packed with its primary cargo. Fifty large solar panels in this hull alone, each four feet by two feet and packed in a slim cardboard box. All of the brown boxes still appeared to be dry, a testament to the catamaran's solid construction.

The Seabago had been built a decade earlier in Key West to Coast Guard specs, qualifying her to carry twenty-five day-tripping passengers on deck between the two hulls. She'd been built both tough and light, of carbon fiber, Kevlar and epoxy. After the tropical tourism trade died, Carson had picked her up cheap in Saint Barts for a smuggler. Cheap, because her narrow hulls were built without consideration to permanent live-aboard habitation, not even providing standing headroom in the hulls. There was no enclosed bridge deck cabin between the hulls, just flat space for passengers to sit during their excursions, and only webbed netting between the hulls forward of the mast. He'd purchased Seabago for cash money without a vessel document or legal title. As time went on this became less and less of a problem. In the free ports Phil Carson had frequented from Brazil to Belize, possession equaled ownership—as long as a boat skipper paid his yard bills promptly.

What a run of bad luck he'd had! His comfortable home in Porto Bello had been confiscated after the last Panamanian coup d'etat, when "rich" gringo expats had been scapegoated by the new regime. He'd been lucky to get out of the country aboard Seabago with most of his gold, which had been just enough to finance this latest smuggling venture. Now if he returned to Panama, he would risk prison—or worse. Well, that was a moot point anyway. How could he return to Panama or anywhere else in the Caribbean? His remaining wealth was locked within the two hulls of this catamaran, in a most illiquid state. He had no other base of operations left in the Caribbean, no home or even a home port to call his own, no refuge beyond where he stood. Eight years after fleeing the United States on another sailboat, he had returned on a smuggling venture. Now he was shipwrecked and stranded.

He climbed up the two teakwood steps from the hull and into the wide cockpit, to inspect the damage outside. The sun was blazing over-head, between the whip ends of storm clouds escaping north. The mast was gone from its familiar spot in the sky. Looking forward with a hand shading his eyes, he stared at the rusting bow of a steel fishing vessel or tugboat. Seabago's twin hulls had straddled the tug's bow on impact, and the immovable wedge of rusting iron had destroyed the cat's forward crossbeam. His boat was finished. Seabago would never sail again, even if she could find saltwater to float upon.

When the crossbeam was destroyed upon impact, down had come the mast. Unsupported by its forestay wire, the aluminum mast fell straight back, and now it lay across the cockpit and far astern of the cat in a snarl of tangled stainless steel rigging wire. Other than the crushed forward crossbeam, the two hulls appeared to be intact. What really finished the boat was its location: it was buried deep in a debris field left by the receding storm surge, with no ocean or bay in sight. Smashed houses, telephone poles, overturned cars, shattered pine trees and random lumber and trash extended in all directions, even lapping over Seabago's trapped hulls. Everywhere in between was sand and mud and rubbish, laced together with half-buried wires, cables and ropes.

Closer examination of the debris revealed an even more interesting fact: most of the surrounding destruction wasn't new. The steel tugboat he'd challenged with the cat's fragile forward crossbeam had not recently come to rest on this spot. It was a mass of rust—it had obviously lain in this place for many years. A small tree, recently stripped of leaves, grew from its windowless pilothouse. All around the catamaran, pieces of weathered gray plywood and other broken construction materials were stained by old dirt and mildew. Saplings grew from within half-buried cars, sprouting through missing windows. He was in a place that had been hurricane-blasted at least once before, and had not been cleaned up since. A new layer of trash had settled over the old when last night's storm surge receded.

The catamaran was a total loss, but his cargo was not. There were a hundred Japanese solar panels he'd picked up in Recife; each was worth more than an ounce of gold in Texas. Packed over and around the panels were 700 two-kilo plastic containers of Brazilian coffee, a luxury currently unavailable in the United States at almost any price. Both cargos were worth a small fortune if they could be sold, but the boat was trapped in a labyrinth of storm wreckage.

His watch told him it was 11:50 a.m. on Tuesday, December 11. At least the cheap digital timepiece still worked. He removed his sextant from its mahogany case in the navigation station, and prepared to shoot a noon sun sight. GPS was gone, but the sun and the stars remained—at least when they were not hidden by thick clouds, as they had been during the storm. Low marshland provided an inexact horizon, but it would be enough to make a rough fix today.

Back in the navigation station, he sat at his desk and entered the sun's mid-day height into his pocket-size celestial navigation calculator, and his numbers were quickly converted to latitude and longitude. A water-stained chart of the Gulf of Mexico lay unfolded on the small table. He ran his finger up the longitude line to where it intersected the coast: he was in Alabama, between the Mississippi state line and Mobile Bay.

This was much, much further east than he had hoped, and his spirits sank. His cargo was destined for Port Arthur in East Texas, the so-called Texas Republic...but here he was in Alabama. Alabama was under some kind of martial law or emergency rule, from what he'd heard. Even western Louisiana would have been better. He would be lucky to get himself out of Alabama, much less find a way to sell his cargo. Salvaging the cargo would require hundreds of trips on foot, across tricky broken terrain. Even if he could salvage it, selling the cargo in Alabama would be difficult to impossible without local contacts—contacts he didn't have.

He had to face the new reality: his cargo was of no value to him if he couldn't sell it, or even move it. What were his alternatives? He had enough food and water to remain aboard the trapped catamaran for a few weeks, but then what? Eventually he'd be discovered, and his cargo would be found and taken away, either stolen by bandits or confiscated by government officials.

If he couldn't stay, and he couldn't sell or salvage his cargo; if the Seabago was a total loss and would never float again...what then? Could he somehow find another boat and transfer the cargo? How far across the debris field and the marshes was it to deep water, and could this movement be made without discovery? Unlikely. No...impossible.

Sixty-four years old, and shipwrecked again. Sitting on a fortune in cargo that was useless to him. Like a homeless pauper resting on a solid gold park bench, as they said in Brazil. So what options remained? Could he make his way across the debris and marshland to the bay, and then find some craft to sail back down island while leaving his cargo behind? As quickly as he thought of this idea, he dismissed it as fantasy. What seaworthy craft would be left floating and intact after a hurricane, just waiting for a stranded sailor? Sailing back down island was not a realistic option.

And even if he could find a way to escape back down to the islands, he just didn't have the heart for it. With his home in Panama confiscated, his remaining fortune consisted of the cargo beneath his feet; and without selling it, he had no means to fund another smuggling voyage. He had to face the fact that at age sixty-four and boatless, he was too old to start again at the bottom of the sailing-for-profit game.

So, where else could he go? He had an address book, a list of a few friends and old military buddies that he might be able to use, but it had not been updated in a decade or more. The person he had been closest to in recent years was Ranya Bardiwell. They had been fugitives together in South America, when their misadventures in Virginia had forced them to flee from the United States. After she had flown out of Colombia, headed back to the States to have her baby, Ranya had dropped off the face of the earth. None of their plans to reestablish communications had come off, especially not since the internet had been put under tight censorship and control. She might be alive or dead, a fugitive or a prisoner. He had no way of knowing. He hoped that she had found a new life for herself. It hurt that he had lost contact with Ranya, his onetime surrogate daughter. For a time they had even shared last names, on their false Canadian passports. She was the closest thing he had to kin, and she had disappeared without a trace.

Ranya. A lot of water had passed under the bridge since those days, whole oceans, but he had never forgotten. Who else remembered their wild adventures? Did their sacrifice amount to anything if nobody else remembered? Good men had died on that crazy night up the Potomac River, and for what? He placed his sextant back into its mahogany case and closed its lid, then turned his eyes back to the chart showing the Gulf Coast.

Where could he go? The entire Southeast was under martial law, according to the shortwave radio. The Northeast and Great Lakes states were a socialist nightmare. California and the Southwest weren't even states anymore. That left the Northwest, a region he'd visited a few times, decades before.

Back in Colombia, he had constantly discussed the future of America with Ranya, and they agreed that this region was probably the most freedom-oriented part of the country. If she was alive and free in the States, that's where she would have gone. Sitting at his chart table, Phil Carson pondered his options and plotted strategies. Looking through a plastic file box of random charts and maps, he found a well-worn highway map of the United States, more than ten years old. He unfolded it across his table and traced his finger along possible routes. He wasn't completely broke, he still had a few ounces of gold not tied up in cargo. He could carry enough carefully hidden coins to pay his way.

Carson had often thought of traveling back to the Northwest someday, but the distance and the obstacles were formidable, and now it was winter. From occasional shortwave radio news reports, he knew that Colorado was in a state of perpetual turmoil bordering on civil war, torn between "Aztlan" and what remained of the United States. Phil Carson had already experienced enough ethnic and social turmoil in Panama: he would have to make it beyond Colorado. Maybe to Wyoming, which was the closest of the so-called free states. He might even travel further, perhaps to Montana or Idaho, but for now he would set Wyoming as his goal, even though it suffered fearsome winters.

Wyoming. It was what, over a thousand miles away from the Gulf of Mexico? That should be possible for a sneaky old bastard, a smuggler and a onetime Special Forces snake eater, he told himself without enthusiasm or conviction. He'd done harder things—but as a younger man. Still, he was in good shape for his age. He would prepare today and start out tomorrow. What else could he do? Stay, and wait for a miracle? Miracles didn't happen. Only fools waited for miracles to save them.

Phil Carson spent a considerable part of the first day considering the question of his future identity, which was intertwined with the choice of his travel strategy. He wasn't naïve. He understood that it would be impossible simply to walk from the Gulf Coast and across the South, all the while evading official detection. He already knew from listening to the shortwave that much of the South was under martial law, and travel restrictions were severe.

His Virginia driver's license was expired, and his old U.S. passport not only was out of date, it also was a paper artifact, a relic of simpler times gone by. Technologically it was several generations out of date. Worse, he was unsure whether he was on any official government watch lists. On the plus side, he had not been fingerprinted since his induction into the Army over four decades earlier. He hoped that those ancient paper fingerprint records had never been scanned into a modern computer database.

He had a Ziploc bag full of false identity papers and foreign passports on the catamaran, none of which would stand up to serious scrutiny, not in the USA. Careful, serious identity checks were rare in the Caribbean and South American ports that he frequented. Gold was the universal door opener when his paper documents were put to question. In the end, he decided to carry no identity papers or ID cards at all, settling upon a different stratagem.

More difficult to decide was the question of weaponry. He realized that in the new America, harsh penalties were handed down for a long list of "gun crimes." Still, he hesitated to go completely unarmed. Eventually he decided to take his tiny Kel-Tec .380 caliber pistol. It was only three-quarters of an inch thick, and concealable in a pocket or even in the palm of his hand.

Next, he had to decide whether to conceal the pistol on his body or in his pack. If he kept it on his body it would be ready for self-defense, but it also was more likely to be found in a close search. After changing his mind several times, he broke it down into its components and hid them within the seams and bottom padding of his old brown backpack. If he were ambushed by bandits on the way out, he'd be done. That was a calculated risk he would have to take. There were no perfect solutions that covered every possible contingency.

Financing his travels would be less of a problem. For that, he would carry the currency that was accepted worldwide: gold. Full one-ounce coins were too large and difficult to conceal, so he limited himself to those of one-quarter and one-tenth ounce. He concealed a total of ten ounces of gold within his leather smuggling belt, his old running shoes, his pack and other places. In his experience, negotiations with police and public officials always went more smoothly with the timely application of gold to greedy palms.

He studied the digital atlas on the laptop computer in his navigation station, planning his route. It had not been connected to the boat's electrical system, and so it had been spared the lightning surge. The computer atlas also provided some overhead imagery, a few years old. The sky photos indicated that the Seabago had landed in a marshy estuary between Pascagoula, Mississippi, and Mobile Bay. He figured he could walk north to a coastal state road in only a few hours or a day, depending on the terrain and water obstacles.

He studied maps and satellite photos and planned his possible escape routes for an hour, until the computer's battery died. For navigation on the march, he would take only his folding road map of the United States; reading glasses, for studying the smallest details on the map; and an innocuous miniature compass on his watchband, to keep him aimed northwest. Everything he carried had to be something credibly in the possession of a destitute hurricane survivor. He had no individual state maps on the boat anyway; he'd had no need of them for years.

In the afternoon, he camouflaged the catamaran's decks with a covering of random debris. Old pieces of plywood, tattered and faded blue plastic tarps, tree branches and other wreckage broke up its outline as it might be seen from the air. The best hiding place for his cargo of solar panels and coffee was within Seabago's twin hulls. When he was finished covering the cat's decks with flotsam and trash, he was satisfied that even a low-altitude aerial reconnaissance would not lead observers to examine the area more closely. The dismasted ocean-sailing catamaran was now just more storm wreckage, lost and forgotten among miles of ruined coastline and marshland.

Without GPS, it would be difficult even for him to find it again, so Carson carefully plotted fixed landmarks with the boat's cockpit-mounted compass, and marked their azimuths on his own cryptic treasure map. He left the rusty eighty-foot stranded tugboat off his hand-drawn map. It would be the unerring final marker, should he ever return for his cargo. The tug also concealed his other guns and five one-ounce gold coins deep within its corroded hull. He had learned the hard way not to carry all of his eggs in one basket. Someday he might return for the weapons and the gold, and with luck, even the cargo if it went undiscovered.

Sidney Krantz guessed what President Tambor wanted the instant he was summoned from his small office in the Old Executive Office Building. It had to be about Tennessee. Meyer Ignacio, the president's young special assistant, intercepted him before he reached the Oval Office waiting room. As usual, Krantz would not be signing in at the Oval Office secretary's desk. No record of Krantz's visit would appear on the president's calendar. Instead, Ignacio guided him via a narrow private corridor to the rear entrance of the president's special reading room. On the way, Krantz handed Ignacio his cell phone and BlackBerry.

To the few persons who knew of the place's existence, President Tambor referred to it as his "reading room." Sidney Krantz understood the truth: the president had had the private room specially constructed to be utterly soundproof and bug-proof. Two heavy airtight doors sealed the rear entrance, one opening outward and one inward. A separate entrance permitted the president to access this room from the Oval Office via a tiny "service corridor." This allowed meetings in total secrecy, without third-party witnesses even to the fact that the meetings had ever taken place. Ironically, some of the same White House floor space had once been used to contain President Nixon's taping equipment.

No kind of eavesdropping or recording device, no matter how sophisticated, could be brought into the president's reading room undetected, much less be made to function without immediate discovery. There were no phones, no computers and no cameras of any kind. Nothing electronic was in the room except for the built-in bug detection system. Even the climate control unit was separate from the ventilation system of the rest of the White House, with its own power supply. Anything said by the president in this room could later be denied. A disgruntled visitor could not even prove that a meeting had ever taken place.

President Tambor was justifiably paranoid. Sidney Krantz understood the value of creating audiotapes of questionable conversations, for blackmail and for insurance. He had made such recordings for both reasons, and he knew of other blackmail tapes, including some unimaginably damning ones. But he also understood that if Jamal Tambor suspected that Krantz might be taping him today, he could become another "assisted suicide" victim like Vince Foster, a presidential adviser in an earlier administration.

This possibility didn't concern him, because Jamal Tambor and Sidney Krantz were longtime allies and confidants, and they understood each other perfectly. He didn't need or desire to tape their private conversations. Politically, they were of one mind. Despite their utopian public vocabularies, power was their shared private creed. And the truth was that his close access to the president was the sole source of Krantz's current power in Washington. How else could a short, fat, balding former political science professor wield so much influence? Politics had always been Sidney's forte, but with his squeaky voice and lack of manly charisma, he had always understood that his position would be in the background, shaping events.

This public distance was satisfactory to him. The people who mattered to Krantz knew of his closeness to the president. Now the decades of his cultivating Jamal Tambor's trust and friendship were finally paying off. His offshore accounts were swollen with Swiss francs and gold bars, all due to his close contact with the President of the United States. When Tambor's term in office was finally over, Sidney would be ready to enjoy the life of wealth and ease that he had earned.

President Tambor was already in the windowless walnut-paneled room when Krantz entered. The president's special assistant closed the two doors behind Krantz, and left them alone. Not even the Secret Service entered this private space during one-on-one meetings. They objected strenuously that this was a dangerous security risk, but the president overruled them.

The president stood with his back to Krantz, staring at a large pull-down map of the United States. The map showed the boundaries of every county, colored in shades from bright crimson to deep blue. He was staring at the middle of the country.

Krantz cleared his throat. "Mr. President?" Twenty-five years he'd known Tambor, but he no longer called him by his first name. Now that he was the "leader of the free world," as they used to call the job, Tambor demanded that everyone kowtow to him, even his old friends. Underlings retreated into their offices at his approach and never dared to look him in the eye as he swept past, lest they incur his cold wrath. Sidney Krantz and Tambor had known each other far too long for him to adopt that level of servility, but he did call him Mr. President.

"Hey Sid, thanks for dropping by on short notice."

Krantz thought, *What else can you do when you're called to the White House?* He waited every day in his Old Executive office for such calls. "No problem, Mr. President."

"I heard you were up in the village last weekend. Did you see our mutual friend Robert?"

The president meant Greenwich Village, in New York City. *The president is keeping tabs on my travels*, thought Krantz. *That's good to know.* Robert was Robert Waylen, an old friend to both of them. Waylen was now professor emeritus of American History at Columbia University, but he had been famous decades before as a radical anti-war activist and some said, a terrorist bomber. Krantz responded breezily, in the spirit of conversation-opening small talk. "I did see Robert. He sends his greetings. He's sorry that he can't see you anymore. He said he misses your old conversations."

"How is he doing? I hear that his health is failing."

Krantz wondered how much the president really knew about Waylen these days, to ask that question. If the president had even an inkling about a certain videotape in Waylen's possession, both of them could wind up in public parks like Vince Foster, or wrapped in chains at the bottom of the Chesapeake Bay. Was the question about Waylen's health sincere, or something more, a hint of suspicion or a hope that Waylen would soon be departing for the great beyond? "He doesn't look too well. He's lost a lot of weight and he doesn't get out much anymore. He walks his little dachshunds, and that's about all he can manage."

Robert Waylen lived alone in a posh three-story brownstone on West 11th Street. Jamal Tambor had been a student at Columbia when he came into Waylen and Krantz's orbit. Now Waylen was in his seventies and battling cancer, while Jamal Tambor had just celebrated his fiftieth birthday in the White House, in nearly perfect health. Tambor could thank his Malaysian mother for his youthful demeanor, good looks and overall fitness. He had been born in California, but raised mainly in South Asia, while his father worked a series of jobs as an engineer. Only a rapidly receding hairline and a few lines around his eyes and his mouth betrayed the age of America's first mixed-race president. He was in decent health, even considering his pack-a-day cigarette habit. At least smoking kept him thin. He wasn't as cute as he had been when Krantz had first known him at Columbia, but he was still a very handsome man.

The president dropped his discussion of their old acquaintance and turned to current affairs. "Sidney, we need to finish our recovery operations in the earthquake zone before summer, or the Northwest campaign will have to be pushed back until next year. And if we can't bring the Northwest back into the fold this year...well, we may lose it for good. The Chinese are not waiting. We can either be their partners, or watch them make their own arrangements. The Northwest may even formally secede, and frankly, we won't be able to prevent it."

"Well," Krantz responded, choosing his words carefully, "the Chinese Navy is already there. Officially, the Chinese naval vessels are only visiting Seattle and Vancouver. There's nothing permanent about their presence, nothing official—"

"But how long can we maintain that fiction? Friendly naval port visits don't last for months on end and stretch from one fleet to another." The president turned from the wall map, sighed, and slid down into his black leather recliner. Krantz took the matching leather wing chair across from him. The president opened a silver case from the side table, extracted a long cigarette and lit it with a matching silver lighter. He snapped the lighter shut and took a deep drag. He was never photographed smoking: this was another reason for the private reading room, with its special ventilation system. Maybe the main reason.

"The Chinese aren't asking for my permission, no matter what we pretend. It's Hong Kong all over again, only this time, China is playing the role of Great Britain and we're the old Mandarins. Sidney, we have to regain actual control of all forty-five states this year, and to do that, we'll need help from the Chinese. And not only from the Chinese… It won't be popular, but there's no other way. We need international help.

"But we have to start in the East. If we can't reestablish permanent control of the earthquake zone, we won't regain control of the Deep South. And if we can't regain control of the Deep South, we can kiss the Northwest goodbye—for good." His voice rose. Normally melodic and controlled in public appearances and on television, it cracked when he was under pressure. "And then the United States won't even be a continental power anymore. We'll have lost our only remaining Pacific ports—and on my watch!" He took a deep drag from his cigarette, then laid his head back on the recliner and closed his eyes. "And that…cannot happen," he said in a whisper, before exhaling a long stream of smoke. "Not on my watch."

Sidney Krantz replied in a soothing voice. "The Republic of Texas is going to do what it wants. But I'm still confident we won't lose Washington and Oregon."

"Sidney, if the Chinese get permanent bases and trade concessions in Long Beach and Corpus Christi, that's out of my hands. That's Aztlan. We lost the Southwest with the new constitution. It was a fair trade to get the new constitution, and now it's settled business. And I agree, what's left of Texas is a special case. The Texas partition was part of the Aztlan treaty, so our options are rather limited there. But now President Yao is making direct overtures to General Mirabeau for port visits in Louisiana. Louisiana might become a new gas station for the Chinese navy."

"You know," replied the president's adviser, "You can never trust the military, none of them. Mirabeau's the worst: he's a religious fanatic and a fascist."

"Be that as it may, at least for now he runs the Deep South, that so-called 'emergency zone' of his. And at least he can feed his people." The president paused, turning away from Krantz to look over at the wall map. "On the other hand, what if Mirabeau were to be…removed?" He took another pull on his cigarette, and then stabbed it out in a glass ashtray on his side table.

"What do you mean, 'removed'?" asked Krantz. He knew, they both knew, that General Mirabeau was polling much higher than the president was. "We can't fire him, we can't retire him, and we can't just replace him with another general. He'd ignore your orders, and that would be even worse than pretending that he's still part of your National Command Authority. It would just clarify our…impotence if we tried to fire him and he refused to go."

"I'm not talking about his resignation, or his replacement. I'm talking about something more permanent."

"Something like…an accident? Or an illness?" Slow-acting poisons that mimicked debilitating diseases were a hobby of Sidney Krantz. It wouldn't be the first time that this special knowledge had been called upon to quietly eliminate a rival.

President Tambor paused, staring at the wall map while drumming his fingers idly on the arms of the black leather recliner. "That might be our best option, if we could arrange it. If we had operatives close to him…but we don't. Otherwise, I was thinking about a *truly* permanent solution. Maybe even a kinetic solution."

"Not now, Mr. President. Later perhaps, but not now. Exercising a kinetic option at this point would be almost as bad as calling for his resignation and being publicly rebuffed. It would cement the perception that we're not in control down there if we had to do that."

"Even if we black-flagged it?" Tambor asked.

"Even then. Who could we blame for it? It would take time to create a plausible anti-Mirabeau group to blame it on. If we did it now, it would point straight back to us. Nobody would believe that we weren't behind it if Mirabeau was suddenly taken out. Certainly we couldn't drop a missile on him like he was some garden-variety domestic terrorist."

The president sighed. "Well then, in that case I think our only option is to sway the general back over to our side. We need to convince him that we're going to win back complete control of the Union, and that if he wants to retain his position as the *el supremo* of the Deep South, he needs to get on board with us. Openly and publicly. He needs to come to the White House for a photo op. Or to Camp David, if he'd be more comfortable there. Kiss the presidential ring, as it were. Now, we can send him offers and overtures to that effect, but in the end, the only way to convince him to get aboard will be for us to wrap up the Mid South, and do it quickly. Why would he feel a need to obey Washington, when we can't even pacify the earthquake zone? Once all of Tennessee and Kentucky are back under our control, he'll see the light."

"I agree, that's our best course."

"So we need a victory. We need Tennessee to be a success. A visible success. But Sidney, I'm gathering that things are not going so well down there."

"They're getting better. We're gaining traction; we finally have the right man in charge of rural pacification. He knows how to get results, and he's not hamstrung by old-fashioned moral qualms."

"Do you mean Robert Bullard?"

"Yes, he's the one."

Quietly the president said, "You know, he'll have to be eliminated when this is over. Along with every trace of his rural pacification program." He whispered this, as if he didn't fully trust the soundproofing of his "private study."

"Of course." Krantz had selected Robert Bullard from a small pool of potential directors of rural pacification. This was a classified position atop a classified directorate. The rural pacification program was a black operation from start to finish. Rural pacification was Krantz's solution to the Mid-South insurgency, and it was wholeheartedly embraced by the president…but never formally in writing. All of the funding was covert; officially, it did not exist.

Robert Bullard, the former Southwest Region Director of Homeland Security, was already under informal non-judicial house arrest when Krantz had discovered his dossier. To call Bullard an unsavory character was to sugarcoat his life history. The man was a thug, ruled only by his lust for power, wealth and young women. But he had a proven track record as an effective leader of other groups of thugs. He knew how to get things done when nobody particularly cared how. In short, Robert Bullard was the perfect man to crack the whip in the rebel areas of Tennessee and Kentucky. Once the mission was complete, he would be tossed out like the garbage he was. Bullard's group was in effect a cutout, a circuit breaker between the foreign mercenary units and the White House. If the foreign units were successful, the president would take the credit. If they were not, then Bullard's rural pacification group would be made the scapegoats and take the blame.

"You know what's ironic?" asked Krantz. "Bullard thinks he's first in line to be the director of our new Department of Internal Security, or whatever we finally name it. He thinks rural pacification is his audition. He really does. I've got him convinced."

"Then he's a fool. Every trace of rural pacification has to disappear when this is over, starting with him. Even with our influence over the media, using the foreign troops…it's still controversial. It's unpopular. Not even using them to suppress the racists in Tennessee."

"But it works," Krantz replied. "Our own soldiers couldn't get the job done—they were much too soft. Foreign troops don't bring all of that sentimental baggage with them. And Tennessee is the perfect test bed for using international peacekeepers in the United States. Especially the North American Legion. The Legion troops are practically Americans already—North Americans, anyway. Most of them were living here for years before the NAL units were even formed. It's perfect: they're gainfully employed, they're serving our country, they're earning full citizenship, and they're demonstrating how well the North American Union can work."

"But they're not all from the North American Legion," the president observed. "There are Pakistanis, Kazaks, Nigerians, Albanians…"

"That's different. Those are just contract battalions. They come in, get a specific job done, and get out."

"What do you mean, 'get out?' We're giving them free land and citizenship, aren't we? That's how we're paying them, correct? In homestead acreage and citizenship?"

The president was well versed in the details, Krantz had to admit. Free land in America was the only 'currency' remaining that could entice and motivate the foreign contract mercenaries. That, and fast-tracked citizenship for themselves and their families. But the president was supposed to keep his distance from these pacification operations in the South, in order to maintain plausible deniability in case things went badly wrong. "I meant that the foreign contract battalions will be out of the Mid South," said Krantz. "They'll be sent out West after Tennessee and Kentucky are fully pacified. The North American Legion will handle the long-term occupation of the Mid South, and then the resettlement of the evacuated regions."

"How can we ever pacify Tennessee if we can't get food in or get the power turned back on?" asked President Tambor. "It's been a year! The plan was evacuate, relocate and reconstruct, and we're still stuck on evacuate."

"It's not our fault. Nobody can blame us for the damned earthquakes. The transportation infrastructure is still in ruins. It's especially bad in West Tennessee because of all of the infrastructure damage. It's systemic, it's pervasive. And it would be hard enough to fix it all if they weren't still shooting at us, but they are. On the other hand, there are certain benefits to not getting enough food relief in. At least, not to the insurgent areas."

Tambor asked, "Advantages? Explain what you mean."

"Well, it's the old carrot and stick. As the counties on the edges of the earthquake zone are pacified, we fix the bridges, we open the feeding centers, and we reconnect the power grid. This increases local cooperation, county by county."

"But some counties are still cut off. No bridges, and no electrical power."

"That's absolutely correct, especially in West Tennessee—but that's not all bad for us. Think about it: outside of Memphis, most of those counties always voted the straight ticket against our party. The fewer of those racist rednecks that are left, the better it is for us. We'll resettle those areas with the North American Legion troops and their families. When it's done, Tennessee will never vote against us again. It'll be as blue as Massachusetts."

The president said, "Never let a good emergency go to waste, right?"

"Exactly," Krantz agreed.

"And the death rates are still high in West Tennessee?"

"Long-term starvation tends to do that," Krantz replied flatly. "Especially when people are freezing cold and sick. But we have a ready explanation that covers us: we can't bring in food where the people are shooting at us. So it's their own fault if they're starving, and even the media see it the same way. Eventually, they'll be too hungry to fight. Screw 'em—they're just Bible-thumping racist reactionaries anyway. We all saw what they did to the African-American refugees coming out of Memphis. That was genocide—so to hell with them."

The president's eyes narrowed. "My God Sidney, this is almost like the Ukraine in the 1930s." The corners of his mouth subtly turned upward, to form the icy smile that only his closest confidants recognized as an expression of true joy. His broad public smiles and easy television tears were as false and calculated as any masks of wood or plastic. This was the real Jamal Tambor, a sphinx with the political brain of a chess grandmaster and the cold heart of a crocodile. Only a handful of people had ever seen this private side of the president, and Sidney Krantz was one of them.

"You do know your history, Mr. President. I wouldn't say that it was exactly the same but…yes, there are parallels. Hunger can be an effective weapon. And as you know, we have established dozens of feeding centers in the relocation areas to draw them out of the evacuation zones. The problem is that too many of the local people are still holding out. They won't leave their homes, even without electric power. So thousands of them are staying in place and resisting our relocation and reconstruction efforts. But that's all right: there are less of them every month. It's winter. They'll either come into the FEMA relocation centers or they'll starve."

"I'm not seeing any starvation on television."

"No, of course not. The earthquake-damaged areas are under emergency law, and that means the media are kept out. It's a fairly simple matter to control the news flow, to spin it our way, because this time the insurgents really are shooting at our troops. If it's too dangerous for our troops, it's too dangerous for reporters."

"*Our* troops?" the president corrected. "Don't you mean the NAL troops, and the foreign contract battalions?"

"Well, you know what I mean. Technically, they're 'our troops,' even if they're not American citizens—yet."

"But using starvation as a weapon…Sidney, if it ever gets out…"

"Don't worry, it won't. Back when Stalin was starving them by the millions in the Ukraine, the *New York Times* even won a Pulitzer Prize for reporting how great things were there. And the *Times* is still on our side. They hate those inbred snake-handlers down South just as much as we do. And what the *New York Times* reports, the rest of the media are happy to parrot. Don't worry, it'll never get out. The major media are behind us. There's nothing in writing about this food policy. We have perfect excuses; we're covered in every direction. It's all because of the earthquakes, and the rebels who are shooting at our troops. I just don't see a down side for us."

"Well I do—time," retorted the president. "Starvation takes time, time we don't have. We need Tennessee wrapped up before summer. Before we can move our forces to the Northwest we need to have complete control everywhere east of the Mississippi River."

"I agree."

"Then tell this Robert Bullard to light some fires down there! He needs to motivate those foreign troops and get this thing over. Finish it! I want to visit Memphis and Nashville by the time the magnolias are blooming. You can do this for me, can't you, Sidney? It's very tricky, this strategy. There are many perils, many risks…"

"Don't worry, Robert Bullard has a handle on it. We'll make your schedule."

Actually, Sidney Krantz wasn't sure if the starvation strategy would work in time, but he didn't tell the president that. And he certainly didn't tell him about the one ace left up his sleeve; this option was a little too radical for Jamal Tambor to hear about. If the foreign mercenaries, freezing temperatures and starvation couldn't clean out the last rebel pockets in West Tennessee, he had another ally ready to bring to the battle. From old university contacts he had obtained a research vial packed with tiny germs called *Yersinia pestis*, more commonly known as the bubonic plague, or the Black Death. Plague was long endemic among wild rodents in the American Southwest, but at a very low level. A few infected rats could have hitchhiked into the earthquake zone on trucks, and then nature would have taken its tragic course…yes, that was plausible.

Coming on the heels of Cameroon fever and the avian flu, nobody would be too surprised by an outbreak of the Black Death in Tennessee. With the remaining population already compromised by stress, cold, hunger and illness, the plague would rapidly finish them off. Even among a healthy population, the untreated mortality rate was well over 50 percent. Yet because plague was easily treatable with standard antibiotics, it would pose little danger of spreading across the river boundaries of West Tennessee, beyond the quarantine zones and into the rest of the federal states. Once the plague outbreak was publicized, the last stubborn holdouts in West Tennessee would rush to the FEMA relocation centers in order to gain access to the lifesaving antibiotics. Even if a relatively small percentage of the remaining population were infected, blind fear of the plague would drive them into the welcoming arms of the government.

Krantz had done his homework. He had learned that the plague germs needed a local species of immune rodents to serve as a reservoir, in order for them to become a long-term problem in a given region. Once the infected rats and humans died off, the epidemic would wind down. At temperatures above eighty degrees Fahrenheit, fleas infected with *Yersinia pestis* did not transmit the disease. When they died, the germs died inside them and the cycle was broken. Warm, dry summer weather would finish off the plague outbreak. With no pool of immune rodents to contain the disease until the following autumn, the danger would disappear after one killing season.

Foreign troops operating in the Mid South, with ready access to antibiotics, would be at almost no additional risk. And if any of them did contract the disease and die, well, they were just foreign soldiers anyway. In the end no tears would be shed for dead mercenaries, no matter what the cause of their demise.

Probably, though, it wouldn't come down to using bubonic plague as a weapon. Sidney Krantz could give starvation, cold and the foreign soldiers a few more weeks to finish the job. But if they were still stuck in this Mid South quagmire next year…then he'd do whatever it took to accomplish the president's mission on time. People didn't whisper that he was the president's Rasputin for no reason.

2

Phil Carson left Seabago for the last time at dawn on the second day after his shipwreck. The occasional bloated bodies of the recently drowned were beginning to stink, and he was glad to depart the catamaran, jumping from the starboard hull over onto rotten timbers and rusted cars. Feral dogs, rats, crows and vultures, already at work on the dead, scurried or flapped away at his approach. The bodies must have been carried in on the surge tide; there were no signs of nearby human habitation. Scattered bones, some partial skeletons still wearing scraps of faded clothing, reminded him that this landscape of death and ruin was not new. In sharp contrast to the death and decay around him, it was a beautiful winter day along the Gulf. The sky was clear blue, streaked with high cirrus; he guessed the morning temperature was in the fifties. A fine day for a walk, he told himself.

His tan pack weighed only about thirty pounds. Almost half of that weight was drinking water contained in various recycled plastic bottles. For now, he was wearing old Reeboks, stained khaki work pants, and a torn green T-shirt. He knew that he would eventually be confronting officials, and his outward appearance was carefully considered. He was unshaven since Brazil, and the gash at his hairline was obviously new, as were his black eyes and other bruises and contusions. He carried the bare minimum, only items that would plausibly be in the possession of a recently shipwrecked mariner.

Climbing up, over and around the jumbled debris with thirty pounds strapped to his back, Phil was grateful for his recent weeks of sailing. The constant exercise involved in sailing had left him strong, agile and fit, especially compared to most men his age. His knees bothered him less now than they had a decade earlier. The constant searching of distant horizons had actually honed his vision. His old blue eyes betrayed him only at close range, when reading fine print or working with tiny parts. Reading glasses were a small but indispensable crutch, a nagging reminder of his age. He had gray hair to be sure, and permanent crow's-feet and laugh lines on his face, but most of the time he felt no different than he had at age fifty—or at forty, for that matter. Aches and pains were more frequent and longer lasting, but what else could be expected after sixty-four hard-lived years? Only his face betrayed his decades. Sun, wind and weather made him look his years, and with his cut and bruised face, he looked even worse.

By noon, the marshes and creeks had turned into a swampy forest of skinny pine trees. Many of them were snapped or cracked halfway up by previous storms, forcing him to climb over and through the deadfall. Like the marshes, these woods were jammed with trash and debris. Just after 1:00 p.m., he climbed up a final steep bank and found railroad tracks, running east to west. They were unused, if the rust on top of the steel rails was any indication. A hundred feet beyond the tracks was a paved state road. He walked the tracks for an hour until they diverged away from the road, heading back into the marshes to the southwest. This presented him with a choice. After pausing to drink water from one of the plastic bottles in his pack, he quit the elevated berm of the railroad for the asphalt road, and continued west. The two-lane road was covered in many sections by sand and mud left behind by the storm surge. Where its surface was uncovered, he walked on the left side of the cracked asphalt. There was no traffic. Not a single car.

Trees, billboards, utility poles and wires were down across the road, but even two days after the storm nobody was working to clear the obstacles. The scattered houses still standing were roofless and long abandoned. An old cinderblock gas station and an even older roadhouse bar were windowless and empty.

"Put it down right there, on this side of the barn." Robert Bullard liked to sit up front in the empty copilot's seat. His four-man personal bodyguard detail sat behind him in the chopper's passenger compartment. The choice of seats was a perquisite of his Senior Executive Service rank. He had never been in the military, but sitting up front, he felt like an Apache or Blackhawk pilot, racing across Western Tennessee. Wearing a headset, he could listen to air traffic control or switch over to other military and law enforcement radio nets.

It was great to be working again, after that fiasco in California had sidelined him for almost two years. Sidelined hell—he had been under virtual house arrest. At least the views had been terrific from his bayside penthouse condominium in downtown San Diego. The important thing was that he had not been indicted. Actually, he considered himself fortunate to have avoided a stretch in Club Fed. His first month under house arrest, he had expected to be served with an indictment on an hourly basis. Now he understood why he had been kept in the deep freeze, under investigation instead of arrested. When the highest echelons of the federal government needed the most difficult and dirty jobs handled, they needed men like Bob Bullard. Well, he really couldn't bitch. Even though he had lost his millions in gold back in California, at least he had not been arrested or imprisoned. Now he was just glad to be back in the saddle. After two years of house arrest, he would have accepted a posting to Alaska, just to get out of his condo in San Diego. It was all relative.

"Those are stables, I think," the pilot answered on the intercom. They both wore headsets over ball caps and sunglasses.

"Yeah, whatever. Put her down." Bullard pointed to the spot. He was wearing his usual unofficial uniform of khaki pants with a matching khaki windbreaker.

"But we'll spook the horses if we land there."

"And do I look like I give a shit? No, I do not. Just put this chopper down where I tell you." Bullard knew from experience that the Kazaks could spend entire days galloping back and forth on these mile-wide fields. The chopper would run out of fuel long before they finished playing their game of goat polo.

Bullard's pilot flared out for the landing and brought the machine down. He set the blue-and-white executive helicopter on the grassy field, scattering horses and riders, a few rearing or bolting off at a full gallop. While the rotors were still turning, Bullard stepped down from the helo, accompanied by his bodyguards. They all wore black combat vests and matching ball caps over black uniforms and were armed with compact assault rifles. Alongside another barn was a row of military trucks and a separate line of ASVs, menacing four-wheeled Armored Security Vehicles with little tank turrets on top of their angle-faceted bodies.

The helicopter's jet turbines were still winding down when the leader of the Kazaks trotted up on his white Arabian. The horse was nervously tossing its head in fear of the chopper, and it was tightly reined in by its rider. Colonel Yerzhan Jibek was also accompanied by his own squad of horse-mounted bodyguards, Kalashnikov rifles slung across their backs. The horses and riders made visible breath plumes in the frosty air. Colonel Jibek was dressed in the earth-brown garrison uniform of the Kazak Battalion, with knee-high leather riding boots. A leather pistol holster with a cover flap and a leather Sam Brown belt matched his boots. He was tall for a Central Asian, at least a six-footer. On horseback, he positively loomed over Bullard and his bodyguards. The man exuded health and confidence. Bullard guessed he was quite a lady-killer, with his thick mustache, high cheekbones and dark eyes. (Not that the local girls had much choice in the matter of romance with the foreign peacekeepers.)

Bullard wasn't nearly as handsome, but he thought he looked pretty good for his age. Some of the ladies still said he looked like Robert De Niro, and he had been practicing the actor's mannerisms and facial expressions for so long that they had become second nature. If he had to dye his hair black, so what? *You talkin' to me?*

The Kazak leader said, "Ah, General Blair, always with the dramatic appearance."

Colonel Jibek knew Bob Bullard only by this alias. These Asiatics had no respect for titles other than military ranks, so Bullard adapted. A Kazak colonel would answer only to a general, so Bullard became one, nominally. In Third World hellholes like Kazakhstan, mysterious "generals" who seldom wore uniforms were standard issue. This custom was useful when dealing with the foreign military units, under the auspices of the rural pacification program. He was the director of the program, and he made up his own rules. He had been hired because he got results. Besides, Jibek wasn't a real colonel either, not in the sense of belonging to a sovereign nation's military. The Kazak Battalion was really just a mercenary outfit manned by contract soldiers—like most of the foreign units under Bullard's command. "*Kontraktniki*," they called themselves. Their contracts stipulated that battalion leaders were colonels, so there you were.

"By what grace do we thank the appearance of our general?" Colonel Jibek spoke with a vague Limey accent, and his English grammar was always humorously mangled. It was all Bullard could do to keep a straight face. He guessed that Jibek (if that was his real name, and he suspected it was not) had probably learned the language while listening to tapes made by English defectors to the Soviet Union. Back in the Soviet era, their special operations officers were trained to operate behind enemy lines and usually learned a foreign language, so it fit his bio. He was one of only a handful of Kazak officers with any knowledge of English whatsoever. This language insularity was one of the key attributes of the Kazak Battalion, making them particularly well suited for certain missions. That and their casual, ingrained brutality.

"Climb down, Colonel, and let's go for a walk."

"But we are not completed of our game."

"Don't worry; you can finish after I'm gone. We need to talk."

"I will bring you horse. We may riding go together. I am for certain that you will enjoy."

"Not today." Bob Bullard had not sat on a horse since a county fair pony ride in the third grade, and he did not intend to get on a horse at this point in his life. "We really need to talk, colonel. Now."

The colonel sighed and dismounted his horse, which was immediately led away by an enlisted Kazak soldier, who then followed behind them just out of earshot. "Would you like something to drink, general? We have made most excellent *kumis*."

"Koomis? What the hell is that?"

"Fermented milk of female horse. It is tasting very delicious, and increase manly capability with woman." The Kazak winked broadly and nudged him with an elbow.

Bullard couldn't decide if Jibek was pulling his leg. Well, it didn't matter at this point. Jibek could do all the teasing he wanted. "I'll pass on it this time. I'm going to make this brief, and then you can get back to tearing that goat to pieces. Colonel, I'm worried about your battalion. They don't seem to be obeying your orders."

The Kazak officer shot him a hard look. "Not possible. My soldiers are obeying orders to one hundred percent, or they are shot like dogs."

"Well, if that's the case, maybe we have a bigger problem than I thought. Why are all of your men still in Clark County? Fillmore and Radford County are going to hell in a basket, and last week I asked you to conduct punitive raids. Those counties should be empty of all unapproved people by now, but they're still full of rebel holdouts. I sent target folders and operations plans. So far we haven't seen anything but...goat polo. Your battalion hasn't moved, not even a platoon. Even your checkpoints are not manned."

"Ah, General Blair, winter now is time for my men to enjoy fruits of their work. They are busy on new farms, with new American wives. It's not simple you know, subduing a rebel province. To win the hearts and brains of the people takes much attention. As for checkpoints, Mexicans of North American Legion are good enough for checkpoint duty. It is not for my battalion to do such low work. My men are all *Spetznaz*, trained for special operations."

"Have you even read the target folders I sent you? I made a simple request, and I was ignored. I don't like being ignored, Colonel."

"I am not ignoring your wishes, but we are, you might say, in a period of reformation and regrouping here. When we are ready—"

"Your men will never be ready, not if they think they are going to turn into farmers and land owners here in Clark County. I'm telling you Colonel, that's not how this is going to work. No way in hell."

"My men were promised land. I was promised land! Land, and citizenship. What are your government's promises, empty wind?"

"You were never promised land in Tennessee. This county is not the end of your mission tasking, Colonel. We have more important missions for your battalion before you will receive your permanent land titles."

Jibek made a sweeping gesture with his riding crop at the hundreds of acres of rolling fields and woods surrounding them. "So this estate, the horses...are not mine to keep, as I was understanding? Pity. I've grown, how do you say...rather fond of the place."

"I'm sure you have, but it's not going to be yours for much longer. Your battalion has been tasked with population evacuation and relocation operations in Western Tennessee. Once this region is pacified, your battalion will be heading far to the west. The Mexicans will be adequate to hold what you have gained for us in Tennessee, but your mission here has not yet been finished. You need to bring your men back into fighting form.

You need to get them back into training for war, not games. You need to get them ready for more operations now, not sometime later."

"Ah, my dear General Blair, you must understand...that is not Kazak way. Kazak men must see rewards along path. I promise you, we will be ready for more operations in spring. Until then..."

"Listen Colonel: don't forget who provides the fuel for your trucks and your generators. Don't forget who provides you with the overhead images and videos that let you know where to find the rebels, and the helicopters that allow you to catch them. I don't think you understand your position—"

"Nor do *you* understand my position! I have told you, my battalion will be ready for new operation—*in time of spring.*"

"That's not soon enough; we have a schedule of operations to keep. I'll stop your fuel allotments; I'll stop your helicopters. And I'll let the *Mexicans* have this farm."

Colonel Jibek stood face to face with Bullard, slapping his riding crop against his leg. "We don't need your supplies or your helicopters; we are capable of sustaining ourselves. We are not soft like you Americans. My men are hard like steel. They can take whatever they need, or do without. As far as *Mexicans* taking this farm, well, send them—and *let them try.*"

Bullard contained his reaction to the Kazak's rising anger. "That's your final answer? You need a few months of rest and recuperation before beginning a new phase of operations?"

"Yes, that is correct. I have many friends in Washington, very high in Department of State. They have given me explicit guarantee that my battalion will not be overtasked with missions. In fact, the Assistant Secretary of State gave me such as promise in writing on paper before even we came to Tennessee. Would you like to see document? We have already performed above our part of agreement."

"The State Department, huh? Well, why didn't you say so?" Bullard put his hands up in apparent resignation. "Well, I guess I know when I've lost an argument. Okay Colonel, you win, have it your way. Keep me informed, and let me know when your battalion is ready. But in the meantime, if I send you some small mission taskings, the occasional ambush or rebel farm liquidation, do you think perhaps you could work them into your training schedule?"

"Well, of course, General Blair, I am a reasonable man. Are you sure you won't try cup of fresh *kumis*?"

"Maybe next time." Bullard turned and walked back to his helicopter, still surrounded by his bodyguards. Colonel Jibek hissed an order to his trailing adjutant, and another lackey brought his white stallion up by its reins. Jibek mounted with a flourish, whipped his mount, and tore off at a gallop to where dozens of his men were still tossing the remains of a dead goat from rider to rider.

By 2:20, Phil Carson could see a distant sign by the road, and beside it a tent colored desert tan. The sign was a sheet of plywood, horizontal. It read MISSISSIPPI in hand-painted letters. As he walked closer, he could make out a subscript: "No entry without official permission." Beyond the sign the road doubled in size, from two lanes to four, with a median strip between the eastbound and westbound lands. A handful of figures moved around the tent as he walked onward, and they paused to study him as he drew near. They were soldiers wearing camouflage uniforms, carrying M-16s. They finally reacted when he was a hundred yards away.

"Hold it right there!" came the shouted command. "No further! Put your hands up and kneel down."

The simple checkpoint consisted of a canvas Army tent, with all four sides rolled up, and a porta-john. A green military pickup truck was parked by the tent. This checkpoint was about what Carson had expected. He did as he was ordered, and dropped slowly to his knees.

A pair of soldiers approached to within twenty yards. Both were clean-shaven Caucasians in their twenties, wearing matching camo patrol caps. These were similar to ball caps but flat on top, with a shorter bill. The taller of the two asked, "What were you doing over there? Couldn't you read the sign? That's a prohibited zone." Both carried their rifles across their chests on slings, but they were not wearing body armor.

"I think he's a looter," suggested the smaller troop, leveling the barrel of his M-16. "Look at that pack—it's probably just crammed with loot."

"What prohibited zone?" asked Carson. "I don't know anything about a prohibited zone."

"Are you blind? Can't you read? This sign says it's a prohibited zone—you can't just go strolling on into Alabama."

Carson looked at the crude four-by-eight plywood sign, and back at the soldiers. "I can't see what it says on your side. I just see Mississippi, and I guess I'm here asking for official permission, like it says. I don't know what the sign says on the other side."

"How'd you get in there, then?" asked the squad leader smugly. "Coastal Alabama's a prohibited zone. It's a no-go area. Nobody can cross the state line without a special permit. So how'd you get over there if you didn't sneak around us?"

At least they were keeping their distance, Carson was grateful for that. They weren't making him lie face down on the asphalt. "I don't know, I was just *there*, that's all. I've never been here before in my life. I've never seen your sign before. At least, I don't *remember* any of this."

"You don't *remember*? What is that bullshit? What's that supposed to mean?"

"I'm not sure what *anything* means. I woke up back there somewhere. That's all I know—I don't remember anything else."

"Where's your ID badge?" demanded the squad leader.

"ID badge? I don't know, am I supposed to have one? I don't remember anything about ID badges."

"Oh, bullshit! What's your name and social security number, then?"

Carson feigned a helplessly bewildered look, alternately staring at each of the young soldiers. "You know, I can't remember that either!"

"Well, you just can't remember *anything*, can you?" stated the shorter soldier.

The squad leader asked, "You're not from around here, are you?" He had a strong Southern accent.

"Where's here?" asked Carson, seemingly perplexed.

"Here's Jackson County, Mississippi, that's where. So you're not from Alabama then?"

"I don't know. Maybe. I can't remember. My head hurts real bad, that's about all I'm sure of."

The shorter soldier spoke to his squad leader. "If he came all the way from Florida, he might be carrying the bird flu or the monkey pox..." Both soldiers backed away.

"You just stay right where you are," ordered the squad leader. "I'm going to call higher and get a QV team down here ASAP. I'm not taking any chances. No sir, I'm not."

"What's a QV team?" asked Carson timidly.

"Huh? QV—Quarantine and Vaccination. If you don't have an ID and a vaccination card, then you have to go to QV. They'll sort it out."

Both soldiers eased further away from Carson, back toward the rest of the watching squad. The taller of the two spoke into a walkie-talkie. Carson shifted from the painful position on his knees to sitting Indian-style on the asphalt.

Bob Bullard instructed the pilot to maintain 4,000 feet of altitude above ground level for the flight from Clark County back to his headquarters at Fort Campbell, on the Tennessee-Kentucky border. This was above effecttive small-arms range, but low enough for him to give the land a good looking over. He had a paper air map unfolded on his lap, and he made notes directly on it with a felt-tip marker as he watched the ground slide beneath. He had already put a giant red X across Colonel Jibek's confiscated thousand-acre estate. The helicopter flew a straight track above the gently rolling countryside. It was still a beautiful region, in spite of the widespread points of destruction. Clark County was horse country, with many farms dedicated to equestrian pursuits.

It had been one of the last openly defiant counties between Nashville and Memphis. The roots of the insurrection went back many years, but as in many other areas, it really took off after the semi-automatic rifle ban. The Tennesseans had openly flouted the ban, and the repeal of the Second Amendment had only hardened their defiance. These Southern rednecks were both crazy about their guns and full of hate for the federal government, which was an explosive combination. Before the two earthquakes, internal ATF reports estimated that Tennessee was at less than 50 percent compliance with the new gun laws. This was a disgrace compared to states like Maryland and New Jersey, but what else could be expected? The South was the South, and rebellion was in their blood. Too many of these hillbillies just would not adapt to the new constitution and its socially progressive laws. Washington could pass all the laws it wanted, but increasingly, it could not enforce them in any meaningful way.

Then, without warning, the New Madrid fault had broken open with a monthlong series of quakes, including two massive ones. The population of Memphis had spilled out into the surrounding countryside, foraging for food and shelter. Across the Mississippi River, St. Louis and Little Rock had not fared much better. A bloodbath resulted when the waves of urban refugees were violently resisted in the countryside. The bloodshed after the quake revealed just how unrealistic the gun law compliance estimates had been: the suburban and rural folk were still armed to the teeth.

After the quakes, the countryside around Memphis was initially pillaged by the starving refugees, until the locals had organized and fought back, killing thousands of purported bandits and looters. Well, as far as Bob Bullard was concerned, every ghetto dweller killed out in the sticks was one less refugee mouth to feed back in Memphis. Even better, every death could be conveniently blamed on the quake aftermath and the white aversion to black refugees.

Phil Carson sat on the road, using his pack for a backrest. While he waited, he sipped water from a plastic bottle that had once carried Gatorade. After half an hour, a pickup approached from the west and briefly paused by the tent. The checkpoint soldiers spoke to its driver while standing well away from the vehicle.

Finally, the truck rolled slowly up toward Carson and stopped. The vehicle had been painted in day-glo safety orange. The letters QV were written in yard-high black letters on both doors. A gray box occupied all of the truck bed except for a little space at its front. It reminded Carson of a portable dog kennel, only bigger. It was made of gray metal, with a window on each side covered with heavy wire mesh.

The driver and a passenger stepped out onto the road, and Carson stood up to meet them. The driver was a Caucasian whose face was horribly scarred. The other soldier was a black man with a smooth complexion and alert, intelligent-looking eyes.

He had seen these facial scars before—on monkey pox survivors. It was like pitting from the very worst teenage acne, twice over. In many of the islands and ports he'd passed through, people with the scars were prohibited entry, banned like modern-day lepers. Carson knew this was merely foolish superstition: monkey pox survivors didn't carry the germs in an active form, and couldn't catch or spread the disease. The only dangerous period was the week after infection, until after the skin boils erupted and scabbed over. Still, victims were often made pariahs, as living reminders of the horror that was monkey pox, with its 20 percent mortality rate and hideous survivor scars.

The pock-faced driver pulled on a surgical mask as he approached, and stopped a few yards from Carson. Three chevrons on a square rank badge on the front of their shirts meant both were buck sergeants. Both wore holstered pistols on web belts. On the opposite side of the passenger's belt was a small green gear pack with a medical caduceus on it. Instead of patrol caps, these two soldiers wore black berets.

The driver said, "So, let me see if I got this right: you've got no ID badge and no vaccine shot card. You just appeared out of nowhere, and you don't even know who you are." His Southern-accented voice was slightly muffled by the filter. He had bright blue eyes above the mask.

"That's about right."

"Empty your pockets and dump out your pack on the ground," the driver instructed without emotion. He seemed to be in no hurry to approach more closely.

Carson did as he was ordered, crouching down and emptying the pack. He spread out its innocuous contents: water bottles, a green poncho, and other very basic gear.

"Any weapons?" asked the medic.

"Just a pocket knife," answered Carson, pulling a small folder from the rear pocket of his pants. He had judged that having no weapon at all would not have been believable, and he was prepared to sacrifice the cheap knife, hoping this might save him from a closer inspection.

The driver eyed the short blade and said, "No weapons in the QVC. Sorry, that's the rule. Leave it on the ground and load the rest back up. You might get it back later, you might not."

Carson repacked the bag while kneeling on the asphalt, moving slowly, as they would expect an old man to do. When he was finished, he struggled up as if he had a bad back. It wasn't a difficult act: after two weeks at sea, the day of hiking over broken ground had worn him out.

The truck's square cage stopped short two feet from the cab. "Put your pack in the truck there," the driver ordered, indicating the open space.

Carson did as he was told, walking close by the scarred man and dropping the pack over the side. The medic backed away from him, maintaining more than a yard of separation.

"Now pull up your shirtsleeves, all the way to the shoulder." Carson did so, revealing on the left side a barely visible smallpox vaccination scar, more than six decades old. Beneath the vaccination was a faded blue two-inch-wide tattoo of an open parachute with a pair of wings curling up on either side.

The driver studied the vaccination mark and the tattoo, then looked again at Carson's face. "That old smallpox vaccination might have saved you. We almost never saw Cameroon fever in people your age. But you'll still need to get the complete battery of new shots." He dropped the tailgate and swung open a chain link door at the back of the cage. "Okay, get in. Don't worry; this is just routine. Anybody who's going to the QV center rides back there."

"Am I under arrest or something?" asked Carson.

"No, it's just SOP. Standard operating procedure. Consider yourself lucky: last year we were running busloads. You'll probably be out as soon as you're medically cleared. It's just unusual these days to see somebody with no ID badge and no vaccine card, that's all. Okay, go ahead and climb in."

Carson looked at the open cage, the driver with his pistol, the other checkpoint soldiers with their rifles. It was too late to change his mind about his plan. At this point running was not an option, and fighting would be worse than useless. He could only do as he was ordered. Now, at the actual moment of being detained, he felt that he'd been a damn fool just to walk into Mississippi. From this point on, what happened to him would be beyond his control.

The floor was of the same gray metal as the rest of the cage. He could see now that the entire box could be lifted out of the truck, prisoners and all, by a metal ring bolted on top. He swallowed hard and climbed up and inside the cage. The driver swung the two back doors closed and then raised the tailgate, locking him in. He imagined the box, carrying infected human cargo, being lifted out of the pickup by a hoist. The people inside the box could be put through a decontamination station...or the box could be lowered into a river or pond, drowning the hapless human debris locked within like unwanted stray cats or dogs.

He could see out of the wire-screened side windows of the box. According to the miniature compass on his watchband, they drove southwest until they entered the town of Pascagoula, and then turned right, heading north. Surrounded by so much metal, the little compass spun erratically, but after many ocean voyages Carson was comforted by its north-seeking needle. Road signs said they were on State Road 63. There was very little traffic, and almost no private cars passed the pickup in either direction. Infrequent buses and trucks made up most of the motor vehicles on the road. Stake-side farm trucks carried dozens of standing men crammed into their backs. A surprising number of people walked or rode bicycles on the shoulders of the road. Some were riding horses or used horse-drawn wagons.

The truck ascended a high concrete bridge over a wide river. Carson could see rusty commercial fishing boats tied up to piers below him. Back down on land, the road continued running straight north, two lanes on each side of a wide median. More people lined the road. It looked like a permanent flea market or swap meet, spread out on both sides.

Everybody the QV truck passed had a card-size plastic badge clipped to a collar, shirt pocket, or belt. The people stopped and stared blankly at the bright orange quarantine truck. A black child scowled, then hurled a rock that bounced off the side of the cage as the truck passed. Soon the truck left the heavily populated coastal zone. Half of the countryside was forested with oaks and pines, and half was in farmland. Businesses and homes were spread out a few to a mile, clustered mostly around infrequent crossroads. The truck drove swiftly northward. Rusty cranes, bulldozers and backhoes were stranded by the roadsides at random intervals, covered with creeper vines and sprouting bushes like ruins reclaimed by the jungle.

At an intersection outside a small town, Carson stared at a man's body hanging from a telephone pole by a thin rope. There was a dark mask over his head, and his hands were bound behind his back. He was dressed in jeans and a red T-shirt, with a sandal on one foot. The man was black, or perhaps his corpse had turned black after his death. A single word was printed on a cardboard placard fixed to his shirt: COUNTERFEITER. Carson moved from the side window to watch the surreal scene through the chain-link rear doors, until the man disappeared in the distance behind them.

Roadside billboards, instead of carrying commercial advertisements, were devoted to government announcements. The messages alternated between boasts of public services restored and stern warnings to potential lawbreakers. A billboard featured a cheerful multiracial group all giving the thumbs-up sign. The text above them gave thanks that electric service had been restored to 82 percent of Mississippi. Other signs featured portraits of a military officer, a stern-faced but rather handsome Creole-looking man. Beneath his portraits were slogans such as "Together we will finish what we have begun!" and "We will rise together, or fall apart!"

A half hour into the drive, the QV truck made several detours through residential areas consisting of badly dilapidated mobile homes and shacks.

Many nicer homes were in ruins, roofless and open to the elements, with tattered blue plastic tarps lifting above them in the breeze. Almost every inhabited dwelling had some type of makeshift fence surrounding it, made of rusty chain link, wood slats, or simple iron rebar posts woven with barbed wire. Simple wooden crosses marked graves in many yards.

People holding an assortment of water containers lined up at a communal spigot. Barefoot children played in the dirt while around them pigs, chickens and goats competed for what fodder they could find. Mississippi seemed to have regressed to Third World standards. All except the smallest children wore the black-and-white ID badges clipped to their shirts.

The land was a checkerboard of small farms, woods, villages, residential areas and open space. Carson could see that it would have been impossible to hike overland without being detected. Every other mile he would have been forced to cross a wide creek, a road, or somebody's field or backyard. Without an ID badge, he would have been spotted and reported before he made it ten miles, and he felt a little better about his chosen strategy.

The orange pickup crossed an ancient two-lane bridge over a sluggish brown creek, then wound its way back up to the main road, and continued at higher speed. The truck entered a posted National Forest and soon was driving along a fenced military base. It slowed as it turned past a cement guardhouse and was waved ahead by the soldier on duty. Carson read "Camp Shelton" on a sign by the open gate. The fence around the perimeter of the base was chain link, topped by multiple strands of razor wire.

Camp Shelton covered a vast expanse, miles and miles of forests and ranges and training areas. The truck drove past barracks, offices, housing areas, warehouses and motor pool lots full of military trucks and humvees. Most of them appeared to be out of commission, rusting and cannibalized for parts.

Beyond a series of unmowed sports fields they came to another fenced enclosure, more chain link and razor wire, and another vehicle gate. A waiting soldier opened the gate at the approach of the orange pickup truck. A painted plywood sign attached to the gate read "QVC 5." The truck passed a row of general-purpose tents, old olive drab canvas relics, which stirred long-dormant memories of Vietnam in Phil Carson's mind. They finally stopped by a U-shaped cement structure that resembled an open-air handball court. The driver and passenger stepped from the truck, dropped the tailgate and opened the cage. The black soldier carried a green medical bag on his side. Both men now wore filter masks over their noses and mouths.

"See the baskets?" the medic asked. "Strip down to your skin and put everything in there." A stack of white plastic laundry baskets stood near the open end of the enclosure.

"What about my stuff? Will I get it back?"

"Sure, don't worry," replied the driver.

Carson undressed, dropping everything into a basket. In the center of the cement floor were painted-on footprints, three rows by three, enough for nine people at a time. He'd last seen footprints like that in boot camp, more than forty years before. Even after all of the intervening years, some-how it seemed familiar. He already had the short haircut, but this time it was gray. He felt like he was processing back into the Army.

The black medic said, "Okay, stand in the middle. Don't worry, it's SOP, routine decontamination. We've all been through this plenty of times. Nothing to it." The driver walked to the front side of the cement wall. Rickety galvanized pipes extended from the ground and along the insides of the enclosure. He turned a valve, and after a few seconds a series of nozzles extending from three sides of the enclosure blasted Carson with cold water. The black medic said, "Here, catch this," and tossed him a small plastic bottle filled with brown liquid. "It's disinfectant. Use it for shampoo and everything else. It stinks, but it'll clean you up good."

Phil Carson did as he was told, sticking to his plan of trying to appear as compliant and non-threatening as possible.

"Okay, give it a minute to work, and then we'll rinse you off." When Carson finished washing, he was sprayed again. The driver cut off the water and threw him a threadbare white towel, saying, "That wasn't so bad, was it?"

Since approaching the checkpoint two hours earlier, Phil Carson had been increasingly worried that he had made a grave error in strategy. At each step he had been rendered more powerless, first at the checkpoint, then in being ordered into the cage on the truck, and now finally in being disinfected, naked. All that was missing, he grimly noted, were the indoor "showers" and the Zyklon B poison gas pellets. At any rate, he had no choice but to follow their orders. He was unarmed, deep within a military base and surrounded by armed soldiers. He tried to imagine that he was simply reenlisting in the Army, instead of being processed into some kind of concentration camp. He had chosen his plan for reentering society, and now he had to ride it out to its conclusion, whatever that might be.

He stood naked and toweled off while the driver and the medic chatted casually. When he finished, he was handed a set of pale blue hospital scrubs and green flip-flop shower shoes. It took only a minute to dress. He was grateful to be covered again, even in the thin cotton.

"Grab your pack and your clothes basket and follow me," ordered the pock-faced driver. "You know, you're lucky—you'll have a tent to your-self. You should have seen this place last year: our daily census averaged almost a thousand, and the dead were stacked up like cordwood. Now we mostly just get stragglers like you, except when a hotspot flares up." A black family with small children occupied one other tent, but they avoided eye contact and said nothing as the three walked past. Rectangular areas of dead grass showed the locations of previous tents, interspersed among the dozen still standing in this one fenced-off section of the quarantine camp.

They stopped halfway down the row of tents. "Okay, this is it, your home for the time being. You're lucky to have a roof over your head tonight. We just put them back up after the storm yesterday." The tent front was rolled up and tied off, allowing in sunlight and fresh air. The ground was still wet from the recent tropical rains, but the area under the tent was raised above the ground level on wooden pallets. "You can close the flap if it gets too cold for you tonight."

The medic said, "Take your pack and your clothes basket inside; we've got to check everything."

"You already checked it," Carson complained, but he did as he was told, entering the tent and setting down his load. The medic put on rubber gloves, opened the top and side flaps of the pack, and dumped the contents out on the white plastic table in the center of the tent. He lifted the basket holding Carson's clothes and dumped them out as well, and then felt the pockets with his gloved hands. He paid no particular attention to the seemingly ordinary one-inch-wide leather belt looped into the khaki pants.

"This all your stuff?" asked the driver. "Everything here is yours?"

"Yeah, I think so. My memory is…"

"Well…look at what we have here!" The driver picked up a large one-time peanut butter jar filled with a dark brown powder. He unscrewed the red lid and took a deep breath through his mask. "Coffee—*real* coffee! Man, it's been like forever since I smelled real coffee…"

The medic joined his coworker at breathing in the aroma of ground coffee, going so far as to lift the bottom edge of his filter mask. Their attitudes reflexively softened, they seemed to lose interest in checking the rest of his belongings: sweater, poncho, extra water bottles and so on. The reason for the second search in the tent was obvious to Carson. They had seen the jar of coffee back at the checkpoint, but they had not wanted to draw attention to it around the other soldiers: they might have had to share its contents. The pockmarked sergeant said, "Okay, mister, we'll just take this little present here, and you can keep the rest of your stuff. After the doctor sees you, after your blood work is done, you should be cleared."

"You mean I'll be able to leave this place?"

"I don't know—that's way above my pay grade. I mean you'll most likely be *medically* cleared. What happens to you after that, I don't know."

The black medic removed a rubber tourniquet and a syringe from the green service pack hanging at his side. "Okay now, sit down and stick out your left arm, and let's see what kind of veins you've got."

"What about this cut?" Carson pointed to his forehead as the medic put the tourniquet around his arm just above his elbow.

"What about it?"

"Will I get to see a doctor or something? It might be infected."

The medic laughed through his filter mask. "What's the matter, princess, you think this is the emergency room? Don't worry: it's not bleeding. I'll give you a little Betadine. You'll live. You'll see a doctor eventually, when the lab results are back. Ask him what he thinks." He lowered his voice, nodding over his shoulder at the white driver with his ravaged face, standing a few yards behind. "We don't worry too much about scars anymore. Especially not for…older folks. They'll put in nice stitches for kids sometimes, but not…you know. I mean, it's a matter of priorities."

"Priorities?"

"Right, priorities. Age triage, they call it. And, well, let's face it— you've aged out. You're in the third category, agewise. Anyway, I'll be back in a little while with your vaccination shots: they have to be kept refrigerated. For Cameroon fever, what everybody calls the monkey pox, and the avian flu. Plus a few more. Then you'll be good to go, assuming you don't get sick in the next week, and you pass your background check. Speaking of which, the MPs will be by to collect your fingerprints later on. Somebody from the camp staff will bring you a sleeping bag, and you'll get fed around six. They'll bring chow around to the tents in a cart. You have to stay in your tent or right by it. No wandering around, okay? Curfew is curfew, even here on base. If you're out after dark, you might get shot, and I'm not joking. We're not trying to be hard-asses—that's just the way it is."

Stanley Fromish slept fitfully, tossing beneath his tangled blankets. He was alone, as he'd been for a year. His wife, Molly, had been on a shopping trip over in Memphis when the first quake struck, and he had never seen or heard from her again. In his dreams he saw her trapped between pancaked concrete slabs in a collapsed shopping mall, calling out to him for help. That was his worst nightmare from the quakes, seeing his beloved wife partly crushed and trapped in debris, unable to escape, dying of thirst, pain and shock. Fortunately, his two young daughters had been home with him on that fateful day, and so they had survived the quake and all that had followed.

What saved them from the even more terrible aftermath of the quakes was his gas station in the crossroads town of Carrolton, five miles west of the Tennessee River. By some fluke of geography and engineering, the State Road 214 bridge had been deemed repairable after the quakes, while the much longer I-40 bridge twenty miles to the north had not. Interstate

40 was the main route connecting Memphis, Jackson and Nashville, but after the quakes sleepy State Road 214 became a detour route of strategic significance. Stanley Fromish owned the first service station on the west side of the river with large storage tanks, which overnight had made his gas station critically important to the state and federal governments.

Several of the concrete spans on the high 214 bridge had toppled from their towers after the first quake. In the weeks following the first of the two major earthquakes, a one-lane steel truss had been thrown across the still-standing bridge supports. This one-lane replacement bridge went down in the second big shaker three weeks later and was eventually replaced with two lanes of metal grating over steel I-beams. Trucks had to cross the narrow jury-rigged span at low speed.

State Road 214 was the only remaining route into western Tennessee, not counting the roads coming up from Mississippi. Little help could come from that direction, since the state of Mississippi was already a disaster area even before the quakes. All of the other bridges crossing the Mississippi and Ohio rivers into western Tennessee were still wrecked. So the rickety two-lane temporary bridge had assumed strategic importance, and along with it, so had Stanley Fromish's gas station.

Through hard work and some luck, Fromish had maintained personal control of his service station and mini-mart throughout the year of unending emergency. Food from the mini-mart had helped to see them through the early months of the crisis. After the first quake in December, he'd had the foresight to move every crumb of food and beverage bottle from the mini-mart to his home's basement. The first waves of looters found an open store that was already empty from ceiling to floor, and they moved on. Thereafter, National Guard troops and later the Mexicans had been stationed right at the gas station. As a result, he had not been forced to fend off bandits or roaming gangs.

Because of his station's critical location, it had been chosen to receive fuel allotments. These deliveries came from tanker trucks driven across the Tennessee River under military escort. No matter how it came, the important thing was that his station had been selected to receive the precious gasoline and diesel. A military generator was used to power his pumps, and while it was running he was able to electrify his service station, his garage, and his home.

The fuel was needed not only by the local civilians but also by the American, Mexican, and other foreign troops struggling to keep the peace and guard the reconstruction crews. For the first three months, the station operated under military control, with Stanley Fromish simply following orders, taking the gas deliveries and pumping it out to military and law enforcement vehicles. Eventually the gas station was put onto a cash basis, and limited civilian sales were resumed. He was paid by the military government in red Temporary Emergency Dollars. Real paper money.

The credit card machines had stopped working the day of the first quake, when the power and the phones went down. The electronic credit system had never been restored, not in a way that he could use to run a business. That was all right, paper TEDs were fine. Assuming, of course, that he would be able to redeem them for whatever permanent currency was ultimately issued by the federal government, once the banking system was back up and running in Tennessee. Until then, he was quite satisfied to cooperate with the authorities and accumulate growing stacks of crisp red $100 and $500 TEDs. A mental image of his hidden money comforted him. Stanley straightened his covers, adjusted his pillow, and settled back down to sleep.

Something shook him and he awakened, believing for a moment that another quake was rocking the world. He opened his eyes, disoriented by bright lights around him. A rifle's muzzle was aimed at the bridge of his nose, just above one of the high-powered beams. Another light shone in his face from the right side of the bed, from beneath a pistol with a long silencer. His blankets had been snatched off him, leaving him exposed in the brown sweatsuit he wore for pajamas. His own Smith and Wesson .38 revolver lay only a yard away from his right hand. It was in the top drawer of his bedside table, but with two guns aimed at him, it might as well not have existed.

It was painful to try to look at them in the crossed glare of their beams. Reflected light illuminated his attackers, if he squinted and looked carefully. The man holding the pistol and leaning over him was dressed in camouflage, his face hidden behind a black ski mask. At first, as the conscious segments of his mind clicked into place, his brain rejected the presence of bandits in his second-floor bedroom. He had a high chain-link fence around his entire two acres, behind his gas station. His idiot brother-in-law lived in the gas station itself, and was armed with a shotgun. Hansel and Gretel, his two German shepherds, were given free run of his property at night. There were solar-powered motion detectors hooked to lights and silent alarms at his gas station, his mini-mart, on his fences, and on his house.

Additionally, his gas station and home were only a half mile down State Road 214 from the company of North American Legion soldiers that had been posted to the town. The Mexicans were living in the old Rite-Aid drugstore, a motel, and the empty Ford dealership next door. More than a hundred NAL troops were only a few minutes away, yet two armed intruders were in his bedroom—how could this be? Stanley Fromish had solar-powered lights and alarms, he had his revolver and his dogs, and he had his brother-in-law sleeping inside the gas station with a shotgun. None of them had protected him.

How could these men have penetrated these defenses to his second-floor bedroom, unheard and unseen? Were they some kind of police? His .38 caliber revolver was properly registered under the new law. He had been granted a rare handgun license because of his critical position as a gas station operator. The revolver was his only remaining firearm besides his double-barreled over-and-under 20-gauge shotgun, and that was a legitimate hunting arm that was also legally registered. He had a valid firearms license and the correct permit papers for both guns—so why were the police here? If they *were* police…

After what seemed like several minutes of silence, the man standing over him with the pistol whispered one word. "Stanley." Then he was quiet again.

"Are y-you the p-police?" Fromish asked hopefully.

"No. We're not."

"Then, w-what do you want?"

"We just want to talk to you."

"Who are you? What…do you want?" He was thinking about the three million TEDs he had in his safe, concealed behind a false wall in his basement.

"Stanley, we just want your help," said the man with the pistol.

"My help?"

"Your help."

"What…what can I do?"

"Stanley, we want some help at your gas station. We want you to give us fuel when we need it. Off the books."

"That's all?" he laughed nervously. "Look, I would, but I can't. Every gallon is accounted for, I—"

"Don't give us that bullshit, Stanley, it won't play with us. We know you too well. We know when you get your deliveries. We know how much goes to the Mexicans, how much goes to the traitor police, to the Kazaks, the Pakistanis, the Albanians, the Nigerians—all of them. We're just asking for a few extra gallons of gas and diesel now and then. Without ration cards, without anything put in the record."

"You don't understand, that's impossible. I—"

"No, Stanley, *you* don't understand. You don't understand that we can come back here anytime we want to. We killed your two worthless dogs without making a sound—do you really think you can stop us? No, of course not."

"But I have no choice in—"

"Shut up, Stanley. You're happy to collaborate with the foreign troops, so I guess you're profiting very nicely out of this occupation. You could even feed those two great big German shepherds, while Americans are starving all around you. It's even nice and warm here in your house; what is it, oil heat? Well, that figures, I guess it would be. Yeah, you're doing okay for yourself. You're living mighty high on the hog, selling gas to foreign troops and the traitor police. But that's okay—like you said, you have no choice. Now all we're asking for is a little help, a tiny little patriotic gesture now and then. So that we won't have a reason to come back here and visit you again."

"There's no way, I can't—"

"Oh, yes you can, and you will. Stanley, think about it. These foreign mercenaries won't be here forever. Sooner or later they'll be gone. But this won't ever be over for you—not if we mark you down as a collaborator. We'll remember you for the rest of your life, Stanley, no matter what you do or where you go. Even if you move back to Illinois or try to hide somewhere else. You might not even live long enough to see the foreign mercenaries leave Tennessee. Then who'll take care of your daughters? Maybe the foreign troops will get them, if you're not around. Who will get your daughters if you're gone? The Albanians? The Nigerians? The Kazaks? I hear they all like young girls, the younger the better. The Nigerians even think that screwing virgins can cure AIDS. Virgins are big magic back in Africa."

"Stop it!"

"Think about it, Stanley. Think about your girls. You have to plan for the long term. You need to get on the right side of this war before it's too late. You have to come over to the patriotic side, right here and now. Tonight."

"How? I can't do what you're asking."

"Don't worry, Stanley, we won't stop you from doing business with the foreign mercenaries. We understand, you have to live. You have your daughters to take care of. We understand that, it's perfectly normal. We just want our fair share of the gas, and some logistical support now and then. Car parts, engine work. Tires. Things like that. Easy stuff for you."

Fromish was beaten. He thought rapidly while the man talked about his dogs, who were probably dead, as they claimed, and his children, who he prayed were untouched. "How will I know what you want? I don't even know who you are."

"You'll know when we send somebody to your station. They might have a ration card for two gallons, but you'll fill them all the way up instead. You, personally, not one of your employees. Or they'll catch you in your office, almost at curfew time. They'll give you a sign, like this." The man in the mask held his left hand against his chest, crossing his fingers and tapping them against his heart. "The man who makes that sign will be your contact. He'll give you more instructions, and you'll obey them. Later on, we might ask you to put somebody on your payroll—a mechanic. We'll let you know who and when.

"But if you pull anything smart, if you try any kind of double cross…then we'll send another team right back here to your house, and we won't be in such a forgiving mood. Remember, Stanley, you're choosing sides, right here, tonight. Double-cross us and…well, I'm sure you love your daughters too much for that. And always keep this in mind: no matter what happens this year, or next year, or ten years from now—when this occupation is over—we'll remember you, and the decision you made tonight. There are hundreds of patriotic Americans all around you, Stanley, and we'll remember you. There'll be no forgive and forget. One way or the other, we'll all remember how you acted while Tennessee was under foreign occupation. So there's really nothing to think about, because you don't have a choice. You want to get on the right side of this war, don't you?"

"Yes, yes, of course…"

"Good. So, you understand what we want, and how we're going to contact you?"

Stanley Fromish was amazed that they hadn't dragged him out of his bed, to torture him, to force him to open his safe and hand over his thick bundles of red TEDs. Promises of future cooperation were easy to make. It was all the same to him: he cooperated with whoever was holding the guns at any given moment. "Yes, I understand. I'll help you; I'll be on your side."

"Good. Very good. We're leaving now, but we have somebody with a night scope who will be watching you through that window—so don't do anything stupid. Wait ten minutes, and then go check on your daughters. Lovely girls, your wife Molly must have been beautiful. Okay, ten minutes." The two masked bandits flicked off their painfully bright lights, and Stanley Fromish was plunged into utter dark, white flares pulsing where the lights had been.

When his eyes regained their normal functioning, he looked at his watch. Its illuminated face told him that it was 12:43 a.m. He wanted to leap from his bed and check on his children, but he looked at the open shades of his window and remembered what the man had said about a watching sharpshooter. He spent the next ten minutes horrified that the intruders might be doing terrible things to his daughters. He also considered ways to finagle the accounting on the fuel deliveries and adjust the flow meters, in order to divert gasoline off the books to whomever the masked men sent to his office. He wondered if he would have the courage to falsify his paperwork, to run bogus accounting past the military government. If he was caught, they would hang him in Jackson for black marketing or for helping terrorists. Literally hang him from the marble arch in Unity Park, where they hanged rebels, terrorists and bandits almost every Saturday at high noon. That was dead certain. But only if he was caught. On the other hand, these masked men could come back at any time, and his girls...

At exactly 12:51 he slid out of his bed, his heart thudding, and padded silently down the cold hallway to his daughters' bedroom with a flashlight in his hand. They shared a bedroom now, to conserve precious heat. He slowly opened their door and scanned the twin canopy beds. Grace and Emily were both sleeping, undisturbed. He walked closer, crossing the carpet in his stocking feet. Thirteen-year-old Grace was sleeping on her side, facing him, her angel eyes closed, her lips a perfect bow. Across her neck was a wide red line, and he stifled a scream with the back of his left hand. His light's beam swung to eleven-year-old Emily, sleeping on her back across the room, and to another crimson trace across her delicate throat. He closed the gap to Grace's bed in an instant, the light bright in her face, and she awakened and then shut her eyes tightly against the blinding glare.

"It's me, pumkin."

"Daddy? What's wrong, Daddy?"

Across the room, Emily stirred and rolled onto her side, facing him, her eyes opening in little blinks.

He breathed again, kneeling by her bed, touching Grace's throat, smearing greasy red paint—no, it was red lipstick—on his fingertips. An open tube of lipstick was standing on her little bedside table. Next to the lipstick stood a rifle bullet, copper tip over golden brass. He recognized the red lipstick by its silver-and-black cylinder; it was his wife's, taken from atop her bureau in their bedroom. Stanley had left the bureau as it had been before she was lost in the first Memphis quake. The intruders must have been wandering freely around their upstairs bedrooms before waking him up. And that, after defeating his security systems and killing his dogs. If their intention had been to terrorize him, they had succeeded.

"Nothing. Nothing's wrong princess, nothing at all." He switched off his light, leaned over and hugged her. "Nothing at all, Gracie."

Diverting the gasoline would be no problem. Not compared to the danger of another midnight visit from the masked men, if he failed to cooperate with them.

3

It was Carson's first morning in the quarantine camp. He was already awake when he heard the national anthem playing over a distant loud-speaker at 0800 hours. Temperatures had dipped to near freezing over-night, and he had slept with his clothes over his scrubs, in a green Army sleeping bag on a cot. The cot and sleeping bag had been brought to the tent the evening before, after he'd been fingerprinted and had his photo taken by a pair of MPs in masks and rubber gloves.

He tied back the two narrow door flaps to let in some daylight; the sky was leaden and the air heavy with cold mist. Breakfast had been brought around on a handcart after reveille: oatmeal and grits in a plastic bowl, and some kind of orange drink in a plastic cup. He was told to keep the cup; he would not get a new one at each meal. In the future, his cup would be refilled from a jug on the handcart.

He could have easily slipped away from the quarantine center over-night, but what would that have accomplished? He would still have been inside a huge military reservation, without any of the forms of iden-tification necessary for traveling. As he paced around outside his tent, he reconsidered the wisdom of his chosen strategy. Two other options had been available to him yesterday: stay aboard the wrecked catamaran and try to find another escape vessel, or travel overland covertly, moving only at night. Well, he'd chosen a third strategy, and now he was stuck with the consequences.

At 10:15, a camouflage-uniformed visitor approached while Carson was outside the tent doing stretching exercises. He was about Carson's age, which meant he should have been too old to be serving in the military. The oak leaf rank on his chest indicated that he was a lieutenant colonel. The nametape over his right pocket said FOLEY and over the other pocket it said U.S. ARMY. He was wearing a black beret like most of the soldiers Carson had seen on the base. The man's hair was just as gray as his own but a bit longer, a good inch past strict military regulation length.

The lieutenant colonel kept a polite distance and made no offer to shake hands. Carson wasn't offended. This was a quarantine camp, and the man wasn't wearing a mask or gloves. He had a round, pasty face, and brown eyes beneath gold wire-rimmed glasses. He spoke slowly, as if he was addressing an utter moron. "Well, good morning, 'John Doe.' I'm Doctor Foley. My medics brought me up to speed on your case. I came by to check your cut, and see if you've regained any of your memory."

Like hell you did, thought Carson. But no matter the reason, the appearance of the doctor was a good sign. Carson said, "You know, I think I do remember these Army tents, and that beret you're wearing seems sort of familiar, but that's about all."

"The medics that brought you in said you had an Airborne tattoo on your arm. Army jump wings. You must have been in the service at some point. If you were in the service, then your fingerprints should be on file, though I wouldn't be surprised if they don't get a match. A lot of the old paper records never made it into the modern databases. But if I had to guess, I'd say you must have been in the Army to get an Airborne tattoo."

"I suppose so, but I'm not really sure. It's all kind of hazy. I'll tell you what, though: I got a flash of something when I put my cot together last night. Sort of like déjà vu."

"Good, that's something at least. Somewhere to start." The doctor paused, and then set out on a different line of conversation. "Say, I've got to thank you for something."

"Excuse me? Thank me for what?"

"For the best cup of coffee I've had in months."

Carson kept his face blank as he replied, "Coffee?" The old peanut butter jar he'd filled with ground Brazilian coffee had been intentionally left in his pack as bait. When passing through customs he sometimes left racy magazines or a carton of cigarettes packed inside his bag. Whatever was rare, forbidden or valuable in that country—it always paid to throw the low-level inspectors a bone. Once they had their own pilfered contraband to spirit away, they were much less interested in conducting a more detailed search.

"Best coffee I've tasted in years," continued the doctor. "Sure beats the hell out of that damn chicory. I'd almost forgotten how much I love real coffee. You don't remember how you happened to come by it? Sometimes tastes and smells can trigger memories."

"No, I don't remember. I just remember waking up in a pile of wreckage, and walking out."

"Just waking up, and walking out?" The doctor looked skeptical.

"That's right."

"Well then, okay. Now, let me take a look at your cut." The doctor approached to within a yard and leaned forward. "Hmm, not too bad. It's going to be a beauty of a scar, but it's not infected. If you let your hair grow, it should cover it up. I'll give you a little antibacterial ointment, that's the best I can do."

"Thanks."

"Any headaches? Blurry vision, double vision, ringing in the ears?"

"I've had a headache. It comes and goes. None of the other things you said. Doctor, how long do I have to stay here?"

"All of your blood tests were negative—normal. Usually that means you'd be able to leave in two weeks, if you don't have any reactions to the shots they gave you yesterday. That is, medically you'd be able to leave. But you're a tricky case."

"What's that mean?"

"You've got no ID. I don't think they'll let you go until they find out who you are. You can't just go walking around without an ID badge. You need it to prove you've had all the vaccinations."

"I don't see you wearing a badge, doctor."

"Military personnel in uniform don't have to wear them. Our uniforms are our badge," he stated a bit pompously. "Everybody else has to wear the badges at all times when on public property."

"I...see. But what if I don't remember? What'll I use for ID?"

"Maybe they'll get a hit on your fingerprints."

"What if they don't?"

"I don't know. Let's hope your memory returns. It usually does."

"So, doctor, let's just say I do remember, what then?"

"Well, you might be able to go home, if you remember where that is. After they check out your story. But if they charge you with traveling without identification, with being in a prohibited zone...they might sentence you to labor. To be honest, that's probably the most likely outcome in any case."

"Labor?"

"Sure, a labor battalion. Reconstruction, or maybe agriculture. That'd be my guess."

"What do you mean, 'labor battalion'?"

"If you don't already have a critical skill or an approved job, they'll assign you one. Reconstruction, cleanup, or farming. Depends on your age and your physical condition. If you have a skill they need, they'll assign you. Mechanic, electrician, things like that."

"Whether I want a job or not, I'll get assigned to one?"

"That's right."

"Doc, Mississippi is still in America, isn't it?"

"Don't get testy—I don't make the rules. It's martial law, what can I say? Nobody gets a free ride. But since you're a John Doe, you'll stay here—at least for a while. I never heard of the tribunal charging an amnesiac, but you never know. Like I said, you're an unusual case."

"Well, thanks, Doc...I guess."

"No problem. Odds are your memory will come back; it usually does. No doubt you've had a concussion, and probably some post-traumatic stress as well. I'll check back on you in a few days."

"Thanks."

"You know, I'm 65, and you're probably close to my age. If you earned jump wings in the Army, then you were probably in the service about the same time I was. Do you remember going to Vietnam?"

Carson hesitated. "No."

"Well, I sure do. I was a door gunner on a Huey. In the 101st Airborne Division."

Carson let the references to Vietnam pass; it was too early for that discussion. "Doctor, if you're 65, what are you still doing in the Army?"

Foley laughed and rubbed his head, combing blunt fingers through his gray hair. "Great question. I was drafted last year...for the second time. Considerably older this time around! That's one more problem with being an MD, I guess. When Uncle Sam needs you, he finds you. You might say he made me an offer I couldn't refuse." The doctor gave a shrug of resignation. "So now I'm doing my patriotic duty...whether I want to or not. Just like everybody else."

Bob Bullard hadn't forgotten Colonel Jibek. He hadn't forgotten his outright refusal to conduct raids outside of Clark County, while his men were playing goat polo and chasing American girls. Well, if Jibek didn't understand the chain of command, there was every reason to think that his second-in-command would, if an appropriate lesson was administered. There was growing pressure from above to finish the pacification and evacuation of western Tennessee, and the Kazaks were supposed to be taking the lead, not taking time off. Sidney Krantz, the president's special adviser, was breathing down his neck to get the job finished. Krantz had been responsible for Bullard being picked to head the rural pacification program, and had let him know that he could also fire him.

A dozen foreign contract battalions in Tennessee and Kentucky provided the fist behind rural pacification when nothing else would work. The holdouts were beginning to understand that overt resistance would result in several hundred Kazaks sweeping in to conduct massive cordon-and-search operations. The horse-mounted Kazaks were particularly impresssive, galloping across the countryside on raids. The Mexicans and the other lesser troops in the North American Legion provided the manpower at the checkpoints and performed routine occupational missions.

The foreign troops on the ground were a vital part of the force equation, the visible face of rural pacification, but the real incentive for cooperation came from the sky. When it came to instilling fear, nothing provided more bang for the buck than the UAVs. Unmanned aircraft—from airplane-sized Reapers and Predators to drones no bigger than model airplanes—kept a watchful eye above Tennessee around the clock. In the areas slated for complete evacuation, the holdouts could be located by the UAVs and targeted for special action as needed, county by county.

While the foreign troops worked on the ground in the problematic regions, the UAVs, helicopters and fixed-wing assets were strictly an American-run show. Bob Bullard enjoyed visiting the UAV operations center in the middle of Fort Campbell. The center was only minutes away from his current residence, a four-bedroom senior officer's house near the base's golf course. In the UAV center, up to sixty flight technicians at any given time were busy monitoring screens, remotely flying twenty to thirty drones and keeping a watchful eye on their assigned regions. All of these flight technicians were federal agents, assigned to the task of rural pacification in Tennessee and Kentucky.

The UAVs were the tool that had broken the back of the incipient rebellion in these two states. On an hour-by-hour basis, the drones were much more expensive to keep aloft than patrolling with police cars. But while police cars and military vehicles were subject to the constant risk of ambush by snipers and roadside bombs, the silent, invisible UAVs were virtually invulnerable to ground attack. Just as important, they were not hindered by the downed bridges and impassable roads resulting from the earthquakes.

Each drone was controlled by a two-man crew, sitting side by side behind their screens and consoles. The pilots and flight technicians monitored their screens in the main room of UAV flight operations, aligned in rows like a low-budget version of NASA's Mission Control. Bullard walked quickly through the area, the gym of a converted Army physical fitness center. He passed through several interior rooms and halls and finally approached an unmarked locked door. The door was covered with a plate of thick steel and was scanned by several video cameras. The cover name for this office was Surveillance Oversight, but not even that innocuous name was written anywhere near the entrance. Bullard punched in a number code, the door buzzed open, and he went inside. Two of his black-clad bodyguards remained just outside, while two others, who also performed staff duty, entered with him.

Inside this smaller room (formerly a coaching office) were four senior UAV crew sitting at flight monitors and two managers at desks, behind their own computers. These six men, as well as those on the other shifts, had all been picked by Bullard, chosen because of their personal loyalty and their understanding of the difficult but crucial nature of their mission.

"Good morning, Director Bullard," the bearded senior technician greeted him. He was wearing a blue plaid flannel shirt and jeans. The men in this room were all dressed casually, in slacks or jeans and long-sleeve shirts, without ties or jackets. Each wore a laminated security badge pinned to his shirt.

"Good morning, Harry. Anything interesting since yesterday?"

"Oh, we had a few good shoots. Popped an A.I. and nailed a few curfew violators."

A.I.s were armed insurgents, curfew violators and boundary jumpers observed carrying weapons. "Let's see the video," said Bullard as he was handed a cup of coffee by one of his entourage, whose duty it was to fetch a cup immediately upon entering any office with a coffee maker. Offices with genuine coffee were rare, but the inner sanctum of UAV flight operations was one such place.

Bullard sat in the senior technician's padded swivel seat as the video was cued up on the monitor. He sipped his coffee and watched. In the first video clip, the infrared image of a man was clearly seen flitting in and out of the brush along a tree line. The man, hotter than his surroundings, was seen as a white figure walking against a dark background of trees and bushes. The scene appeared to have been filmed from only a hundred yards away, even though the slant range from the UAV was several miles.

This night creeper was clearly a curfew violator, with no legitimate reason to be out after midnight. The image of a crosshair appeared on him, and a few moments later the crosshair was surrounded by a flashing box. The flashing box meant that the target was being painted by coded pulses of invisible laser energy. Within a few seconds there was a silent explosion of white light. When the picture was reacquired, the man was gone, replaced by scattered white hotspots on the ground.

The senior tech said, "Night shift dropped one of the new thirty millimeters on him."

He had seen the prototype 30mm rockets. They were not much thicker than a rake handle, and only a yard long. Smaller even than the baseball bat–sized Viper missiles, with their four-pound charges. Being dropped from altitude, they didn't need much propellant. Once a target was designated, GPS guidance would send the missiles into the correct area, usually to within twenty meters. The UAV operator kept the crosshair on the target, painting it with the laser target designator. When a missile was coming down its seeker head locked on that reflected laser energy, and its fins steered it to the exact impact point. Now the 30mm rockets were entering active service, saving the government money by conserving the larger and much more expensive missiles. "They follow the laser just like the old model Hellfires, right?" asked Bullard.

"Every damn time. Only a pound of explosive. Cuts 'em in half. Much better than the Hellfires or Vipers on exposed insurgents. We can use the thirties a lot closer to structures and friendlies. We used a thirty millimeter on this guy because he was over the line."

"Over which line?"

"Northern Mississippi, but inside the buffer zone. Practically on the state line, actually."

"Aren't you supposed to run that by my office? We don't want to get General Mirabeau in an uproar. We need his cooperation down there."

"There wasn't time. It was take the shot or let him go. The UAV was almost out of fuel, and nothing else was close enough to pick up the coverage. He was in the buffer zone anyway."

"Fine, just use your discretion. Look, let's skip the rest of the review. Everybody else, why don't you go out for a break? Smokes, whatever. Take ten, okay?" When the room was clear except for Bullard and the senior UAV tech, he said, "Harry, I've got a special mission for you today. Here are the coordinates." Bullard handed him a scrap of paper with the GPS numbers recorded on his visit to Colonel Jibek's estate a day earlier.

Harry sat at an adjoining monitor and entered the digits on his keyboard. "Clark County. Let's see what we've got up that's nearby. Okay, we've got an armed Predator. The easiest way would be to just drop a thirty on him."

"Listen, I don't want to drop a missile on this target, not even a thirty millimeter. Do you have a SniperHawk available?" Bullard already knew that one was available. He'd personally been down to the "bird farm" a mile away, where the UAVs were launched and recovered, and had ordered one sent up. The small and stealthy SniperHawk had to be used together with a Predator, using the bigger drone as its data link and main visual reference provider.

"Oh, going for plausible deniability, are we?" Harry raised a conspiratorial eyebrow and winked. Harry had worked with Bullard on special projects in the past.

"Something like that." If the Kazaks blamed an insurgent firing a long-range sniper rifle for the death of their commander, their hatred for the locals would intensify, which was a good thing. On the other hand, a missile dropping down from the sky and taking out Colonel Jibek would lead their suspicions elsewhere.

"You're in luck—we've got a SniperHawk just a few minutes away. Sounds like you've already got a target in mind, am I right?"

Bullard handed him a photograph of Colonel Yerzhan Jibek, a portrait from the chest up, wearing a Russian-style uniform tunic with medals. "This guy. He's not working out quite as well as we'd like."

"Oh, I see—we're going to have a kinetic change-of-command ceremony. Got it. Any idea where we're going to find him?" Jibek's confiscated equestrian estate came into view on the flat-screen video monitor, in full color and rich detail, as the Predator UAV steered itself over to Bullard's coordinates.

"He's usually riding a horse this time of morning," offered Bullard. "A white stallion."

"Well then, let's start over at the stables." Harry steered the camera, and in a few minutes of searching he found a mounted party. He zoomed in the camera until the men were vaguely recognizable.

"That's him, in the middle. With the mustache and the brown beret."

"How do you want to do this?"

"Well, you can just shoot him, can't you?"

"Right now?" asked the senior UAV tech.

"That's what I'm here for."

"Kind of unusual, taking out one of our loyal allies from the People's Republic of Kazakhstan."

"I wouldn't exactly say he was so loyal," replied Bullard.

"Hey, it's your call, chief. Okay, here's how we'll do it. I'll line the SniperHawk up for a straight glide-in, right at his back. As long as he doesn't turn too much, this should work just fine."

"They won't hear the drone?"

"A SniperHawk? Hell no. No way. Silent but deadly—that's our motto. I'll bring her in low and just pop her up for the shot. They'll never see it or hear it." Harry cracked his knuckles and went back to his keyboard while staring at the screen. "Okay, watch a pro at work, see how it's done. We'll use both screens: this one is the Predator, this one is the SniperHawk. This'll take a minute to sync up. Okay, I'm cutting the Hawk's engine now, and arming the rifle."

"What's that thing shoot?" Bullard already knew; he was just testing Harry's level of knowledge.

"What caliber? It's a special round, very fast. A 6.5 millimeter. Fully suppressed, so there's nothing but sonic crack, and that doesn't give a directional reference. Okay, here we go, just watch your man on the horse." Harry used his track ball to put a white crosshair on Colonel Jibek's back. "Fully stabilized. Once I designate the aim point, it'll lock on and fly the bird. There, it's done. You want the honors? Just push this button here when the crosshair is where you want it."

"Sure thing. This is great." Bullard leaned across and pushed a red button on its own small keyboard. A second later he was rewarded with the image of Jibek slumping forward and sliding from his horse to the ground. Around him, the other horsemen wheeled and reared their mounts.

"Okay, I'll take her back around now. Nice shot, chief."

The director of rural pacification chuckled. "Yeah, I'm a natural."

Lieutenant Colonel Foley returned for another visit on Friday after lunch. Phil Carson met him outside the tent this time. Carson had been exercising, jogging around the dozen tents in his section of the quarantine center, trying to get into shape for a possible escape. Once again Foley was wearing his unpressed camouflage uniform, with his beret worn like a rag and his hair over his ears. Like many military doctors, he lacked any semblance of military bearing, and looked anything but sharp. Carson attributed this sloppiness to the doctor being drafted into the Army for a second hitch, only this time four decades later, at retirement age.

The weather was unseasonably warm, in the low seventies. Carson had rolled up the tent's back wall. The doctor brought a promising-looking brown paper bag. They entered the tent together without exchanging greetings, and Foley sat down at the white plastic table. He removed his beret and dropped it on his lap, then ran his fingers through his gray hair. He gestured to the other chair, and Carson took a seat opposite him. Carson was wearing cutoff shorts, sneakers and a tan T-shirt with the logo of a bait company on the front. The three T-shirts Carson had packed from the catamaran were chosen to be disguises of one type or another, including a commercial fisherman with amnesia.

"Good afternoon, *John Doe*. I brought you some snacks." Foley opened the bag and pushed a can of Coke across the table. "There's some cookies in there too."

"Thanks, doctor, I appreciate it." It was the first can of pop Phil Carson had seen since the catamaran was halfway up the Caribbean, when their stock of sodas had run out. There should have been plenty for the entire voyage from Brazil, but Paulo had been sneaking extras on his watch. He imagined that soft drinks must be quite precious in Mississippi under the present conditions. In the quarantine camp, all he'd had to drink was tepid water that smelled of sulfur, and weak Kool-Aid. The Coke was a rarity, something that was not grown or produced locally.

"Are they treating you all right?" asked the doctor, removing his wire-rimmed glasses and wiping them off with a cloth from his pocket.

"I suppose. I hardly ever see anybody, except when they bring the food around."

"You're getting enough?"

"Peanut butter sandwiches? Yeah, great protein—I'm not complaining. So what brings you around today?"

"Well, I was hoping maybe there was some improvement in your condition. Your head injury looks fine. The wound is closing, and the swelling is gone. Definitely no infection. Any more headaches?"

"Some, but not as bad as before."

"How's the memory, any change?"

Carson had to measure his words carefully; a slip before a trained medical professional might betray his false amnesia. "Well, I'm getting some flashbacks now and then, but it's mostly old stuff. I think it's from when I was a young man. I'm fairly sure I was in the Army. Maybe I'm just mixed up—maybe I just saw too many war movies—but I think I was in Vietnam. Sometimes I think I was in the Special Forces. It's all kind of floating around in my head. Maybe I'm just getting confused by being on this Army base. Maybe I'm just inventing false memories, I don't know. Nowadays practically everybody around here is wearing a beret, but for some reason I think I used to wear one too, way back when. Most soldiers didn't used to wear berets, did they?"

"No, only the elite units. Personally, I hate the things; we have to wear them in garrison. Off base, we can usually wear patrol caps, depending on what we're doing. So, is anything more recent coming back? Any places where you might have been, any faces of family members?"

"No, it's all pretty vague, kind of swirling around."

"Hmmm…okay. Well, I'll leave you a pen and paper; a notepad. When you remember things, anything, write them down. That'll help get your thoughts organized."

"Thanks."

"You mentioned 'Nam," said the doctor. "You know, I did a tour over there, in '69. As an enlisted man—college and medical school didn't come until later. I wound up as a Huey door gunner. Not something I'll ever forget, I can tell you that. We hauled Special Forces around sometimes…doing insertions and extractions, medevacs. You must have taken quite a whack to the noggin to knock *those* memories out of your head. Too bad I can't send you out for an MRI or a CT scan."

"Don't worry about it." Carson took another grateful sip of his tepid cola, eyeing the doctor. The flavor was off; it didn't taste like a real Coke.

"Hey, there's another reason I'm hoping you get your memory back."

Now we're getting to it, thought Carson.

"It's no big deal, but…I was sort of hoping you'd remember where you came by the coffee. Maybe there's more where that jar came from." Doctor Foley locked his eyes on Carson, and the stare was reciprocated.

"Doc, I'm not sure of anything. I just remember stumbling around in wreckage that went on forever. It's almost like I was *born* there, somehow. I couldn't remember anything before it."

The doctor paused, subtly casting doubt on Carson's story. "Do you think the coffee was already there? On the land, I mean. Like you just happened to find it out there somewhere? Or if you were shipwrecked in the hurricane, maybe it was on your ship, or on your boat? You have a sailor's hands, and better muscle tone than most men our age. Could you have been on a fishing boat?"

"I guess it's possible. Maybe it'll come back to me."

"Well, if it did come back to you, that'd be a good thing. Let me tell you, I wouldn't mind getting my hands on some real coffee of my own. I only managed to snag a few cups from what my medics took from you. It's already gone."

"I'm sorry I can't help you out."

The doctor stared heavily at him across the white plastic table. Carson wondered if he believed the amnesia story at all.

"Well," continued the doctor, "just FYI, real coffee is worth serious money these days. Coffee doesn't grow anywhere in the emergency zone. It has to be imported, and, well—it's not. At least not that I've seen. Not in Mississippi anyway."

Carson smiled inwardly while maintaining a poker face. "The emergency zone? What's that?"

"Most of the Southeast. Eastern Louisiana and Mississippi, over to Georgia and South Carolina, and the top part of Florida. We're under martial law. That's how I got drafted…again."

"Martial law? When did that happen?"

"After the hurricanes. A year and a half ago. Two in July, one after the other. Then a real monster hit in October—a category five. Matilda, the mother of all hurricanes. Hundred-and-ninety-mile-an-hour sustained winds. The whole country was already in a depression, and those hurricanes just broke our backs down here on the Gulf. Especially Matilda. She dumped twenty inches of rain on most of the South in one day. Floods like you would not believe. And practically nothing came from FEMA or the federal government. We were on our own."

"What about the hurricane last week?" asked Carson.

"Ricardo? Oh, that one was just a baby. Hardly a hurricane at all, just a December freak. Anyway, October a year ago we got hit by Matilda. Hooked in across Louisiana and zigzagged right along the Gulf Coast. 'Waltzing Matilda,' they called her. Took out most of our reconstruction, what we'd managed to put back together after the two July hurricanes. Then six weeks after Matilda, that's when the Memphis quake hit. You don't remember hearing anything about the quake? Nothing?" The doctor was wide-eyed, incredulous at Carson's flat affect.

"No, nothing, I can't remember anything about a quake," Carson lied. He'd heard about it on shortwave radio news broadcasts, and from individual ham radios he was occasionally in contact with. There was a high percentage of propaganda and rumor on the official and unofficial radio news, but he'd heard about the devastating quakes that followed the killer hurricanes.

Doctor Foley eyed him doubtfully while sipping his own cola. "Memphis got hit by a Richter eight on December the 15th a year back. The aftershocks went on for weeks, and there was another big one in January. That was just about the worst part. The aftershocks kept everybody living outside in the rain and cold. Memphis just about got flattened. Nashville and St. Louis were slammed hard too. The whole Mississippi Valley, really, but Memphis was the worst. It was practically cut off from the world. Most of the bridges went down. Barges couldn't move because the bridge wreckage blocked the rivers. Coal and grain couldn't move on the rivers, and the highways were cut all over the place too. Bridges, over-passes...they all went down."

"All of the bridges?"

"I'm not sure how many, but enough to stop just about anything from moving." The doctor smiled wistfully. "Railroads too: they got all twisted up. And pipelines. Most of the pipelines that took natural gas from the Gulf up to the Northeast got taken out, right in the middle of the winter."

"Damn..." Carson had never heard these details before.

"Then without the coal barges on the rivers, most of the power plants shut down—the ones that weren't already knocked out by the quake. So people froze, and *more* power plants went down, one after the other. It was like dominoes, a chain reaction. The quake came right after Matilda, so it stopped the hurricane relief effort...what little there was anyway. The South was written off by Washington. Triage, I guess. Then after the second big quake, everything just spiraled out of control. Religious folks called it God's judgment. The people in Memphis went crazy. It was like a race war up there when the power went out and there was no more food coming in. They were starving in no time, but where could the refugees from Memphis go?

"We sure couldn't take them here in Mississippi...we already had enough of our own problems. So we kept them out: we held the line. We could do it, since the state National Guard was already in control down here after Matilda. The refugees couldn't cross the Mississippi River either, not with the bridges down, and Arkansas wouldn't take them any-way. Arkansas was almost as bad off as Memphis was, so they couldn't help even if they wanted to. We were on our own. One problem just fed off the other, it was a cascade of disasters. Anyway, that's what happened. But I'll tell you what—martial law beats what we had before it. Beats it by a mile."

"And that's why coffee is so hard to come by a year later? Martial law?"

"That's part of it."

"What's the other part?"

"Well, the economy is a wreck. And not just because of the hurri-canes and the earthquakes. We were already in a depression before them. The disasters just put the final nails in the coffin. Here's how it goes now. Things like coffee can only be sold for an official price that's set by the government, plus a percentage for 'reasonable profit.' That probably comes to something like fifty bucks for a two-pound can of coffee, except I haven't seen any coffee being sold for months. I'm just guessing."

"Why would they do that? Price controls never work."

"It was to be *fair*, so that everyone could afford things, right? Everybody was against hoarding and gouging. Maybe right after the hurricanes and the earthquake, maybe it made sense, for a while. But the price controls never went away, since we're still in a state of emergency. So now, a year later, who's going to sell coffee or anything else for the official price? Nobody. And who's going to bother to import it if they can only sell it at a dead loss? Nobody. That's why we've got no coffee. The government tried to fix the economy and make it fair for everybody, but instead they just about totally wrecked what was left of it. Plus, coffee comes from South America, and they won't sell it for New Dollars."

Carson knew most of this perfectly well; it was the very reason for his latest smuggling venture. He had planned to sell the coffee for a 400 percent profit in East Texas, where there was no martial law and no price controls. He paused, and asked the doctor, "So...what if somebody could get coffee, let's just say. What would it be worth...unofficially?"

"Hell, I don't know. Maybe five or ten times the official price. But that would be illegal, because of the maximum laws. You can only sell for the maximum price that's set by the emergency government. Price controls, like you said. They have an entire new branch of government now called the OPA, the Office of Price Administration."

"So, what happens if somebody had something like coffee and he tried to sell it for more than the official maximum price?"

"Oh, he'd be in a world of trouble. They'd get him for price gouging, profiteering, black-marketing, hoarding, illegal importation...you name it."

"Are these price controls only here in the South?"

"It started here, but now the government sets all the prices, even up North." The doctor smiled. "They say it's the only way they can make the economy *fair* for everybody. Share the wealth. Share and share alike." Then he muttered, "Idiots..."

"But the situation in Mississippi is getting better, though. Right? I mean, 80 percent of the state has electrical power now."

"Who told you that? Oh—you saw the billboards. That's just propaganda. Feel-good stuff for the unwashed masses. And I do mean unwashed—there's almost no soap. Eighty percent with electricity? That's a joke. Less than half of the state has power connected at all. If you live in the boonies, forget it. Even the towns that have a power connection only get it six or maybe eight hours a day—and that's on a good day. They have to keep rolling the power around. Rolling blackouts."

"What about backup generators?" asked Carson.

"Sure, they work, but who has gas? There's no fuel—well, hardly any. Gas is rationed. For civilians it's $59 a gallon at the official rate. But even with ration cards, it's almost impossible to find. You have to park your car in a line a mile long and wait just about forever. And when the line moves, you have to be there, ready to move. It eats up all your time trying to get gas. It's a Catch-22."

"Where's the gas coming from, when it comes?"

"From Louisiana and Texas, and some from Venezuela and Mexico," answered the doctor. "But there's barely enough fuel for the Guard, much less for civilians."

"On my way here I saw a lot of people walking, and some people were even riding horses."

"Yeah, that's how it is these days. Back to the future."

Carson gave him a slightly conspiratorial look. "Come on, a doctor must be able to make some extra money...on the side. Maybe do some trading for medical services rendered, right? You're telling me you can't get gasoline?"

Foley laughed. "You're dreaming. The flip side of price controls is wage controls. An Army doctor doesn't make much, that's for sure, but I can't take money for working on the side. Not a single dollar. That's against the law—that's a *big* no-no. Health care is all rationed by the government—to make it fair. Fair!"

"What about gold?"

"Gold? You mean, would I accept gold for private medical care? Well, first, it's illegal to own gold, unless it's a ring on your finger, and second, if you tried to buy anything with it, they'd hang you. Literally. If anybody offered me gold, I'd think it was a setup, a sting operation. Then I'd have to report it, just in case it was a sting. If I didn't report it and it was a setup, well, they'd get me for that. You're screwed either way."

Carson paused to let this sink in, and then said quietly, "I saw a man hanged from a telephone pole, back on the highway on my way here. He had a sign that said 'counterfeiter' on his chest."

"Yeah, the emergency tribunals are tough. They're run by the Public Safety Commission, and they don't mess around. Economic crimes like counterfeiting will get you hanged fast. They call it 'economic sabotage,' and that's a hanging crime these days. Black-marketing, hoarding, price gouging, buying or selling with gold or silver, counterfeiting: they say all of that threatens the economic recovery. The only way the government can fix the economy is if everybody uses the TEDs, and only the TEDs. 'Everybody has to play on the same level field,' that's the new mantra. And when they say everybody has to play on the same field, they're not joking. You either play on their field, or they'll hang your ass above the field from the nearest tree. And that means you use the TEDs and you pay the official prices."

"TEDs?" asked Carson.

The doctor pulled out his worn leather wallet, extracted a $500 note, and held it up. It was bright red, with an engraved likeness of John F.

Kennedy. "These are TEDs. Temporary Emergency Dollars. Theoretically, they're going to be exchangeable at one-to-one for North American Dollars, but you have to get special permission to convert them to NADs. You can't take the TEDs outside the e-zone. It's supposed to help the recovery and eliminate speculation and black-marketing. Of course, that's all bullshit, like everything else they say."

"I'm surprised they're still using paper money at all. What about credit cards, money cards, digital dollars, electronic money?"

Doctor Foley shook his head. "They're still around some, but not too many places use them. The electric power is too unreliable. When it goes out, electronic transactions get screwed up like you wouldn't believe. You see, the phone system is all shot to hell, and the internet is maybe 50-50 at best, even if you have power and the phones are operating. Which they never are, at least not all at the same time. So when you have a credit card problem, getting it straightened out is just about impossible. Most people just use the TEDs now. They're paper. They don't need electric power, or phone lines."

"What about paying bills, like mortgages and credit cards?"

"It's so messed up, you wouldn't believe it. Lots of folks just don't pay them. What can the banks do, foreclose on everybody's house at once? But they couldn't anyway, because the federal government put in 'temporary' mortgage relief, and it's still going. The banks were nationalized, and then they froze everything in place. They halted payments and collections. If you're a landlord, you're shit out of luck. It's a real can of worms; nobody knows how they're going to untangle it all. First, they need to get the power back on all the time, and the phone system too."

"The power grid is that shaky, huh?"

"Like you wouldn't believe. Every big storm, we practically have to start over. Half of Camp Shelton is still out just from last week's little Category One. Forget the twentieth century, sometimes it feels like we've gone back to the nineteenth. I've done surgery by candlelight so often…"

"Doesn't the base have emergency generators?"

"Sure, and they work—when there's fuel. But there's never enough, and they need it to run truck convoys. If they used it just to power the military bases it might be enough, but then the Guard would lose control of the rest of the e-zone again. Food convoys and security patrols are the top priority. If we don't show the flag out in the sticks, law and order breaks down in no time. Fuel and electric power are still our biggest problems."

Carson paused, appearing to mull over this information. Then he quietly offered, "What about solar panels? Aren't there any solar panels?"

"Not enough. They're the best: completely quiet, and they don't need gas. If you used your own gasoline or diesel generator at home, you'd be reported by a jealous neighbor in about five seconds. If you couldn't show the proper gasoline ration card stubs, you'd be in deep, deep trouble."

"Even a lieutenant colonel like you?"

"Even a full bird colonel. General Mirabeau has had colonels hanged for black-marketing. He's big on making examples. He's a real hard case when it comes to corruption, I'll say that for him. He can't put soap or coffee on the shelves or gas in our cars, but by God, at least we're all equal!" The doctor looked around nervously after this outburst. "Equally poor," he mumbled.

"Who's General Mirabeau?" Carson guessed he was the stern Creole face on the roadside billboards.

"You're kidding, right? No, I don't suppose you are." The doctor spoke quietly. "Lieutenant General Marcus Aurelius Mirabeau, the Savior of the South. He who restores the power, feeds the starving and smites the lawless. As we used to say, he's the head mo-fo in charge. The big boss man of the Southland, all the way across the e-zone from Louisiana to South Carolina. He's the final authority down here next to God almighty—who is a Baptist, in case you didn't know. Mirabeau keeps his main headquarters where he's most comfortable, at Fort Benning, Georgia, but he travels all the time. He can pop up anywhere, and his wrath is legend. His word is law, expressed through the Public Safety Commission and the tribunals."

Carson slowly shook his head. "This doesn't sound like America."

"Tell me about it. Maybe you're lucky you lost your memory."

"So anyway, just hypothetically…what would a solar panel be worth around here? A big one, say…120 watts." Carson indicated the two-by-four-foot size of his panels with his hands. He knew he was taking a chance, being so up front about the panels, but he needed to get something moving. He needed a contact on the outside to work a trade with, and for now, Foley was the only game in town.

The doctor whistled an exhalation. "Something that big will charge golf cart batteries, or a bunch of car batteries wired together. Then you'd get quiet, secret electrical power from the batteries around the clock. You could run computers all the time, have some reading lights all night—and run shortwave radios at night, when they work better. Solar panels would be worth a hell of a lot of TEDs, I can tell you that. A boatload of money. But nobody could sell them without government permission, that's the problem. You'd need import licenses, and you could only sell them for the official maximum, whatever that would be, so what's the point? It'd be a huge hassle if you did it legally, and it probably wouldn't pay. Remember, in the e-zone we're guaranteed never to be price-gouged or overcharged. That's the theory. In practice, it means we just can't get a lot of things.

Sugar, vegetables, milk—stuff we produce locally—that we have, thank God. Coffee, razors, new shoes, solar panels? Forget it."

"Doctor Foley…"

"Please, call me Ken. We're the same age. The doctor thing gets old. Like us."

"Ken…I can't believe what I'm hearing. You and I, we fought the communists in Vietnam. Now look at us…" Carson stopped himself short. He'd let his mask of false amnesia slip, but the doctor appeared not to notice.

"I know, it's terrible. But what can I do, what can anybody do? It's martial law, so it's all a military situation…and here I am, right back in the military. You can't say no—orders are orders! But it's better now than it was last year. Imagine six straight months with no electric power, none, I mean zero! And not a drop of gasoline. Mississippi was going back to the Stone Age. We were living like savages, drinking dirty water, afraid to leave our houses because of the looters and cutthroats. Never mind Cameroon fever and the avian flu: plain old cholera and typhoid killed thousands. Let me tell you, after living through anarchy, starvation and epidemics, martial law is a big step up. A *big* step up! As bad as it is now, it's better than it was. General Mirabeau…he's a hard-ass, but at least he's gotten control. It's harsh, but it's getting better. We're organized now. If he hadn't kept the Tennessee refugees out after the earthquake, I don't know what would have happened. Once we're on our feet again, they'll end the martial law and lift the wage and price controls and drop the travel restrictions. We'll have elections again in two years, they say—"

"Ken, listen to yourself! I mean, is this really America? Temporary Emergency Dollars, curfews, martial law, hanging people from telephone poles for counterfeiting? You have price controls but nothing to buy. And everybody is wearing an ID badge, what's up with that? How long has that been going on?"

"Hey, the badges are for a damn good reason! You'd know why if you remembered the epidemics. Once people are vaccinated, the badges are the only way to keep track of who's safe."

"But why does everybody have to wear them?"

"It's just easier that way. They can be seen from a safe distance."

"Well, the people I saw looked like prisoners in a big outdoor penitentiary."

"Look, I don't like it either. But the Supreme Court ruled that people don't have an expectation of privacy in public places. The badges are necessary to prevent the spread of disease, and to control the criminal element. It was the only way—"

"Doc, Ken, do you hear what you're saying? We fought the communists in 'Nam, we fought them in the Cold War, we beat the Soviet

Union, and now look at us! I'm sorry, but it just seems like…well…like communism to me."

The doctor coolly regarded Carson through his wire-rimmed glasses. "Communism? Maybe so. I mean, I guess you have a point to a certain extent, but what else could they do? There was no other way to get control and restore order, not when people were starving. And it's all legal, so there's no use opposing it."

"It's all legal? Making everybody wear badges, like convicts? Assigning people to jobs and making them work for bullshit Temporary Emergency Dollars?"

"The Supreme Court has already ruled it's all constitutional, right down the line. Under the Economic Justice and Democracy Amendment, the federal government can pass any laws it deems necessary to assure an 'equitable distribution of the wealth of the nation.' That's what it says, right in the EJDA. And with martial law in the e-zone, it even goes beyond that, because people were starving, people were dying! The government had to be given emergency powers; there was no other way. So yes, it might seem like communism to you, but honest to God, it's a lot better than it was before."

"I still can't believe we've come to this in America! I can't believe people don't fight it."

"Fight it?" The doctor seemed to take offense at this challenge to the courage of Southerners, and he rose from his chair, bumping the cheap table. "Fighting it won't put food on your family's table! I don't know where you were the last couple of years, but around here, people were starving to death, right here in Mississippi, in the USA! Look around you, this camp is down to only twelve of these big tents now, from sixty-four. Our daily census is down from over a thousand, to only you and that black family over there. A year ago we were losing a hundred a day, in this very camp! We lost more than half of the medical staff, most of my colleagues, including a lot of old friends, and including my only son and most of his family. I can take you to see the mass graves! So please don't tell me about fighting it—we *did* fight it! We're *still* fighting it. Cameroon fever, bird flu, cholera, dysentery, beriberi…you name it, we fought it. We even lost thousands to pellagra. Pellagra! Do you even know what that is?" He dropped back into his plastic chair.

"That's, um, from a vitamin deficiency?"

"Right, no niacin, which you get from protein. We had pellagra beat in the South after the Great Depression, and now it's back. It brings the four Ds: diarrhea, dermatitis, dementia and death—just from a lack of niacin, because of a shitty starvation diet with no protein. We were right back to square one, we went back a century in medicine, but now we're turning the corner—and with almost no help from the federal government,

I might add! So we did what we had to do to survive. We have nothing to be ashamed of, nothing." The doctor was red-faced with emotion, and out of breath.

Carson was reduced to temporary silence, and then said in a hush, "Listen, I'm sorry, I really didn't know how bad it was here." And this was true. Carson didn't know. He knew the vague outlines, but he had not heard the dire details. After hearing Doctor Foley's description of life under martial law, he understood how news reports from the Southeastern emergency zone could be tightly controlled. With the electricity out and travel restrictions in place, this would not have been hard to accomplish.

The doctor added, "I guess you'd have to remember living through the last couple of years to really understand just how bad it was. Or maybe it's part of the reason for your amnesia. I know we've seen PTSD like you can't imagine. Post-traumatic stress. We have thousands of young orphans. Sometimes they just don't talk, not a word. Shocked into silence. Catatonic. People commit suicide, people just plain give up. And not a few—thousands. People can't adjust to living without electricity, to living poor, dirt poor. Being hungry all the time, with no end in sight. And where they're putting the elderly is just a disgrace—it's a wonder they don't *all* kill themselves. Nobody gives a *damn* about the elderly anymore, *nobody*.

"That's why I don't mind working again. *Nothing* is worse than being old and unemployed these days—nothing. These days, if you can't work, you don't eat. Society has just...*changed*. In some ways, the psychological impact has been worse than the physical, and it's all tied together in tight little vicious circles. Here's just one: a bad diet leads to pellagra, and that causes dementia. So whole villages wander around like idiots, starving, killing each other over *nothing*. People would fight over a shovel to dig a well, and then kill each other with the shovel! So we might not eat too well these days, we might not have coffee or bananas or new shoes, but at least we're not starving anymore. Little kids aren't drinking water from ditches and dying from cholera. And one more thing: at least the Mississippi National Guard is *us*. I mean, it's our own. General Mirabeau is one of us, he understands us. Not like up in Tennessee and Kentucky and some other places."

"What's going on up there?"

"You really don't know? You're not just putting me on?"

"No."

"Well, after the quakes it was too crazy up there, too wild for their National Guard to handle. Everything just fell apart after all the bridges went down and the power went out for good. In most of Tennessee and Kentucky, the Guard wasn't...reliable. It didn't respond to federal authority. The Guardsmen just went home, or never reported for duty.

The chain of command collapsed. There was something like an eighty percent desertion rate in the Tennessee Guard. Almost nobody reported for duty. Police? Gone. There was no General Mirabeau in charge up there, that's for sure. The president had to ask for help…outside help. He had to bring in outsiders—there was no other solution. Foreign troops, foreign volunteers. Six months after he signed the new U.N. global security pact, he's bringing in foreign soldiers…"

"What about other U.S. troops?" asked Carson. He'd heard rumors of so-called foreign peacekeepers, but it still seemed implausible. "What about the Regular Army?"

"They tried, but it didn't work. Americans couldn't do the job, they wouldn't…"

"Wouldn't fire on fellow Americans?"

"That's right. That was a part of it. They couldn't do what had to be done. So they needed fresh soldiers from outside. Motivated soldiers, who could go in there and sort things out, really knock heads. Shoot people. Most of them are in the North American Legion, the NAL. Mexicans, Salvadorans…men that used to be illegal aliens. It's all so confusing. With this North American Union crap coming down, I don't really understand what's going on up there. From what I hear, they're none too gentle, those NAL troops. And they sure don't get along too well with the native Tennesseans, I know that much. They're getting paid with land, homestead grants, so you know that's not going down easy. God, Tennessee is a mess! So, no matter how bad it is in Mississippi, at least we know we're being taken care of by our own. Sure, it's rough, but we're handling it on our own, in our own way. If we lost control, like up in Tennessee…well, then, I think we'd find out how bad it could really get."

"Foreign soldiers on American soil," said Carson, shaking his head. "I never thought I'd live to see the day."

The doctor continued. "Foreign troops…you'd think that's about as bad as it can get. But you know, there's one thing worse: anarchy. Up around Memphis, you can't believe how bad it was after the quake. Mass murder, mass suicide…from what I hear, just about an all-out race war. Thousands of people froze to death up there last winter. There was starvation, and with lots of frozen bodies, there was even *cannibalism*. And not just a little of it, here and there. It was common. They even had a name for human meat: 'long pig.' That's how desperate people were, after a month with no food, no clean water, no electricity, no gas and no heating oil. When people are starving to death, when they figure out that the government can't wave a magic wand and save them, they turn into animals. Wild animals, savages. I've seen it—it happened in Mississippi too.

"But it got so out of control in Tennessee that even when the government could finally bring the supply convoys in, they were attacked and looted before they could get the food distributed. My God, it was a hundred times worse than after Katrina in New Orleans. It was even worse than after Matilda down here. Inviting in the foreign troops was the only option the president had left. Well, if you count the North American Legion as foreign. We're all supposed to be one country pretty soon, so maybe the Mexicans aren't really foreign anymore. It's pretty confusing." The doctor scratched his head, looking down, bewildered. "Well anyway, they needed troops to guard the relief convoys, they needed troops for everything. Troops who wouldn't balk at shooting native-born Americans. At least here in Mississippi, martial law is run by Americans, and it's only temporary."

Carson replied in a subdued manner. "Well, now I guess I understand what you've been through down here, I really do. But it's still not anywhere I want to live. I'd rather not stick around and find out how temporary the martial law is going to be."

"I don't see how that's up to you. Until we find out who you are, you'll be staying right here. And after that, you'll probably be assigned to a work crew."

"What if my memory doesn't come back?"

"Then eventually you'll be classified and assigned to a work brigade. Everybody works for his food in the emergency zone. Nobody rides for free. No work book, no ration cards. No ration cards, no food."

"I'd have no choice in the matter? About leaving, I mean."

"None that I can see. Unless..."

"Unless what?"

"Well, unless maybe your memory just happened to come back." The doctor walked over to the open side of the tent, looked around outside, then continued in a softer voice. "Let's say you remembered where you found that coffee, and then you remembered where you might just find some more. That would go a long way to getting a positive disposition of your case. If it was handled...carefully. Privately. I mean, if it was a significant amount of coffee, the right people might be more...favorably disposed toward your case. So you see, 'John Doe,' a lot depends on your memory."

"Do you think I'll get my memory back? I'm already remembering some things more clearly, like Vietnam."

"That's a good sign. Now see if you can remember things that are more up to date. Keep in mind, I'm your doctor." He smiled. "If you can't trust me, who can you trust? We were both in 'Nam, and you know, we're sure not getting any younger."

"No, we're not," Carson agreed.

"I can hold you here for two weeks without raising any eyebrows. That's the standard quarantine period these days. After that, some flags will go up. Then it'll get tougher for you, a lot tougher. Pretty soon some other officers will come around, asking hard questions. Some officers who might not believe in amnesia, let's say. So if your memory is going to get better, maybe it had better happen sooner rather than later. Before you're standing in front of a military tribunal."

"I'll remember that, Ken."

"I hope you do. I won't be around again until early next week. Try to stay out of trouble here in fun city until I'm back." Lieutenant Colonel Foley rose from his plastic chair, put on and adjusted his black beret. "I always hated these damned fuzzy things. A little round blanket for a hat? Like a Frenchman? It's sure not my style. They soak up the rain, and they don't even keep the sun out of your eyes. Berets are about the most useless damn thing the Army ever issued, especially in the South."

"Well, the berets used to mean something," replied Carson. He thought that the doctor might have been trying to provoke a visible reaction, indirectly ribbing him about his possible past service with the Special Forces. "At least, I remember that the green ones did. Back in the old days."

"Yes, they sure did," said the doctor. "Here, keep this pencil and paper and work on your memory. Jot down those fleeting thoughts, and try to organize them. That'll help a lot."

"Thanks."

"And a word to the wise: time is not on your side, John Doe.

4

Lieutenant General Marcus Aurelius Mirabeau flew into Fort Campbell
on his own Blackhawk helicopter, escorted by an Apache gunship. The
sprawling Army base straddled the Kentucky-Tennessee border, just east
of the Tennessee and Cumberland rivers. Bob Bullard had requested this
Friday meeting, but it was not a command performance. Mirabeau came
only because it suited his purposes; he was not under Bullard's control. Or
under the control of anyone in the federal government, for that matter. As
a courtesy, Bullard had sent two Suburbans and two pickup trucks to the
landing zone, for the general and his staff and bodyguard detail.

The meeting took place after their luncheon on the patio deck outside
the base golf course's clubhouse. The entire golf course had been cleared
of players for the day to accommodate the meeting. Bullard thought that
General Mirabeau looked like a young Harry Belafonte, the popular singer
of calypso songs in the 1950s. He looked very sharp in his starched camouflage uniform, polished jump boots and perfectly set black beret.

It was warm, over sixty degrees, but the officers and soldiers accompanying the general wore their camouflage uniforms with their sleeves
rolled down, exactly matching the way the general wore his. Each wore
his beret at the same angle, just touching the right eyebrow and ear.
Bullard smiled at what a flock of ass-kissing clones they were. Only their
skin tones varied, running across the racial spectrum.

Bullard, as usual, wore his unofficial field uniform of generic khaki
pants and a matching long-sleeved shirt. After lunch, General Mirabeau
suggested a private ride on a golf cart, to which Bullard readily agreed. A
meeting room in the "19th Hole" clubhouse had been prepared, but Bullard
could well understand that the general would not want to be covertly
filmed and recorded. Mirabeau selected one of the carts at random and slid
behind the wheel, leaving Bullard in the passenger seat. Their bodyguards
fit into a half-dozen more carts, and followed their bosses down the fair-
ways at a respectful distance.

On a cinder path in a small hollow between fern-covered banks they
came upon a cement bench, and Mirabeau stopped. The two leaders left
the golf cart to sit in the shade beneath willow trees, facing a brook. Very
importantly, they were in cover, out of the line of sight of any distant
sniper, a consideration even within the protection of the surrounding miles
of Army base. Both men took such precautions instinctively.

"Beautiful day for late December, just beautiful. Thanks for inviting
me up. We flew up the Tennessee River the last part—that was my first

good look at it since the earthquakes. Kentucky Lake is gone…it's amazing to see. Just the old river running down the middle of a mud valley. Any idea when the dams will be fixed?"

"If it's even being discussed, I haven't heard about it."

"Well, Fort Campbell looks the same as ever. I spent a few years here as a junior officer, and I've visited many times over the years. I'd imagine you can almost forget the state of emergency here. Do you golf? What's your handicap?" They sat on opposite ends of the six-foot bench.

"No, I don't golf, but I like getting out here. Nature, and all that good shit. My house isn't far from here." Bullard leaned back and stuck his legs out, feet crossed at the ankles. He was wearing low-cut leather hiking shoes. "Listen, General, you didn't fly all the way up here for small talk—if you don't mind, I'm going to get right to business. First of all, I'm having serious problems feeding our FEMA relocation camps. Your deliveries have been dropping off for weeks. If you can't supply the amount of food that was agreed upon, well, then we won't be able to keep all of these folks in Kentucky and Tennessee. We'll have to turn them loose, and you know where they'll be heading: south. If we can't bring the food to them, then they're going to go to where the food is. It's as simple as that."

"Well, Bob, you might let them walk out of the FEMA camps. That's Tennessee, so that's your call. But that doesn't mean they're going to just stroll on down into Mississippi and Alabama. There'll be no refugee camps waiting for them. No food, no medical, nothing. I won't allow your refugees into my states, and that's non-negotiable. We have our own problems, plenty of them." Mirabeau coughed, clearing his throat. "But at least *I* can feed my people—and *I* can control them with my own troops."

"Listen, General, if you're referring to our foreign peacekeepers…all I can say is I don't make policy, I just carry it out. But if a few million hungry refugees from Tennessee come walking down your way, well, it might just lead to a level of chaos your troops couldn't handle. In that case, President Tambor might feel a need to send some fresh foreign peacekeepers down into Mississippi and Alabama, to help restore order."

General Mirabeau smiled. "Help restore order? Do you mean like they've restored order in Tennessee?"

"There's no need for sarcasm, General."

"We have a signed agreement. The president would not—"

"He'll do whatever it takes if you can't keep order in your states. Agreements can and will change, as new circumstances dictate. The president is still the president of *all* of the states. It will be *his* decision. So, what I'm saying is that if you don't want to feed and house a couple million new refugees, you'd better get the rice and pork and beef moving north again—as we agreed on in Mobile." Bullard leaned forward and scooped up a handful of pebbles.

"You can't order blood to come from a turnip. We still have people on the edge of starvation in my states—it's not like we're rolling in milk and honey."

"Well, compared to Tennessee and Kentucky, you are. And if my people don't get fed, I'm going to hand them maps and point them south."

Mirabeau gritted his teeth and said, "We'll do our best. We're between a rock and a hard place as it is."

"We all are." Bullard took careful aim and threw a pebble at a blue jay perched on a branch a dozen feet away, neatly hitting it. The bird squawked and flew off.

"Now I've got an issue of my own," declared the general. "The black markets in the buffer zone are getting out of control. I know we agreed not to make any moves in the buffer areas without consultation, but the free markets are becoming a serious problem. We can't police them effectively. People are beginning to carry guns openly, and they're not just bartering anymore, they're trading with gold and silver and North American Dollars. It's causing a massive devaluation of the Temporary Emergency Dollars, and I just can't tolerate that. The TEDs are shaky enough as it is. Plus, the markets are a magnet for criminals and refugees coming down from Tennessee. I'm just giving you a heads up: I'm planning on a major crackdown on the swap markets, starting at Corinth."

Bullard said, "I understand the problem, but I still want you to hold off for now. The free markets are one of our best sources of actionable intelligence on the resistance in Tennessee. Shut down those free markets and you'll shut down our best source of information."

"How long are you talking about?"

"Just a few months. Summertime, maybe. We'll let you know."

"I don't like it, Director Bullard. Those free markets are trouble: people are getting their backs up. We can't even send the Guard into some of them—they'd be lynched. The local sheriffs in some of those northern counties are getting mighty independent-minded. They put their own deputies around the markets, but they don't stop the illegal activity, they protect it. It's not healthy; it's causing erosion in respect for our authority. We're not ready for free markets yet, not until the economy is stabilized around the TEDs. If we lose control of the currency, if people stop using the TEDs, we'll lose top-down control for good. It'll be anarchy. The food supply chain will break down again, and everything we've worked to rebuild will collapse. God only knows what might happen then. We'll never get the banks functioning again if people are using any damn kind of money that they please."

"Well, it's not up to you. The buffer zones are under shared control, so I'm asking you not to do any sweeps into them without consultation."

Mirabeau stood up and turned, glaring down at Bullard, who was still sitting at the other end of the stone bench. "Bob, that's not what our memorandum of understanding says. I'll take this back to the White House if I have to. The buffer zones are in Mississippi and Alabama, and that's my bailiwick, not yours. You only have approval for hot pursuit of terrorists and fugitives."

Bullard smiled. "General, that's your interpretation. Let me put it another way. If you shut down those free markets, a lot of folks in southern Tennessee are going to be cold and hungry. If they're cold and hungry, they might get a mind to just walk right on through the buffer zone and keep going."

"You keep threatening me with refugees. We've already demonstrated that we know how to stop them—in case you've forgotten what happened after the quakes."

"General, please. I'm not making threats; I'm just stating the reality of the situation. Provide the food in the tonnage we agreed on, and leave the free markets alone. That is, if you don't want a few million extra mouths to feed." Bullard smiled again. "I don't know why we're even discussing it. We already agreed on all of this last October in Mobile."

Mirabeau took a deep breath and exhaled through flaring nostrils. "Okay, we'll hold off on the sweeps for now, and we'll do the best we can with the food shipments. But for my part, I want to be in the loop when you go dropping rockets into the buffer zone. Let me remind you: Mississippi is not Tennessee, and we don't enforce the curfew with rockets in Mississippi."

"Maybe you should."

"And maybe you should just keep your UAVs out of our air space."

"So that terrorists can just wander back and forth? I don't think so. But I take your point. Let's beef up the liaison effort, and we'll get on the horn before we run armed UAV missions on your side of the line. Of course, if we're in hot pursuit, we're going to come in. There won't be any sanctuary states, not while I'm director of rural pacification." Even with the general looming over him, Bullard affected a posture of nonchalance.

"Hot pursuit or not, don't send any of your foreign mercenaries into my states. Not even one foot into the buffer zone. That's a redline I won't tolerate being crossed."

Bullard stood up and playfully punched the Creole "Savior of the South" on the shoulder. "Aw hell, General," he joshed. "What have you got against a little multinational outreach? Diversity is our strength, didn't they teach you that in your Equal Opportunity classes? God only knows I heard it a million times in mine." Then Bullard quickly walked to the golf cart and slid behind the wheel, gesturing to the open passenger seat. "You coming, Marcus?"

"So, how was your weekend, Mr. Doe?" Doctor Foley returned to the quarantine tent at 10:30 Monday morning. The weather had turned cold again and Carson had rolled the tent sides down. Once again, the doctor entered without asking permission.

Carson was sorting out his meager possessions on his cot, and tried not to appear startled as the canvas door flap was pushed aside. "The dancing girls just left. The maid is due any minute." They both sat down at the white plastic table.

"I can imagine. Your forehead is looking a lot better. Have you seen yourself in a mirror?"

"There are no mirrors in the latrine."

"Well, your cut is looking fine, and almost all of the facial edema and bruising are gone."

"Thanks for the update. When can I get out of here?"

"You already know the answer. After two weeks—depending."

"Great. Another week of peanut butter sandwiches and Kool-Aid."

"Peanut butter is loaded with protein, and the Kool-Aid is fortified with vitamins," said the doctor. "It's almost a complete meal."

"I'm not really complaining. It's not so bad here, just boring as hell."

"There are worse things than being bored, trust me."

"Well, I could use a radio or a newspaper. Even an old magazine."

"It's all just official news and propaganda. Believe me, you're not missing much."

"That's easy for you to say, Doc. You're not stuck in here."

"So, how's your memory? Do you remember what we talked about on Friday? If you have anything to say, you might want to get right to it, while there's still time. Once your two weeks are up, there'll have to be some kind of a review. After that, I won't be the only one taking an interest in your case. You'll be out of my hands, out of my small circle of influence. You might be moved from here to some other camp, or you might be assigned to a work brigade. So, if your memory is coming back, tell me now."

Carson had made his decision over the weekend. "As a matter of fact, Doctor, it is."

"Good. How is your memory about coffee? If you want help from me, you'll need to offer something in return."

"A special fee for your services? I thought that was against the rules."

"Don't give me any crap, John Doe—I'm just about out of patience. If you want to know the truth, I've never bought the amnesia act for one minute. So stop acting cute with me. If you have something to offer, lay it out. Otherwise, you'll be on your own."

Phil Carson had spent the entire weekend thinking about this coming confrontation and the subsequent negotiation. "Doctor, it must be your bedside manner, or maybe the diet or the fresh air, but most of my memory has returned."

"Yeah, I thought it would. So tell me who you are, and where you came from. You didn't get that tan or those calluses in an office."

"Sorry, but I don't remember everything. You might say that my memory is kind of...compartmentalized."

"I'm sure. So just tell me, *John*, what's in the coffee compartment?"

"What's in it for me, Doctor?"

"That depends on how much coffee there is and how easy it is for me to get it. Get it without attracting attention."

"A lot, and very easy."

"How much is a lot?"

Carson paused. "Seven hundred kilos of Brazil's finest. Packed in two-kilo plastic cans."

"Seven...hundred...kilos?" The doctor whistled softly.

"That's right. And that's not all. There's more." Carson withdrew a compactly folded sheet of paper from the breast pocket of his blue hospital shirt. "Do you know what this is?"

Doctor Foley opened the page, spread it out on the plastic table, and peered at it through his glasses. "It's some kind of a schematic. 'Kyocera 120 photovoltaic array.' Where did you get this?"

"They're packed in each box with the solar panels, where else? I've got a hundred brand new panels. They're hidden the same place where the coffee is."

"A hundred solar panels?"

"That's right. Kyoceras. Big suckers. The best there is."

"And seven hundred kilos of coffee?"

"Correct."

"What else?"

"That's it," said Carson. "That's everything."

"Did you ever have any amnesia at all?"

"No."

"I didn't think so. Were you in the Special Forces?"

"That part is true. I was."

"What's your real name?"

"I'd rather not say. John Doe is fine."

"Have it your way...John. Now, let's cut to the chase. What do you want for the coffee and the solar panels?"

"I want to get out of here."

"Naturally; who wouldn't? I can help with that."

"Not just out of here, I want to get *way* out of here. Out of the emergency zone. I want to go to the Northwest. To Idaho, Montana or Wyoming."

"That's not possible."

"I want an ID badge, and whatever papers and permits it takes for traveling freely. I want a car with extra gas tanks, everything I'll need to go all the way without stopping. I'll give you a list."

"This is not based in reality, John."

"Sure it is."

"Just what do you think your bargaining position is? Even if I believed your story about the coffee and the solar panels—"

"Where do you think I got that Kyocera 120 schematic?"

"Even if you do have the stuff, let's talk about what's possible, not your fantasies."

"All right, Doctor, tell me what's possible."

"I can't get you an ID badge and documents. Well, not by myself, not without help. At the very least I'd need to bring in somebody I know at the Personnel Support Detachment, and probably somebody higher. That means at least a two- or three-way split, and more risk. And it's a big risk: they hang people for black-marketing, and for forging identity cards."

Carson smiled. "But it's a risk you're willing to take, right, Doctor?"

"You know, there's something low and disgusting about people who profit off the misery of others. There's a good reason they hang profiteers and smugglers."

"That's no way to talk to a business partner. And for what it's worth, Doc, I never had any intention of coming to Mississippi. Believe me, this is the *last* place I wanted to wind up. I'm only here because of the hurricane. I was heading to East Texas, where there's no martial law and no price controls."

"East Texas, huh? Now, you might be able to make it to Texas from here, but Montana? Montana might as well be on the moon. I could probably arrange travel papers to Dallas—Dallas is in the so-called Republic of Texas. If you got to Dallas, you'd be on your own after that. From Dallas, you'd be able to travel north into Oklahoma and maybe Kansas at least. After Kansas, I don't know what you'd need for travel papers."

"If I can make it to Texas, I can make it the rest of the way. East Texas is still free. Well, at least compared to here."

"Good, I think we can do business then. So, tell me where the coffee and the solar panels are, and we'll work on getting you to Dallas."

Carson smiled. "I don't think so. My memory is kind of slipping in and out. I'll tell you where they are later—once I'm in Texas."

"No way. I'm not going to put my neck in a noose for a promise."

"Nor am I, Doctor. I'll tell you where they are when I'm in Texas."

"Sure you will. Do you take me for a complete fool?" Doctor Foley began to rise from his chair.

"Sit down, don't be dramatic. We can work something out, something that works for both of us."

The doctor sat down heavily and paused, reflecting. "You really do have seven hundred kilos of coffee and a hundred solar panels?"

"They're in a safe place."

"In a place where I can get them, secretly?"

"Yes, for sure."

"You have a map or something?"

Carson touched his right index finger to his temple. "Right in here."

"But you could draw a map, a map that would work? Something one hundred percent certain?"

"Once I'm in Texas I will."

"Not Texas, I can't go that far."

"You're going with me?" asked Carson.

"Damn right I am. If we're going to do this, I'm going to protect my investment. I'll be with you until you give me the map and the directions. How about in Louisiana, on the other side of the Mississippi River? With a vehicle and travel permits, you can make it from there to Dallas easy. Draw me a good map and directions once we're on the other side of the river. Then we'll say goodbye."

"I'll think about it."

"No, don't think about it, you don't have time! You don't have anybody else you can deal with. All right? Do we have a deal?"

Carson hesitated, then said, "For now."

"Good. But let me take the Kyocera schematic. I'll need to convince somebody to help me with the travel papers and the ID. Somebody higher up. The solar panel diagram will help."

"Be careful—both of our necks are on the line," said Carson.

"You think I don't know it?"

"I'll need papers, travel permits, a real ID badge, and a good car with extra gas. Enough gas to make it to Dallas nonstop. The right clothes, and winter gear for up north—I'll give you a list. You get all of that and get me across the Mississippi River, and you have my word of honor: you'll get the coffee and the solar panels. Can you do all of that?"

Phil Carson extended his hand across the plastic table toward Doctor Foley, and they shook on the agreement while maintaining eye contact.

"It's a deal, then," said the doctor. "I can arrange all of that. But it'll take a little time."

"When?"

"A few days, maybe more. I'll send somebody with a razor and soap: keep yourself clean-shaven. You'll need to look presentable to pull this off. We might need some more pictures too, for the IDs."

"Okay, Doc, I'll be right here."

"The man who brings you the razor, give him your shopping list."

Carson stroked his stubbly beard, suppressing a smile. "You'll be a very rich man, Doctor."

"Rich…yes, I suppose so. And you'll be free, free to go. Either that, or we'll both be very dead—and swinging from the same gallows."

5

Bob Bullard dropped the personnel file on his desk and leaned back in his black leather executive chair. Christmas Eve was just another working day as far as he was concerned, and it gratified him that the new man had reported to Fort Campbell as scheduled, without any whining about the holidays. His new recruit, dressed in coat and tie, stood uneasily across the desk from him. "I've looked over your résumé, Agent Zuberovsky. It's damn good. Only four years out of the Army and you made the CAGE Unit—Chicago Anti-Gun Enforcement. Great arrest stats. Picked up your college degree on your own time, just like I did. Then three years with the ATF, before coming over to Homeland Security. That's all fine, top notch. Between the military and your law enforcement background, you're more than qualified. But there's one more thing I have to know, and don't bull-shit me: can you really ride?"

"Excuse me, sir?"

Based solely on his professional background, which had been flagged by a computer search, Martin Zuberovsky had been sent from Chicago down to Fort Campbell. Bullard was giving him the once-over before sending him out into the field. Zuberovsky was thirty-seven, a good two decades younger than Bullard, but in many ways he reminded Bullard of himself in his younger days. Zuberovsky had gotten his undergraduate degree via internet correspondence courses while still in the Army and later while working full time as a cop. The degree was required to become a federal agent, but why waste time going to college with a bunch of commies and faggots?

Martin Zuberovsky was no pansy—that was obvious. The new man was only average height, but had a powerful physique that couldn't be concealed under his jacket. His build, along with his intense black eyes and black hair combed straight back, gave him the presence of a larger man. Mid-afternoon and Zuberovsky already had a five o'clock shadow on his square jaw. A real no-nonsense hard-ass like Bullard was. He'd have to be, for what he was getting into.

"This file says you spent a year with the Chicago Mounted Police before you went to the CAGE unit. So does that mean you can walk an old police department nag down a parade route—or can you really ride? You know: gallop, jump fences and all that shit."

"I don't understand what—"

"If you're going to be my liaison with the Kazak Battalion, you have to ride. *Really* ride. The Kazaks practically live on their horses. Kazak is where the word Cossack comes from. Kazaks, as in Cossacks. They don't respect anybody who can't ride horses. They'd rather screw a mare than a woman any day. If you're going to go out with them on operations, you'll have to be a damned good horse rider. Are you?"

"Sir, I was raised on a farm in downstate Illinois. Yes, I can ride. Gallop, jump fences and all that shit."

"Well, if you can't…I guess we'll find out soon enough. Here's the deal. You're going to be my new liaison to the Kazak Battalion. The Kazaks are a royal pain in the ass, very hard to work with. Central Asian prima donnas. They all think they're Genghis Khan. But for RPP ops they can't be beat. I'm not going to sugarcoat it, Agent Zuberovsky: the rural pacification program can get ugly. And the Kazak mercenaries do ugly better than just about anybody I've ever seen."

"Sir, I haven't actually been briefed on the program. I've heard some back-channel talk, but I haven't seen anything in writing. I couldn't find an ops manual. In fact, I couldn't find any formal references for the RPP."

Bullard leaned back, lacing his fingers behind his head. "And why do you think that is, Agent Zuberovsky?"

"I really wouldn't want to guess…"

"Go ahead, guess."

"Well, I suppose some of the methods that are employed in the RPP are a bit on the…ah…*ugly* side, as you mentioned."

"Ugly is an understatement, Agent Zuberovsky. But Tennessee is very, very ugly these days. Western Tennessee is the worst of all, because it was cut off by the rivers after the quake. That's where you're going. Most of the locals in the unpacified counties are beyond redemption. They're still holding onto the old days and the old ways. They're dead-enders. They totally reject the new constitution and the emergency laws. We went in to try to help them, and they shot at us. Shot at us! So be it. We're not bargaining, and we're not negotiating. We're way beyond all that. Either they obey the emergency laws, straight up, or they're pacified the hard way. We have a zero tolerance policy for assholes down there. The president has made this clear: we don't have any more time to screw around in Kentucky and Tennessee. He wants it done. Over. Finished. And that's where the Kazak Battalion comes in."

"Sir, I don't speak any Kazak…"

"Of course not." Bullard cracked his knuckles and laughed. "Who does, except for Kazaks? But you speak some Russian, don't you? Isn't your father a first-generation Russian?"

"I speak Russian okay. Good enough to get laid. And I traveled over there a few times—that's where I met my second wife."

"Your file says you're divorced."

"She flew home to Mother Russia when our economy tanked. But yeah, I speak Russian pretty good."

"Well, that's great, because the Kazaks speak Russian too, mostly. You'll be okay. Most of their enlisted men can't speak a word of English, but their officers speak it well enough. But not well enough to go blabbing to reporters, if you catch my drift."

"I do, sir."

"Not that there are any reporters down there, but you know what I mean. It's good for operational security that the Kazaks can't speak English. They can't get close to the locals. Rural pacification is kind of a dark and foggy subject, and that's not by accident. That's why we're using foreign troops in West Tennessee. Once it's done, they'll be shipped out or sent home. We're not keeping written records. It's an ugly chapter, one that won't go in the history books." Bullard leaned forward, elbows on desk, and stared hard at his new liaison. "Do you understand me, Agent Zuberovsky?"

"Perfectly."

Bullard sized up the new man. The "CAGE," the Chicago Anti-Gun Enforcement unit, was famous for its brutal efficiency at gun confiscation. This had been a perfect introduction to the ATF and then to the DHS for the agent. Like Bullard, Zuberovsky was divorced, with a messy trail of domestic violence complaints against him that had been papered over as he had shifted assignments, duty stations and agencies. The fact that Zuberovsky spoke Russian and could ride horses made him a perfect fit for the liaison assignment.

"The Kazaks have a new commanding officer," stated Bullard. "We've discussed the plans for their battalion's redeployment to the West; this is going to take place next summer. In the meantime, I want you to ride herd on them in West Tennessee. They think their job there is over, but we want Kentucky and Tennessee fully pacified before springtime. They need to clean out the dead-enders and the holdouts. The Kazaks know how to do it—they just tend to be lazy between ops. They need somebody to keep them on task until they're redeployed out West. I'll be sending you specific mission taskings; it'll be your job to motivate the Kazaks to do them. Tell them about all the land out in Montana we're going to give them. How it's just like back home in Kazakhstan, only better. Promise them the moon, I don't care. But let me be frank: you're going to get your hands dirty, Agent Zuberovsky. Does that bother you?"

The agent didn't hesitate or blink. "No sir, not at all. We can't rehabilitate the fanatics. I saw the TV reports about what they did to the Memphis refugees after the earthquake. That was genocide, mass murder. In my book, those Tennessee rednecks aren't even human. We don't need their kind in the new America."

"That's good, Zuberovsky, very good. Keep that attitude and it'll see you through. That, and the double differential pay you'll be making in the RPP. Oh, and one more thing: we've got some new gear we want you to test out. It's a microwave device for crowd control. You'll be briefed on it, but it seems simple enough. I want a full report on how it works in the field, under real-world conditions."

"No problem."

December 24. Christmas Eve. Outside the tent, light rain was falling as twilight faded to black. The interior of the tent was dimly lit by a single 15-watt bulb, hanging from the center pole. The electricity would be cut off promptly at 10:00 p.m. Every day and every night was the same, the only slight variation in the routine coming in the handcart that brought the meals. Tonight's supper had been a bowl of sweet potatoes and corn. Carson wondered if the menu would improve on Christmas Day. Maybe there would be meat.

It was two weeks since he had been brought to the quarantine and vaccination section of Camp Shelton, a week since he'd last been visited by Doctor Foley. A vehicle pulled up close to the tent, and its engine shut off with a clatter. Bad fuel. The entrance flap to his tent was pushed aside, and a black enlisted man in his mid-twenties entered, carrying a large cardboard box. Carson recognized him from the day he had been detained at the Alabama-Mississippi border. He was one of the soldiers who had collected him in the orange pickup and brought him to the QV camp. He was the medic. Later he had brought Carson a used disposable razor and a sliver of bath soap for shaving. His nametape and three chevrons identified him as Sergeant Amory.

"Tonight's the big night, Mr. Amnesia. I'm going to be your driver. There's a uniform for you in here, everything you need. I hope I guessed right on the boots."

"You're coming?" Carson was momentarily flustered.

"I'm driving you to Vicksburg and over the river. That's the plan, right?"

Carson didn't let on that he had not known the details until this moment. "What about Doctor—I mean Lieutenant Colonel Foley?"

"He's coming too. He's outside in the truck. Hurry up and get dressed. We're getting out of here just as soon as you're ready."

Carson wasted no time changing. The box contained a pressed Army Camouflage Uniform, including a black beret, a patrol cap, and a wide-brimmed boonie hat. The boots fit well enough, about one size larger than his feet. He used his own brown leather belt. A thick field jacket in matching camouflage went over his uniform blouse. The boonie hat was rolled up and stuck into the left cargo pocket of his pants. The beret went on his head, flooding him with memories at its touch. The patrol cap was too small, and he left it in the box. The cloth nametape over his right pocket read BRICE; over the left was U.S. ARMY. The black eagle on his rank device and on his beret made him out to be a full colonel. The rank insignias were attached to both the blouse and field jacket with Velcro, and Carson smiled to think how simple this made it to impersonate an officer. His short-cropped gray hair matched the assumed rank, and as instructed, he had kept himself clean-shaven.

When he had dressed, he picked up his pack, which he had kept loaded in readiness for this moment. With his back turned to Sergeant Amory, he slipped his diminutive Kel-Tec .380 caliber pistol into the right front pocket of his camouflage pants. Since he had been brought to the quarantine camp, none of the guards or medical personnel had shown any interest in him, much less searched him or his few belongings. In the uniform of a colonel, he would be even less subject to search. The Kel-Tec was thinner than the width of a finger and invisible in a pocket.

Carson briefly flipped through a bundle of cards and folded papers in the box, after removing the rubber band from around them. There was a laminated Army ID, a folded yellow cardboard vaccination record, several black-and-white plastic ID badges with metallic shirt clips, and a few other cards. He slipped on his reading glasses and gave them a cursory examination. He was now Colonel Jonathan T. Brice. He put these ID cards into his angled left shirt pocket, along with his reading glasses. "Okay, Sergeant, let's go." He deliberately referred to the medic by his rank, in order to establish their officer-enlisted relationship. To noncoms, colonels were close to God. Even a fake colonel might give pause to a man used to saluting officers.

Outside the tent was a green crew-cab military pickup truck. A heavy black tarpaulin was stretched taut across the bed. Amory slid behind the wheel. Doctor Foley sat in the front passenger seat. Carson got into the back behind the driver and set his pack on the seat beside him. The interior light came on briefly when the doors were opened. Doctor Foley turned and glanced at Carson.

Carson spoke first. "Sergeant Amory said we're crossing the river at Vicksburg. How far is Vicksburg from here?"

"About a hundred fifty miles, the way we're going," replied Foley.

"What's in the back? Everything I asked for?"

"Everything on your list. Right, Amory?"

"Yes sir," answered the medic. "Everything."

"I'll have enough gas to make it all the way to Dallas?"

The doctor hesitated for a beat. "There are six jerry cans. Thirty gallons. It's plenty."

"I'd like to check it."

"There's no time for that—it's all there. Go ahead, Amory, let's get out of here."

The medic started the engine and pulled ahead. The pickup's head-lights illuminated the rain. The dashboard lights barely revealed the doc-tor's face. Carson could only faintly see the skin of Amory's neck and his black beret. They stopped when they neared the fence surrounding the quarantine camp. A soldier wearing rain gear stepped out from a sheet metal guard shack and swung open the gate. They drove across the base by a route Carson didn't recognize from his way in, but that had been two weeks ago, in the daytime, and he had only been able to see out the sides and back of his cage on that trip. Now he was completely lost, depending on these two practically unknown soldiers to get him off the base, across the state, and over the Mississippi River.

He asked, "Why Christmas Eve?" He thought he knew the answer, but he wanted to hear the doctor speak—primarily to gauge his sincerity.

"It's after curfew," answered the doctor. "Only military and police are allowed on the roads, so we won't be stopped. On Christmas Eve everybody will be a little slack at the checkpoints, maybe even sneaking a few nips of liquor. For that matter, the checkpoints will be undermanned, or even just left open for the night. I have papers showing that we're carrying critical vaccines in coolers. Nobody will hassle us, nobody ever checks vaccines. It's perfect. It's even raining. Nobody will be out."

"But Texas isn't part of the emergency zone, is it?"

"No, but it's not hostile to us either. We have decent relations. Texas won't be a problem, not with your IDs. You have everything you'll need to be a colonel returning home to Texas on Christmas leave. It's com-pletely normal."

Carson was suspicious. "So how are you getting back, if I'm driving all the way to Dallas in this truck?"

"No, we're coming back in the truck. You're going the rest of the way in a civilian car, once we're over the river. That's where we're going now, to pick up the other car. Sergeant Amory will drive you to Louisiana in this truck, and I'll follow in the car. Once we're over the river we'll switch vehicles, and you'll go the rest of the way on your own."

"What about the curfew, won't that be risky with a civilian car?"

Doctor Foley answered after a hesitation. "Don't worry. In Miss-issippi it'll be okay, since we're all in uniform and I'll be following right behind this military truck. Amory knows what to say at the checkpoints, and he has the right papers. Once you're in Louisiana, just wait until day-light when curfew's lifted before you take off in the car. Louisiana is much more relaxed than Mississippi. Then it's a straight shot across I-20. It won't be a problem."

"What about crossing into Texas? I didn't see a driver's license in the ID cards Sergeant Amory gave me."

"You won't need a civilian driver's license: your military ID is all you'll need. You're an Army colonel traveling on official leave orders. You won't get any trouble from police. One of the fringe benefits of martial law. Rank hath its privileges, Colonel Brice—especially when you are in uniform."

Carson wondered about this, but he changed the subject and asked the doctor, "What's your family think about this, your going out all night on Christmas Eve?"

"What family?"

They drove in silence after that, through pitch darkness, passing no other vehicles, finally leaving Camp Shelton and heading along a small state road under a canopy of rain-soaked forest.

"Where is the other car?" asked Carson, his hand resting on the pistol in his pocket.

"Just a little further up," replied the doctor.

The truck stopped at an unlit, unmarked intersection, turned right, continued for another minute at slow speed, and then turned left down a muddy dirt track. Branches brushed both sides of the truck until they entered a clearing. A long mobile home stood on the opposite side of the small open space between the dripping pines. Carson slipped the tiny Kel-Tec pistol from his pocket and placed it on the seat alongside his right thigh. He could conceal it entirely beneath the palm of his hand. Their headlights shone across the boxy white trailer and a dark compact car parked in front.

Doctor Foley said, "Pull behind the Toyota and stop." Amory did as he was told, driving slowly through high, unmowed grass. When the front of the truck was a few yards behind the car, he parked and turned off the headlights. The pickup was even with the small stoop and side door of the mobile home. A dim porch light illuminated the trailer and the vehicles.

"This is where I'm getting out," said Doctor Foley. "I'll follow right behind you in the car. Sergeant Amory knows the way to Vicksburg." He opened his door, turning on the overhead interior light, and stepped out into the drizzle—then unexpectedly jerked open the back passenger door of the truck. "You're getting out too, John Doe." The doctor held a full-sized pistol, a military-issue Beretta M-9.

"Oh, you...bastard," Carson swore. He turned sideways facing Foley, his left hand on the back of the front seat, his right hand over his own pistol. "We shook on it. I would have kept my end of the deal."

The doctor shrugged. "Well, Mr. Doe, I was willing to go with the plan, but I was outranked at the last minute. That's how it goes." The door of the trailer opened, and two other men walked down the steps and stood on either side of Doctor Foley. The mist-shrouded porch light above the trailer's door backlit the three. The men wore camouflage military rain parkas, with their hoods pulled up over their heads, hiding their faces. "Get out, asshole," barked the taller of the two, standing on the left. He held a pistol leveled by his side. "If you really do have coffee and solar panels hidden somewhere, we're going to find out tonight. Right here, right now. And if you don't," he snickered, "well, then you won't have to worry about what Santa Claus is bringing you."

Carson could think of nothing to say. He had been double-crossed. Whether he talked or not, he'd be done for once he was put under inter-rogation. If he revealed the location of his hidden catamaran, they'd exe-cute him, probably after forcing him to lead them to the boat. If he didn't talk, they'd wind up torturing him to death. Either way, it was game over if he complied with their demands.

"Come on, get out," said the doctor, waving the pistol. Carson put his right hand on the seat beside him, as if to help push himself toward the open passenger-side door. The three men stood shoulder to shoulder just outside the cab, the doctor in the middle, his Beretta's muzzle only a yard from Carson's chest.

"Okay guys, you win—no need to get rough." He began to slide over, then swung his left arm across to deflect the doctor's barrel while at the same time pulling up his little .380. He extended the gun like a striking snake and put one shot into Doctor Foley's forehead almost at contact distance. He moved the pistol's aim a foot to the right and fired again, into the center of a shadowy hooded face. He brought the pistol back to the left and fired just as the taller man dropped beneath his line of vision.

Frozen in the front seat with his hands still clutching the steering wheel, Sergeant Amory yelled out, "Don't shoot! Don't shoot!"

Carson grabbed the handle of the door behind him and pushed it open while covering the open passenger-side door with his pocket pistol. He slid out and fell back onto the wet grass just as the third man reappeared across from him. The man's Army Beretta exploded with a booming flash that flared across the interior of the pickup. The shot passed through both open doors as Carson hit the ground and rolled onto his side. The big military pickup had high ground clearance, and Carson could make out a pair of legs on the other side, backlit by the glow of the trailer's porch lamp. More bullets impacted the inside of the partially open door just above him.

Lying on his side, Carson took a two-handed grip, the gun horizontal. He aimed as well as he could by feel and instinct, his little pistol's sights invisible. He fired twice at the nearest shin, and heard the tall man cry in pain. The man dropped to the ground clutching his leg, and Carson fired two more times at what he could see of his enemy's torso, and on his next trigger pull he heard only a click. The little Kel-Tec was finished, empty. Without pausing, he bounded up, threw himself into the backseat of the truck, and grabbed the doctor's Beretta from the floor, where it had fallen. He aimed it toward the back of Amory's head and began to squeeze the trigger. Fear and excitement flowed like lightning through his veins—he was running on killer instinct, going for a clean sweep, eliminating every threat one after the other.

"I didn't know sir! I swear I didn't know!" The medic's hands were now straight up, palms pressed against the roof of the cab. Slight movement in Carson's peripheral vision alerted him, and he whipped the Beretta back to the right. The tall man, the one he'd shot beneath the truck, groaned and pulled himself up to a sitting position. His rain parka's hood was pushed back, revealing a bald head glistening wet with rain. He looked inside the cab at Carson, and with an unsteady arm, he lifted his pistol above the seat. Carson was faster. He rapid-fired the Beretta, hitting the wounded man two times in the middle of his face. The bald man fell backward against the wooden steps of the trailer and didn't move again.

Carson's adrenaline was pumping so hard he could barely form words. He swung the pistol back around to the driver, jamming its warm muzzle into his neck. Amory's hands were still up, palms against the pick-up's roof liner as he stared forward with bulging eyes, his face lit by the truck's interior light. "Where...are...we?" Carson panted, pushing the barrel of the 9mm hard into the medic's neck.

"I don't know sir, I don't know! I've never been here before!"

"Liar! You knew we were coming here! Foley didn't tell you where to turn—you knew it was an ambush!"

"I didn't, I swear it, please don't shoot me, I didn't know! I swear, I thought we were going to Louisiana tonight! As God is my witness, believe me!"

"Is there really extra gas in the back? Or was that a lie too?"

"It's true sir, it's true! Lieutenant Colonel Foley, he gave me your list yesterday, your list and a pile of money, and I got everything, everything on it, I swear!"

"Okay, okay, now shut up. Let me think. Just let me think." Carson slumped back in the seat, his chest heaving, his ears ringing, the pistol held on his lap. He knew he should check the bodies, check to make sure they were dead, but he didn't dare turn his back on Amory. He had no handcuffs or flex cuffs or rope, no way to quickly secure him. He considered his immediate escape transportation options. "Are there extra gas cans in the trunk of the car?"

"I don't know, sir, I don't know—I just know everything from your list is in the back of this truck, I swear it is. Winter clothes, a sleeping bag, everything on your list! I drew it from supply and packed it all myself. I think those men just got to Doctor Foley and made him change the plan. This morning he told me we were going to Vicksburg—I know him, and he wasn't lying. Not this morning."

Maybe that was true, but it didn't matter. They were dead. He knew he could be making a fatal error by not policing up the scene, checking the other car, checking the house trailer, checking the bodies to make sure they were well and truly dead. He could find the other pistols. He could drag the bodies into the brush at least, into the woods, to conceal them from rapid casual discovery. He could search the trailer and maybe locate some more weapons, possibly a rifle or shotgun.

But what about Sergeant Amory? He didn't want to shoot him now. That moment had passed. Plus, Amory would know how to deal with the checkpoints. He would know what passwords and procedures were needed to get through them without drawing suspicion. Carson knew he'd probably make a mistake and give himself away if he tried to escape on his own. A colonel being driven by a sergeant would appear quite natural, and he would only have to flash his military ID as they stopped at checkpoints. Maybe not even that. What soldier would ask to see a uniformed colonel's ID, in an official Army vehicle? Nobody in the old Army he had known.

His brain couldn't handle the permutations, the options, the variables. Not with his bloodstream awash with adrenaline, his ears still ringing, and the snapshot memories of his deadly close-range headshots filling his mind. Each muzzle flash had left a sharp picture printed in his mind. Obviously, it had never occurred to Doctor Foley or his partners that their victim might be armed at the very moment of their double-crossing him. Not at that fateful moment, which had led to the final minute of their lives. Carson reasoned that the water-saturated pine forest surrounding the trailer would have swallowed up the sounds of their shots. Nobody would be outside to hear them anyway. His mind fixed on the thought of gunshot sounds radiating outward into the wet forest, and then it froze up, his mental gears jamming stuck. Finally he just said, "Drive."

"What?"

"Drive. Just get us the hell out of here."

"Yes sir." The medic lowered his hands to the steering wheel.

"Sergeant Amory?"

"Sir?"

"Merry Christmas."

"What?"

"We're still alive."

6

Carson held the doctor's Beretta in his right hand. He guessed it still held maybe ten or so 9mm bullets in its double-stack magazine. He slid the empty Kel-Tec back into his pants pocket. Ten or twelve bullets, to make good an escape across the state of Mississippi and the Mississippi River, and then across Louisiana over to Texas.

"Sergeant Amory, do you have a map?"

"Yes sir, but I don't need it. I know the roads."

Carson raised his left arm to within a few inches of his face. His watch had a mini-compass the size of a nickel fastened to its strap. A tiny firefly light glowed dimly in the dark cab beneath his eyes, a green triangle pointing forward. He rolled the compass horizontally until he had some confidence in its orientation. "We're heading north. How long until we hit a checkpoint?" Inside of the steel truck, he trusted the button compass to within maybe 45 degrees, either way. It was a rough instrument, but he didn't want Amory to think he could fool him about their direction.

"No way to tell how long. There's no permanent checkpoint around here, but sometimes they set up mobile checkpoints."

"On Christmas Eve?"

"No, probably not. With the curfew, nobody's out anyway. And no-body's got gas to go anywhere, so why bother putting up a checkpoint? Rainy night like this is a night for staying inside, close to a fire. Close to a bottle, if you got one. Or a woman. Soldiers and civilians both."

"You can talk your way through a checkpoint, right, Sergeant?"

"I think so…"

"You have to do better than just think so. I'll be aiming this Beretta at your back every single second. If we get stopped—well, you'd better not blow it, that's all I'm going to say."

"I…I won't sir. I won't."

They drove in silence for several more minutes. Then Carson asked, "What's the bridge at Vicksburg like? What kind of security do they have on it?"

"That bridge is guarded all to hell, both sides and the river too. They check everything."

"Did you see my ID cards?"

"What?"

"Did you check my ID cards, the ones you brought to my tent? Do they look right, are they perfect?"

"I just picked them up, that's all. Doctor Foley, he had them made at the Personnel Support Detachment. He had to bring the XO of the base into the plan to get it done. I think that's probably where...where it all went wrong."

"You think that was the base XO back there, by the trailer? The executive officer of Camp Shelton?"

"I don't know, sir, maybe. No, not maybe. Probably it was."

"Shit, what's an XO—a colonel?"

"Yes sir, he'd be at least a full bird colonel."

"Who was the other man?"

"I don't know. Another high officer, I expect."

"Shit. Well ain't that just great. So tell me about my ID cards. Will they stand up?" Carson knew he'd have to get rid of them fast. Once the bodies were discovered, the connection from the dead base executive officer through the Personnel Support Detachment to his bogus ID cards could be made very quickly. On the other hand, the three double-crossers had no reason to tell anyone else of their plans, and no reason to provide easily traced ID cards. If the cards were ever traced, it could only lead back to their involvement and incriminate them in the conspiracy. The conspirators would have every reason to provide clean, untraceable cards. The cards might work out...at least for a few days. He just didn't know. But who else would know about the creation of the bogus cards? Some clerk at the personnel detachment, probably. And, of course there was Sergeant Amory...he certainly knew.

"I think they're okay, I mean, they look right to me. They're real, if that's what you mean. Made on real machines from real ID card paper. That's what Lieutenant Colonel Foley said anyway. They're real cards, made out for a dead man, that's what he said. Somebody who died in one of the epidemics, but without a proper death certificate or anything. Somebody real, somebody Doctor Foley knew. He said nobody would ever know the difference."

Carson digested that for a while. He was carrying a dead man's ID cards...he grimaced at the thought. "So, Sergeant, if we're the only ones out here driving tonight, and we're driving a pickup truck, don't you think that any checkpoint troops will think we're civilians out after curfew?"

"They will sir, until they see the Army numbers on the truck, and our uniforms. We're military all the way. We're good to go. Nobody's going to stop a colonel, sir. Nobody."

"I'm not a colonel, Sergeant."

"You are tonight, sir. You are tonight."

Carson grunted and let the remark pass. After a minute he asked, "Vicksburg is on I-20, right?"

"Yes sir, Interstate 20. Jackson, Vicksburg, Shreveport, then Dallas."

"Where's the road map? Pass it back here."

Carson pulled a penlight from a side pocket on his pack, and Amory handed him the map. Carson unfolded it across his lap, put on his reading glasses and studied the map for several minutes as they drove north through the drizzle. The houses they passed were barely lit, if lit at all. Long stretches were obviously without electricity. During sections of road where there was electricity, only dim lights were visible inside homes, or just flickering firelight. Christmas Eve or not, plainly there wasn't enough power to squander on holiday lights. "Okay Sergeant, just how well do you know these Mississippi roads?"

"I'd say excellent, sir: I've lived here all my life. I got all around the state—I used to drive a moving truck, summers during college. Back when I was in college…"

"Good. We're going to give I-20 and Vicksburg a pass. Maybe somebody else got the word about our route, I don't know. If the whole thing was a setup, the whole plan might be blown. I don't like the idea of driving right to where we might be expected. So, what's the next bridge across the Mississippi River, above Vicksburg?"

"Above Vicksburg? I don't rightly know, sir, probably up in Illinois somewhere."

"What? Illinois? Don't bullshit me, Sergeant—I wasn't born yesterday."

"No sir, it's the truth! That's why they guard that Vicksburg bridge so tight: all the bridges north of Vicksburg went down in the New Madrid quakes. Down or busted, and they're still busted."

"No shit?"

"No shit. So you really do have amnesia, sir? You really don't know about the bridges?"

Carson didn't answer him. No bridges above Vicksburg? Doctor Foley had mentioned the bridges, but the quake was more than a year ago, and the bridges were still down? That meant most of the state of Mississippi and all of Tennessee, with no bridges across the river? Then how would he get across? On a raft, like Huck Finn? His situation was growing worse. He checked his wrist compass again, with his penlight. They were heading basically northwest on a rural two-lane highway. The overhead traffic signals at the infrequent intersections were unlit, and no streetlights were working. It was black outside except for the meager light from fireplaces or lamps inside of widely dispersed clusters of homes. Carson checked the map, matching it with the road signs and the names of the small villages they passed through. They approached a four-lane divided highway that headed more east than north.

"Stop up ahead, in the gas station by the pumps."

"Sir, they ain't got any gas."

"I can see that." The station's windows were smashed in, the store an empty shell. The other crossroad businesses were all closed and dark. They were either out of business for good, or shut tight for the nightly curfew and the Christmas holidays. The intersection was fifty yards ahead. Its unlit traffic signal faintly reflected back their headlights.

Amory pulled into the station. Their headlights caught a small bill-board across the parking lot. The sign showed General Mirabeau in a khaki shirt, in front of a multiracial team of workers and farmers, all carrying tools over their shoulders. Beneath them was the slogan "We will rise together, or we will fall apart!" Grim determination was written on their faces.

"Cut the engine, Sergeant, and turn off the lights. The fuel gauge says we've got two-thirds of a tank left, so let's put in a jerry can right here. I want to check how much gas we really have in the back so I can plan where to go. I'll be right behind you—and there'd better be gas, like you said there was. You got that?"

"Oh, I got that, sir."

"Now take out the keys and give them to me. Come on, get out, grab a can and pour it in."

Amory did as he was told. They both stepped out, sheltered from the steadily falling rain by the wrecked gas station's high metal roof, which extended above the pump island. Carson held the Beretta in his right hand and the penlight in his other. Amory untied the front corner of the tarp on the driver's side. There were six jerry cans beneath the tarp, in a row across the front of the truck bed. Amory lifted out the closest metal jug, set it on the ground, and attached a spout. He poured the diesel fuel into the truck, gurgling and thumping as the can emptied, the odor pungent.

While Amory finished up, Carson became aware of a new sound. He couldn't see very far down the four-lane road ahead—trees and the low buildings of closed businesses blocked his view—but he could clearly hear the hum and rumble of approaching engines. "Throw the can back in and fix the tarp. Come on, be quick!"

Amory tied down the rope attaching the corner of the tarp and, covered by Carson's pistol, slid back behind the wheel and closed his door. Carson got in behind him. They both hunkered down low in their seats; the engine sounds were now audible even from inside the cab with all of its windows rolled up. Many headlights stabbed through the darkness, coming from the south, from their left. A humvee rolled past at about fifty miles an hour, blowing through the intersection without slowing down. A hundred feet behind was a five-ton military truck with a canvas roof, then a school bus painted a dark color. More vehicles came rolling on, one after the other.

"What is it, Amory? Where are they going?"

"Supply convoy, sir, I don't know exactly where they'd be going. I'm just a medic at Camp Shelton—supply routes and convoys aren't my thing."

Carson put the penlight on his map, holding it close and shielding it. "That's the way to Meridian, right?"

"That's right, yes sir, Meridian, and then Tupelo."

A dozen vehicles moved by at even intervals: humvees, eighteen-wheel fuel tankers, tractor-trailers, pickups, another bus, and finally a last humvee.

"Here, take the keys. Do *exactly* as I say, all right?"

"Yes sir."

"Turn on the engine, but don't turn on the lights."

"Okay…" The warm engine came instantly to life.

"Good. Pull ahead slowly…slowly. There! That's the last of them! That's the tail-end Charlie. Go ahead now, swing out and get in line."

"What? Sir?"

"You heard me, get in line, fifty yards behind the last one."

"But…"

"Just do it!"

Amory shook his head as if in great doubt. He had a rigid grip on the wheel, almost cringing as he gently accelerated out of the gas station, leaving by the exit on the northeast-bound divided road. It had a flat, grassy median strip, but it was not a limited-access road. He slowed again when he was fifty yards behind the final vehicle, a humvee with an all-weather metal roof. After a minute, the highway made a left-hand curve and Carson said, "Now, switch on the headlights while we're not aiming at them."

"But they'll know we don't belong, they'll…"

"No they won't. In this rain that driver is staring straight ahead at the truck in front of him, and anybody else in there with him is either asleep or bored to death and trying to stay warm. Stragglers fall behind and catch up all the time." Carson chuckled softly. "It's one of the oldest tricks in the book: convoy hopping. It's a matter of psychology. It's the same thing that makes it so easy to sneak onto military bases. What keeps most people from trying is pure psychological intimidation, nothing more than that. You get past that fear, and you've got it made."

"You've done this before?"

"Yep. A long, long time ago. If I told you where, you'd never believe me. Now as long as they keep driving, we'll keep following. If the convoy stops, we'll peel off. Let's hope they're going a long, long way."

"What about the Mississippi River, going to Texas, all that?"

"Not tonight, Sergeant. We just left three dead officers back there, colonels, and if anybody else knew about the plan, that bridge is where they'll be looking for me. We don't know when those bodies are going to be found. Maybe not for a couple of days, or maybe they already have been. Either way, I don't want to be trapped against the river. Not at that Vicksburg bridge, and not looking for a boat. Not if anybody alive knows that's where I was heading. So we're going where nobody would expect us to go."

"Where's that, sir?"

Carson paused, then asked, "How far is it to Tennessee?"

"Tennessee? About two hundred miles. But Tennessee's even worse than Mississippi!"

"So I've heard."

"Tennessee is practically a war zone. Tennessee is occupied by foreign troops."

"Does the Mississippi National Guard go into Tennessee, Sergeant Amory?"

"What? Go into Tennessee? Hell no sir, no way! It's full of foreign peacekeepers; it's a mess. There's fighting up there—Kentucky too."

"Well, that's why we're going there. Foreign troops I can handle— but I just killed three Mississippi Guard officers. I mean, they hang *counterfeiters* in this state! I've seen it." Carson chuckled. "If they hang counterfeiters, what do you think they'll do for three dead colonels, shot right in their faces? You think they're going to just let that go, let it slide? No big deal, let bygones be bygones?"

The driver shook his head slowly. "No sir, never. Never. I think you poked a big stick in a hornet's nest back there, killing those officers."

"So do I, Sergeant Amory. And that's why we're going to Tennessee."

The truck convoy rolled northward up the eastern flank of Mississippi on Highway 45. The dual-lane road was almost like an interstate highway, running ruler-straight while ascending and descending long gentle slopes. Every few miles they passed in and out of rain showers, including some hard downpours. Their headlights occasionally shone across billboards, many featuring General Mirabeau in different heroic poses among workers, farmers and children. Sergeant Amory maintained a distance of fifty yards behind the humvee that was the last vehicle in the convoy. Without turning his head the medic quietly said, "You're going to kill me, aren't you?"

By the dash lights, Carson could see Sergeant Amory's white eyes flickering in the rear view mirror, trying to get a look at his captor in the seat behind him. "Keep your eyeballs on the road, Sergeant, or you're going to kill both of us."

Amory slammed a fist on the wheel. "You think this is a damn joke?"

"Am I laughing?"

"You *are* going to kill me," the medic stated flatly.

"Is that really what you think?" said Carson.

"Of course it's what I think. You shot three officers, what do you think I think? You're gonna just let me go? You must think I'm some kind of stupid. You've got a gun at my back, and we're going fifty miles an hour following a military convoy. That means you're crazy too."

"Listen, Sergeant: it wasn't my plan to shoot anybody tonight. I made a deal with Doctor Foley. We shook hands on it, man to man—and he pulled a gun on me. What do you think they were going to do to me back there at that trailer? Throw me a Christmas Eve surprise party? Before that scene at the trailer, I thought I'd be across the river in Louisiana by now—and you'd be on your way back to Camp Shelton with the doctor. So okay, Foley double-crossed me—and he paid the price for it—but that doesn't mean I'm going to kill you. After we get to Tennessee, you can go. You can have the truck and the rest of the gas. Twenty-five more gallons will get you all the way back."

"What, you think I can just drive back to the base now? Just show up, turn this truck back into the motor pool like nothing happened tonight, when three officers have been shot dead? Including probably the base XO? Man, what do you think is gonna happen to me now, no matter what I do? I'm screwed any way you cut it. And besides, we can't just drive into Tennessee anyway. The state border is closed except for official business—which we ain't—and they check every damn thing going over that border with a microscope. And only in the daytime."

"Then just get me close, and I'll hump it the rest of the way."

"Huh, you think you're some kind of geriatric Davy Crockett? Or Rambo maybe?" Sergeant Amory glanced at Carson in the mirror, and shook his head.

"Don't you have family somewhere in this state that could put you up?"

"Yeah, but so what? What good would that do, except bring heat on them? How am I gonna hide out under martial law? How can I stay hid when they're looking everywhere for the black medic who signed out a truck for Lieutenant Colonel Foley, who just happens to be dead now? I can't wear my uniform while I'm AWOL, and if I'm wearing civvies, I gotta wear my badge like everybody else. First time I'm scanned, I'll be busted. Then I'll hang for sure, just for desertion—even if they can't get me for the three murders."

Carson mulled this over for a while, ready to dispute the medic's assertion that what he had done constituted murder. He dropped the thought: it was pointless. To the Mississippi Guard, the three dead officers would certainly be seen as victims of foul play, and their deaths would be investigated as murders. He could shout self-defense from the gallows platform while the noose was cinched around his neck, for all the good it would do. Instead, he refocused on more practical matters. "How do the badge scanners work, Sergeant?"

"Scanners? Oh, I think just like the supermarket things that used to scan your groceries—back when the supermarkets were open. Back when they had electricity all the time. Now they got a portable laser scanner at the checkpoints."

"Portable, so it runs on batteries?"

"Yeah, what else? I mean, I guess. They look like a square flash-light."

"So how does it know who's who, there at a checkpoint? It must be hooked up to a central database somewhere. It has to get updated, and compare the badges to a central list." Carson was thinking aloud. Then he asked, "How's the wireless network in Mississippi these days?"

"What do you mean?"

"The cell phones, all of that."

"Oh, we don't have cell phones anymore, hardly. Not for regular folks, anyway."

"What about the military, the government?"

"Yeah, they got it, some places. Not everywhere. Jackson, Hatties-burg, Greenville…around the cities they got it."

Carson removed the stack of ID cards from his left pocket and examined a black-and-white scan badge by penlight. It had a small, grainy photograph of his face, a thumbprint, a bar code, and a data bit field on the front side. The name on the card matched his new military ID card: Jonathan T. Brice, but the face was his. A spring-clip on top allowed it to be attached to a collar or shirt pocket. "How often do they check the thumbprint?"

"Depends on where you are. Up here, things are kind of loose—until you're right close to the border. They don't check your thumbprint hardly ever. Seems like a waste they even got the thumbprint on it. Most times, they just look at the picture and your face. If you're in a big line of folks, getting food or water, say, then they don't hardly check at all. Just so they see you got a badge, that's all they're looking for most of the time. Least that's how it was in October, last time I was up here on leave."

Carson reflected some more, and asked, "How many people died in the epidemics? Must have been thousands, right?"

"Thousands? Thousands was an average week. Almost three hun-dred thousand died in the whole emergency zone, that's the number I usu-ally hear. Nobody really knows for sure."

"Then there must be a lot of ID badges from dead folks, right?"

"I see what you're getting at, but it won't work," said Amory. "When folks die, they take the badges. They keep track. And a lot of those folks didn't have badges when they died—the badges came later."

"But the point is, they can't keep track of everybody all the time. It's impossible. It's a bluff, basically. Put badges on everybody, and they'll conform like sheep. It's simple psychology."

"Man, you don't know what you're talking about."

Carson asked, "Okay, so what do you want to do? If you have any bright ideas, I'm all ears. Seems to me like neither of us has a whole lot of good options. If you can't go back and you can't hide, what are you going to do?"

"I don't know. Guess I'd go back to Pontapola, where I got family, lots of cousins. Maybe use my cousins' scan badges when I gotta be out and about. Things are a little more chilled out up around there, especially away from the main roads. I might be able to blend in with the scenery, you might say. And maybe I could pick up a badge from somebody who died, like you said. Sometimes whole families died, and nobody checked. Nobody counted them. Death records are still a mess, you're right about that much."

"Where's Pontapola?"

"West of Tupelo."

Carson studied his road map. "If I jump out near the Tennessee line, then you'd just disappear?"

"What choice would I have? I'd have to. Otherwise they'll connect me with those officers you shot back there."

"You could be a witness against me. You could save your ass by going to the police."

"Oh man, what planet are you from? Think about it—this is still Mississippi, and some things don't change. No matter what I said, I'd hang for those three dead officers, one way or the other. With you or without you."

Carson leaned over his map, studying it closely by penlight, thinking aloud. "We're about fifteen miles from Tupelo—the convoy might stop there for gas. Or it might just stop there for the night, or it might just stop there period, end of the mission. It's been almost two hundred miles since we hooked on. We've pushed our luck far enough. So right now is probably our best chance to split off, and go for the Tennessee border on our own."

"Whatever. You got the gun."

"State Road 61 is coming up in a little bit. Slow down now and drop back a little, just ease off the gas. No turn signal. That's good, that's good, there's the turnoff, ready?"

"Are you sure? I don't like taking these back roads, especially not at night."

"It's not a back road; it's a paved state road. It should be all right. Okay, go ahead and take it."

Sergeant Amory asked, "You see a road on the map a few miles from the Tennessee line? Runs right along it on the Mississippi side?"

"I see it. State Road 72. Goes most of the way across the top of the state. What about it?"

"It's a security zone north of it. From 72 to the state line is called the 'buffer zone.' Like a no-man's-land, a few miles wide. No way can we drive across State Road 72. We have to stop this side of it, and then you're on your own. Then it's maybe three or four miles from there to the Tennessee line."

"Why can't we drive across 72? It's Christmas Eve and it's raining. They can't be watching it all."

"Look, if there's any checkpoints in this whole damned state on Christmas Eve, it'll be up there. They don't want refugees from Tennessee coming into Mississippi, and 72 is the line the Guard patrols. You want us to get caught? You want to get shot or hung? Then you just try to make me drive across State Road 72." Rounding a downhill curve, Amory hit the brakes, screeching the pickup to a stop. A tree lay across the road. Another moment of observation revealed that it was a tree trunk, with most of its branches crudely chopped off. A hand-painted sign, black letters on a scrap of plywood, was nailed to the trunk: "BRIDGE OUT AHEAD."

Carson looked between the road blockage and his map. "What bridge?" He examined his map with the penlight. "It doesn't show a bridge on this map, it barely shows this road. You know what bridge is out?"

"Hell if I know, it must be further up ahead. I can't see anything past the tree but more road. But we're getting closer to Memphis, and that earthquake shook everything up but good. Even before that, it was the floods from Matilda. Lot of bridges got busted up or washed away. I don't know this road. We have to turn around. Go back and find another way."

"Go ahead, pull a U-turn."

Sergeant Amory did as he was told. The road was only two lanes wide, with narrow shoulders and steep slopes down to swampy lowlands on both sides. He accomplished the turnaround in three cuts, using great caution on the slippery pavement.

"This map doesn't show any roads smaller than this one we're on," stated Carson. "We might have to go back ten or twelve miles to pick up another road big enough to be on this map. Or we can try one of these local roads and just use my compass. Kind of feel our way north."

"Use the back roads? Feel our way north? Are you serious?"

"Why not?"

"Because this is Mississippi! I don't think that's such a good idea."

"Turn right here, Sergeant, this one looks okay. The pavement is just as wide as the road we've been on. It looks like it runs about northwest, so that should work for us." There were no homes or buildings visible, nothing but dripping trees surrounding their small area of headlamp illumination.

"You sure about this?"

"Come on Sergeant Amory, we'll be all right. When we get to State Road 72, we'll know it. If this map is right, it'll be a big road. Dual lane, like 45 was. We'll know it when we reach it. Then I'll bail out, and you can backtrack on your own. You'll be in Pontapola before daybreak."

"Look, these back roads don't run straight like the big ones, they run more like spaghetti. See? We're turning already. Which way are we going now?"

"Northeast. That's still okay. Just go slow, we'll be okay. Thirty-five is fast enough…"

"We're still turning, so if that was northeast, now we gotta be going east."

"Okay, we'll try the next left turn that looks like it's going north."

After ten minutes of winding and weaving through more woods, swamps, small farms and smaller properties, their headlights occasionally sweeping across scattered house trailers and homes, they were heading almost south again. Few of the houses showed even the least glimmer of light within. Almost all of the dwellings had some crude fence or wall between them and the road. Homemade palisades protected against unseen night dangers.

Carson said, "Okay, turn left here, we'll try this one."

"Seriously, I don't like this, I *really* don't like it!" They were driving on a narrow one-lane asphalt road, between overhanging pines so thick they formed a solid canopy. Beyond their headlights was the darkness of the tomb, with only a slight fire glow from the windows of some houses set back among the trees.

The curving road rolled downhill and ended without warning at a T intersection, and they stopped. Carson looked at his wrist compass again. "I guess right takes us more north. Let's try it."

Amory pulled out, ruefully shaking his head. The road narrowed again, the asphalt badly cracked on both sides, the tree branches sometimes brushing the sides of the truck. Both of them were peering hard into the darkness beyond their headlights. "Shit!" the medic yelled and hit the brakes.

"What the hell is that?" asked Carson. They stared ahead at a plank of rough two-by-ten lumber lying completely across the road, with dozens of long and short nails protruding upward from it. The board was tied to trees at both ends with heavy wire. Driving over the improvised spike strip would cause four flat tires.

"Somebody's own private night barricade," said Amory. "They do that up here nowadays. That's one of the reasons why I didn't want to try these back roads, but you wouldn't listen, you..."

A single shot rang out, and a muzzle flash flared through the under brush to their left.

Carson yelled, "Back up, back up!" but Amory already had the truck in reverse, skidding backward on the slick road. The truck lost traction and fishtailed sideways, the rear wheels going over the shoulder into a shallow ditch, stopped hard by an unseen tree behind them. They had not made it a hundred feet from the defensive barrier of nails.

"Come on Amory, show me what you can do!"

"I'm trying!" The truck grabbed traction as he downshifted to low and slowly goosed the accelerator. They dragged through brush on the other side of the narrow lane, found the pavement again, and were soon sliding through S turns at better than fifty miles an hour. They were totally lost, completely disoriented, the map useless. They blew past the last T intersection, and the road curved several more times while dipping and rising.

Carson peered at his dim mini-compass and laughed. "Well, at least we're heading north again—for the moment anyway. Oh, and nice driving, Sergeant Amory."

"Yeah, anytime. Be sure and tip your driver when I let your white ass out."

"Don't you worry about my white ass."

"Believe me, I won't."

"So, Sergeant Amory, it seems like not everybody in Mississippi got the word about the new gun laws."

"You noticed that too?"

They both laughed in relief.

Carson said, "Imagine that, shooting visitors coming around tonight. They might've hit old Santa Claus himself. Good thing they missed."

"Missed? No, Colonel, they didn't miss. They weren't shooting at us."

"How do you figure that, Sergeant Amory?"

"These boys out here? If they were shooting *at* us, they'd be stretching us out on the road right about now, and going through our pockets.

They wouldn't have missed, no sir. I know—I grew up with these Mississippi crackers. Deer hunting and fast cars are about their two most favorite things in the world. You think they'd miss if they were aiming right between our headlights?"

"No, I guess not."

"That was just a neighborly warning back there. Pure Christian charity. Next time we might not be so lucky. Next time, they might not be in such a friendly mood. Not at all. Colonel, I do believe we have used up all of our good luck tonight."

"Well, Sergeant Amory, it is Christmas Eve. You gotta believe in something."

An hour later Carson sat with his pack against a thick tree, watching State Road 72 from a few yards inside the woods. He'd chosen the tree carefully, so that he could lean back against his pack, his butt on a wide root-branch, keeping him above the mud. The tree's branches were winter bare above him. His green poncho covered his up-folded knees, protecting him from the cold drizzle. Only his face was exposed, peering out of the poncho's hood. Beneath the vinyl poncho was a gore-tex camouflage Army rain parka with its own hood, part of the gear that Sergeant Amory had assembled from his list. Beneath the parka was his field jacket and uniform, and still he was chilled to shivering.

The four-lane road ran east to west in a shallow valley. During the half hour before two in the morning, not a single vehicle had passed by in either direction. Carson already missed the warm, dry interior of the truck. He wondered if he was up to the task of walking the next few miles out of Mississippi, and then more miles into Tennessee. A lot depended on his knees holding up. Hiking well into Tennessee before dawn was his goal. With the addition of the items from the back of the truck, his backpack now weighed at least forty pounds. It was also much bulkier, with the sleeping bag in its waterproof compression sack strapped beneath it and his foam ground pad rolled up and lashed on top.

With its wide median strip and generous shoulders, the state highway before him constituted a danger zone almost a hundred yards across, open to long-range surveillance from either direction and from above. On both sides, the land climbed into woods. The shoulders and median strip were overgrown with brush up to waist height, which would provide some concealment for his passage.

The highway was the last major obstacle in his path before Tennessee. He was determined not to be captured in Mississippi. He rejected the thought of standing before a military tribunal attempting to explain the deaths of the three Guard officers. Two weeks in the quarantine camp had already tested his patience, and being thrown into a cell to await hanging was not an option he would choose. He'd go down shooting, rather than be arrested in Mississippi. If he could make it to the free states of the Northwest, great. If not, well, he was sixty-four and he'd already lived an interesting life. Several lives, in fact. He'd visited over thirty countries in his time, and he'd seen combat in three of them.

Directly ahead of him was Tennessee, an American state, but a state at least partially occupied by foreign soldiers. He'd seen foreign militaries in many countries. He'd fought with them as allies and fought against them as enemies. More recently he'd simply watched them strutting down a tropical street while he sipped a beer at a shady outdoor café table. But this had always been overseas, far from America. Drunk or sober, Phil Carson had never dreamed, never imagined, that he might live to see the day when armed foreign troops were standing on American soil.

The idea of foreign occupational troops in Tennessee both angered and intrigued him. Who had decided to invite them into America, President Tambor? It wouldn't have surprised him. Jamal Tambor had always been a one-worlder, a proponent of global solutions to every perceived problem. Well, whatever the reason, the idea of foreign troops in America stuck in Phil Carson's throat like a rusty hook. Sure, the America he'd known as a young man was long gone, after being debased and defiled for decades. Still, he never imagined that in the end, foreign soldiers would be standing on American soil.

His arms were inside the poncho, across his chest for warmth. He shook the water from the plastic covering and shivered, staring into the wet darkness. Maybe he'd see some more combat in this country he scarcely recognized, these United States of America. United? America was anything but united these days. The Disunited Regions of America was more like it.

At 2:10 a.m. a single humvee passed below him, driving westward at about forty miles an hour. It was hard-topped, with no visible gun mounts, running with subdued headlights. Routine patrol, the bare minimum. Probably making a token patrol run from Corinth in the east to the northwest corner of the state. Memphis was about sixty miles west. Directly across from Memphis was where the Mississippi Guard would patrol heavily, not out here in the boonies.

Carson gave the humvee five minutes to depart, then snapped the straps across his chest and his waist, securing his pack tightly to his body. He leaned forward to take the full weight on his back, and rose stiffly. Getting up had always been the hardest part, and it was much harder at age sixty-four. The straps bit into his shoulders, the poncho snagged on thorns concealed in the overhanging limbs, but after a struggle he was on his legs and away from the dripping branches. It was forty feet to the asphalt through the unmowed grass and weeds, hunched over to lower his profile.

As a soldier, he might have done it at a low crawl, but not now, not at his age, not with this pack on his back. He held the Army M-9 Beretta pistol in his right hand out of habit, realizing it provided no more than token security under the circumstances.

He put his head down and hustled across two rain-slick lanes of pavement, then down and up the ditch at the center of the wide median strip, through more high grass and weeds growing into brushy trees. Then there were two more lanes of wet asphalt and another highway shoulder dipping down and then rising toward the northern tree line. He was breathing heavily with the effort as he pushed through the vegetation, the clods uneven beneath his feet. He slipped and fell heavily onto his face when he was almost into the woods. He crawled the last fifteen feet, the pack trying to flip him over as it slid to the left off his shoulders. Finally he was under the cover of forest, and he rolled onto his back. His pack was beneath him, poncho and straps and belt and gear and gravity twisting and pulling him in all directions at once, tying him to the earth like Gulliver as he panted for breath, rainwater dripping from unseen leaves onto his face.

But at least he was once again in the protective cover of the woods. No hidden sniper with a night vision scope had been watching this remote stretch of highway. He still had several hours of darkness ahead of him, and it was only three miles to Tennessee. He just had to catch his breath, reorganize his pack's straps and his rain gear, roll back over and force himself to his feet again. Just get to his feet…after he took off the poncho. The poncho was a mistake; there were too many loose ends and flaps for sliding easily through the branches and brambles. He sat Indian style, slung off his pack, and pulled the poncho over his head with difficulty. Then the pack went back on, over his gore-tex parka. The dripping poncho was clumsily rolled up and hung over the bottom of the pack's strap on his left side. All of this was done by feel, with cold, wet fingers. In the dark, drippy woods, even trivial tasks like rearranging his gear were ordeals. During this process, he had lost track of his pistol, and he groped like a blind man in the sodden forest litter until he felt the familiar Beretta.

I'm way too old for this shit, he told himself as he struggled onto his muddy knees, which unerringly found a sharp stone, and then up onto his legs, grunting and wheezing with exertion. He remembered a time when he had carried much heavier packs, plus a rifle with a grenade launcher attached, along with a special combat harness loaded with extra ammunition magazines and 40mm grenades, plus mortar rounds, and claymore mines, and LAAWs rockets, and C-4 demo charges… Where had that young warrior gone? It was so, so long ago…

They had dropped out of low-hovering Hueys in Cambodia and Laos, with more than seventy pounds of gear and ammo and demo and commo and water and rations strapped onto their bodies. Now he had a much lighter pack, and only a 9mm pistol for a weapon, and he was winded after the first few hundred yards. *A man my age should be in a dry, cozy house by a fireplace*, he thought. Near a crackling fire, with a blanket over his legs, a whisky in one hand and a cigar in the other. Maybe a dog at his feet, and a woman nearby.

Where is my warm fireplace? Nowhere, he thought with bitter regret while pushing wet, thorny branches away from his face. All of the roads not taken. The women not married (despite two near misses), the children not raised. Well, he'd never been one for settling down; he'd known that since he was a young man. This solitary end game was the price one paid for being an incurable wanderer, an eternal misfit. The Army had been the only place he had ever truly fitted in, but the Southeast Asia War Games had soured him on the prospect of a military career. Now at the age of sixty-four, he was homeless and unmissed by anyone, anywhere. There was not even a stray dog or a cat somewhere to lament his passing.

Stripped down to its essence, his life story was a catalog of one loss after the other, full only of colorful tales he could tell no one, no one who could even begin to understand. The only ones who knew the truth of his stories were either dead or otherwise lost to him. Just as lost as Paulo, his last crewmember, who was lost at sea, which was as lost as lost gets. Tonight Phil Carson was rich only in aches and scars and memories, all of his worldly possessions packed in his old rucksack and concealed within his belt. He laughed as he inventoried his few possessions. There was still an ammo can containing $25,000 buried back in Virginia, but the currency was in the old greenbacks, as worthless today as Confederate dollars. As worthless now, in the greater scheme of things, as his life. A canceled check from a defunct bank. Void where prohibited, which was anywhere and everywhere.

So why go on? Why stack more struggle and hardship on top of his already overflowing account of desolation? He could simply lie down on the sodden forest floor and give in to inevitable nature. Let the rain fall on his face and surrender to the big chill, the final, unending sleep. It would be easy and painless, simply merging with this forest until roots ran through his remains. Why continue putting one boot in front of the other, tripping through brambles, collecting only cuts and scrapes on his hands and face from invisible thorns?

Why? He slowly shook his head and laughed again, stooped over beneath his heavy load, forcing himself through snagging brush and over leg-trapping deadfall. The doctor's pistol was now jammed under his belt; he needed both hands to navigate these choking woods. Why did he go on? He knew the answer, he'd always known it: because he was not the type to give in, to lie down and surrender to fate. He was a fighter, win or lose. He was a Southerner, born a Virginian, and fighting was a natural part of his heritage. Even for lost causes. Maybe especially for lost causes. He wouldn't lie down and submit to nature, not while he was capable of moving on.

The third alternative to quitting here or going on was even worse. If he was captured in Mississippi, the alternative was a rope or a firing squad. That would be a disgraceful and anticlimactic ending for an old jungle fighter, real estate wheeler-dealer and occasional smuggler. They hanged pirates, traitors and murderers, and he was none of those. Which meant that his first order of business was getting the hell out of Mississippi. Then he could figure out just how he would make it all the way to the Northwest, and maybe to some kind of freedom.

But first he had to hump the last three miles out of Mississippi and lose himself in Tennessee. His parka's hood brushing against his ears diminished his sense of hearing, so he pushed it back and pulled the rolled-up boonie hat from his left pants cargo pocket. Except for its modern digital camo pattern, it wasn't much different from the ones he had worn in Asia forty years earlier. It felt exactly the same in his hands, and on his head, protecting his ears and neck as he slid through the dripping foliage.

7

The deer stand was one of Zack Tutweiler's best thinking places. The rain had masked the sound of his climbing up the tree's nailed-on steps and into the plywood box an hour before dawn. The blind's roof sheltered him from the rain. For as long as seventeen-year-old Zack had been allowed to go hunting by himself, the blind had been a place he could go without being hassled for choosing solitude. He brought home enough meat that nobody bitched about his disappearing with his compound bow into the forest. Now there was nobody left to bitch at him for anything. He was the last one still living at the end of Bear Trail Road, the last inhabitant of their refuge from the world.

The Tutweilers had hidden very well, but not well enough. The troubles of the world had sought them out in spite of their preparation, their camouflage and their faith. All the praying in the world had not prevented the flu from choking the life out of his twin sisters Becky and Annie last winter, the winter of the hurricane floods and the great earthquakes. Becky had died first and Annie a day later, both drowning in their own lung fluids. Zack and his family had prayed continuously, to no effect.

And praying hadn't stopped the raging infection from killing his eleven-year-old brother Sammy last September. He'd gashed his knee with a hatchet while helping to trim the branches off their winter firewood. The most powerful antibiotics in their family medicine chest couldn't stop that infection, and poor Sammy had died in horrible pain. Zack had helped teach Sam how to use the ax, but he had not taught him well enough. And now his little brother was buried in the cold ground forever.

After Sammy died, the praying had stopped, even Mom's praying. This was some months after Mom had run out of her blue pills, the ones for her depression. These days when pills ran out, they ran out for good.

All along Mom had been waiting for the Rapture and praying for the Rapture, and in the end it was all for nothing. "We sure got the tribulation," she'd often say, "But when, oh when, are we getting the blessed Rapture?" It wasn't long after Sam died that she took the baby up to the bridge. "Rapturecide" is how Zack often thought of it.

Dad said she must have had an accident, probably baby Sarah had slipped and Mom had tried to save her, the river all swollen and running fast…but in his heart Zack had never believed this. He didn't know if Dad believed it either, but he'd never challenged his father on the issue. It would have brought nothing but pain, and pain they already had to overflowing. They found Mom stuck in the rushes along the bank, but they never did find little Sarah. Dad said it had to have been an accident, but even he didn't sound convinced.

But Zack knew what had happened, in his mind he knew. It was Rapturecide. He'd heard the term whispered at the swap market, at the crossroads town of Walnut, Mississippi, a half-hour bike ride away. Sometimes whole families had gone that way, in their exhausted desperation challenging God to put up or shut up, once and for all. If they were not among the chosen, selected to fly up to heaven and avoid the tribulations, then who was? They were true believers, and God had forsaken them. Zack didn't believe in the Rapture business, but he knew that many others did. When their deepest belief was finally shattered and crushed, the life quickly went out of them.

Zack had a clear mental picture of their final moments, gleaned from a thousand imaginings. Mom standing on the low steel trestle of the railroad bridge over the Little Hatchie, clutching baby Sarah to her heart. The dark creek running high and swift on the floods just beneath her feet. Staring heavenward through the clouds and making the final leap for everlasting glory. Giving God one last chance to carry them up on angels' wings, to relieve them of their unending earthly travails. This was on the tenth of October, after it had rained for forty straight days. Mom had hardly spoken a word in weeks, not since little Sammy died, and she hadn't smiled in even longer. And then she carried baby Sarah down to the river, in the never-ending rain. One of the few remaining bridges around, and it was her launch pad to heaven, according to Zack's reckoning.

So if God was watching, He'd flat missed His chance to perform a miracle. Or maybe not, maybe God had snatched up their eternal souls anyway, because of her great demonstration of faith in Him. Maybe God had simply allowed their mortal bodies to fall into the swift current. Zack often wondered about this point: was faith alone enough to cancel out the sin of suicide? Mom just couldn't bear living anymore. It was too hard, much too hard, especially after losing Becky and Annie and Sammy—and after running out of her blue pills.

Their lives had been hard before the hurricane floods and the earthquakes, but Dad had prepared them well, moving the family from Tupelo up to the Holly Springs National Forest near the Tennessee line. Moved them from the city to the hidden dead-end Bear Trail Road, to the cinder block house he'd built with his own strong hands. Dad was a survivalist even before the crash, before the Greater Depression had set in. He'd had foresight; he'd been one of the few mad Noahs who had seen the great flood tide of misery coming, back when there was hardly an unhappy cloud to be seen in the then perpetually blue Mississippi sky.

Against every friend's recommendation and well-meant word of family advice, they'd left their comfortable home in Tupelo and moved to their own five acres on the uppermost edge of Mississippi, backed right against the National Forest. They had water from their own well, they had firewood and chickens and enough stored rice and beans to last for years. Even after the dollar crashed to nothing, they hadn't starved. They could survive, even without electricity from the power grid this last year, since the quakes. They had hidden from the looters, robbers, and gang rapers after the quakes, they had survived all of the visible dangers, but Bear Trail Road was not hidden from the epidemics. Their refuge was not hidden from infections that no antibiotics could defeat. And Bear Trail Road was certainly not hidden from the affliction of despair, not when the flooding Little Hatchie River whispered its siren song to Mom's beaten-down soul.

Then it was just the two of them, father and son, and even then they could survive. They had buried all of the rest of the family, had shed rivers of tears, but quitting was not in Dad's vocabulary. Zack had grown up hearing that and he knew it was true. Dad would never quit—Dad was the rock. His father prayed, but he didn't believe in the Rapture, and he would not hasten his way to joining his family on the Other Side. Father and son would continue to struggle, they would push on, and they would survive.

They would emerge intact on the other side of the long emergency, if it were in any way possible. Zack was nearly eighteen, almost "of age," Dad had said. Zack Tutweiler would find a girl to marry, and the family would not die. Tutweilers had survived wild Indians, the Civil War, the Spanish flu and the Great Depression, and they had not yet been pushed out of Mississippi. Tutweilers had fought in every American war, but enough of their men had returned to Mississippi to carry on the name down through the generations. They were people who knew when to lay low and when to push back and when to fight with animal ferocity. Quitting was not in their vocabulary, which is why Dad clung to the threadbare belief that Mom had gone into the river to save baby Sarah.

And so it had been only the two of them these last months, until a week ago. Dad had gone out after midnight. He had people to meet over the state line in Tennessee, trading partners who couldn't come to the swap markets in Walnut or Corinth. Sometimes Zack accompanied him on these walks, but more often not. When Dad went out alone, Zack stayed up waiting, although he pretended to be asleep when Dad slipped out of the house. But that last time he'd heard a single echoing bang, and his father had not returned.

He didn't find his father—what was left of him—until the middle of the next day. He was in the National Forest a mile northwest of their home, almost on the border. His father had been blown to pieces, his powerful body shattered. Even his shotgun had been blasted into a bent piece of junk. Zack hid in the woods near the human fragments of his father, shaking, crying, and wondering what to do next. He also found pieces of rocket casing and what was probably part of a rocket tail fin knifed into a tree near the body. His father had been killed by one of those little missiles that dropped down from the unseen drones. He knew of them from his dad, who had heard of them from the men he met in Tennessee. He'd never imagined his father would be killed by one, not in Mississippi.

So now Zack was the last of the Mississippi Tutweilers, who the Indians and the Yankees and the Spanish flu couldn't kill off. The end of the line. He'd sometimes considered following Mom and Sarah into the Little Hatchie, but even in death his father's voice was stronger: Tutweilers don't quit. They might get knocked down, but they always get back up. But what was the point of remaining in Mississippi now? The men who had killed his father were in Tennessee, he thought. This was why Zack was up in the deer stand on Christmas morning, thinking, watching the first hint of false dawn appear above the treetops, where the dead power lines cut a swath through the forest leading up into Tennessee.

Now was the time the deer moved. Night fog hung low over the ground. Sometimes he'd see antlers before he'd even see a deer, but more often the bucks pushed the does out ahead: no dummies they. Well, a doe would serve him just fine, he could trade the fresh meat to the Mississippi Guard soldiers stationed at Walnut. His eyes strained to see down the game trails that ran in the brushy terrain beneath the hanging power lines, beneath his deer stand of green-painted plywood. It didn't need to be camouflaged. Deer weren't made to think about odd shapes, like the square green box nailed to the branches twenty feet above their trail.

Movement in the shroud of mist attracted his eye. Most of his face was hidden behind the square shooting hole in the south side of the blind. He saw the tan-gray color of a deer, moving cautiously in the underbrush, pausing, and moving again. Zack silently shifted to one knee and brought his compound bow up, an arrow ready, his right hand gripping the string's trigger release.

The shifting tawny shape slowly emerged through the ground fog, but it soon became apparent that it was not a deer at all—it was a man. A man coming up one of the game trails, northbound. A man with a pack on his back, a man wearing the camouflage uniform of the Army, a matching wide-brimmed hat concealing his face. Zack shrank away from the shooting port and put his eye to one of the peepholes. Deer would not pay attention to a plywood box suspended from a tree, but a soldier would. The solitary soldier could be a point man. He could be a few yards ahead of a squad or a platoon, probing for booby traps or ambushers.

But as Zack peered at him, he noticed some things that didn't fit. The man had no rifle or machine gun; in one hand he held a pistol. No point man would come this way armed with only a pistol. But the lone man was wearing the new camouflage pattern uniform of the Mississippi Guard and the United States Army, and it was forbidden on pain of death for civilians to wear it. So the man was a member of the Guard, or he was an Army soldier—or had been.

The drone that had dropped a rocket on his father had been fired by such men. His father was out after curfew, of that there was no doubt. And he was carrying an illegal pump-action shotgun. The government had, he guessed, every legal justification to blow him up with a rocket for violating those two laws. That's the way the world worked under martial law. Zack understood this, but it didn't make him feel any better about it.

This soldier was alone, Zack finally decided. He was one of the soldiers who helped to fly the drones, who dropped the missiles on the curfew violators. Men like him had dropped the missile on his father. Was he out checking the results of another missile drop, like the one that had killed his father? No. Alone and armed only with a pistol, he was more likely either a spy or a deserter. He could be a military spy from Tennessee, on his way back to make a report. Maybe he was even one of the foreign "peacekeepers" in an American uniform.

The man paused for a solid minute, looking in all directions, and stared up at the boxy deer blind. Zack knew it must be clearly outlined against the pale dawn sky. But the man had no heat-sensing infrared scope, so Zack trusted that he was invisible in his box—as long as he remained motionless and made no sound.

Finally, the man looked around in a wide circle and continued walking a few steps at a time, passing less than thirty feet away, directly in front of the blind. Zack slowly shifted to another peephole in the long side of the blind, and he saw the man going away now, walking north up the game trail below the power lines, with brush and saplings and bushes up to his shoulders. It was winter and the shrubs were mostly without leaves, so he could easily see the soldier through them.

Without thinking, operating on automatic, Zack twisted around in the box and rose to a one-knee crouch, his compact bow rasping against the interior plywood, almost but not quite silent. The arrow was nocked into the string, his trigger release was ready in his right hand. He rose to a crouch and took aim through the square cutout on the north side of the box. He took in a breath and held it, drew back the seventy-pound pull string, and put the glowing orange plastic bead sight on the man's back as he reached full draw. The compound bow's wheels rolled to a stop, held for a moment—and then he let fly.

Phil Carson heard something scrape behind him and he turned to his right, just beginning to twist and dive when he was struck. He fell onto his face in the wet underbrush, rolled onto his right side, his pack preventing him from rolling onto his back. He saw the arrow buried in the ground just ahead of him, feathers aiming back at the tree stand behind him. Already his leg was going numb, and his hip and backside burned. What an idiot he'd been, taking the easy path, stumbling up the power line right-of-way, not even sure if he was in Mississippi or Tennessee. The moment he was hit, he'd known the arrow had come from the wooden blind he'd just passed. He had studied the boxy deer stand but he'd ruled out that it might be occupied. He'd disregarded the potential danger, eager to make time and get as far as possible into Tennessee before full light.

Now he'd been skewered by an arrow, and he knew the unseen hunter would be drilling him again any second, would nail him to the ground. He'd been sneaking up a game trail, surrounded by bushes that were head high or better, so perhaps he was now invisible from the blind, hidden down among the dripping ferns on the forest floor. The arrow seemed to have sliced through his left thigh or buttocks, gone all the way through and out again. There was no way to know how badly he'd been injured, and no time to examine the wound.

Carson knew the hunter would be coming down out of the stand, following his wounded prey, looking for another shot, eager to put a fatal arrow through his vitals. If he was going to survive even the next few minutes, he had to move, regardless of the pain, no matter how much he was bleeding. The backpack was too heavy; he released the chest and belly straps and awkwardly slid his arms out. He kept the pistol in his right hand, and using his elbows and his uninjured right leg, he began to push himself away from the game trail into an evergreen holly thicket. He wormed his way into the almost clear space at the very bottom, and out again on the other side into an area of roots and wet leaves and bushes and small pines like Christmas trees.

Seconds counted. He ignored the pain and low-crawled ahead a dozen more yards, fully aware that he was leaving a trail of blood and broken vegetation a blind man could follow. His creeping path brought him alongside a massive deadfall pine trunk, bare of bark to its yellow core. It had fallen long ago, and once it became rotten it had broken into segments following the contour of the ground. When he reached the end, where its roots had once upended the earth, he turned sharply around it and pushed his way rapidly back in the direction he had come, racing against time, against the bow hunter he knew was coming. The earth was lower on this side of the trunk, lower and eroded, and he pushed his body into the hollow space alongside the bottom of the log. When he came to a break where the rotted log had broken into two pieces he stopped, his face pressed against the pungent mud and wet wood punk and loose forest litter, and he waited, with just one eye looking up through the gap.

He didn't have long to wait. The hunter was dressed in camouflage raingear, the pattern he recognized as something like Mossy Oak, so similar to the background of the wet winter forest that he almost appeared to melt into it each time he stopped. He carried a small camouflage-painted bow, an arrow at the ready but not drawn back. He was walking in a crouch, pausing to snake his way through the underbrush and, it appeared, to stoop down and touch Carson's blood trail. The hunter's parka hood was pulled up, covering most of his face, a puff of vapor visible with each breath.

The hunter approached in short, quiet steps, until he was on the other side of the rotten trunk. In spite of the pain and steady blood loss, Carson felt a measure of satisfaction. The hunter was used to following the blood trails of herbivore game like deer, animals that went deeper and deeper into cover until they found a place to rest, and then to bleed out and die. Deer didn't double back. Deer didn't fishhook their own path, to lay an ambush for a pursuing hunter.

The bow hunter moved silently, pausing to listen and look, then took a few more steps, the wet forest litter masking any sound. He reached the break in the log on the other side of Carson's head; Carson's body was still hidden in the hollow beneath the log against the wet earth. The bow was carried with the arrow pointing at an angle to the hunter's left, away from his hiding place. Carson held his Beretta alongside his cheek, pressed against the dirt and leaves. His head was turned so that he could peek from under the brim of his boonie cap, up through the break in the deadfall log. The hunter's face slowly turned toward the foot-wide break in the rotted trunk, his arrow still aimed away, and he stared downward. Carson saw in the hunter's altered expression the very instant that he recognized the uniform in the forest litter on the other side of the log. In that moment of mutual recognition, Carson thrust his arm and pistol upward through the break in the spongy log and began to squeeze the trigger, the Beretta's first shot requiring a long double-action trigger pull.

The hunter's bow swerved around, but the arrow snagged on a sapling branch and stuck. In the next moment Carson saw a boy's wide-eyed face looking back at him, and he stopped the tightening of his trigger finger in mid-squeeze. The young hunter jerked at his bow, trying to free it, still staring into Carson's face with huge brown eyes, his mouth wide open.

"Don't you do it, boy! Don't move, if you want to live."

The young man froze, then seemed to relax, his posture sagging. His open mouth formed into something like a smile, revealing crooked front teeth. He said, "Shit. You doubled back and ambushed your own blood trail. My father showed me that trick. He said men and mountain lions will do that, but I never hunted mountain lions. Or men, till now. I should have been ready. I should have seen it coming." The half smile faded, but did not entirely disappear. In a soft voice the boy asked, "So, are you going to shoot me now, mister?" He did not seem overly concerned about the possibility.

Carson replied, "Put down the bow, and then I'll decide."

"I found your blood trail and I followed it. You've lost a lot of blood already. I don't think you're going to last very long. You're going to get weaker, then you'll go into shock, and then you'll die." The young hunter slowly lowered his bow toward the ground, keeping his gaze on the black pistol a few feet away, aimed at his chest.

"Do I look like a whitetail deer, boy? I've been shot before, and I ain't died yet."

"Not with a hunting broadhead you ain't. That's four razor blades through your guts. You ain't got long. Better make your peace, mister."

"You only shot me in the ass, through and through. I'll live."

"I found your pack, back up your blood trail. You turned, and the arrow went through your sleeping bag. You're damn lucky to be alive: I can hit a rabbit at that range."

"Not today. I heard you up there in the box, that's why I turned."

"Yeah." The boy was still smiling wistfully. He didn't seem entirely bothered by this sudden twist in outcomes. "So, what now, old man?"

"Old man, is it? Well this old man has you dead to rights, boy. I can shoot you, that's what." Carson eased his gun hand over until the back of his wrist was against the broken trunk, to steady his pistol. "Huh. Some hunter you are."

Still almost smiling, the boy said, "I think if you were going to shoot me, you'd have done it already."

"Maybe. Or maybe I'm deciding if you're worth killing. If you're up to my own high standards." Carson sighed audibly, thinking of the three dead Mississippi Guard officers. "Or maybe I've had enough killing for one night." Carson pushed himself up onto his left elbow, getting a better look at the young bow hunter, trying not to wince from the pain. The boy couldn't have been over twenty years old, with just a wispy adolescent mustache and smooth cheeks. But he was right: Carson was going into shock from blood loss. If he passed out, the boy could simply finish him off with an arrow or a knife at his leisure. Or just leave him to bleed out and die.

So if he was going to shoot the boy, he had to do it right now or lose his chance forever. But already he knew he wouldn't. He'd been unintentionally truthful: he'd had enough killing for one night. He wasn't going to begin this new day by shooting a smiling boy, an American kid. Not even one who had just tried to put a hunting arrow through his brisket and had very nearly succeeded. "You know, boy, I can shoot you right now, if I want to. Right...now. Keep that in mind...when..."

With that Phil Carson's vision grew dark at the edges, diminishing like the end of a Looney Tunes cartoon down to a single point of light, and then the light blinked out.

General Mirabeau sent his chief of staff out of his large but Spartan office at his Fort Benning headquarters. They had discussed the case of the three murdered officers in Mississippi, and the general had briefly reviewed the preliminary case files. Because of the sensitivity of the murder case involving three senior officers, he had kept a tight leash on the investigation. He had assigned the CID investigators, two majors who were personally loyal to him. The Criminal Investigation Command in the emergency zone answered only to him, he had made damn sure of that. After examining the personnel files of the dead officers and reading the preliminary CID investigative report, he pushed the intercom button on his desk and told his secretary to send in the medic.

Three sharp raps on the outside of his doorframe.

"Enter."

Sergeant Amory, in his pressed ACU camouflage uniform, marched the four paces to a position in front of the general's desk and locked his eyes upon a spot on the wood paneling above and behind the general. General Mirabeau sat upright in his executive chair and gestured at the gray-and-green government chair across the desk from him. Amory was a shade or two darker than himself. His hair was freshly shaved up the sides and back. High and tight, in preparation for what he must have assumed would be the final stage of his inquisition. Quinton Amory was a fine-looking black Army Soldier; he was almost recruiting-poster material. Almost. "Take a seat, Sergeant." The enlisted man was almost trembling, no doubt wondering if by the end of the week he would be shot or swinging from a rope.

"Thank you, General." Amory dropped rigidly into the chair, his hands neatly laid on his knees, his eyes still fixed on the wall above the general.

"I have a few questions, Sergeant. I just want some background information. Maybe something that's not in this stack of paper."

"Sir?"

"Go ahead, Sergeant, speak freely. Tell me what you think I really should know. Something that's not in this official report."

"I...well...I just don't rightly know what you might mean by that, General, sir, I..."

"Don't try to run that jive routine on me, Sergeant Amory, it won't work. You had two years of college, before everything went to shit. You're a smart guy, so let's get on with it. I want to understand some of the intangibles. What didn't make it into these reports."

"Yes sir, I'll do my best, sir."

"That's better. Now, this John Doe, AKA 'Colonel Brice.' You first met him when he came walking out of Alabama, on the coast road."

"He had already been detained when I first saw him, but yes sir."

"He had amnesia."

"So he said."

"And what did you find in his pack that's not mentioned in your report? Did you forget to include something?"

Sergeant Amory paused, his facial muscles flinching, his eyes unsteady. "Uh...yes sir. Just some coffee, sir. In a plastic jar."

"Real coffee, Sergeant Amory? Not fake stuff? Not chicory?"

"Yes sir, real coffee."

"Fresh coffee, not a-few-years-old instant coffee?"

"Fresh. Very fresh." Amory reflexively smiled at the memory.

"When you found it, where did you think he had obtained the coffee, Sergeant?"

"I didn't think about it, sir. I couldn't guess."

"And Lieutenant Colonel Foley, he knew about the coffee?"

"Yes sir. He had some of the coffee that we made."

"And after that, Doctor...I mean, Lieutenant Colonel Foley, he took a personal interest in this 'John Doe'?"

"Yes sir."

"And he included you in a plan to drive this man across the Mississippi River at Vicksburg?"

"Yes sir."

"Did you think this was an authorized military operation, Sergeant? On Christmas Eve?"

Amory lowered his eyes and hung his head. "I...no, I didn't think so. But—"

"You brought the new ID cards to him, in quarantine at Camp Shelton. Colonel Foley gave you money for black-market gasoline and camping gear. And most of the gear was Army issue, including a current-issue uniform?"

"Yes..." Amory replied, his voice hushed. Under emergency rule, these could be hanging crimes.

General Mirabeau said, "And then it all went wrong."

Amory was still looking at his boots, shaking his head, quivering. "Yes, all wrong, sir, all wrong. He had a pistol—"

"John Doe had a pistol?"

"Yessir! Colonel Foley and the others, at the trailer, they pulled guns on him, they said he wasn't going anywhere, that they were going to find out where his coffee was hidden, right then and there, that night." Amory looked up, wild-eyed. "And he shot them, all three of them!"

The general paused, studying the sergeant's face. "How old would you say he was?"

"John Doe? Colonel Brice?"

"Stick with John Doe, Sergeant. There's no Colonel Brice. He does not exist."

"I'd say he was about sixty, or maybe a little older. But very, very fit."

"He must be pretty quick for a man his age, wouldn't you say? Pretty quick, to shoot three Army officers like that? Three officers with drawn pistols."

"Very quick. I think he was just so pissed off at being double-crossed, I mean he was angry, raging angry! I thought he was going to kill me too, and then he made me drive him north."

"I understand, Sergeant. He had a pistol aimed at your back, and you had every reason to believe that he would kill you if you didn't obey his orders. Now, describe his tattoo."

"Sir?"

"You saw John Doe's tattoo during his quarantine washdown, didn't you? It's in your report." General Mirabeau tapped the file on his desk.

"Yessir. Army jump wings. Airborne wings." Amory pointed to his left upper arm. Right here, about an inch wide."

"Can you estimate how old it was? The Airborne tattoo."

"Very old, sir. Decades old at least. They get that look, faded and blurry."

General Mirabeau paused, staring beyond Amory at one plaque among the many on the opposite wall, a plaque that incorporated an outsized replica of silver Army jump wings on mahogany. After almost a minute of reflection, during which Amory remained frozen in his chair, the general asked, "And when you left him at the buffer zone, he was walking north, toward Tennessee, correct?"

"Yes sir."

"And you marked the drop-off location on the map in this report correctly?"

"Yes, exactly correct."

"So where do you think he is now, Sergeant?"

"Really, I wouldn't know. I suppose he's in Tennessee."

"Thank you, Sergeant Amory. That's all. You're dismissed."

Amory stood at attention, about-faced smartly, and marched out of the room.

General Mirabeau leaned back in his chair and slumped down, thinking. Sergeant Quinton Amory would present no problem. The medic could be transferred to some distant post, kept in quarantine work and effectively isolated. Fortunately, the media were no longer a consideration, not under the emergency laws. The doctor, the colonel and the major were already dead. The entire case could be slammed shut on his word alone. A plausible explanation was readily available: the three officers had been killed in a falling-out among thieves, a crossfire over some black-market double-cross.

The next question was: should he notify his counterparts in Tennessee that an unknown subject, a dangerous killer, was probably loose in their territory? It wasn't only a question of justice. From what he had gleaned, John Doe had killed the three officers in self-defense, after being betrayed. The three dead officers were dirty, involved in some black-market dealings. If he had caught them at it, they might have been hanged. At this stage in the economic and political recovery of the emergency zone, it wouldn't be good for public or military morale to publicize this bizarre case of senior officers involved in black-market deals and shootouts. They were already dead.

General Mirabeau examined the duplicate ID card on his desk, made from the backup file on the computer that had made the original. The conspirators hadn't managed to erase every trace of the creation of their fake ID card. "Colonel Brice" looked like a very serious man, with pale blue eyes and a scar across the top of his forehead. It would be simple to have the entire file sent to his civilian counterparts at Fort Campbell, along with a summary of the case.

But why should he? He despised the new rulers to the north, especially what they were doing in Tennessee and Kentucky. Using foreign soldiers on American soil to round up and relocate Americans...that was something he could not understand and would never consider. The Deep South emergency zone had its problems, to be sure, but Americans were solving those problems. In a year, two at most, they would hold new elections and he would step down. Possibly even run for governor of Georgia, his home state. In time, that could even lead him to the White House, as a candidate with a proven record in crisis management and disaster recovery.

In any event, life would eventually pick up and then go on in the Deep South, with or without him. But what the civilian leadership was doing in Tennessee and Kentucky was beyond the pale. Using the Mexican troops of the so-called North American Legion and, even worse, the foreign contract soldiers of the mercenary battalions, that was simply unimaginable. Why should he help them find an old American soldier on the run, even if he had killed three of his officers? Three corrupt officers. Well, he wouldn't do it, he finally decided. To hell with the traitors up north. Let them find the old soldier on their own—if they can.

The fingertips of the general's right hand went to his left side and gently touched the wings that he had worn since graduating from the Fort

Benning jump school thirty years before. He spun around in his executive chair and stared out his window at the massive jump tower across the green fields, where even during the long emergency trainees still made their first controlled descents under canopy. *Airborne, all the way*, he mouthed silently.

Carson was dragged, bumping and scraping along a path, sunlight flickering between trees. He was pushed and rolled and jabbed, and with every movement came stabbing pain he could neither grasp nor evade. His world was a swirling cavalcade of faces and places, remembered or imagined. Jet and prop fighter airplanes flew above him as he heard desperate radio calls for air support, screams and explosions.

Eventually there was stillness, and when he awoke he was in a small, dimly lit room. He was lying on his side on a narrow bed, covered by a quilt, wedged into position with cushions and rolled-up blankets. Besides the pain, he was possessed of a great thirst. Above him, model airplanes locked in frozen dogfights hung by threads, suspended from the ceiling. Posters of rock groups and professional athletes covered the walls.

The young hunter entered the room and sat on a wooden chair near the bed. He was wearing jeans and a gray sweatshirt. Thick brown hair nearly covered his brown eyes. The boy said, "Welcome back to the world of the living."

"Who are you?" Carson had to work his lips and tongue to speak, seeking saliva and finding none.

"I'm Zack Tutweiler."

"The kid who shot me. Zachary? Okay, Zack. When...how long?"

"That was Christmas morning—Tuesday. It's Friday now. You've been in and out, but this is the first time you made sense. You talked a lot, but it was mostly crazy talk."

Phil Carson stared at the boy, blinking, working his jaw, licking his lips with a dry tongue. "Well, Zack, thanks for not putting another arrow through me."

"Yeah. And thanks for not shooting me."

They stared at each other.

Carson broke the silence. "Zack, where are your parents?"

"Parents? My parents... They're dead. Both dead. I'm the only one left."

Carson continued to stare. "I'm sorry."

"Yeah. Me too."

"Is this your house?"

"My father—I mean—yes. It's mine now, I guess."

"Are we far from the place...I mean...how did I get here? Did I walk?"

"No, you lost too much blood. You were out of it. I wasn't even sure you'd live. I dragged you here in a travois."

"A what?" The word, which rhymed with "boy," was unfamiliar to Carson.

"You know, two poles, with a blanket tied between. Like the Indians used. Only I used your poncho instead of a blanket, and two saplings."

"Where did you learn *that* trick?"

"The Boy Scouts. And from my father. And from reading a lot."

Carson pondered this, his mind still swirling with dreams, fragments of nightmares, and half-remembered images of trees and sky, of being pulled through the woods. "Zack, have you got some water?"

"Right there in the cup. You've been drinking plenty already. It's juice, made from powder. You don't remember?" He pointed to the small table set up near the head of the bed. There was a purple sports bottle with a long flexible straw protruding from its cap, and he handed it to Carson.

"I'm not sure what I remember. I'm not sure of anything." He took the cup and drank from the plastic straw. The room-temperature grape-flavored drink was delicious.

The boy asked, "So, what's your name? I think we can rule out what's on these ID cards, *Colonel Brice*." Zack Tutweiler held up Carson's stack of identity cards, fanning them out like a hand of cards. "These are brand new—they never spent a day in a wallet. So, where did you get them? Your uniform is brand new too, and so is your nametag and rank. And why were you running north? Most folks are trying to get out of Tennessee. You're the first one I've met going the other way."

"It's pretty...complicated." Carson set the water bottle back on the table.

"Well, go ahead anyway. I've got time. Why don't you start with your name? Your real name."

Carson stared at the blue Spitfire prop fighter hanging above him. Red and white shark's teeth decals had been carefully applied to the plastic model's nose. He dropped his eyes back to the young man who had shot him with an arrow and then brought him home and nursed him. The kid could still finish him off or turn him in if he so desired, that was a given. He was lying on his side in a strange bed, in an unknown house, completely at the boy's mercy.

He had nearly been killed when he'd shot the three Army officers back near Camp Shelton on Christmas Eve. Then he'd been shot with an arrow on Christmas morning. If he were arrested now, they'd hang him for sure. He wasn't just living on borrowed time; he was far beyond that stage. There wasn't even a term for his current precarious state of existence. Playing charades with this boy seemed pointless. "My name is Phil

Carson. I'll tell you the rest, anything you want to know, but tell me about my wound first. How bad is it?"

"The arrow went through your left butt cheek at an angle and out your left thigh, on the outside. Split your butt open pretty good. So I put on the coagulating powder—lucky for you I had a pack of it. I always carry Quik Clot when I'm hunting, in case of an accident. That stopped the bleeding, but you'd already lost a lot of blood. You must be pretty tough: I think most people die when they get a wound like that. Maybe it's because you're old, or maybe you're just lucky...I don't know."

"Lucky? If I was lucky, I wouldn't be here at all."

"Maybe. So, who's Paulo? And who's Ranya?"

"Long story..."

"Do you really have a treasure boat worth a million dollars? You were trying to sell it to me, but I needed a helicopter to get it." Then Zack laughed, showing his crooked front teeth. The teenager needed braces, which seemed as unlikely under the present circumstances as his sprouting wings, or owning a helicopter. "Was that all crazy talk, like all that jungle fighting stuff? I mean, a treasure boat—what's up with that?"

Carson exhaled and stared at the Spitfire model above him. "Well, Zack, let me tell you what happened. I was bringing a sailboat, a cata-maran, up from Brazil. I was aiming for Texas. It was loaded with Japanese solar panels and Brazilian coffee. I put everything I had into that cargo after I got chased out of Panama."

"You're making this up, right?"

"Nope, it's all true. A bad storm caught us rounding Cuba, and the boat went ashore just over the line in Alabama, down from Mobile. The boat was wrecked, driven way up into a marsh. There was nothing I could do but walk away from it. The Mississippi Guard picked me up and put me in a quarantine camp. While I was there, I made a deal with an offi-cer—a military doctor. He was going to help me get out of Mississippi, and I was going to tell him where my boat was. That was the deal we made, but I was double-crossed. That was on Christmas Eve. There was some shooting...they didn't know I had a pistol. I didn't start it—well, maybe I did. But they pulled guns on me first, and then a couple of them wound up dead."

"That's why you have an empty .380, and an Army nine millimeter Beretta."

"That's right. I didn't figure it'd help to stick around and try to ex-plain how it was self-defense, so I took off in an Army pickup truck. I was trying to get out of Mississippi as fast as I could. The last part of it I was on foot—and that's where we, ah, met. So, how close was I to Ten-nessee?"

"About a quarter mile from the border."

"Shit. I almost made it."

"Yeah. Almost."

"And now what? What's next? Are you going to turn me in, Zack?" The boy paused and then replied, "Naw, I don't reckon so."

"Why not? You could get in a lot of trouble for harboring a fugitive."

Zack snorted, almost a laugh. "Like things are so great around here already? You know what I was really doing up in that deer stand? I was wondering if I ought to do what my mother did and jump off a bridge. Or maybe just walk into Tennessee and try to kill the first foreign S.O.B. that I saw. Things haven't exactly been going so well for my family—they're all dead. If I told you about it, you'd understand what I was thinking about up in that tree stand. Nothing good, let me tell you. Then you came along and, well, after you didn't shoot me when you could have, I figured that was some kind of a sign. Christmas morning, and everything. So, no. I won't turn you in."

"Well, I appreciate that."

"Hard to figure why you'd want to walk into Tennessee, though. When I was thinking about doing it, I figured it for a one-way trip."

"Can't be much worse than getting hanged for murder, here in Mississippi."

"You've got a point there. But you ain't going to Tennessee or anywhere else real quick, not till your hindquarters heal up. You try and walk too soon and it's going to bust wide open."

"Thanks for taking care of me, Zack. You're a pretty good medic."

"Thank my father, he taught me. But there's some other reasons I figure to keep you around a while, besides pure Christian charity. I found some interesting things on you when I was playing nursemaid."

"Such as?"

"Well, your belt seemed sort of heavy, and it's not the kind of a nice leather belt you often find on a soldier. Not even on a fake colonel, I'd reckon. That was another giveaway—no real colonel would wear a non-regulation belt. I split it open with a razor and I found your gold. Then I checked the sneakers in your pack, and I found some more."

Carson stared at him. "I see." The boy was formidable.

"And I found a little bitty list of names and addresses, written real tiny with a sharp pencil."

"You found that too, did you?"

"I did. Piss-poor security, Phil Carson, carrying around a list like that. You know, if the wrong people found that list, everybody on it could wind up skinned alive. Or sent to a relocation camp, which probably ain't much better."

"Where'd you get ideas like that, Zack Tutweiler? Your father?"

"That's right. Plus I read a lot—there's not much else to do out here."

Carson smiled. "Except to go out bow hunting, right?"

"Well, there sure ain't no TV or video games, not when there's no electricity." Zack smiled back, revealing his twisted front tooth.

"You're right about it being bad security, my having that list. I know it's a poor excuse, but when you get to my age, you have to write things down. My memory isn't what it was."

"I see. So, were you really a soldier in Vietnam? Or was that just more crazy-man dream talk? You know, all that 'Sneaky Pete, Roger Dodger, over and out' stuff?"

"What do you think, Zack?"

"I think it matches up with that old parachute tattoo on your arm. The Army jump wings. And all them old scars you've got—and some not so old. Like that beauty on your noggin."

"Yeah. And don't forget the one you gave me."

"Don't mention it."

Neither said anything for a long minute.

"So, what's next, Zack Tutweiler?"

"I don't know. It's going to be a while before you're up walking. Your butt cheek is all torn up, and I'm not much of a surgeon. I hope that broadhead didn't clip anything important, like nerves or something. Can you lift your leg? Wiggle your toes?"

"Let's see...damn, that hurts! Maybe I'll wait a while on that." Carson went slack, breathing heavily while fixing his eyes on the diving Spitfire above him.

"Suit yourself." Zack stood and idly rearranged small knickknacks on top of his dead brother's bureau.

"Zack, how safe is it here?"

"Safe? Are you kidding? It ain't safe at all. Everybody in my family died here."

"I mean, do they ever come to check this place out?"

" 'They' who?"

"The Mississippi Guard, the police, the sheriffs...any of them."

"No. We're at the end of a dead-end dirt road, and it's made to look like nothing's back here. I hardly ever run the generator, and I never show lights at night."

"How are you set for food, without your parents?"

"I'm okay. My father stocked us up pretty well. We've—I've still got food left over from before. There were six of us. Now there's only me—and you."

"How do you get drinking water?"

"We have a hand pump in the backyard. Our own well. Every day I pump water into a gravity tank. Filtered rainwater goes into it too."

"Your father was smart."

"Yeah, that's for sure. But smart wasn't enough. It didn't save his family, or him."

"Zack, do you have a mirror? I'd like to see my wound."

"Not yet, it's all bandaged up. Don't worry, it's not infected, or you wouldn't be talking right now. You'd still be out of your head. I've seen what happens. You know, this was my little brother's room. Maybe I shouldn't say this, but you wouldn't be the first to die in that bed." Zack began to tear up, but pushed the display of emotion from his face. "Your wound is clean. I used a real suture kit and lots of antiseptic. There's no infection, at least not so far. The miracle is you're still alive after all the blood you lost."

"Thanks."

"It was Christmas Day. I guess I felt generous."

"I'm not a freeloader, Zack. I can pay you. For what I eat. For all your trouble."

"It's no trouble, don't worry about that." Zack held up a gleaming coin the size of a dime between his thumb and index finger. "I've never seen these little gold ones before. They'll come in handy—you can buy just about anything with gold at the free market down in Corinth. Gold is worth twenty times silver, that's what they say. We had some old silver coins, but they're all gone. Hey, don't worry: I'll only take what we need. I'm not a thief."

"You said you're a Boy Scout."

"I *was* a Boy Scout. Eagle, in fact. But that was before all this. Now I don't know what I am. The Last of the Mohicans, I guess. The end of my tribe."

Lieutenant General Lucian Armstead detested Bob Bullard. He would have preferred to sit on a filthy rug in a Bedouin's tent for a luncheon of goat's eyeballs than to share a table with the so-called director of rural pacification. Their eleven o'clock meeting had been requested by Bullard, who, predictably, would have his hand out. The general had agreed only because these meetings gave him some measure of oversight of Bullard's civilian-run operations in Tennessee and Kentucky. These meetings were a bare fig leaf hiding the general's lack of authority in the two states. The informal get-together was for the two of them only, with no aides in the room. The general deliberately wore his pressed ACU combat uniform. Wearing his blue Army Service Uniform would show too much respect for a man for whom he had no respect.

Now Bullard was standing him up, already ten minutes late. This simply was not done to lieutenant generals!

They had agreed to meet at the Cole Park Buffet, which in long by-gone years had been the Fort Campbell Officers' Club. "Classist" officer–enlisted rank segregation was no longer permitted in military clubs or dining facilities. The location was neutral territory and convenient for both of them. At least his general's rank had allowed them to have a small private dining room set aside for their one-on-one meeting.

The civilian club employees even managed to find a clean white cloth for his table, unlike the gray, stained ones in the adjoining main dining room. A dented stainless steel pitcher of sweetened iced tea was put on the table, along with two empty glasses, two glasses of tap water, and a basket of stale dinner rolls, without butter. Oh, how standards had declined over his long career! While he waited for Bullard, the general studied the military oil paintings hanging on the walls around him, depicting battle scenes from the Revolutionary War to Iraq. He wondered how much longer these unabashedly heroic paintings would escape the attention of the new commissars of political correctness.

General Armstead had privately met with Bullard only a few times before, even though they both lived in Senior Officer Housing by Fort Campbell's golf course, less than a mile away from where he was sitting. How had Bullard qualified for one of the few generals' houses on Fort Campbell? Bullard was certainly no general, despite his Senior Executive Service federal supergrade position.

Armstead liked nothing about Bullard. He disliked his cocky over-familiarity, his lack of manners, and perhaps most of all his affectation of a faux uniform of khaki slacks and shirts. Bullard, who had never served in the military, liked to pretend he was some kind of mysterious CIA operative. In reality, he had only been a senior BATFE official before moving up to Homeland Security. Nevertheless, the general had been ordered to cooperate with this civilian "to the fullest extent possible." This kind of non-traditional relationship gave General Armstead an ulcer. He had graduated from West Point fifth in his class, and had served his country for thirty-one years, across the globe from Korea to the Middle East. He had attended the War College and had a PhD in history from Georgetown, and now he was in the demeaning position of taking orders from a civilian thug with mail-order baccalaureate and masters degrees!

General Armstead understood that this pitiful state of affairs was largely the president's fault. It all came back to Jamal Tambor and his inner circle of crypto-communists and one-worlders. He was deliberately trying to hamstring the United States military, while entangling the nation in adverse treaties that served only to destroy what vestiges remained of American sovereignty. Lucian Armstead had considered resigning his commission a hundred times since Tambor's election. Only his knowledge that many of the generals coming up behind him were left-wing perfumed princes, groomed and selected for their politically correct views, had kept him in uniform for the last three years. Under U.S. law, the president nominated generals for promotion, and the Senate approved them. It had traditionally been done that way, in accordance with the doctrine of civilian control of the military. But what happened to the very nature of the military when the White House and the Senate were dominated by Fabian socialists, America-hating internationalists who had even managed to overturn and rewrite the very constitution he had sworn to defend?

General Armstead was the Commander of U.S. Army North, NORTHCOM, the Fifth Army, sometimes referred to as the Homeland Command. On paper, he was charged with responsibility for the defense of America, plus Canada and Mexico. In reality, his so-called Army had no permanently assigned combat troops to call its own. He was the leader of six hundred staff chiefs but no Indians. Active and reserve military units were assigned to NORTHCOM on an ad hoc basis as needed, the need determined by the president and the Joint Chiefs. He was a paper general with a skeleton command.

This phantom army had been headquartered at Fort Sam Houston in San Antonio, prior to the ratification of the new constitution and the passage of the Aztlan Agreement. Then his virtual army's staff headquarters had then been shifted out of Texas to Fort Campbell, on the Kentucky-Tennessee border. The logic of the move had been sound: Fort Campbell was half-empty after the last round of troop cuts had decimated the Regular Army once again. God had one hell of a wicked sense of humor was all General Armstead could think about the timing of the move, coming only seven months before earthquakes devastated the region. No matter. Command of NORTHCOM was meant to be a meaningless sunset tour for a soon-to-be-retired three-star general from the Old Army. At least that was how command of NORTHCOM had been seen, before the earthquakes and the virtual secession of the Deep South and the "free states" of the Northwest. Now, finally, his paper command was going to be fleshed out and called upon to deal in fire and steel in the American homeland.

But not in the Southwest. The Aztlan Agreement took care of that. And not in the Deep South. His former colleague Lieutenant General Marcus Aurelius Mirabeau was effectively the unchallenged ruler from the Mississippi River to South Carolina, Georgia, and North Florida. NORTHCOM had no operational control in these Southern states, although General Armstead personally maintained cordial relations with General Mirabeau. Of the quake-damaged states, NORTHCOM had a field presence only in Arkansas, Missouri and Illinois, consisting mostly of attached National Guard units. The general had genuine authority only in these three states, which had been the least severely damaged by the quakes and where central authority had not entirely collapsed.

This certainly could not be said for Kentucky or Tennessee, which lay on either side of Fort Campbell. After the devastating back-to-back earthquakes that had practically leveled Memphis and wrecked the transportation and energy infrastructure in the area between Nashville, Little Rock and St. Louis, the National Guard had been the first responders. At least those who had mustered for duty. Almost a quarter of the Guardsmen had failed to report, and another quarter of them slipped away over the following weeks. Three months later, the remaining troops were ordered withdrawn by the president for "lack of performance." His National Guard regiments had been sacked, fired for failing to demonstrate sufficient zeal at forcing the evacuation of the stricken regions. President Tambor had lost faith in the military's ability to pacify the area, in particular Western Tennessee and Kentucky, between the Tennessee, Ohio and Mississippi Rivers. NORTHCOM had been ordered out.

Now the civilian administrator, Robert Bullard, was the person charged with restoring federal government control of Kentucky and Tennessee. Worse, he was using foreign soldiers to subdue and occupy the region. "Peacekeeping volunteers," the president called them. Most of them belonged to the hastily formed so-called North American Legion, a ragtag passel of miscreants led by Americans more loyal to the United Nations than to the United States. The NAL troops had literally been picked up off the street corners of American cities. Until recently they were illegal aliens, who had been strong-armed into enlisting with the promise of citizenship and a homestead land grant. Many of the North American Legion recruits were convicted felons, taken directly from prison and put into uniform under the president's "Operation Fresh Start" initiative. Their prominent gang tattoos didn't lie about their origins, or their true loyalties.

At best, the barely trained NAL troops could man checkpoints and conduct very basic cordon operations. The real hammers in Tennessee and Kentucky came from much further away than North America. The true enforcers were the "contract battalions," recruited abroad from the militaries of Nigeria, Pakistan, Bolivia, Kazakhstan, Turkey, Albania and a dozen other nations. They wore their own uniforms and served under their own officers, attracted by the promise of United States citizenship and free land. Bringing in foreign mercenaries and calling them volunteer peacekeepers had been President Tambor's idea. "A grand experiment in new levels of international cooperation," he had termed it. "The first major test of the new U.N. military cooperation treaty." Well, it was surely that.

Considering the ongoing horror show that had evolved in Tennessee and Kentucky, General Armstead was in many respects glad *not* to have

NORTHCOM involved in those two states any longer. It was an interesting case study in the development of an insurgency. From the first weeks after the earthquakes, a small percentage of the locals had developed the nasty habit of taking potshots at anybody that they perceived to be trespassing on their land—including uniformed members of the military. This had begun shortly after the first of the devastated counties were reached by emergency response units.

Following the arrival of National Guard troops and out-of-state law enforcement teams, a strong effort had been made to enforce the new federal gun control laws. The reasoning was that ordinary citizens, living under conditions of hunger and fear bordering on hysteria, could not be safely relocated and fed if they were armed. The unintended consequences of this policy had been calamitous. Once the word spread that the government was collecting guns at every checkpoint, relocation camp and feeding center, thousands of Tennesseans had resolved to reject any assistance that came with the quid pro quo of mandatory disarmament.

The situation worsened when ATF agents conducted confiscation raids on a few well-known gun collectors, using the National Guard for extra muscle and perimeter security. These raids had been intended to serve as draconian examples—and examples they had proven to be! The first raids had limited success, only because they retained the element of surprise. After that, they had been met with bullets, lots of bullets, from point blank to extremely long range.

Being met with armed resistance by fellow Americans, Regular Army and Guard troops had in most cases refused to apply the necessary level of tactical firepower, and the situation had stalemated for three months. Everywhere the Army went in Tennessee and Kentucky, it was suspected of supporting firearms confiscation raids. The bond of trust between the local people and the military had been shattered. The result was invariably casualties lost to snipers, who typically fired one deadly shot from hundreds of yards away, and were rarely found. Without security, reconstruction teams could not enter the contested areas. Bridges over the Mississippi, Ohio and Tennessee rivers still lay in twisted wreckage, and the critical pipelines, power lines, railroads and highways that crisscrossed the region were still shattered in a thousand places.

Instead of reevaluating the policy of gun confiscation, the president had invited the U.S. military to leave Tennessee and Kentucky, for, as he put it, "demonstrated lack of performance." Tambor then put those two states under civilian control, most recently in the person of Robert Bullard, a DHS super grade. He was an SES-2, a member of the Senior Executive Service, the civilian equivalent of a two-star general. Bullard's last federal posting had been as the Southwest Region Director of Homeland Security. Bullard and his ilk had done such a bang-up job there that the United States had lost the entire Southwest to the Mexican nationalist "reconquistas." Naturally, this stunning failure qualified Bullard for another posting within the DHS. Shortly after the civilians were put in charge of Tennessee and Kentucky, the first foreign contract battalions had been brought in by President Tambor.

Bullard finally arrived at the former Officers' Club twenty minutes late. Armstead used the time to get some work done on his laptop. The general did not stand to greet Bullard. Even though he would have enjoyed the opportunity to tower six inches above the troll-like civilian, he did not want to show the respect that rising would convey. If Bullard noticed the slight, he showed no sign of it. He simply sat down and poured himself an iced tea, then took a sip while glancing around at the military artwork on the walls. His bodyguards (dressed all in black like the Gestapo), waited in plain sight, just outside the open double door to the main dining room. As the general expected he would, Bullard dispensed with pleasantries and launched directly into his requests for equipment and support. The man somehow had connections directly into the Tambor White House, and despite his lack of a military rank and his generic unmarked khaki pseudo-uniform, there was little doubt that in purely political terms Bullard out-ranked him.

"General, we're down to only sixteen operational Predators. We need at least a dozen more of them ASAP, to get our coverage up to anything like it needs to be."

General Armstead ignored the request. "Well, it's nice seeing you again, Mister Bullard." He refused to dignify the man with any other title. There was no "department of rural pacification" that he could find in any register of federal agencies or table of military organizations. He would not refer to this Robert Bullard as "director." Director of what, exactly? In equivalent federal service terms, he was clearly senior to Bullard, but today he found himself the subject of demands from this subordinate in rank. To Armstead, this was reminiscent of the inverted power relationship between the Red Army and the KGB in the old USSR, a sorry state of affairs he had never imagined he would experience at first hand in the USA. Or perhaps under President Tambor, now it was the USSA?

"Yeah, likewise, good to see you too. Listen, General, we need more UAVs. We can't accomplish our mission—the president's mission—without them."

"Well, you're not going to get them from me. Not without something in writing from the NCA."

"The NC who?" asked Bullard, popping a roll into his mouth. "What are you talking about?"

Armstead sat fully erect, hands folded on the table, and stared downward at Bob Bullard. "The National Command Authority. That's the White House, Mister Bullard. The president. Our mutual chain of command. I cannot honor your request. We are down to less than a hundred fully mission-capable Predators and Reapers for the rest of CONUS—that's the continental United States—"

"I know what CONUS means."

"I'm sure you do. Well, the military also needs UAVs. The actual American military. I'm not signing any more of them off to you on just your say-so. Particularly when you're managing to lose one just about every week."

"This winter weather sucks around here for flying, as you well know. The terrorists don't take time off. We need to push the weather envelope with the UAVs, otherwise the insurgents would have free rein half of the time. We can't let that happen."

"Well, I won't transfer any more Predators just on your word."

"I guess we'll see about that, won't we? And while I have my wish list out, I need more aircraft. Helicopters, to be specific. Blackhawks, Chinooks, Little Birds, Hueys: we need them all. At least thirty more, right away. With crews, maintenance, fuel—the whole package. I'll send you a complete breakdown of what we need."

"There's no chance of that." General Armstead knew that all of the aviation assets that could be mustered were being readied for operations in the Northwest, to commence in the summer. Operation Buffalo Jump was the president's top priority. Admittedly, securing Tennessee and Kentucky was more than a sideshow—it was a bleeding ulcer—but it was not the main event. Pacified or not, the Mid South was not going anywhere. And it was, blessedly, now Bob Bullard's problem. This was one positive aspect of having Kentucky and Tennessee transferred to civilian control: General Lucian Armstead was off the hook for future success or failure in the region. Any more aircraft would be given to the so-called "department of rural pacification" only if the orders came from the president himself.

Bob Bullard finished his glass of iced tea and rose to leave. "I'll get right back to you, after I talk to the White House. Then I'll get my helicopters, and my UAVs."

"Perhaps you will. Just bring me authenticated orders—in writing—and we'll talk about it again. Orders from *my* chain of command—the president, through the JCS. You know who they are, don't you?"

8

Almost two weeks had passed since the arrival of the stranger. Phil Carson was napping on the sofa near the wood stove after a tasty dinner of canned pork and beans. A book lay open across his chest while he snored softly. The iron stove warmed the living room and kitchen, and it heated their water and cooked their food. It also provided a substitute for television as the center of their indoor lives. The stove door was often left open, the glowing coals comforting them.

They were eating better the last few days, since Carson had given Zack two gold dimes to take down to the free market, which was held on the former Wal-Mart parking lot outside of Corinth. The purpose of the trip was to collect information on conditions in Mississippi as much as it was to buy a variety of canned food and other needed items. The roads were dry and the trip took only an hour and a half each way on his mountain bike. Zack had tied a plastic milk crate to the bicycle's rear cargo rack to bring home his purchases.

These days State Road 72, which ran parallel to the Tennessee border, was safe enough for a daylight expedition. On the road Zack wore his ID badge visibly, as the law demanded, clipped to his jacket collar. He was not hassled at the permanent Guard checkpoint at the big intersection by the town of Walnut, or at another temporary one halfway to Corinth. The Guard soldiers had no badge scanners, and merely looked him over, asked a few basic questions about his home and his destination, and allowed him to proceed. The few cars and trucks on the road were given closer scrutiny at the checkpoints.

Like most of the other shoppers and traders, Zack slyly concealed his ID badge while he was in the actual free market area. He reclipped it so that it hung down inside the upper left pocket of his camo hunting jacket. If questioned, he could plausibly say that this was to prevent it from being accidentally lost while riding his bike. He cautiously showed the tenth-ounce gold coins to the clandestine moneychangers lurking under the trees, just beyond the Wal-Mart parking lot. Their ID badges were also hidden, and for good reason. Trading gold or silver could be a hanging offense, depending on who caught you and if there was a push on to stamp out black-marketeering. That day there were no Guard soldiers stationed around the free market, which was a sign that the martial law currency regulations were being relaxed—at least for the time being.

The best offer had been 450 TEDs for both gold dimes, which Zack accepted, exchanging them for nine of the red-and-yellow fifties. He was also offered 350 pink-and-blue North American Dollars. These bills were also called ameros, but to Zack Tutweiler they were just NADs, a slang word for gonads. Instead of portraits of dead presidents, the NADs featured famous landscapes in their central position. The Grand Canyon, Canadian Rockies and Mexico's Mayan pyramids were on different denominations. The NADs were harder to spend in Mississippi (you were supposed to use only TEDs in the emergency zone), but they were needed if you traveled to the North, to the federal states. At least that's what the moneychangers told him.

Zack's father had said that the NADs would eventually replace the Temporary Emergency Dollars in the South. People were beginning to hoard them, in case the red TEDs were suddenly replaced, as the blue bucks had been, and the old greenback dollars before that. Paper money being devalued or even becoming worthless overnight was a constant threat. When paper currencies were switched, you took whatever the government offered at any rate it set, which could be ten or even a hundred to one. If you didn't exchange your paper money within the official grace period, it became totally worthless, which was why many folks were beginning to accumulate North American Dollars whenever they could. Zack had no use for the NADs. He was only interested in money he could spend easily here and now, in Mississippi, so he took the 450 dollars in red Temporary Emergency Dollars.

Nobody bothered with the old blue or green dollars, which were given away to small children to play games of pretend. Some adults folded them into intricate origami birds and flowers and gave them away as curiosities, or even tried to sell them as art.

Four hundred TEDs had filled the plastic crate on his bike rack with canned goods, a bottle of lamp oil and a few other items. An additional thirty TEDs bought Zack a huge pork sandwich (with a side of Texas fries and a large apple cider) from a barbeque joint being run outside a former gas station. This was, he thought, fair payment for his long and somewhat risky bicycle trek to Corinth and back. He returned before dark with the food and the information, which Carson extracted detail by detail, asking him many questions while they ate their pork and beans.

That night, while Carson slept, Zack dressed head to foot in his rainproof hunting camouflage. Then he took his compound bow and slipped out of the house. Leather gloves protected his hands and especially his fingertips. He only used the trigger release when hunting, for super accuracy. Tonight in the dark, distances would be close and speed would be much more important, so he would just use his fingers on the string. Four arrows were clamped in brackets along the right side of the bow, feathers down. A fifth arrow was nocked and ready to launch. Nine more arrows were in a leather quiver on his back. Without electric lights, the interior of the house was already dim, so his eyes quickly adjusted to the blackness outside. Somewhere above the low overcast, the new quarter moon was setting, providing no light for night stalking. No stars were visible above the gloom.

In the past year spent without electric power, Zack had become so attuned to the lunar cycles that they were as familiar to him as the rising and setting of the sun. With only minimal use of oil lamps for nighttime indoor lighting, he had developed uncanny night vision. The subtle distinctions in illumination resulting from different combinations of moonlight, cloud and tree cover became in their way more important to him than the more obvious difference between day and night. With sufficient moonlight, Zack could easily find his way. Without it, he was blind. Batteries were too rare and expensive to waste on regular flashlights, except in a dire emergency. He also knew that any drones flying above them could quickly zero in on artificial light sources.

Zack's secret weapon for these dark times of the month was a tiny red LED flashlight no bigger than a finger, which would run almost forever off a single AA battery. It cast only a faint puddle of dim light, but this was sufficient for him to follow familiar paths without tripping or walking into stumps or logs. The penlight was attached with rubber bands to the front of his compound bow. Where his eyes looked, the light and the bow followed in synchronization. Outside that small circle of faint illumination, the entire universe was utterly black.

Zack Tutweiler had spent the last year following game trails at all hours and under every light condition, so it was not hard for him to find his way. The steady drizzle dampened the woods and quieted his footsteps. Wet leaves didn't rustle, and sodden sticks didn't snap beneath his boots. Even so, he walked into Tennessee carefully, ever mindful of his father's fate, creeping along fences overgrown with weeds, streambeds, wood lines and windbreaks. Skills developed in stalking wild game hid him from the eyes of terrestrial watchers, unlikely as they were on a cold, wet night. He wondered if the drones with their deadly missiles could fly in the rain, or see him through the misty clouds that hid the moon and stars. His father had said no, but his father was dead.

Moving cautiously along a circuitous path, it took him two hours to reach his destination. Zack gently placed his bow on the ground and prepared the signal exactly as he had seen his father do it, while holding his LED light in his mouth. He tied a strip of red cloth to the top strand of a barbed wire fence, where in daylight it could be seen from Tennessee's State Road 57, which ran parallel to the state line two miles north of Mississippi. Thick woods provided good cover on the south side of the fence. He made his final approach in a stalking crouch, arrow nocked and ready to draw. On the far side of the fence, grassy weeds along the shoulder of the road grew almost as high as the top strand of wire, and he wondered if they would obscure his signal from view in the daylight. He knotted the strip of red cloth securely, letting it hang down a foot. He had cut the strip from his dead brother's pajamas, a talisman intended to include poor Sammy in his stealthy night work.

This place was one of the "dead drops" his father had used to communicate with some of his Tennessee trading partners—and some others who probably were involved in more than illegal commerce. It was slow and cumbersome to communicate this way, but safe and sure. His cargo was contained in a black plastic container small enough to conceal within his fist. According to his father, it had once held old-fashioned picture film, the kind used before digital cameras. Zack knew only that the little cylinder was easily hidden and perfectly waterproof.

His hand-written report of his father's death and the arrival of Phil Carson was already folded to nut size and jammed inside the black film can, along with a meticulously copied duplicate of Carson's list of names and addresses. The film can went into a hole at the base of the wooden fence post beneath the signal rag. He had watched his father load the dead drop, and he had been briefed on the procedure. He would return to another location in two days to look for another signal and a hidden message giving a reply. Zack had now done his father's secret night work. He wondered whether his father was in a place where he could watch over him. He hoped so. He wondered again about his mother's final destination, and if she had rejoined his father in heaven. Had she indeed killed herself and taken the life of his baby sister? If so, would God ever forgive her for it? Just how much earthly suffering could He expect anyone to bear? Zack headed toward home wondering about these mysteries, resolving none of them, and arriving as dawn was breaking. There was at least some consolation in carrying on his father's night work.

Carson was already up, crouching by the iron stove in the middle of the kitchen, feeding it small chunks of wood. "No luck with the hunting?"

"Nope, not this time."

"Looks like you went stalking, instead of sitting up in your tree stand."

The old codger was observant. Zack had to be on his guard. "Well, I thought I'd try something different. It didn't work out." Did it matter if Carson was suspicious? Or was he merely curious, in an innocent way?

"Yeah, well, you'll do better next time. One way or the other, I'm sure we won't starve."

"Jenny, why didn't you go to the swap meet?" The two seventeen-year-old girls talked on the porch of a modest one-story house. It was chilly but dry outside for a change. The visitor was a short redhead, wearing green-framed eyeglasses and dressed in jeans and an orange University of Tennessee sweatshirt.

"I'm supposed to stay behind to watch the house. And besides, you know I've got nothing to sell or trade." Jenny McClure was almost a head taller than her visitor. She was wearing baggy gray sweatpants and several oversized men's sweaters piled on top. Tussled straw-blond hair spilled over her shoulders. In the front, her hair was cut in bangs that stopped just above light cinnamon-colored eyes.

"That's no excuse, girlfriend. Come on with me, we'll have fun."

"I don't feel like walking two miles for nothing." Jenny yawned and stretched, extending her arms and rolling her shoulders.

"Jenny, the sun is shining, and that's a rare thing lately. Come on, Hope Baptist puts out soup and fresh bread on Saturdays. That's worth a little walk, ain't it?"

"Not to me. Anyway, I can't. I told my uncle I didn't want to go to church just to get free soup, and he said, fine, stay home then. If I don't go to church, I can't go to the market. It wouldn't be right. And I still have to fetch today's water. Twenty gallons, that's my job."

"Oh come on, he doesn't own you, you're not his slave. Don't make me walk up there by myself. Listen, if you go, the boys will check you out—they always do. Then I might get noticed just by accident. I'll take your rejects any day."

Jenny blushed, trying not to smile. Her friend Sue Bledsoe wasn't exactly pretty, that was true enough. Pretty or not, she was unfailingly cheerful, considering the hard times. She'd lost her chubbiness over the last hungry year, but she still wasn't pretty, with her curly red hair, round face, and an overabundance of freckles. Cute maybe, sort of. Not that looks counted for much anymore. What mattered were practical things like food, firewood, and gasoline. Especially food. Jenny's blond hair and eyes the color of wild honey wouldn't fetch any of those items—not unless she was willing to trade more than a pretty smile. Sleeping with somebody might win her a few good meals. It might buy her temporary protection under the roof of some single man, but that was about all.

Now Jenny had enough protection, here at her aunt and uncle's house on Ben Duggin Road. The road ended in a loop, where a developer had built twenty modern homes on one-acre lots. The rest of Duggin Road was taken up with a mixed lot of trailers, small farms, and older homes. Uncle Henry, a former Marine Corps captain, was a popular leader of the neighborhood defense team. Their house was well situated near the end of the loop, which was almost a half mile back from County Road 144. No one could come into their isolated neighborhood without passing scrutiny at Duggin Road's single entrance. A palisade wall of ten-foot-high sharpened pine logs had been erected on either side of Duggin Road where it met

the county road at a T intersection. The opening was the width of one vehicle. At night, a junker panel van filled with dirt and topped with barbed
wire was pushed across the single narrow entry and chained in place at
both ends. No stranger casually approached Duggin Road. As long as
Jenny was under the protection of her aunt and uncle, she had no need to
meet any other men, and certainly not teenage boys with only one thing on
their minds.

So she replied, "Boys? I don't care about any boys—not unless
they've got rich daddies. Rich enough to get me right the hell out of Tennessee. What good are boys? Anyway, it's not too bad here. I get fed.
I'm just so tired of being cold and hungry and dirty, that's all."

"Well, who isn't? You should count your blessings. You're lucky
you had kin here, folks willing to take you in. Lots of refugees didn't have
anybody at all."

"Somehow I don't feel lucky. Not with all that's happened." Like
losing her family after the Memphis earthquakes, for starters.

"You're alive, aren't you? You're not the only one who's suffered.
Jenny, I refuse to let you drag me down. It's too nice a day." Sue Bledsoe
lifted her arms and forced a wan smile. "Make hay while the sun shines,
didn't you ever hear that? Well, it's Saturday, the sun is shining, and
everybody for miles around is going up to Mannville for the swap market.
Come on, try smiling once in a while—it's free and it doesn't hurt. Have
some fun when you can. Life goes on, Jenny McClure, and you have to
keep living too."

"This isn't living—this is just surviving."

"Welcome to reality."

"Reality sucks. I'm too dirty. My hair is revolting…and I smell like
a hound dog."

Sue Bledsoe stared at her friend for a moment and then said, "This
was going to be a surprise for later on, but look what I found." She
reached into her jeans pocket and pulled out a few coins. "Two quarters
and three dimes. Old ones—real silver."

"Where'd you get all that money? You steal it? Who had it?"

"Nobody had it. I found it."

"Oh, *sure* you did," exclaimed Jenny. "So, who'd you have to sleep
with?"

"Get out! No, really, I found it. I was getting firewood. I was taking
apart an old shed in the woods back behind our place. I knocked down a
glass jar that was hid up in the rafters. It busted on the ground right between my feet."

"And that's all that was in it?"

"No, the jar was full of change, but the rest wasn't silver. These were
the only silver ones—and believe me, I checked every single coin. The

newest were from 1970, so that's probably how long the jar was up there. From 1964 on, they're just fakes painted silver—you can tell by their brown edges. These old ones are real silver all the way through. Come with me to town, we'll splurge. We'll get something good to eat; oh, we'll have a fine day." She slipped the money back into her pocket.

Jenny knew that a genuine silver dime could sometimes buy a small can of vegetables. A silver quarter might buy a can of soup or ravioli, according to her uncle. But that had been months ago, and canned goods were getting hard to find at any price. Her uncle used to have some old silver coins, but they had all been spent. "I don't want charity, Sue. I'll come, but I don't want you to think it's just because of your silver. Okay?" She reached out and took her friend's hands in her own.

"Okay. Just wash your face and brush your hair. Maybe throw on some of your aunt's perfume."

"Have you got your gun?" asked Jenny.

The redhead pulled her Tennessee sweatshirt up a few inches at the waist, revealing the butt of a revolver. "You better believe it. I don't leave home without Mr. 38."

"All right, I'll get ready. Come on in, it won't take me long."

For Jenny McClure, bathing was a once-a-week proposition at best, but fortunately her last bath had been only two nights before. Their washing water came from the roof, so with all the recent rain there was plenty of it. To bathe properly, she'd have to get the fire going in the kitchen stove, heat a big pan of water to boiling, and then pour that boiling water into a tub of cold water. The process would take too long. Instead, she took a basin of drinking water into the bathroom to wash up at the sink. Drinking water came from one of the subdivision's communal wells and had to be carried home in jugs, one of her daily chores. The new wells had been dug by hand, after the earthquakes had destroyed most of the old ones belonging to each house. Without electricity to run their submerged pumps, even the wells that had not cracked were useless.

In the mirror Jenny's winter-pale face looked bony. Her cheekbones were much too prominent, her wide-set eyes sunken, the result of her involuntary diet. Her narrow chin looked a bit longer with less flesh on her cheeks. Still, she was tall and leggy, and that helped—sometimes. Tall, slim and blond, with eyes like dark golden amber. Perfect for some lost California dream, like those she'd seen in movies—if she could only get to California. Or to anywhere else.

She'd arrived at her Aunt Rochelle's house last March with just the clothes on her back. They were torn and filthy from weeks of walking and sleeping by the road and in the woods, wherever and however. These days Jenny's wardrobe consisted of her middle-aged aunt's outgrown hand-me-downs. Since Jenny McClure was several inches taller and much slimmer, she couldn't wear any of her aunt's jeans or slacks. She peeled off her gray sweatpants and selected a red, black and gold plaid wool wraparound skirt, which extended halfway down her calves. To go with it she chose a yellow cashmere cardigan sweater, topped off with a black insulated vest with gold buttons on the front. The yellow sweater and gold buttons accentuated her eyes.

Tatty gray running sneakers and not very white socks completed her ensemble. Shoes were a constant source of aggravation for Jenny. Her feet were several sizes larger than her aunt's. She had to wear old castoffs from her cousin Paul, who had succumbed to the flu before her arrival. Before the earthquake, Jenny would have considered this outfit to be a Halloween party costume at best. A Salvation Army or Goodwill Store special. Well, beggars couldn't be choosers, she told herself once again.

Jenny inspected herself in her aunt's full-length bedroom mirror, turning from side to side. Not too bad, considering. As long as you ignored the torn, dirty sneakers. She still wasn't quite a stick figure, despite losing almost thirty pounds over the past year. Five foot ten, and only a hundred twenty pounds, according to the bathroom scale. She was an involuntary anorexic, runway model thin. Thin but strong, from the constant carrying of water jugs and firewood. Almost a stick figure, but not quite—thanks to Henry and Rochelle's kindness in providing for her. She had been developing a very nice figure by the time she was fifteen, but now at seventeen her development was, if anything, going in reverse. She was getting skinnier by the month. Jenny turned sideways to the mirror and thrust out her chest: there were still a few curves left. Just.

Oh, what she would give for a double quarter-pounder with cheese, French fries, and a Coke!

The swap market was held every day except Sunday, but by far the biggest crowds attended on Saturdays. For most of the several hundred county residents who came, transportation meant walking, or maybe riding a bicycle. Many pushed shopping carts both ways, sometimes for miles. They would make the effort only once a week, when the most wares were offered. Some fortunate ones arrived on horseback, or aboard horse-drawn wagons. The Saturday swap market brought out enough shoppers that a few well-off sellers even drove their wares to town in cars and pickup trucks, using up a bit of their precious gasoline and diesel.

Jenny and her friend accepted a lift for the second mile of their journey, climbing atop a wagon loaded with firewood. The unpainted wooden wagon had four rubber tires from an automobile, but it was pulled by a mule in a proper old-fashioned leather harness. The driver was an elderly black man with white hair, one of the few blacks still regularly seen in the county. He wore bib overalls and smoked tobacco in a corncob pipe, like a picture of old Tennessee. Jenny was willing to accept the ride only because of his advanced years and decrepitude. She was still too full of fear and rage toward younger blacks, after what had happened following the quakes. The old man had a different delivery route for his firewood, and the girls jumped down at an intersection on the outskirts of town.

Unlike the past few weekends, this Saturday was clear and cold and the roads were dry. By late morning, hundreds of the remaining inhabitants of the town of Mannville and the surrounding countryside were strolling about and enjoying themselves, at least as much as they could under the present conditions. Besides the opportunity to find some needed item or foodstuff, the market was a chance to meet friends and exchange wild rumors, scant news, and divergent opinions. For young people, it was an occasion to connect with friends of both sexes—a rare opportunity, with school canceled for the year. Just being in a crowd of friendly people was a pleasure after spending so much of the last year isolated and often virtually in hiding.

The informal swap market's location had shifted several times since the earthquakes and their cruel aftermath. For the last few months, it had been held on the high school's big parking lot and outdoor basketball courts. Before that, it had been held in front of the Mannville Shopping Center, after the stores had run out of sellable stock and closed one by one. The high school's location on the south side of town, nearer to the subdivisions where most people lived, had proven more convenient. In addition, being surrounded by a high chain link fence, the school parking lot had much better security. Tables covered with plastic tarps could be left there overnight; the enclosed lot was locked up by the sheriff every afternoon before darkness fell. A deputy remained on the premises, sleeping somewhere in the high school. By nightfall, almost nobody ventured outside. Night was a time to be locked inside one's house, trying to stay warm, hopefully fed, and as safe as humanly possible.

Susan Bledsoe and Jenny McClure entered the parking lot through the open vehicle gate. Both girls would have been seniors at Mannville High, if the county schools had been open. They were not questioned or hassled by the lone sheriff's deputy who stood there, keeping watch. The tall deputy was in uniform, wearing his duty pistol on his hip. Some of the civilian men coming and going wore holstered handguns as well. Those who had no visible sidearm were assumed to be carrying a concealed firearm. A year after the earthquake, such protection was considered a natural part of life. Even in Radford County, seventy miles east of Memphis and not far from the Tennessee River, marauding bandits were still occasionally a threat. Carrying mere pistols actually reflected an improvement in the level of public safety. Until a few months before, most residents of Radford County would have been carrying carbines and shotguns, if they risked traveling the roads at all. Even in daytime.

Many of the men were wearing elements of old combat fatigues and hunting outfits. The surplus BDUs were highly valued, because they were tough enough to hold up without much care. Rarely if ever washed, most of these outer garments were dark with dirt and grime. Since just about all of the local men had quit shaving a year before, they made a fearsome sight: bearded, armed and generally wearing some mix of military or hunting camouflage. A significant number of people wore homemade rag facemasks, either to hide pox scars, lend dubious protection against germs, or perhaps to conceal their identities. Masks worn in public were simply unremarkable, after all that they'd lived through.

The single deputy represented a remnant of the old civil order, but it was obvious that he was there mainly to unlock and lock the gates to the parking lot. Otherwise, he was unneeded. Certainly he was unpaid, at least in the old sense of the word. Mannville's Saturday swap market was a classic example of Robert Heinlein's famous saying, that an armed society is a polite society. An adult voice was rarely raised in anger, even when grimly haggling over trades. Loudest among them were the children, welcoming the opportunity to run and holler and play in groups. A guitarist sang and strummed folk tunes near the parking lot gate, hoping that something of value might be dropped into the open guitar case at his feet.

An odd assortment of tables were left permanently on the parking lot, to be covered with wares on Saturday. There were kitchen tables, picnic tables, office and school desks, warped gray plywood sheets over sawhorses. With every table already in use, late arrivals spread out their goods on the asphalt, on old blankets. Jenny and Sue strolled among them all, shopping with their eyes. Some traded a bit of everything; others specialized in specific categories of items. There were sellers of used clothing (including underwear), stacks of old telephone books (for toilet paper), jumbled boxes of eyeglasses, batteries of every size, freshly baked bread and biscuits, rusty canned goods, fruit preserves in glass jars, vegetable seeds, moonshine corn whisky, gasoline of doubtful octane in random containers, wood stoves made from old metal drums, empty five-gallon water jugs, and antique non-electric tools such as hand saws and drills. Several tables were dedicated to trading guns, ammunition and reloading supplies.

Nobody bothered to bring televisions, microwaves, stereos or cell phones for trade. Unless and until electrical power was restored, electronic gadgets were worthless. A sixty-inch hi-definition flat-screen plasma TV would not fetch half a cord of dry firewood.

Jenny and Sue finally stopped at a table featuring an assortment of canned goods. The fiftyish couple sitting behind the table paid no attention to the two teenage girls, until Sue produced her silver coins. After a few minutes spent examining the meager goods and dickering, Sue exchanged one silver quarter for a can of peas, plus a second unlabeled rusty can that was promised to contain peaches in syrup.

The girls retired to the aluminum bleachers by a basketball backboard to partake of their feast. Sue had brought a tiny GI can opener and a plastic spoon, and the girls took turns enjoying the peas and peaches, washed down with the syrup and water. Even trying to take their time to extend their pleasure, they emptied and drained the cans in minutes.

The arrival of two helicopters a thousand feet overhead didn't particularly frighten anyone at the market. Helicopters flew over the county every few days, sometimes dropping leaflets containing official news and proclamations. If the government knew that the town existed, it seemed in no hurry to bring relief supplies to the cold and hungry residents, who were still practically cut off from the world by broken roads and bridges. For their part, the remaining locals seemed in no hurry to be saved by the government. Government salvation came with too many conditions attached.

For one thing, carrying guns was not permitted in the counties under military control. Not that the military government could provide protection from the bandit gangs that came prowling at night. Particularly not when those daytime soldiers often were those very same bandits by night. Day or night, the soldiers at the military checkpoints outside the county were reputed to shake down travelers for bribes and accost and abuse women and girls. Worst of all, guns were always confiscated at the checkpoints, and frequently the travelers who risked the checkpoints never returned. A few smugglers seemed to have no problem passing through the checkpoints, undoubtedly by paying bribes. Many of the rumors about conditions outside the county came from these roving merchants. According to the leaflet drops and official radio broadcasts, there were "emergency relocation centers" further north. Anybody who truly believed that was already gone.

So the remaining residents of Mannville and the surrounding area were stuck in an uneasy equilibrium, by now accustomed to the status quo of government abandonment. The folks still living in Radford County were of the hardest and most durable stock. They hadn't been killed in the gang attacks following the quakes, they hadn't died from the flu, or the pox, or the cholera, or the cold, or of simple starvation. Nor had they fallen to the quiet death by despair that defied medical categorization. Cold, hunger, illness and depression had proven to be a fatal combination for hundreds of their neighbors, who had simply stayed in their beds under warm blankets until they perished. Nor had the remaining survivors quit the other way and walked out of the county to the military checkpoints, abandoning their homes for the unknown promise of a distant FEMA camp. The remaining residents had endured every hardship. They had adapted and overcome and never surrendered to any of the numerous fatal perils so common to their time and place.

Those desperate enough to seek government help knew where to look for it; the information was in the airdropped leaflets and on the portable radios that broadcast official news. The radios had been dropped from helicopters after the second earthquake. They were black plastic, the size of a paperback book. Each came swaddled in bright orange bubble wrap, to protect them when they hit the ground. The emergency radios were pre-tuned and received only two stations: one with official talk and news, the other with music and news. One side of the radios had a card-sized solar collector to keep their built-in batteries charged. Some of these emergency radios were still used in their original configuration to keep abreast of official news and government pronouncements. Many others had been stripped down for their parts and converted to charge AA batteries or for other uses. These FEMA radios and their many derivative forms were available for barter at the swap market.

So the residents of Radford County fully understood that their open carrying of firearms was in violation of the new emergency decrees, de-crees that they simply ignored. The government, state or federal, had not brought them safety or food or fuel or medicine or electrical power, so what was the point of obeying their new gun laws? To be fed by the gov-ernment, one had to leave his home, walk out of the county, abandon everything, become a refugee and throw himself on the mercy of the unknown. Rumor had long since established that approaching any govern-ment checkpoint meant at a bare minimum permanently surrendering one's firearms, and firearms were crucial for survival.

Life was hard in Radford County, but it was lived on terms that the remaining residents could understand. Beyond the mayor, sheriff and de-puty, there was no law, no government in Mannville. The local police sided fully with their neighbors, and did not attempt to enforce any of the emergency laws they had heard about on the radio and read about on the leaflets. Taxes, rents and mortgages had not been collected since before the first earthquake, yet no one spoke of foreclosures or evictions. What would have been the point? Half of the homes were at least partially quake damaged, and many of them were abandoned. Their former owners and tenants were either dead, or they were refugees living elsewhere unknown.

Then there was the thorny issue of peaceful refugees known to be squatting in homes belonging to the dead or disappeared. Finally, there would have to be some kind of legal accounting for the many shootings that had taken place between starving city refugees and the terrified locals. Killings that had seemed entirely justified during the desperate weeks of anarchy and starvation after the quakes might now appear to outsiders to be murder. Many people had been killed when they were caught trying to steal livestock, during a time when a pig or a cow was seen as a source of life itself for its owners. The fear had been so great during the exodus from the cities that people were shot just for trespassing, after ignoring or bypassing dire warning signs. For all of these reasons, the remaining residents of Mannville looked upon the prospect of the return of outside government agencies with a mixture of hope and dread.

The locals had been through so much deprivation and terror that they were almost shockproof. So the two circling helicopters, ancient CH-47 Chinooks, were regarded with wary caution but not much alarm. The dual-rotor choppers assumed opposite poles of a half-mile-wide orbit, descending to five hundred feet above the swap market, causing all eyes to look skyward out of animal curiosity. Would they drop new leaflets or radios, or perhaps, finally, some food and relief supplies? Even more of the blue plastic FEMA tarps would be welcomed. Or was this purely a reconnaissance mission, some kind of a census-taking? Maybe the helicopters would land and bring an official delegation from the state or even the federal government. The clattering of their dual rotors and the incongruity of their airborne mechanization, in an increasingly nonmechanized world, held everyone at the swap market spellbound. They were like suspicious foxes staring up at a pair of circling eagles.

The helicopter noise masked the sound of the approaching column of five-ton Army trucks; no one heard them until they were only a quarter mile away. The olive-drab trucks stopped on the state road alongside the swap market, and platoons of soldiers immediately tumbled out of their canvas-covered cargo areas. A pair of armored cars with oversized wheels and little gun turrets, like small tanks, guarded each end of the line of trucks. Then an amplified voice split the morning, immediately reducing the helicopter sounds and truck engines to background noise.

"Attention! This is an unlawful assembly!" came booming from a refrigerator-sized speaker on the last truck, which was absent the green canvas roof of the others. "All inhabitants of Radford County were ordered to evacuate three months ago. All persons remaining here are in violation of emergency evacuation orders." The disembodied voice spoke slowly and clearly, pausing for the echoes to die between each pronouncement. "This illegal black market is in violation of currency regulations. Many persons here are in violation of firearms laws. Place all firearms on the ground and move back to the fence, away from the street."

There was activity on the sound truck as soldiers in the back swung a black rectangle up to vertical, facing the crowd from a hundred yards away. It looked like a giant flat-screen TV, turned off. For a moment Jenny wondered if they were going to show a movie. The black screen on the truck was higher than the top of the chain link fence along the side of the parking lot. What was it? Another giant audio speaker? The first was more than loud enough to be heard clearly.

"Move now!" the voice sternly ordered. "You have one minute to put any weapons on the ground and move back to the fence."

Confusion and fear bordering on panic swirled through the market crowd. Men grabbed wives and children, and then glanced at one another, unsure what to do. They had learned to drive off gangs of marauding bandits, but they were not prepared for this new situation. The noisy Chinooks continued circling above them, beating the air while lifting to a higher altitude. Eyes darted between the helicopters, the armored cars, the military trucks and the platoons of soldiers standing by them—and then they saw the horse troops.

A company of cavalry appeared from the thick woods behind the Hope Baptist Church, horses in two columns that divided into separate lines, hooves clattering, mist steaming from flaring nostrils. The columns diverged, right and left, until the street outside the fenced market was lined with mounted soldiers, Kalashnikov rifles across their chests, attached to the soldiers with slings. The mounted troops wore brown-speckled camouflage uniforms and brown berets. The two columns of horses left an open space in front of the truck with the raised black screen.

Nobody moved back to the fence, as they had been ordered to do. Children cried and women wailed as families and friends drew into tight clusters amid the market tables.

The disembodied voice boomed out again. "Place all weapons on the ground, including knives, and move back to the fence. Spread out in a line. You now have thirty seconds to comply. Move back to the fence now. You have thirty seconds to comply."

A few began to walk backward, some guns appeared on the ground, but most of the crowd remained frozen in place, huddled in trembling groups as stragglers hurried to rejoin their families.

"Your time is up," declared the voice. A second later Jenny felt her skin burning; it was as if she had been thrown naked into a bonfire. All of her body felt the searing burn but especially her face and bare hands. She screamed in agony along with the rest, and after an indeterminate time the pain suddenly lessened to something like very bad sunburn. Around her, the screaming and crying continued as the people began to move back in a body, falling down and overturning some tables in their haste.

The voice came again, slow and deliberate. "Because you did not follow my instructions, we have been forced to apply a non-lethal crowd control measure to ensure your compliance. If you follow instructions and move to the fence, we will not be forced to use it again. Now, put down your weapons and move to the fence. Move now!"

The high school parking lot's chain link fence had provided welcome security to the swap market, and it had formerly been considered a great advantage. Now it turned the same parking lot into an instant holding pen. The people almost ran back to the fence to avoid another blast of the invisible burning rays, which they now understood had come from the black panel on the last truck.

Most of the local men were with their families, and they were afraid to resist for fear of another shot from the heat gun hitting their wives and children. The invisible rays had partly blinded the people who had been looking directly at the speaker truck, and these people needed to be led by those whose eyes had not been affected. The crowd subsided from among the tables like an ebbing tide, until it caught up along the ten-foot-high chain link fence.

"Put all weapons on the ground! Spread out, spread out along the fence!" came the voice again. Men quietly cursed and groaned, miserable at having been taken so easily, but what else could they have done? Not a thing—not mixed among a crowd of unarmed women and children.

"Weapons on the ground, all weapons on the ground. Pistols, knives, all weapons on the ground, or you will feel the heat again!" This time the citizens did as they were ordered. Even Sue Bledsoe placed her revolver at her feet. With the tall fence behind and the heat ray in front, they already were effectively imprisoned. The people backed up to the gray steel fence and spread along it until they were in a hundred-yard-long line only a few persons deep, facing the trucks.

"Good. Now, all men: take ten steps forward. All men and teenage boys, walk ten steps forward, away from the fence. Do it now!"

The crying and wailing was universal. A few boys began to walk forward but were pulled back by their families. Then they were all blasted again by the heat ray that sent out an instantaneous wave of burning agony. It seemed incredible that their clothes didn't burst into flames. As Jenny again writhed in pain against the fence she wondered, what was this horrible black device that burned like fire, without light or sound?

"Now—let's try again, people," boomed the amplified voice. "All men: take ten steps forward, away from the fence. Move now!"

The hopelessness of their situation became clear. The crying and moaning continued. A few men, then most of them, walked forward forming a rough line, individuals turning back to their families imploringly and then looking again at the truck containing the black burning machine, at the horsemen, at the soldiers, and up at the still circling Chinook helicopters.

When the men were divided from the rest, a column of about fifty horse troops cantered their mounts through the vehicle gate, their steel horseshoes clattering on the asphalt. Most of them had an Asian appearance, or Eurasian. Many of them were unshaven, with hair much longer than would ever be tolerated on any American soldiers. They approached the left end of the fence and turned their horses to ride between the line of men and boys and the line of women and children still along the fence.

"Okay, that's better," came the slow, deliberate voice again, pausing between each phrase. "I think we understand each other now. The Mannville area should have been evacuated several months ago, with the rest of Radford County. I'm sorry that your actions forced us to take these measures. Soon you will understand that it's for the best. You will be moved now to a relocation center, where you will be fed and provided with free medical care. School is open there for your children. Reconstruction jobs are available, for those who can work. You will be reunited in your family groups after you are in-processed at the relocation center. Okay now, men: turn left, and walk forward."

The line of cavalry was between the men and boys and their families. It didn't occur to them that the heat ray couldn't be used now without also roasting the soldiers and horses. Two searing blasts from the heat ray had taught them to follow orders immediately and without question. The line of disarmed males, more than a hundred of them, walked forward while calling and waving back to their wives, girlfriends, mothers, and children.

The men were not marched out to the street; instead, they were herded toward the double doors of the high school gymnasium. As they approached, the gym doors were opened from within, where more camouflage-clad troops were already waiting inside. An order was given to the men that their women couldn't hear. The men as a group put their arms straight up in the air as they marched out of sight into the gym, and the doors closed behind them.

The amplified voice spoke again, slightly more gently this time. "I'm sorry, but we don't have enough buses to take you all in one trip. For everyone's security, your men will wait here while you ladies will take your children on ahead to the relocation center. Now, ladies, everybody turn around to your right and walk out to the street in single file. Come on, ladies—the sooner we go, the sooner you will arrive at your new temporary home. Warm showers and hot meals are waiting for you. Warm showers and hot meals."

Jenny and Sue were near the head of this line, once they had been turned to face the other way from where the men had gone. The fifty cavalry troops inside the fenced parking lot, having returned from herding the men into the gym, formed a column alongside the women and escorted them out. Once outside the parking lot, the line of women and children was turned to march down the sidewalk, the equestrians riding parallel to them on the street. The fence was now on her left side as Jenny walked on the cement sidewalk. The cavalry moved between the line of women and children and the half-dozen Army trucks. A yellow school bus drove slowly up the street and parked near the truck at the head of the column. The armored cars moved back and forth nervously, their crewmen keeping watch on the proceedings.

More squads of these Eurasian-looking soldiers wearing brown berets stood by each truck. The front of the line of women and children approached a separate group of soldiers, who seemed to Jenny to be in charge. These five men were clean-shaven except for dark mustaches. They were older and somewhat more intelligent looking than the rest. Jenny had no idea where they were from, or what their alien rank insignias meant. They were smiling and chatting away in a language she could not understand. All the other foreign troops carried AK-47-type rifles, but this nearest group had only holstered pistols. Were they officers? One of them raised his arm and pointed at her as she was passing by only a yard away. Unexpectedly, he spoke to her in perfect American English. "You—the blond—get in the first truck." He was dressed identically to the others, in the same uniform. The foreign camouflage pattern was distinctive, with jagged black zigzags over brown, tan and green, the brown predominating. He held a slender black wireless microphone in his hand and used it almost as a pointer.

Jenny stopped to face him, causing the line of women and children to pile up behind her. "You're an American?" She had recognized his unaccented voice at once. "That was you on the loudspeaker, wasn't it? My God, an American, doing this to other Americans! I can't believe it!" She glared at him, her chest heaving, nostrils flaring, a surge of anger overriding her fear.

"Believe it, blondie. Just get in the first truck. Right now—I won't ask you again." He pointed with his microphone behind him to the street.

"It was you on the loudspeaker. An American—a traitor!" Her mouth was almost dry from fear, but without thinking, she managed to spit a fleck of saliva directly onto his face. Then she froze and stared at him, shocked at what she had done, cringing to await the blow. The American stood equally frozen, glaring back at the tall girl eye to eye. He slowly wiped the spit from his reddening cheek with the back of his sleeve. His comrades stared at both of them, wide-eyed and open-mouthed, hands moving to their holstered pistols.

"Shut up, you bitch!" The American in the foreign uniform struck her backhanded across the face, knocking her nearly to the ground. Then he grabbed her by her shoulders, pulled her back up, spun her around and kicked her hard in the backside, propelling her forward. "First truck—and I'll see you later, blondie!"

Young soldiers, their Kalashnikov rifles slung on their backs, stood by the lowered rear tailgate of the truck. A wooden crate had been set behind the truck for a first step. Steel rungs on the hanging tailgate served as other steps. Her mind still reeling, Jenny climbed up into the open back of the truck, "helped" along by hands that grabbed and squeezed at her rear end and breasts. Wooden benches ran along both sides of the truck's cargo area, beneath the heavy fabric roof. She immediately found a place at the very front, behind the cab. A dot of light caught her attention, and she peeked out of a rip in the tightly stretched canvas. Across the road from the high school, she noticed that another troop of cavalry had surrounded Hope Baptist. She shrank down into her corner in horror, trying to absorb the events of the fifteen minutes since the arrival of the helicopters, piled on top of the horror that had been her life for a year since the earthquake.

More girls were forced up into the truck, perhaps a dozen or fifteen in all. Then a squad of the foreign soldiers climbed up after them, and the giant tailgate was raised and latched into place with a metallic bang. The engine was started with a rattle of noise and a burst of black diesel smoke from the exhaust pipe above the cab. The truck lurched forward, the gears grinding audibly. Jenny dared to turn to look behind her at the other girls, and the soldiers, and gradually a new reality came into focus. She was not in a truck with a random assortment of toddlers, old women, and small boys. She was in a truck loaded exclusively with young women and teen-age girls. She looked from crying face to crying face and tried to picture them in happier times. Even underfed and unwashed, they were all at least attractive—or so it seemed to Jenny after a quick assessment. The soldiers sitting behind them grabbed at the closest girls, laughing and smiling, semi-Asiatic eyes narrowed to slits. Who were these troops, and what was this relocation camp they were going to?

The space above the tailgate was left open, to allow light and air into the cargo area. The military truck passed a pair of yellow school buses parked one behind the other in the middle of Main Street. A long line of women and children was being led to the waiting buses by soldiers forming a gantlet. Sudden shadow extinguished the day's bright sunlight, and the temperature dropped as a line of iron-gray clouds moved in from the north.

9

Dwight Granger was a supervisor at the UAV Operations Center, located within a former fitness center on a closed part of Fort Campbell. With so many Army units decommissioned since the last election, almost half of the base was a ghost town, available for other uses. His retirement pay from twenty years in the Air Force should have been enough to live on, but now it wouldn't even buy his groceries. Not after being "adjusted" and converted to North American Dollars at the new ten-to-one rate. So here he was at the age of fifty, back working for Uncle Sam.

It wasn't all bad. At least he wasn't being paid in red TEDs, like the locals. The Temporary Emergency Dollars were not exchangeable and had no value outside the South. In addition, he was able to shop at the Army commissary on Fort Campbell, which at least had regular food deliveries. Not only that, but he also was eligible for free military health care on an "as available" basis. The government even paid for his eyeglasses, and he didn't even mind their ugly black plastic frames: free was free. Dwight Granger was well beyond the years of caring about his style or appearance.

On Saturday he was overseeing four Predator Bs on routine patrol over Middle Tennessee, the region around Nashville and south to Alabama. Once launched from the flight line two miles away on a secondary runway of Campbell Army Airfield, each Predator was controlled by a two-person crew, consisting of a pilot and an ISR technician. ISR for Intelligence, Surveillance and Reconnaissance. Each Predator B filmed the earth below in both color and infrared video.

They also soaked up the electromagnetic spectrum, listening for insurgent radio communications on walkie-talkies and CB radios. Outside the Nashville-Clarksville metro area, there was still practically no cell phone coverage, so any radio transmissions from the ground were immediately pounced upon, analyzed, recorded, and RDF'd. Radio Direction Finding was an automatic function. With this information, ground teams could be vectored to the site of any suspicious unauthorized transmissions. At the same time, paradoxically, the Predators provided a secure radio relay for the government forces on the ground.

With no more low-earth-orbit satellites, the surveillance function provided by the Predators had become more critical than ever. Last year's undeclared and practically unacknowledged space war with China and Russia had seen to that. It was still an open question as to which country had fired the first hostile shot into space. Most people believed the government line, that it was China, since they had less to lose through the destruction of their much smaller and less sophisticated satellite fleet. Many believed they had taken out America's lumbering low-orbiting spy satellites to cloak their preparations for last year's invasion of Taiwan. Whatever the reason, tit had led to tat, until everybody's spy sats had been destroyed up to almost four hundred miles into space, and many had been rendered inoperable at much greater altitudes.

"Open skies" for satellites, which had been the unofficial policy of both sides during the old Cold War, had fallen by the wayside with the advent of ground-based gigawatt chemical lasers and kinetic killers traveling at 18,000 miles per hour. The kinetic weapons took out the low satellites, and the lasers fried or blinded the ones further out. Only the GPS birds and commsats orbiting above 12,000 miles had been left intact. But those distant communication and navigation satellites could not stare down at the earth with an eagle's all-seeing eye. Uncle Sam's fleet of low-earth-orbiting spy satellites had been destroyed or rendered useless. Millions of pieces of satellite debris now littered low space, making their replacement a futile exercise. Even if new spy sats could somehow avoid the welter of hyper-velocity space debris, China or Russia would simply zap them the next time they flew above their territory.

After the unexpected demise of most of America's space fleet, the Predators and the other UAVs had surged to the position of primary importance for regional ISR. It also didn't hurt that UAVs cost only a tiny fraction of the old spy satellites and their launch rockets, a key consideration during the Greater Depression. The USA could no longer rely on outspending its enemies in order to retain military supremacy, not with the dollar relegated to peso status. America was no longer the uncontested global superpower it had been for most of Dwight Granger's life. In the new downsized America, UAVs were the affordable replacement for satellites, at least over American territory.

Jam-proof encrypted broad-spectrum digital microwave beams sent the data collected by the Predators back to the ground data terminal, located on a tower a mile away from UAV Flight Ops. A fiber optic cable brought the data to the ops center, and then to the flight control teams operating each Predator and the other smaller UAVs. This Saturday the sky over Tennessee was clear, with visibility unlimited for a change, and the pictures coming in were unusually crisp. When the weather turned bad, as it often had this winter, the video quality was greatly reduced. Often the Predators were simply grounded, unable to record anything worthwhile. They were far too valuable to put at risk by flying them in extreme conditions. Predators lost to weather or system failures were not replaced. Even when they could fly above the weather, they could not see through thick cloud cover, at least not with video or infrared lenses. Their narrow-aperture radar could sometimes detect large objects like moving trucks through cloud cover, but the radar could not see people.

Granger knew that an especially sensitive operation was going to take place today, when he watched Director Bullard and his team enter the building and disappear into the hall leading to the ISR Oversight offices. The controllers in the ISRO monitored all of the flights in the Ops Center. Whenever they wanted to, they could assume control of a drone, temporarily blanking out the screens of the technicians in the main room on the gym floor.

It amused him when Bullard visited flight ops and went directly to Oversight, believing that they were operating in complete secrecy and isolation. Obviously, they failed to understand that he had personally configured and installed most of the data link hardware in flight ops. But even after all of his hard work in setting up the Ops Center six months ago, he had not been invited to join the so-called elite team of controllers in Oversight. Twenty years in the Air Force with a Top Secret security clearance apparently wasn't good enough for them.

Naturally, Granger had provided his own undetectable backdoor access to the computers and monitors located in the ISRO office. Networks, hardware, fiber optics and computer code were Dwight Granger's passion. So what if he had not been selected for the Oversight team? Of course, he had set up his private channel into the ISRO to work in one direction only, and to be completely undetectable.

The only supervisor on duty this Saturday above Granger in the chain of command was busy reading magazines and drinking ersatz coffee in his own cubicle fifty feet away. The man was clearly appointed based on political connections; he didn't know a sheep from a RAM. Typically, he would not emerge until the end of his shift at three o'clock, asking just enough off-point questions about the day's operations to verify his cluelessness.

Granger typed in his own private command, and accessed the monitors in Oversight. There was little risk of being found out while clandestinely checking into ISR Oversight. Because he was in charge of four Predator teams today, it was routine for him to click from UAV to UAV on his own monitors. He could not control the data throughput from the Predators once they passed over to the control of Oversight, but he could watch their video and digitally record it. The team in Oversight didn't have a clue about his backdoor access. Dwight Granger had designed and practically installed the entire UAV flight control network on Fort Campbell, from the off-site Ground Data Terminal via optical cable to each monitor in flight ops. The guys in Oversight thought that they could operate in secrecy from him? They thought that they could exclude him from their secret business? Morons.

Seen on his monitors, the UAV flights controlled by Oversight didn't appear to be any different from the standard ISR missions controlled in the gym, the main room of flight ops. But their armed Predators and smaller drones as often as not ended up dropping missiles on insurgents. Granger enjoyed observing them at their work. It gave him a sense of satisfaction to know that they could not keep him out of the ISRO with a heavy steel cover on their door and special keypad code locks. He had even compiled personal "best of" clips of their missile strikes and shootings from the smaller UAV SniperHawks. Like the one that had killed the former commanding officer of the Kazak battalion.

It was a distant and sterile way to conduct a counterinsurgency, but this was nothing new to Granger. He had spent years controlling UAV missions all over the globe from Nellis Air Force Base, outside Las Vegas. Pull a shift out there with the 3rd Special Ops Squadron, and you could drop a Hellfire missile on a terrorist safe house in Afghanistan one hour and be playing blackjack in a casino the next. Surreal is what it was. Of course, in those days they were using satellites to communicate with UAVs spread around the globe.

Typically these days in Tennessee and Kentucky, three or four white blobs would be seen crossing a field or walking along a road. These were the heat signatures of human beings, usually sneaking around at night after curfew. Zooming in would reveal more details of size, dress, and items being carried. If they were out after curfew or were seen to be carrying weapons, they were often targeted by the team in Oversight. The big Hellfire rockets would blow insurgents into tiny bits, leaving a hot crater in the ground to mark the point of impact. The Hellfires could level an entire house and make vehicles disappear.

The new miniature 30mm laser-guided missiles did much less damage. They would leave their human targets in scattered pieces on the ground, gradually lightening in color as they cooled off. Cars hit by them would often continue rolling, usually on fire, until they ran off the road or impacted something to stop them. Nobody ever crawled out of the burning wrecks, even when they were hit by the smaller missiles. From 20,000 feet up, it was difficult to tell one car or truck from another before they were blown to Kingdom Come. Dwight Granger could only suppose that the deadly missile strikes were based on some kind of solid intelligence work, but target selection was outside his area of responsibility.

Today the armed Predator controlled by Oversight was operating in the bottom of West Tennessee, not far from where the Tennessee River touched the corners of Mississippi and Alabama. Granger split his screen and selected a topographical map of the area, zooming it down to the same scale as the video coming from the Predator. The UAV was orbiting 20,000 feet above the small crossroads village of Mannville in Radford

County, a town he had never heard of before. Black squares on the computer-generated topo map represented each house and structure.

Granger clicked the Predator video back to full screen and saw columns of horses with mounted troops moving in from the west. These were probably the Kazaks, the first cavalry unit seen in Tennessee since the first Civil War, a century and a half earlier. Against all expectations, horse cavalry had come to fill a unique niche in the pacification of Tennessee. Many roads were still blocked by earthquake damage, and bridges were down across the region. Horses, plentiful in both Tennessee and Kentucky, could move with great stealth where no mechanized units could go. Even better, they operated with almost no logistical tail. The horses fueled up on grass, hay and water from the innumerable streams crisscrossing Tennessee. They could even swim. To Dwight Granger, the reappearance of horse soldiers was one of the more colorful and interesting aspects of the counterinsurgency in the Mid South.

M1117 Guardian armored security vehicles and heavy Army trucks filled with more troops approached the town from the north, and stopped. The wrecked bridges, which had cut off large areas of West Tennessee from outside help, also provided those insurgent-controlled areas with a sense of security against outside interference. Military bridging equipment was sometimes used to cross a series of small rivers, in order to penetrate an unpacified county with government forces. Sometimes the foreign troops would throw a vehicle-mounted scissors bridge across a creek or stream, allowing them to arrive in force with little or no warning. This was probably the case today. Of course, helicopters were used when they were available. Today a pair of Chinooks was orbiting around the village, looking like a pair of horseflies when seen from four miles up.

The Kazak soldiers were readily identifiable by the blinking infrared Phoenix firefly strobes that squad leaders wore on the shoulders of their uniforms. The rest of the soldiers wore reflective strips on their shoulders. On a clear day, when the Predators were filming in both the visible and IR spectrums, the tiny strobes and reflective tape allowed the UAV crews to distinguish the military forces from the local civilians.

Today appeared to be the day that this part of Radford County was coming back under government control—like it or not. Granger didn't know how the locals had done it, but they had managed to hang on through an entire year without electric power, heating oil, gas stations, banks, or supermarkets. You had to give them grudging admiration, even if they were resisting the government's very best efforts to assist them.

The admiration stopped cold when you pondered the horrible acts of racial genocide they had inflicted after the Memphis earthquakes. Dwight Granger had seen the murderous aftermath of their racist hate crimes on many national news programs following the quakes, and he had little pity for them. These holdouts would now be transferred to a location where they could be properly housed and fed, while heavy equipment crews moved in to repair their roads, rebuild their bridges, and reconnect their county to the power grid. Once the Mannville residents were moved to the relocation center, their post-earthquake crimes against humanity could finally be given a full legal accounting before the Truth and Reconciliation Commission.

A few hundred local civilians had gathered on a black-paved parking area near some large intact structures. A quick click back to the electronic map told him it was Mannville Senior High School. This was not unusual, especially on a Saturday. These small towns, almost cut off from the outside world, had turned to barter to provide for their needs. What they managed to find to eat, he couldn't imagine, but then again, it was rich farming country down there. But how did they grow anything last summer without fuel for their tractors and harvesters? Someday, experts would have to conduct a field study of how these rural Tennessee folk had adapted so readily to life without fuel or electricity. They had "gone Amish" and actually survived.

The Predator's video view slid around, panned, and zoomed. Dwight Granger couldn't control the camera; he was a passive observer. Columns of mounted troops entered the parking lot, where the people had assembled in a line near a fence. The file of people then separated into two long lines. One line walked toward the east and then disappeared into a large rectangular building and out of sight. It appeared that the horse-mounted troops were guiding them, like sheepdogs moving livestock. Then the remaining line of people walked the other way, out of the parking lot. The horsemen led them to the state road where the Army trucks were parked, and where more foot soldiers stood in groups. Their reflective tabs and IR strobes easily distinguished them from the townspeople.

The video panned in a blur, refocusing to show two school buses emerge from another large building. Their roofs were painted white, with large black numbers clearly visible from above. The buses were numbered R37 and R22. They drove to the area near the high school and parked, one behind the other, in the middle of the road.

The people herded from the parking lot stood waiting in a long line, at least three or four hundred of them. When the buses stopped, the people walked toward the first one, R37. Fifty or sixty people disappeared inside, like little bugs disappearing inside a hive. Another group disappeared inside R22. The buses then departed, leaving the long line of people assembled between columns of horse soldiers. The buses were followed by one of the Army trucks.

The camera slid over to another set of buildings across from the high school. A steeple on top of one building identified it as a church. Next to the church was a larger rectangular structure. The two buildings were surrounded by soldiers both on foot and on horseback. Their IR strobes blinked the Morse code letter K: dash-dot-dash, which identified them as Kazaks. Granger clicked back to the computer map: the troops were around the Hope Baptist Church and its adjoining church hall.

The video then followed the two buses and one truck as they drove east out of Mannville on State Road 158. The townspeople were being involuntarily relocated. Dwight Granger switched screens to observe what his own Predator teams were doing above Middle Tennessee. They were on routine patrol patterns above Nashville, Murfreesboro, Columbia and Shelbyville. Still curious, ten minutes later Granger clicked back to his private channel into Oversight. One of the buses was winding its way along a narrow, twisting road. The trees were bare of leaves, so the bus remained visible almost all of the time. The latitude, longitude and elevation data in a box on the bottom of the screen changed, following the Predator's cross-shaped aiming curser. The second bus was not in the frame; he assumed it had stopped somewhere else after leaving Mannville.

Bus R37 finally parked in a small clearing. Granger had assumed the people were going to be taken to a relocation center north of Radford County in a pacified area, so this remote location confused him. Most of the FEMA relocation centers were built around former "big box" retail stores. Their parking lots and subsidiary shopping blocks were fenced off, creating instant internment and feeding facilities. There were no such re- tail shopping centers east of Mannville. The computer map indicated that it was farmland and woods clear over to the Tennessee River, a few miles to the east.

The Army truck stopped behind the school bus. Soldiers exited from the back and went to the front of the bus. The people, more than fifty, emerged from the bus one at a time. They walked toward a prominent stripe cutting across the clearing, where the ground changed from grass or brush to some other kinds of shrubs and dirt. The landform was indistinct, but the straight line across the clearing where the terrain changed was apparent. He clicked the screen back to the topographical map of the area and zoomed down. The gash across the clearing was a ravine. Ravines, creeks and sinkholes crisscrossed and pockmarked this part of the country.

Dwight Granger sat transfixed, unable to move. The small dots that were people walked forward until they were in a line spread along the color shift on the ground. A dozen somewhat larger dots with their distinctive IR reflectors formed another line behind them. These soldiers were widely spaced apart, perhaps twenty feet from the line of civilians. A dozen or so soldiers for fifty or sixty civilians. Then the people suddenly moved for- ward a few yards, and instead of being small dots as seen from above, it was apparent that they were on the ground, in different orientations, one upon the other. The Predator B was filming both the visual color spectrum and IR, so Granger switched views to try to gain clarification of what he was seeing. From each soldier sprouted a vivid white line. Rifles. Very hot rifles. When seen on infrared, rifles fired on full automatic went from ambient temperature to hundreds of degrees in seconds, turning them bright white. The soldiers moved toward the edge of the ravine; it appeared that they were continuing to fire.

Dwight Granger checked his own computer, to be certain he was capturing all of this action. He had seen individuals and small groups rocketed, but it had always been at least plausible that they were in fact rebel AI's, armed insurgents. That was one thing. This was another. This was sickening. This was mass murder—there was no other possible explanation.

The school bus departed empty, taking several turns to reverse its direction in the small clearing. Fifteen minutes later, bus R22 arrived. It must have been parked far enough away so that its passengers couldn't hear the gunshots and become alarmed. A few miles would be sufficient. The horrific process was repeated. The passengers were marched from the bus the short distance to where the clearing broke in a sharp line at the edge of the gully. Clicking to the infrared view, he could see that the hot white shapes that were the people taken from the first bus were already turning a cooler shade of gray. Dead. The new line of victims, that's what they were, he understood that clearly now, the new victims were again lined up and mowed down, falling forward, down the ravine's edge and on top of the earlier victims. Again the soldiers moved to the edge of the ravine, and continued to fire down into the warm bodies until there was no more movement. Empty, the second bus departed the scene.

A hundred feet away from Dwight Granger's work station, Bob Bullard and Harry, the senior UAV tech, were also closely watching the events unfolding at the nameless ravine in Radford County. The director's staff, bodyguards, and the rest of the Oversight team had been sent out for an extended lunch, leaving them alone to follow the events around Mannville. The movement of school bus R22 as it departed the clearing seemed to snap Bullard out of a trance. "Harry, where's the other bus?"

The tech had put the Predator into a programmed circle pattern, so that he could concentrate on controlling the sensors. He pulled back the zoom lens, widening the field of view until R37 was visible, approaching the departing bus on the rural lane leading to the ravine. "There it is. Like clockwork."

"Harry...we need to turn this off. I don't know what I was thinking."
"What?"

"Kill the video, and get that Predator out of there. Then erase everything that was recorded today. This is bad. This could be a problem. We can't have this saved anywhere. I never authorized this. My new liaison officer to the Kazaks must have gone out of his mind."

"Okay...you're the boss," said Harry, stubbing out a cigarette.

"I'm serious. Erase it all. This could bite us in the ass, big time. Get that Predator out of the area. Erase everything."

"The weather's getting shitty anyway. I'll bring it back to the bird farm."

"Good," replied Bullard. "The Kazaks don't need our help to finish this job. They know what to do. They can take care of business the old-fashioned way, without UAVs or helicopters. I just don't want any video of it. Got it?"

"Loud and clear, chief. There, it's done. It's all deleted and overwritten a thousand times. It can't be recovered."

"And there are no backups?"

"Hell no. It's gone. Trust me—I zapped it good. Just forget you ever saw it."

"And no more UAVs or helicopters down there until I tell you otherwise," Bullard instructed.

"I understand. No problem. Nothing flies over Radford County until you say so. Like you said—the Kazaks know how to take care of business the old way."

The five-ton Army truck drove no more than twenty minutes, rumbling along narrow country lanes into a section of the county Jenny had never seen before. At least not as far as she could tell from her limited rearward view out the back of the truck and through the tear in the canvas roof behind her. Since arriving in Mannville, she had only gone on a few short car rides. Gasoline was too precious to use for anything but the most essential trips. Even with unlimited gas, it was impossible to cross the Tennessee River to the east or the Mississippi state line to the south, and nobody in their right mind would go west, back toward the hell that was Memphis. A checkpoint allegedly manned by Nigerians prevented free travel over the one remaining bridge to the north.

Today's involuntary truck ride was the farthest she had traveled from Mannville toward the east. She guessed they were traveling east, based on what she could tell from the remaining road signs. The surrounding country was a mix of bare winter farmland, patches and strips of thick woods, and some isolated homes. The green truck wound up a narrow asphalt road through trees, then between rows of bare oaks straight to the top of a hill. She saw a gray squirrel hop along the ground and she thought, *We're all searching for food, even you.* Jenny had eaten plenty of squirrel in the last year. It tasted something like dark chicken meat.

On the bald knob of the hill, encircled within a ring of oaks, was a grand old house with four white pillars in front. A mansion, Jenny supposed, but probably not old enough to be an authentic antebellum plantation house. It was three stories high, painted plain white, with a slate roof and protruding dormer windows. Smoke curled up from partially ruined stone chimneys at either end. The gray slate on the roof was missing in sections. The mansion was built of wood, she supposed: most of the big multistory brick homes had collapsed during the earthquakes last winter. Funny how things had changed after the quakes, she reflected. Brick and stone houses used to be favored by the wealthy. But masonry couldn't hold up to prolonged shaking as well as plain old nailed-together lumber. And for some reason, the older houses seemed to have endured better than the newer ones.

The driveway looped in front of the house. The truck jerked to a stop, the engine still running. The soldiers stood and began yelling in their incomprehensible tongue, but their intent was clear: get out, get down! The tailgate was thrown back with a bang, the girls were pulled and shoved and forced off the truck. The troops jumped down with them, no box for a step this time, and it was a long way down.

The soldiers formed two ragged lines leading up to the big home, and gestured and prodded the dozen girls up the stone steps, onto the veranda that ran the width of the house and toward the massive front door. There was fresh red blood in puddles and splotches on the steps and across the front of the wide landing. There were splintered bullet holes in the varnished wood front door. Bright golden shell casings littered the porch. The three-story home was enormous, at least eight or ten bedrooms, Jenny guessed. The door opened into a hallway with a Persian rug laid over hardwood, and more blood.

The girls were pushed at rifle point into a living room that looked like an art museum, then through an opening into another room with a pool table and more art on the walls, then through a door to a large old-fashioned kitchen and down stairs into a cold cellar. Finally, they were herded into a separate room that appeared to have been hastily emptied; there were still paint cans, rags, and trash on the bare concrete floor. The soldiers didn't accompany them into this room, but merely pushed them inside, slammed the heavy wooden door closed, locked it and left them alone.

Weak winter light entered the room through a high casement window. The room was cold enough to store meat. A bare light bulb hung from the ceiling. A girl gave its string a pull, and as Jenny expected, no light came on. There was no electricity, not even in this mansion. There was no electricity anywhere, not unless you had your own generator and enough fuel to run it.

The room was about ten or twelve feet on a side, with two walls of bumpy stone and concrete, and two interior walls of rough timber planks. Jenny counted; there were fourteen girls jammed into the space. All of them appeared to be terrified, and so was she. None appeared to be older than about twenty-five. They were all white girls—but this was no sur-prise, since almost everyone in the county was white. A helicopter flew somewhere nearby, rotors clattering, turbine engines whining. When it was gone, she could hear popping sounds, some in ripping sequences: distant gunfire.

She had been in the Mannville area since fleeing from the Memphis suburbs, but she didn't know any of these girls by name. A few whispered to each other, a few wept, others appeared to be in shock, beyond any nor-mal reactions. Her friend Sue had not been picked for the truck ride. Jenny wondered: who was the lucky one? And what was happening to Uncle Henry and Aunt Rochelle? She had not seen them at the market; more than likely they had been in the church hall when the foreign soldiers came.

Jenny asked no one in particular, "Does anybody know where we are?" Several of the whispering girls turned to look at her, and finally a petite brunette with short-cropped hair said, "This place is called Barton Hall. It's not very far from Shiloh, the battlefield. I've been to horse shows here. Sometimes they hold Civil War reenactments. What's going on, do you know what's happening? Why are we here? Where are our families? Why didn't they let us go with our families? Why did they make us get on that truck? What's going on?"

Jenny remembered her tenth-grade Human Geography course and its chapter on the Balkan civil wars of the 1990s. She had a very good idea of why the girls had been brought to this old mansion on the hill, but she kept these ugly thoughts to herself. Instead, she placed an empty paint can under the casement window; leaning against the damp wall, she stood on it and peered outside. Even balanced on the can, she could look outside only at an upward angle. Pale afternoon light was filigreed by fingerlike tree-tops, silver and black. The grimy window was set into solid wood frames and appeared unmovable.

If they broke out the window, maybe they could boost and pull one another through. Outside, the window was set below ground level, down a deep and narrow slot. But even if they could squirm their way through and up and out, then what? There was more than a hundred feet of clear lawn between the mansion and the trees, and soldiers were almost certainly posted as guards outside. If escape were possible, the attempt would have to be made after dark. However, it was already near freezing, and none of them were dressed to endure a night of bitter cold. And where could they go, even if they could run away from the soldiers, with their horses and their helicopters? Their families were being relocated, that's what the American traitor had announced. He had promised them food and warm showers. Maybe they should just wait and see what happened next. Whatever happened in the mansion, they would just have to endure it and pray that they would be reunited with their families later. She had been through worse.

A few snowflakes as wide as cotton balls drifted down and settled at the bottom of the casement.

Mid-January, and it was dark early. It had been a wet couple of weeks since Phil Carson had come to be living under Zack Tutweiler's roof, but today had been uncharacteristically clear and cold as a front blew in from the northwest. The small living room was their winter quarters because of the cast-iron potbelly stove, set on bricks in the center of the floor. The kitchen and adjoining living room were the only well-heated spaces in the house. Carson half-reclined on an old sofa facing the black stove, dressed warmly and covered with blankets, reading in the soft light of a hurricane lantern on the end table behind him. Zack was out stalking around with his compound bow.

He was almost through an old biography of General Nathan Bedford Forrest, and he was savoring every page. Many of the general's raids and battles had taken place within a hundred miles of this very house. Between the foul weather and the Tutweiler library, he had spent most of his time indoors and immobile, allowing his wound to heal. The last few days he'd been going on walks, up to several miles at a time. Tonight he was grateful for the chance to read by the heat of the fire. His activity was confined to turning pages and occasionally prodding the hot embers in the stove or adding a chunk of wood.

Neither Phil nor Zack was a gushing fountain of conversation. After their life histories had been shared to their mutual satisfaction, they had become content with long periods of silence. Both men preferred quiet reading. Without electricity, there was no television or music. Zack had a portable Sony AM/FM radio that ran on four rechargeable AA batteries. The batteries had a charger that could be powered from a solar panel, but they were not holding their charge, and so they could listen to the radio only for brief periods. The only daytime radio with a clear signal was government propaganda on two AM stations.

At night, they could tune in stations from much farther away, Chicago and other distant cities, but the news reports were confusing and contradictory. Every night they tried to tune in Radio Free America from Laramie, Wyoming, but an oscillating and chirping tone usually covered its frequencies. Jamming. Tonight Phil listened to old country tunes on the Nashville frequency. When they ended, a male announcer with a folksy Southern accent began speaking.

Now, friends, it's time for some official news. In response to questions from concerned citizens, Mayor Antoine Zaragoza has released the following statement that I'm going to read now. Here it goes, so listen up. "Nashville has ample food supplies; however, these food supplies are still being hoarded by the rich. Anyone who is found to be hoarding food will be prosecuted to the utmost severity of all applicable emergency laws, not to exclude capital punishment in exceptional cases. A two-week supply of food staples for each household is the most allowable under the anti-hoarding laws. Anyone in possession of more than a two-week food supply must register the stockpile with his or her neighborhood food distribution committee—this is the law. It's unfair and unjust that many of our neighbors are still going hungry while the rich profit from selling their illegal stockpiles of food on the black market, food that they don't even need. Anybody who reports an illegal food stockpile will receive a generous cash and food reward for doing his or her civic duty. Only if we all pull together can we make it across the..."

The old nicad batteries abruptly lost power, as they tended to do, and the radio faded to dead silence. It wasn't much of a loss, just more government propaganda. Carson closed his book and set it on the floor, put his reading glasses in his shirt pocket, and folded his hands across his chest. Gradually he nodded off.

The final afternoon light steadily diminished, until it was black inside the basement room. The girls sat shivering on the cold floor, huddled together away from the damp stone outer walls, waiting to learn their fates. The empty paint cans became their toilets. Some of the girls prayed quietly, reciting the Lord's Prayer and the 23rd Psalm. In the darkness, Jenny's hearing became hyperacute. She heard several vehicles coming toward the mansion, accompanied by shouting, and a few gunshots not so far away. The girls froze at the sounds, and the praying ceased.

The vehicles stopped near the mansion. Their diesel engines went silent, but the shouting continued. Boots stomped on the floor above them, making the old wooden ceiling creak and groan. A generator came on with a low, vibrating rumble, and their hanging bulb suddenly flashed on, causing them to blink at the unexpected light. Overhead, they heard loud voices, the sound of furniture being scraped about on the hardwood floor, and...music? Yes, music. Soon there was shouting, singing, crashing and banging. Jenny had no idea what was going on above them, but she instinctively knew that it would eventually involve the girls huddled in this room. She had survived a deadly home invasion after the first big quake, and the stomping and loud voices over her head made evil memories flash through her mind. Jenny had no hope at all that their presence in the cellar had been forgotten. The girls went back to praying, more fervently and rapidly than ever.

After a too-short period, perhaps ten minutes, they heard heavy boots tromping down the basement steps. The girls automatically moved away from the door when they heard the approaching footsteps. Then the door was unlocked and jerked open. In the doorway were four of the foreign soldiers, holding bright flashlights. "Come here, girls," Jenny understood one to say. The "here" sounded rasping, as if the man had something stuck in his throat. He said "girls" as if there were two syllables: "gay-rils." The rest of what they were saying Jenny couldn't make out. Soldiers grabbed the closest girls by their arms and yanked them toward the door. "Come, gay-rils! Now you come: vee havink big party, yes!"

The first two were pulled out of the room and shoved toward the steps. The other girls shrank back and pressed together in the corner opposite the door, milling like penned sheep in the presence of wolves.

"No, no, gay-rils—everybody comink now! Everybody out, comink big party, yes!" Two enormous soldiers entered the cellar room and roughly began grabbing and pushing them toward the entrance, brutal shepherds. Two other soldiers waited outside the door and herded the last girls out of the room and up the dark wooden steps, back upstairs into the game room.

Jenny was the third in line as they entered. A stereo was playing loud rock music, with fast guitars, a men's vocal chorus and accordions. She'd never heard that kind of song before; she assumed it was in the same foreign language spoken by the soldiers. A roaring fire blazed in an arched stone hearth, and a glance showed that broken furniture was being fed into the flames. More than twenty men stood around the perimeter of the big room, mugs and liquor bottles in their hands, laughing and grinning and whistling as the girls were pushed into the open space in the middle. On seeing them, the soldiers broke into a drunken song, slapping one another on the back, swaying together, and holding out their cups as they closed the circle on their quarry. Some of the men had on their camouflage tunics; some were wearing only brown T-shirts over their uniform pants. Jenny saw that they were glassy-eyed, filthy and unshaved, and well on the way to getting stinking drunk.

The song ended after a verse or two, and some of the soldiers began demanding, "Drink! Drink, gay-rils! Havink big happy party now—you drink, have good time!" There were enough men to double up on each girl, putting arms around their shoulders, grasping their arms, squeezing breasts and forcing full glasses to their lips. The girls, terrified and confused, put hands to the cups to steady them, and coughed as the hard liquor bit their throats. Jenny was extremely thirsty after hours with no water, but still she resisted the whiskey a soldier was trying to pour down her throat. Another man grabbed her from behind and pinched her nose closed with his other hand. She was so surprised by this that after she gasped for breath, half a cup of whiskey was forced down her throat, leaving her coughing and gagging. The soldiers laughed as if they had heard a great joke.

In the next room, the front door slammed open and a few more soldiers entered the party room. The soldiers already present stood at sloppy positions of attention and momentarily quieted down as four newcomers entered. There were greetings and chatter between them in the unknown tongue. More loud laughter and backslapping, and after a brief interchange the soldiers returned to forcing alcohol into their young victims while groping, pinching and rubbing against them.

Then, unexpectedly, Jenny heard an American voice call out from the unintelligible din.

"Hey, blondie! Well, we meet again. I promised you we would—and I *never* break a promise to a lady."

The speaker was one of the new arrivals, who were all wearing Russian-style fur hats. The four had just come from outside, and melting snow clung to them. The one who spoke to her was also dressed in the brown camouflage uniform, with a pistol in a black holster on his wide military belt. On his back was a medium-sized green backpack. The new soldiers were clearly higher-ranking than those already in the house. They were a bit older, they had shaved more recently, and their uniforms looked more complete and less dirty. In fact, it occurred to Jenny that all of the troops in the mansion were officers, or at least sergeants of some kind. It made sense that they would be the high-ranking soldiers, if they could simply seize a mansion—and kidnap girls for their "party" as well.

The American spoke in the foreign tongue, and Jenny's most recent pair of captors pushed her from behind, through the revelers and the other captive girls, to where the new arrivals stood in the opening to the living room. She straightened up to look the American in the eye, not wanting to cower or cringe in his presence. In spite of herself, she was almost glad to see him. At least he was an American, someone who spoke her language. This took away just a bit of her fear, somehow.

"So, blondie, you've learned better manners now?" He raised his open hand as if to strike her, and Jenny reflexively flinched but held her ground. He guffawed, and his companions laughed with him while he translated his remark for them. She was just as tall as this American traitor, who was no more than her five foot ten, even with his fur hat and combat boots on. Although no taller, he was much larger; Jenny guessed that he outweighed her by at least eighty pounds. Wherever he came from, there was certainly no famine. All of the soldiers had thick, fleshy faces while the girls were gaunt and hollow-eyed.

The American spoke again in their foreign language, slowly and loudly, and the men in the room burst out laughing and raised their cups in toast. Then he reached out to Jenny with his left hand and slid rough fingers behind her neck, pulling her in close, nose to nose, eye to eye. He had the beginning of a bristly mustache like most of the others, heavy whisker stubble, and cold, dark eyes. He could have passed for one of the foreign soldiers except for his unaccented English.

While looking into her eyes with his hand still squeezing her neck, he said quietly, "I just told them that I have chosen you, blondie, and that now I'm going to teach you better manners. You know, believe it or not, I'm doing you a favor—it'll just be you and me tonight. The rest of these babes are going to pull trains, all night tonight and on into tomorrow. Do you know what that means? Once the officers have had their fun, the rest of the battalion will march through and take their turns. Fifty North American Dollars a pop, all for the battalion recreation fund. There's hundreds of troops in the battalion—just do the math. So if you're smart, blondie, you'll want to make me *real* happy tonight. If I'm happy enough, maybe you'll be the one special girl in this house that doesn't get laid twenty times. Who knows, maybe you'll even get to be my Tennessee sweetheart. Maybe. If I like you good enough." He grinned a chipped-tooth smile and winked, close enough for her to be repelled by his bad breath, stinking of garlic, onions and liquor.

"Okay," he finished. "Enough small talk. Enough polite chitchat. Come on, blondie, let's go upstairs and find the master bedroom in this dump before the colonel grabs it for himself." Still smiling, he pulled her through the opening into the living room by her neck and then pushed her toward the front hall and the stairs. Behind them the soldiers roared their approval, whistling and stomping their boots, then once again they broke into a verse of their drunken song. He pushed her upstairs with one hand clamped around the back of her neck and the other clutching her left upper arm tightly enough to hurt.

He shoved Jenny through the door, toward a king-size four-poster bed. He pulled out his pistol; a bright mini-flashlight was attached beneath its barrel. He scanned the room with the light until he found an oil lamp standing on an antique bureau. He gave Jenny one more hard push, and she landed on her face on the bed. The bed was piled high with quilts and blankets; the room temperature was nearly comfortable, not bitterly cold. He pulled off his fur hat, dropped his pack, and kicked the bedroom door closed behind him with a boot. He lifted the lamp's glass and lit the wick with a butane lighter. With the wick adjusted, the room was suffused in a soft glow. It was burning real lamp oil, with a nice scent, not the foul smelling motor oil she was accustomed to. He reholstered his pistol, its harsh electric light no longer needed.

Expensively framed antique oil paintings of pastoral equestrian scenes hung on the walls. The room had a white brick fireplace across from the foot of the bed. A large painting of horses and riders preparing for a fox hunt hung above the fireplace mantle. It was a working fireplace, not merely decorative. There were half-burnt logs on an iron grate, and fireplace tools in a rack on the side. She carefully noted the iron tools: she might get a chance to use them as weapons if her captor let down his guard. There was a large window on either side of the fireplace, their shades pulled down. Between the fireplace and the windows were low bookshelves. The sounds of the bacchanal came up through the floor: men singing and shouting, and girls screaming. Jenny wondered if she was indeed luckier than the girls remaining below.

Her captor breezily said, "You have to admit, they really knew how to build these old places. More earthquake-proof than houses built ten years ago. It must have been built before they had central heat—lots of fireplaces." He grabbed some bound books from the low shelf to the right of the fireplace, ripped pages out and threw them into the hearth, and then threw in entire books. He ignited the paper with his lighter. He picked up an antique mahogany chair, and using only his upper body strength, broke it into pieces by pulling the legs apart. He tossed its solid wood legs and arms into the fireplace, and repeated the process with another antique chair, and then the four mahogany posts from the bed, which lifted easily out of slots. The paper was already burning brightly, and he fed additional open books into the flames until the wood began to catch fire.

"There, that should do it. It'll be warming up in here in no time." He went to his pack, opened a side compartment, and extracted a thick sausage wrapped in plastic film, already opened at one end. He waved the long reddish-brown cylinder in the air. "Here's what you're playing for, blondie. Make me a happy man, and we'll have a nice romantic dinner to-gether—afterwards." Jenny could smell its greasy, spicy aroma and her mouth began to water. He said, "Summer sausage, from Wisconsin. Not too many problems up there—the cheeseheads have all they want, just about. Not like down here in Tennessee. I'll bet you're just *starving*, eh?" He laughed at his own joke. He set the meat within her sight, on the edge of the bureau under the lamp, then removed a plastic bottle from his pack, unscrewed the cap, and took a drink.

Jenny lay on the bed on her side, her knees drawn to her chest, look-ing at him as he first unbuckled his outer belt with its pistol and other gear, then unzipped his camouflage jacket and dropped it to the floor, followed by his uniform shirt. He left on his brown T-shirt. He sat on the edge of the bed and unlaced his boots, taking his time, staring at her with his mouth agape. Finally he stood and unfastened his belt, and let his pants drop to the floor. He was a huge, thickly muscled man, with hairy gorilla arms and short bandy legs.

"Okay, blondie, your turn now." He stood above her by the edge of the bed and clapped his hands together. "Come on, honey; get with the program. Take off that vest—let's see what you're hiding under there."

Jenny wondered if he was possibly a foreign soldier, trained to speak flawless English. He was wearing the foreign uniform, but his English was perfect. Maybe he was a foreigner who had lived for a long time in America. She had also heard him speak the foreign tongue. There were so many groups of foreigners living in the USA, it was hard to keep track of them all. She was repulsed by him and didn't want to join in his one-way conversation, but she felt compelled to ask him a single question. "Are you really an American?"

He smiled, his face softening slightly. "As American as apple pie, blondie. Born and raised in the Land of Lincoln. Now, here's the deal: I'm getting cold waiting for you to get in the mood. I want you naked under the covers, right now. Got it? Come on, it's still too chilly in this room. Don't worry, I'll be gentle," he laughed. "You're going to love what I'm going to give you, I promise. Then if I like it too, well…I'll try to forget what you did back there in Mannville. That was rude—you *really* pissed me off. You embarrassed me in front of my colleagues from Kazakhstan. Now I'm giving you a chance to make it up to me. Then we'll have dinner."

Jenny crossed her arms tightly and looked away. "No."

"No? You don't understand. 'No' is not an option for you tonight."

"No—I won't," she repeated, quietly but with conviction.

"Oh, yes you will! He gave her a cruel smile and then launched hiself on her, still wearing his brown T-shirt, boxer shorts, and socks. She rolled quickly to the far side of the wide bed and half slid off it, but he crawled after her, grabbed her by an ankle and easily dragged her back into the middle. He laughed and playfully smacked her on her rump, then pulled the sneakers off her feet and tossed them aside. Jenny rolled onto her back, trying to get into a defensive posture where she could fend him off.

"So you're a fighter, are you? Well, I like spirit in a girl, but don't push your luck." Without warning, he turned and slapped her hard across the face and Jenny's hands flew up. Still laughing, he grabbed the edge of her plaid wraparound skirt in both hands and yanked it upward until she rolled out of it. Then he straddled her bare legs at the thighs, grabbed both sides of her black insulated vest and yanked them apart, sending the gold buttons flying, and then pulled up the bottom of her yellow sweater.

He was extremely powerful, but Jenny clutched her arms to her chest tightly and for a moment they were at an impasse, until he gave her another open-handed blow to the other side of her face. The shock of it stunned her, and in that instant he forced the sweater and open vest up over her head and off. When the sweater came up, it took her cotton undershirt with it. She wore no bra, she did not own one anymore; bras that fit her were impossible to find. He flung her clothes aside and she clasped her arms back across her bare breasts. She had never been exactly busty, and after a year of near starvation, she was even less so. Naked now except for her panties and socks, she felt furious, powerless and terrified all at the same time. Her face was scarlet both from humiliation and from his slaps.

He carefully grasped both of her wrists, easily peeling her arms away from her chest, and pinned them under his hands against the mattress, on either side of her head. "Come on, blondie, I like a frisky little filly now and then, but enough is enough. Make it easy for yourself—I don't want to mark up your pretty little face. You can't be my Tennessee girlfriend if you look like you just went ten rounds in the octagon." All of his upper body weight now bore down upon her slender wrists, his hips crushing hers, his knees battering her thighs, forcing her legs apart.

Then he lowered his chest against her while Jenny squirmed and thrashed to no effect, his greasy whiskered face only inches away, his breath stinking, his tongue darting out and wiggling like some perverted lizard. He licked her neck, her cheeks, probed her ear as she turned her head to the side and clamped her eyes shut. She was crushed, pinned and helpless. While he licked and kissed her neck, his whisker stubble grating like sandpaper, the back of his ear brushed against her lips. Without thinking, she bit into it as hard as she had ever bitten anything in her life. It was like biting a dried apricot, with a piece of beef jerky inside. She held onto his ear with her teeth, like a crazed pit bull clamping down on a rawhide chew toy.

He shrieked in pain and released his hold on her wrists, his meaty hands going for her throat, but she maintained her bite on his ear. His thick fingers snaked up to her neck, one hand found her windpipe and began to clamp down, but her hands were now also free and her fingernails flew to his eyes like ten daggers. Then his head was suddenly loose from her and he pulled away. Most of his ear was still in her mouth, and she spat it out on the bed between them, their eyes locked together. He rolled away from her to gain some distance from the source of his pain, then raised himself up on one arm and drew his other hand back in a fist to strike her.

His face was a twisted contortion of blind rage, there were deep red scratches running from his eyes down his cheeks. The ragged stump of his ear gushed hot red blood down his neck and onto her. His right fist came down, but Jenny darted away toward the side of the bed as the punch narrowly missed. He pursued her, hitting her on her buttocks, grabbing at her flailing legs as she went over the edge, kicking backward at him. He was right behind her as she shot head first down to the floor, but she just managed to scramble ahead of him toward the foot of the bed, slipping on the small rug in front of the fireplace.

He sprang up to leap on her, and as she rolled onto her back she grabbed at the brass fireplace poker that leaned against the bricks, point upward. There was no time or space to swing it as a weapon. As he came hurtling down, she turned slightly, guiding the poker's iron tip. In his rage and animal excitement he focused on her naked body, not seeing what she held in her hands.

As he threw his bulk onto her, his full weight came down on the poker. The bottom of the brass and iron spear held fast where the hardwood floor met the raised bricks of the fireplace hearth. The harpoon point tore into his throat, piercing his windpipe. The poker's outward curving hook, the complement to its spear tip, prevented it from completely impaling him. His forward motion vaulted his body over Jenny into the fireplace. The top of his head slammed into the bricks at the back of the hearth, his face, chest and shoulders landing across the blazing wood. His still-pumping feet and legs found no purchase on the small rug and smooth hardwood. He jerked and tried to roll out, but he was trapped in the fireplace by the iron poker jammed deeply into his neck, its shaft caught backward among the burning wood and the iron hearth grate. His back arched and stiffened, his legs gave a few more kicks and shivering spasms—and then he was motionless, with his black hair and T-shirt already aflame.

Jenny crabbed away from him on her back, hyperventilating, finally sitting against the pillaged bookshelf, staring at her would-be rapist's prone body. She was naked except for her panties and socks. Downstairs, she could still hear the music, the yelling, and the screaming. Nothing had changed except that her attacker was apparently dead. Dead and now on fire, already smelling like burnt hair and roasting meat. But he wasn't the meat she was interested in. She stood and snatched the sausage from atop the bureau and tore into its open end with her teeth while still watching his body for signs of movement. She washed down half-chewed chunks of the sausage with gulps of water from his plastic bottle; it was flavored with some kind of citrus. Something like Gatorade—sheer heaven. Within minutes, she had consumed almost a foot of the sausage. She belched with great pleasure, her stomach already rumbling agreeably.

It took no deliberative planning, there was no moment of eureka, she simply saw his uniform pieces on the floor and went straight into action. As long as the "party" continued downstairs, she hoped she might have time. On went her undershirt and sweater and vest, then his pants, his boots, his uniform blouse and insulated outer jacket. His pants were baggy on her, but they fit tolerably well with the belt cinched tight, and the strings at the bottoms of the legs tied. It took a minute to figure out how to adjust the wide pistol belt that went on over his jacket, around her waist.

The holster was made of black plastic. A special button had to be pushed to release the gun. The pistol was a big one, a Springfield XD .45, according to the inscription on the slide, but her fingers were long enough to get a good grip around it. One thing she knew was guns: Uncle Henry had shown her how to operate all of the most common models. There wasn't enough ammunition to waste on much practice, she'd fired only a few real bullets, but she was confident that she'd be a good shot when the time came. She knew how to line up the sights, she'd dry-fired her uncle's pistols without ammunition hundreds of times.

This Springfield XD pistol was similar to her uncle's Glock. That meant there was no manual safety catch—you just pulled the trigger to fire it. The XD's hinged safety was right on the trigger, like on a Glock. She mentally thanked her uncle for teaching her about guns, something her own father, a non-shooter, had never done. This lapse had cost their family dearly when Memphis had been transformed into hell on earth by the earthquakes. The silver barrel extended a half inch beyond the front of the slide, and it was threaded like a bolt or screw on the outside. A small light was attached under the barrel, in front of the trigger guard. From the grip's length and thickness, she estimated that it carried at least ten bullets in its magazine. Two extra magazines fit into a black plastic pouch on the opposite side of the web belt. There was no time to examine the gun further, so she holstered it.

There were twenty or thirty armed soldiers downstairs, along with a dozen local girls she didn't even know. She pushed mad thoughts of a rescue from her mind. What was impossible was not worth wasting time thinking about. Jenny was a survivor first and foremost: it was why she was still alive a year after the quakes, when so many others—including her parents—were dead. She knew that there was a time to fight and a time to run. Anybody could die for a pointless, futile gesture. Thousands had. Maybe millions. Not Jenny McClure.

She went to the window and rolled the shade halfway up. After she figured out how to unlock the old-fashioned clasp, the bottom section of the wood-framed window slid up and open. Cold air blasted in, along with snow. The snow was really coming down now! She looked outside. It was too dark to see much except that the world was now blanketed in white, but she could make out a small angled roof just a few feet below the windowsill. She put a leg over and then had a thought, looking back into the room. She climbed back inside, grabbed the would-be rapist's pack, and put the rest of the sausage and the water bottle into the side compartment and snapped it shut.

It was heavy but manageable. She'd carried heavier. It weighed maybe twenty-five or thirty pounds. She heaved it over the windowsill and then let it go. It dropped onto the lower roof, slid for a second, and disappeared from sight. One last look: on the floor by the bed, the dead traitor's fur cap caught her eye. She scooped it up and put it on her head, looked at herself in the mirror above a low dresser, and pulled the fur earflaps down on the sides and back. The inside of the hat was as soft as mink. It would protect her head almost like a helmet when she landed.

She paused on her way to the window to look again at the traitor's body, its upper half now sizzling and burning in the fireplace. A sudden idea overtook her. She looked around the room, yanked comforters and sheets from the bed, and shoved them partway into the blazing fireplace. Next, she slid the low bookshelf sideways away from the wall and tipped it over across the traitor's back. The way the drunken soldiers were carrying on downstairs, the sound would never be noticed. The flames were already dancing along the bed sheets into the jumble of open pages beneath the overturned wooden shelf. Finally, she climbed over the windowsill and lowered herself downward until her boots touched the angled roof, its wet slate covered with a thin layer of snow. She let go, slid on her fanny down to the edge, and was launched into space.

10

Phil Carson was on another sailboat, but it was not a catamaran this time, and not on the ocean, or even on water. The boat was somehow mounted on wheels, and he was trying to negotiate a mountain road. The vessel's mast was as tall as the surrounding trees, and he worried about how he would navigate the boat through overhanging branches and under electrical power lines that he could see ahead. He was steering the boat from behind the wheel, high up in the cockpit; somehow, the boat's means of locomotion was not important. Gravity, he vaguely understood. It did not seem at all strange to him that he was driving a big sailboat down a mountain road. Then the boat began swaying beneath him. The dirt shoulder at the edge of a turn began crumbling away, the boat slid toward the edge…

He was awakened by harsh words and cold steel against his cheek. His eyes opened to see pistol and rifle barrels inches away from his face. There were two guns, and behind them, two men. One man held a large black pistol with a suppressor fixed to its end. The other had an M-16 carbine across his lap, its barrel casually angled to aim at his chest. The men were dressed in dark rain gear, their faces hidden behind black balaclava masks. Both were sitting on kitchen chairs, their backs to the iron stove. Zack was nowhere to be seen. The man holding the pistol said, "Sorry to wake you up. We're on a tight schedule, and we need to talk." He had a Southern accent, but not overly strong.

"Who are you?" Carson had spent the last three weeks dreading a sudden and unhappy end to his peaceful convalescence, and here it was.

"That doesn't concern you. We ask, you answer—that's the only program tonight. Got it?" The mask had one slit across his eyes and another across his mouth.

Carson tried to sit up on the couch, but was jabbed down by the carbine's muzzle in his ribs. He had to address his tormenters while lying helplessly on his back.

The man with the pistol asked, "What's your name? I mean your real name."

He sighed. What was the point of holding out, or lying? Presumably, they'd already interrogated Zack. "Phil Carson."

The second masked man with the rifle asked, "So who is this Colonel Brice?" He held the laminated military ID card in front of Carson's face.

"He's a dead man, or at least that's what I was told. The card was made for me."

"By who?" asked the pistol wielder.

"It's a long story."

"So start telling it."

Carson repeated the truthful version of his shipwreck, detention and escape from Camp Shelton, as nearly as he remembered telling it to Zack. The two men listened quietly, occasionally asking questions about details.

The man with the pistol changed tacks while Carson was describing the Christmas Eve drive up the eastern side of Mississippi. He held up a sheet of loose-leaf paper. "Where did you get this list?" Its many creases showed that it had been recently folded to postage-stamp size. Carson recognized his list at once, but it was not in his handwriting. It was an exact copy of his hidden personal contact sheet. Zack had sold him out.

The masked man shook the page in Carson's face. "What are you, deaf and dumb? We're not playing around. Where did you get this list?"

"It's my own—I didn't 'get' it anywhere."

"Who is on this list? I mean, who are these people? What's your connection to them?"

Carson's mind spun. Now he risked compromising more people, endangering them through his carelessness. What a huge mistake it had been to carry a copy in clear text, uncoded, even if it was in miniature and—he had thought—well concealed. "They're old friends."

"So you say. Don't play stupid. Let me ask you again: what do these *old friends* have to do with you?"

Carson hesitated, considering his words. "I knew some of them in the military, a long time ago. Some I met later."

Now the two masked invaders were quiet, and exchanged glances. The man with the pistol held the paper with his gun hand and pointed to a single line written near the bottom. "This one, right here. Can you read this name?"

Carson fiddled on his narrow reading glasses, squinted at the list, and sighed. "Eric Vikersun. Viker, rhymes with biker, not Vikker rhymes with liquor." The ditty giving the pronunciation of the name just popped into his head, after lying dormant somewhere in his brain for decades.

The masked pistol holder nodded almost imperceptibly. "How did you know him?"

Carson exhaled again, and continued. "Vietnam. He was in one of my my recon teams for a few months. Before he was medevacked out."

"When did that happen?"

"Oh…that would have been in 1970, I think."

"Where did it happen? His getting hit, I mean. Be specific, and don't even try to bullshit me."

"Officially, or in reality?"

"Try both."

"Officially, up around Dak To. We were staging out of Kontum. In reality, we were in southern Laos. Those cross-border missions were part of Operation Prairie Fire. That was all classified back then. It was classified for years and years after the war."

"How was he wounded?"

"Mortar frag in his legs and back. They caught us on the LZ, on insertion. We barely got out. I caught some too, but not as bad. It was almost normal to get hit on the LZs by then. The NVA had most of the likely LZs indexed and wired—it was grim. Prairie Fire was just about finished by 1970. A lost cause, the way we were fighting it."

"Who else was on that mission?"

Carson closed his eyes, thinking. There had been so many cross-border ops, and the recon teams frequently changed as men were wounded or killed. Typically, there would be three or four Americans and six or seven 'Yards. "Let's see...I think...Chuck Miller, and Dick Fielding. They were the only other Americans on that one, I think. I could be wrong—there were a lot of missions like that, and it was a long time ago."

The second man leaned over and whispered into the masked ear of the man holding the list.

"Tell me something else. What was Eric Vikersun's nickname?"

Carson replied without hesitation. "Eric the Red. But usually we just called him the Viking."

The man with the pistol nodded. "Describe him."

Carson closed his eyes again, remembering. "Real tall. At least six foot four. Kind of reddish-blond hair, I think, but it was usually cut short, of course. Blue eyes, for sure. What's all this about Eric Vikersun? Why do you want to know?"

The man dropped the list and pulled off his mask. He had long dark blond hair, a thick chestnut beard, and piercing blue-green eyes. "Eric Vikersun was my father. I'm Boone Vikersun."

"Viker, rhymes with biker," Carson murmured.

"You got it. But folks call me Boone."

Phil Carson stared in wonder for a few moments. "You know what? I think I met you before. You were just a kid, not even ten. It would have been at Fort Bragg, at the SOG reunion. I remember seeing Eric at the reunion, and that he had his boy with him—so that would have been you. I'm guessing it was in the late '80s. How's your father?"

"My father's dead. He died five years ago. Heart attack."

"Damn..."

"Yeah. Look, I don't remember meeting you at the reunion, but I heard of you. My dad thought a lot of you. You were in some of his best stories. I heard them since I was a kid. Maybe that's why I joined up too, all of my dad's old war stories. I put eighteen years in the green machine before this current shit storm came down. Airborne Ranger, Green Beret. The whole nine yards, from Kuwait to Kandahar. You know the drill. You were in it too, back in the day."

Carson nodded, looking at the face of the man who so strongly resembled his old recon teammate. It was like seeing a ghost in the flesh, except for the long hair and the beard. "You only did eighteen years instead of going for twenty? Did you voluntarily separate? Or did they RIF you out, get you during a reduction in force?"

Vikersun grinned. "Neither. They wouldn't let me separate, so I just walked away. I'm not sure what they call it these days, but they're not sending me a paycheck anymore, that's for damn sure. From their point of view, I guess I'm a deserter; they didn't give me permission to leave. But the way I see it, most of the ones that stayed on active duty are traitors—at least the ones operating with the foreign troops sure as hell are. I walked away, so yeah, technically that means I deserted. But when foreign soldiers are running around Tennessee, well, I sure as hell ain't staying out of that fight! This is *my* state. Eighteen years or no eighteen years. And I don't care if our own president sent them in—Jamal Tambor's a traitor too, as far as I'm concerned."

The second man pulled off his own mask, revealing the face of a young man in his mid-twenties, with medium-length wavy black hair and dark eyes. Unlike his older companion, he had only a week's worth of stubble on his pale face.

"I'm Doug Dolan. Nice to meet you, Mr. Carson. Boone told me some of his father's war stories, after we got the message and decided to come down here. We just had to be sure you were the real thing, and not a plant." He held out his right hand.

Carson sat up on the sofa and shook the offered hand while studying the younger man's features. Dolan seemed like a decent enough guy, at least on first impression. It stood to reason that the Viking's son wouldn't hang around with any slackers or REMFs—Rear Echelon Mother F'ers. Zack had also quietly entered the room, looking sheepish, as if he wasn't sure if he should apologize for bringing these armed visitors to the house without giving any warning.

Boone stood up and stretched, holding his pistol straight out, and rocked his head from side to side, neck bones audibly cracking. He was wearing a long unzipped parka that extended almost to his knees. The hood was pushed back, revealing wild hair that covered his ears and stuck out in many directions. Like his equally tall father, Boone was an imposing figure with electric blue eyes and a reddish-blond beard. His rain parka was printed with one of the commercial hunting camouflage patterns, which looked like actual leaves and branches in a wet forest.

He lowered his arms and unscrewed the suppressor from his pistol, rotating the metal tube seven or eight times before it came free. He pulled his parka aside and slid the pistol into a black holster beneath a compartmented combat vest. The black suppressor went into its own small pouch. His coat covered the vest and weapon when it fell closed. Then he looked down at Carson and said, "We can finish our little stroll down memory lane later on, but right now you've got to get up and get ready to leave. We're moving out. I hope your ass is healed well enough so you can ride a horse. That's what we'll be doing tonight—a lot of riding. This house is blown. It's not secure."

"How do you know?" Carson pushed the blanket off and swung his legs to the floor.

"I really don't see any good reason why you need to know that." Boone paused, staring at Carson for a moment. "Ah, what the hell. Your getaway driver was picked up right after Christmas. The black medic. They know where you were dropped off, and that you were heading north, straight through here. If the word made it to me in Tennessee, there's no telling who else knows. We can't risk it, not after what happened to Zack's father. It's only a matter of time before they're connecting the dots and kicking down that door over there. Or just dropping a rocket down this stovepipe, on general principle."

"What about Zack?"

"He's coming too. He understands. We had a long talk while you were cutting Z's. It's no good, him hanging around where all of his family died. And he knows how to contact us, so that makes it too much of a risk for him to stay, even if he wanted to. A risk for him, and for us too. This house was very useful, while it lasted. Great location. Zack's father was a real patriot, an ideal courier, but shit...I guess his luck ran out. His getting nailed on this side of the border by a missile—that took us by surprise. We thought that was against the rules of engagement, but we're figuring out that there aren't any rules in this shitty little war. So we're taking what we can carry on horseback and getting out right now."

"We're moving tonight? The sky is clear...isn't that risky?"

"Have you looked outside lately? It's snowing."

"Snowing?"

"Yeah, snowing hard, low overcast. So we have to haul ass. Once it stops..."

"Tracks."

"Exactly. And infrared—that's even worse. As long as it's coming down, we should be fine. They won't put the drones up when it's this bad. I hope."

Carson stood up and stretched. He said, "Okay, Boone, you're the boss." Then he put his hand out. "This is for your father—the Viking."

Boone Vikersun smiled and accepted the offered handshake. In his face Carson saw Eric the Red, decades before. Viker, rhymes with biker. The son was now probably pushing forty, about the age Eric was the last time he had seen him, over twenty years earlier at Fort Bragg. Boone the son was now older than the Vietnam memories of his father, eerily blurring and merging the two men into one in his mind. "So where are we going, roughly?"

"Roughly?" Boone laughed. "Straight up into Tennessee, where else? That's my state, and that's where the whole shit storm is coming down. You'll see for yourself, soon enough."

Jenny landed on her back hard, knocking the wind out of her. She moved each limb in turn and then her head; nothing seemed to be broken. She lay motionless for a moment, listening, and then she slowly sat up. The backpack lay a yard from her feet; the fur hat was still on her head. She was at the side of the mansion. A raised patio deck with snow-covered outdoor furniture was just a few yards to her right. She had narrowly missed landing on the wooden railing around the deck. If she had, she'd have certainly broken something, so she counted herself lucky.

She slowly stood upright, looking all around as she brushed the snow off her backside. The closest of the bare oaks surrounding the mansion was about fifty yards down the slope. No soldiers or vehicles were visible on this side of the house. Pumping with adrenaline, she easily hefted the pack onto her back and walked straight downhill toward the trees, not looking back—hoping that any guard peering in her direction through the falling snow would see only another soldier.

In half a minute Jenny reached the nearest oak, and once behind it she turned for the first time to stare back at the house. Flames leapt skyward from the windows on either side of the chimney, coloring the falling snow orange. The side of the house and the overhanging roof above the two windows were on fire. A pair of doors on the back of the mansion flew open, there was shouting and yelling. Soldiers stormed out, then turned to look up at the burning roof while throwing on their coats and hats. Jenny could see some girls mixed among the troops, all of them lit by the orange glow reflected off the blanket of snow. The soldiers' attention seemed focused on the roiling flames above them. At least now the girls had some small chance to take advantage of the confusion caused by the sudden fire. While she watched, more fire exploded out of the third-floor bedroom windows. No one turned away from the fire to look downhill toward her hiding place.

Jenny pushed the straps of the backpack further up on her shoulders and walked away. She continued down toward a stand of woods that grew in what appeared to be a small depression or valley. There was an inch of new snow on the ground, nearly covering the lawn of unmown grass and weeds. Her footprints were not obvious in the snow among the protruding tufts, as far as she could tell. If it continued snowing, her tracks would be erased after only a short while.

Walking in the open, she tried not to think of a guard's night scope being aimed at her back. In a few more seconds, she reached the covering line of bushes and low trees. Because it was winter, the thickly twined vegetation had receded enough for her to find a trail, and Jenny began to think that she might live to see another sunrise. She took one more look back up the hill. The entire top of the mansion was fully engulfed in dancing waves of fire reaching dozens of yards into the sky, outlined by the black fingers of the oak branches.

Four horses were tied outside, saddled and ready to ride. Zack and the two visitors hurriedly loaded what supplies they could carry into bags and packs, and slung them across the horses in front and behind the saddles. The horses were huffing excitedly, stamping and blowing vapor through their nostrils while biting impatiently at their steel bits. The men were all dressed warmly in multiple layers, plus thick wool hats and gloves. Carson wore his complete military camouflage uniform, with long johns underneath, and the military-issue gore-tex parka on top. Doctor Foley's 9mm Beretta was holstered on a web belt around his waist. Days earlier, he had found the web belt among the gear at Zack's house, and modified a generic black nylon holster to take the Beretta. A velcro strap he had sewn onto it would hold the pistol securely in any position. Even while resting and recuperating, Carson had been preparing to leave, always improving his kit, and he was glad that he had been ready when Boone Vikersun arrived without advance notice. The unseen moon illuminated the clouds and the inch-deep snow on the ground, providing just enough light for them to see through the blowing flakes.

"Do you need help getting up in the saddle?" asked Boone.

"I'm about to find out," replied Carson, lifting his left boot into the stirrup, and pulling himself up using the saddle horn for a grip. There was no easy method for him to mount the horse; he had to push and strain. The tight skin of his wound didn't tear as he swung his right leg over the wide saddle and found the opposite stirrup with his right foot. The other three men had smoothly mounted up while he struggled aboard. "Okay, I'm ready."

Boone addressed them all in a loud voice. "I'm leading. Carson, you'll be second, then Zack, and Doug is going to be rear security. Phil, your horse knows what to do—you'll be okay if you don't mess up too bad. These are quarter horses, and nothing much spooks them. They don't get ridden much in the winter, so they're awful frisky. I'll warn you now:

they're just dying to take off in a gallop, so hang on. I assume you know the basics of riding?"

"I'm rusty, but yeah, I know what to do. Steer with the reins, like this. Pull back for slower, and kick for faster. I'll be okay." *Just as long as my ass holds together*, Carson thought. From this point on, he wouldn't bitch or whine aloud, even if he bled to death. They'd know he couldn't ride any further when his dead body fell from the saddle. Would he show weakness to the Viking's kid? To another Special Forces operator? Never, not as long as he was alive. That's just the way it was, within the ancient code of stoicism that defined their tribe. Even at his age. He'd die first.

"Keep your head down and be alert," instructed Boone. "We're going to be riding under a lot of low branches, and a few bridges and tunnels even. If I holler duck, don't wait to see what I'm ducking. Your horse will do all right—you just stay on the saddle." While he was talking, Boone slipped night vision goggles over his face, and then pulled a bulky Icelandic knitted wool cap onto his head and over the NVG's straps.

Carson asked, "What's his name?"

"Who, your horse? Hell if I know. They're not mine."

"You stole them?"

"Of course not," replied Boone, laughing. "I borrowed them—with permission. Sort of. Zack, are you ready?"

"I'm ready." Zack's compound bow was strapped across his back; a Winchester 30-30 lever-action was jammed into a saddle scabbard. The four horses wheeled and turned together.

Boone asked the boy, "You remember everything else I told you?"

"I remember."

"Your father would be real proud of you. Okay, that's it. We've got a long ride ahead of us, and it's not going to snow forever. Let's go." Boone reined his horse's head sharply to the side and made a loud clicking sound with his tongue, kicked his heels and his horse broke into an easy loping canter, eager to be moving. Carson turned his horse to follow, digging with his heels.

Boone kept the horses moving at a steady walk most of the time, which was easier on Carson's wound, just a long, slow, back-and-forth heaving motion. He remembered the gaits: walk, trot, canter and gallop. Bumping up and down while trotting was the worst, and they avoided it. Sometimes the trail went uphill and the horses broke into a run. Often he had to rein back his mount as it tried to pass Boone's horse and gain the lead.

Carson couldn't tell a quarter horse from a thoroughbred in the darkness, but it was obvious these four were keen to run. Just a few hours earlier, he had been reading about General Forrest's cavalry dashing around the Tennessee countryside. Now, improbably, he found himself astride a horse with a gun on his hip. The transition was surreal but exciting, and welcome after three weeks of forced indolence while he recovered from his wound. Horses were nearly ideal for this country and this type of low intensity conflict, he mused. They were not restricted to the roads, where checkpoints might be encountered, and were not bothered in the least by weather that grounded hostile aircraft. He remembered seeing a picture of Special Forces riding horses in Afghanistan. I'll have to ask Boone about that sometime, he thought.

He wondered how Boone knew their way, even while wearing night vision goggles. For long stretches, their route seemed to wind through labyrinthine passageways below overhanging branches, so low the riders needed to hug their mounts' necks. Other times they went right up streams, splashing through water and mud, clattering over rocks, their horses struggling to find sure footing. Once they rode thirty or forty feet through a tunnel beneath some kind of elevated roadbed. Boone shouted back for them to stay low and they did, leaning forward and down until their faces were buried in their horses' manes. Water streamed through the tunnel, and Carson's horse balked and needed encouragement to move forward in nearly pitch darkness.

Occasionally they traveled on asphalt country roads, the sound of their horses' steel-clad hooves muffled by the snow. They crossed countless fields, Boone opening gates ahead of them and closing them behind, then galloping ahead to resume his position at the lead. Some of the "gates" were clandestine openings, with sections of wire fence cut but left tied in place, pulled to the side for their passage and then returned to their everyday position.

The dead man's boots were not too bad a fit. That had been one of Jenny's biggest worries, that blisters might force her to stop walking. She knew from painful experience that this was always a risk when going for a long hike in untested shoes. There were a few hot spots, one on her right heel, but they did not get any worse during the first hour. After a year of enduring ill-fitting castoff shoes, she felt as if she had won the footwear lottery tonight. For once, her bigger than average feet were a benefit, matching the dead man's in size.

It figured that the traitor would have top quality boots. He had even broken them in for her. Now he was burnt meat, and the boots were hers to keep. This thought gave her no small satisfaction as she trudged along beneath his pack, crunching through the soft snow. *Hey, asshole—I'm walking out of your nightmare! Keep right on burning forever—in hell!* She smiled in spite of herself. No matter what happened next, she had won the victory of outliving him. He was dead, and she was alive and free, at least for now. She was even wearing his uniform, and carrying his pack and his gun.

The Russian-style fur hat was perfect with the flaps turned down, keeping her head, neck and ears warm in the blowing snow. She had even found insulated gloves in the pockets of the camouflage parka, another gift from the dead would-be rapist. She walked with her gloved hands gripping the pack's straps, at chest level. When she finally had to stop, she would search his pack for more of the food she felt sure was inside. Until then, the sausage she had wolfed down would hold her over.

Jenny McClure had had plenty of experience as a walking refugee, but never dressed so well for cold weather. She had a close familiarity with hypothermia: last winter she had almost died of exposure on several painfully memorable occasions. She had escaped from the ruins of Memphis, from home invasions, road ambushes and night attacks, from the worst horrors imaginable. Her odyssey had covered only eighty straight-line miles, but her route had been anything but direct, and she had walked several times that distance. It had taken her almost two hellish months to reach safety in Mannville.

After what had happened in Memphis, she would never again trust any happy status quo. The quakes had taught her that the earth could literally tumble off its axis without warning. The world could suddenly tip and spill all of the baby birds out of their cozy nests, onto the cold ground. Ground teeming with hungry predators. A year ago, she had been one such baby bird, blinking in shock at finding herself unexpectedly alone on the hard ground. No more. That innocent girl was gone forever.

Unlike during her trek from Memphis to Mannville, this time she was not only better dressed, she was also carrying a big damn pistol. A .45, no less. Those big fat bullets would put anybody down with one shot in the chest, that's what her Uncle Henry had told her. "Aim for center mass," he had said. Uncle Henry knew what he was talking about: he had been an officer in the Marine Corps. He had been to Beirut, Lebanon, and the first war in the Middle East, the one that he called Desert Storm, back before she was born.

If anybody tried to stop her, tried again to attack or rape her, Jenny was determined that she would test that 45-caliber theory, personally. Then if one bullet didn't work, she'd keep shooting. Two to the chest and then one to the head, in case they were wearing body armor or were doped up on drugs. That's what Uncle Henry said. No more dirty stinking men were going to lay their disgusting hands on her, punch her, and tear her clothes off. From now on she would carry the pistol 24/7, and she would avoid sucker traps like that fenced-in pen at Mannville Senior High. She would get out of Tennessee entirely. Mississippi had to be better. They were turning back refugees at the state border, that's what she had heard, but she wouldn't cross at a road. She'd cross somewhere in the middle of the boondocks. She'd get into Mississippi or Alabama, where there were no foreign enemies, only Americans. Things there had to be better than in Tennessee. They had to be. And if they weren't, she'd keep going all the way to Florida. Or maybe to Texas: she'd heard that most of Texas was still free, almost like the old America.

Tonight the most important thing was to put miles between herself and the foreign soldiers behind her. Would those soldiers ever be pissed off if they knew that she had burned down their house and ruined their little rape party! They had probably all gotten out of the house, since it started on the floor above them. Jenny wondered about the other girls. Most likely, they had been taken to the next big house down the road. The foreign troops obviously could take over any home they wanted, and nobody could stop them. Maybe some of the girls had managed to escape after they exited the house, but it was unlikely. Well, they could survive being raped, just as she had survived it last year, on the way to Mannville.

Jenny quickly stabbed out those evil memories, shoved them back down into her bad memory hole, and dropped the iron lid of hate over them. She knew that she had gotten lucky tonight, in being taken upstairs first. Well, it was about time—she was seriously due some good luck. The rapist had said it was her lucky night. He was surely right about that, but not in the way that he had intended!

It was inconceivable that the foreign soldiers might have extinguished the house fire. She had seen it spreading from room to room and up the wall to the roof. How could they possibly put it out? With what? A bucket brigade, from a water well? Or snowballs maybe? Snowballs, to put out a roaring house fire. She laughed at the idea of them tossing snowballs through the windows, into the burning house. Fires still happened, and these days, houses usually burned to the ground. With no more 911 to call for help, there was almost no other outcome possible. With everybody jury-rigging homemade wood stoves and chimney pipes, there were probably more house fires than ever. The switch from gas, oil and electric heat to wood-burning stoves had not been made without an increase in danger.

The snow continued falling at a furious rate; Jenny could only follow the edge of the first road she had literally stumbled upon. Downhill from the burning mansion, the bramble-filled woods had ended where a stream disappeared into a small culvert. Above the concrete pipe was a narrow paved road. Without a compass, Jenny knew that she could wind up walking aimlessly in circles if she stayed off the road, crossing fields and streams and tree lines and woods. The snow might stop, and she might still be near the area full of foreign soldiers. While it was snowing, she had to make tracks, literally. Tracks that would quickly be erased behind her by the falling snow.

So she had studied that first road, and some inner sense of direction told her to turn left, which was slightly downhill. Downhill might take her toward the Tennessee River, or the Mississippi state line. It was really just a guess, but without a map or a compass, she had no choice but to pick a direction and walk fast. Even with the pack on her back, she knew she could make four or five miles an hour. It was less than fifteen miles from Mannville to the Mississippi line, but she didn't know where she was in relation to Mannville. To the east, she thought. She hoped she was walking south. The sky was no help. Somewhere up there, the moon was sending down just enough light to allow her to walk without tripping over every obstacle, but it gave no hint of direction. The road ran in curves and hooks, and at each rural intersection she had to decide again: which way should she go?

At least the blowing snow kept visibility to only a hundred feet or less, and the smooth white blanket on the ground silenced her footsteps. There were no tire tracks from any vehicles, and no other footprints on the road. She approached and passed infrequent homes with trepidation, her head down, steadily marching on. There were no lights on inside any houses, no curling smoke rising from chimneys. If anybody was in them, they were hiding tonight.

At an intersection, a sign reading "Shiloh National Battlefield 7 Miles" gave her fresh hope. She knew that Shiloh was not far from the Mississippi state border. The sign also confirmed that she was on the southeast side of Mannville.

After what she guessed was at least two hours of steady walking, Jenny heard an engine, and a moment later she smelled diesel exhaust. She dashed from the road, almost slipping down the inclined shoulder, and hid behind a car abandoned in the drainage ditch. One of the enormous Army trucks approached from the opposite direction, driving slowly, its headlights illuminating a swirling pool of snowflakes ahead of it. She crept around the side of the derelict automobile as the six-wheeled truck passed her, praying that they would not notice her footprints in the snow.

The sudden appearance of the truck made her appreciate the danger she was in, walking on the side of a paved road to make better speed. Jenny waited for perhaps ten minutes after it passed before continuing at a slower pace, with more caution. A half mile on, she smelled wood smoke and then saw two moving orange dots. A bit further and the glowing spots illuminated faces behind lit cigarettes. Only soldiers would be smoking out in the middle of a snowstorm. They had probably been dropped off by the truck that had rumbled by.

She was already too close to them to be safe. She moved away from the side of the road to take a position behind a small fir tree, and observed them. Four soldiers wearing fur hats identical to hers were standing around a metal barrel. Tongues of flame licked up from the barrel like a blazing well from the underworld. Staring at the fire would have ruined their night vision, which meant less chance of her being seen. The four looked like witches or warlocks huddled around the flames.

They were positioned at a crossroads, where a small store had a tin roof extending out from its front. A hundred feet opposite the store was a boarded-up tavern. The men had set up the metal drum in the shelter of the overhanging roof, where they could watch the intersection while staying out of the falling snow. They were not carrying rifles, at least not that she could see in the flickering light from the flames. They were talking quietly and smoking, keeping warm around their fire, unconcerned about the remote chance of anyone passing their sentry position while it was snowing at night. Still, there was no way that she could possibly sneak past them on the road unseen.

It was probably already around midnight, and she could not stop for the night anywhere so close to a position guarded by enemy soldiers. Reluctantly, she decided to backtrack and find a place to strike out cross-country to maneuver around them.

A few hundred yards back she came to a small lane, probably a dirt road beneath the snow, judging by its unevenness. She thought it ran eastward, based only on her previous guess that she had been walking south. In actuality, she had no idea which direction she was going; she just hoped that this narrow lane, with two low ruts, one on either side of a central hump, might take her around the foreign sentries.

The narrow road could have been a long private driveway. No street sign named it, though the lack of a street sign didn't mean much in itself. Many if not most street signs had been scavenged or removed over the past year. The steel pipes and aluminum plates were useful for do-it-yourself projects, such as constructing wells or building stoves. In addition, many people felt that street signs only helped bandits, who used paper road maps to find their way to overlooked neighborhoods, targeted for looting or worse.

This narrow road just didn't feel like a public thoroughfare. Fifty feet in, a heavy chain hung across the path, shackled around trees on both sides. The trees were the beginning of thick woods, spaced too closely together to allow the passage of vehicles. Whoever lived in here didn't want uninvited guests.

If she was caught on private property, she was likely to be shot as a trespassing bandit. This was the normal response in West Tennessee, after the earthquakes. You just did not trespass on private property, period.

Especially not after dark. She understood that not one single step she took was without risk. There was just no risk-free option for traveling on foot during the long emergency. Not last year on the way from Memphis to Mannville, and not now.

After a few minutes of walking through the woods there was a clearing, and she passed a long single-wide trailer, set a hundred feet back from the one-lane road. It appeared to be uninhabited or even abandoned. Cars were parked randomly in front of the mobile home. They could have been abandoned hulks, but under a fresh layer of snow, it was impossible to be sure. Tall weeds grew around them, protruding high above the snow. There was no way to tell if people were inside the trailer without breaking in. Many people intentionally made their houses look like wrecks; pre-looted, and not worth robbing. If they were inhabited and she forced open the front door, odds were good she'd be meeting Saint Peter with a stomach full of buckshot.

The land gradually rose before her. She walked up a long hill with about a hundred-foot gain in elevation over a winding half mile. The terrain here wasn't as flat as it seemed back on the paved county road. That paved road's path had probably been chosen long ago because it crossed the easiest ground. Two hundred years ago, many such Tennessee roads had been Indian trails. Now this snow-covered dirt road forked, and once again Jenny had to guess her next direction. She was in an area that looked like a Christmas tree forest, composed of little firs that ranged from five to ten feet high on both sides of the road. The trees closed in until they were only a yard from her shoulders on both sides. Still, it was a road. A jeep or even a pickup could drive it. It went somewhere with a purpose.

The gentle uphill shifted abruptly to a much steeper down slope. The land didn't run in steady, even undulations. Then the road went back uphill again, until it unexpectedly ended at what seemed to be either a junkyard or a landfill, or perhaps just a local dumping spot. There was sufficient moonlight filtering down to make out a landscape of wrecked cars, kitchen appliances, old tires and a thousand kinds of trash, all covered with a smooth patina of new snow. She had no desire to cross the dump; it was too easy to imagine all sorts of psycho monsters hiding behind every piece of abandoned junk.

She had to circle around its perimeter, between the derelict machinery and household scrap on her left and the small trees on her right. The dump was a few acres in size, seemingly dug into the base of a bluff. Perhaps the hollow was a natural terrain feature, perhaps not. Old cars and washing machines trailed off into the gnarled and twisted pine woods, and the going became more difficult.

It had to be after midnight by now. Jenny recalled that the moon was not quite full tonight, so it would go down before dawn. She had done enough night traveling to know that when it was overcast and the moon set, the world would become as black as the inside of a coal mine, and she would literally have to move by feel. So she had to keep walking, and find another road or path before the moon went down.

The junkyard finally petered out, and the land rose on both sides of her. Her path turned, the sides of her valley became steeper, until she recognized that she was in some kind of a cut or cleft in the face of a steep bluff. With visibility at less than a hundred feet because of the blowing snow, she was traveling by instinct as much as by sight. At least there were no more houses up here, neither empty nor inhabited. There was little chance of running into anyone in this desolate landscape—not a bandit, a property owner, or a soldier.

Her path narrowed and became more constricted as it rose, until there was almost a cliff on her left side. It was nearly as steep on the right. Trees could be vaguely seen on the top of the overhanging precipice. The slope below the top was too steep and eroded to support much in the way of vegetation. Snow was not sticking on the vertical surfaces, and she could see where the sides were cut with smaller erosion gullies at right angles to the main faces. Jenny continued up the dry watercourse at the bottom of the ravine. She had to be vigilant with her footing, because the frozen dirt beneath the snow was cut and chopped by old runoff channels. She found herself waist deep in tight little mini-canyons, using her hands to climb up, over and through them. It was slow, hard going, but she hoped that when she gained the summit, she would be rewarded with a flat plateau or a gradual down slope, and a safe way around the outpost of foreign soldiers.

The ravine turned again, and she believed she was nearing the summit. She was working so hard that she had to unzip her parka to avoid breaking into a sweat. Using her gloved hands, she climbed onto an uneven area, lumpy and quite different from the narrow and deep erosion channels she had been negotiating with such difficulty. There were logs or trash bags piled under the snow. She thought back to the dump she had passed a half hour earlier, before entering the bottom of this ravine. Snow was three or four inches deep now, obscuring the uneven obstacles under her feet. She put a boot down carefully, and her right leg slipped between two logs. She tried to wrench it free but lost her balance and went over, pulled down by the weight of her backpack.

She flung out a hand to support herself and grasped something odd. It was a shoe, but it was a shoe that was…still attached to a foot, and a leg! She rolled onto her side and saw a man's face staring back at her, from only a yard away! An arm reached above the snow, splayed fingers outlined against the sky. Jenny grabbed for her holster, fumbled to push the release button, and drew the gun. The pistol's light had a switch like a rubber bump on its back end. She pushed it on and the harsh white glare revealed that she had fallen down among people, dead people, dozens of them frozen in every posture, all covered with a coating of white snow.

Jenny McClure had seen great cruelty since the earthquakes, and dead bodies were not unknown to her, but the scene before her now was far beyond the scope of anything she had witnessed. Everywhere she aimed her light she saw more of them, as the irregular shapes she had been treading upon were transformed under her light's beam into scores of bodies, bodies on top of bodies, all under a blanket of white. But these were not rotted old cadavers, with scraps of skin stretched over dried skeletons. Nor were they bloated and blackened corpses, dead a few days.

The snow and darkness softened the picture, but could not hide all of the horror. Many of them still had their eyes open, with mouths agape in silent screams. Horrific body-shattering injuries were visible on many of them. The head wounds were the worst, with grisly, cracked skulls and split faces. One man's half-missing face in particular grabbed her attention. She snapped off her light and vomited. She crouched motionless for a period of several minutes at least, until she began to feel the spectral presence of the people around her, almost hearing their urgent whispers.

Growing very cold while lying still in the snow, Jenny finally sat up in the middle of the slaughter field, and she *knew* what had happened. There was no blood on top of the snow. These people had been killed today, before the snow. They were the people taken away on the school buses. While she was in the back of the Army truck, she had seen them being loaded onto the buses. She knew who they were. Not as individuals, but she knew them. She was sitting on top of hundreds of people, many of whom she had seen only half a day earlier. Friendly people, who had been laughing and smiling just yesterday morning. Tough and practical people who had endured one of the worst years in American history, people who had been maligned and rejected and abandoned by their own government, and yet had turned the corner from bare survival to creating new lives.

Now they were in this God-forsaken ravine, dead and covered with newly fallen snow. They had not been taken to their promised relocation center for hot meals and showers, after being caught by surprise and rounded up by their foreign enemies. Instead, they had been bused to a ravine in the middle of nowhere and shot. Jenny stood carefully, the heavy pack fighting her rise. It was impossible not to step on them. She had to walk directly across their bodies to get out. There was nothing else to walk on but dead people!

She steeled herself, and switched her light back on. The snow had accumulated unevenly on the bumpy landscape of corpses, here and there revealing random faces and hands. Jenny's beam of light revealed something else: most of the bodies nearest the cliff and on top seemed to be men. Their swollen hands were all cinched tightly behind their backs with black plastic ties. Many of their heads were blown apart, skulls split, faces gone. She knew what bullets did to people's heads; she'd seen it. If the men were on top, and if they had been tied up before they were shot, then they must have been brought to the massacre site last. After the women and the children had been murdered.

Back in the high school gym, they must have been searched and disarmed, and then had their hands secured behind their backs with the plastic ties. What must these men have been thinking, on that final bus ride? They would have been as helpless as sheep being trucked to a slaughterhouse—but at least sheep didn't understand their preordained fates. What must they have thought when their bus drove further and further into the boondocks and finally stopped up there? Then they must have been forced at gunpoint to the top edge of the ravine, and machine-gunned from behind…while looking down upon their already murdered families. Jenny shuddered to consider that somewhere in this ravine were Uncle Henry and Aunt Rochelle, and Sue Bledsoe.

She realized that this probably would have been her final destination, after being raped by the American traitor and probably by the rest of the battalion of foreign soldiers. What did the traitor call their country, Kazakhstan? What was that, part of Russia? What in the hell were soldiers from Kazakhstan doing in Tennessee anyway? Just who had invited them here? Well, it was brutally clear what they were doing. They were murdering innocent civilians and dumping their bodies in ravines. If there were truly any "relocation centers," then they were not meant for the residents of Radford County. It was unimaginable what had happened today, but it was here all around her, revealed in the beam of the light mounted under her pistol. Without even being conscious of it, she found herself stammering, "Oh my God…Oh my God…" She couldn't look down anymore, afraid of recognizing a face, and she tried to walk, but she couldn't walk without tripping, unless she looked down…

Before she had taken many steps, she heard a soft, keening wail. For a few moments, she imagined it was her own voice, or simply her imagination. Then she stopped to listen, wondering if she had heard a distant cat or perhaps a baby goat. Kid goats made that same plaintive cry. Only gradually, she realized it was not her own voice, or a cat or a goat or the wind in the trees, but someone else's voice, someone alive in this ravine full of bodies. She stopped and listened carefully, and the sound grew. It wasn't an adult voice that she heard, but the sound of crying. It was an infant, a little baby, a live human baby, somewhere beneath her!

Jenny scrambled, fighting for balance, moving toward the sound. She had to twist and push several stiffly frozen men away, weeping and apologizing to them for disturbing their resting places, as the sound grew louder.

She laid her gun down in the snow on top of a man's back, in a position to light the area from where the crying seemed to be originating. The pack on her back made it too cumbersome to work, and she slipped it off. It took an eternity to push and drag apart the rigid bodies with their intertwined arms and legs, until finally she could see the source of the crying.

She saw a baby lying on its back, a baby wrapped in a bloody yellow blanket, pressed against a woman with dark hair who was lying on her side. Jenny sat on one body, worked her feet between others, and reached under and pulled out the infant, who was swaddled tightly in layers of blankets. She had to tug the baby out; its outer blanket was frozen to the woman's coat. Blankets covered the baby's head like a papoose, exposing only its face. Even well bundled the infant must have been terribly cold, but it was undeniably alive, crying out to heaven for rescue. Jenny pulled the baby out from beneath the woman with dark hair, clutched it tightly to her chest, and its wailing faded to a whimper. The blood splotches soaking part of the baby's yellow blanket were frozen, and had stuck the blanket to her mother…

Jenny could tell the woman with the dark hair was the baby's mother, by the pink diaper bag looped over her shoulder. Pink, so the baby she held was most likely a girl. The baby had been sheltered between its mother, who was lying on her side, and the padded diaper bag, which was as big as an overnight valise. Other bodies had fallen crosswise over them, sheltering the infant from the falling snow.

Oh my dear God, she thought, I can't take a baby with me! It's already hard enough to travel alone—how can I possibly carry a baby and still evade the foreign enemies? She's probably already hypothermic, she feels so cold, and she'll die anyway. She should just stay with her mother, and remain with her family where she belongs…

All of these excuses ran through Jenny's mind, and were rejected one by one. There was no choice: she had to take the baby with her. She had to. How could she possibly place the baby back down in the snow, among the icy corpses? But if she took the baby, how could it survive? There was no 911 operator to call. There was not even a cell phone to call with. Jenny looked back down at the mother, and she suddenly realized that the pink diaper bag was the key. It was almost as if the baby's mother willed the idea into Jenny's head. She had done enough babysitting to know that diaper bags meant not only diapers but also usually baby bottles, milk, and formula. She placed the blanket-wrapped baby gently back on the ground to remove the diaper bag, and it began crying again, its tiny eyes tightly closed. While she extricated the pink bag's shoulder strap from around the mother's head, Jenny spoke aloud to her. "I'm so sorry that this happened, so sorry, but I promise, I promise I'll take care of your baby. I'll do the best that I can for her. I'll do my best. That's all I can do, but I'll do it."

Jenny picked up and reholstered the pistol, after switching off its light. Because she was working on her knees while sliding around in the snow among frozen bodies, the backpack was very hard to lift and swing onto her back, but she was filled with new resolve that gave her the necessary strength. She looped the diaper bag's canvas strap over her head and across her right shoulder, so that it rode against her left hip, keeping her pistol and gun hand unencumbered. Finally, she picked up the swaddled baby and pulled her against her chest, and began the clumsy and difficult process of getting up onto her feet. She had to stand on their frozen bodies. There was no other way. She tried not to look down, tried not to see if she was stepping on faces. Fortunately, the snow covered most of them. How she had found the baby, and managed to pull the bodies away from her and extricate her, it still seemed impossible, it must have been a miracle. The people around her were all so hard and cold and frozen so tightly together...but she had done it.

Jenny couldn't stomach the thought of climbing uphill over hundreds of more bodies. She was closer to the beginning of the mass of corpses than the end, so she gingerly backtracked down the ravine, slipping several times to her knees. Once she was off the massacre site, off the bodies, the frozen dirt beneath the snow made for easier going. This time, the sides of the narrow erosion channels actually steadied her, giving her something to lean against when she lost her footing on the slippery snow.

The baby was no longer crying, but Jenny could feel its breath against her neck, could feel it squirming inside its blanket wrappings. It was too difficult to hold her this way, and Jenny needed her arms for balance and support while moving through the labyrinth of frozen flood channels. She unzipped her outer camouflage jacket, placed the bundled baby against her chest, and zipped it inside. Even wrapped in a blanket, the infant was so tiny that she fit between Jenny's neck and the web belt that fit snugly around her waist. The belt kept the infant from sliding down. Now it was easier to move, because she could use her gloved hands to grasp at the sides of the gully channels, and catch herself when she slipped.

Images of the massacre site in the ravine filled Jenny's mind, and she was hardly conscious of walking through the Christmas tree forest, until she passed the edge of the junkyard and found the twin parallel depressions of the snow-covered dirt road.

But how far could she walk now, with a baby? Realistically, it was a hopeless situation. If the odds were against her before she had literally stumbled across the massacre site, they were impossible odds now. But what kind of odds had the helpless baby faced? What were the chances that she would have been rescued, found buried alive in that massacre ravine? Yet here she was, still alive, and so was Jenny McClure. If God had gotten them this far, alive, then He must have a reason. The baby's rescue was a miracle; there could be no other explanation. If that was true, then Jenny was part of that brushing of God's hand. Why would God send her out, lost in a snowstorm, to find one living infant buried in a massacre pit, if it was not part of a larger plan? The thought kept Jenny moving forward. God has a plan; this is no time to give up. Just keep hope alive, thought Jenny, almost laughing at the madness of it all. Just keep a spark of hope alive, and God will do the rest.

I hope.

11

Carson guessed their average speed on horseback to be about twice a man's walking pace. This might have been eight or ten miles an hour, but he knew his estimate could be far off. A straight-line distance would have been almost impossible to estimate, and their route had been anything but straight. After two hours, Boone led them along the edge of more woods, along and then through a wooden fence, and into a small barn. Boone climbed down, and the others followed his lead and dismounted. Carson was bone-tired and sore in places he hadn't remembered, happy just to put his boots on the straw-covered floor of the barn. Until they entered the stable, he had feared that they might ride all night.

A dark compact car was parked in the center of the musty barn. Without talking, the men unloaded the packs from the horses by flashlight. They transferred some of the loads into the back of the waiting four-door mini-wagon, beneath its raised hatchback. The rest of the bags went on the wagon's roof, and were lashed down to its luggage rack.

"How did your ass hold up?" Boone asked in a loud whisper.

"I'll live." The recently healed gash was outside of his weight-bearing areas, and his posture in the saddle had not stretched the wound apart.

"I think you'll find this a bit more comfortable. You ride in the back, with Zachary. Doug, you're riding shotgun. Keep your weapons ready: if we come across a checkpoint or an enemy patrol, we're not stopping."

They slid into the dry interior of the car and Boone started the engine, but left the headlights off. In fact, no lights came on at all, not even when the doors were opened. With night vision goggles over his eyes, their driver had no need for lights. The vehicle was small for a four-door wagon, and with all of their gear, weapons and bags it was a tight fit. Carson thought he saw a shadowy figure enter the barn, probably to take care of the horses, but it was too dark to be certain. They left the barn, bumping and jouncing cross-country over snow-covered fields until they encountered the first dirt track.

They drove for miles on rutted gravel and dirt roads hidden by snow, and sometimes on asphalt, by the feel of it beneath their tires. Overhanging tree branches often formed a ceiling above their path. There was enough moonlight penetrating the low overcast and reflecting off the snow for Carson to make out the basic contours of the gently rolling terrain, but no more. With NVGs, Boone had no difficulty keeping the car's speed up, even when Carson saw nothing ahead of the windshield but swirling flakes in the darkness.

The baby began crying again, struggling within its blanket wrappings. Jenny could do little to comfort the infant tucked inside her parka. She knew that she had to find a place to get out of the blowing snow, to check the diaper bag for milk and try to feed the infant. To come this far, to find the baby and save it, only to then lose it to death seemed too cruel a fate. If God had sent her to save the child, well then, she had to be up to the task and do her best to keep her alive.

Jenny passed the junkyard, and approached the trailer home. If she could just get out of the snow and check the diaper bag for milk or formula, the baby would have a fighting chance. Inside the house, she could use the mini-flashlight attached to the pistol to see what was in the bag, and perhaps find something to make a fire. If there was any formula or milk in the diaper bag, it would be too cold to give to the baby. She prayed that there was formula in the bag. If not, the baby would cry until she died. It had been at least twelve hours since she had been fed, and almost as many hours that she had been alone in the freezing weather.

Jenny walked directly across the snowy yard to the wooden porch built along the front of the trailer. She could see that the snow was now about three inches deep on the edges of the steps up to the porch. First, she would just try the door, to check if it had been left open. The white door didn't appear to have been damaged by looters, who often used crowbars or battering rams to get inside. There were no hinges visible, so it opened to the inside. The knob was on the right side. Above it was a separate keyhole for a deadbolt lock. She would give the door a good strong push, and then shoot the lock out if she had to.

Before trying the door, she stepped to the window that was on the right side of the porch, and tried to look into the mobile home. A heavy curtain was pulled across on the inside, blocking her view. Not even a faint glimmer of light was visible. She drew her pistol, just to be ready. She held the big gun in her gloved right hand and switched on its light. With her left hand, she grasped the knob and slowly turned it in both directions. It stopped after only a few degrees of travel. It was locked. Still, she might be able to slam her hip or shoulder against the door and force it open. After all, it was only an old mobile home. She pulled and pushed as hard as she could, using every bit of her strength while turning the knob. The snow on the wooden deck hindered her efforts, preventing her from getting a solid footing while she tried to slam her 120 pounds against the door. It didn't budge.

Okay then, she thought, *let's see what a .45 caliber bullet will do.* She stood back with her right arm extended and turned her body to the left, to shelter the baby from any ricochets. She carefully aimed an inch to the right of the deadbolt's keyhole. The compact gun light protruded a bit beyond the end of the pistol barrel above it. The light was almost touching the white door, reflecting a brilliant glare down onto the snow. She knew the shot would be loud, and she steeled herself against it. She had walked several miles, and she hoped that she was far enough away from the burning house so that the foreign soldiers would not hear the gunshot. With her uncle's Glock, she only had to pull the trigger back a little way, maybe half an inch, for it to fire. Her right index finger continued to squeeze the trigger by fractions of a millimeter. Jenny didn't know at what point she would hear the booming shot, cringing at the thought of metal fragments and wood splinters flying back at her.

Instead of the expected earsplitting explosion, the door swung open away from her! Jenny's heart skipped, her index finger froze in mid-squeeze, and then she released the trigger. A boy about ten years old, dressed in an oversized red mechanic's suit, stared for a moment into the bright white light on her gun. Then he shrieked incoherently and ran away hobbling awkwardly, hands clamped over his eyes.

A female voice came from within the trailer. "Ramsey, you quit your fooling and get back inside! Arthur, I didn't hear your truck; what took you so damn long? The fire's gone out, and it's freezing in here."

Jenny quickly scanned inside the trailer with her gun light. There was a black stove in the center of the room, with a chimney pipe going straight up through the roof. The interior of the full-width living room was cheaply paneled in fake wood; the kitchen was off to the left. A bed was against the opposite wall in the far corner, with someone lying in it. The boy who had opened the door was leaning over the bed, wailing. He was wearing bright red and black coveralls, covered with patches and letters. It was a promotional version of a NASCAR racing driver's jumpsuit, made for a child. An old woman was on the bed, her body covered in quilts. A simple cross was nailed to the wall above the head of her bed.

There was no one else in the room.

Jenny said, "I'm not your Ramsey or your Arthur. Is anybody else at home with you, ma'am, besides the boy?"

"Ain't Arthur? Ain't Arthur? Well then, who are you? You sound like you're just a girl." The old woman stared up at the low trailer ceiling, only her pale white face visible above her bed covers. A blue knitted nightcap was pulled down almost to her unblinking eyes. Her elderly voice was quavering, but not weak. She was at least eighty, by what Jenny could see and hear. The boy in red moaned an unintelligible question to her, then ran clumsily into another room and slammed the door.

"My name is Jenny, ma'am." The temperature inside the mobile home was not much above freezing, but still it felt wonderful to be inside, out of the wind and blowing snow.

"Jenny is it… Well, Jenny, can you please tell me what time it is? I can't see, except I can tell you got a powerful strong light."

"I don't know, ma'am, I don't have a watch. It's late, probably sometime after midnight I'd guess."

"So what're you doing out traipsing around the countryside after midnight, young lady?"

"I don't think you'd believe me if I told you."

The old woman cackled. "Oh, I'd believe most about anything these days."

"I found a baby, ma'am." Jenny hardly had to say so; the foundling was crying again.

"I can hear that plain enough—I'm blind but I still got ears. It's not your own baby?"

"No ma'am."

"So where did you find this lost baby?"

Jenny couldn't form the words to describe the ravine massacre. She had to think of something else to say first. "Ma'am, were you expecting someone to come home tonight?"

"I still am. My son and my nephew. They should have been home before suppertime."

"Were they in Mannville today, at the market?"

"That's right, they were. How did you know that? They were selling good usables, like they do every Saturday. Stoves and such, made from our junkyard. Did you see them? Did they send you here?"

"No ma'am. That's what I have to tell you. I was in Mannville today too. Foreign soldiers came, on horses and in big trucks. I'm so, so sorry to tell you this, but…but the foreign soldiers put everybody onto school buses, and took them to a ravine not far from here. Then, well—they shot everybody, ma'am. Everybody. If your kin was in Mannville today, then I'm real sorry to tell you this, but…they're probably not coming home."

The old woman was silent, staring up with unseeing eyes. She sighed audibly and said, "I was afraid it was something like that. I heard the shooting today. Five or six big volleys like crackling thunder, about a half hour apart. Or maybe more than that. I can't see, so I can't tell time, but that's my guess. It was a powerful lot of shooting."

"Yes ma'am."

"And you got away, with a baby?"

Jenny answered in just a whisper. "Yes ma'am, I did." She stood very close to the stove, where it was a few degrees warmer.

"God must love you more than most, Jenny. Is it a boy or a girl baby?"

"A girl, I think. I just found her. She's tiny, maybe less than a month old."

"Well, she's hungry, that's certain. What do you have to feed her?"

"I don't know. I found a diaper bag near her. Do you have a lamp that works? I don't know how long this flashlight is going to last."

"On the table. There's a lighter by it."

Jenny lit the big oil lantern with an old-fashioned silver Zippo. She took off her fur hat and dropped it on the table, then pulled off the diaper bag and let her pack slip to the floor. The infant remained snuggled in its nest, between Jenny's torso and the parka, supported by the pistol belt. She unzipped the diaper bag on the table, and checked inside it with her gun light. There were folded diapers cut from old cloth rags, a pair of clean outfits, a crocheted blanket, rattles and toys and a pacifier...but no baby bottles, and no baby formula.

"Ma'am, there's nothing to feed the baby in this bag. Nothing!"

"No? Well, of course not—the baby was breast-fed. Where would a momma find such as baby formula these days? These days, it's the old way or no way. Listen Jenny, don't give up quite yet. We have a box of instant milk, and I can tell you where to find a baby bottle. Look for a big orange box in the cabinet over the sink, that'll be the milk powder. And there should be a baby bottle or two left in...in...let me think... Okay, if there's a baby bottle left, it might be in the bottom cabinet on the other side of the fridge. Probably way back in the corner, past all the plastic cups and Tupperwares. Way in the back, if it's still there."

Jenny found the carton of instant milk first. It was the size of a small cereal box, and judging by its weight, it was more than half-full. Then she went to the bottom cabinet and began pulling out plastic pitchers, bowls and cups. She cradled the baby inside her jacket with her left arm while she crouched down to search, using her gun light to push and probe through the forgotten glass and plastic relics. When she located the simple treasure standing in the beam of her light, she called out, "I've got one!" It was a tall, clear plastic baby bottle, with a golden rubber nipple still attached to its neck

"The Lord be praised!" the old woman joyfully replied. "Okay Jenny, we're in business. Let's make some milk for that baby, and it has to be warm. First, you'll need to stoke the fire. I can't do for myself, and the boy ain't right. He can't mess with the fire, so when it goes out, it's out. My son and my nephew, they build up the fire in the morning, and let it go until they get back. Now I guess they ain't never coming home... Well, that's that. The Lord's will be done. I've seen it coming for a long time. Now my time on this mortal world is small. I can't see and I can't walk, so I don't reckon I have much time left. That's all right; I've lived a good long life. I'm not afraid, not for me, oh no. One door closes, another opens. A better one... Oh, listen to me prattle on! There's wood for the stove by the door."

In the last year, Jenny had encountered similar hopeless situations. People who were doomed when their medicines ran out, or who couldn't get kidney dialysis, or who were simply too feeble to gather firewood and keep from freezing. It was the way the new world was: merciless toward the weak and helpless. The elderly more often than the young seemed to accept their fate with equanimity.

Jenny opened the stove's iron door and felt inside. It was still very warm. A metal teapot lay on the flat stovetop, also warm. She hefted it, and determined that it was half-full of liquid. She fetched an armload of split wood and fed the pieces into the stove's open belly. Once stirred, the coals were hot enough to ignite the new fuel. Soon, heat began to radiate from the black stove, pushing back the chill.

On the kitchen counter next to the sink was a five-gallon water jug upended into a ceramic crock with its own spigot. Jenny found a spoon in a drawer and scooped milk powder into the bottle, then filled it with water and shook it up. Then she placed the baby bottle into the open teapot on the stove to heat it. Every few minutes she tested the milk formula by squirting it on her wrist. When the bottle was warm enough, she sat down on a padded kitchen chair near the stove, unzipped her jacket, and put the bottle's nipple into the crying baby's mouth. The tiny girl instantly began sucking; her eyes flicked wide open and she looked up at Jenny. The room was silent except for the crackling of the wood in the stove. Jenny thought, *I'm so sorry, little one. I know that this doesn't taste anything like your momma's milk, but it's the best I can do.*

"Does the baby have a name?" the old woman softly asked.

"A name? Does she have a name?" Jenny stared down into the bright eyes above the rosy button nose and the busy little angel lips. A tear fell onto the baby's forehead and slid into her eyes, so that she blinked but did not remove her gaze from her savior. "Yes ma'am, she has a name. Her name is Hope."

Through the Subaru's windshield, Boone Vikersun's night vision goggles turned the darkness into a green day. The Tennessee countryside was covered in a shimmering blanket of lime-colored snow; the windblown flakes were a million sparkling fireflies. He had spent so many nights of his military career peering into this alternate universe that its strangeness no longer struck him, but falling snow was still something special. The last time he had seen the bright green snow was in Afghanistan's Hindu Kush Mountains, above 10,000 feet. On that occasion he had been chasing Taliban insurgents, and the Predator drones had been on his side.

The PVS-7 goggles were Army issue, one of the many tactical tools he had taken with him when he left active duty without official permission. But even with night vision, Boone could not have navigated the Subaru wagon through this labyrinth of back roads and dirt farm tracks without extensive local knowledge. Especially with his peripheral vision severely restricted by the goggles. Boone drove mainly by memory, steering from landmark to landmark. He had grown up in this part of Western Tennessee, not far from where the Tennessee River left its excursion through northern Alabama and rejoined the state of its origin.

He had roamed these hills, creeks and ravines as a boy and hunted among them as a teenager. Although he was a high school football standout, a knee injury his senior year killed several college scholarship offers. He enlisted in the Army a week after finishing high school, graduated from Ranger school while he was still a teen, and earned his Special Forces Green Beret when he was twenty-three. The badly timed knee injury that aborted his college aspirations never bothered him again. For most of the past two decades, he had been away on his country's military business, but he had not forgotten the nameless hidden places of his youth. The past six months of operating in this region had renewed his old familiarity, and revealed many new trails, back roads, caves and thickets to move through and hide in.

Two centuries of European settlement had left Tennessee with evidence of habitation from every period of American history. The current generation preferred to build on bare hilltops. This had not always been so, particularly in the much longer era before climate controlled central heat at the push of a button. It was rare to find a parcel of land without overgrown foundations, forgotten chimneys, and tumbledown shacks, even deep inside woods and thickets.

On his mother's side, his Tennessee roots went back nearly two hundred years. Forgotten dwellings and barns were some of his most dependable hiding places, besides providing him with a constellation of back-road signposts to guide his way. Everything from pioneer cabins to millennial McMansions had been abandoned over time, and Boone had committed the locations of hundreds of them to memory. Even forgotten water wells and stone springhouses covered by eons of vegetation had their uses.

The ten-year-old Subaru Outback wagon was well suited to his nocturnal travels. Its four-wheel drive kept it moving in mud and snow, even up the few steep slopes. If it got stuck, it was light enough that its four passengers could push it free. In daylight, the mini-wagon looked like a beat up and worn out piece of junk, with its faded and rusting forest green paint job. Only a close look at the deep and knobby treads on its tires or a close listen to its smoothly revving engine might have revealed its secret. The Subaru's performance upgrade was a gift from a service station owner, an American who had recently been encouraged to support the patriotic side during a nocturnal visit. The gas station operator supplied the foreign occupiers; he had little choice in the matter. This was acceptable, as long as the man also supplied Boone with fuel and other logistical help. There were few clear lines of division in this guerrilla war. It hadn't been much different in the first Civil War, when Tennesseans had been bitterly divided in their loyalties between the Union and the Confederacy.

Boone Vikersun was a longtime student of unconventional warfare and counterinsurgency, both through reading and in actual practice. He understood the many advantages the foreign enemies (and the American traitors allied with them) enjoyed in pursuing the freedom fighters. These advantages were never to be underestimated. But he also understood their limitations. The foreign soldiers had no local knowledge and few reliable guides to lead them to the thousands of potential guerrilla hiding places and caches. The UAV drones operated by American traitors were a fearsome weapon; there was no point in denying that obvious fact. However, they could not be everywhere at once, and they could not fly in the gusty winds beneath the turbulent clouds that were so common in the Tennessee winter and spring.

He knew that unless the traitors who controlled the UAVs were acting on specific intelligence from informants, their drones patrolled randomly only above the cities and the larger towns, and along significant roads and highways. There simply were not enough UAVs to cover more of Tennessee than that without pinpoint targeting information. To be a guerrilla in Tennessee today, one had to acknowledge the odds and accept the chance that a deadly missile might plunge down without warning at any time. Zack Tutweiler, sitting behind him, certainly understood the danger after what had happened to his father. It was a gnawing fear that ate at all of them. But a hungry mouse could not live forever in its burrow, despite the existence of unseen hawks and owls. To live and to fight in Tennessee was to court sudden death.

Tonight's snowfall was not going to last much longer. An accumulation of more than a few inches was a rare event in Western Tennessee. Every fresh inch of snow would obscure and then erase the car's tracks. Their timing was tight, but they would make it to one of his best hideouts before dawn. He knew from information passed on to him from Fort Campbell that the Predators were grounded during the passage of these cold fronts. Better still, he knew that once they were grounded, they were never relaunched at night.

Like most rear-echelon troops, the UAV crews tended to fight this war like postal clerks who were working on a schedule under union rules. Once the birds were hangared for inclement weather, their crews would be sent home. The next shift would not report for duty until 0700 hours, and they would not launch new UAV missions until mid-morning. That was only if the weather cleared. The traitor UAV operators at Fort Campbell were responsible for covering all of Tennessee and Kentucky with only twenty functional Predators, along with a variety of smaller tactical UAVs. The smaller UAVs had even shorter ranges and tighter weather restrictions than the Predators. They had lost two Predators over the past month, and now their prime directive was to safeguard them, and not put them at any unnecessary risk. This was war as fought by bean counters, and it gave the patriotic forces one of their only exploitable operating margins.

It was much the same with the traitors' helicopters and other aviation assets. They were spread too thinly to give them effective coverage of their entire operational area. With the national economy and its industrial base in a shambles, spare parts and aviation fuel were in short supply. It was true that the drones and helos occasionally found freedom fighters out after curfew and killed them. This is what had happened to Morgan Tut-weiler. These missile attacks were unquestionably demoralizing, and they dissuaded many potential fighters from joining in his efforts, but they were too random and unlikely to deter Boone Vikersun from conducting his own guerrilla war. Foreign enemy soldiers were operating in Tennessee, and he would harass, snipe and bomb them—and the American traitors—for as long as he could.

There were only a few more hours of darkness ahead of them. There was always the remote chance of encountering a night ambush, but it was not the way the foreign troops preferred to operate. It just wouldn't have been productive: almost nobody moved at night, and even less frequently on these scarcely known dirt tracks. Civilians were afraid to be out after dark; they preferred to hunker down behind fences and walls. Nighttime patrolling was performed from high above, by the unseen UAVs—but not in bad weather.

Daytime movement in force was the standard operating procedure of the foreign troops. They preferred to conduct cordon and search oper-ations, and set up mobile checkpoints. But as happened so often, the inevitable drift toward routine limited the effectiveness of their operations. They returned consistently to the same patrol patterns and checkpoint locations. Boone knew where almost all of their most regular checkpoints might be, and he avoided them, rarely moving on the main roads. Instead, he traveled on foot or even on horseback. When he used a car, it was mostly off the pavement, on private farm tracks that appeared on no maps.

Now it was time to put the Subaru wagon back into hiding, and move on foot to their next laying-up position. With snow on the ground and warmer weather coming they would hide, and wait for another frontal passage before they made their next move. In Tennessee during January, fronts blew through every three or four days almost like clockwork. Snow was uncommon but it rained frequently and for long periods. The enemy soldiers hated to spend time outside in the raw, bone-chilling weather.

This was especially true for the Mexicans and the other Central Americans of the North American Legion—their combat effectiveness went down with the mercury.

The compressed parallel tracks left behind the four-wheel-drive Subaru could not be prevented. It was still snowing hard, and the new accumulation would soften and obscure the tread marks, but not wipe them out entirely. Enough new snow to accomplish the complete erasure of tire tracks was unlikely. But this part of Radford County was only rarely patrolled on foot by any foreign soldiers. It was almost a sanctuary zone for the few remaining rebels, a buffer between Mississippi and the occupied counties to the north, where the real guerrilla war was taking place. Like the horses, the old Subaru Outback wagon was a link in his transportation chain, but Boone could not drive it much further north without risking an enemy checkpoint, even at night and in bad weather.

He approached the hiding place at crawling speed, in low gear. He followed a dirt farm road into thick woods, turned off at an unlikely looking trail, driving on a left-leaning slant on the side of a hill, and then he turned downhill and took aim directly between two massive holly trees. Boone stopped the vehicle and said, "Everybody out. Get everything off the roof first." They stripped the baggage from the Subaru's rack: the ceiling of the car's hiding place would clear the roof rack only by inches. A minute later, the lower branches between the two holly trees were raised as Doug hauled down on a concealed rope, which was attached to a pulley far up one of the trees. With the bottom branches up and out of the way, Boone pulled the Subaru forward a dozen feet, sharp holly leaves scraping down the roof and sides.

The holly trees were enormous, each covering a diameter of more than thirty feet with dense, waxy leaves, which were opaque to visual or IR observation by day or night. The prickly-edged holly leaves would also deter any unlikely passersby on foot from exploring deeply within their domain. But the holly trees were not the only element of this vehicle hide. A small roof of corrugated fiberglass greenhouse panels had been erected over scrap lumber corner posts, just high enough to conceal the car. The makeshift roof was piled with a layer of dirt, and intentionally overgrown with weeds. The dirt and weeds would further obscure the IR signature of the metal car hidden beneath the fiberglass roof. Military camouflage netting hung down from the sides of the car shelter, and all of this was hidden beneath the opaque holly leaves.

This was one of a half-dozen vehicle hides Boone used. Others were less elaborate. Serviceable cars could often be left in woods disguised as abandoned junk, with their charged batteries removed and hidden nearby. This four-wheel-drive Subaru mini-wagon was his first choice for nighttime off-road driving, so it earned his best hiding spot. Tonight they would leave the car's hiding place quickly, while it was still snowing. If their fresh tire tracks were discovered, enemy patrols might follow them and, holly trees or not, the car would be discovered.

The last leg of their journey would take place on foot, while it was still dark. He had two new recruits in tow, but at least they had proven quiet and stealthy. Phil Carson had been a Special Forces operator, even if his experience had been decades before. Boone's only concern was that Carson might not be physically able to make the last mile-and-a-half hike. He was over sixty, and if he slipped, he could sprain an ankle or break something. Well, the old man had walked out of Mississippi as far as the Tennessee line, and he had made a rapid recovery from an arrow wound. Even so, he was old, and that meant his strength could fade quickly and without much warning. It would not be wise to overburden Phil Carson by regarding him as the man from his father's war stories.

Boone knew he could trust Zachary to be quiet and sure-footed. The teen was a natural hunter, trained by his father and raised in the Mississippi woods. Stealth was a skill better learned in the forest in pursuit of game than on any military training ground. Getting within bow-and-arrow range of a deer was much more difficult than finding and shooting men, even soldiers of above-average skill.

Since Boone was the only one wearing night vision goggles, he knew that to the others, it would appear that the Subaru had just driven into a black bush. The branches and prickly holly leaves scratched and creaked down both sides and the roof of the car. When the car was all the way inside, he killed the motor. He pushed open his door against the camouflage netting, and slid down the side of the car and out the back of the hiding place to where the others were waiting. He spoke quietly to Doug Dolan and his two new volunteers. The snow-covered woods would swallow his whispered words.

"I'm going to scout around the area before we leave. I'll sweep up our tracks, back to where we turned off the last trail. Then we're going somewhere else on foot. It'll take us a half hour or forty minutes, depending on how fast we can move. Then we'll reach a safe place where we can lay up for a few days. We'll move out of here as soon as we unload the rest of the gear. We'll carry as much as we can, and leave the rest inside the car and get it on another trip. I'll be back in a few minutes. Doug will show you what to do."

Leaving the warm trailer was difficult, but Jenny knew that she couldn't stay there, not so close to the ravine. There was no way that the people who had committed the massacre would allow any witnesses in the area to survive. The old woman was already resigned to her fate. Jenny had seen it before. She could do nothing to help her, besides making her some warm tea and building up the fire in the wood stove before she left. Jenny offered to take the boy, but she had been rebuffed. "If you want to take him, you'll have to tie him up and carry him. He won't leave this place. He don't understand any other life." There was no point arguing; Jenny knew the old woman was right.

After changing the baby girl's cloth diaper and outfit, she prepared another bottle of formula from the milk powder and put the box into the diaper bag. She heated the bottle so that it would be drinkable for a few hours. She packed two folded bed sheets in the diaper bag, to cut up for extra diapers. The old woman told her where to find some road maps, and told her how to get around the checkpoint she had seen by the store. "Take the other way around the junkyard, go to the left, it takes you up a steep path but you won't have to go up the ravine." Jenny put a county and a state road map into the left cargo pocket of her trousers. The Tennessee state road map showed a strip of the northern edge of Mississippi. It would be enough. She closed the trailer's door behind her, with baby Hope tucked again inside her camouflage parka. It was still snowing, and the accumulation had built up to perhaps four inches.

No tearful goodbyes, not after what Jenny had seen tonight. She didn't know the old woman. Maybe her son Arthur was still alive. Maybe he had been somewhere else yesterday and not at the swap meet. He could still come home. In any event, it wasn't Jenny's problem to worry about the old woman. Stopping at the trailer had been a lucky break for her, but that was all. There was no need to grow overly sentimental; no good would come of it. Sentimentality would only slow her down, make her hesitate. The woman was elderly; she'd lived a very long life. Not so Jenny McClure, who would be fortunate if she could live half as long—or if she could even make it through another year. Not to mention the baby, who had not lived much of any life at all, and who was already an orphan without ever knowing her parents.

Time was of the essence. It was early morning, and when the moon set, Jenny would be blind. Even hidden by unseen clouds, the diffused moonlight made it possible for her to move fast. She had to go now, and make rapid progress to the south. At least the old woman had been able to give her a starting direction. She even had a pair of road maps to study tomorrow in daylight. If she could just get five or ten miles away from the ravine before dawn, she'd find somewhere to hide during the day.

After she closed the door behind her, she used a trick her uncle had taught her. It had seemed like a silly joke when he had showed her how to do it on a muddy trail. She walked off the porch and away from the trailer backward, carefully lifting her feet and leaving prints that pointed back to the mobile home. Uncle Henry had told her that an expert tracker could easily detect the fakery, but ordinary folks could not, and experts were rare. She had never imagined actually using this ploy, much less in snow.

As the old woman had informed her, the path to the left side around the junkyard was better than the route that had led her up to the massacre site. At the bluff behind the junkyard, a jeep trail ascended the steep slope, and then she was on top of a plateau. After laboriously crossing a tightly strung barbed wire fence, placing her pack, her bag and the baby on the other side and climbing over, Jenny sensed that she was on some kind of a farm. She struck out at right angles from the fence. The trees thinned and turned to pasture on a slight downgrade, and then she encountered a stream, shining black between two curving borders of snow. Unable to determine its depth, and unwilling to risk soaking her feet in ice water, she backtracked and turned roughly parallel to the watercourse, walking downhill.

Within a half hour, Jenny was lost again, with no residual sense of her direction. She found what she thought might be another jeep trail. Once again, her choice of directions came down to a mental coin toss. Something told her that right would take her south, so she kept walking that way, depending again on fate. Fate had brought her this far. Each of the night's directional coin tosses had been in her favor. Even being selected for the rape house had turned out to be lucky, because it had led to her escape.

For Jenny to live to see her next birthday would require a miracle. The old woman in the trailer had already lived at least fifty or sixty years longer than she had. There was no reason to pity the old lady. She had lived a full life, and raised children and grandchildren. She had outlived hundreds of younger, healthier people who had been killed today in the ravine. No, there was no reason to pity her, even as she thanked her for the gift of shelter and the milk powder that had fed the baby. Jenny kept walking through the snow, which now was up to her ankles. The dead traitor's boots were excellent. Inside, her feet were still practically dry, and not too cold. She just had to keep moving south.

She left the sloping pasture near the stream, when it passed back into woods. The bare trees allowed most of the moonlight to reach the snow and gave the world a soft glow, but gradually the light dimmed until her eyes strained to see where she should place each footstep.

The cloud-hidden moon must be setting. Soon it would be too black around her to see her gloved hand in front of her face. Then she would have to use her pistol's bright flashlight, and risk being seen by the foreign troops. Either that, or try to move forward much more slowly in the darkness, almost by feel. Jenny McClure had experienced both forms of night travel during last year's escape from Memphis. On that journey she had not been afraid of foreign soldiers, but of the desperate, starving refugees pouring out of the city, and of the thousands of inmates who had escaped en masse from prisons, jails and insane asylums after the earthquakes.

Boone pulled his Randall fighting knife from its sheath. It had been a gift from his father when he had completed the Special Forces qualification course. The blade was eight inches long, and sharp enough to shave a clean swath of hair off his arm like a razor. He selected a pine bough, sliced through it at an angle, and resheathed the knife. The branch was six feet long and thick with pine needles, a natural broom. Walking backward, he used the feathery end to sweep away the tire tracks and his footprints back to where the car had left the trail and driven into the holly thicket. The tracks were clearly visible in the bright green image seen in his night vision goggles. The moon was setting, but his light-amplified view was more than adequate.

Snow was still falling, and with luck, there would be enough fresh accumulation to obscure the Subaru's twin tire tracks. He knew that there was no way to elude professional trackers, if they were searching hard after them. So much was a matter of chance, based largely upon the vagaries of tomorrow's weather. Tonight the snow was a blessing, but tomorrow it could be a curse if the car's compressed tracks were preserved by a hard freeze. The odds were good that the foreign troops were inside on a night like this, staying warm and probably getting drunk. They rarely mustered the motivation for night patrols, relying instead on the missile-armed UAVs to deter curfew violators. Bad weather at night left a seam in the enemy posture that Boone had learned to exploit. Tomorrow this luck could turn against him, if their tracks froze solid.

Once the tracks were obscured back to the trail and a few dozen yards further on, he would circle around to the other side of the holly thicket, sweeping his footprints behind him as he went, and leaving a confusing pattern left by backward and forward walking. None of these tricks would stop a professional tracker or a tracking dog, but they might be enough to confuse ordinary troops, and buy them a head start. If it kept snowing for a few more hours, the swept tracks would disappear altogether. So much depended on tonight's and tomorrow's weather. The snow might melt completely, or freeze hard. Clear weather tomorrow would also mean Predators aloft and new aerial surveillance. Seen on the UAV's infrared, warm human bodies would stand out against the snow like blazing torches.

Boone was standing next to a bare maple tree, scanning his head side to side and evaluating his efforts, when movement to his left caught his eye. Peripheral vision was almost nonexistent with the night goggles. He slowly turned his head to focus his vision in that direction. This was beyond where he had driven the Subaru off the trail and into the hiding place. Even in the open areas, his vision was limited to no more than two hundred feet because of the falling snow. With the winding of the trail through the evergreens and bare hardwoods, in many directions his vision was limited to only a dozen yards. Again, the movement caught his eye. What was it, a black bear or a deer? No, they would not be moving on such a night. His heart churned—someone was coming! He had been paying too much attention to the snow beneath his feet, and so he had missed the silent approach of an intruder. Boone slid against the foot-thick maple beside him, putting its trunk between himself and the person approaching.

A single foreign enemy meant a recon scout, or a point man for a patrol. The man was wearing a Russian fur hat and a uniform, and was walking toward him, now less than a hundred feet away. In Tennessee, only the Cossacks wore those hats and that uniform. But the man was not wearing any night observation device, and he appeared to be carrying no rifle. To an enemy without NVGs, it would be difficult even to follow the path without tripping over obstacles. Boone knew that he would be invisible as the soldier passed by. He looked back up the jeep trail. He could now see a hundred feet beyond the single trooper, but there was nobody following behind him. In this wooded terrain, in this darkness without night vision, soldiers following one another would have to be no more than a few feet apart, or they would quickly lose each other.

That's what must have happened, Boone decided. This solitary soldier must be a straggler, separated from his squad and lost. Or perhaps a deserter, although he had never heard of a Cossack deserting. To whom could he desert? Except for a few officers, the Cossacks couldn't speak a word of English, and they were universally hated by Americans. The officers spoke Russian and some English. This solitary soldier must have become separated from his unit, but that did not take away from the danger. His unit must be nearby, certainly within hearing range of gunshots. A platoon or more of Cossacks might even be laying up for the night in this very same area!

If the Cossack continued beyond the Subaru's hiding place, even without NVGs he'd be bound to notice the two fresh tire tracks in the snow. The car had compressed the four inches of white powder down to a slippery hard-packed crust. Even in the last moonlight that filtered through the clouds the parallel tracks would be noticeable. He might even feel the compressed tracks with his feet, and then examine them further with a flashlight. When the soldier eventually found his unit, he would report the fresh tracks, and his comrades would easily be able to follow their trail straight back to the car's hiding place.

All of these thoughts ran through his mind in the time it took the soldier to walk to within twenty feet of Boone's bare maple tree. He slowly revolved around the thick trunk, keeping it between the two of them, until the soldier passed by and walked onward. There was no way to alert the other three men by the car. He looked back toward the hollies and could see the side glow of Doug's dim flashlight. Even without night vision, this straggler would see the light in a few moments.

When the soldier was just a few yards past him, Boone silently drew the Randall knife from its sheath. The blanket of snow would silence his footsteps. The enemy soldier was not stopping to listen and look around, but was marching at a steady pace.

Boone stepped from behind the maple and began taking long but stealthy strides forward. He matched his steps to the enemy soldier's pace, further hiding any slight sound of his approach. An unwanted memory from Afghanistan invaded his mind: hot arterial blood gushing from the throat of a Taliban sentry. He steeled himself mentally to do the deed. In the last meter, slam him from behind with a hip while the left hand wraps around the face and pulls the head back sharply. Then the blade goes around in a flash, and with one deep backslash it will be done, his carotid and his windpipe severed. The man will be too shocked and have too little time left alive even to make a shout. Then he will be dead in the snow where he drops.

Only six feet separated them now. Boone's steps matched the lost straggler's in cadence, but each of his steps was a little longer. Covering more distance, gaining ground, a few inches closer with each stride. Knife held in the right hand, the left hand up and a little forward for the head grab. A few more steps, a few more seconds to contact, and it's throat-cutting time—again.

Jenny had to walk ever more slowly, because of the diminishing moonlight. Her pupils were already dilated to their maximum, only the white snow was still faintly visible. Trees around her dissolved into blacker obscurity and then disappeared altogether. She put out her left hand, to keep from walking directly into an unseen trunk. She set each foot down carefully, lest she put her weight down on a hole or trip across a root or a rock. She knew she must try to find a stick or a pole, to probe ahead of her like a blind person. Part of her wanted to simply draw her pistol and turn on its light, but it was one of those super-bright police lights, and anybody within a mile might see it. She wished she had an ordinary small flashlight, just enough to faintly illuminate her path a few steps ahead.

For all she knew, there might be one in the pack on her back, but she had departed the old woman's trailer in too much haste to inspect its contents. Perhaps she could jury rig a filter for the gun's light? A glove perhaps? For now, a blind man's stick would have to do. When she walked into some bushes, she'd break one off by feel and strip off its leaves. If she wandered into thick cover, she'd use the gun light to explore the rest of her backpack, and search it for a weaker light. Or she'd try to rig a filter over the gun light. At least the baby was sleeping warm against her chest, resting in the hollow pouch between her pack's straps, where the pistol belt pinched in the dead man's big parka. Every few minutes she had to pull down the front of the parka beneath the belt; otherwise, the baby was no real bother to her. Pregnant mothers carry a baby for nine months, she thought. I can carry one for a day or two.

12

Boone was half a head taller than the enemy he was stalking. The unlucky Cossack had no idea he was being followed by a hardened killer with a razor-sharp Randall fighting knife in his hand. According to his father, the knife had been used to kill several Viet Cong and NVA fighters. Decades later, it had dispatched one Taliban. Now it was going to cut a foreign enemy's throat right here in Tennessee. The wars were sure getting closer. They couldn't get any closer than this one—this one was walking distance from his old childhood haunts. No Air Force transport plane or chartered jet airliner was needed to deliver him to this war. At least he had the home field advantage for a change.

Just a few more steps now. Without night vision goggles, the enemy was nearly blind. His hands were outstretched to feel ahead for unseen obstacles. He was walking slowly, tentatively. Boone focused on breathing silently, and matching the Cossack stride for stride. Only one more yard, he was close enough to touch the soldier's pack. His right hand held the knife blade forward, ready to strike. He visualized his next moves: left hand over the face, pull back his head, and slash the throat.

It was almost too easy, like a jungle panther stalking a lost suburban poodle. Boone matched another step and held his breath, now less than a yard behind his oblivious victim. The man was several inches shorter, so the reach for the head and the cut across the throat would be easy. Boone had every possible advantage, the foreign soldier had none. The soldier's pistol was holstered, his hands groping blindly in front of him. He had a pack on his back and was carrying only a pistol, not a rifle. Only a pistol…

Boone looked again and saw three small stars arranged in a triangle on each soft shoulder board, just outside the straps of his pack. And the pack: it was not in the Russian flecked-camouflage pattern, it was a plain-colored model, an American commercial type that he recognized, similar to those purchased privately by American soldiers and SWAT cops. The exterior gear attachment system was of the current American standard. And there was another small kit bag, riding by the soldier's left side, that did not look military at all. To his green night eyes, it appeared to be bright, shiny plastic.

The pistol and three stars meant he was not just a Cossack or even a Russian soldier, but an officer! But a foreign officer with an American-style pack? This man was a find, a prize, worth far more alive than dead. Boone reached over the pack to its front, between the pack and the enemy's collar, and jerked sharply rearward while stepping back and to the side in an aikido pirouette. The soldier, thrown off balance and totally surprised, flew past him and thudded onto his back, landing across his pack like an upended turtle. Boone followed and pounced down on him, straddling his body at the hips. The cutting edge of the knife was laid across his enemy's throat in a second.

Any Russian words that Boone had ever learned did not rise to his lips tonight. Not "stop" or "surrender" or "hands up," which he had learned to say in a half dozen languages over the years. But he didn't need to speak—the enemy spoke first.

"Don't hurt the baby!"

"What the *hell*?" Boone replied, stunned by the sudden turn. The soldier's face was smooth, not bearded or whiskery. "You're not one of them? You're not even a man!" Clearly this was not an ordinary Cossack officer. The person below him was a female—that was becoming obvious. Boone was not expecting to hear English, and he was certainly not expecting a woman. Once they were both still, her face was clear to him in the green light of his NVGs. The soldier was a woman, and a young one at that.

"You're—an American?" returned the female voice, struggling for breath beneath his weight.

"Yes, I'm an American." He pulled the blade back away from her throat, but only an inch. "What are you doing here? Why are you wearing a Russian uniform?"

"Do you mind getting off me? I'm carrying a baby, and you're crushing her."

"You're pregnant?" Boone relaxed a fraction and lifted up some of his weight, while kneeling in the snow over the prone form pinned beneath him.

"No I'm not pregnant, I mean I'm *carrying* a baby. Right here, under my jacket." The baby, roughly jostled and pushed, began to cry.

A white light flashed on above them, shining down on Jenny's face. She was blinking upward against the sudden glare. From above Boone's shoulder Doug said, "Well, now I've seen everything. An American girl, in a Russian uniform, in a snowstorm, with a baby."

Boone tipped his NVGs from his face up onto his forehead, then pushed himself up and pulled Jenny to her feet. Doug covered her with his M-4 carbine, its muzzle a yard from her torso.

Boone ordered, "Just keep your hands up until we figure out what's going on."

"I can't keep them both up—I have to hold the baby with at least one arm." The infant was visibly squirming inside her parka, and began to cry.

She was not following the script. Who was this girl in a Russian uniform, with a gun and a baby, out in a snowstorm? "Okay, then keep your right hand up, up away from the pistol. You're alone?"

"No, I told you about this baby."

"But nobody's following you?"

"God, I sure hope not. You're *really* an American?" She looked back and forth between the two men.

"Yeah, I'm really an American. Okay, let's get you out of the snow." They were not far from the holly trees, and with Doug holding a flashlight they were able to walk back in less than a minute. The rifle was aimed at the girl's back.

Phil Carson and Zack Tutweiler were waiting by the holly trees when the others returned. Their weapons were leveled, Carson's 9mm Berretta and Zack's lever-action Winchester 30-30 rifle. Boone said, "We found a pair of strays. Relax, put up the guns." They stood under the raised holly branches, at the back of the Subaru. Its hatchback was lifted, showing the packs and bags stowed tightly in the rear cargo area. Boone had to adapt his plan on the fly. Doug held his flashlight pointing at the ground, but it provided enough light, reflecting back up off the snow.

Boone said, "Okay, let's start with your name."

She couldn't speak again until she had caught her breath. "Jenny McClure."

"All right, Jenny, first, take out your pistol very slowly and hand it to me."

"Oh, no. No way. It's mine. I'm not giving it to anybody. You guys already have guns—I need one too."

"You don't have a choice," Boone answered curtly. He was accustomed to being obeyed by prisoners.

"You know what?" she replied. "The last guy who said I didn't have a choice tonight is dead. This used to be his pistol. This was his uniform too. I killed him a few hours ago."

She was clearly serious about keeping the gun, so Boone let that go for the time being. "Let's back up, Jenny. Where are you from?"

"I used to live with my family in Germantown, that's just outside of Memphis."

"So where do you live now?"

"I've been staying with my aunt and uncle, just south of Mannville."

"Where exactly? Be specific."

"Ben Duggin Road, on the south loop. The new houses."

"I know the place. Hank McClure is your uncle?"

"Yes, they took me in after the earthquakes. Hank and Rochelle."

"Good man."

"Very," she agreed.

Boone was satisfied with her story, at least for the time being. Hank McClure was a former Marine Corps officer who helped train and organize the neighborhood defense teams around Mannville. They had met, and Boone remembered hearing something about his young niece, who had trekked solo from Memphis to Radford County after the earthquakes. "So Jenny, what's in the pack? Is it yours?"

"It is now. It belonged to the guy I killed. Now it's mine—so don't get any ideas."

"He was a Cossack officer?"

"No, he was an American, but he was working with them. He was a translator or something. It was his pack. Other than a sausage and some water, I don't know what's in it. I haven't stopped to look—I've been in too much of a hurry."

"Well, we need to look, right now. Doug, help her take it off. Jenny, where did you get this pack, and the uniform? And what's that, a diaper bag? And what about the baby? Is it yours?"

She looked between the men. "You're really Americans? You're not working for the…the Kazakhstans or whoever they are?"

"I already told you we're Americans," said Boone, "And no, we're not working with the Cossacks. We're fighting against them and against all of the other foreign enemies. And against the American traitors too, for that matter. Foreign, domestic, we don't care."

"So you're fighting against the Kazaks?"

"Kazaks, Cossacks, same difference. That's what we do, every day," said Boone.

"Well, I escaped from them tonight." Jenny sat beneath the hatch-back, on the wide rear bumper. "I've been walking for hours, since before I found the baby. That's what I need to tell you, about where I found the baby. If you're fighting the foreign soldiers, I need to tell you a lot. I was in Mannville today, at the Saturday swap market. You know the place?"

"At the high school. I'm familiar with it," said Boone.

"Well these Russians came, or Kazaks or whatever they are. It was an ambush, a trap. We were penned up inside the fence, on the high school parking lot. I can't believe how stupid we were! They came on horses and they had trucks and helicopters, and little tanks on wheels. They had a ma-chine that burned our skin like fire. Then they put everybody on buses and took them to a ravine, back there, back where I was coming from. That's where I found this baby. Everybody else there was dead, dead in the snow. Hundreds of them, I think. They were all shot."

"Hundreds?" asked Boone, perplexed. He'd seen a lot of death in his years of war fighting, both abroad and lately at home, but this was a new level of atrocity—if it was true. Only some of Saddam Hussein's old mass graves in Iraq had been on that scale. And some in the Balkans that he had read about, but not personally seen.

"Yes, hundreds. Everybody who was at the swap market, and at the Baptist church across the street. They were taken away on our own Radford County school buses. Taken to a ravine…and shot."

After a brief silence Boone asked, "How did you get away? Did they miss you when they were shooting? Did you play possum?"

Jenny shook her head, "No, no, it wasn't like that, not for me. I didn't go there with everybody on the buses. I was with—well, there was a group of girls. We weren't taken to the ravine. We were put on an Army truck, an American Army truck, and taken to a big house, a mansion like they have on a plantation." She paused, remembering. "It was called Barton Hall."

"I know the place."

"The Russians were having a party…"

"Kazaks, they're Kazaks," Boone reminded her. "I just call 'em Cossacks, their old name. Most of them speak Russian, but they're from Kazakhstan, in Central Asia. It used to belong to Russia, back when it was the Soviet Union. There's almost a thousand of them in Tennessee now."

"Well, we were the main event. At the party, I mean. There was an American with the Kazaks. He dragged me upstairs, and he tried to rape me. That's what the party really was: a rape party. Now he's dead. There was a fireplace in the bedroom, and I lit the whole house on fire before I climbed out the window. Now I'm wearing his uniform and his boots. I was hoping he had food or valuables in his pack, but I couldn't stop to check. I had to keep running away; I was trying to get far away before the snow stopped, and before daylight. Then I found the baby in the ravine. You know the rest."

There was silence as the men digested the incredible tale. Boone began mentally ticking off the names and faces he would have expected to be in Mannville yesterday morning, at the church, the swap market, or both. Most of his local network was probably wiped out. Most of his half year of working to organize a guerrilla insurgency was gone. Mannville was a vital linchpin. It was the center of a small region where he could occasionally surface and live a semi-overt life, find support, and slip in and out of the areas under the traitor government's control. It would be difficult to recover from this blow, if she was telling the truth. His last operational sanctuary was gone.

After a period of silence, Carson asked Jenny, "Is the baby all right?"

"I think so. I'm not sure. I hope she is. I gave her a bottle of instant milk. I stopped in a house trailer by a junkyard that's not very far from the ravine where I found her. There was an old blind lady there. That's where I found the milk powder. She gave it to me."

"I know the place you mean," said Boone. "Lots of old refrigerators and washing machines."

"That trailer is real close to where the people were shot."

"And it's not very far from here either. Listen, Jenny, we need to see what's in your pack." Doug held the flashlight while Boone spread out a green poncho on the ground between them, mostly beneath the Subaru's hatch. Boone removed the contents from the side and back pouches, and then the main compartment. The holly branches above their heads blocked most of the falling snow. "This pack belonged to the American, the traitor with the Cossacks?"

"Yes. He was the one on the loudspeaker back at Mannville, when they attacked the swap market. He was the one that gave the orders, and told us what to do. When we didn't move fast enough, he burned us with some kind of a heat ray that looked like a big TV screen. Later he showed up at the house they took us to—the girls, I mean. Then he dragged me upstairs and tried to rape me, but I killed him instead."

After a pause, Boone redirected the conversation. "Jenny, those three stars on your shoulders mean he was an officer. Like a senior lieutenant or a captain, or maybe a major. At least I think that's the Russian rank system. I don't know what his American rank was. He was probably assigned to the Cossack Battalion as a liaison, not just as a translator. That means he was a go-between, to take orders to the Cossacks. They gave him a Cossack uniform so he could blend in with them. Too bad he's dead—he's the kind of traitor I'd *really* love to talk to. But I'm glad you got away, even if it meant killing him. Don't get me wrong, we would have killed him too. I just wish we'd had a chance to interrogate him first—before hanging him. That's what we do with traitors when we catch them alive."

Carson asked, "But who was giving him his orders? An American, or a foreigner? Who's in charge of this thing?"

"Americans are in charge, I'm fairly sure," said Boone. "I think the foreign troops are being run under Homeland Security, so it would go from there to the president. But just in Tennessee and Kentucky, I think. And I think it's being run out of Fort Campbell, that's on the Kentucky state line a hundred miles north of us. Now, if somebody else is giving orders to the president—I mean somebody foreign—well, that's *way* above my level of knowledge. I wouldn't have a clue about that."

Boone removed a black plastic waterproof Pelican case the size of a big shoebox. The case was the largest item in the pack. He opened its latches and removed a black brick-sized walkie-talkie. The bottom third of the radio was a removable battery pack. A thick rubber-coated antenna was detached from the radio so that it could fit within the waterproof container.

In the Pelican case there was also a portable GPS unit with a small LCD screen, a digital camera, a cell phone, an infrared aiming laser the size of a television remote control, a small tactical flashlight and a clear Ziploc bag full of AA batteries. There was also a small plastic container full of exotic batteries for the other electronic devices. There was nothing else in the Pelican case. In a separate plastic case, there was a pair of night vision goggles identical to his military PVS-7's. The backpack also contained dry socks and other spare garments in a waterproof bag, ammunition, folded paper maps, candy, a water bottle, another sausage and two MRE military ration packs.

Boone held the walkie-talkie, turning it over and showing it to the others. "This is a PRC-148; it's used for talking ground-to-ground or ground-to-air. And for communicating anywhere else too, using an airplane or a drone as a relay. This was the traitor's radio for contacting his headquarters, and for receiving his orders."

Doug said, "We'd better pull the batteries out of all of this stuff. Any of these things could be used as tracking beacons."

"The cell phone and the radio, for sure. But let's turn on the GPS. I haven't had a working unit for a long time." GPS was now encrypted, and the encryption was changed frequently, so old GPS devices without current chips were useless. GPS had become a tightly restricted tool available only to the military and certain civilian industries, after terrorists began programming airplanes to fly bombs into government buildings. GPS plus an airplane flying on autopilot allowed almost anybody to create a poor man's cruise missile. Besides the government, only airlines, shipping lines and a few other authorized users were now granted access to GPS. The position signals for these authorized civilian users were degraded to only quarter-mile accuracy, to prevent misuse. Only the military had access to the real thing, GPS signal accuracy down to a few meters.

Boone pushed the power button, and the LCD screen lit up. In a few moments it had acquired its position. He scrolled the menu through screens until he found the map page. He zoomed in until it covered the area surrounding them. "See the dotted line? The trackback was programmed. Jenny, it shows every step of your path tonight. It might even show how the traitor got here, and where his headquarters is. This thing could be a gold mine of information. It's even got a night vision mode, so the screen won't be too bright to use with NVGs. It's a damned good piece of gear."

Doug Dolan was already removing the battery packs from the handheld radio and the cell phone. "What if the GPS can be activated as a tracker?"

"Not likely," said Boone. "Out of the box, it's set up to receive only. There's no reason for it to be modified to transmit a homing signal—the

American traitor that Jenny killed wasn't on that kind of a mission. He had the radio for sending out his position."

Boone knew that Doug was right to ask about the GPS. It was an old Special Forces trick to leave weapons, radios or other gear with electronic trackers secretly embedded in them, where guerrillas would "find" or "capture" them. The Americans could then use these covert tracking beacons to locate the enemy base camps. Boone had done this himself, in Colombia, Peru, Iraq and Afghanistan. Removing batteries provided little assurance of safety. A tracking device could be concealed anywhere, even within the backpack's frame, or for that matter in the boots that Jenny wore. The bugs could then lay dormant, not turning on and emitting any detectable signal for days or weeks.

The only assurance he had that no tracking devices were being carried by this girl was the fact that she had killed the previous owner to acquire them. That is, if he accepted Jenny's story at face value. But it was just too far-fetched to believe otherwise. The infant was the deciding factor. Jenny's arrival with a baby was too elaborate and bizarre to be a planned operation, designed to locate his tiny resistance cell. Her story of being Hank McClure's niece fit what he already knew. Finally, he told Doug, "I suppose anything's possible, but it's a chance we have to take. I need this GPS for what I have in mind. Okay, here's the new plan. Can you find Charlie Two without me?"

"Yeah, I think so…" Doug sounded less than certain.

"That's not good enough—can you, or can't you? Be sure, one way or the other. You've made the trip with me a few times: can you find it at night, without me?"

"With night vision goggles, yes." Doug pulled the new NVGs from their case and turned them on. A single light amplification tube in the center split into two images and poured green light from both ocular lenses. He held them to his face and adjusted the straps around his head.

"You'd better—you have to. Okay, here's what we'll do. I'm taking the GPS and the cameras, and I'm going to find Jenny's ravine. No pack, and no long weapon—I'll be moving fast, and I might have to move in daylight. The bodies were left uncovered in the open, and that was a big mistake by the Cossacks. We need to take advantage of it. I'm going to take pictures and try to collect some forensic evidence. Wallets, ID cards, that sort of thing. Hair for DNA, maybe. Solid, undeniable proof. If they've massacred hundreds of the people from around here, then they've crossed a big red line and they can't go back. They're taking their counterinsurgency to another level: total scorched earth, no holds barred. This changes everything. After this, it's a whole new ball game, with new rules. But I need to get the proof, so this is our new top priority."

"I'll go with you," offered Phil Carson. "I can cover your back."

"No, this is a solo mission. No offense, but I'll be traveling too fast, and I can't risk your getting injured and slowing me down. That area will be thick with enemy soldiers, and one man means fewer tracks and less chance of compromise. I'll be at the cave before dawn, day after tomorrow. If I'm not, well...it's over. What I mean is resistance in Radford County is finished. We can't operate here any longer, not if Mannville was wiped out. If I don't make it to the cave, head for Mississippi, to Corinth. But with a little luck, I'll see you at the cave by tomorrow night, or Monday morning at the latest. Doug, make sure this place is squared away. Sweep your tracks behind you as best you can on the way out, and around the cave. We can't do anything about the car tracks back behind us, but you don't want to leave footprints leading from here to the cave. Don't rush it, be careful, but don't waste any time either. Doug, listen to Zack and Phil, they're both good in the woods, right? But you're in charge." Boone looked at each of their faces. "Right. That's it then. I'll see you tomorrow night, or by Monday morning at the very latest."

Boone quickly did a rapid mental inventory of what he was already carrying, and what he needed to take from the car. Night goggles, and both digital cameras. Two frag grenades, with trip wire rigs for hastily setting across his trail in case he was pursued. A small bag of beef jerky and his camelback full of water. His mini escape and evasion kit, as always. For close, quiet work, his .45 caliber Glock 21 pistol, with a threaded barrel ready for its suppressor. His backup weapon was another Glock, the compact version without a threaded barrel. Both weapons took the same ammunition and magazines. He considered carrying an M-4 carbine, but decided that its advantages in range would be outweighed by its lack of concealability. No matter how he was armed, he could not win a firefight against a squad of Cossacks armed with Kalashnikovs and belt-fed machine guns. The key to survival on this solo operation was keeping a low profile, and that meant using only fully concealable weapons, in case he was forced to cross open ground or skirt the edge of a village.

The camouflage parka hung nearly to his knees, completely covering his pistol holster. This was an advantage to winter fighting: he could never hide his combat vest, gear and weapons on his body when dressed for summer. The tradeoff was that in the summer, the far thicker foliage and the leaf-covered woods kept him better concealed, even while dressed more lightly and carrying weapons on the outside. Boone didn't need to carry much, because he was operating practically in his backyard, and he had secret caches of necessities, including firearms, located around the county. It was impossible to walk a mile without crossing a source of water that he could drink through his charcoal filter straw. He could live off the land practically forever in this country. Boone pulled his NVGs down over his face and punched the GPS unit's backlight down to its dimmest night vision–compatible setting. He clicked the map to the trackback mode and set off at a brisk pace, following Jenny McClure's GPS trail. Her footprints were also clearly visible in the bright green snow.

Phil Carson reluctantly accepted Doug Dolan taking the point position. Boone was gone, but he had unambiguously left Doug in charge. Doug had the new set of night vision goggles, he knew the way to their hideout—and he was a lot younger. But what kind of an operator was he? How good was he at night patrolling, how quietly could he move? Would he find a good path, or would he lead them blindly into impassible obstacles, or worse, lead them into an ambush? Well, they'd find out soon enough. Except for the girl, they were going to be carrying extra heavy loads: their own packs, plus sacks of food and gear brought from Zack's house.

They stood in the little clear space behind the Subaru, packing what they would take and leaving the rest cached in the back of the vehicle. The dome light inside the car had been turned on, providing the little area with just enough light to work. The baby was squirming and restless, fussing, threatening to break into a full-throated cry at any time.

"Maybe I should feed her here?" suggested Jenny. "I've got a bottle ready."

"Not yet," Doug answered in a loud whisper while strapping extra bags to his pack. "It's less than two miles to the cave. The snow might stop anytime, so we have to move out fast and hope it covers our footprints. Save the bottle for if she really gets loud. Zack, help me get my pack on." Once his load was on his back, he slid his rifle's sling over his neck.

Zack said, "Doug, you've got night goggles and you know where you're going, but we're going to be tripping all over the place behind you. The moon's down, and even with the snow it's too dark for us. Once we turn off the car's light we're going to be as blind as bats. We'll be lucky if we don't get split up and lost. Let me hang this on the bottom of your pack. Your flashlight is too bright, but this one is just right." He showed them his finger-sized light, removed from his compound bow. Its single LED bulb cast a small pool of red light on the ground. "It'll let us see where we're walking, and we won't lose you. I don't like to use lights at night, but this is an exception. Nobody else will see this light unless they have night vision or they practically walk into us. We have to take the chance. It'll be worse for us if we get separated and have to call to each other, or if we're falling down and making noise."

"I don't know about using a visible light…"

"Zack is right," said Carson. "Without a light we'll have to move too slowly. We'll be stumbling around like blind men and that means noise, and somebody might fall and get hurt. Then we'll have a bigger problem, because there's not enough of us to carry somebody with a busted leg. The red light's a small risk, but we have to take it. What's your name again, honey?"

"Jenny."

"Sorry. Jenny, you walk right behind Doug there, close enough almost to touch him. Then Zack—and I'll bring up the rear." Carson didn't ask; instead, he used a positive, commanding voice. It was essential that they not lose one another in the dark. Zack clipped his cigarette-sized penlight to Doug's pack. If enemy soldiers were out on ambush patrols tonight, the light would give them away. But if they were patrolling with night vision or—God forbid—infrared thermal imaging scopes, they'd be seen anyway, red light or no red light.

Zack asked Jenny, "Do you want me to take your stuff? You're carrying the baby. I can take your pack, I can carry it in front of me."

"No thanks—I've got it. It's not that much. Really, I can deal with it, if it's only a couple miles. That's nothing. I'm used to it."

Doug adjusted the dead traitor's night goggles and pulled his black watch cap back on his head, over the straps. "All right, we need to go. Is everybody ready?" The others nodded their assent. He reached inside the car and switched off its light, and they were plunged into darkness, except for the dim pool of red light behind his feet. He whispered, "I'll take you across the trail now. Wait for me there right where I leave you. I'll get the car ready and close this place up, drop the branches again, and I'll sweep our tracks out. It'll take me a few minutes. Then we'll get going. Once we're out of here, no talking unless it's an emergency, and then only whisper right into an ear."

"Like we're hunting," suggested Zack. His small compound bow was tied vertically to the back of his pack, but he held his lever-action rifle at the ready. A pair of daypacks full of food were tied to the sides of his main pack, a compressed sleeping bag was strapped below it, and a ten-pound sack of rice was lashed on top. They were all heavily laden for their short trek, but none more than Zack.

"Right, like we're hunting," agreed Doug, who had grown up in the Maryland suburbs and had never stalked an animal in his life. "That means no shooting unless we absolutely have to. Not unless somebody shoots at us first, and they're damn close. And don't shoot just because you hear rounds popping. The bad guys might be shooting at somebody else, or they might be doing recon-by-fire. Don't fall for it. Don't kid yourself: once we go loud, we're probably screwed. There's hundreds of Kazaks, and only four of us. Make sure you keep that thing on safe, Zack. An accidental discharge could get us all killed."

"Do you think I don't know that?" he responded coolly. Under his breath he muttered to Carson, "Damn Yankee, givin' me gun advice…"

Doug ignored him and continued. "We know the Kazaks are around us, it's just a question of whether they're running patrols tonight. I'll be stopping once or twice a minute to listen. Stop when I stop. I'm going to take you guys a little way off from here now, then I'm coming back to sweep up our prints and let the holly branches down to hide the car. Okay? Let's go." He led them out into the darkness. The three waited a hundred feet from the vehicle. Doug's light disappeared under the holly trees, and then reappeared. No one without night vision would be able to see the small circle of light on the ground, unless they were very near.

Doug returned in a few minutes to where the others waited. He approached them walking backward, feathering their snowy tracks with Boone's pine bough, then he handed it off to Carson, who was going to walk at the rear of their file. "The car is booby-trapped now: don't go back for any reason. Not unless I'm with you to disarm it. I'll try to keep us out of deep snow so we don't leave too much of a trail. Mr. Carson, clean up what you can of our tracks, but don't fall behind or lose us. Okay? Okay. Follow me." They kept an interval of only a yard or two between them, almost touching distance.

Carson had placed the girl at the second position, where she would benefit the most from the tiny red light. Carrying a baby inside her parka against her chest and a pack on her back would be a challenge, he knew. If she fell, the baby could be hurt, or at least it might start crying loudly. She must have been made of strong stuff, though, to have endured the past day's events as she had described them. For that matter, she had to be tough just to have survived the last year in Tennessee.

Zack needed no help or advice about how to follow along silently; the boy was a born hunter. They made steady progress. Most of their route was under tree cover, zigzagging from woods to tree line to woods, occasionally crossing unavoidable segments of open fields. Most of the terrain was slightly hilly, folded land, up and down a couple hundred feet of elevation. Some of it was steep enough to require bending forward and using hands for balance, or to pull up on roots or saplings. At times they had to slow their pace almost to a crawl when climbing steep, slippery stream banks, or while negotiating thickets and clambering over fences and through deadfall trees.

After almost an hour, they were ascending a steep slope, the higher side of a small valley. The snowfall was diminishing; the snow on the ground was heavy and wet. Their boots compressed the snow to slush, through to the frozen mud below. Carson knew that four sets of boots would leave a trail a blind man could follow, in spite of his sweeping their tracks when he could. Fortunately, most of the time they were walking through underbrush and bushes, which were obscured beneath bare trees and some evergreens. Otherwise, their trail would be readily visible from the air once daylight came, if aircraft were up and looking. Another inch of snow was what they needed, to obscure their back trail, but that was looking doubtful.

Doug slowed again, stopped, looked around, then whispered, "This is it. Come on up close so you can hear me. The opening is pretty small, so take your packs off here. We'll have to push them in, one at a time. I'll go in first. Wait here, and give me a minute to get inside and get some lights turned on. Zack, take your light back now. Use it out here to make sure nothing gets left outside the cave, and see to it our tracks are swept up around here. Okay?" Doug stripped off his pack, went down onto his knees and then onto his stomach. Then he snaked his way forward and out of sight, his boots the last thing seen in the red glow of Zack's light. The others gratefully downed their own loads and waited, stretching their necks and shoulders. The cave opening was at the bottom of a rocky cliff, which extended vertically about twenty feet from the tree-covered slope. Thorn bushes grew thickly around the base of the rocks, concealing the cave's irregular angled entrance, which was only about four feet wide and less than two high. The only way in was on one's belly, the way that Doug had gone.

Dwight Granger lived in the Unaccompanied Personnel Quarters on Fort Campbell, not far from Gate One. A generation ago at the start of his former Air Force career, it would have been called the Bachelor Officers Quarters, but two of those three terms had fallen prey to political correctness. The sprawling three-story structure was built of reinforced concrete, and it had come through the earthquakes with no more than cracks. Granger occupied a single room, with a bed that converted into a sofa, a table, a desk, and a connecting bathroom that he shared with the next room. It was not much more than his own cell in the low-rise building, one of hundreds of identical cement-walled cubicles, but at least he had a key to the door. This bachelor's room was a far cry from the three-bedroom home outside Las Vegas that he used to own. Own? That was not the correct word. In the end, the bank owned it. It always had, really.

During his current employment contract with the Department of Homeland Security, it was a much better deal to live on the Army base than off it. At least his room in the UPQ had reliable electricity and heat, unlike most of the housing opportunities off base. Granger currently did not own an automobile, and gasoline was practically unobtainable anyway. The UPQ was within walking distance of the Post Exchange store, the food commissary, and the Cole Park Buffet, where he could pay for his meals with voucher cards. A free shuttle bus was usually available to take him to and from his job at UAV flight operations, but most of the time he walked instead of waiting for it.

Tonight he lay on his sofa bed, staring up at the constellations of bumps and holes in his stucco plaster ceiling. The dots doubled and merged as he stared into and beyond the yellow paint. He was still unable to focus on anything beyond the Predator video he had captured today. He had the entire Mannville massacre recorded on several thumb-sized USB drives, but he was afraid to load the images onto his personal laptop computer. He didn't need to view it on his computer screen: the massacre at the ravine in Radford County played itself in his mind over and over again.

The flash drives containing the video files were fairly well hidden, taped to the back of a drawer, but in his mind's eye, they glowed and pulsed like radioactive isotopes. His tiny room could be searched to its concrete walls, ceiling and floor in mere minutes. He wanted the drives out of his room, but he did not want the information contained on them to be lost. He considered hiding them in one of the UPQ's common areas or laundry rooms, but even there they might inadvertently be discovered. Conversely, if something happened to him, the flash drives might lie unnoticed in the laundry room for years, or they might be thrown away in the trash unviewed.

Regardless of where he temporarily hid the flash drives, what could he do with the information contained on them? He supposed he could take them and leave Fort Campbell. But to go where, without a car? He would have to leave Tennessee and Kentucky, but to do that he would need official authorization, and travel papers for boarding an interstate train or bus. He'd have to go to the national media centers in Washington or New York, he thought. He'd need to take the flash drives directly to one of the big television networks or newspapers.

He quickly reconsidered that idea. In reality, there was no truly free press in America anymore, not during the long emergency. National security was invoked so freely that the First Amendment had become an empty promise. The major media outlets would never broadcast the Predator video, not without first running it past the Department of Homeland Security for approval and official clearance. Under the emergency laws, he would probably be arrested on charges of...well, something. They would secretly arrest him for conspiracy, sedition or the new catchall, "advocating violent radicalization against the government." Then he'd disappear into a detention camp...or worse.

He could make multiple copies, and try to mail them in the blind to various media outlets and hope for the best...but the mail was carefully scrutinized these days. Even small parcels required a trip to the Post Office, where he would be filmed. A flash drive would easily show up under an x-ray, the file could be opened by the security services, and then he would be arrested. Perhaps he could send it out to the so-called free states of the Pacific Northwest? He promptly dropped that idea. He had no contacts out West. When he lived in Nevada he was still on active duty in the Air Force, and he had no local friends outside of the military. When he left Nevada, that state's presence upon him evaporated like the desert's morning dew. To Dwight Granger it was no more than a hot and arid geographical location that he had occupied for a few years, and he had not put down the shallowest roots.

Five years ago he could have simply uploaded the video onto the internet, but no more. There was no free, unmonitored internet as there had been even a few years earlier. It was impossible to anonymously upload videos onto the net. It would be simpler and quicker just to walk over to base security and confess his unauthorized copying of the Predator video than to try to disseminate it on the internet. The result would be the same: arrest. Trying to mail or merely to release the video images would be too dangerous. Perhaps he should just wait, and hope that someday the political situation in the United States would change enough for the video to be shown on broadcast television. Someday Americans will need to know what happened in Tennessee during the long emergency, he thought. The true and complete history of the past year will have to come out, eventually—not just the politically correct version preferred by the government and its allies in the media.

It was part of the official history that hundreds of thousands of people died because of the twin earthquakes and their aftermath. We have all understood that, thought Dwight Granger. There was no denying the obvious. We have also been repeatedly told that the earthquakes and the fires that followed them were tragic events, but that they were unforeseeable and unpreventable acts of nature. The government even reluctantly admitted that thousands more were killed during the complete breakdown of civil order that followed the quakes. Many more froze to death or died from drinking foul water, or from disease or even in some cases from starvation.

And of course, it was well known that thousands of black refugees were killed by white racists when they fled Memphis and other urban areas, seeking food and clean water in the countryside. He had seen the television news footage of helpless blacks shot down on the roads and in the fields. Entire documentary films had been produced about the racial killings. So who would have sympathy for the white racists in Western Tennessee if in turn a massacre had been perpetrated upon them? Everybody remembered the televised images of the African-American bodies piled up on the roads leading out of Memphis, where they had been shot dead by racist whites. White people like the ones who had in turn been shot in the ravine outside of Mannville. There was almost an eerie symmetry to today's massacre. Perhaps it put last year's bloody events into some balance. Payback.

Even so...even so...this thing that he witnessed today could not be excused, no matter what terrible racial crimes white Tennesseans might have committed following the earthquakes. Yesterday's massacre was not committed during the weeks of starvation, anarchy and panic immediately following the earthquakes. This slaughter was done a year later, by foreign soldiers who had been sent in by our own government to "pacify" the region. This new mass murder was done in cold blood. This was the stuff of Hitler's Nazis. No matter what some of these rural whites had done to the black earthquake refugees a year ago, the massacre he had witnessed today could not be justified or rationalized. But what could he do with the information he possessed? To whom could he show the video proof? How could he disseminate the truth in a way that would make any difference? No television network or newspaper would touch the video—that was a certainty. They would pass the video on to the Department of Homeland Security for vetting, and there it would stay. And then he would be arrested.

So in practical terms, what could he do with the evidence? Every day that he kept the flash drives hidden in his room he risked their discovery, and then he would be arrested, and their information might be lost forever. Anytime he reported for duty at flight operations, his room could be covertly searched, and if that happened the flash drives would be found. What, then, could he do with them? What? He stared up through the blurring and merging dots on his ceiling, and found no answers there.

13

Jenny was too exhausted to feel much surprise, but entering a cave in the black of night promised to be a singular experience. The opening was no more than a yard wide. The bottom was not smooth or level, but more diagonal. Rocks protruded through the snow, where the man they called Doug had already crawled in. When Zack helped take off her backpack she became lightheaded, and she had to reach for his shoulder to steady herself. Zack aimed his little red light at the cave's mouth, and she watched as her pack was dragged into the hole in the rocky hillside.

Carson, the older one, asked, "Can you carry the baby inside where you have him, or do you want to slide him through like your pack?"

"Her. She's a girl," replied Jenny.

Doug's face appeared from inside the cleft in the rock wall. He had dark wavy hair and a thin stubble beard. The night vision goggles he had worn on their hike to the cave were gone. Instead, he had a headlamp on his forehead, a row of white LED bulbs that illuminated the mouth of the cave from within.

She asked him, "Does it get tighter than this?"

"No, this is the narrowest spot right here. It gets higher and wider just a few feet inside."

"I'll bring her in, then. She's still sleeping, if you can believe it." Jenny knelt in the slushy snow and ducked under the rocky opening, coming face to face with Doug.

"Okay. Here, let me put this on you. You need these to see inside." Doug slid an elastic strap over her fur hat. Her hat's side and back flaps were already down, and the band fit snugly around the leather top. He depressed a button and the light came on. They were almost nose-to-nose, and he lingered just a moment to brush a loose strand of blond hair away from her face.

Jenny lowered herself almost onto her belly in the snow, propping herself up with her left elbow. Her right forearm cradled the infant, who was still tucked against her chest within the nest of her parka. She twisted slightly onto her left side to accommodate the angle of the cave mouth, and wriggled her way through, hunching forward like a caterpillar. It was not completely dark inside as she had expected, but was lit by, of all things, a line of white and red miniature Christmas lights. Doug slid backward just in front of her, gliding over boulders and cracks like a snake, guiding her in. The floor of the cave was dry once she was inside.

After a couple of yards, Doug stopped and said, "Okay, you can sit up here. Just move slowly, and watch your head." Then he crawled past her, back toward the cave opening. "Okay, Zack, shove all the packs in now." Doug hauled them in as they appeared. The teenage boy was the next to creep inside, followed by Phil Carson.

When they were all sitting together inside the cave, Doug told them, "It's not standing headroom yet, but you won't have to crawl anymore. Just watch your heads. During some of the way in, you'll have to hold onto a yellow rope. You'll see it when we get there. The rope is already bolted along the wall in the places where you need a good handhold. Just watch what I do, and follow this string of lights. Take your time, and be careful where you put your feet. I'll come back and collect the gear once we're all the way in."

Through it all, the baby was sleeping against Jenny's chest, the little bundle secure inside her parka. How could she sleep through such commotion? Was the baby tired, or weakened, or perhaps actually sleeping contentedly? Jenny rose carefully to her feet, until her fur hat touched the cave ceiling. The line of Christmas lights was attached to the right side of the cave at shoulder height, and disappeared upward and around a curve.

Boone reached the bottom of the ravine by following Jenny's electronic cookie crumb trail on her GPS, and her footprints in the snow. These were easily seen with his night vision goggles. The snow was turning to sleet. During his walk, he encountered a few other foot trails, softened at the edges and partly filled in by newly fallen snow.

Jenny McClure was an interesting enigma, and he hoped that he would meet her again. He would, if this morning's operation was successful, and he was able to sneak back to the cave undetected. She was only a teenager but she was already tough, both mentally and physically. She was a survivor. On the other hand, her rescuing the baby showed that she had a soft and human side as well. These days many people would see the orphaned infant as simply a liability. A baby was dead weight that required constant feeding, and might betray your location at any time by unstoppable crying. She was a survivor with a heart, a rare combination a year after the train of disasters that had befallen Western Tennessee.

Boone understood the added danger he faced in traveling to the massacre site, but he felt that the stakes were high enough to risk his life once again. It was likely that the place would be under guard, or at least some kind of observation. Over the past six months that the foreign mercenaries had been operating in Tennessee, he had seen casual cruelty and random murder, but nothing like what the girl had described. This was something new, an elevation of their brutality by an order of magnitude. If he could collect irrefutable proof of the massacre before the bodies were removed or buried, it might make a real difference.

It was darkest in the period between the moonset and dawn. Any hint of starlight was blanketed by unseen clouds. Even the NVGs gave only a dim image, but he was reluctant to turn on their IR illuminator. Foreign soldiers with night observation devices would see the infrared light as clearly as a white flashlight. Once he found Jenny's path leading upward through a tight little canyon, he was in excellent cover. Small erosion channels rose chest high. Soldiers standing watch on top of the opposing bluffs would be sky-lighted by the coming dawn, and he would probably see them first, in time to hide himself.

He was glad that he had come alone. Doug Dolan had become a fair soldier for a city-born Yankee, but he was no SF operator. He had his strengths, but stealthy night patrolling was not among them. Phil Carson was still an unknown quantity. He had been an operator, but that had been many decades ago in Vietnam. Even if they were gung-ho, old guys were too brittle and prone to injury, and carrying out an injured man was not always possible. You just didn't start a mission by taking on that kind of added risk. Zack Tutweiler was probably the best of his motley band of recruits. His father had bragged about Zack's ability to stalk deer with a compound bow. If you could sneak up on a deer close enough to use an arrow, humans were no problem. But Zack's physical stamina was needed to help carry the extra food and gear from the car to the cave.

No, it was best that he came alone tonight. By himself, there was no issue of communicating, either with hand signals or by whispering. By himself, there would be nobody falling down, coughing or noisily banging into things. If Boone could manage to hide his own considerable frame, then he had no worries about anyone else being left exposed to enemy observation, compromising them both. It took weeks of operating together for two men to be able to move fluidly and silently in tandem. It was even harder to learn how to disappear from observation in any terrain. Doug was getting there, he was improving, but tonight he was needed to guide the others to the cave.

And there was one other undeniable reason why Boone felt it was best to go solo tonight: if he was killed, the others might still escape. There was no reason to risk more than one of their lives for a simple photo recon mission. In Iraq and Afghanistan, when he was operating with friendly forces in the area, and with a Quick Reaction Force on standby and Army helicopters above, it was always possible to slug it out in a firefight and wait for rescue. Even if heavily outnumbered, you might fight your way back to a friendly position, or hold out until the cavalry arrived. But this was not the case in Western Tennessee. Now the only cavalry belonged to the damned Cossacks, and all of the air assets were operated by traitors.

If he was engaged in a shootout, he could expect no help, and would find no sanctuary. He would escape clean, or he would die. Having one or two extra shooters along would make little difference when going toe-to-toe against a platoon or more of Kazaks. If he were compromised, the only reinforcements arriving would be more enemy platoons, setting up cordons and sweeping the woods and trails. But one man might avoid detection where two or more might not. And one man could do a photo recon as well as a squad. Or do it even better, since one man left only a single set of tracks.

He wormed his way up the gully, the main walls rising thirty feet above him on both sides. His next task was to find a hidden location to wait for the dawn. Taking pictures before daylight was out of the question. He might as well fire off parachute flares as take flash photographs.

A persistent buzzing woke him up. Bob Bullard fumbled for the red secure phone on his bedside table, and finally grasped it. The glowing digital clock behind the telephone informed him it was 3:47 a.m.

"Talk."

"Director Bullard? John Andretti. I'm the duty officer at Building 1405 tonight."

Andretti? Bullard vaguely recalled the man. Another new guy, Andretti had come over to rural pacification from Customs. For the purposes of paperwork, he was assigned to a non-existent planning commission within Homeland Security. Officially, there was no department of rural pacification. 'Building 1405' was their name for the rural pacification operations center, a name that appeared on no plaque or sign, nor in any directory. The buildings on Fort Campbell were all numbered, and they had taken over building 1405 when the phantom department had been commissioned. "Okay, John, what have you got?"

"I have the commanding officer of the Kazaks on another line, patched over from secure HF radio. You might want to take this one."

"What's it about?"

"Our liaison to the Kazak Battalion is missing. Special Agent Martin Zuberovsky. The Kazaks know him as Major Zinovsky. I had to check the alias file to find that out, but I'm cleared for it."

"You woke me up to tell me somebody's missing? Call me when they find him." Bullard began to put the phone down, yawned deeply, but then started to pull the fragments of his mind together. "Wait a minute. Tell me that again." Bullard's groggy brain was throbbing, one of the aftereffects of half of a bottle of Canadian whisky mixed with a bad imitation of Coca-Cola. What was the security level of this red phone over to the operations center? Andretti had just used a real name and an operational cover name in the same telephone call, a serious breach even on a supposedly secure line. There was no point in making the security lapse worse than it was already during this phone call, but Andretti would get a royal reaming out in person, come Monday morning.

"There was a fire, something like that. Zuberovsky is missing. I have the new commanding officer of the Kazak battalion on the horn. His name is Colonel Burgut. He sounds kind of excited, but it's hard to understand him. His English isn't so great."

"Okay, I'll take it." The phone clicked in his ear, and the Kazak was on the line. "Colonel, who is missing? A fire, you say? I don't understand... Listen, I'll fly down in the morning. Radford County? Give the location to my duty officer. Yes, yes, all right, I'll see you in the morning. Seven o'clock. Good night." He set the red phone back in its cradle. Zuberovsky was missing after a house fire, in Radford County. Bullard did not want to hear anything from that place, not after what he had seen today in the UAV flight center. What could this call mean? Zuberovsky was missing? Parts of his brain were still not working at full speed, the cylinders were not all firing, but he was filled with a sense of foreboding. He remembered watching another house fire at night, years before, near the Potomac River in Virginia. Colleagues had died in that fire. He flopped back into his bed and tried to sleep again, but he could not find rest. Instead, he got up and microwaved a cup of yesterday's leftover coffee. Radford County. He tried to put the place out of his mind.

Zack had been in a few caves before, but none like this. He was in the biggest room of any cave he'd ever seen. It was irregular and oblong, about forty by twenty feet at the bottom, its craggy roof arching above them. The rocky floor was sloped at an angle, not exactly difficult to walk on, but you had to watch your step or you could slip. The floor of the cave consisted mostly of jumbled boulders, from shoebox size to mailbox size. It looked like someone had moved a lot of the smaller stones, filling gaps between the larger ones. This made the surface a little more usable. Planks and pieces of plywood filled other spaces. The ceiling was more than fifteen feet above them, and it was not hard to imagine more boulders falling loose and crashing down. Zack reckoned that short of another major earthquake, the ones still overhead would stay up there for a few million more years. It smelled of rock dust, but otherwise the air was fresh.

This big room was nothing like the narrow tunnels they had crept through to get to it. In some of them, you had to hold onto the yellow guide rope and walk along a narrow ledge. His flashlight had showed that water was running in a slot ten or twelve feet below them. If you fell into one of those cracks, you might not get out. A string of miniature Christmas lights hung below the yellow hand rope, illuminating the way. Moving deep into the cavern was a little frightening, but also, somehow, exhilarating.

The main room felt safe and secure. It was cool but not cold, and as silent as a tomb. A level area had been built of scrap lumber, mostly from wood pallets and pieces of plywood. This floored area was about the size of a large living room, maybe fifteen by twenty feet. There was a dome-shaped two-man tent set up at the far end. Most of the area was stacked with metal and plastic boxes and crates. Four folding chairs were set up around a folding card table. A bare electric bulb hanging above the table provided the primary illumination in the room. A stationary bicycle and some heavy dumbbells and free weights could be seen just off the wooden floor.

Doug Dolan addressed them, once they were all inside the main room. "Okay, this is it, the end of the line. This is going to be our home for the next few days at least. It won't get any hotter or colder. It's about 60 degrees, and it stays like this pretty much all the time. We can't build a fire big enough to heat this place. We'd just smoke ourselves out anyway, so instead, we'll heat ourselves from the inside out. I'll get a pot of water boiling. After the baby is fed, then we'll get something warm inside us. We've got some instant coffee, instant hot chocolate, instant soup, and instant freeze-dried meal packs. Civilian stuff, and military MREs. I'll boil the water, and you guys can decide what you want to have. I'll show you where everything is.

"Once you've had your fill, you can sleep if you want to. Day and night don't have any meaning in here, so rest whenever you can. I'll set up a watch rotation; somebody has to be awake all the time. Jenny and the baby can take the tent. There's already a foam mattress in there, and a sleeping bag. It's a lot cleaner in the tent, and you can have some privacy. The rest of us will sleep on the wood floor, on camping mats. They're rolled up over there. Sleeping bags too. Oh—there are some spare uniforms and some other clothes in that metal bin. They're not exactly the cleanest but they should be dry. Take your pick, whatever fits you. The house batteries are at full charge, but with the lights on, somebody will have to ride the bike later on. That's how we make electricity: we ride the bike. Any questions?"

"Yeah," asked Zack. "Are there bats in here?"

"Nope, no bats, but there are some bugs. Some beetles, and centipedes sometimes. You can't rule out snakes either. I haven't seen any, but Boone said he has. Shake your shoes out before you put them on, and try not to drop any crumbs or we'll get rats. That's one of the reasons Boone built this wooden floor: the bugs and rats."

The maze of erosion channels at the bottom of the ravine hid him perfectly from every direction except directly overhead. Boone moved only a few steps each minute, then stopped and sank down, listening and watching. He intentionally dragged his feet to obscure his footprints, trying to cause his tracks to appear to be the product of natural snowmelt running down the gully. He reached the bodies just as dawn was beginning to lighten the sky in the east. After a few minutes spent looking at the killing field from below, he stripped off his night goggles and placed them into his vest's big left side cargo pocket. It was sleeting by then, terrible weather, but perfect for him. Nobody in his right mind would be out in such icy rain. Ninety-nine out of a hundred soldiers ordered to stand watch in these conditions would find a way to hide in vehicles, or would at least crouch under improvised lean-to poncho shelters. Only with officers or NCOs right behind them would soldiers even pretend to stand watch in such weather. In his long experience, this was true even of well-trained and disciplined troops. Some might consider his outlook cynical, others would call it realistic.

Trust did not come easily to Boone Vikersun. He had come to this isolated ravine based on the barely credible story of a girl he had met just a few hours before. He knew that his actions over the past six months had hurt the foreign invaders, and they had more than sufficient reason to concoct a ruse to lead him into a trap. Boone could not shake the lingering suspicion that he was being lured into some kind of an ambush—until he saw the bodies. Jenny McClure had told the truth. Where it widened out, the bottom of the ravine was full of intertwined layers of bodies, from one side of the gully to the other. It was obvious that they had been shot while standing up on the west rim of the ravine, to his left as he looked up it. The snow did not cover them evenly; here and there torsos, arms, legs and some faces were partially visible.

It was still too dark to take decent non-flash pictures with the digital cameras. Meanwhile the cold rain was making millions of tiny craters in the snow, melting it away. Crazy temperature swings were typical in Tennessee, and he wasn't surprised by this rain at dawn. There were still a few inches of slushy snow. It could be washed away entirely, or the temperature could plunge again and leave a frozen crust of ice on the bodies. He knew that if he tried to collect physical evidence from the bodies right away he would have to disturb the snow. Fresh tracks among the corpses would make his presence obvious, if guards examined the area after daylight. He would wait a little longer, until there was more daylight for the cameras and, he hoped, less snow left on the ground for leaving footprints.

The temperature was hovering right around freezing. He was well hidden in the bottom of a narrow erosion gully, his gore-tex parka and pants and boots keeping him dry enough and relatively warm. Warm enough. He'd live. It seemed like he'd spent half his life shivering on the edge of hypothermia. The other half he'd spent broiling in the Middle East. A professional soldier did not choose an easy or a comfortable life.

Nobody could see him in this spot, unless they literally stumbled over him. Only an eye in the sky could find him. He could wait a while longer; it would be worth it to take sharp photos in natural light just after dawn. A thick coil of root protruded from the mud bank for him to perch his butt on, and he settled down to wait, his arms folded across his chest, gloved hands buried under opposite armpits. Cold rain trickled off the front of his hood and down his face, so he pulled the drawstring tighter. Inside theoretically waterproof and insulated boots, his feet ached.

Discomfort was an old acquaintance he knew all too well. He mentally subdivided and compartmentalized the various regions of cold and hunger his body felt, and pushed them away from consciousness. This allowed his thoughts to roam free of his physical constraints. If he stayed in this position for too long, he'd begin shivering uncontrollably, an early sign of hypothermia. He calculated that he would be okay for another half hour, until full light. At least his head was warm, inside of his thickly knitted wool hat and beneath his parka's waterproof hood.

Not too many people had his knack for isolating and ignoring pain. The past year of widespread deprivation had proven this true. The vast majority of Tennesseans had demonstrated a willingness to cooperate with anybody who would promise to bring them gasoline, home heating oil and electricity. Many of his fellow soldiers had stayed on active duty, even if it meant collaborating with the foreign enemies. Special Forces NCOs were being recruited to serve with the foreign units as guides and liaisons. To their credit none willingly volunteered, at least not before Boone had slipped away from Fort Campbell. The president himself had invited in the so-called foreign volunteers. Jamal Tambor gave collaboration with the foreigners his official blessing, and most of America's soldiers and police stayed on for the ride, and the guaranteed paycheck.

It wasn't hard to understand their motives. Most of them were married and had families to worry about. Boone's wife had divorced him a decade before, finding the long separations caused by his constant deployments too much to endure. Thankfully, this had happened before they had children, and he had never remarried. It was easy to understand why soldiers with families did not go AWOL, the way he had done six months before, when the first foreign battalions were sent into Tennessee. Even in the midst of the Greater Depression, soldiers and police were paid regularly, and they received top priority for food and gasoline coupons, housing permits and medical care. Instead of shivering in a rainy ditch, they could retain most of their old lifestyle, put food on their families' tables, and sustain the illusory promise of an eventual government pension. It was easy to understand how they could rationalize their decision to work alongside the foreign occupiers, or at least to tolerate their presence.

Anyway, for the most part the Special Forces had been sidelined during the present low-intensity civil war. The A-teams had been benched. The Green Berets were considered "unreliable" by Washington. If they were sent into the so-called unpacified areas, it was an open question as to whether they would fight for the government or for the rebels. But if these unpredictable specops warriors were forced out of the military, they might put their skills to use in ways that ran counter to Washington's aims. So the Green Berets and other special operations units were parked on base in garrison, paid on time in almost worthless currency, and asked to do nothing.

Last summer Boone had been in North Carolina, at Fort Bragg's Special Warfare Center for a three-week leadership course, which was in reality a mandatory political correctness indoctrination class. The course title was "Special Forces in the New Global Cooperation Structure." The class gave him an ulcer; it was almost the last straw, and it helped him to make his decision. After the course, he returned to his home in Clarksville, Tennessee, outside Fort Campbell. He quietly began to put his plan into action, stealthily accumulating needed equipment, telling no one. He departed Bragg after he had seen the televised images of Pakistanis, Kazaks and other foreign soldiers being trucked and bused into Tennessee. The mainstream media television programs showed these "peacekeeping volunteers" rebuilding bridges and schools, operating health clinics and passing out food supplies.

This was propaganda, meant for the naïve masses outside the earthquake zone. Boone knew from his web of active and reserve military contacts that the foreign troops were sent in because American soldiers would not fire on their fellow Americans, not with enough gusto to bring Tennessee and Kentucky back under solid government control. American soldiers wanted nothing to do with searching for illegal firearms and rounding up fellow citizens for internal exile away from their home counties. Half of the National Guard and active duty forces ordered into Tennessee either had failed to muster for the deployment, or had deserted soon after.

Boone misinterpreted this reluctance among American soldiers to obey the president's orders as the beginning of an active resistance movement. He had naïvely believed that after the introduction of foreign soldiers into Tennessee, he would soon be leading his own guerrilla band of patriots. He thought that by this point in the war he would be leading a rebel operational detachment consisting of at least a dozen former specops troops, one of many similar groups of freedom fighters taking on the foreign enemies. But he had never mustered more than four semi-qualified troops at any one time, troops who were willing to take part in offensive direct-action missions. His tiny pick-up squads had conducted successful sniper attacks, set roadside bombs, and made a few snatches of foreign troops and American traitors. He knew that other American patriots had been sniping at foreign targets of opportunity. He heard the echoes of their high-powered rifles, and later he heard the rumors of foreign soldiers and domestic traitors who had been shot from afar.

This unorganized resistance had faded away when the revenge attacks began in the early autumn of last year. Now sniper attacks brought immediate harsh reprisals, which alienated the local population against the few remaining resistance fighters. The Cossacks and other foreign units were not restricted by genteel American rules of engagement. When a foreign soldier was shot, his mates went into the nearest occupied dwelling and dragged out its inhabitants. Sometimes these unfortunates were executed on the spot as suspected terrorists or as terrorist sympathizers, and sometimes they simply disappeared. Five Americans killed in reprisal for every dead Cossack, Nigerian or Pakistani was too high a price to pay. If an insurgent fired a shot from near his own property, he risked the lives of his family. If he took a shot from somewhere else, he only transferred the danger to the innocent inhabitants of the nearest dwellings. The undeclared policy of reprisals led to terrible moral and ethical dilemmas for the few active insurgents. Most of them gave up the fight rather than see their neighbors murdered in reprisal attacks.

In the end, Boone's guerrilla strikes were merely a series of uncoordinated pinpricks, largely because there was no way for different rebel groups to communicate effectively, or even to know of each other's existence. Their enemies, both the foreign occupiers and the domestic collaborators, owned the entire electromagnetic spectrum. Hand-delivered messages and dead drops were too slow and unreliable a method of communication. The problem of establishing timely and effective communications between insurgent groups was a nut he had failed to crack. Without secure communications, Boone had not been able to mount more than isolated nuisance attacks. This was a factor he had been unprepared to deal with. During his military career, he had taken the ready availability of secure communications for granted. It was a very different ball game to operate as an insurgent without logistics, resupply or secure radio communications.

Six months after deserting the 5th Special Forces Group at Fort Campbell, Boone was down to leading one drafted Army private, one old Vietnam veteran, and a couple of teenage civilians. He laughed, scattering sleet from his beard. When crunch time had come, most Tennesseans had been content to wait in long lines for a booklet of government ration cards. Apparently, fighting for freedom was not high on many people's lists of priorities, compared to assuring themselves a supply of food and electricity. Maybe this should not have come as a surprise.

Radford County and the surrounding area had been among the few exceptions. After the earthquakes the federal government had put the region dead last on the list for recovery assistance, and the locals had said screw you right back, and gone on living without government help. And now look what their stubborn independent streak had brought them: death in a ravine. The proud nails that had stood up to the government...had been hammered down flat.

Even in Radford County, people for the most part were only willing to defend their own neighborhoods. Very few were willing to take the next step, to go on the offensive and violently resist the foreign "peacekeepers." It was too risky. Wives and children needed their fathers. Basic survival needs consumed all of their waking attention. There were too many random checkpoints, and always the threat of an unseen missile-armed UAV staring down at them, or an attack helicopter popping up over the next rise. Guerrilla attacks were countered with bloody reprisals, and gradually most of the people turned against the handful of active insurgents, blaming the rebel fighters for the revenge attacks instead of the foreign soldiers who carried them out. Boone thought of this as the Stockholm syndrome in reverse. Fewer and fewer doors were open to him, while his fear of being ratted out by informants grew. It took only one weak member of a family to go to the enemy, seeking to collect a blood-money bounty payment, paid in red TEDs or gasoline ration coupons.

Over time, the people had become worn down by hunger and cold, and had slowly bought into the government propaganda. They came to believe that active resistance to the foreign occupation would only mean a delay of the day that the bridges would be reopened, the roads graded and repaved, and the electricity reconnected.

Despite the steady diet of propaganda, some of the Radford County locals had supported his cause with food, and a place to hide and rest up when he arrived at their back doors after midnight. And as a reward for their defiant patriotism, most of the members of his network were dead now, lying frozen in the snow a few yards above him. So that's it, it's finally over, he thought. Active resistance is finished in Western Tennessee. If there was anyone else still actively opposing the foreign enemies in Western Tennessee, he had no way of knowing it. Sitting in the icy rain below the bodies of his neighbors, Boone Vikersun was the last guerrilla fighter.

Bob Bullard's blue and white Eurocopter was waiting on the runway apron when he arrived at 6:30 a.m. He was dressed in a khaki thermal snowmobile suit, the pants tucked into calf-height black rubber boots. The sleek civilian helicopter was dwarfed by rows of Blackhawks and Chinooks stationed at Fort Campbell's Sabre Army Airfield. His pilot was waiting in the right seat; the helo's turbine engine was already spooling up. As usual, he sat in the empty left front seat. There were no copilot controls in the civilian Eurocopters. It was a mystery to him why pilots sat in the right seat in helicopters but on the other side in fixed-wing aircraft. He handed the pilot a slip of paper with the GPS coordinates provided by the Kazaks, and when he slipped on his headset he told him, "No filming today, Jack. No video, no audio, no GPS tracking—nothing. No record." The Eurocopters could automatically be set to record everything beneath them, with both visual and infrared cameras, and that was the last thing Bullard wanted on this day. Three bodyguards in black and Jeff Sinclair, his assistant, sat behind him in the passenger area, and they lifted off.

The 150-mile flight from Fort Campbell south to Radford County roughly followed the course of the Tennessee River in reverse. The helicopter crossed the river several times as it meandered northward across the state on its final big looping turn back up from Alabama, on its way to meet the Ohio River. With the twin failures of the Tennessee and Pickwick dams after the first big quake, the water level in the western part of the Tennessee River had dropped more than fifty feet. Six hundred square miles of artificial lake had disappeared downstream in a calamity of Biblical proportions, washing away bridges already damaged by the earthquake. This left only the original Tennessee River channel snaking between wide mud banks that in places stretched for miles across, revealing entire drowned forests. The two earthen dams were designed and built during the Great Depression of the 1930s, and they had lasted three-quarters of a century. Well, Bullard mused, eventually they'd be rebuilt during the current Greater Depression. Once the region was fully pacified, those two reconstruction projects would mean work for thousands of men that would last for years. Pacifying the region so that the work could begin was his contribution to the overall mission.

The helicopter banked and swept inland from the river, with dawn just breaking in the east. The Kazaks had sounded both guarded and uncertain in their radio calls, last night and this morning. The only thing he was reasonably sure that they had communicated accurately were the GPS coordinates of this flight's destination. Like most of his foreign battalions, the Kazaks were practically useless without their American liaisons. Martin Zuberovsky had just been assigned to the contract battalion, and now he'd gone missing, only a few miles from the scene of yesterday's events around the town of Mannville. Bob Bullard hated these kinds of coincidences.

The pilot flew toward the GPS coordinates provided by the Kazaks. He had not even entered the latitude and longitude numbers into the helicopter's onboard navigational system as a go-to point; instead, he clipped the slip of paper to his console and flew manually. Evidently, he had taken the admonition about no flight records seriously, and Bullard was pleased with his attention to detail. Icy rain clicked against the helicopter's windscreen and streamed back. Their destination was a snow-covered hilltop, where an old house was finishing the process of burning down into its foundation. A plume of gray smoke and steam marked the location. Bullard ordered his pilot to orbit the knob a few times while he studied the situation from a thousand feet up. A circle of twenty or so widely spaced oak trees made a bull's-eye a hundred yards across, with the burned-down house in the center. The pile of timber and charcoal was still smoldering, hours later. The snow had melted near the ruins, exposing a ring of brown grass. Obviously, any response from the local fire department was out of the question. There were no more operational fire departments in this part of West Tennessee.

A pair of four-wheeled armored security vehicles was parked near the top of the destroyed home's driveway. A large green military truck with a canvas-covered cargo area was parked below it. Last night's snow had accumulated to a few inches, but even though it was still overcast, the day was warmer and it was already melting away in patches. The wind had swung around to the south, and it was raining. He could not figure out Tennessee weather to save his life. It wasn't San Diego, that was for sure.

The pilot set the helicopter down between the oaks and the former home site, where the ground was nearly level. Snow and ash whipped outward from the chopper's downdraft. His retinue of bodyguards and his assistant climbed down with him onto the snowy field, and spread out around him.

The Kazak officers stepped down from one of the green camouflage-painted ASVs; it was a stretched-out commander's version without a turret, but with plenty of extra antennas. They walked halfway around the burned home to meet the Americans. Their new commander, Colonel Arman Burgut, did not have any of the problematic Colonel Yerzhan Jibek's dash or charisma. Colonel Burgut suited Bullard much better. Burgut was shorter than his former commander, at no more than five seven or eight. This meant that Bullard could look down at him, unlike the taller and, frankly, more handsome Colonel Jibek, now deceased. Burgut had a half-Asian face, and a long mustache that covered his upper lip and reached nearly to his chin on both sides, in the Kazak style. He was wearing the Russian-style camouflage uniform and jacket, mostly brown with bold black zigzags, topped with a fur hat. Unlike the late Colonel Jibek, his successor made no pretense of culture or refinement. Burgut's English was rudimentary at best, and his knowledge of American customs and culture was nil.

Never one for small talk, Director Bullard got right to the point. "Colonel Burgut, where is my liaison officer, Major Zinovsky?" This was the alias that Special Agent Martin Zuberovsky was using while attached to the Kazak battalion.

Burgut spoke haltingly, struggling to form comprehensible sentences. "Ah, General Blair, good it is to seeing you again. After very succeeded operation as we conducted yesterday, it is much I regret to inform to you that your officer is…he is missed. Missing. I am thinking that he is there, under." The Kazak officer indicated the smoking heap of timbers and ash with a hand sweep. They were standing near enough to the pit to hear steam hissing from the still-burning main beams somewhere below. The harsh stink of burnt paint and plastics assaulted their noses.

"Are you sure that he was inside the house during the fire?"

"Yes, I think…very sure."

"How many of your men were lost?"

"Praise be unto…that is…thankfully, we lost no men. All my officers were able to remove selves from house quickly."

"I don't understand. Then why is my liaison officer missing?"

"He…Major Zinovsky was first to go up steps to number two level of house. The fire had begin—had began—on number two level. I saw this with my two eyes, standing where now we stand. There were places on number two level to make a fire, with small parts of tree, that is to say, wood. To give heat to bedrooms. Word in English is fire place? Yes, fire place. Big fire in house, I think came from small accident of fire place. I do not know why Major Zinovsky not did remove self from house. Frankly, General Blair, some of my officers were taking much strong drink. I think perhaps Major Zinovsky have taken too much whisky made from corn." Colonel Burgut mimed lifting a bottle to his lips, grinned and rolled his eyes. "White thunder is called this whisky, you are knowing of?"

"White lightning. The homemade corn whisky is called white lightning. Thunder is the noise. Tennessee is famous for it. The whisky, I mean."

"Yes. Too much of this corn whisky can make even the strong man go blind of eyes."

"Colonel Burgut, have you found any remains in the fire?"

"Remains? I am not understanding."

"Human remains. A corpse. A dead body."

"General Blair, you must understand, is not possible to examine into fire. Even now house burns, and we have no machines for such work."

Bullard could see his point. Looking for human remains in that mountain of smoldering debris would be useless. "Okay, Colonel, let's discuss yesterday's operation. Your mission was to remove the remaining population from the southern part of Radford County. How would you evaluate your progress so far?"

"Well, first day of operation was big success. Very big success. We shall conclude operation through next two or maybe three days. Problem is now not to having liaison officer. That makes big problem for radio communication with headquarters of Fort Campbell. Other problem is ammunition. Kazak armored vehicles are having almost no 40 millimeter linked ammunition. Last week was sent not correct ammunition, was sent 40 millimeter for American rifle grenade launcher. We are needing correct 40 millimeter linked grenade ammunition for armored vehicles."

Bullard ignored these last requests. The M117 Guardian armored security vehicles also had a .50 caliber heavy machine gun on their turrets—that was enough firepower for running roughshod over a few barely armed rebels. Supplying them with any 40mm grenades was a mistake; that level of destructive ordnance was clearly beyond their role as volunteer "military police." Anyway, he wasn't concerned about what the Kazaks wanted; that wasn't why he had flown down here. "Where are the people from Mannville now, Colonel?" He already knew where they were, he had watched the operation via video feed from a Predator UAV, but he wanted to study the Kazak while he answered. He wanted to test Burgut's ability to withstand any problematic questioning in the future. Two Kazak commanders dying in rapid succession might make it difficult to find the next replacement, but there was no doubt that Burgut would have an accident when the time was right. Until then he needed to be able to keep his mouth shut tight.

Colonel Burgut answered nonchalantly, "They are…not far from here."

"Really? I would like to go there now, and see them for myself."

"General Blair, there is not need to see them."

"But I insist. We can fly there in my helicopter, right now. We'll be back in half an hour. Let's go, Colonel." Bullard whispered to Jeff, his assistant. As planned, his bodyguards physically blocked Burgut's two staff officers as their commander was shepherded toward the aircraft. Bullard had read the situation correctly, surmising that the new Kazak leader would not want to cause a face-losing scene by resisting his entreaties to go for a ride on the executive helicopter.

Only the Kazak and Bob Bullard climbed aboard the chopper for the short trip; the pilot had remained in his seat. For this hop, the two men sat in the plush rear passenger seats. His pilot had also come up from the ATF, "Agents That Fly," and Bullard trusted him as much as he trusted any man. Which was not much, but hopefully, enough. Because the pilot was about to see what had happened in a gully outside the small town of Mannville.

Once they were aloft, Bob Bullard envisioned a freak aviation accident taking place a month or two in the future. Perhaps when the same pilot was flying Colonel Burgut to a rural pacification program meeting at Fort Campbell. It could easily be explained as a "lucky shot" from a rebel .50 caliber sniper rifle, fired from the ground. The famous "golden BB" was always a threat to helicopters flying too low over rebel territory. If Burgut and the pilot both went down in flames, that would be taking two birds with one stone. It would not be the first time Bullard had planted a small bomb to solve a problem. Sometimes the old ways were the best.

Boone was suspended in a semi-trance, sitting on his root-chair with his back against a wall of frozen mud. He was still more or less dry in his gore-tex parka and trousers, but not warm by any stretch. The snow had turned to sleet and then to rain by the time it was light enough to see. For more than two decades, he had spent nights like this, hovering between dreams and memories, cataloging his life's joys and regrets, ticking down the slowly dragging minutes and hours until the earth's turning would bring another day. Most of the snow was dissolving before his eyes, and water was beginning to trickle down the erosion channels under his feet. When daylight finally came he carefully stood, turning very slowly, scanning above him for any watchers.

He had put his night goggles away for the day, but it was still too early to take decent photographs. The ravine was in deep shadow. He stood at the bottom of the massacre site, looking uphill. He would have to climb a final slippery wall of mud and ice to get right among the bodies. As the snow had begun to disappear, the extent of the massacre was becoming clear. There were hundreds of dead in the ravine. The count would never be more than guesswork until the bodies could be removed one by one. It was impossible to know how many were buried in layers beneath the ones he could see.

The victims were killed in whatever clothes they had been wearing when they were captured. The men were on top. They had their hands bound behind their backs with black nylon flex-cuffs. They must have been brought to the ravine last. He could see well enough to begin to collect some wallets for identification purposes, if these had not been removed before the victims had been shot. He would have to move bodies to search for any of the new ID badges or old driver's licenses or credit cards. Radford County was an "unpacified" region, and for the most part the people had never submitted to wearing the ID badges.

Boone was climbing among the bodies at the lower end of the killing site when he heard the diesel engine and recognized the sound of Army five-ton trucks. These heavy-duty all-wheel-drive monsters would have no problem negotiating the slippery dirt roads he had walked while following Jenny's GPS track. It enraged him to think that somewhere, American Quislings helped to maintain these U.S. Army trucks, and then turned them over to the foreign occupiers. Turned them over for use on operations like this massacre. Many Americans would accept any kind of paying employment during this economic depression. No doubt, if questioned they would deny any knowledge of what their trucks were being used for. They would pretend to have clean hands. Many, Boone knew, were active duty soldiers putting in a few more years toward their pensions. Sometimes he hated them more than he hated the foreign enemies. But then, he didn't have a family to feed.

The trucks were not far off, less than a mile away and getting closer. Most likely they were back on the asphalt two-lane road that led to Shiloh and then down into Mississippi. If they were carrying platoons of soldiers on a return trip to the massacre site, he might be trapped in this place, hemmed in on both sides by icy mud walls. The trucks might even follow the route he had taken, and if so, they might see his tracks. A few hours had passed since he had walked that path, and the snow had turned to rain since then. Instead of his prints being filled in with new snow, the rain could actually wash through his compressed tracks, leaving a perfect trail for the enemy to follow.

One of the two truck engines stopped. He guessed that the motors belonged to five-ton, six-wheel-drive Medium Tactical Vehicles. These military trucks could be relieving sentries at a checkpoint, or dropping off a patrol. Five minutes later the noisy diesel started up again, and gradually the engine sounds diminished until he could no longer hear either truck. He had to assume that more troops had been dropped off, and not far away. Perhaps a full platoon of Cossack mercenaries.

14

The short flight took only five minutes. The countryside was pleasantly rolling, with dozens of fingerlike streams dividing woods, pastures and farmland. There was still some snow on the ground, melting under steady rain. Smoke curled from a few chimneys. Cows and horses continued their difficult grazing, ignoring the helicopter. They were not far from the Shiloh battlefield, on the Tennessee River. To Bob Bullard, it almost looked like one of those Currier and Ives dinner plates showing a New England scene from long ago. The blue and white Eurocopter set down in the clearing above the ravine, where the buses had brought their passengers for a one-way trip. Bullard had seen it already, from 15,000 feet up, bounced back from the Predator's cameras. The helicopter's downdraft blasted wet snow in all directions until the rotors stopped.

Bullard hopped down lightly, walked directly to the edge of the drop-off, and looked over into the gully. Most of the bottom was still in dark shadow, and not much of the snow had melted down there. The bodies were half-covered in a white mantle, revealing a random landscape of arms, colorfully dressed torsos and some shattered faces and heads. The bodies had rolled and fallen down the steep slope, and accumulated in heaps at the bottom. There must have been hundreds of them, in a continuous mass that was at least fifteen feet across, running more than thirty yards along the bottom of the gully. The snow had fallen after the massacre, so the scene was still partly masked from direct observation. He imagined that from high altitude, it might appear to be a trash dump.

Sidney Krantz, the president's special adviser and liaison for the rural pacification program, had said that Jamal Tambor wanted results, and he wanted them fast. The president wanted Western Tennessee completely pacified or completely empty, one or the other. Mannville was the central node of resistance in Radford County, and with it depopulated, insurgency in the rest of the region would crumble. Well, there was no faster way to depopulate a rural county, Bullard had to admit. The results below him in the ravine spoke for themselves. Striking at the town on market day was the logical way to accomplish the mission.

He had assumed that Special Agent Zuberovsky was going to have some of the residents forcibly relocated to the FEMA camp in Jackson, Tennessee, and the rest scattered and harassed into leaving the county...but not murdered wholesale. Of course, for obvious reasons, these types of instructions were never put into writing or transmitted electronically, so there was always a risk of miscommunication.

Raiding the illegal black market had been Martin Zuberovsky's overt mission, and with it put out of business, the dead-enders in Radford County would have been forced to come to the government relocation centers for food. That had been one of the basic plans that had worked quite well over the last few months, if not quite as quickly as President Tambor desired. Zuberovsky and the Kazaks had clearly taken his order to wipe out resistance in Radford County as rapidly as possible much too literally and had far exceeded his orders. Well, what was done was done. He couldn't personally control every detail of every operation in every unpacified county in Tennessee. But the bodies remained…hundreds of bodies. They were a problem.

The Kazak commander stood beside him, a look of disgust on his round Eurasian face.

"Colonel Burgut, you do understand that your battalion was never instructed to do this…thing we see here."

"But General Blair, your liaison officer, it was of his instruction. He said that it was of your order to smash the market and destroy the rebels—"

"No, that's wrong! All wrong. He was not given those orders. It was a mistake—*his* mistake. This is America, dammit—not Chechnya or Kosovo!"

"But General Blair, you told us we must finish job, and permanently remove all peoples from County of Radford. Permanently. Major Zinovsky said to me that—"

"But not this way. Not this way!" Bullard gritted his teeth and stared down over the edge. "Well, what's done is done. It's finished. It can't be changed. But Colonel, there is a problem: these bodies. Why haven't they been covered? The snow is already melting; soon they will be completely visible. I don't understand why they were not covered. What was your plan for covering them, and why was it not completed?"

"Before operation, we located earthmover at business near Mannville town. Was big part of plan. Caterpillar; very good machine, number one earthmover. It is already on special lorry—on truck-trailer. We had plan to cover bodies yesterday, but Kazak driver could not start this special truck to bring Caterpillar to here location. Yes, we had very good plan for complete operation. Horses and trucks for Kazak soldiers, two autobus for transport of peoples, Caterpillar earthmover, everything to as needed. A very good logistic. But important parts are removed from truck engine, needed for to bring earthmover to here location. Was impossible to know this problem before operation. Impossible."

"Well, you need to get the job finished, and get them covered up. Bury them deep, very deep, and plant grass and trees on top. Move some small pine trees like those over there. This place must disappear."

"We are finding necessary parts for engine of big trailer truck. After, we will bring Caterpillar and push earth over this...small valley." Colonel Burgut extended his arms forward level with his shoulders, and made a smoothing gesture with his hands. "When job is finished, small valley will be flat, and peoples will be many meters under earth."

"Good. And when will this happen, Colonel?"

"Perhaps tomorrow. Perhaps next day after. We must locate parts for truck engine, for bringing earthmover." Colonel Burgut gave a foolish smile and pointed his finger down, indicating the dead below them. "Owner of business of earthmover and special truck, he is perhaps down there now, with other dead peoples. Now he cannot help us in finding important engine parts for earthmover truck. We must have to discover missing engine parts in Jackson, Tennessee, if possible."

"Tomorrow is too late, Colonel. I want it all covered by tonight."

"I will try, I will—"

"Colonel Burgut, you will do more than try! You will personally see to it that this job is finished today. I'll have the parts flown down to fix the truck right away. One way or the other, this ravine—this small valley—it will be covered with dirt today. Covered with dirt, and planted with trees like a forest."

"I have factory number of parts from truck motor. If we obtain correct parts, we can repair truck very quickly, and bring earthmover today to here."

"That's good, that's very important. And no more jobs like this one, all right? Make people leave, frighten them. Shoot a few of them if they don't obey, burn their houses... Do what you have to do to make them run away. But no more 'small valleys' like this one. Do you understand?"

"Yes, I understand. As soon as Caterpillar can bring here on special truck, valley will be covering with much earth, and many small fir trees."

"Notify me as soon as it's done."

"I shall call to you with secure radio. But to be sure, this...this was complete idea of Major Zinovsky." Colonel Burgut swept his right hand toward the corpse-filled chasm, and let it drop to his side. "From words of Major Zinovsky, we thought operation was also idea from you."

"Okay. What's done is done. And Major Zinovsky is dead in the fire, right?"

"Yes, very dead. Very dead." Burgut slumped his shoulders and sighed. "General Blair, I am wanting to finish job in Tennessee. When Kazaks are leaving Tennessee? When we are leaving, to go to Montana and Wyoming, as was said before?"

"I don't know. June, I think. When we're completely finished here in Tennessee."

"Good. Good." Colonel Burgut slowly shook his head. "Kazaks not so much loving Tennessee. Very too many small farms. Very too many small forest. Very too many rifles, very too many snipers. Truth, General Blair. I am not thinking is possible to, as you say, *pacify* Tennessee to one hundred percent. Only with many small valleys, like here today, can we pacify Tennessee to one hundred percent. If no more small valleys possible, then best if Kazaks are to leaving Tennessee. Montana, I think better is for Kazaks. Big wide country, like Kazakhstan."

Boone was on his knees crouching between frozen bodies, looking in purses, patting for wallets. Even today, with no credit cards or ATM machines, and with paper money damn near useless, people still carried wallets and identification cards. At least the adults did. Between collecting IDs, he snapped pictures with his own digital camera, and with the dead American traitor's camera for insurance. He snapped wide-angle shots of the entire ravine, as well as close-ups of individual victims. Most had been shot through their torsos, but there were also many limb and head wounds. As a soldier, he was used to seeing the many ways that rifle bullets could destroy a human body. At least in this cold weather the bodies did not smell, and they had not even begun to bloat or blacken. They were blue-gray against the white snow, but otherwise perfectly preserved. He gently brushed a little snow away when he needed to take a face shot for positive identification.

The bodies were frozen in place, locked together like a 3-D puzzle. He estimated that they were piled five or six deep at the center of the ravine, with more on the western side, where they had tumbled down the steep bank. The zone of death was perhaps twenty feet wide by a hundred long, running up the length of the gorge. He thought he could climb up the left side of the ravine, to where the shootings had taken place. He could collect spent brass shells for forensic identification, and take some better pictures of the entire scene from a downward angle. He was considering a route up the steep slope of frozen earth and snow when he heard the distant whine of a turbine and the faint beating of rotors. The sound was not that of any military model that he was familiar with, but it was growing in strength, rapidly flying closer.

He was fifteen feet up into the zone of death, and he had to make a decision. Infrared detection was an ever-present fear. If the helicopter made a direct overflight and it was equipped with an infrared camera, his warm body would glow like a burning torch against the frozen bodies. Perhaps they would think he was a wounded massacre victim, who had been shot but not killed. He stepped as carefully as he could, his feet slipping between bodies and limbs. He was nearly at the bottom edge of the field of corpses when the chopper appeared among the leafless tree branches, scattering crows before its approach. Now visual detection by the aircrew was the greatest danger. Motion would give him away, so he could only drop between bodies and play possum, hoping they were not using infrared at all in the daylight.

Boone turned on his left side, facing uphill. Most of his body was below the level of two male corpses. He had not recognized them. Their swollen, blackened hands were tied behind their backs. The helo continued on a direct course, came to a hover, and landed just out of sight above him. Snow being blown over the top of the ravine indicated the nearness of the helicopter. The blades wound down as the turbine engine slowed. He didn't move, trying to blend in among the bodies, feeling conspicuously uncovered by snow. He wondered if his footprints in the slushy snow were obvious.

The morning temperature was just above freezing, a light drizzle was falling. Once the helicopter had shut down, the ravine and the surrounding country were perfectly quiet. The remaining snow dampened any sound. Boone lay absolutely still, relying on his position between two bodies to conceal him.

Then he heard the voices, two male voices. He could not make out what was being said, but he could tell that they were speaking English. One voice was plainly American, the other unmistakably foreign. But not Spanish, so he was not from the North American Legion. Perhaps a Kazak, as Jenny McClure had said. Boone slowly raised his head, just enough to observe the top of the western slope with one eye. He was no more than a hundred feet from where two men were talking. His camera was already in his left hand, open and ready. Did he dare to risk it? The wide-angle lens could be pointed in their general direction and it might capture the outlines of the two men, from the shoulders up. The high-resolution camera image could be blown up and cropped, and might even reveal something about these two morning-after visitors. Their uniforms at least, and perhaps some identifying insignia.

Boone gradually raised his forearm at the elbow, and slowly turned the camera. He depressed the shutter button with his thumb. The camera seemed ridiculously loud as it clicked and readied itself for another picture. He took another photo, and a third. The voices stopped, the men disappeared. After a minute he could hear the helicopter engine spinning, the blades coming up to speed. Then it lifted into the sky, briefly crossing the ravine as it departed. He snapped another picture, hopefully freezing the blue executive helicopter in mid-flight above him.

He waited ten minutes before moving, and then he very slowly sat up and looked around him. The big ravens had returned. They were now making exploratory flights into the ravine, flapping and hopping among the corpses with wings outstretched. He checked the camera. It was hard to be certain judging by the miniature digital images, but he might have captured usable pictures of the two men, and their helicopter. This was enough; there was no point in continuing his inspection tour of dead bodies. He had collected more than twenty driver's licenses and other ID cards, and he had an even greater number of photos stored on the two cameras. It was enough to prove that the massacre had taken place. Boone was at the point of preparing to stand and depart, to backtrack down out of the ravine, when he heard voices again, louder this time.

They sounded foreign, that was certain. They were definitely not speaking English, so they were not Americans. He dropped back into his slot between the two male corpses, in time to see more visitors peering down upon the little valley of death, their heads clearly skylighted. They were loud, boisterous, making no effort at all to be stealthy or tactical. He would have to wait until these gawking troops left before he could continue his exfiltration.

Then he saw the rope flung out, uncoiling in midair. Green rope, military rope. It came to rest not a hundred feet away up the ravine, hanging down from the lip of the steep western slope. Oh, crap—a rope could mean only one thing: they were coming down! Boone watched the first soldier descend. He wrapped the line around his back and over his shoulder, a field-expedient method for rappelling short distances. From the lip of the ravine to the first bodies was maybe thirty feet, at a fifty- or sixty-degree angle. He had a Kalashnikov rifle slung barrel down across his back, and was wearing the Russian camouflage pattern uniform, brown body armor, and a brown beret. Cossack mercenaries: the worst, just as Jenny McClure had described them. The soldier leaned back over the edge, slid and walked down the icy slope, then unwound the rope from his body and called up to the others.

Snow and ice covered the ravine's sides in patches and streaks. The second soldier used just his gloved hands, without wrapping the rope behind his back. This one wore a fur hat like Jenny's instead of a beret. He quickly scrambled down the cliff, and then both men called up to the third Cossack soldier. Boone couldn't understand what they were saying, but the two soldiers at the bottom seemed to be challenging the last man to hurry down into the ravine. The third man also wore a brown fur cap, the flaps tied up on the sides and front. This soldier descended hesitantly. He had wrapped the rope around his body incorrectly, and halfway down the line became twisted. This clumsy rappeller attempted to unbind himself, but he fell against the slope and then spun upside down, the rope between his legs. Then without warning, he came free and slid the last ten feet to the bottom headfirst. The waiting soldiers laughed, shouted, and threw snow on their comrade, who had landed in a heap among the corpses at their feet. Boone thought that it would have been funny, except for the fact that they were standing upon the bodies of murdered Americans.

The last man righted himself and stood up, brushing snow and mud off his uniform and rearranging the rifle slung on his back. The soldier wearing the beret pulled a clear bottle out of an ammo magazine pouch and took a long drink. His grimace and cough indicated that it was full of some kind of high-octane liquor, probably local moonshine. He passed the pint-sized flask to his buddies, and the three took turns slugging it down until it was empty. The soldier wearing the beret then threw the bottle up the side of the ravine at a tree, causing a pair of crows to take wing, protesting with loud caws. Most Kazaks were nominally Muslim, thought Boone. When it suited them. At other times, liquor suited them even better. God love Tennessee: in good times or bad, there was never a shortage of fine corn whisky. Maybe these were Russianized Cossacks, who had been raised outside the Islamic faith. Not that it mattered, not when they were taking part in the foreign occupation of his state.

The three soldiers continued to laugh and push one another, but shortly they quieted down and went to work. The snow was rapidly melting; the temperature was already well above freezing and getting warmer. They turned and rolled bodies, twisting limbs to gain leverage, looking for wallets and purses, extracting paper money and dropping the rest. Watches and bracelets went into the pockets of their parkas and trousers. Peering over the shoulder of a frozen man's dead body, it was obvious to Boone that the three soldiers knew exactly what they would find in the ravine. They were not here by happenstance; they were here because they *knew*. And they knew—because they were the killers.

The soldier wearing the beret pulled a long fighting knife from a sheath on his belt, crouched in the snow, and lifted a woman's bare arm, her long fingers extending skyward. Boone clenched his teeth as the soldier grasped her frozen hand and prepared to remove several rings in the most grisly manner possible. Boone's right hand slowly pulled aside the bottom of his parka, and went to his holster. With his left hand, he extracted the pistol's suppressor from its compartment on his combat vest, after gently peeling back the velcro flap. He moved as quickly as he dared, afraid to attract the attention of the three-man looting party, who were busy only fifty feet upslope from his partially concealed position.

One fur-hatted soldier vomited loudly, and his mates yelled abuse at him. They began arguing, then pushing and shoving, and one of them fell down. The disgusting job was proving to be a stressful ordeal even for this crew of ghouls. At least the frozen bodies had no odor, Boone thought. Come back in a few days, it won't be so pleasant... The three soldiers continued to search bodies, not going much deeper than the first layer. They hastily removed rings, watches, silver coins and paper money, occasionally kneeling or even lying prone to reach deeper into the mass of corpses. Sometimes they slipped among the thawing jumble of intertwined torsos and limbs, and fell down between them.

The soldier wearing the brown beret, the first to descend into the ravine, was working his way down toward Boone's position. His two comrades were about thirty feet away from the beret wearer, upslope from him. These two were working as a team now, taking turns at snipping off rings with a pair of wire cutters. The beret-wearing soldier was only twenty feet away from Boone, efficiently removing rings with the blade of his combat knife, and then casually dropping the bloodless severed digits into the snow. The serrated edge of his knife was audible as it sawed through their finger bones. He was approaching the area that Boone had recently searched for IDs. The soldier stood erect and looked at the bodies around him, a quizzical look on his face, the gory knife gripped in his right hand. He seemed to be considering the snow, the corpses, and their somewhat different appearance from those above, the ones that he had already looted.

He wiped the blade of his knife on his pants, sheathed it, and began to rotate the slung Kalashnikov rifle from his back, the barrel slowly coming up under his arm to the ready position. His right hand found the rifle's pistol grip, in front of which was a wickedly curved thirty-round magazine. The soldier studied the well-stamped slushy remnants of snow, then turned and looked back upslope, raising an arm toward his two comrades, who were still intently pillaging bodies as a team.

Boone's pistol was a Glock 21. It held 14 rounds of .45 caliber ammunition. The bullets were heavy but slow as pistol bullets went, which had the critical benefit of making them slower than the speed of sound. It was a stock Glock pistol, except for the threaded barrel. He had bought the aftermarket barrel years earlier, when they had been perfectly legal to own. No coincidence, the threads matched those of the military-issue suppressor he had taken with him from Fort Campbell. His suppressor would reduce the muzzle blast to the sound level of a loud handclap, and the slow subsonic bullets would not make a telltale sonic crack while passing through the air. The snow would further dampen the sound of a shot, and the ravine walls would reflect any remaining noise skyward.

When the soldier turned upslope and raised his left arm, Boone sat up, twisted sideways, took aim using a two-handed grip and fired. The pistol's sights were barely higher than the top of the suppressor, but he had practiced enough to be dead certain of his aim at this close range. The soldier was wearing body armor over his coat, so Boone aimed higher. The bullet took him at the base of his skull below his beret, destroying the medulla oblongata and dropping him like a steer in a slaughterhouse.

Boone immediately took aim at the next soldier. He was fifty feet upslope, a much more difficult pistol shot against a moving target. The two soldiers took no immediate notice of their finger-hacking comrade suddenly falling prone, or of Boone sitting up. The three Cossacks had been slipping and falling since descending into the ravine and treading among the packed bodies. They were too intent upon their own looting to wonder about their mate going down again, probably to reach for the promising golden glimmer of a ring or bracelet.

A head shot was too risky at this range, so instead Boone aimed beneath the body armor for the pelvis area and fired. The man twisted and dropped to a sitting position, in total shock and amazement. Boone sprang to his feet and continued to take aimed shots at both men, alternating between their heads and hips. One of his bullets connected with a skull inside a fur hat and Boone was certain the second man was dead. The third man had meantime fallen among the bodies and was lost to view.

Boone changed magazines and charged upward, ignoring the fact that he was running over frozen bodies, instinctively weaving and ducking until he saw the third soldier. The wounded man was lying on his back and groaning loudly, trying to unsling the Kalashnikov rifle from behind him, where it was pinned under his own weight. Dark blood was soaking his camouflage trousers and staining the snow scarlet beneath him. He had been shot in the groin area, or perhaps the femoral artery. He glanced up at Boone and they locked eyes, brown staring up into blue. The color rapidly drained from the man's face. He stopped trying to free his rifle, and slowly raised both hands in submission. Boone aimed carefully, squeezing the Glock's trigger slowly, and sent a final bullet into the soldier's forehead just below his fur hat. From the minute that he had seen the three soldiers rappel into the ravine to pillage the bodies, there had never been a question in his mind of taking prisoners if it came to this point. His only momentary regret was that the three had suffered far too little in comparison with what they had done.

There was not a minute to waste, but Boone still forced himself to take a moment to think. If any other foreign soldiers were watching the drama in the ravine unfold, they would have opened fire. He quickly scanned both ravine tops, but saw nothing, only the crows returning to the tree branches, waiting their turn. The three looters were probably operating on their own, out of pure callous greed. It was not the kind of mission that you invited your entire platoon to attend. For one thing, more participants meant a smaller share of plunder.

He could either take off now or spend a minute hiding the fresh bodies. He decided to take the time, after quickly photographing them in their Kazak uniforms, with their weapons. He pulled and dragged the last Cossack he had shot into an open slot between two dead Americans, and pulled a bearded man partially over the soldier's warm body. Boone scrambled down the ravine and repeated the process with the other two dead enemies. He left their rifles under their corpses, not bothering to take one. There were already plenty of captured AKs back in the cave, and hidden in other caches. He could not conceal a rifle with a non-folding stock during the next part of his escape and evasion. Being seen with a rifle would pronounce an instant sentence of death upon him from any unseen enemy sniper, or even from a missile-firing drone possibly circling high above. The easily concealed sound-suppressed Glock pistol was ideal for close work, the only type of combat he could hope to win as one man against the world.

He did remove the matchbox-sized infrared firefly strobes from the body armor shoulder straps of the last two. They were already switched off, indicating to Boone that the three Cossack looters had been operating on their own, not wishing to be tracked from the sky. Since he could not be completely certain that the infrared strobes were turned off, he buried them deeply inside a vest pocket. The tiny strobes' invisible infrared flashes were so bright on thermal IR that they could be detected even through a shirt pocket.

The snow was already melting. Soon their helter-skelter footprints among the corpses would be meaningless, and then their message would disappear altogether. In an hour, the three Cossack bodies would be too cool to be noticed by a helo or a drone equipped with thermal infrared. It might be hours before the soldiers were missed, and more hours before they were found. That was all the time Boone needed. From here, he could make it to the cave in two hours, if he was not impeded. Without a doubt, there were many more foreign soldiers patrolling in the area. He could not play it safe and hide nearby, waiting for them to leave. When the three bodies of their missing comrades were discovered, the Cossacks would go wild seeking revenge. There would be helicopters, UAVs, and tracking dogs. He had to move now.

15

"**The young ones sure need a lot of sleep,**" said Phil Carson. He wasn't quite whispering, but he was speaking very quietly. In the silence of the cave, he didn't need to raise his voice to be heard.

"Thank God for that," replied Doug. "The only time that baby is quiet is when she's sleeping."

"I meant Jenny and Zack." Jenny and the baby were sleeping in the blue dome tent at the other side of the wooden platform. Zack was in a green sleeping bag, sprawled on a foam mattress pad next to the tent. Carson was across the square card table from Doug, sitting on one of the four wooden folding chairs, one for each side. Both men were nursing mugs of instant coffee. Doug had his AR-15 carbine disassembled on the table, and he was wiping down the bolt carrier with an oily rag.

The handheld radio and some of the other electronic devices from Jenny's pack were also lying on the table, after having been carefully examined. Both men had changed into dry camouflage BDU fatigues, part of the cave's stockpile. They were the old woodland pattern BDUs, curvy splotches of green, brown and black, not the digital gray and brown of the newer ACU pattern. A single bare light bulb was suspended above them. Doug had washed his face and hair in a basin and given himself a shave, and his black hair was combed straight back. Carson looked at his watch. "It's almost noon. How long do you think until Boone gets here?"

"There's no telling. If there are foreign troops around, he might decide he can't move in the daylight, and then maybe he'll wait until tonight."

"You have a lot of faith in him?"

"Oh yeah. I'd of been dead a few times if it wasn't for him. He'll make it."

A murmur came from within the blue tent, the start of a baby's cry, followed by a soft reassurance from Jenny. When the sounds quieted, Carson whispered, "You know, Doug, that baby can't live on instant milk powder. At least I don't think it can."

"What if we grind up vitamins and things to add to it?"

"I don't know. I just don't think babies can live on instant milk. You know what that means?"

Doug whispered back, "Is it going to die?"

"Maybe, but that's not what I meant. It means we can't stay hidden in this cave for a long time. Not if we want that little orphan baby to survive."

"Let's wait until Boone gets here. We don't have to decide anything today."

"What's the longest you ever stayed in here?" asked Carson.

"You mean without going outside at all?"

"Yeah."

"More than a week. We wait for bad weather to go out. The worse the better, that's what Boone says. The worse the better. He calls it good operating weather. It keeps the enemy inside."

Carson lowered his voice in order not to be heard by Jenny, in case she was awake. "Well, I don't think that baby can last a week on instant milk. Not a newborn. I hope I'm wrong."

"Let's just wait until Boone gets here, okay? He's the boss. He decides these things."

"Fine by me." Carson sipped from his cup of weak instant coffee. He was surprised that a luxury item that could not be found in the state of Mississippi was available in a cave in Tennessee. The coffee was from an old MRE meal pack—government-issue Meals Ready to Eat. Carson had seen only one cardboard case of the plastic meal packs. They'd split a single coffee packet and made two mugs, but at least it was hot. "So, Doug, you already heard me tell my story, back at Zachary's house. What about you? Where are you from, and how did you wind up here?" If they were going to spend the next few days or even longer in the cave, they were going to become well acquainted.

"Me? I'm from Maryland. The Baltimore suburbs, north of the city."

Carson had placed his accent as coming from somewhere in the Northeast, maybe Philadelphia. Maryland was a close guess. "So how did you wind up fighting a guerrilla war in Tennessee?"

Doug smiled wistfully. "It's a long story. To start with, I was drafted. I was going to the University of Maryland, majoring in communications, but I had to drop out after my junior year because I couldn't afford the tuition. Unfortunately I'm just a Category 7—a healthy heterosexual Christian white male. That's the bottom, the baseline. My tuition was tripled with no warning, so that was that. They pulled my student loan and I couldn't get any kind of extension, so I was back at home living with my mom. That made me draft bait—except they call it National Service now."

"The draft is back?" asked Carson. "How's that work? Do they still have college deferments?"

"There's a lottery. They can get you anytime between eighteen and twenty-five. College doesn't get you out of it, but it puts it off, and if you're lucky they might not call you up at all."

"How long do you have to serve?"

"It's supposed to be two years in the military, or three years in the Conservation Corps or the Urban Corps. The CC's quota was already filled for the year—at least that's what they said—and forget the Urban Corps. That's all Jamal Tambor fanatics. We call it the Tambor-Corps. So it was the Army for me. To tell you the truth, I would have picked the Navy or the Air Force, but I didn't get a choice in that either. I did basic training at Fort Dix. Then I was assigned to an engineering battalion at Fort Leonard Wood. So I was already in Missouri when the first earthquake hit."

"What are you, about twenty-four?"

"Twenty-five. I thought I'd have my master's degree by now. Well, so much for *my* plans—Uncle Sam had some other ideas for my future." He went on cleaning his rifle, ramming a small cloth patch on the tip of a metal rod up the inside of the barrel.

"Tell me something, Doug. You're obviously a smart guy. I've been out of the country for seven years. What the hell happened to America? I always thought Americans would fight to keep their freedom. What happened? How could Americans just roll over and give up their rights?"

"Well, we didn't just 'give up' our rights. It wasn't like that. Not at all. It's more like they were stolen in broad daylight, at the constitutional convention."

Carson asked, "How did *that* happen? I was down in the Caribbean then. American news wasn't so big down there. Panama was going through its own troubles, and I was keeping a low profile. I didn't have cable TV, that's for sure."

"I'll tell you what happened—I watched it happen. When the convention was over, that's when we knew that the old America was gone. It was over. Finished."

"The convention was in Philadelphia, right?"

Right. I was in Baltimore when it happened, but it was televised wall-to-wall. On television, the talking heads called it the con-con, like it was a big joke or something. Maybe constitutional convention was too hard to spell, or maybe it took them too long to say it. Too many syllables. You know—time is money. I think a lot of the people behind the convention couldn't even pronounce it, much less spell it, so it just became the con-con."

"It was two years ago?"

"Yeah, two years ago in September. You have to understand how bad things already were, even before the earthquakes, and before the big hurricanes hit the Gulf Coast. Even back then, the economy was so bad that people were calling it the Greater Depression. People were desperate. And not just welfare types—I'm talking about solid middle class citizens. Or formerly middle class, like my family. Nouveau poor, we called it. I think people were ready to try just about anything to get the economy moving. Nothing the government tried was working; everything was in a downward spiral. We were still using blue bucks then, what they called 'New Dollars.' Banks were failing left and right, only the Fed wouldn't let them fail—they pumped in trillions of dollars in new money to keep them open. Nobody wanted to hear that it might take years to unwind the economic mess we were in. That it took us decades to ruin the economy, and it would take a long time to fix it. Everybody wanted a quick fix, like pulling a rabbit out of a magic hat. But everything the president and Congress tried just made things worse. Especially printing so much new money."

Doug set his rifle barrel back down on the table and continued. "The country was already a mess, and that was undeniable. Everybody and his brother were proposing constitutional amendments, supposedly to fix the economy, or make everything fair for the poor, or whatever. That's how Congress came up with thirty-four state legislatures calling for amendments. There were seven or eight totally different amendment proposals, but it didn't matter. Once Congress had thirty-four states on record proposing amendments, they went for it. I think they were just waiting for the chance. Once they had thirty-four states, it only took a 51 percent vote in Congress to call for the convention."

"Congress? I don't understand. What do *they* have to do with the convention?" asked Carson.

"Everything, under Article Five. It all came down to Article Five of the old constitution. Congress runs the whole show for constitutional conventions."

"It does? I didn't know that."

"Yeah, well, join the club. That was a major surprise to almost everybody, since it had never happened before. Not in over two hundred years, since it was written. So nobody knew much about Article Five," said Doug.

"I guess that changed in a hurry."

"You're not kidding. It was shock therapy. Especially when the Poor People's Party marched through Baltimore. There were already about a million of them camping out in Washington on the National Mall before the convention. When they took off walking to Philly, it was like a dam bursting. That was on Labor Day. Mile after mile of people with flags, signs, drums, musical bands on trucks—everything you can imagine. Police cars were escorting them, leading them up I-95. They closed the northbound lanes of 95 for something like twenty miles, for the whole time it took them to walk to Philly. They kept moving that closed section of 95 north, to keep up with the marchers. There was nothing else on television, practically. It took them two days just to get through Baltimore, and when they came through, they spread out like locusts. I was in Baltimore then, back in my mother's house. I'd quit college and gotten my draft notice. I was waiting to report for basic training."

Doug took a sip of his instant coffee, and went on. "Naturally, our own locals got into the spirit and joined the march. They took whatever they wanted from any stores along the way, and the police just watched. There was nothing they could do anyway, or it would have caused the biggest riot in history. It was legalized looting, that's all it was. Legalized looting, all over Baltimore. 'Redistributing the wealth,' they called it. We stayed locked in our house and watched it all on television. It would have been suicide to go out and see it in person."

"So it was, ah…racially polarized?" asked Carson.

"Extremely. Everything was black and white when they came marching through Baltimore. Blacks marching, and whites hiding. I never saw anything like it in my life. Well, not until Memphis, but that was after the earthquakes."

Carson asked, "How far is it from Washington to Philly? Two hundred miles?"

"That's about right. It took two weeks for them to make it all the way, and when they arrived, the constitutional convention was just starting. Perfect timing. What a coincidence, right? It was all planned in advance, that's obvious now. They held the convention in Philly's new sports arena, the one that was named for a bank. I think that bank is out of business; I don't know what they call it now. The delegates were down on the floor, and the rest of the stands were full of twenty thousand 'spectators.' Yelling and screaming like maniacs—and outside it was worse. They said there were over a million of the Poor People's Party in Philly by then, coming from everywhere, not just Washington. Probably another million just from the Philadelphia area. They were banging on buckets and pans, turning over cars, barricading streets and smashing store windows. They kept interviewing the rabble-rousers on TV—it was like pouring gasoline on fire. 'No Justice, No Peace,' that's all you heard. That was one of the big mantras. They called the looting 'street reparations.' They said if they didn't get the economic justice amendment, they'd burn the city down. It looked like they would, too. Every street in downtown Philly looked like Times Square on New Year's Eve, that's how crowded it was."

"Jeez, that had to be pretty rough, with that many people packed into downtown," said Carson. "There couldn't have been enough public bathrooms."

"Almost every store and restaurant was broken open. Needing to use the restrooms was always a good excuse to force their way in. That, and needing food and drinking water. And after that, everything was looted."

"And the police didn't stop it?"

"They *couldn't* stop it. How could they?" asked Doug. "The police just stayed back on the edges and tried to herd them. Even that didn't work. A mob that big makes its own rules."

"Like a human tidal wave."

"Exactly. A human tsunami. So, with that mega-mob outside the arena, you can guess what kinds of radicals were being let in to fill the twenty thousand seats. The real cream of the crop. It was a total farce. That's when they started to call it the 'kangaroo convention' on talk radio. That was back when we still had AM talk radio."

Carson asked, "What happened to talk radio?"

"Two things. First, a couple of years ago Congress passed the so-called 'fairness' laws. That meant that every point of view on a radio station had to be balanced by another radio host or by other callers from the other side. It got incredibly complicated. They literally had to count how many minutes were said for this and for that on every subject. Trying to keep up with the fairness laws made talk radio a money loser, so most stations went to sports or music. Then Congress passed a law against 'hate speech on the public airwaves.' Anybody could take a radio station to court for just about anything that they claimed was hate speech. They'd cherry-pick a left-wing judge and jury, and it was a slam-dunk every time. After a few million-dollar judgments, the last talk radio stations threw in the towel. Now radio is practically all music and sports, with happy talk in between government PSAs—public service announcements."

"This must really be up your alley, if you were majoring in communications."

"Yeah, I picked a great time to choose that career path, huh? Now all we get on television and the radio is government propaganda."

"I've heard it," said Carson. "We could get Nashville radio at Zack's house at night. So, you were up to the start of the convention."

"Right. So to start it off, the Aztlan Coalition said they wouldn't vote for any other amendments unless they got their regional autonomy deal first. That was the Southwestern Justice and Compensation Amendment. That was the first amendment they voted on, and it passed on a voice vote. Next, it was reparations for slavery. Five hundred thousand New Dollars for every African-American man, woman and child. Right after that, it was reparations for 'survivors of the Native American genocide.' Another half million for everybody with Indian blood."

"How was that paid?" asked Carson in astonishment. "Where did the money for all of that come from?"

"Didn't matter," Doug replied. "It was just instant money from the Treasury...or the Federal Reserve. What's the difference? Ten trillion brand new blue bucks, right out of thin air. The checks came in the mail, or the money was just direct-deposited straight into their bank accounts. It was all just electronic digits, but it was real money just the same. It was just as spendable as any other money."

"And that brought on the hyperinflation?"

"Among other things, like fraud on a scale never seen before in human history. People were collecting reparation payments right and left under false identities. I think there were about a million double-dippers who claimed they were black *and* Indian…but it didn't matter. Congress said that the reparations money would stimulate the economy. It would 'prime the pump and even the playing field' at the same time. It was 'the mother of all stimulus packages.' That was another of those clichés you heard all the time. The convention was already way out of control by the time they passed reparations for slavery and the Indians.

"Next came the Freedom from Gun Violence Amendment, and that's when the Second Amendment was annulled. So you see, we didn't want any of it. Not regular Americans. We didn't ever vote for it; it was all done at the con-con by mob rule. It was a complete circus by then—the kangaroo convention. But it didn't matter what average Americans thought, the amendments all became law. They became the new constitution. When the Second Amendment was repealed, the delegates in the arena had a mass orgasm. We watched it all on TV. It was surreal, like a bad dream you get after food poisoning."

Carson asked, "What did the gun amendment ban?"

"Just about every legal firearm that was left. After the Washington Stadium Massacre, the semi-auto rifles were already outlawed. The ones they called assault weapons."

"I remember that," said Carson. "I was here for that one."

"Well under the Freedom from Gun Violence Amendment, there are no more privately owned handguns, none. Um, except for the police. The police and the military. And no pump or semi-auto shotguns. Only single shot and double-barreled shotguns—and you need to get a federal license to keep one in your house. Oh, and you have to take a federal firearms safety course and pass a background check to get your license. And if they don't like your background—meaning your politics—no license."

"Gun control was never about safety: it was just about taking power away from ordinary Americans," said Carson. "It's to make it safe for the police, in a police state."

"Exactly. And that wasn't all," continued Doug. "No rifle scopes, only assassins need them, right? No rifles bigger than thirty caliber, period. And all of the bolt- and lever-action rifles have to be licensed and registered, just like the shotguns. Everything that's registered has to be kept in officially approved gun safes, and they're subject to inspection at any time. They even have to be kept disassembled, with the bolts stored separately in another room. And God help you if they come in to inspect and they're not 'properly stored' according to the law. That was another part of the amendment: if you manage to get a gun license, you agree to random 'safety inspections'."

"What about ammunition?"

"You have to fill out about a yard of paperwork and get police approval to buy a box of hunting ammunition, and then it's taxed at around 500 percent. And you have to turn in your fired brass before you can buy more ammo. Oh, and forget about reloading—that's illegal. You can't even own gunpowder—that's 'bomb-making material' now."

"And this was all in the gun amendment?" asked Carson.

"Hell, yes. I think the FFGVA is something like thirty pages long."

"Damn—the whole Bill of Rights was only a couple hundred words."

"I hear you. It took the Founding Fathers four months to write the original constitution. That was in the summer in 1787. Some of the greatest minds in history. The new constitution is about fifty times longer, and they cranked it out in a week. Of course, they shortened it here and there. Like by cutting out most of the Bill of Rights."

"And American shooters just went along with it?" Carson asked with a look of incredulity.

"No, not most of them. I mean…oh hell, I don't know. I didn't believe any of the polls I read on it. But you'd be amazed by the number of so-called hunters and sportsmen they found to say it was all actually *quite reasonable*. They were on TV all the time, telling shooters to be *reasonable* and comply with the new laws. They could still go hunting, and a *bit of inconvenience* was a small price to pay for public safety."

"They can always find sellouts and traitors."

"Yessir they can," Doug agreed. "Jamal Tambor was all about *reasonable* gun laws, until the guns were all gone. But any way you cut it, the Second Amendment was finished, dead and buried after the constitutional convention."

Carson sighed, and slowly shook his head. "The end of two centuries of American gun rights."

"Yep, the end." Doug smiled, and patted the lower receiver of the AR-15 carbine lying across the table. "Legally, anyway. That is, if you consider anything that came out of that abortion that was born in Philadelphia to be legal."

"I take it you don't."

"Nope, I don't, not at all. But the con-con didn't end with the gun amendment. The economic amendment was the last one. That was on the final day of the convention. It was a rubber stamp, another voice vote. By then the con-con was like a religious revival meeting, so of course the EJDA passed. That's what they call the Economic Justice and Democracy Amendment, the EJDA. It was another mass orgasm in the Philly sports arena. We were in shock by then, watching it on television at home. It all happened so fast! Only a few months before the con-con, everybody thought the Poor People's Party was a joke. We thought the constitutional convention would never happen, and even if it did, it wouldn't really count somehow. But it did, and nobody's laughing now."

"What's this economic amendment do?" asked Carson.

"The EJDA guarantees jobs for everybody; it guarantees a living wage, it guarantees affordable housing, free health care, free college and free child care. I'm sure I left out a few things it guarantees, but you get the idea. Almost any freebie or handout you can think of, it's in the EJDA. Basically, it's communism, written into the constitution. And believe it or not, they sold it as the best way to fix the economy! The new constitution was going to get us out of the depression, and make life fair for everybody at the same time. With the new constitution, the president could enact the 'New New Deal' and get us out of the depression. Fat chance! That's like taking arsenic to cure a stomach ache."

"Back up a minute," said Carson. "How did they ratify these amendments? What does the old constitution say? Don't they need something like three-quarters of the state legislatures to ratify an amendment?"

"That's what we thought," replied Doug, "but they used the backdoor clause. In Article Five, it says new amendments have to be approved by three-fourths of the state legislatures, '*or by conventions in three fourths thereof.*' That was the fuzzy part, the part nobody could really explain. That became just about the most famous sentence in the old constitution. But what the hell does it mean? Who makes up these state conventions? Who nominates the delegates, what are the rules, and where do they hold them? There's nothing in Article Five that spells it out. You'd see ten so-called constitutional experts on television, and you'd get ten different explanations. It was all up to the Congress to determine what *conventions in three fourths thereof* meant. At least according to the Congress it was, and Congress is three-quarters Democrat now."

"It sounds crazy," said Carson disgustedly. "It sounds like something that would happen in Venezuela or Zimbabwe. Making up the rules as they go along."

"It *was* crazy, especially because the whole thing started with eight Western states that wanted a states' rights amendment. It was mostly over coal and gas revenues, and water rights. They wanted to cut back on federal control of their resources, and then they were joined by seven Southern states. That was the original group of fifteen states. But pretty soon lots of blue states jumped on the bandwagon, when they thought they might be able to turn a convention in their direction. Nobody really thought it would actually happen, it seemed so far-fetched—but in less than a year there were thirty-four states calling for a constitutional convention. For six or seven totally different amendments, mind you.

"Nobody saw the train wreck coming. Well, almost nobody—the radical Democrats in Congress saw it. They wanted it…they saw the potential. It was a setup, a scam from day one. A big scam to turn the country hard-core socialist in one big jump. We all know that now. But by the time we figured out what they were up to, it was too late to stop it. Congress had complete control of how to run the convention, and that meant the Democrats. The train had left the station, and it couldn't be stopped. Then the Poor People's Party was organized, and the next thing you know, we had Philadelphia. They held these so-called 'state ratifying conventions' right there in the big sports arena in Philadelphia, right after the constitutional convention. It was such a joke! That's why we called it the kangaroo convention."

"And the Supreme Court didn't stop it?"

Doug said, "Oh, the Supreme Court—I forgot that one. There are twelve justices on the Supreme Court now. That was another amendment: twelve justices instead of nine. President Tambor nominated the three new justices as soon as the convention was over, after the amendments were passed. Congress confirmed them the same day Tambor nominated them. The old Supreme Court with nine justices was our last hope: that they'd throw the whole thing out. Just invalidate the whole thing. But they didn't stop it. They voted five to four that the Supreme Court had no standing to overrule the convention results. The majority said that Article Five conventions are up to Congress. That was the last ruling by the nine-judge Supreme Court. Most people think the five liberals on the old court liked the new constitution better. They agreed with the new amendments, so that's why they voted to stay out of it. Now that there are twelve justices, the liberals win everything. Three of the conservative justices resigned in protest, but that just gave Tambor three more seats to fill. Since the convention, it's like living in Venezuela, or Russia. It's Alice in Wonderland."

"What about Congress?"

"What *about* Congress?" Doug asked back. "The Democrats had unbreakable majorities. The whole convention was their idea. Oh my God, the Democrats were all in heaven—and the Republicans were just as gutless as ever. The RINOs rolled over for the new constitution, most of them anyway. They never had the numbers to stop it. You know, as long as they can keep their snouts in the hog trough, that's all they really care about. A few Republicans challenged the basic legality of the con-con, but they were shouted down and called fascists and racists, all the usual stuff. They took an unholy beating in the media. So most of them caved in, and shut up."

"Typical," agreed Carson.

"Very. It works every time with RINOs. Growl at them, call them racists or homophobes, and they'll run for cover with their tails between their legs. They just want to stay in Congress—it's like being royalty. I think most of the RINOs in Congress like being in the permanent minority—it's easier. Just keep your head down, shuffle along, make your votes, and get invited to millionaire parties every night of the week." Doug spat on the floor of the cave. "Bunch of pathetic losers."

"But I take it that not all of the states accepted the amendments."

"You can say that again," said Doug, laughing. "Most of the North-west, some of the South, half of Texas...but not enough to kill the new constitution. The president, the Congress and the Supreme Court accepted the new amendments, and that's who counts. They control most of the military, and all of the federal law enforcement agencies. And they're in charge in Washington, D.C., so they make the rules for everybody."

"Only they can't enforce it out West."

"Well, that's right," agreed Doug, "They can't enforce it out there in the free states. Their state legislatures rejected the new constitution out-right. They said that everything that happened in Philadelphia was illegal and invalid because their so-called state delegates were stooges and im-posters. So now the Northwest is using the old original constitution. They even got rid of the federal income tax, because they said it was uncon-stitutional. They say that the Sixteenth Amendment was bogus because it was passed by some kind of a fraud back in 1913. They use a 12 percent sales tax instead, and it's the same tax for everybody. Rich, poor—every-body pays 12 percent. And they keep it in their own states—they don't send any money to Washington."

"I'll bet Washington can't stand *that*," said Carson. "Washington, D.C., I mean."

"Can't stand it is right. Especially with the federal states still stuck in the depression. Yeah, the feds opened up a real can of worms with this new constitution. The states that rejected the new constitution didn't just stop there; they started what they call the 'rollback.' That's how they got rid of the federal income tax. They even got rid of New Dollars out there. Now they use gold and silver instead. They're hard-core on the original constitution."

Carson was intrigued. So the Northwest was going back to the gold standard. That was how he had been doing business in the Caribbean, and he still had a few ounces hidden in his belt, and more stashed in the derelict tugboat near his wrecked catamaran. He said, "Politicians can't just create more gold and silver out of thin air, like they do with paper and electronic money. Taking away their printing press is like cutting off their balls and putting a ring through their nose."

"Exactly right. It cuts the power of the government right off at the knees. People are finally starting to figure this out, and boy, do the politicians up in D.C. ever hate it."

"What about the South, the emergency zone?" asked Carson. "Which constitution are they following?"

"Basically, General Mirabeau speaks for the emergency zone. He *is* the e-zone. He's the only law down there that matters. They haven't had an election in three years. I don't know how he really feels, I don't think anybody does, but I don't think he's committed one way or the other. As far as I know, he hasn't rejected the new constitution, but why should he? He rules like a king from Louisiana to Georgia. He makes up the laws as he goes along, under his own emergency powers act. It's easier for him to avoid making trouble with Washington. What would it gain him? Washington can't force him to do anything, so it's a standoff. Personally, I think General Mirabeau is just for General Mirabeau."

Carson said, "The folks here in Tennessee can't be happy about the new constitution."

Doug asked, "What difference does it make if they're happy about it, when they're under martial law?"

"Did people really turn in their guns?" asked Carson.

"Here, or up in the federal states? Up north, people didn't have much choice. The police already knew where most of the guns were, from all kinds of computer records and registration lists. Most people up north turned them in. At least it looked that way on television. People had no alternative. It was either turn them in or get arrested. Or take a chance on having a SWAT team make a midnight visit. Maybe some folks up north buried their guns, I don't know. If they're buried, they're still buried, I guess. But they're not much good when they're in the ground."

"Nobody fought back?"

"Some hardcore types went down shooting, but not many. I was right there; I was still up in Maryland then. There were a few shootouts on the news, but not a lot."

"What about you, Doug? What did you do with your guns?"

He grinned sheepishly. "I didn't *have* any guns to turn in. My family was pretty liberal, and they were always against guns in general. You know, growing up in Maryland, my family blamed guns for violence in society. I never touched a real gun until after I was drafted." Doug finished wiping down his rifle's barrel assembly, rejoined it with the lower receiver, and pushed the two cross pins through.

"What about here in the South?" Carson asked.

"Oh, it was way different down here. Even after the new constitution was passed, the local sheriffs wouldn't cooperate with the feds, not when it came to gun control. They wouldn't set up collection centers like the city cops did up north. Then they had the hurricanes and the earthquakes, so things just worked out differently down here. The local police down here could barely find enough gasoline to drive around, much less to go out on gun raids. Not that they wanted to anyway. With all of the looting, people needed their guns—the local police understood that. Taking people's guns away wasn't a priority down here. After the earthquake, the feds couldn't even bring food in, so they sure as hell couldn't come in looking for guns. So anyway, folks down here are mostly still armed, just like before the Second Amendment went down the tubes. And with what happened after the earthquakes, people damn sure wouldn't give up their guns. Guns mean survival—life or death. If people didn't understand that before the quakes, they sure know it now. They won't give up their guns now, no matter what the law says." Doug Dolan picked a loaded thirty-round magazine up from the table and slid it into the rifle. He stood the weapon up on the table, pulled down the charging handle, and let it fly home with a rasping metallic snap, chambering a round. "And I won't either. At least not while I'm alive."

"And that's why the feds are coming down so hard on Kentucky and Tennessee?"

"That's what most folks think," replied Doug. "If the feds can't get Kentucky and Tennessee and the Carolinas whipped into shape, they'll never be able to get control of the Deep South, what they call the emergency zone. That'll leave General Mirabeau in charge, except he's not really under Washington's authority. All Washington really controls now is the Northeast and the Midwest, from Maine to Minnesota and down to Virginia—and Virginia is shaky. There's a lot of mountains in Virginia, just the same as eastern Tennessee, Kentucky and the Carolinas."

"Mountain folks are a different breed of people, that's been my experience."

"Mr. Carson, the federal government is just an empty shell anymore, and that's how I think it looks in most of the country. It's hollow, it's all rotten inside—it just hasn't collapsed yet. Why should General Mirabeau obey Washington if Washington can't even get a handle on Kentucky and Tennessee? And if they can't get Kentucky and Tennessee under control, then they can forget about the Northwest. They'd never have a chance of getting control out there. Not while the East is still divided. That's why Kentucky and Tennessee and the Carolinas are so important. If Washington can't even get their own backyard cleaned up, they can forget about the Northwest. I think that's why Tambor was willing to bring in foreign troops. He doesn't care what anybody thinks—it's make-or-break time. The whole world is watching. If he can't get control east of the Mississippi River, then the federal government is finished, and everybody knows it."

"Well that's sure something to ponder," said Carson. "The end of the United States of America."

"Maybe America died a long time ago, and it just took us this long to realize it." Doug shouldered the reassembled rifle, aimed it at the ceiling of the cave, and sighted along its barrel. "Hell, we already lost the Southwest without a fight. Yeah, I think the America you knew is long gone."

"That might be right. You know, you've got a lot of ideas, a lot of insight for a young man. Maybe someday you could write a book about all of this."

"I've thought about it." He propped the rifle against a crate behind him, within easy reach. "Did you ever hear of a book called *The Black Swan*?"

"No, never."

"You ever read about chaos theory?"

"Sure, a little."

"It's related to that. Risk, randomness, fractal geometry…it's sort of where mathematics meets philosophy. Anyway, a black swan event is something nobody thinks is possible, like a black swan in nature. All swans are white, right? That was a certified known scientific fact forever—until they found black swans in Australia. You can't even imagine a real black swan, until it hits you between the eyes. Planes taking down buildings on 9-11, that was a black swan. The constitutional convention coming out of nowhere—that was a black swan. The global financial collapse, that was one too. After they happen, everybody has an explanation, but never before. Hindsight is twenty-twenty, but foresight is blind. The twin earthquakes sure as hell were black swans. All the experts said that a big Midwest earthquake should happen only about every five hundred years. They said that like it meant we had another three hundred years to go, counting from the last big New Madrid quakes. Like earthquakes follow human schedules. So much for experts!

"Hell," said Doug, warming to his subject, "we got attacked by a whole damn *flock* of black swans, and the experts didn't see a single *one* of them coming. Nobody believed any of this could happen. But it did! When it comes to predicting these off-the-bell-curve events, the experts were all wrong, wrong, wrong. Speaking of bell curves, some people call these black swan things 'fat tails.' That means a big fat bulge out on the skinny edge of the bell curve, where things should be astronomically rare. Fat tail events happen all the time out in the real world, but the experts can never see them before they hit, because they don't fit their probability models."

"Like the 'hundred-year floods' that happen twenty years apart," said Carson.

"Exactly. I read *The Black Swan* back at the University of Maryland for a statistics course I was taking. I'd love to read it again someday. When I read it back in college, it seemed kind of far out. Not anymore. I'm a big believer in black swans now. What you can't see *can* kill you. What you can't even *imagine* can kill you—or wreck your country. You think that just because your country has been chugging along pretty well for two hundred years, it'll keep on going forever, nice and easy. Like some kind of American birthright, or natural law. But black swans are out there—even if you can't see them, or predict them. And they can change *everything*."

"Doug, you have got to write a book about this."

"Maybe I will. But who's going to read it?"

"I would."

"Thanks. I'll start tonight. Or today, or whatever time it is."

Carson checked his watch. "It's half past noon."

"It never changes in here. It's easy to get disoriented and lose track of time."

"You were telling me how you dropped out of college and got drafted. So, how did you wind up in Tennessee with Boone Vikersun?" Phil Carson understood that this might be a sensitive topic if the young man was still supposed to be serving on active duty in the Army.

16

His weak coffee long since finished, Doug reached under the table for a plastic water bottle and took a drink. "Well, I was stationed in Missouri at Fort Leonard Wood when the first earthquake hit. It was December 15, at ten o'clock in the morning. Saturday. I was outside the barracks, throwing a football around with some buddies. It lasted for almost five solid minutes. The first really big shaker, I mean. There were aftershocks that went on for days, and you never knew if they were the start of another big one. We were two hundred miles from the epicenter, and it was still almost strong enough to knock you off your feet. You couldn't stand up, you had to sit down. I was outside, and you could see land waves, like rollers on the ocean. Not that high, but you could actually see them, see the land rolling. It was pretty amazing. When you can't trust the old terra firma under your feet, what can you trust? Anyway, most of the troops at Leonard Wood were put on buses and sent to St.Louis. St. Louis didn't have too much direct earthquake damage, but the power was out and the gas and water were down. A lot of fires started, and they just kept getting bigger. And as soon as the power and lights went out, you might say that the civil order fell apart pretty fast."

Carson said, "When I was down in Panama, I saw some video of the damage. It hit between St. Louis and Memphis, right?"

"Closer to Memphis. It's two hundred fifty miles from St. Louis to Memphis, and the quake's epicenter was fifty miles north of Memphis. Just below Missouri's 'boot heel,' but across the river in Tennessee."

"Is that near New Madrid? The news I heard said it was almost as bad as the big New Madrid quake, back in the early 1800s."

"It was in 1812. New Madrid is in Missouri, just above the boot heel. But it doesn't matter exactly where the center was. It was almost an eight on the Richter scale for about a hundred miles around the epicenter. Midwest earthquakes are a lot worse than California ones. I mean, they're wider; they cover a lot more territory with the full power. We sure felt it at Fort Leonard Wood, and we were two hundred miles away. Like I said, most of our available troops went to St. Louis, to try to restore civil order. My battalion was held back because we had the assault bridges. We were staging up for bigger and better things.

"While we were waiting around, we were watching television every chance we got. Cable news. Some of the base was on generator power, so we could watch satellite TV. There was rioting and looting in St. Louis and Nashville, but the video coming out of Memphis was the worst. Video shot from helicopters. It was like the end of the world down there. It seemed like half of that city was unreinforced masonry—brick—and most of it went down. Even regular wood-frame houses were shaken to pieces. All kinds of natural gas lines go through there; it's like a big energy corridor from the Gulf to the Northeast. Well, at least it *was*. The gas pipelines broke in a million places, and a lot of Memphis burned to the ground. Then it was the chemical plants. They had all kinds of chemical plants and fuel farms along the Mississippi, and the ones that didn't burn spilled. It was a mess! And smack in the middle of all of that, a million people. No electricity, no drinking water, no gas stations or supermarkets open, roads blocked, bridges down…you couldn't imagine such a place. And that's where we were going."

"It sounds like Hurricane Katrina in Louisiana," Carson said.

"Oh, it was much worse. New Orleans wasn't on fire after Katrina. And New Orleans had a big rescue effort going in after just a few days. FEMA was ready and waiting to go into New Orleans, because you can see hurricanes coming a week out. Earthquakes catch you totally off guard. The worst earthquake damage went for more than a hundred miles around the epicenter, and it just *nailed* Memphis. There was damage everywhere, from Little Rock to Nashville to St. Louis. Memphis was just the worst-hit major city, so it got the most media attention.

"My unit spent until Christmas at Fort Leonard Wood. We were watching television news reports all the time we weren't on duty. Most of the film was shot from helicopters. It was too dangerous to land in Memphis. Any helicopters that landed were swarmed with people trying to get out. So many people would grab on that they couldn't lift off the ground. And when they did airlift people out, where could they put them? You can't just drop them off in a field—that just moves the problem from A to B. They dropped pallets of food and water bottles, just hovered and threw them down, but that caused riots. Every time they dropped pallets of food or water in Memphis, it was like *Mad Max*—survival of the fittest. The law of the jungle. Every man for himself, and the devil take the hindmost. Women and children last. They did hundreds of airdrops, but it was just a drop in the bucket, and the meanest thugs got it all anyway. No way could we land and set up distribution centers, not right after the first quake. We had to wait to go in with a big enough force, that's what my battalion was gearing up for. It was just dog-eat-dog on the ground in Memphis. And it was freezing cold, remember. A lot of the city burned for days, and some chemical dumps burned for weeks, so the air was horrible."

"And no food, and no drinking water," said Carson. "I can't imagine what it must have been like in there. It must have been hell in Memphis."

"Apocalyptic, that's the word. When you thought it couldn't get any worse, it got a lot worse. I was in the headquarters company, so I had a little better idea about what was going on. Some of my friends were in communications; they let me know what was really happening. The whole earthquake rescue operation was totally botched. FEMA was just over-whelmed, and they did almost everything wrong. It didn't help that so many highway bridges were down. You just couldn't get relief convoys in. People coming out of Memphis had to walk, because their cars were out of gas or they were stuck in massive gridlocks. Too many roads were cracked, and too many bridges were down. Anyway, not very many people got out of Memphis in cars, not after the first big quake. It's not that every single bridge collapsed, they didn't. But enough did that it turned the evacuation into a permanent gridlock. Thousands of people got out by walking…but they weren't exactly greeted with open arms out in the country. A lot of the black refugees were shot on sight. At least I think they were black. Everybody looks black after they're lying on the ground dead for a few days. That was what we saw on television, back at Fort Leonard Wood. The TV networks all had their news anchors up in helicopters, filming it. Dead black people on the ground, everywhere.

"Well, we finally got our orders to move out the day after Christmas. We went with our equipment on trucks, and worked our way down into Arkansas in a two-hundred-vehicle convoy. So many highway overpasses were down that we had to keep making detours, which was a real problem because every time we slowed down, we'd get swarmed with refugees. And that was in Arkansas, which wasn't half as bad as Tennessee. We crossed the Mississippi north of Memphis, on barges. Tugboats pulled us across, going back and forth like an amphibious landing. Some of the chemical plants were still burning, two weeks after the quake. The air was so bad it burned your eyes and made your lungs ache. It was like D-Day meets *Apocalypse Now*."

"Is it true that all the bridges above Vicksburg are still down?"

"Down, or unusable. Well, there's a new cable-stay bridge at Cape Girardeau that came through the quakes, but that was the only one."

"So, what was the problem? Why didn't you cross there?"

"The problem is the river doesn't go under it anymore. There's just a lake there now. The river cut a new channel, a few miles west of the bridge. The quakes made a lot of new channels. The Ohio and Tennessee rivers too. Paducah was wiped flat when the Kentucky Dam failed. That sent all of the water in Kentucky Lake down into the Ohio like a tidal wave, straight through Paducah."

"Kentucky Lake is huge," Carson noted. "It goes practically all the way across Tennessee."

"It *was* huge. But not after the dam collapsed. It was just an earthen dam, built way back during the Great Depression. Cairo, Illinois, is gone, just plain gone. And I don't mean just the buildings, I mean the land *under* the buildings—it's not there anymore. It's under water. That's where the Ohio meets the Mississippi now, right where Cairo used to be. That happened after the first earthquake, a year ago on December 15."

"Damn…"

"So our battalion made it across the Mississippi on barges. Our mission was to put a temporary bridge across the Wolf River, and another one on Nonconnah Creek. Have you ever heard of them?"

"No."

"Well, they both run into the Mississippi. The Wolf runs along the north side of Memphis, and the Nonconnah along the south side. Most of Memphis lies between those two rivers, and of course the Mississippi River is on the west. Memphis was practically an island once those bridges went down. All of Western Tennessee was basically an island when the big river bridges went down, so that made Memphis an island on an island. The only way out of Memphis across dry land was straight to the east between the Wolf and the Nonconnah, through suburban towns like Germantown and Collierville. Our mission was to open a supply route from Memphis straight south into the state of Mississippi. Getting a bridge over the Mississippi River was out of the question, that'd take years. The Ohio and Tennessee rivers weren't much better, those bridges were down too. Interstate 55 was going to be our main supply route from Mississippi into Western Tennessee. The highway runs straight south from Memphis to Jackson, Mississippi, and then New Orleans. Our mission was to bridge the Wolf and then the Nonconnah, to open up the route down into Mississippi."

"I thought General Mirabeau sealed the state border."

"He did, to refugees coming out of Memphis. We were opening up a route to bring in relief supplies. I have no idea what kind of coordination happened between Mirabeau and Washington, or what kind of deals were made. At the time, we were just operating under our original orders: put temporary bridges over the Wolf River and Nonconnah Creek, and open up I-55 from Memphis down into Mississippi."

Doug sipped his water and continued. "The Memphis airport is south of the Nonconnah too, near I-55. Between Nonconnah Creek and the Mississippi state line. Once they got the runways fixed, they were bringing transport planes with relief supplies into the airport, but they could only get it from there into Memphis by helicopter. It was the mother of all bottlenecks. Once we fixed the bridges, FEMA and the military could bring the stuff into Memphis on the roads. As it was, thousands and thousands of refugees were crossing the Nonconnah in little boats, or even swimming. Pedestrians could get across some of the wrecked bridges. All of these people were swamping the airport, turning it into a giant refugee camp, and that made the bottleneck situation there even worse. Without a working road from the airport into Memphis, all they could do was helicopter airdrops, and that wasn't enough. FEMA was stuck way behind the curve. The situation in Memphis was getting worse by the day, not better. But first we had to bridge the Wolf River, north of Memphis."

"How did that go?"

"We set up a series of assault bridges. We had the Wolverine bridge system at Fort Leonard Wood; it can extend out across an eighty-foot gap. The Wolf River averaged about two hundred feet wide—over the water, I mean. The bridge was much wider, to get the roadway up onto high ground. Sections of the old bridge were still usable. We got a lane open with our Wolverines, plus what we could pick up out of the river with cranes. We broke every safety regulation there ever was putting old bridge sections back up, but our mission came first: open a lane over those two rivers ASAP, no matter what! Our welders and riggers really kicked ass, they were just amazing. The work they did! We had our own operating engineers, so when we needed bigger equipment than what we brought, we just commandeered what we could scrounge up and we got to work. Big road cranes, mostly, plus 'dozers and backhoes."

Carson asked, "What do you mean, commandeered?"

"We just took what we needed. Emergency law, it was all under emergency law. We could take the crane operators and mechanics too, when we could find them. Sometimes they helped us willingly. I mean, it's their city, and they wanted to fix things even more than we did. Plus, they'd rather run their own equipment than see it driven off by strangers and maybe get ruined. We usually got help with the heavy equipment, one way or the other. We had our own fuel tankers, and we were armed, right? We had plenty of qualified equipment operators in our battalion. We could run any machines we could find. Well, it took us three days to get a single lane open across the Wolf. We left a reinforced company for security, and the battalion pushed on south to Nonconnah Creek with the rest of our equipment.

"It took them two days to make it ten miles as the crow flies. Whoever decided our battalion should cross the Mississippi River above Memphis should be shot. We should have come across the Mississippi further south, into the state of Mississippi, and then gone up into Memphis. Instead, we did it ass backwards. Typical Army planning—go the shortest way, not the best or the easiest. I think they did it because the Mississippi River was blocked by the fallen bridges: they had to use the barges and tugs where they were, north of Memphis. Anyway, we ended up driving clear around the city in a big zigzag circle, trying to get to the Nonconnah.

We couldn't use the highways, I-40 or 240—that's the beltway around Memphis. Too many overpasses came down in the quake, so we had to use the surface streets. It took us two days of moving telephone poles and pushing through rubble and fending off refugees. It was a nightmare. We were supposed to put up bridges to bring in relief supplies and allow refugees out. In the end, it was *us* who needed to be rescued, along with everybody else.

"We had to use live ammo—fire warning shots, then shoot to kill, the whole nine yards. Our mission was considered that important. We lost a third of our convoy along the way: ambushed, split off, looted or burned. Our battalion CO had orders to press straight on to the Nonconnah, but she kept detaching elements to rescue people. It was a horror show. It was hard to drive on by when you saw little kids begging for help, drinking ditch water…starving and freezing. We had our own rations, but it was tough keeping our minds on our mission. You just wanted to stop and help people everywhere, but you couldn't. We had to get the highway down into Mississippi open. We had to open the way to the airport. By then we had some big road cranes that we'd picked up along the way. Anything we could use, we took it if we could. Just took it, under emergency law. Finally, on January 7, we opened up the bridge over the Nonconnah. The interstate highway down to Mississippi was open, and that meant the Memphis airport was open too. Only one lane, but it was open. Technically open, anyway. Then my company was sent back north, to bring down more supplies from the barge crossing point north of Memphis."

Carson asked, "The state of Mississippi was already a disaster area from the hurricanes, wasn't it? Did they really expect Mississippi to come and rescue Memphis?"

"That kind of decision was way above my pay grade. I was just there to help open the highway down into Mississippi. But it didn't matter in the end—it was a moot point. On January 9, the second big quake hit. *Nobody* expected it! At first, we thought it was just another aftershock. Our temporary bridges fell into the rivers. Our best cranes went over too, both our own and the big civilian cranes that we'd commandeered. It was the best heavy equipment we could find around Memphis, and down it went. When a crane goes over, you need another crane to lift it back up…but there were no more cranes. And their booms and lifting cables were totally fubared. You don't just go down to Home Depot and get more of them. They don't stock cantilevered booms for hundred-ton cranes, or spools of one-inch rigging wire. Not to mention that all of the Home Depots were looted anyway. So all that work we did to get heavy equipment to the rivers was wasted. After the January quake, all of that equipment wound up getting stuck. Stuck, trapped or ruined, and the bridges were back down in the river. And here we were, an active duty

Army battalion, and we basically needed to be rescued. Our rations ran out. We didn't bring any heavy weapons, just our rifles and a basic load of ammo. That was almost all expended just getting through Memphis."

"Didn't the Army use choppers to fly food and ammo in to you?"

"Some, but hardly enough. Remember, there were millions of people in a bad, bad way, from Nashville to Little Rock. We were just a battalion of soldiers, so I guess they expected us to be able to take care of ourselves. We were a low priority, just one of probably hundreds of military units stranded all over the place."

"How big was the second quake?"

"I've heard all kinds of numbers. At least an eight on the Richter scale, about as strong as the first one. I don't truthfully know. It was big. The second earthquake hit after dark, seven thirty at night. There was a curfew. No more vehicle traffic at night except for the military—not that anybody obeyed the curfew. It was a madhouse, nobody was in charge, there were no police. We had camps on both sides of the Wolf River, guarding the bridge, manning refugee checkpoints. There were refugee squatter camps on both sides of the river, trying to get protection and begging for some of our rations, our MREs, and our clean water.

"Anyway, I was walking across the bridge with a couple of my squad buddies when it started moving, slow at first, then bucking real hard. I tried to run for the land, it was about fifty yards in either direction to get off the bridge and onto solid ground—our steel Wolverine spans and the concrete sections that came through the first quake, or that we'd lifted back up with cranes. I couldn't run; the bridge was going wild. I tried to hang on to a girder; it was like trying to hang on to one of those bull-riding machines. Felt like it went on forever, minutes anyway. *Very* long minutes. Our cranes all went over. One came down right across the bridge and almost nailed me.

"You can't even imagine how freaking scary it was. Thousands of birds were going insane, screaming and flying in every direction, just flying straight into things and breaking their necks. Lightning was striking all around us. The sky was kind of a sickly yellow from the chemical fires that were still burning over on the Mississippi River, and there was a new sulfur smell just to remind you that hell was opening up. You could smell it: the sulfur was so strong it burned your nose. It was apocalyptic, super-natural, anything you can think of like that—times ten.

"The steel bridge girders were grinding and wailing, up and down, side to side, back and forth, and then it all let go. I was sure I was going to die. I went down with the bridge section; it was about fifty feet down to the water. I went underwater, and then I was like a goldfish in a blender full of black paint. I thought, 'Well, it's my turn now.' I'd seen so many dead bodies since I'd crossed the Mississippi River into Tennessee…it was hardly a surprise that my time had come. I was on the verge of just taking a great big breath of Wolf River when I was spat up into the air, and then I was just carried along like on whitewater rapids. Mind you, this was on the Wolf River that most of the time barely moves. But there I was, just getting swept along for the ride with trees, cars, telephone poles, I can't even imagine what. It was pitch black except for the earthquake lightning and the chemical plants back on the Mississippi River that were still burning.

"I grabbed hold of a door or something that felt like a door and just held on for dear life. Everything was just tumbling and rushing around me, and I thought I was going to be killed, only this time I'd be crushed first and then drowned. But as sudden as it started, all of the crap I was surrounded by became still, and the water rushed out from under me. It was still almost totally dark, but there was no more lightning, just that stink of burning chemicals and sulfur. And dead bodies…there was always the smell of death since I'd gotten to Memphis. That was my last memory, being buried in a mountain of trash while the water was sucked away. The whole thing from the first shake to going into the river, to washing up high and dry maybe took ten minutes—but who's counting minutes in the middle of a freaking nightmare from hell? My watch was gone anyway. I was wearing ACUs and combat boots; they were still on me anyway, thank God. My pistol, my wallet, my watch, they were all gone. But I was alive. Freezing cold, soaking wet, but alive. During that entire ride, from the bridge and down the Wolf River, I was sure I was going to die. Positive. So even freezing cold, cut up and bruised all to hell, I was happy. I was going to see another dawn. At some point I passed out. From shock, probably.

"The sun woke me up. I was in a giant tangle of trash and debris. Broad daylight. Lucky for me, it wasn't too cold for January, and I didn't die of hypothermia or something. I was so packed into trash that maybe it kept me warm overnight. Insulation, you know? Otherwise, I don't know how I didn't freeze. When I came to, I was just shaking like a leaf. Shivering. It took me an hour to get myself untangled and work myself loose. I was weak, I had no energy. After I climbed out of my tangled-up nest where I'd spent the night, up on top where I could see a little ways, I saw things I never imagined. Cracks and crevices in the ground that were deep enough to fall into, and too wide to jump across. Huge trees, oaks even, split right up the middle from bottom to top. Half a tree on one side of a crevice, half on the other, just ripped apart like a celery stalk. And all around there were big white sand hills that formed during the quake. I found out later they're called 'sand boils.' It's like quicksand under-ground, then it shoots up like a geyser during a quake. Some of those sand boils were twenty or thirty feet high.

"A lot of the land around there liquefied: houses and cars just sank into it like it was instant quicksand. You might see the corner of a car, or a man's bare foot sticking out, and the mud all around it was just as smooth as a beach after a wave passes over it. I didn't see much of anything during the quake; it was dark and I spent most of it in the river. Afterwards, the next day, I saw plenty. I saw people half-buried in mud, dead. Almost everybody was already in a bad way after the first quake, so it was like the second one came along three weeks later to finish the job. I saw dogs, wild dogs, dogs gone feral, feasting on corpses. Just chowing down on human bodies. That was commonplace. You saw that everywhere.

"I had my uniform shirt and pants and my boots, but that was all. My wallet was gone, my M-9 pistol was gone from my holster, my watch was gone…and I had no idea how far I'd been swept by that flood. I couldn't see the bridge supports, or the bridge. I was dehydrated, I was in pain all over, I'm sure I wasn't thinking straight. I thought I was carried downstream of the bridge, toward the Mississippi River, so I started walking east, trying to get back to my unit. It wasn't until later I figured out the quake had turned the Wolf around. That flood had already swept me way to the east, so I was just walking farther and farther away from my unit. Or what was left of it.

"And it wasn't easy going. It took all my concentration and effort just to make a little progress, weaving my way over and through piles of debris. I kept running into dead ends and backtracking. The Wolf was running the right way again, toward the west, but the banks were all washed out, and they were covered with every kind of debris. It looked like a picture I saw after the Johnstown Flood. Wreckage on top of wreckage, all tangled together and coated with mud. Eventually I couldn't go any further. The debris had piled up against another wrecked bridge, almost like a solid wall or a dam. I had to try to go around it the only way I could. The river cut through more or less open country, but after I left the river I wandered into the edge of some suburbs, or what had been suburbs. There were survivors, digging into rubble.

"It was all black people, African-Americans. It was a black area, I have no idea where. Small one-story detached houses, mostly tumbled down in heaps. Some apartment buildings pancaked down, they were probably three- or four-story buildings, but I'm just guessing. I couldn't tell if they collapsed during the first quake or the second. No police, no ambulances, no paramedics, no sirens—no nothing. Just quiet, except for people cursing and crying over their fallen-down homes and their dead family members. And a few random gunshots, that was about it. No cars were moving. Even if you had gas, there was no way to drive with trees and poles and cables all over the roads. And there I was, Mr. White Boy, in my muddy Army uniform and boots. My empty military holster had a flap, so maybe it was hard to tell if I had a gun in it, but it was a weak bluff. I got a real bad feeling that I had better not go any further south, into Memphis. People were looking at me with pure hate in their eyes, or at least it seemed that way to me. Like the earthquakes were *my* fault, some-how. Or like it was my fault that they hadn't been rescued by the federal government already. I turned around and headed back to the Wolf. It's not as if I was going to get to a telephone and call in to my unit. Who had a phone that worked? There was still no electric power since the first quake, three weeks before.

"I edged my way back toward the river, got around the big debris field piled up against the other bridge, but it wasn't my bridge, it was a different one, with a few big round concrete pilings in a line instead of lots of square pilings in pairs. That's when I finally figured out I must be on the wrong side of my unit, walking further away instead of getting closer. That's when it came to me, the way all the debris was piled up: the flood had swept in from the Mississippi, right up the Wolf River against the regular current. But hell, everything in the whole world was so strange by then…that it almost seemed natural that a river could flood backwards. Why not?

"I didn't know if I should turn around and head back west, or what. I hadn't eaten or had anything to drink in probably eighteen hours. I was getting ready to drink straight from the Wolf, and I knew that was a bad idea. Everything from oil and chemicals to dead bodies was in that river. Anyway, I didn't have to think about it long. I was pushing along between chest-high bushes and an old chain link fence, and I ran smack into a dead end. The fence ran right into the side of an old wall from a warehouse or something, and I had to turn around.

"That's when I was captured. It was just casual, easy, no problem at all. I turned around and there were three black guys trailing me about ten feet back. Two teenagers, and one maybe about thirty years old. He had a revolver, and he just waved me out. He was the tallest, my height, about five eleven, with a big pile of dusty dreadlocks bundled together up on top. That made him seem taller, maybe. The other two were carrying machetes, like Mexicans use. These two had spiky dreadlocks and they were very dirty, but they were all dressed pretty well, considering. Nice jeans and jackets, not ripped or filthy like you might expect, not three weeks after the first earthquake. Stolen or looted, probably.

"Anyway, there was nowhere for me to go, and I was too weak and out of my head to try anything. They put me on the ground and tied my hands behind my back so tight that I thought that would kill me all by itself. Then they tied a noose around my neck, and pulled me back up on my feet and jerked me along like a goat or a cow. They kept pinching me and laughing, but I couldn't really understand them. For some reason they seemed glad that I wasn't too skinny, I gathered that much, but I didn't make anything of it at the time. I'd trip and they'd pull me, drag me along on my face, until somehow I'd get back up on my feet. I could hardly understand a word they were saying, but I got the strong idea my problems were only just beginning. Obviously, if they had wanted to kill me where they found me, they could have.

"They led me back along the chain link fence to a gate, down a few weedy paths and alleys, and finally to a concrete slab, next to a big rusty steel warehouse that was half falling down. They had set up kind of a camp there, under part of the warehouse's roof that was still intact, giving them a dry spot. I guess they were used to catching stragglers like me who were working their way along the riverbank. The old warehouse was maybe a hundred yards from the river, all surrounded by weeds and trees.

"And that's when I saw the absolute worst. That's when I gave up my last hope: when I saw the burnt body parts. There were legs and arms hacked down to the bones, and a fire pit, with the big iron grill over it. There were even decapitated heads, set in a row. I was lying on my side, and I looked over and saw a severed head that almost seemed like it was looking back at me. Dead eyes, wide open. The cooking grill was a wrought-iron gate, propped up on angle iron legs that were driven into the dirt. There was a square hole in the cement, where they had built their fire. Now I could understand what they had been talking about. That's why they had been pinching and squeezing me. That suddenly became perfectly clear. Three weeks after the first earthquake, that was three weeks without supermarkets or fast food joints. Hunger makes people crazy, and some people are crazy to begin with. I guess it doesn't take much for the ones that are already crazy. An earthquake will do it, that's for sure. It'll push psychos right over the edge.

"They tied my ankles together, and then they tied my hands to my feet behind my back. They trussed me up like a hog. I was lying on my side then, tied to some kind of a pipe that came up out of the concrete. By then I was way beyond shock. I could only hope that they were going to kill me fast and not torture me too much beforehand, but really, I didn't have too much hope of that. Sometime in the afternoon, two of them left. They said they were going out hunting for more meat. It was like a joke to them. They laughed and said, 'Honky, the other white meat.' Or maybe I just imagined that. By that point, I couldn't tell what was real and what was a hallucination. But I was sure that I was a goner. I had no doubt about that at all.

"The one that stayed to guard me couldn't have been more than fifteen years old. I tried to talk to him. I told him I was in the Army and they'd come looking for me, all of that, but he wasn't buying it. He wouldn't even look at me. I told him he'd get a reward for helping me—nothing, no reaction. He was smoking some kind of homegrown reefer wrapped up in sheets of telephone book paper. He had dead eyes, stone cold dead eyes that looked right through you like you were a ghost. The leader gave him some chores to do while they were gone. His job was collecting firewood and cleaning up, taking body parts and bones down to the river in a wheelbarrow. Heads, hands, feet…he was pretty casual about it. The way he acted, they could have been beef or pork scraps he was picking up and tossing into the wheelbarrow. The whole thing was right out of a grade B horror movie.

"This was January, like now, and it got dark early. The other two came back after sunset with another teenage boy that they seemed to know already, and two black girls about twelve or thirteen. Black or Hispanic, or maybe somewhere in between. They were just numb with fear, it seemed to me. Or maybe they were in shock, almost catatonic. I can only imagine what hell those girls had been through in the three weeks since the first earthquake, and what they thought after another big quake hit. They weren't tied up, but I couldn't tell if they were going to be on the menu with me or if they were going to be on the other side of the dinner table, so to speak. It was about twenty-four hours since I'd had anything to eat or drink, and I must have been delirious. The older guys brought back a big cardboard box, and they were drinking wine from bottles. They must have had a good afternoon of looting. They built up the fire in the hole under the big iron grate, and I thought, 'Well, this is it: curtains. Just let it be quick when it's my time.'

"When the fire was up and burning hot, the two biggest guys came for me and untied me from the metal pole—but they kept my feet and ankles bound. I'd lost all feeling in my hands. I was waiting for one of them to take a machete to my throat. I figured that they'd do it that way, but no, they just dragged me over by the fire like a slab of meat. There was a square hole in the concrete, where they had the fire going, with the grate over the top. The two girls were sitting together on a log a few feet away, getting warm by the fire. They weren't tied up, but they weren't trying to get away either. What else could they do? They were just young girls. The whole thing was surreal: the half-tumbled-down warehouse, the cooking fire, everything.

"Then the leader, the older guy with the dreadlocks tied up in a bundle, he seemed to gradually notice that I was still in my Army uniform. I got the idea that he was comparing his size to my uniform. Staring at me, sizing me up. This presented a problem, because my wrists and ankles were still tied. I think if I wasn't wearing the uniform, they would have just thrown me over that iron grate and burned me alive then and there. Or maybe hacked my arms and legs off with the machetes and just cooked them, I don't know how they were going to do it. I think that he was so drunk and stoned that he couldn't figure out how to get the uniform off of me without burning it up or getting it soaked in blood. I got the impression that this was a serious mental challenge for him, a real puzzle. He'd been smoking weed pretty much the whole time I'd seen him, and drinking wine, a lot of wine. Bob Marley meets Frankenstein—in hell.

"By now it was dark out, except for the fire under the cooking grate. The tallest one, the leader, he pulled me up on my feet, but they were still tied together, like my hands. He was wearing a bright green Urban Corps jacket. He had his pistol shoved in his belt, a machete in one hand, and he was holding me by the shoulder with the other. I was sort of hopping around with my feet tied together, trying to balance, while he held me up and considered his next move. I thought he was just going to push me over the fire. We were nose to nose. He looked like the devil himself, his eyes glowing yellow in the firelight. He said, 'White boy, I'm gonna untie you, and then you gonna get all naked and give me them Army clothes.' I knew that once I was out of the uniform I was a dead man, so I was thinking of something to say, to stall him. I was going to try the 'earn a reward from the Army' pitch again, and see if it worked on him. I knew it was a long shot, but I couldn't think of anything else to say. He was their leader, so probably he was the smartest, and maybe he'd go for it. He looked right in my eyes; I can't imagine what he was thinking.

"And then he just let me go without the least bit of warning. I hit the ground right by the fire pit, fell on him and rolled off. For a second I couldn't understand why he'd dropped me, but then I saw that most of the top of his head was gone. Smashed apart, blown open by a gunshot, it looked like. I heard thumps and cracks, and sounds I didn't recognize, and all of my captors went down, one-two-three. They were so stoned and drunk they didn't know what was happening, and then they were dead. I wondered what the hell had just happened, and what can possibly happen next? It was three weeks since the first earthquake, and I thought I'd seen it all—but I hadn't seen *anything* compared to what I saw in the twenty-four hours after the second quake. The horror just kept ratcheting up, like a nightmare that keeps accelerating until you fall into a bottomless well or off a cliff and then you wake up screaming. Only this was no dream, this was all happening. Even as delirious as I was, I knew all of this was for real.

"So there I was lying on the ground, still tied up hand and foot, close enough to the fire pit to feel the burning heat, right next to Mr. Brains Hanging Out, and then I heard a friendly voice behind me. 'Well, soldier boy—this appears to be your lucky night. It looks like your dinner plans have been unexpectedly canceled." A white voice. He had a Southern accent, but he sounded educated. Somebody knelt behind me and cut the rope off my hands, and then my ankles. I could barely tell I even had hands by then, until that pain came ripping back into them. I guess I was wincing or yelling, and the man behind me said, 'That's a good sign. If they hurt, that means your blood is moving again. Do you think you can walk? No offense, son, but this is not the kind of dining establishment that we generally prefer to patronize.' I'll never forget that. I laughed in spite of everything.

"I rolled onto my back, now that my wrists were free. I could look up and see who was talking to me by the orange firelight. There were four guys in camouflage BDU uniforms. Not the regular ACU Army camouflage; the old pattern, like we're wearing now. Woodland, I think it's called. Green and black face paint, not a bit of skin showing, but I could tell they were white men by how they talked. They all had rifles, and different kinds of load bearing vests and magazine pouches. The one who had been talking had a suppressor on the end of an M-4 carbine. It was a flattop rifle with a scope on top, a night scope. They were very well equipped. Everything was first class.

"He hoisted me back up to my feet, and two of them half-carried me down along the riverbank and into a boat. A big squared-off Jon-boat like they use in the South, with an outboard motor. A big enough boat to have a steering wheel on a console in the middle. Then we were out of there, but moving slowly—to keep quiet, I suppose. Plus, I knew the river was full of floating debris. One of the guys had night vision goggles, so I guess he could see well enough to drive, and avoid the debris. It was as black as a coal mine to me, once we were away from the cooking fire.

"They told me they were on a rescue mission. They were coming down the Wolf River the day after the second quake, trying to get to some trapped relatives. They couldn't get past the wrecked bridge that was blocked up with debris. They had to give up on their rescue mission and turn around, and that's when they saw me about to become the main entrée. My luck had changed a hundred eighty degrees, just like that. All of this happened in the space of about twenty-four hours, from the second earthquake to my rescue. Crazy, but I couldn't complain about how it ended. Not when I'd been about to be thrown on a fire and eaten by cannibals.

"The only thing that bothered me was that my rescuers shot the two black girls along with the three men. The guy with the silenced carbine was using a night scope, and I thought maybe he couldn't tell the good guys from the bad guys, I don't know. Maybe they all looked like bad guys to him in his night scope, except for me, the tied-up guy about to be thrown on the fire. I gave them the benefit of the doubt about those two girls, when they rescued me. Hell, I don't know, maybe they saved those girls from getting gang-raped and going onto the fire after me. Or maybe those girls would have been gnawing on *my* bones in another hour. I'll never know what would have happened to those two girls if they hadn't been shot by my rescuers.

"But I'll tell you this: a lot of people died *after* those earthquakes, and most of them didn't die *from* the earthquakes, if you know what I mean. It's hard to tell who died from dehydration or hunger or disease, from those who were shot or stabbed or clubbed to death. Dead is dead—and dead men tell no tales, right? You could kill anybody after those earthquakes, and who would ever know what really happened? Dead bodies were all over Memphis, and I didn't see any cops or CSI's around them, that's for sure. Just buzzards and feral dogs. Anyway, those two young girls died right there by the fire. If my rescuers had any regrets about that, they didn't show it. Not one little bit."

17

Both men heard the zipper of the tent slide open, and turned that way. Jenny emerged, still wearing the brown camouflage trousers, but with a green wool military sweater for a top.

"The baby's sleeping?" asked Carson.

"Yes. At least she's taking the instant milk, and keeping it down."

"Did we wake you up?" asked Doug.

"I slept a little. I was listening to your story." She sat down on a folding chair between the men. Zack was still snoring softly in his sleeping bag, blessedly oblivious.

Carson said, "There's hot water in the thermos. You want something?"

"Hot chocolate?"

Doug went to a box and returned with a brown paper pouch. He tore it open and made the cocoa, mixing it in a mug on the table. Jenny sipped the warm liquid and stared into the space between the two men. Her long blond hair, mussed and matted on top, spilled across her shoulders in the absence of the fur hat. Her bangs hung almost to her honey-colored eyes. She spoke quietly, because Zack and the baby were still sleeping. "I found something in one of my pockets."

Jenny placed a small Ziploc bag on the table. Inside was a thin black rectangle: a pocket-sized notebook. Carson opened the plastic bag, withdrew the spiral-bound booklet, and opened it. She looked at Doug and said, "I'm glad you got away—that was an incredible story. It brought back a lot of my own memories. Do you guys want to hear it?"

Carson nodded and Doug said, "Sure."

She sipped her cocoa, then took a deep breath and began. "You were describing the January earthquake. I was already away from Memphis for the second one, but I was there for the first. My family lived in Germantown, that's between where the two rivers almost come together. The Wolf and the Nonconnah, like you were saying. It's about twenty miles southeast of downtown Memphis. That meant it was one of the only ways out of the city when the bridges went down. Our house shook but it didn't fall down, thank God. We had some cracked walls, but we were lucky: a lot of houses did collapse. It was Saturday morning, or I would have been at school. My school pancaked...so we were lucky it happened when it did. In Germantown, the earthquake shook us around and broke some things, but I didn't see it kill anybody. Not directly. Roads were buckled and cracked all over the place, so you couldn't drive very far without making a lot of detours. The main thing was the gas and electric went out, and the water. That was all right at first. We've had tornados and ice storms that knocked out the power. We weren't too worried. It always came back on in a few hours…or at least by the next day.

"Only this time, the power didn't come back on. Not a blink, nothing. The whole system was down—telephones, cell phones, ATM machines, gas stations—everything. On the second day, when we were lined up at the Safeway supermarket, that's when it started to get crazy. The store employees said you had to pay with cash. But the ATM machines didn't work, so how could you get cash? People who didn't have enough cash started to get angry, real angry. And all of the ATM machines I saw were smashed open anyway. Looted.

"By then the refugees from Memphis were starting to walk out to Germantown. I'd been waiting in a line all the way around the block with my father, and then these people walking out of Memphis just started cutting in line and pushing right to the front. Mostly black people, and Germantown is mostly white. It got ugly fast. There was a lot of pushing and shoving and yelling.

"People started saying we were stupid to wait while everybody else cut in line, and then they started pushing inside too. Police were there trying to keep order, but they gave up. What could they do? Shoot everybody? The police were a joke, useless. We waited in that line for six hours, my father and I. We were probably about number five hundred in the line to get inside the Safeway, and then the mob just pushed ahead of the line anyway. The supermarket was stripped bare to the walls by the time we got inside. There was nothing left. Nothing you could eat or drink, anyway. We felt like fools for wasting half of a day waiting in line, but who could you complain to? Nobody. We *were* fools…for acting civilized.

"We figured the electric company would get the power back on in a few days, or a week at most. Water became a big problem right away. Our neighborhood was on city water, and it stopped during the earthquake. We were lucky because we had a swimming pool, so it wasn't so bad for us. It cracked during the quake, but it still had a few feet of water at the bottom. We shared it with our neighbors on each side of our house; we let them dip it out with buckets. We used our propane grills for cooking, and for boiling the water to drink.

"And then on the third day more and more refugees started coming. That was Monday. Little groups at first, then big crowds, and then just continuous, like a parade. Mostly blacks from Memphis. Lots of them were pushing shopping carts full of stuff. Their own stuff or looted stuff, who knows? Our street was only one block off Poplar Avenue, it ran parallel to it. Poplar's a big street; it goes all the way into Memphis, and the other way it goes out to the country. We had a lot of people walking through our neighborhood. I mean thousands, like a stadium letting out, and we were a block off of Poplar.

"At first folks came up and knocked on the door, fairly polite, asking for water and food. They thought we were rich or something, because of our neighborhood. Somehow they found out we had a swimming pool, and they wanted water. That sounds pretty reasonable, but then some of them started sitting all over our yard. At first we hoped they were just 'resting,' but then it went from a few people to dozens to hundreds. We had whole families sitting all over our yard, camping out almost. Then our car disappeared. We could only fit our Expedition in the garage, so our Acura was parked in the driveway. Then it was gone, and the people sitting all over our yard just shrugged. They didn't say anything; they just glared at us like *we* caused the earthquake or something. I peeked out through the curtains—only my father went to the door to talk to them. On the third day, the refugees went right into our backyard too, and then we couldn't get water out of our own pool. We were too afraid to go outside, not even in the backyard to get water. I was never a racist, I had black friends at school, but this was different. I was scared to death every minute. The people outside didn't seem grateful for the water, they seemed more angry. Resentful, I guess, because we had a little swimming pool. Smaller than this platform we're on.

"In the afternoon of the third day it started raining hard, cold hard rain, and people started banging on our doors. Women. There were men too; in fact, it was mostly men outside. I think they sent the women to knock on the door, just to play on our sympathy. They were pleading for us to open up, and let them come inside and get some shelter. They said they had babies and children with them, please God have some mercy and let them in! And about then there were some loud bangs around the neighborhood, and I just knew they were gunshots.

"My father didn't have any guns. He *didn't believe* in them, can you imagine that? Didn't believe in them! That's like not believing in rocks, or hammers or knives. He *didn't believe* in guns! I mean, guns are reality, so not believing in guns is like not believing in reality. Well, some of our neighbors must have believed in them, because we started hearing gunshots, and it was pretty obvious that no matter what happened, 911 wasn't coming. Not with the phones out. The police were not even a factor. I don't know if they all ran away to look after their own families, or maybe they were guarding something more important than our street. Whatever it was, we never saw them around our neighborhood after the second day, during the riot at the supermarket. After that, they evaporated. Disappeared.

"My mother said, maybe we can just let the women and the children in for a little while, as long as it was raining? My father said no, we can't let them inside, not even for a minute. If we do, we won't be able to keep the men out, and once they're in, they'll never leave. They'll take over. We had an ax and a baseball bat for weapons. We barricaded the doors with furniture. The window curtains were already closed tight. Some of the windows were cracked from the earthquake, but the glass was still in the frames.

"My dad told me to get ready to run away if they broke in. I was the younger of two children, and the only one still living at home. My sister, Julie, was away at college in Nashville. I still don't know what happened to her. I don't even know if she's alive… Well, my father said that in case they come in the house, I should be ready to hide, or to run away. He didn't have to tell me why. We all remembered what happened to those kids who were carjacked and kidnapped in Knoxville. They were gang-raped and tortured to death. It was hard not to think about that, because I'm blond, like that girl in Knoxville was, and about the same age she was.

"So I got a hiding place ready in the cellar, and I got a cellar window ready just in case. I had a big meat-carving knife too. Without gas and electric, the house was so cold that we were already dressed like we were outside, so I was ready to run away if I had to. I was wearing jeans and sneakers, and a waterproof green parka with a hood over a couple of sweaters. My father said that we were going to try to get to my uncle's house in Mannville. Uncle Henry. That was our plan. We packed our SUV in the garage for the trip, but with hundreds of refugees from Memphis camped out on our yard and our driveway and all over the street, we didn't think we could make it. We'd have to run over too many people, if they didn't get out of the way—and they wouldn't. It just wouldn't work, there were too many of them. Plus, there were telephone poles and trees all over the roads.

"We were waiting for the refugees to go away somewhere, but it just seemed like more and more were coming every day, walking out of Memphis. And all of them were cold and wet and hungry—and mad. We kept waiting for the police or the National Guard or FEMA or somebody to show up and save us, but they never came either. We listened to a radio that ran on batteries, but they just said, 'Wait in your homes until the authorities arrive.' What authorities? I think the authorities ran away too, like the police. Totally worthless. So we were trapped inside our own home.

"It was terrifying every minute. You couldn't sleep a wink, even after three days. We were hoping and praying that the people outside would just go away and leave us alone! It was raining hard, and the people outside kept yelling and demanding that we let them in. They were banging on the front door and kicking on it, getting madder and madder because we wouldn't let them in. My father yelled back that he had a shotgun and he would shoot if they came in, but it was just a bluff. He didn't believe in guns, remember? Not until he really needed one—and then he only had a make-believe gun. It was quiet for a little while after he said he had a shotgun. We thought his bluff had worked, but then big rocks came crashing through some of our windows, paving stones from our walkway and our garden. Right after that, our front door was smashed in with a metal pole, I think from a street sign. They demolished the door and pushed right over the table we had against it. My father was standing there with his ax raised, and that was the last I saw of him. He never had a chance. A whole gang of men rushed in at once, and they were climbing through the smashed windows too. They all had knives and spears and clubs. I ran for the cellar, praying that nobody saw me. I think they were all focused on my father because he had an ax.

"I ran down the steps and crawled backwards into my spot behind the old oil furnace. The furnace was cold because we didn't use it anymore since we switched to gas heat, and of course the gas stopped during the earthquake. So we had two different furnaces that didn't work. Anyway, I'd found some plywood scraps to cover my little hiding place behind the furnace, like a false wall. I was sitting on the floor in a little ball, not moving an inch. All I could do was pray. Hold onto my carving knife, and pray.

"The worst part of it was I could hear my mother upstairs screaming. The sound came down through the air ducts to the old furnace right next to me. She screamed and cried for at least an hour, until her cries grew weaker and then they stopped. I felt like such a coward, hiding in the cellar. I could hear them stomping around upstairs, knocking things over and raising hell, looking for food. They must have found the liquor cabinet, because when they finally came down to the cellar, they were drunk. I don't think they even realized there was a cellar in the house; they were probably just checking closet doors and found it by accident.

"I could just tell that they were stinking drunk coming down the steps by the way they laughed and carried on. I don't know how many came downstairs, I couldn't see from my hiding place where I was curled up, but I know there were at least a few men looking around the cellar. I could see their flashlight beams through the cracks of my hiding place. I was never half so scared in my entire life. Not a quarter, not ten percent. I turned the knife around, pointing it at my own heart, holding it with both hands. That's how scared I was. I thought I was having a heart attack the whole time. I had an ache inside that I'd never felt before in my life. Physical pain. Pure fear, absolute terror. I kept remembering what happened to that blond girl in Knoxville...and to her boyfriend.

"I was just petrified that they were going to find me, and drag me out and gang-rape me and torture me to death. I didn't know if I should try to kill myself with that carving knife if they pulled back that plywood and found me, but they didn't. It wasn't a big cellar, it was old and rough and very dark even in the daytime. It wasn't a fixed-up rec-room kind of cellar, especially not on the side where the furnace was. Anyway, they didn't find me, or I wouldn't be here right now telling this story. My mother and father were upstairs when our home was invaded. I was certain they were dead, and there I was, hiding like a scared rabbit behind the old furnace. That was the low point of my life, up to that time. I think my parents stayed upstairs to save me. If they had run downstairs with me, we would have all been killed. Instead, they stayed upstairs and died…died for me, I guess.

"After midnight, when the house finally got quiet, when the party upstairs died down, I eased out of my hiding place and snuck over to the basement window that I'd gotten ready. I didn't even have a flashlight, so I had to move across the cellar all by feel, like a blind person, about an inch a minute. I was so afraid that I might bump right into somebody who might be hiding there in the basement in the pitch dark! My God, that was so, so scary. I was glad I'd gotten the cellar window ready, and that I knew the way by heart. There were bushes outside the window, so nobody could see me climbing out. Once I was outside, it was just barely light enough to see, if you knew your way around. I knew my neighborhood better than anybody, so I could sneak around in the dark, and I made it to a little woods behind our street without being seen. That was the very beginning of my journey to Mannville.

"I had an old boyfriend who lived just a few blocks away. Bobby Buchanan, he was in my ninth-grade homeroom, and our families went to the same church. His neighborhood didn't connect to Poplar Avenue. You had to know your way in; his whole neighborhood was like a big loop, with only one entrance road. You could only drive into it from another direction, not from Poplar Avenue. It was on the other side of a creek and a city park that ran along the creek, so I was hoping it wouldn't be overrun with refugees yet. Once when we were going together, Bobby told me that if there were ever riots in Memphis, his father and his friends were going to guard the road into his neighborhood. I laughed at him and said he was paranoid. I know better now. There were no refugees on his side of the park, at least none that I saw, thank God.

"I knew all the shortcuts, even in the dark. Like the little footbridge over the creek that cuts through the park, so I made it to his street okay. His parents still liked me, even though I kind of dumped him. His father was a real gun nut, a deer hunter and all that. He had an entire room in his basement that was full of guns and stuffed animal heads and Army stuff.

He even had a little machine to reload his own bullets down there, which I used to think was crazy. I hoped the Buchanans would still be there. Prayed, actually. They had a big property, about an acre. There were two trucks in the driveway. It was so dark I practically had to feel my way, like tonight. I'm lucky, I've always had cat's eyes, and I've never been afraid of the dark.

"I was only about twenty feet up the driveway when somebody shoved something hard in my back—a gun. He said, 'Stop right there. Where are you going?' I didn't recognize the voice. I said that I was coming to see Bobby. Like it was any normal night, but there was nothing normal about it. He asked if anybody was with me, I said no. He whistled, and Bobby came down. I told him what had happened at my house, how it was taken over by refugees, and that my parents were dead. I'm sure I was hysterical. It was kind of a blur, what had happened the last three days since the quake.

"Bobby said they were leaving that night, just as soon as they finished packing. He brought me into their garage through the side door. They were packing their SUV, a Suburban or something big like that. They had lots of lamps and flashlights turned on in there. In their garage it was so bright, it was almost like the regular electricity was still working. Bobby's father listened to my story. Then they made me wait in the laundry room while they talked about bringing me along on the trip. Only it wasn't just Bobby's family that was going that night, it was three families.

"I could hear what they were saying through the wall. They were arguing about me because they had all agreed not to take anybody outside of their group. They had already turned people down, left friends behind, so it wasn't fair if I went. That sort of argument. All of the seats were taken. Their trucks were jammed with stuff inside and up on their roof racks. They were going to some hunting place down in Mississippi, and they knew from the police radio that the Mississippi National Guard was going to close all the roads the next day, to keep out the Memphis refugees. The Buchanans had police radio scanners, night vision goggles, and guns all over the place. This trip down into Mississippi was their bugout plan. That was the first time that I ever heard that expression, 'bugout plan.'

"They had all agreed to a plan, and that meant no outsiders, none at all, but Bobby and his father were on my side. I think the hunting place belonged to one of the other families; at least that's what it sounded like to me. They compromised, and agreed to take me about twenty miles out past Germantown, but not to their place in Mississippi. They said it would already be too crowded at the hunting cabin with three families. They wouldn't budge on that. They were even yelling at each other about it. They were not happy to see me show up, that's for sure, but they took me.

"I rode in the middle seat of the Buchanans' Suburban, squished in with Bobby's two younger brothers, with his little sister on my lap. She was about seven or eight, not really so little. Bobby's mom was in the front middle, and Bobby was on the right side, by the passenger door, with his rifle. Literally riding shotgun, except with a rifle. The third-row seat and all the way to the back was piled with boxes and bags right up to the ceiling. I mean, from right behind my head to all the way back was just full up to the roof, every inch. When we pulled out, the Suburban was the front vehicle of the three trucks, like the convoy leader. Bobby's father drove with night goggles on, and his headlights turned off. They put little green chemlites on the front and the back of each truck, that's how they saw each other. The ones without night goggles, I mean.

"It was wet and cold out, nobody was walking around, thank God, and there were almost no cars moving, at least not from what I could see with the streetlights out. A city is a completely different place when the lights go out. I guess all the Memphis refugees had found houses to take shelter inside of—one way or the other. There were a few cars driving, but not many. Sometimes we put our headlights on, but most of the time they were off. They had walkie-talkies to communicate between the three trucks. Sometimes the trucks had to go slow and kind of weave around telephone poles and things, but at least the wires didn't have any electricity in them. For once I was glad about no electricity—funny, huh?

"I was hoping that they'd just sort of forget that I was there, or maybe take me along to be a babysitter. I was being quiet, just a perfect nanny with the little kids, keeping them calm. It felt so warm and safe in the Suburban that I never wanted to leave it. I couldn't believe that they would put me out, no matter what kind of agreement they had with their friends. And all the time I was trying not to cry about my parents and my friends back on my street. But what could I do to save anybody? It was everybody for themselves.

"We almost made it out of Collierville. That's the last real town in Shelby County, the county Memphis is in. After Collierville, it's mostly open country. I'd been on that road lots of times, so even in the dark I kind of knew where we were. We were almost through Collierville, but a bunch of wrecked cars were smashed together in a tight spot between some buildings, and we had to backtrack. We messed up the convoy order turning around, and our Suburban ended up in the back of the line, number three. I couldn't see much of anything outside, it was too dark. All I could see was the green chemlite on the truck in front. We were driving down a small side street between houses, and somebody started shooting at us. No warning, no nothing: just shooting. I almost had a heart attack again, and everybody started screaming at once.

"And not just one gun was shooting at us, there were at least two of them, you could tell by the different booms and bangs they made. The truck in front was hit. They were yelling in the walkie-talkie that they had people shot. It was pure panic. Bobby's father stopped real fast, and he and Bobby jumped out with their rifles and ran up to help their friends. A bunch of stuff that was loaded behind the middle seat fell all over us when he hit the brakes. I stayed in the Suburban with the kids and Bobby's mother; we got down as low as we could.

"There was a lot of shooting, and it was close, very close. Shooting and yelling, and the bright flashes from guns going off. I mean hundreds of bullets—I was just hoping they were *our* bullets, going *out*. It's funny how you can think of something like that, at a time like that. It was the loudest thing I ever heard in my entire life, it sounded like machine guns. Bobby had an Army rifle like yours, one that takes thirty bullets at a time in the clip—I mean magazine. So did his father, and they both had lots of extra magazines in pouches. Bobby's mother had a big pistol. She was scared to death, I could tell. She kept saying, 'We should have left yesterday, we should have left yesterday, I told him and told him, we should have left yesterday!' The boys were crying, the little girl was hysterical—it was basically a nightmare. *Another* nightmare.

"After just a few minutes, or maybe just one minute, Bobby and his father came back to the Suburban. They had two people with them from one of the other families who were shot and wounded. Or maybe they were just hit by glass, I'm not really sure, but they had blood all over them. The truck that had been up front after we got turned around couldn't drive anymore. Its motor was ruined, and it had flat tires. That's what they said. The men were all yelling and screaming at each other, and they were yelling that I had to get out. Just like that. I wasn't part of their group. They had a deal, and it was the group first, and no room for strangers, period. Bobby's father said, 'I'm sorry, Jenny, I'm so sorry.'

"There was no room for me, not when they had to put two more people in the Suburban and two more in the other truck that wasn't shot up too bad but would still run. And there were all the boxes and backpacks that fell over onto the middle seats when they stopped so fast. It was all yelling and screaming and crying, it was another nightmare from hell. They had people bleeding, but they were too afraid to stay there and do first aid. They had to get moving, and they had to fit two extra people into each truck. They were screaming and crying and yelling at me, like I had brought them bad luck or something. I had broken 'the plan.' I guess I was their Jonah, that's how they saw it. I can't blame them, in a way. I *felt* like bad luck. Jonah, that's me." Jenny sniffed and wiped away tears with her sweater's sleeve. After a deep sigh, she continued.

"And so...I was put out on the side of the road, right there near the end of Collierville. Bobby gave me a flashlight and a pistol, a little .38 revolver, just put them in my hands and got back in that Suburban, and his father hit the gas pedal. They took off, just like that, heading down Route 86 toward Mississippi, trying to get across the state line before the Mississippi Guard blocked off the roads. I was pretty damned depressed about not going with them to their hunting cabin in Mississippi, but at least I'd gotten past Collierville, and now I had a gun and a light.

"There were railroad tracks that went along our road heading east, and I figured less people might be on them than on a real road, so I just started walking. At least I had a good head start over most of the people walking out of Memphis: I'd made it all the way to the outskirts of Collierville. I heard later that most of the refugees couldn't drive out of Memphis. Most of the roads were blocked because of earthquake damage, and when everybody tried to drive out at the same time, it just gridlocked and then it turned into a gigantic gun battle. They used to call Memphis 'Mogadishu on the Mississippi.' After the earthquake, I guess it really was. So most of the people in Memphis had to either walk out, or just stay where they were and take their chances finding food and water. At least I was ahead of most of the walkers. It was something like seventy miles to Mannville. I figured that I could hike there in a few days, and get to my uncle's house. Boy, was I ever way off on that guess! It ended up taking me over a month.

"So I just hoofed it down the tracks, walking slow and careful, not using the flashlight because I was afraid people would see it coming and then they'd lie in wait for me. I knew the railroad went way, way to the east, because when I'd gone that way with my family, I could usually see trains running parallel to the road. I actually liked it better walking at night; nobody could see me, and nobody was out wandering around. Nobody jumped me or anything—at least not on that first night. I kept the revolver in my hand the whole time, and I would have shot anybody who came at me, but nobody did.

"By morning, I had made it to where a two-lane road crossed the tracks. Down to the south I could see a little town, sort of a village. Just some houses, really. I was starving by then, literally starving, and I needed water bad. It was worth a try. I walked about a mile south on the road, between bare fields, and then I came to the town of Brandonville. It had one of those cute little welcome signs, with the population and the elevation. Just a few hundred people, I think.

"I walked up to the very first house I came to; it was set way back from the road on a few acres. They had some religious things outside, crosses and Jesus and Mary statues, so I hoped they would treat me nice. An old couple lived there, and they opened the door for me. They could see from way off that I was only one girl by myself. I explained that I was walking all the way from Germantown to Mannville. They let me in, I think because they wanted to hear what was happening back in Memphis. They had a radio that ran on batteries, but they couldn't get any local news and the national news didn't make any sense to them. All they knew from the radio was that an earthquake had hit above Memphis. Well, shoot, they didn't need a radio to tell them that—they felt it! Everybody did for hundreds of miles around. And there were aftershocks all the time too, and every time you thought it might be another big one starting. You could *never* relax.

"They let me sit in their kitchen, and I told them my story after they gave me some lemonade, and biscuits with butter and jelly to eat. They had an old-fashioned cast-iron hand pump right behind their house that went straight down to its own water well. Let me tell you, there's nothing better than a hand pump when your electricity goes out, or your city water pipes get broken. You'd know what I mean if you ever had to haul twenty gallons of water back from a community well almost every day for a year. Even if you had a wagon to carry the water like I did, it's still hard work pulling up that bucket rope forty or fifty times and handling all those jugs. But I'll bet I'm stronger now than most of the boys at my old high school. Sorry, I got sidetracked. Simple things like water pumps leave a strong impression on you when you have to use a bucket well for a long time.

"While I had breakfast the old man walked over to the next house, and then some kids ran around to fetch all their neighbors. I told my whole story again to about twenty people who were standing in their living room. Everybody knew everybody else by their first names. Not like in Germantown, that's for sure. They were all friendly, but I could tell they were afraid. I told them that no matter what, they couldn't let the refugees from Memphis into their town. If they did, they'd get overrun with people, and the refugees would just flat take over and probably end up killing them. I told them what happened on my street, and what happened to my parents in our own house once the Memphis refugees broke down the doors. You could have heard a pin drop in that living room. They were all staring at me like I was from outer space.

"Most of the houses in Brandonville were just a little ways north of Route 57, maybe a quarter mile. That's the road that runs just above the Mississippi border, all the way back into Memphis. The railroad tracks were about a mile to the north side of the town, running parallel to 57. They discussed what I said, and they argued a little about Christian charity and whatnot, but in the end, they decided to barricade the Brandonville roads and not let any strangers in, no matter what. Except for maybe a few folks like me, that came in ones or twos, but no gangs or big mobs. They'd keep them out—*no matter what.*

"And that was no empty threat. The men were all carrying rifles and shotguns, and some of the women too. The people in Brandonville put up warning signs on the road coming into their little town, and they parked hay trailers across it and blockaded it. Bobby's escape convoy had probably driven straight into a barricade like that the night before, and that's why they got into a gunfight. Anyway, it was daytime now, a nice clear day. A few cars passed by down on 57. Then there was a group of four cars that went by, but they stopped and came back, very slowly. Like they were deciding something. Hunger and thirst can make people do desperate things. Stupid things. Or maybe they were almost out of gas. The gas station was at that end of the town, down by Route 57. They drove on the bare field around the roadblock, past the warning signs, and the towns-people didn't wait for them to get any further. They just opened up on those cars. I was watching what I could see of it from the front porch of the house where I was staying with the old couple. The men from Bran-donville just riddled those four cars with rifle bullets, like a turkey shoot. Their rifles all had scopes, so I'm sure they could see exactly what they were shooting at. Mostly deer rifles, you know the kind.

"A man came back to our house, and I heard what happened. There was a lookout hiding down near the barricade, and when he saw that the four cars were all full of young black men, he called back a danger warning on a walkie-talkie. There were probably twenty rifles scoped in on those four cars, so it was just a massacre. But nobody felt too bad about it after they checked the car registrations, and found out the cars were from Germantown, not Memphis, and the dead men didn't match the car registrations. They had stolen the cars, probably carjacked them or taken them after home invasions. The cars were full of stuff that had obviously been looted, including fancy hunting rifles and expensive liquor. I had no trouble believing this at all, not after what I'd been through. I didn't feel one little twinge of pity for those dead gangbangers. Not one little bit. They probably couldn't get their own cars out of Memphis, so they walked out, and stole cars along the way. Probably after killing their owners, like my parents had been killed.

"Somebody in Brandonville had a radio with a giant antenna that could reach pretty far across the country. The folks I was staying with said he was on a ham radio network with people all over the place, including lots of people in Tennessee. He said Nashville and St. Louis were in bad shape too. That's also when I heard about the dams breaking, and wiping out Paducah and Cairo and flooding over the levees all down the Miss-issippi.

"The radio guy reported what I said about what happened in German-town, and about keeping the city refugees out no matter what. He said that the word was already getting around. He'd already heard lots of stories like mine from other ham radio operators. That was becoming the normal pattern. Every country house and little town became a fort like the Alamo. The locals would guard the roads, barricade them, and shoot any strangers who tried to get in. There was fear, real fear, of those Memphis refugees. I wasn't the only one who escaped with a story about being overrun by refugees. People learned that they had to keep the refugee mobs out of their houses, out of their towns, no matter what they had to do. And they did. They did what they had to do to defend themselves.

"And that's why they call us racists now, on the national radio programs that I hear sometimes. That's why they call us killers and say we committed genocide on those 'poor hungry African-American refugees' from Memphis. They're all Monday morning quarterbacks now, with nice clean hands. It's so easy for them to call us that when they never ex-perienced what *we've* been through. I *know* what happens when you let mobs of starving, desperate refugees in. They start out just by asking for water, real friendly-like. But they end up taking over your house and killing your family and stealing your cars. Then they go and do it again to somebody else. So, Doug, it doesn't surprise me one bit that your rescuers shot all of the people that were getting ready to cook you on a fire. I'd probably have done the same damn thing. I have no pity and no mercy left for the 'poor hungry refugees.' I've seen what 'poor hungry refugees' will do when they get the chance. Those girls would have eaten you for dinner if your rescuers hadn't shot them first. That's the only thing you can do with those people. Once the shit hits the fan and they're hungry enough to kill you, you have to kill them first. Before they kill you—and they *will* kill you."

There was dead silence around the table when Jenny finished her story. Then Doug hesitantly said, "I don't blame you for feeling that way. If that's all it was—a form of self-defense. But I've seen when it goes too far...way too far. Completely out-of-control too far. Let me tell you what happened after I missed being barbequed. I stayed with my rescuers for two weeks after the second earthquake. Their leader was a man named Web Hardesty. He was the guy who cut my ropes off when they saved me. Wade Ewell Browning Hardesty the Third. They called him Web. He was maybe in his mid-forties, with a beard like Boone's. Well, maybe it was trimmed shorter. Like a big goatee, sort of. And his hair was darker, and he wasn't quite as tall as Boone, but otherwise they could have been related. Maybe brothers even.

"Hardesty had a great setup. His family owns about a hundred acres on a side creek off the Wolf River. Both sides of the creek, all the way down to the Wolf. He's rich, seriously loaded, but I never heard him mention where he made his money. It was family money, I think. I got the impression that this wasn't his only place. Hardesty had his own little band of survivalists staying with him after the earthquakes. There was even a little barracks house with ten bunk beds, just ready to go. Generators and everything. Like your friend's hunting retreat in Mississippi, but on a bigger budget, a *way* bigger budget. He had a nice house there too, where his close friends and their families were living. Hardesty was probably just *waiting* for the shit to hit the fan. His friends and him were ready for anything, and fully equipped. Picture a whole squad of Rangers or SEALs. Maybe a little past their prime, but still hard-asses, and armed to the teeth."

Jenny shrugged. "So, what's wrong with that? That sounds like a good place to me."

"Nothing, not a thing. But these guys were twisted. I went out with them on 'rescue missions.' It sounds plausible. They were going out to rescue their friends who were stuck in dangerous places when the shit hit the fan. They had boats, jeeps, dirt bikes…I heard they even had a Cessna, but I didn't see it while I was with them."

"I wish a group like that had come and rescued *my* family," said Jenny.

"I'm sure you do. But that wasn't the whole picture. The 'rescue missions' turned into something else. Those good old boys, they had night vision scopes, infrared lasers, silencers…everything. They were very intense, very high strung. To listen to them, it sounded like they all knew somebody who had been raped or murdered by blacks, and you know that's just not possible. But maybe they did see some pretty terrible things."

"Like you, about to be eaten by cannibals," Jenny noted dryly.

"Yeah, that's true. That's one example. But I think those guys were just waiting for something like the earthquakes to happen. Not just for earthquakes—they were ready for anything. For the end of the world. Like they were expecting it all along. And if you ask me, they were enjoying it. It was almost like a game for them. They wore camouflage uniforms, they put on face paint, the whole nine yards. When they had that green and black grease paint on their faces, you couldn't tell *what* color they were underneath. Oh, they really got into it. They called black people niggers, of course, but they also called them zombies and goblins. Hardesty's group could just roam around at night and kill people like it was a video game, all in the green light of starlight scopes. I think the 'rescue mission' part was just an excuse.

"At night, refugees would build little campfires for warmth and for cooking, so they were easy for Hardesty to find. You could see them from literally a mile away, and then just stalk in toward them, using night vision. If they were white people, sometimes Hardesty helped them, gave them some food and water, or gave them directions and advice on where to go. Sometimes Hardesty just went on around them and left them alone. But if they were black…most of the time, they were shot. From a hundred yards out, with a night scope and a silencer, it's like shooting fish in a barrel. They said that they were taking out the trash, cleaning up Tennessee while they had the opportunity. They called it 'coon hunting,' they said it was 'open season on niggers.' They said they were culling the herd and flushing out the gene pool. After shooting some blacks they'd say, 'NHI—no humans involved.' I think they enjoyed it, from what I saw.

"And not just blacks. One night on a 'rescue mission,' we found a camp that they thought was white people, but when we got up close enough to come into their firelight, we could tell they were Mexicans. Or maybe from somewhere else in Central America, I don't know. They were talking in Spanish. There were at least eight or ten men, from their teens to their fifties, and two or three women.

"That night there were seven of us out with Hardesty, counting me. We went out in two big aluminum hunting boats. They had special muffler boxes over the outboard motors to make them run so quiet that you almost couldn't hear them. From the front, when they were going slow, you couldn't hear them at all. The boats were painted green and brown camouflage, but they mostly used them at night when I was with them. The Wolf River was their secret highway at night. When we saw campfires, we'd beach the boats about a half mile away, and patrol in on foot.

"The Mexicans were camped in a field between four old cars. Like circling the wagons, you know? It looked like they were sleeping in their cars and under plastic sheet lean-to shelters, but when we approached, most of them were sitting in a circle around their fire, between the cars. It was a wretched, miserable night. Not really raining, but misting, almost drizzling.

"Hardesty could speak pretty good Spanish, I'd heard him, but that night he wouldn't. He could speak French and German too; he was very well educated. He could whip out quotes from famous people for almost every occasion. Lines of poetry too. Just pull them out to fit any situation, and not miss a beat. A real Renaissance man. Great sense of humor, at least with his group. A natural leader.

"So he kept ordering these Mexicans to speak English, speak English dammit, this is still America! He asked them why were they in America. He asked them if they had snuck over the border, or come in legally. 'Where were you born? Show me your green cards! Show me your visas!' They didn't have a clue what he was saying. He called them invaders and thieves and blood-sucking parasites. He said they didn't belong in Tennessee or any part of America, and to get the hell out of his country. He was livid, he was even angrier than when he was just killing blacks. He kept firing questions at them in English, but they couldn't answer him. Remember, this was last January, and that was months before the first North American Legion battalions were formed up and sent into Tennessee. So these were just poor dumb Mexican illegal aliens, not NAL troops or anything like that. That came later." Doug pronounced NAL so that it rhymed with pal.

"They were all huddled around their fire when we snuck up on them. We must have been a terrifying sight, all cammied up, with rifles. I had a rifle, too, by then—this rifle, in fact. Hardesty gave it to me himself. It came with this suppressor, just about all of his rifles had suppressors. He had a weapons room in his river house like a big-city SWAT team might have. This one is a semi-auto AR-15 carbine, but otherwise it's the same as a military M-4. I have a night scope for it, but its batteries died and I couldn't get any more. They're special batteries, impossible to find. You brought some in the dead traitor's pack, so I'll be back in business with night vision now. I just need to put the scope back on."

Jenny nodded, but didn't say anything.

"Since Hardesty rescued me, since he saved me from being cooked and eaten by a gang of blacks, he must have assumed that I'd be thrilled to join his little band of killers. I was another trigger puller in his private army, and obviously I'd be highly motivated, right? At first I was grateful, how could I not be? He had generators, diesel and gas tanks, freezers, meat, ice, beer—everything. All hidden in his own personal survivalist paradise. And I *was* grateful! They had saved my life, saved me from being killed and eaten by cannibals. So sure, I went out on 'rescue missions' with them. After all, we'd be saving more people like me from a horrible fate, right? I thought they were heroes, at first. I really did. For a while, I thought we were doing a good thing. It was like being in an un-official National Guard unit, almost. An unofficial militia, kind of on the vigilante side. The Rescue Rangers. I would stay with them until I found the Army, or the Army found me. I suppose that's how I rationalized it.

"But they were enjoying it, especially killing blacks. They called black women 'breeders.' Hardesty said, 'For Pete's sake, don't let the breeders get away!' His friends laughed and said, 'We're finally breaking the cycle of poverty. We're the best welfare reformers in history.' And they meant it, too. After they shot them, they usually dragged their bodies into the river. 'Sending them down the river,' that's what they called it. 'Mail us a postcard from New Orleans,' they'd say. If they were too far from the river, they'd drag the bodies over their own campfire and burn them. Or they would just leave them where they fell. There were already so many bodies, who would ever notice a few more? Like you said, Jenny, there were no police anywhere.

"Most of the time they just snuck close enough to campfires to see if they were black people. Then they'd start sniping away, with their night scopes and infrared lasers and their sound suppressors. Fish in a barrel. But once we did actually rescue two white girls. They had been raped and beaten for days and days, so it wasn't entirely clear in my mind that what we were doing was just plain out-and-out murder. That night when we found the two white girls was a real rescue mission, no doubt about it. That night, we really were 'rescue rangers.' Hardesty was a perfect gentleman toward those two, and he returned them to their families. One of those girl's brothers joined up with Hardesty's band right on the spot, after Web brought her home. That one mission made me question if what they were doing was more evil, or more virtuous. I was actually proud to be with Hardesty then.

"That, plus we shot plenty of looters, and we found some more evidence of cannibalism. Cooked, half-eaten evidence. Humans were on the menu at a lot of those campfires. In those cases I didn't mind shooting them so much, but murder is still murder. I knew that what Hardesty was doing was mostly wrong...but nothing was completely clear after those two earthquakes. Normal reality had definitely gone off-kilter after those quakes. Nothing was the same after the earthquakes, especially that first month or two when there were aftershocks all the time. There were no police, no military...and no laws. Web Hardesty's law was the only law for miles and miles around. I'll be the first to admit that I went off the deep end. Way off. My hands are not clean, far from it.

"So anyway, that night with the Mexicans, Hardesty thought they were white Americans until we got up real close. And I think those Mexicans thought that we were the real military, or the National Guard or something. At first they were smiling, like they thought we were there to help them or maybe give them some food. Until Hardesty started to rant and scream and shout questions at them in English. He switched from infrared to a visible red laser on his rifle, and he'd put that bright red dot on somebody and ask that person another question, in English. They were just numb with fear, petrified, crying and pleading in Spanish. When Hardesty got tired of it he opened fire, and so did the rest of his team. It was just a pure massacre. Very different than sniping at blacks from a hundred yards away.

"While their attention was focused on shooting everybody around the fire, and getting the ones who were running away or crawling under the cars, I went the other way. Why I didn't shoot Hardesty and his team, I don't know. I was behind them, I could have. Maybe because I owed them my life. But I went the other way, and they didn't find me. I don't know what they would have done if they had found me after I 'deserted'

Hardesty's group, but lucky for me, they didn't. A week after that, Boone Vikersun found me."

When Doug finished, he looked down at the table. His folded hands were trembling.

"So, what's the point of that story?" Jenny asked. "That white people are just as bad as blacks? I can guarantee you that for every Web Hardesty, there were a hundred blacks that did worse, a lot worse. And at least being shot is quick, a lot quicker than being raped and tortured to death at the hands of savages! And then eaten! And you even admitted that you rescued some people, and found more looters and cannibals."

Then Doug was talking, but Jenny was not hearing his words. She was hearing her mother's last screams. Unbidden memories were once again taking her back to her hiding place in the cellar of her family's home in Germantown, and to later painfully evil memories from the long journey to Mannville. When her mind returned to the present she heard him say, "But those two white girls were the only time we rescued anybody, other than me. The rest of the time they were just shooting innocent people in cold blood."

Jenny snapped back, "How do you know they were innocent? You said some of them were looters and cannibals. And Web Hardesty's group rescued you, didn't they? If it wasn't for him, you'd have been roasted over a fire and eaten."

"I know, I know, and that's why I still have mixed feelings about them—but you can't ever excuse cold-blooded murder, no matter what. Or you're no better than the worst savages."

Carson had been a silent listener to this emotional exchange, occasionally glancing between them while examining the pages of the newly discovered notebook.

Jenny was about to tell Doug that she wished that Web Hardesty's group had not rescued him and thus prevented him from becoming a cannibal feast. Before she could utter these words, the line of Christmas lights that marked the passageway back to the cave entrance blinked out, and then came back on. Then it blinked twice, and stayed on as before.

18

Doug said, "Boone's here! That's the signal."

"What time is it?" Jenny asked Phil Carson.

"Almost one."

"One a.m. or one p.m.?"

"P.m. It's Sunday afternoon."

After a minute, Boone crawled beneath the last low portion of the tunnel into the main room, and stood upright. He was wet through and his clothes were streaked with mud, his face red and streaming with sweat and grime above his beard. Huffing and panting, the first thing he said was "Doug, is everybody ready to haul ass?"

"Zack and the baby are still sleeping. I thought it was a good idea to let them rest."

"I'm awake now," said Zachary from his sleeping bag.

Boone hid his minor disappointment. It wasn't reasonable to expect civilians to be as hard-core as he was. "Okay, but we need to make a new bugout plan and be ready to go ASAP. The whole area is swarming with Cossacks. And they're going to be really pissed off when they find three of their buddies that I sent to meet Allah, or whoever they pray to. The snow's mostly melted, but there are still a lot of tracks around the cave's mouth where it's shady. It doesn't look good outside. It's too slushy to do a good job sweeping the tracks. I tried, but the sweeping looks just as bad as the prints. The snow's too wet. Just pray that the rest of the snow melts fast, and doesn't freeze our tracks. A lot of places our footprints melted all the way through, so they're like brown tracks on white snow. You can see them easy. Even from the air, I'm sure."

"Did you make it to the massacre site?" asked Carson. "Was it the way Jenny described it?"

"Yeah, I made it. It was bad, just like she said. There were at least a couple hundred bodies in a ravine. Men, women and children. All shot." Boone pulled a thick handful of ID cards from his parka's upper left pocket, and placed them on the table. "These are all I could grab before I had to take off. A helicopter came and landed on top of the ravine, probably where the people were brought in the buses. The side where their bodies slid down." He unzipped his parka and threw it over a stack of empty crates to dry. He left on his green combat vest, with its numerous pouches and pockets and pistols in holsters.

"Did you get pictures?" asked Doug.

"I did. Even the helicopter. It flew right over the ravine when it took off."

"They didn't spot you? Where were you hiding?" asked Carson.

"The only place I could: right in the middle of the bodies." Boone shrugged. "A few minutes after the helo took off, three Cossacks showed up. Looters. They knew what they were doing: they were there for the rings and the cash. Jewelry, anything they could find. They were about to walk right into me, so I had to shoot them. I hid their bodies in with the rest of them, and I hauled ass. I couldn't come back the way I planned, because a truckload of Cossacks was in the way. Jenny, that trailer you stayed at? They burned it. Troops were out in squads, beating the bushes and torching houses. I hid in that junkyard out back of the trailer, under a car. I figured I could wait until the three Cossacks moved on, but then the damnedest thing happened.

"A kid about eleven or twelve years old was out there, strolling around and jabbering like an idiot. He was wearing a red mechanic's suit, wandering around the junkyard, climbing up on things and hollering. He walked right past me, a few feet away. I thought he was going to lead the Cossacks straight to me. I don't think he was right in the head. There was no way I could help him, no way. The Cossacks started taking potshots at him, but he was pretty good at running and weaving. I think they were having fun with him. They took off after him like hounds after a fox. When the sound of their rifle shots moved away from me a little, I slipped out of the junkyard and made it into a woods full of little fir trees, like maybe eight feet tall. Planted for harvest, I think, but not really in rows."

Jenny nodded, following the story. She said, "The boy was in the trailer last night. I think he's retarded. I guess his grandma is dead now."

"Yeah, I guess so," replied Boone. "All the while I was out there, I was wondering when I'd get blasted. I had no overhead cover at all, so if there were any UAVs up, I guess they were busy somewhere else, or maybe I was just lucky. Or maybe they just had too many targets to deal with. The little fir trees were nice and thick and I had great lateral concealment, so I wasn't too worried about being seen by the soldiers. I was just worried about what was above me. But I never even saw a helicopter supporting the soldiers, except for the civilian chopper that landed by the ravine."

Carson asked, "Is it normal for the Kazaks to operate without helicopters?"

"No, they usually have a couple of Chinooks or Blackhawks on big operations like this. Or even a Little Bird or just an old Huey. I don't know why they didn't today. The helicopters have American aircrews. Maybe they don't want any American eyewitnesses to what was going on—especially at that ravine. If that's why, it was sure lucky for me. I made it from the woods near the junkyard down to the road, and you might say I was pondering my next move. There was no good cover for the next mile of my trip here to the cave; it was mostly open fields. But the road turned out to be okay, because Americans were out walking on it: refugees. They were pulling wagons, pushing carts, taking what they could. I just stepped out of the trees and took my place among them. Actually, I helped an old man push his wife in a wheelchair. I said, 'Let me help you,' and I hunched way over and kept my head down and just pushed her along. I'm not exactly a little guy, and with this vest under my parka I'm basically huge." Boone paced around the wooden-floor area of the cave, animatedly waving his arms.

"The Americans around me must have known something was up, my just popping out of the woods like that, but they didn't say a word. We passed a squad of Cossacks in a pickup truck. It was going the other way, and we weren't hassled. Of course, if we came to a real checkpoint it would have been all over, because as soon as they searched me…well…it would *not* have been good." Boone patted the .45 caliber Glock holstered on the bottom of his vest, and the frag grenades in their own pouches. "A five-ton truck full of Cossacks passed us that had a loudspeaker; it was playing a tape that was looped over and over. 'You must leave the County Radford before night! You cannot be protected after this day! You must leave now, and you shall not be harmed!' Over and over it played. It must have been a Cossack that made the recording—his accent was terrible, and so was his English." Boone pulled a clear plastic water bottle from a box on the cave floor, drained most of it, and then sat down heavily, nearly cracking the fourth folding chair.

"I'll bet my American traitor would have made a better tape for them," suggested Jenny, brightening. "That is, if he was still alive." She was sitting across the square card table from Boone.

"You're probably right. Good work getting rid of that piece of shit. So I pushed granny along in her wheelchair for about a mile, and when we got to a nice tree line that I've used before, I said goodbye and took off again. I think the old guy understood what was going on. He actually said good luck to me, winked and gave me a thumbs-up. Yeah, he knew what was going on, I could tell. He could have ratted me out, and made a scene when Cossacks were around, but he didn't. Nobody did. It wasn't a big column of refugees, just dribs and drabs. There were maybe a few dozen that I saw, heading south toward Mississippi. I guess they're cleaning the leftovers out of the county, after yesterday's big massacre. There was a lot of smoke, too, from houses burning. Oh, and I even passed a lowboy tractor-trailer with a big bulldozer on it. Cossacks were driving the truck, and an Army truck that was escorting it. I'm thinking that maybe it was going back to the ravine to bury the evidence. What else would it be going that way for? Jenny, that's how lucky it was that we found you last night, and that I took the pictures today. Once they bulldoze that ravine, nobody will ever know what happened there, at least not for years and years. They would have gotten away with it. But I've got the pictures, and the GPS coordinates.

"So after I made it into that tree line I had to low-crawl for a while. I'd freeze while trucks full of soldiers passed on the road, and then I'd crawl some more. It wasn't much of a tree line, not in the wintertime. Kind of sparse in the cover and concealment department—that's why I had to low-crawl it. The only good concealment was down low."

Carson laughed. "Low crawling sure beats getting shot. I've got the scars to prove it both ways. Why, I can remember crawling so low, I was looking *up* at snakes—and they were passing me. Of course, that was a *long* time ago, in another war, and I'm a lot older now. Much too old for low-crawling."

"Yeah, well I'm getting too old for this shit too, but like you said, low-crawling beats getting shot anyday. And twice on Sunday, which is today—by the way, God bless you all and hallelujah, amen. The only thing I really worried about was what I couldn't see: Predators. I had almost no overhead cover, and the whole time I was out there on my belly, I was wondering if I was going to get nailed between the shoulder blades by one of those skinny little UAV missiles." Boone smiled, his teeth shining white against his dirty red face and his filth-crusted chestnut beard. "I even thought that if the rocket was a dud, it might pin me right to the ground like a bug. But I'm alive, and I'm here, so I guess I got lucky again."

Carson said, "Yeah, unless they just tracked you here on purpose, so they could find your base camp. For all we know, they're surrounding this place right now."

"Well, aren't you just a ray of sunshine. Hey, old-timer, let me enjoy my fleeting moment of glory, while my adrenaline burns off. Sure, that's a possibility. It always is. And we're going to get started on our new bugout plan ASAP, just in case. There's another way out of this cave. It's not as easy as the way in, but it works. We need to get our gear ready. And let's square away our ammunition and battery situations. Doug, make sure all the rechargeables are good to go, and let's divvy up the new ones that Jenny brought. We need to be ready, just in case we get visitors at the front door. That's the one thing I hate about caves: the thought of getting an unexpected knock on the door from the other team." Boone upended and drained the last of the water from the plastic bottle.

"And even if we're not compromised, we're going to be leaving this cave soon anyway. I've given this a lot of thought, and this is what I've come up with: Jenny and Zack, you're going south to Mississippi, with the baby. A newborn won't last long if all it gets is that instant milk powder crap. I've got contacts all around Corinth that can take care of you and the baby, and Zack knows his way around down there pretty well too. I've got maps that I can mark with the best routes, for walking across the state line away from checkpoints.

"The rest of us are going north, to Fort Campbell. There's no point in staying down here anymore—there's no resistance movement left. It died in that ravine yesterday. We could keep sniping and harassing the Cossacks, but for what? Once they clear the last Americans out, Radford County will be a free-fire zone. Any warm bodies they see on thermal will catch a missile. The most important thing now is what's on these two cameras. This massacre was something new; they're taking the foreign occupation to a whole new level. I have lots of friends up around Fort Campbell. If we can show these pictures to the right people, we might be able to change some minds. These pictures might make a difference."

"Too bad we can't just upload them onto the internet," suggested Doug. "A few years ago, it would have been easy."

"No, forget the internet, that's out, that's over, the government has it all sewn up. We need to do this another way: person to person. That's why we're going to Fort Campbell. Zack and Jenny will be our backup, our insurance policy. They can take the other camera with them. That way we'll have two chances of getting the pictures out. Okay? Great, now let's make some chow. If we're leaving this cave for good, there's no point in leaving all of this food behind. Doug, get our big pot boiling. We'll cook up a great big old mess of Zack's Mississippi rice, enough for a whole platoon. We'll throw in some 'taters and beans, canned corn, whatever you guys want. Even the last can of chicken, the one we've been saving. Let's do it right. When we leave this cave, I want us to leave with full bellies...for a change. And plenty of extra cooked rice for the next couple days."

Phil Carson slid the booklet across the table to Boone. "Jenny's traitor wasn't much for operational security. This thing is full of his cheat sheets. Check it out." The pages of the pocket notebook were arranged by topics. The writing was neatly printed in black ballpoint ink. On one of the first pages, twenty names were listed, across from their aliases and radio call signs. Each of the following pages covered a different subject.

"Bad opsec is right," Boone replied, flipping through the pages. "I guess he never thought his notebook might get lost. Damn, he writes as neat as a girl. I'll bet his checkbook was perfect."

"He wrote down his frequencies, his call signs...even their passwords," said Carson.

"Passwords?"

"Looks like it. 'Challenge and reply,' it says there."

"Let's check the words for tonight—that might be helpful." Boone flipped through the pages until he found the passwords.

Both men laughed. Carrying all of this information in hard copy on one's person was a cardinal sin for a special ops soldier.

"Let's see," said Boone. "It's animals, and they change it every week. This week it's camel and horse. 'Boora and Toolpar.' That must be in Kazak, so there's no chance of an American guessing the right password." He turned the page. "And they use a number code for crossing out of the Kazak areas. That's all done in English. I guess English is the only common language between all of the foreign mercenaries. This week for the password, you add up to number seven."

"You hear five and you say two, you mean like that?" asked Carson.

"Right."

Carson said, "We were doing it like that way back when I was in the Army."

"Well, they probably had American advisers set up the multinational stuff for them."

"You mean American traitors."

"Yeah, American traitors," agreed Boone. "Look, it says they use the infrared lights anytime they're approaching another 'national area of operations.' It's Morse Kilo for the Kazaks. Morse N for the Nigerians, they're the next bunch north of us. It's all in here."

Boone turned another page. "This is a gold mine. Look at this: phone numbers. Fort Campbell Building 1405—that must be the traitors' HQ. That part of the base was closed when they axed most of the 101st. What a dipshit this guy was to write all this down!"

"Even so, you've got to admit that it's pretty impressive when a seventeen-year-old girl takes out a full-grown man. That's not something that happens every day."

"You think everything she said is true?" asked Boone.

"Well, she's wearing his uniform, and she's got his gun and his notebook. If it's not true, it's the most elaborate plant in history. Sure, it must be true, how can it not be? You saw the massacre; she sure didn't make that up. It's just too bad that she wasted him before we could do a little field interrogation." Carson smiled. "Good thing the stupid bastard wrote it all down for us anyway."

Both men snickered, and Boone handed the notebook back across the table. Carson opened it up to the page giving the aliases of twenty or so officials. One name in particular stood out from the rest. The name right at the top of the list. An unusual name, one that he remembered from seven years ago in Virginia.

Director Bullard = General Blair.

Zack Tutweiler was glad to ride the stationary bike. He didn't consider it a chore at all. The older men were busy with their own tasks. The bike's chain drove an iron flywheel connected by a rubber fan belt to an automotive alternator. This whirring mechanical generator was wired to an interconnected rat's nest of car batteries, AC/DC inverters, transformers and small battery chargers, all pulsing and blinking with red and green LED lights. The heavy flywheel and the resistance provided by the alternator made Zack feel like he was pedaling up a slight grade. Staring into the darkness of the cave, he was able to travel familiar Mississippi roads in his mind.

Doug Dolan was packing and preparing equipment while occasionally stirring the big cast-iron stewpot. The pot hung from a tripod constructed from iron rebar. The bottom of the pot was poised a few inches above a burning chunk of what Boone said was C-4 explosive. They had run out of the hexamine and trioxane fuel tablets that they had been using, and now they had to use C-4 to heat water and cook. It looked like a burning marshmallow, only smaller. Phil Carson had explained that this was safe. You could burn small pieces of C-4, as long as you didn't drop anything on it while it was lit. That iron pot hanging over the C-4 would probably do the trick if it fell! Zack wondered what a thumb-sized piece of C-4 would do inside the cave if it exploded. It couldn't be good. Boone had also said that there was enough natural ventilation in the cave to keep the fumes from building up. Well, the three adult men seemed confident, and Zack had no choice but to trust their judgment. They were all professional soldiers, now or in the past. The rice was bubbling and filling the cave with steam. Doug added cans of vegetables and even meat to the pot. Its aroma made Zack's mouth water, and he pedaled harder. Soon they would be sharing a hot "all you can eat" feast.

Phil Carson and Boone Vikersun were whispering over the card table. Between the two of them, they had many years of experience as guerrilla fighters, and Zack was completely willing to accept their leadership. Even though Carson was the older of the two, Boone was unquestionably the leader of this little squad. Boone had announced that Zack would take Jenny south to Mississippi, and that was that. It only made sense. He was heartened that they considered saving the infant's life to be worth some effort and risk. He was glad that even under these difficult circumstances, they still found the life of a single orphan baby to be worth preserving.

It was quite a responsibility, to be entrusted with getting Jenny and the infant she called Hope to safety down in Mississippi. She was back inside the tent with the baby, where she had spent most of her time since they had crawled into the cave. He wondered if Jenny was sleeping, or doing some motherly task with the baby, or just daydreaming like him. In some ways Jenny was familiar to Zack, and in other ways she was a mystery. She had also lost her family, so they had that in common. She had survived the brutal year since the earthquakes, and so had he, when so many others had not. They had both adapted to life without central heat or air conditioning, running water, flush toilets, full refrigerators and microwave ovens. Not to mention no cell phones, television, video games or trips to shopping malls and restaurants. They had all of that in common.

There was a hardness and aloofness to Jenny that did not match her devotion to the orphan baby. Maybe it was a case of compensation. Maybe caring for the baby filled a vacant spot in Jenny's personality. That would be understandable. Maybe the infant was a substitute for her missing family. It was too bad that Jenny was so cold toward him. They were the same age, almost eighteen, but Jenny barely acknowledged his existence. Still, she had not protested Boone's decision for the two of them to hike south on their own with the baby. At least not that he had heard. Privacy was hard to come by in the cave. Maybe she was keeping her feelings about the planned trek to herself, until he was out of earshot.

During the last few months, Zack had not thought much about the opposite sex. Staying alive was higher on his list of priorities. Now, in the relative safety of the cave, surrounded by warriors, he felt the familiar urges return. Jenny was tall and strong, even if she was on the skinny side. Who wasn't, these days? Her face was kind of bony and angular, but her blond hair was still pretty, and matched her wide-set honey-colored eyes. He wondered what a few months of good eating would do for her looks. Her chin and her cheekbones would not be so prominent, but she would be nice-looking either way. Zack could not help the lustful thoughts he felt toward her. He wondered if she was undressed inside the blue tent. Did she have underwear on, or maybe long johns? He tried to imagine her naked, inside the tent. Long legs she had for sure, he could see that even through her oversized Russian camouflage pants. The rest of her body's shape was almost a complete mystery to him, and that was unlikely to change, so he was left to his teenage virgin's imagination.

Zack had little hope of arousing romantic interest in her. Girls like Jenny McClure always went for an older guy, somebody like Doug Dolan. Somebody from a big city, who had gone to college. Like Doug, Jenny was also a city girl. She'll never be interested in me, Zack thought. Especially not with my bad complexion and my messed-up front teeth that keep me from smiling much. She would travel with him until they reached safety somewhere in Mississippi, and then she would go her own way. That was the unfortunate truth. At least he would be close to her for the days that this quest might take. And he was honored that the older men had thought him capable of performing this mission. They consider me a man, Zack thought, or they would not let me guide Jenny and the baby to safety in Mississippi. Perhaps more importantly, they trust me to get the second camera with the massacre pictures to the right people. Zack had seen the photos, on the little LCD screens on the backs of the cameras. He understood how important they were.

The chunk of C-4 beneath the stew pot gradually diminished in size, until the flame guttered blue. Doug Dolan gently placed another thumb-sized piece of the white plastic explosive beneath the pot, and it quickly ignited from the last of the old fire.

"I can't believe all the foreign militaries that are in Tennessee," said Carson, examining the dead traitor's notebook. "There's Albanians, Bolivians, Kazaks, Koreans, Egyptians, Indonesians, Nigerians, Pakistanis..."

"Yeah, those countries have all sent over at least a battalion of 'volunteers.' There's about a battalion of mercenaries in each 'unpacified' county. And the Russians are behind the Kazaks, you can be sure of that. The Kazaks are just Russian puppets. You can bet their officers report straight to Russian intelligence—if they're not Russians posing as Kazaks in the first place."

Carson asked, "And the president doesn't care?"

"Jamal Tambor? Tambo? Hell, my guess is that J.T. reports to the Russians too. He's been a closet Marxist since he was wearing red diapers. He's a good talker, he's smooth, but just look at the friends he picked all his life. Communists and one-worlders. America haters, every one of them. That's no coincidence."

"I don't even recognize this country anymore," Carson replied with a sigh. "What in the hell are all these foreign troops doing here? How could our own president have sold us out like this?"

"Tambo's an internationalist down to his bone marrow. The depression and the earthquakes are his big chance to finally destroy American sovereignty once and for all. That's what the push for the North American Union is really all about; it's not just about the new currency. Hell, there's more NAL troops in Tennessee than all the other foreign contract battalions put together. Anybody that can speak Spanish can join the North American Legion, with no questions asked. That basically covers everybody from the Rio Grande to Cape Horn who wants to move here and become an American citizen. But the Legion troops are mostly Mexican illegal aliens who were already here. Mexicans and Central Americans. There are thousands of them just in Tennessee. Tens of thousands."

Carson asked, "How's that going over with the locals?"

"It's not going over well with the whites and the blacks, but hey, Tennessee has changed a lot in the last few years. Did you know there's more Hispanics than blacks in Middle Tennessee now?"

"No kidding?"

"Yeah, it's true," said Boone. "And not just in Tennessee. That's the trend in almost the whole United States…or what's left of it. Hispanics are starting to outnumber blacks almost everywhere. So now that we've been invaded—that is, now that our traitors *allowed* us to be invaded—we're supposed to just suck it up and become part of the North American Union. Canada, America, and Mexico. One big happy family. Just like the NAL motto: 'Three Nations—One America.' Canamexico, they might as well call it. It's in Congress, and it'll pass. The president already said he'll sign it. Tambo's been pushing the North American Union for years."

"When did we ever get to vote on this bullshit?" asked Carson.

"We didn't. But it's happening anyway. The whole North American Union, it's part of some kind of master plan, it has to be. That's why they've kept the border with Mexico wide open, and that's why we've had all the amnesties. That's why we're going from dollars to that new North American money, the Amero. It's been planned for years. This was no accident."

"Boone, what the hell happened to America? I don't care if they're from Mexico or Timbuktu, foreign troops don't belong here! What was the president thinking, to bring in foreign mercenaries?"

"You have to understand Jamal Tambor; he's a globalist at heart," said Boone. "Has been all his life. There was never a U.N. treaty that he didn't support when he was a senator, and it's worse now that he's president. The same goes for his cabinet and most of Congress. The depression just gave them the opportunity to finally push it through, once and for all. Hell, they probably wanted this damned depression—they'd never have been able to do all of this otherwise. I don't think they even consider themselves Americans anymore: they're 'citizens of the world.' Give them a choice between an American solution and an international one, and they'll choose international every time. Just on general principle. That's who they are."

Carson said, "You're telling me that Americans couldn't handle the earthquakes without foreign help?"

"Probably, at least before the depression. But even considering how weak America is now, the earthquake response was totally bungled. Not that the problems weren't enormous—they were. With all of the bridges down, it was damned near impossible to bring in relief supplies, especially to Memphis. Helicopters just couldn't bring in enough tonnage to make a difference, not when law and order totally collapsed. Not to millions of people."

"Doug and Jenny told me all about it."

"Yeah. So you can understand how hard it was. No bridges meant no fuel trucks could get in. And no fuel trucks meant you couldn't run the equipment to fix the bridges. With the bridges all down, the rivers were blocked. Catch-22. It was just terrible from Nashville to Little Rock, but inside Memphis, it was unbelievable. Memphis went totally *Mad Max* in about the first three days. To the outside world, Memphis looked like a living nightmare. Media from all over were covering it from helicopters. They were calling Memphis 'America's black eye.' All those dead bodies lying all over the place, and where was Uncle Sam? Why didn't the Feds rush in with FEMA and fix everything?"

"Yeah, well, that's what I'd be asking too," said Carson.

"The honest answer is that nobody could wave a magic wand and fix it. Maybe not even *before* the Greater Depression, when the dollar was still worth something, and we could import enough fuel to run the helicopters and the transport planes. But no matter how you looked at it, the Feds were just pathetic in how they responded. There was no hiding it from the cameras up in the helicopters. It was complete anarchy down on the streets. Memphis was just dog-eat-dog. The mainstream networks filmed it all, and every day people were screaming, 'Where's the government? What's taking so long? People are dying and the government is doing nothing!' And that's not all they were asking. People were asking why so many bridges collapsed, why the dams failed, and why all those government housing projects in Memphis and St. Louis collapsed. If you looked at it honestly, it seemed like a lot of the blame really would have to be pinned on the government. Bridges and dams: that's the government's job.

"So, what Washington needed was an excuse for why they couldn't get FEMA into Tennessee and save the people in time. Something more than just natural causes, more than the earthquakes, more than the dams and bridges collapsing. They needed a scapegoat. They needed a bad guy to take the blame, to take the heat off of FEMA and the Feds. Tambo didn't want to wind up like George Bush, getting blamed for what happened after Katrina. Especially not with him being a minority president, and all those black victims in Memphis. That's when they came up with the white racist genocide angle. That was their excuse for everything: they couldn't get the relief in because the white rednecks started shooting at everybody in sight, including the rescuers. And of course with no police around, those rednecks reverted back to their own true white racist selves and just started blowing away every black person they could find. And that's the story that was put out in the media wall to wall."

"And this worked?" asked Carson.

"Hell yeah, it worked! The genocide story got plenty of traction, since the TV networks were beating the drum 24/7. I mean, there were plenty of black bodies to film, that's for sure. Bodies were everywhere, and nobody was organized to collect them. Not to bury them or to burn them. They just lay where they died, in droves. Phil, I don't have to tell you that after a few days almost *every* corpse turns black. So with every passing day, it looked more and more like whites were gunning down blacks wholesale. That was the big lie, and the big excuse for the government not getting FEMA in. And you know what? It worked. The big lie worked.

"Hey, it wasn't the *government's* fault that the rescuers couldn't get into Western Tennessee—it was because of those gun-toting white rednecks! It was perfect. And once that excuse became the official line, well, it's pretty easy to see why the government wouldn't be in a big hurry to go in and rescue those white racist killers, right? Southern whites became the perfect group to blame. Anything that happened to us, we had it coming, because of what we supposedly did to the blacks.

"After the second quake, most of the relief supplies for Western Tennessee were flown into Memphis International. They fixed Doug's bridges again and Memphis got the big rescue operation, at least what was left of it. But in the end more than a hundred thousand people died in Memphis, and who got blamed? Whites! It took the federal government two months to get Memphis halfway under control, and then the relief and reconstruction supplies started pouring in. But those white rednecks out in the sticks? Forget it. They were the racist killers who caused most of the mayhem, right? So forget them! And the rural white folks were mostly from the 'religious right,' so screw them twice, they never voted Democrat anyway. It was perfect. Doug calls it 'the convenient lie.' You know, like the opposite of 'an inconvenient truth'."

Carson quietly said, "Well, to be fair, you can't ignore people like Web Hardesty and his vigilante group."

"Maybe, but they were a drop in the bucket. They were blown all out of proportion. I'll give you an example. I saw a television documentary about a month after the quakes. It was called something like 'America's Shame—The Evil That Walks Among Us.' Documentaries like that made it sound like the KKK was riding again all over Tennessee and Kentucky. That's all you saw on the TV news, week after week: white rednecks with rifles, and black bodies on the ground. A few blacks were hanged by vigilantes, that's true, but so were whites. I mean, there were no police! People *were* hanged for looting, and for cannibalism, there's no denying that. But not just blacks, it was whites and Mexicans too. People did what they had to do to bring back some semblance of law and order when things were totally out of control. It's not easy to get a society back on the rails when it goes *Mad Max* and the police have skedaddled. It takes some vigilante justice, there's no doubt about it. What else can you do when there are no police? But all you ever saw were the blacks that were hanged. Over and over, the same handful of hangings, until it looked like thousands of blacks were lynched just for being black. They never showed the whites that were hanged—never. Just the blacks. The same five or six hangings were shown about a million times on TV. It was like the Rodney King video. They just played those same hangings over and over and over.

"It was classic scapegoating, and it worked. Nobody was pointing fingers at Washington anymore. Anything bad that happened after the quakes was our fault. Rural whites were Public Enemy Number One. So when they finally got around to 'pacifying' us, they sent teams of ATF agents out with the National Guard to collect our so-called illegal firearms. That was only logical, from Washington's point of view. It was because of those illegal guns that we were able to kill all those poor defenseless black refugees, right? Without our illegal guns, we wouldn't be able to slaughter those poor defenseless blacks anymore, right? Well, you can just imagine how the gun confiscation went over in a state where there's more deer rifles than houses.

"The ATF didn't have too much luck, not after the first few surprise raids. After that, the Feds *really* had a reason to be pissed at us, when a bunch of their agents got sniped. Then the National Guard wouldn't even go back in for round two. I mean those Guardsmen that didn't desert in the first place. Regular Army units too—they just wouldn't do it. It was practically a mutiny. They wouldn't go. Hardly any Guardsmen reported for duty. They wouldn't shoot Americans, not to take their guns away. And there weren't enough ATF agents to do squat, not unless they were backed up by soldiers. They brought in some big-city cops from places like Chicago to back up the ATF, but it wasn't nearly enough. Not without the National Guard.

"So it was a standoff from about March to June. The Feds wouldn't come back in by themselves, because they knew damn well what would happen. And if they couldn't come in to enforce the federal gun laws, then they damned sure weren't going to help us—and we damned sure weren't going to give up our guns! It was another vicious circle, another Catch-22: no gun confiscation, then no electricity and no bridges. They said we were in a 'state of insurrection against federal authority'."

"I thought you were at Fort Bragg."

"I'm saying 'we' because I was born around here. Yeah, I was at Bragg last spring, listening to all the government propaganda. If you watched network television, it seemed like it was just going to be a perpetual standoff. Evil gun-toting white racist rednecks, versus the noble multicultural federal agents, who just wanted to stop the violence and restore law and order. But with each week that went by, the federal agents were looking more and more impotent. Then they said that as long as Tennessee was in a so-called 'state of insurrection,' we wouldn't get our electricity back, and we wouldn't get our roads and bridges fixed. We wouldn't get a 'rescue package' like the one Memphis got. Well, we damn sure wouldn't give up our guns. The Feds knew what that meant from the first time they tried, last February. Come into Tennessee and try to take our guns away, and we'll shoot. That was no secret. So it was a standoff, and we thought it would go on like that for a while. We were at an impasse, or so we thought.

"Then in June…then came the big shocker. That's when they started sending in the foreigners. That's when we first heard about the North American Legion. Mostly it was Mexican illegal aliens, and most of them were gangbangers. You know, MS-13, the Mexican Mafia, real dirtbags like that. Illegal aliens who had been given conditional amnesty."

"What about officers and NCOs?" asked Carson. "You can't just pick them up off street corners."

"Their officers are mostly Americans. Americans who volunteered for Legion duty. Mostly Hispanics with prior military experience. And some active duty military transferred over to the NAL."

"Good God, how could they get Americans to do that?"

"Easy," replied Boone. "Just promise them extra pay, extra ration cards, and accelerated promotion. Active duty American NCOs could transfer over and be commissioned in the NAL as lieutenants. As soon as they transferred over, privates became sergeants, and lieutenants became captains. Phil, I'm sorry to say that plenty of young American NCOs and junior officers would just as soon fight for the U.N. or the NAL as for the U.S. Army or Marines. Especially if it meant more pay and a promotion. They've been brainwashed from birth to love anything international. They call it 'a higher form of patriotism.' Can you believe that crap? A higher form of patriotism! They actually say that, and they're proud of it! It's all that 'citizen of the world' crap they've been force-fed all their lives."

"Well, that's damned depressing," said Carson, shaking his head. "Are these North American Legion troops under the U.N., or the U.S. Army?"

"I wish I knew. That's a pretty murky subject, and I think it's meant to be murky. I *think* the Legion is under the U.S. Army, but is the Army under the U.N. now? You'd have to ask Tambo who's really in charge. What do you call it, when the president of your country is handing authority over to international commissions every chance he gets? Who knows what's really going on with the chain of command? I'm just a guy hiding in a cave in Tennessee, so I really have no idea. I'd just be guessing. Maybe it's sort of a test program, to see how Americans adjust to the idea of foreign troops. It didn't make any sense, except that they're getting ready to pass the North American Union treaty. The whole concept of the North American Legion seemed bizarre, until we figured out what was really going on. With the Legion in Tennessee, we'd get relocated *out*, and they'd get relocated *in*. The Legion troops and their *familias*.

Land is just about the only thing the Feds have left to pay anybody with. *Our* land. And that's what the NAL troops were in it for: our land, and our homes. That much I understand. But the chain of command, the real lines of authority? Clear as mud."

Boone continued, agitated. "The Legion troops were a joke at first. Just thugs and clowns, dressed up in old Army surplus uniforms and led by American traitors. Maybe they were big shots in Memphis and Nashville, but that's about it. They were nothing more than a bad joke last summer. A joke, but I guess they did break the ice for foreign troops operating on American soil. Well....sort of foreign. They tried to sell us that whole North American Union line of bull crap. Our North American brothers were coming to our assistance in our time of need. Yeah, right! I wonder if they really believed that line of crap up in Washington, or if they just did it to provoke us. You know, I haven't seen any Canadians down here, but I've sure seen a ton of Mexicans toting M-16s. Only their uniform says North American Legion, not Mexico, and we're supposed to treat them like brothers, like our fellow compatriots from the North American Union. 'Three Nations, One America.' Well, fat chance of that! Other than doing shakedowns at checkpoints, the NALs were worthless—at first. They didn't operate outside Memphis and Nashville.

"And that's where it stood last summer. Our own National Guard wouldn't come in and fight us, and the North American Legion *couldn't* fight, not at first anyway, and the standoff continued. That's when the president took the next step. Tambo needed troops who were ready when their boots hit the ground, troops who didn't need training. Troops who would obey his orders. You know he's been a huge internationalist all his life, so he probably thought bringing in foreign contract soldiers was a great idea. 'We are the world,' all that globalist bull crap. Supposedly the world was returning the favor to America for all the help we've given the world over the years. So Tambo's new idea was to find the right foreign battalions and invite them over on contracts. Offer them citizenship and free land, so it costs practically nothing. They bring their own small arms and tactical gear, and we provide the air assets, military vehicles and some logistics support. Counterinsurgency on the cheap—and they're way better trained than the NALs, right from the start. They bring their own rifles, and Uncle Sam provides the rest—trucks, armored vehicles, helicopters, and UAVs."

Carson asked, "Do they even speak English?"

"Hell no, and since they don't speak English, there's no trouble with things like the Bill of Rights or the Constitution. They never heard of them and can't read them anyway. They've just been told that we're rebels and terrorists and outlaws. That's all they know about us, and we sure can't convince them otherwise because they don't speak English. And they sure as hell don't have any sentimental attachment to Southern rednecks, so they're always ready to shoot any 'rebel' that looks cross-eyed at them. Especially since we were sniping them like crazy when they first got here—before they started the reprisals. It's not a bad strategy, really. Very cost effective. You still have to scrounge up some American traitors to fly the helos and planes, but the Predators are a big force multiplier there. There's no denying it's worked well. Look at us, hiding in a cave, getting ready to haul ass out of the last unpacified county in West Tennessee. Yeah, I'd say the president's strategy is working. Old Tambo's a traitor, but he's no idiot. He's a crafty son of a bitch."

"You said they brought over their own small arms?"

"Pretty much. I think each foreign battalion has its own arrangement. Mostly I think they brought their own small arms, from what I've seen. The Nigerians are using FN- FALs. The Kazaks brought over their Kalashnikovs. The NALs use our M-16s. Most of the foreign groups use some of our weapons. It's all a mishmash. They use their own small arms, but American crew-served weapons and vehicles. Each country has a different working arrangement, different rules of engagement, different SOPs. Mainly, we're talking fifty-caliber machine guns and trucks, and some light armored vehicles. We have plenty in the inventory, since Tambo cut the size of the U.S. Army in half. Hey, you want to see a real pisser?" Boone left the table, rooted around in a wooden ordnance crate, and returned with a small brown cardboard box the size of a pack of cigarettes. He slid it across the table.

Carson slipped on his reading glasses and read what was printed on the exterior. "It says 5.45mm ball ammunition. That's for the new AKs, right?"

"AK-74s. The Russians switched from AK-47s in the 1980s. Same basic rifle, in a new caliber. Great bullets, they're hollow inside the tip. Really tear you up. Everybody still calls the rifles AK-47s, though."

"It's about the same size as our M-16 ammo," observed Carson, removing a round from the box and comparing it to a loose 5.56mm cartridge left on the table.

"Right. But read the rest of the box."

" 'Lake City Ammunition.' This AK ammo is made here in the *States*?"

"Yeah, that's a real pisser, ain't it? Our own dear old Uncle Sam is making the very ammo that the Cossacks are shooting at us."

"Damn…if that's not treason, what is?"

"I can't imagine," replied Boone.

"What about the Constitution, and the president's oath to defend it?"

"*Which* constitution? That's the problem. The traitors claim they're defending the *new* constitution. That's their excuse. That's what my old

Army buddies say—the ones that stayed on active duty through all this shit. They're just defending the *new* constitution. Of course, plenty of them don't believe it. They just want the paycheck and the pension, which they still hope they'll get someday. And even when the dollar is just about worthless, the military commissaries still get food supplies. Plus, they get to stay in military housing for free. It's a pretty good deal—if you can stomach working with foreign enemies. The whole thing is just a mess."

"In a million years, I never would have imagined the United States could have sunk to this."

"You and me both, brother."

"So, when are we leaving?" asked Carson.

"Tonight. How's your ass doing after all this running around?"

"Sore, but it's holding together. I'll live…just don't ask me to ride any more horses for a while."

"I'm not planning to."

"So what's the new plan?"

"We're crossing the Tennessee River in a small boat. It's usually a more, uh, permissive environment on the other side in Middle Tennessee. It's mostly just NAL troops over there. I have contacts on the other side that can get us up to Fort Campbell. But until we can hook up with them, it's going to be a couple of long nights." Boone pointed up toward the ceiling of the cave. "Things are different since you and my father were running around in Southeast Asia. Now it's the eye in the sky that's the biggest danger. But we can't just sit here and hide, not with what's on these cameras. And maybe I'm getting soft, but I can't see hiding in this cave while that infant perishes. What's the point of that? We've had a good run, you and me.

"It's the youngsters I care more about now. Maybe because I never had kids, I don't know. Maybe it's because Jenny's so attached to the baby, and that's touched me somehow. Shit, listen to me, I sound like an old woman. We'll brief it, and then we'll get ready to move out. Once we're ready, completely set to go, we'll sleep. We'll take off later tonight, before midnight. It's about a two-thirds moon, and it won't set until later in the morning. Zack and Jenny won't have night vision; they have to be able to pass as refugees if they're stopped. The moonlight will help them move faster in the dark. They'll have a compass, and a map that I marked with the best routes."

"Have you got a spare rifle I can use?" Carson asked.

"Sure. You want an M-16 or an AK? The M-16 has a red dot sight, an Aimpoint."

"I'll take the M-16. With this much moonlight, a red dot sight will work well enough. Do the Kazaks have night vision?"

"Oh, hell yeah," replied Boone. "They use night scopes and IR lasers and IR spotlights."

"Do they have infrared scopes?" asked Carson.

"You mean thermal infrared scopes?"

"Right, the kind where they see people's heat."

"As far as I know, the only thermal infrared is what's up in the UAVs and the helicopters. I don't think they're giving thermal imagers to the foreign troops: they cost a fortune. But the helos and UAVs, they have thermal for sure. I'm pretty sure the Predators can downlink the FLIR video to the ground units." Boone pronounced the acronym so that it rhymed with near or beer.

"Fleer?"

"Forward-looking infrared," Boone explained. "That's what they used to call thermal night vision. They still call it FLIR in helicopters—I don't know why."

"So, we just have to worry about thermal infrared, *and* starlight night vision."

"Phil, it's not easy being a guerrilla fighter anymore. Hiding in the forest ain't what it used to be. Not when the enemy can see right through it, and your body heat shows up like a lit candle in a dark room. The days of playing Robin Hood and hiding out in Sherwood Forest are definitely over. Especially in the wintertime."

"You make it sound hopeless."

Boone laughed. "Well, look at us: we *are* hiding in a cave, and getting ready to run away. But even so, I've got a few ways to even things up a little. You ever see one of these?" Boone got up from the table, returned with a black nylon case that was a yard long and a foot wide, and set it down on the table. He unzipped the case, revealing a rifle that bore a resemblance to an M-16, except for its scope and the fact that it was randomly painted and taped in shades of dark brown and green. He lifted the rifle and handed it to Carson.

"This is my baby—it's an SR-25. It fires 7.62 NATO instead of 5.56 millimeter like the rifle you're going to take. I can shoot four-inch groups at six hundred yards—at night. It's got a pretty good sound suppressor, so the bad guys can't find you by your muzzle blast or your flash. With this rifle, I can outrange any weapon they've got. Well, their rifles anyway. Not their heavy machine guns. But they can't hit what they can't see…and they never see me. I make a special point of that."

"Do you think you'll be using it tonight?" asked Carson.

"I'm hoping we can sneak through without getting into a scrap, but you never know. Our new mission is getting the pictures on this camera to Fort Campbell—not getting into firefights."

"I'm guessing that fancy rifle is Army property."

Boone grinned. "It was, but I always sort of considered it to be mine. Especially since I did my own custom camouflage job on it."

Carson smiled back. "How do they feel about you taking it?"

"I never stopped to ask. I didn't sign a chit. When I walked off the job, I figured I might as well take the best stuff with me. They can add 'theft of government property' to my charge sheet—if they ever catch me."

"You were at Fort Campbell when you took off?"

"Yeah, 5th Group. Last summer, after the foreign mercenaries were sent in. That's when I, um, switched teams."

"You think the military will ever take you back?"

"Do you mean will America ever get rid of the traitors in Washington and throw out the foreign enemies? I don't know. But what else can a patriotic soldier do when his government is led by traitors? Traitors who trashed the real constitution and ginned up a phony one? Traitors who brought in foreign mercenaries to kill Americans and steal their land?"

The two old soldiers locked eyes, and found no disagreement.

Carson said, "I see we're cooking with C-4. How much of it do you have?"

"Here in the cave? About forty pounds, but I've got more in some other caches."

"Can't you get any more? Can't your friends up at Fort Campbell get some to you?"

"I wish. After they got the new constitution, federal agents came in and locked up all of our armories, and especially our demo bunkers. Ammo and demo are kept under strict federal control. The Army is kept on a short leash, a very short leash. Especially the Special Forces. They don't trust us one inch. They even collected the bolts from our rifles, and took them away."

"The Feds don't trust the military?"

"Hell no, they don't. I heard that they conducted secret polls, and about 90 percent of the military supported the old constitution. So they did as much as they could to neutralize the Army. Ammunition was collected and sent to armories under federal control."

"What about body armor?" asked Carson. "Do you have any?"

"I've got a rifle plate that I usually wear on the front. It fits in a pouch on my combat vest. I figure there's no point wearing soft armor. The bad guys are shooting rifles, and soft armor won't stop rifle slugs. It's the same old tradeoff: speed versus protection. There's about zero chance of getting real medical help, so I try to focus on not getting shot in the first place." Boone grinned. "So far, it's worked like a charm."

Carson asked, "Hey, are you going to booby-trap this place before we go?"

"Yeah, we'll leave some surprises. I camouflaged the cave mouth pretty well, considering all the tracks you guys left. As long as the snow melts and they don't bring dogs, it's not too likely they'll find it. But if they do...well, I've got the charges all laid out, but with an electrical firing circuit that'll go dead in a few weeks. Otherwise, some Tennessee kids might crawl in here years from now and get themselves blown up. We'll take the best stuff, as much as we can carry and still move fast, and we'll leave the rest. You never know, we might have to come back." He turned toward the simmering pot hanging above the iron tripod. "Doug, isn't that stew about ready?"

19

Sunday was seafood night at the Cole Park Buffet on Fort Campbell. Dwight Granger remembered real seafood, and this was not even close. Crunchy breaded fillets of reconstituted mystery fish, "crab" salad and pasta were the highlights of the meager feast. Even so, he knew that it was better than anything available outside Fort Campbell. A ticket to the seafood buffet cost only twenty new North American Dollars, paid cash in advance. This was the price of just a single soyburger and fries off base. As usual, he dined alone, anonymous within the dining hall. After dinner, he moved to the bar in an adjoining room. Granger had not come just for the meal. He had a vague plan and a larger purpose tonight. He could not keep the USB memory sticks in his room, but neither could he bring himself to destroy them. He had to try to get them to people who might be able to use the information they contained.

Granger had narrowed his selection down to two tables of men who were clearly active duty or newly retired senior enlisted, even though they were dressed in casual civilian attire. There were only a few remaining oc-cupied tables in the bar connected to the dining room. An Asian bartender dried glasses with a towel between his infrequent orders. A middle-aged barmaid with bleached-blond hair chewed gum and read a paperback, sitting on a chair near the kitchen pass-through. At eight thirty, one table broke up and the four diners departed, after saying a quick goodbye to the two men at his other prospective table.

Now it was time to either do it, or just forget the whole thing and throw away the memory sticks. His chosen pair consisted of two senior NCOs, or Dwight Granger had never served in the armed forces. They were wearing jeans and sweatshirts, but that didn't hide their identity. After his first career as an Air Force enlisted man, he knew the type on sight. They spoke without moving their lips, or casually covered their mouths as if they were afraid of lip readers. Short military haircuts, and clean-shaven. Broken noses and scarred faces. Broad shoulders, but not overweight like most men their ages. They were the granite boulders that the entire United States military was built upon. It was time to carry out his plan.

He had not considered exactly how he would do this, beyond a hazy concept. Granger took a paper cocktail napkin, unfolded it, and in the middle he neatly wrote with a black ballpoint pen: "PLEASE OPEN THIS FILE—IMPORTANT—NO BS—THANK YOU." Then he slipped the finger-sized USB drive from his pants pocket, and on his lap, he rolled it inside the napkin. His tab was already paid, so he stood up and put on his coat to leave. Once the deed was done, it would be a cold five-minute walk back to his solitary room in the UPQ.

They were sitting in the dimmest corner of the room, under large oil paintings of American tanks and helicopters in various wars. There was no smooth way to finesse this exchange. He looked to the exit door, and back at the two NCOs, still not sure if he could do it. Dwight Granger steeled up his courage, suppressed his fear, and walked across the room.

CW4 Hugh "Hulk" Rogan held his beer glass close to his mouth with the thumb and remaining three fingers of his right hand. The chief warrant officer helicopter pilot had left his pinkie and the tip of his ring finger in Iraq, but counted it as no big thing. He thought that their loss was more than a fair deal, considering all of his other wounds and near misses. Fragments of a machine-gun bullet had clipped off the finger while his hand was wrapped around the cyclic control—after passing through his thigh. The loss of the digit did not keep him from being fully mission qualified on Blackhawks and AH-6 Little Birds with the Special Operations Aviation Regiment.

What made him lose his FMQ status was the loss of flying hours, not fingers. The Night Stalkers of the 160th SOAR were grounded while the regiment was awaiting decommissioning as a unit. To Rogan, this often seemed like a microcosm of the Army in general: grounded and awaiting decommissioning. Tonight he was in a bad mood, and it looked like somebody wanted to make it worse. He shook his head and spoke quietly.

"Charlie, what the hell is up with that asshole over there? He keeps giving us the eye. Is he a faggot looking for a beating, or what?" Rogan had left New York thirty years earlier, but he retained some of the unmistakable accent.

"Who? You mean that geek-looking dude wearing the birth control glasses?" Sergeant Major Charlie Donelson was sitting with his back to the unwanted observer, but could see the man's reflection angled off the bank of mirrors behind the bar. Donelson was a senior noncommissioned officer in the 5th Special Forces Group. He still wore a Green Beret to work, where he rode a desk and seemingly did little more than shuffle papers for a living, while awaiting the end of his nearly thirty-year career.

"Yeah, him," said Rogan. "He must be a faggot. Jesus Mary and Joseph, does he think *we're* homos too?"

"So what if he does? Hulkster, the fags have their rights in the Army now. 'Don't ask, don't tell' is history. These days, the rump rangers get married in the base chapel and move right into base housing."

"Don't remind me. Every time I see a couple of queer lieutenants slow dancing and making out in the All Ranks Club, I want to bash their faggot skulls together. That's why I never go there anymore. That, and the shitty beer."

Donelson sighed. "I sure do miss the old NCO clubs. Can you imagine a couple of queers dancing in an NCO club, in the old days? Hulk, this just ain't the same Army we enlisted in."

"No shit. When we enlisted, Reagan was president."

"That was a different world. So, what about this guy? You seen him around?"

"I've seen him. He's a civilian contract employee, I think. DOD, or maybe Homeland Security. I'm pretty sure he's a Predator jockey. You know, part of that Building 1405 program." Rogan smirked. "Clandestine operation, my ass."

"Then what's he got to do with us? Unless he gets off on getting his faggot ass kicked."

"Hell if I know," replied Rogan. "Why don't you ask him—he's coming over, it looks like."

The two men sat across the small table, unmoving and silent as the stranger approached. The man was walking like he was crossing an unmarked minefield with an unexploded RPG jammed up his fourth point of contact. The two men said nothing, did not acknowledge the presence of the interloper until he was literally at their tableside, standing between them, and visibly shaking. He was the epitome of a tech rep, a technical support puke.

After an uneasy ten seconds, without looking up, Rogan tersely asked, "You want something buddy?"

The man seemed too afraid to speak, but finally he managed to croak out a whisper. "I trust you. God help me, but I trust you." He dragged a shaking hand across the table, depositing a folded piece of white paper. Then the stranger about-faced and scurried toward the exit to the back parking lot.

"What the hell was *that*?" muttered Rogan. " 'I trust you?' What the hell does *that* mean?"

"Hell if I know, but he sure wanted to give us this…whatever it is." Donelson unrolled the napkin, revealing a small USB memory stick. Both men stared at it. "This stinks, this just stinks like crap, this is a setup," whispered Donelson. "Don't touch the thing. No, wrap it back up and drop it in the garbage can."

"I don't know, Charlie…aren't you curious? The guy works on Predators, but he's a civilian. You know about Building 1405, right?"

"Yeah, it used to be 101st's logistics coordination center, until that was axed. Now it's full of civilians, federal alphabet agency types. But there's no sign out front, and no name on it."

"Well, I've heard about it," said Rogan. "It's called the rural pac-ification program—but that's not written down anywhere, at least not anywhere I could find. It's all civilians, mostly feds. They have their offices in 1405 and a few other buildings around there, and they control the Predators out of the old fitness center across the drill field from 1405. Their UAV flight line is over on the old runway at Campbell Field. They're running counterinsurgency ops against Americans, that's what I hear."

Donelson replied, "I knew what it was. You thought I didn't know? Come on, Hulk, you've known me too long for that. After twenty-five years, there's not much happening on this base I don't know about."

"So, why's a civilian who works with Predators dropping a memory drive on our table? What's his angle? Is he setting us up? It doesn't make any sense. 'I trust you'… What's up with *that?*" CW4 Rogan finished his beer with a final swig and set the empty glass down on the table. "Let's get the hell out of here and go to my place, and see what's on it."

"You're not afraid it's some kind of a setup, a sting?" asked Don-elson.

"Charlie, who's going to bother to run a sting on a couple of old has-beens like us? That doesn't make sense. And I don't give a damn any-way—this is still a free country, right?" He laughed. "Don't answer that. We know it's not. Not anymore. So fuck 'em if they think they can pull this KGB bullshit on us—I ain't playing. Free or not, this is still America. I'm done playing bullshit games with the politicos. They want to bust me for putting this computer widget in my pocket? Let them try. They're going to send me to some American gulag? I don't think so. Let's get the hell out of here and go to my place. I want to see what's on this thing."

"You've got electricity at your house today?"

"I did when I left. Let's go find out."

With no warning, the cave thudded as if a hand had slapped the hill above them. Boone froze in place, and a second later he felt more than heard a muffled boom.

"What was that?" asked Doug. Carson looked above them at the cave's roof.

"The car, I think," said Boone. "I'll bet they found the car. Some-body probably tripped my booby trap. Well, I just hope it killed some of them." He stood up from the table. "Okay, campers, that's why we got ready early. New plan: it's time to go. Grab your stuff, we're leaving right now. Everybody get your headlamps on—this backdoor route's not lit, and there's no guide rope to follow."

"What time is it?" asked Doug. "Is it dark outside?"

"It's almost five, so it'll be dark soon. They must have gotten lucky—if you can call detonating five pounds of C-4 lucky. I just hope we nailed some of the bastards, and that it slows them up some. They'll be mighty careful after tripping a booby trap. But we can't count on that, so we can't stay here. If they found the car, they'll find the cave—there's just too many tracks in the snow and mud between there and here."

Carson said, "If we just blew up a couple of their guys, it'll take them a while to get their shit together, and by then it'll be fully dark outside. You think they'll be tracking us here in the dark?"

"I don't know. There's most of a moon up, even with the clouds. Moon over snow means plenty of ambient light. And they have night vision. We just can't take the chance of getting trapped in here. We're leaving now, right now. Jenny, the baby's been fed? You have another bottle ready to go?" The message was implied: the infant had to be kept quiet for their escape.

"We're ready," she replied. "I'm packed." Jenny was wearing a brown fleece jacket over a green military sweater, baggy blue jeans, and the dead traitor's boots. She kept the traitor's pack, it was American-made, not Kazak, and its former owner was not going to report it missing anytime soon. She had to trade her Russian-style fur hat for a hand-knitted gray wool cap, almost like the one Boone wore. Being seen wearing the fur hat would arouse instant attention from the Kazaks. Jenny pulled on a green vinyl raincoat with a hood, from the cave's store of spare clothing items. The others made their final preparations for departure, slipping on coats, hats and packs, and picking up weapons.

Phil Carson and Doug Dolan had changed to their Army ACU-pattern camouflage uniforms and matching gore-tex parkas. This was Boone's idea. It was now illegal for civilians to possess or to wear this current-issue Army combat uniform, and if they were captured while wearing them, they would be considered terrorists or spies. Paradoxically, their very illegality made wearing the ACU uniforms more advantageous. If they could not avoid making contact with their foreign enemies, they would attempt to pass themselves off as a unit of collaborating traitor Americans, and bluff their way out of danger. Besides American traitor units, the North American Legion also wore the ACUs, with different insignias attached. If they could not avoid a fight, their foreign enemies might hesitate to fire on "friendly" troops wearing ACUs, and this might provide them a critical edge. They also carried dark earth-toned brown and green civilian clothes in their packs, in case they had to move through open or built-up areas in the daylight.

With his long hair and beard, Boone could not possibly pass as a soldier. Nobody suggested that he should shave, or have his long hair cut to military length, just so that he could also wear the ACU uniform. Boone was Boone, and he obviously preferred to travel and fight in his own manner. His "Mossy Oak" pattern coat was printed with realistic-looking leaves, sticks and tree bark. This hunting camouflage was like a snapshot of the dark Tennessee winter woods, and he could virtually disappear, simply by melding into the brush and standing very still. As a sniper, his ability to disappear from view was a paramount consideration. His pack and his rifle were likewise camouflaged. Even his thick Icelandic hat was knitted in shades of brown and gray wool.

"Everybody should be ready to pull chocks in five minutes," said Boone. Pulling chocks was military slang, it was done just before aircraft took off. "Now you understand why I was such a hard-ass about getting ready early. A lot of this route is low, hands-and-knees stuff, so tighten up your straps and slings. Take your time and do it all right. The one thing we can't deal with now is an injury. Watch your heads, don't rush it. I'll go first, then Phil, Jenny and Zack. Doug, you bring up the rear. This is it: this is for real. If you forgot anything, this is your last chance—we're not coming back. Jenny, is the baby ready? You can carry her inside your jacket, on your hands and knees?"

"I can do it, that's how I got us in. I just need a minute to get us set." Unlike the men, Jenny carried no rifle, only the pistol on her web belt, concealed beneath her rain slicker. The baby was awake, wearing a white pajama outfit with booties, and a yellow knit cap. She was alert, looking around her, but made no outcry as Jenny swaddled her in a blanket and zipped her inside her fleece parka.

They stood on the rough plank floor, helped each other on with their packs, cinched down their rifles to their chests, and turned on their headlamps. Boone reached above the table and switched off the single light bulb. He said, "When you see the person in front of you get low, you get low. Near the end, there's a little room where we can get organized again. This way opens onto the side of a creek, and we might get a little wet. Any questions? Anybody forget anything? Zack and Jenny, you both have the road maps I marked? Good. I've armed the booby traps, so nobody goes back after we leave. Okay? Everybody is good to go? Okay, let's move out. Follow me."

Boone's parka hood was swept back from his long hair and beard. His headlamp was on an elastic band, stretched around his thick wool hat. His rifle was secured diagonally across his chest, keeping his hands free. He turned and led them out.

Carson hoped that he would be able to keep up with the younger rebels. He was older than Boone by two decades, and nearly four times the age of the teenagers. What he had gained in experience he would gladly have exchanged for twenty-year-old legs. His left butt cheek ached where the arrow had split it, and his right knee was already sore. Boone went to a crouch when the cave ceiling dipped, and Carson followed suit. The path wound downward in a snakelike route. Twice Boone took a branch smaller than the one Carson would have chosen if he'd had to guess their way out. After maybe two hundred hunched-over steps, they had to crawl. The stone walls had been dry, but now they glistened in the headlamps' beams. In some spots, water dripped on the travelers, or pooled beneath them. The light cast by their five headlamps threw bizarre swirling shadows. The barrel of Carson's M-16 carbine was tied to his left shoulder strap, the collapsed butt stock to his right hip. On his elbows and knees, he struggled to avoid dragging the weapon across the rocky floor when the ceiling pressed down on his backpack.

After five more minutes and another unknown distance, Boone turned around in a wide area and sat with his pack against the stone wall. He pulled out his camelback tube and sucked down some water. From a pocket, he removed a small baggie containing a stub candle and a box of matches. He lit the candle and set in on a niche in the rock above him. When all five were in the same small space, he said, "We're close to the final exit to the outside; you can start to feel the draft here. Once we're out of the cave, we're going a hundred percent tactical. Turn off your head-lamps and put them away; the candlelight will be your transition to night vision. We'll just let the candle burn down once we're gone. After this, no white lights and no talking. Hand signals only, or mouth-to-ear whispers. The cave exit is over a creek. There's one more rally point on the other side, and then we're splitting up: three of us north, and two south. Just like we briefed, except we're leaving a few hours earlier. Let me take a look outside—I'll be right back."

Boone was able to walk in a deep crouch, and in a few steps he was gone from their view. Five minutes later, he returned and addressed his little squad, who were sitting back against their packs in a tight circle, feet together. "Okay, we've got a slight problem. The creek is way up, and the water is deeper than I expected. The ledge that I can usually walk along on this side of the creek is under water. It's too narrow to use if you can't see it, especially since you've never done it before. We can't risk it; somebody will fall in for sure. We'll have to cross the creek right outside the cave. It's going to be at least waist deep, so that means you'll get wet up to your chest—and that's if you don't fall down. It's freezing outside, so if you get your clothes soaked, you'll get hypothermia. Then if you have to stop and lay up to avoid the enemy, you'll definitely get hypothermia, and that'll kill you as dead as any bullet ever will."

Zack asked, "Why don't we go back out the other way?"

"We can't. They found the car, so that whole side of the hill is com-promised. For all we know, they found the tracks between the car and the cave. They might be halfway to the cave already. By the time we got back there, they might already be at the mouth."

Doug had another idea. "We all have a change of clothes; why can't we change into them on the other side?"

"You don't want to start out with your best stuff soaking wet and freezing. Your other clothes are for tomorrow, in daylight. Trust me; I know what I'm doing."

"How wide is this creek?" asked Carson.

"When it's this deep, maybe twenty or thirty yards across."

"What's the bottom like?"

"Sand, and smooth rocks. Nothing too sharp."

"Any sign of the enemy?" asked Doug.

"No, and when those guys are around, I usually know it. They use IR spotlights and lasers all the time, and they wear those IR strobes. I didn't see any with my night vision goggles, and I didn't hear anything. There's no way that they know about this cave exit."

"But what about security on the crossing?" Carson asked. "Who's going across first, and how are we going to set up covering fire?"

"Phil, we can't do it by the book. We just have to get across as fast as we can. If the eye in the sky is up there, then the quicker we get across, the better. Stringing it out just means more of a chance for a Predator to see us, if they're flying."

Carson said, "So we're going to bare-ass it?"

"That was going to be my next suggestion. Carry everything across over our heads, then dry off and dress on the other side. There's an old fishing cabin across the creek, maybe a hundred yards down. That was our next rally point anyway."

"What does 'bare-ass it' mean?" asked Jenny. "Does that mean what I think it means?"

"It does," answered Boone. "You're just as cold either way, but bare-assing it means you'll have dry clothes on the other side. But don't worry; I can carry you across on my shoulders. You can stay dressed. Just take off your boots and hang them around your neck, and roll up your pants as high as you can. Okay, boys, just do what I do. Take off your coats, spread them out and make bundles. Put everything inside, and zip them up. If you have drawstrings at the bottom, cinch them off. If you don't, tie your sleeves around the bottoms: just make bundles that won't come loose, the best way you can. Tie the bundles and your rifles into the straps of your rucksacks, hoist them up and wade across. Just make sure nothing gets loose."

"What about our shorts?" asked Zack

"Leave your skivvies on if you want to, but if they're wet they'll be freezing cold and you'll have to ditch them on the other side, at least until you get a chance to dry them out. The whole idea is to keep your clothes dry."

Nobody joked, nobody objected, nobody balked. To be alive in Western Tennessee a year after the twin earthquakes, and six months after the arrival of the foreign mercenaries, meant that they were already adaptable and hardy survivors. The squeamish, the fainthearted and the weak had either died or run away long before.

While undressing, Boone said, "The water's not running very fast, and the bottom isn't too bad. Make sure of your footing and don't slip. Keeping your stuff dry is what this evolution's all about. I'll take Jenny and the baby across first, so the rest of you can follow me, and then I'll come back for our packs. When you're on the other side, Doug will lead you to the cabin. There's plenty of moonlight, so you don't need night vision goggles. You can use some light inside the cabin, just be careful. When you're inside the cabin, use the tops of your socks and the bottom of your pants to dry off, and then get dressed again. I'm sorry, guys, this is guaranteed not to be any fun. It'll be freezing cold no matter how we do this, but at least we'll have dry clothes on the other side, and that's what matters. Okay, Jenny, are you ready? Stick right behind me. When I tell you, you just climb up on my shoulders. If you have to grab my hair, that's fine. Don't worry about hurting me—just stay on, and keep that baby dry."

Boone was wearing nothing but a set of dark boxer shorts when Jenny crouched down and followed behind him. Carson followed behind her, with his pack, the jacket bundle and rifle clutched to his chest. The candlelight disappeared behind them. A few yards on, moonlight reflecting off the rippling creek made the cave opening visible from inside. Carson watched Boone step down into the water, his back against the cave's mouth. The creek made an inside turn against a rocky cliff that concealed the cave opening. The water came up to his hips when he leaned back to the cave exit. Jenny reached out, grasped Boone's head, and swung a leg over each of his shoulders. Boone lurched as he struggled for balance, then he set out across the stream. Carson followed as soon as his gear was ready. He fastened his bundled clothing inside the shoulder straps of his pack. The rifle was also thrust through the straps, the chest strap tying it all together. His entire kit became one tight mass.

Carson put the heavy bundle down just outside the cave opening, then turned and clambered into the icy water. It hit his skin like a thousand daggers that were alternately red hot and ice cold. He had almost no sensation of his feet on the bottom of the creek. The water was running strongly. If he cut a foot making this crossing, he wouldn't be able to hike out, and he'd be finished. He might not even feel the gash or know it until he was on the other side. He turned around toward the rocky ledge, dragged his bundle toward him, and strained to hoist it all over his head. He understood Boone's rejection of heavy body armor for this exfiltration. The pack, clothes, load bearing vest and rifle weighed at least fifty pounds, and Carson had to somehow balance it all above him. He held the pack's straps and positioned the middle of this bundle on the top of his bare head. Like a drunken juggler, he struggled to find his balance beneath the unwieldy load.

Just don't let me drop it, and don't let me fall in the middle of this creek, Carson prayed. There was sufficient moonlight to see by, reflecting off the water and snow. Ahead of him, Boone was already halfway across, the water rising up his back almost to Jenny's bottom on his shoulders. Her feet must be submerged where Boone held her ankles. Give me the tropical jungles any day, Carson thought. Behind him, a concave rocky cliff rose at least fifty feet above the water, ancient layers of rock angling upward where it had been undercut by the current. Ahead of him there was a shallow bank of pebbles, and bare tree branches hanging over the stream. Patches of snow covered the ground in streaks. Boone emerged from the water, and once he was standing on the ground, Jenny slid down from his back, then moved into a moon shadow and disappeared from view. Boone was already returning to the water when Carson reached the middle of the stream

Doug Dolan passed him and was out of the water before Carson. Zack passed him as he struggled up the bank. The younger men were faster, but I'm hanging in there, he thought. The ground was frozen where it was not covered with an inch or two of snow, the air was frosty and revealed their exhalations in the moonlight, but his body was too numb to notice. My goose bumps have goose bumps, Carson thought, shivering uncontrollably. He clutched the entire load of pack, bundle and weapon to his heaving chest and followed Doug. They hustled in their bare feet across an open, easy area along the creek, mostly snow-covered grass, and they quickly came to an abandoned fishing cabin. It was no bigger than a single large room, but it was relatively dry inside and protected from the chill breeze.

Doug set a small flashlight onto a windowsill, aiming at the floor, so they could see what they were doing. The cold drove them to a furious pace of activity, unstrapping their bundles and finding their clothes. Carson used his hands to rapidly swipe most of the remaining water from his body, then found his socks and use them to dry himself as much as he could, and then dressed in seconds. His feet appeared not to have suffered a gash or puncture, but perhaps they were too numb to bleed or to hurt. Once he was dressed, had replaced his equipment vest and strapped his pack back on, he grabbed his rifle and exited the cabin before either Zack or Doug was ready.

He was already standing guard when Boone walked into view, clutching both his own pack, bundled gear and clothes and rifle as well as Jenny's smaller pack. Jenny was in a corner, rewrapping the baby's blankets and getting herself ready to march. Again Boone merely nodded as he passed, going into the one-room cabin.

A few minutes later, they were all assembled in the cramped cabin, everyone dressed and ready to move out. Carson stood watch in the open doorway, the short M-16 carbine comfortingly familiar in his hands, an acquaintance since 1968.

"Zack, where's your Winchester?" Boone asked in a whisper. Carson perked his ears up and looked over from the doorway.

"It…it fell off my bag," he whispered back.

Boone paused before asking, "Where?"

"In the creek."

"Why didn't you get it?"

Zack stuttered, and faltered.

"Never mind. We can't backtrack; there's no time. You've got your bow, Jenny's got her .45…that's enough. You'd probably have to ditch the rifle anyway before you crossed over into Mississippi. Suck it up, Zack; just try to be more careful."

During their patrol briefing in the cave, they had decided that Zack should carry his own Winchester instead of one of Boone's captured Kalashnikovs. The two youngsters were wearing civilian clothes, in order to pass as refugees if they were trapped at a checkpoint. They might be able to explain the ordinary civilian lever-action rifle, but to be caught with a captured Kalashnikov would mean an instant death sentence.

So now he'd have to rely on his compound bow and his hunter's instincts. Plus Jenny had her Springfield XD .45 caliber pistol, with its suppressor. She refused to part with the pistol or the silencer, in spite of Boone's mentioning that if she was captured with them, they could lead to her execution. It didn't matter, she didn't care. She would not part with the gun, but agreed to carry it concealed, beneath the oversized green rain slicker that she had found in the cave's clothing box. Obviously, she couldn't pass as a refugee while wearing the Kazak uniform and parka that she had obtained from the dead American traitor.

Boone whispered to Zack and Jenny, too quietly for Carson to hear his words. The three huddled over a partially unfolded road map held between them, and a pocket compass Boone had provided the teenagers. Zack's tiny red LED light illuminated Boone's finger as it traced their route down into Mississippi. Finished with their final route brief, Zack shook hands with each of them in the cabin as they all whispered good luck. Zack had removed the compact bow from where it was tied to his pack, and nocked an arrow. Jenny followed him out of the cabin, and they headed upstream along the bank. The creek ran northward here, and the teenagers were hiking the other way, down toward the Mississippi state line.

After a quick look around the tiny cabin for anything dropped or left behind, the three remaining men set out directly into the woods, away from the stream. The first part of their journey led to the east, toward the Tennessee River just a few miles away. A hidden Jon-boat with an electric trolling motor would take them across the river to the relative safety of Middle Tennessee. At least, that was the plan Boone had laid out in his patrol order.

Boone walked point. Carson followed, and Doug Dolan was rear security. Boone would have felt better with Carson watching their backs, but Doug was more familiar with night vision goggles. At any rate, there were only three of them, and with the moonlight filtering through the clouds night vision was a bonus, not a strict necessity. During their frequent stops, Boone tipped his goggles up, giving himself a wider angle of view in the ambient light. It was always a tradeoff with night vision: the enhanced brightness came with a restricted field of vision, almost a keyhole view. Years of practice had taught him how to balance natural and amplified night vision. He found his path; it took them mostly through woods for the first half mile, past a few isolated farmhouses now abandoned. The hidden boat was located on another side creek two miles north; he had made this trip enough times to know the way with or without night vision. The side creek then spilled into the Tennessee River, in a stretch where it was less than a half-mile wide.

They moved slowly, but smoothly. Haste would lead to mistakes, to noise, and possibly to their discovery. "Slow is smooth, and smooth is fast" went the old saying. In night patrolling, stealth was everything. Those who were detected first often died. Those who did the detecting could hide in order to allow a superior force to pass by, or they could set up an ambush if the tactical situation permitted. Tonight the risk of discovery was very real. The foreign enemies had found their hidden automobile, and that meant they would soon find the cave. Unseen UAVs circling high above could already be preparing to drop missiles upon them, or the distant UAV pilots could be calling the Kazaks to report the location of the insurgents. It was hard to gauge the cloud cover: was it low enough to keep the drones grounded? Boone only hoped that the C-4 bomb in the Subaru had killed some of the foreign mercenaries, that it had not been discovered and detonated in a controlled explosion. That would have been a waste of valuable C-4, and an insult to his expertise as a demo man.

Little snow was left on the forest floor. Enough moonlight filtered through the clouds and the mostly bare branches above them to create vivid green daylight in his NVGs. The wet ground reflected the moonlight like silver filigree. Even Carson, a few paces behind him with bare eyeballs, had not expressed any difficulty in keeping up. Slow is smooth, and smooth is fast. Tortoise and hare. Boone always kept Carson's lack of night vision in mind, and avoided trip hazards. When this was impossible, he allowed Carson to catch up to touching distance, and by hand-pointing and a few careful whispers he guided the old man across to easy footing.

This part of Tennessee was a crazy-quilt patchwork of fields and woods, attached at the odd corners and stitched together by hedgerows and tree lines. When the paramount object was always to stay in the best cover available, the closest route was never a straight line, but an apparently random succession of zigs and zags. Like capillaries flowing into arteries, a fractal system of streams and creeks spread between the low hills and eventually found the Tennessee River. You could not walk a straight mile in any direction without crossing at least one ankle-deep stream, flowing subtly downhill to join another and another until they all met the Tennessee, then the Ohio, and finally the Mississippi for the last run to salt water in the Gulf.

Western Tennessee was certainly not classic guerrilla country in the way that Eastern Tennessee with its mountains was. This was subtle terrain, shifting and blending, giving barely adequate concealment even to those who understood its hidden folds and textures. But after tonight, he was done with it. The Cossacks had won, and for now it was time to leave. The most important weapon he carried tonight was contained within the memory chip of his digital camera, but that weapon was useless here in Radford County.

They were about two miles north of the cave, so that meant they were almost four miles from where the Subaru had been hidden. If the explosion had killed a few more of the Kazaks, they'd be mad as hornets and out for immediate revenge tonight. Especially if they had found the bodies of their three dead comrades at the massacre site. Any Americans remaining in the area would be targets for reprisal attacks. The faint echoes and cracks of small-arms fire reached the three men, possibly from the other side of the cave. The louder but slower thumping of a .50 caliber machine gun was unmistakable. The Kazaks might be doing random recon by fire, or they could be gunning down American civilians on the road or in their homes. It was impossible to know. Mostly he hoped they were not shooting at Zack and Jenny. The shots were too far away for that, he hoped.

The lack of any helicopters above them puzzled Boone. Normally, helos would rapidly arrive over the scene of a rebel-caused explosion, both for medical casevac and to search for the rebels who had planted the explosives. But there was no faint whine of turbine engines or rotors beating the night sky.

That did not preclude the possibility that a UAV was already high above them, searching in expanding circles around the Subaru for the thermal signatures of humans. The bare branches above them provided cold comfort; they were no barrier to the heat given off by their bodies. Boone kept under and between the occasional evergreens as much as he could. In the pines, they might be missed entirely, or mistaken for deer. Under the bare branches of deciduous trees in winter, they were naked prey, upright walking bipeds carrying packs and weapons. He kept to the thickest cover, bushes that still held some leaves, following a stream as it wound gradually downhill. If they were spotted from above, they would never hear the missile coming.

He consulted the captured military GPS unit, its screen dimmed down to its night vision setting. They were approaching the narrow waist of an hourglass-shaped section of woods. According to his memory, this stream threaded its way across the narrow point of the woods. He remembered often seeing cattle moving through it on their way to lower pasture. The woods ahead of them thinned out until they provided almost no cover, a danger area for sure.

Ahead Boone saw a flash, and he froze in place and slowly sank down. He turned around. Carson was only a step behind, also crouching silently below the level of the bushes that provided their only concealment. Doug closed up the gap, waiting. Boone turned back to his front, and watched. Again he saw the flash, and this time he thought he saw it flicker. It could be someone with a flashlight, moving in the woods, swinging the light side to side. He pushed his NVGs up on his head, straining his eyes, but saw only blackness, his night vision ruined by the magnified light of his goggles. He slid them back down over his eyes, and waited. After a few seconds, there another series of flashes. An infrared strobe?

He crept to within inches of Carson, and with a hand gesture waved Doug in for a conference. "I saw a light ahead. Phil, did you see anything?"

"No. Nothing."

"I can see it," whispered Doug. "Infrared?"

"I think so." Boone didn't need to explain further. Infrared meant foreign enemies. No civilians were out tonight with IR lights. "Let's get a little closer. We have to cross an open area before we get back into some more woods. It's the only way to the boat. If it's blocked, we might have to backtrack for miles, or lay up here until they're gone." He hated to talk so much when they might be approaching enemy forces, but he had no choice. Sometimes you just had to. He gave a thumbs-up sign, which was returned by both men. Boone noted that at this distance, in this light, even Carson could see a thumb. This was important to know. Boone gave the "move out" sign, sweeping his right index finger forward, and continued forward, but in a low crouch, at a slow pace, stopping every few steps to look and listen.

A hundred feet further forward, and he could more clearly make out the light. It was blinking dash-dot-dash. That was Morse Kilo. Kilo for Kazaks. The Morse strobe repeated every ten or fifteen seconds. The signal, invisible to the naked human eye, was meant to prevent friendly-fire mistakes. The Kazaks must be feeling supremely confident, certain that no one but themselves possessed the black magic of night vision in their area of operations. They clearly perceived that the risk of accidental misidentification on their night operation was greater than the risk of being seen by some local insurgent with NVGs.

When the trees began to thin, Boone halted them again, this time using only hand signals. Now they could all hear muffled engines and catch whiffs of diesel exhaust. The infrared blinks and the engine sounds grew as they drew closer. As he had remembered, the trees disappeared at the narrow waist of the hourglass of woods. He hid behind a rotten stump and took in the scene. A stream flowed from the woods, and then ran down into a lower pasture to their left. An armored security vehicle like the ones that Jenny had seen in Mannville was only seventy or eighty meters ahead of him, moving forward slowly to the left. There were four big tractor-sized wheels supporting an angular metal rectangle, the whole vehicle was about twenty feet long. The side and front armor plates angled outward in a sideways V, to deflect incoming fire. On top was a turret mounting both a .50 caliber heavy machine gun and a 40mm automatic grenade launcher parallel to it. Sporadic rifle and machine-gun fire was still audible a few miles away, but this armored vehicle was silent except for its well-muffled turbo diesel engine.

A second ASV was fifty yards further to his left in the lower pasture, not moving. It took Boone a minute of watching to put the scene together. The ASV in the pasture was stuck. The stream came down from the woods, and then fanned out into the pasture like a miniature delta. Cows' hooves had churned the bottomland into muck. On this cold night, with most of the ground frozen hard, the ASV crews were probably feeling good about their ability to drive off-road, but the muddy stream had trapped the first armored car.

Stopped or moving, the ASVs presented a deadly adversary, capable of destroying any unarmored vehicles or people out to several thousand yards with its two heavy weapons. If the three fugitives were detected, they were virtually at point-blank range from the armored car, and his tree stump might as well have been a fern, for the protection it would afford.

Boone guessed that the armored vehicles had been sent sweeping north behind the hills that hid his cave, to cut off their possible escape. This meant the vehicles were heading in the same direction as his hidden Jonboat, their intended means of crossing the Tennessee River. To continue on, they would have to find a way around the ASVs.

The nearer vehicle stopped at the beginning of the lower pasture, having moved ahead as far as it could without getting itself trapped in the bog. A Kazak walked in front of it, gingerly testing the ground under his boots, and disappeared around the front. A minute later he reappeared, dragging a retrieval cable forward, across the bog toward the stuck ASV. These armored vehicles had a retrieval winch built into their fronts, but only their fronts. Because of this, the stuck ASV's own winch was uselessly facing in the wrong direction. They would have to drag the trapped vehicle backward, toward the ASV closer to the three Americans.

The turret on the stuck vehicle was still pointed forward, away from the three men. The turret on the recovery vehicle faced rearward, to their right and uphill. This was standard operating procedure for a two-vehicle patrol, covering their front and rear with their most potent weaponry.

Boone could see only the left side and back of the nearer ASV, so it was impossible to tell if the driver and vehicle commander were inside or if they had dismounted. The driver's hatch was open, flipped out to the left of the vehicle's hull, just forward of and below the turret. The vehicle commander in the right seat wouldn't be out dragging the cable through the mud. That task would probably fall to a junior crewman—the driver. The driver would haul the wire, leaving the turret gunner in place for security. The commander would merely push the button and activate the winch, spooling it out as his driver dragged it forward across the bog. Once the cable was attached to the back of the stuck vehicle, both ASVs would use their combined four-wheel-drive power, plus the winch motor pulling the wire, to try to free their comrades from the mud.

The soldier dragging the cable forward held a small white flashlight in his left hand, casting a brilliant pool of green light as seen in Boone's night vision goggles. The mud was up to the soldier's ankles as he crossed the bog. While Boone watched, the soldier lost his balance, slipped and fell down, dragged backward by the weight of the heavy wire hooked over his shoulder. He tried to sit up and rolled onto his belly in the slime, yelling in what must have been Kazak, obviously cursing his crewmates, who began cursing back at him, as well as laughing. Boone didn't need a course in Kazak to understand the situation; it was one that any soldier could readily interpret. Their lack of discipline in what should have been a serious tactical situation, despite its undeniably humorous aspects, gave him hope, leading to a new idea.

A brighter light switched on from the recovery ASV, causing Boone's NVGs to momentarily flare out, so he pushed them up on his forehead. The recovery ASV had turned on one of its secondary spotlights and directed it forward at the man dragging the wire, and thereby across the pasture to the stuck ASV. The small moveable spotlight was mounted atop the left rearview mirror, which stuck out a yard from the front corner of the vehicle. The man pulling the cable hollered something, and there was an immediate call back to him, probably to shut up and do his job. Another shout came from an unseen voice. The big side door of the closer ASV opened up, with the top section swinging back first and then the bottom part flipping down. Another crewman stepped out from the vehicle onto the ground. Without speaking, he marched forward in the white searchlight's glare, slowing his pace as the firm ground changed to muck. Boone understood the situation: the two ASVs wanted to get out of this mudhole by themselves, even if it meant breaking light discipline. It was typical "Snuffy" thinking: they were probably more afraid of incurring the wrath of their superiors for getting stuck, than of the remote chance of encountering American rebels lurking nearby.

Boone slid back behind the stump, beckoning his two buddies in whisper-close. The noise from the two diesel engines allowed him to speak softly without fear of detection. "New plan: forget the boat. Here's the situation: two men from the close one are dragging out their recovery cable. It's almost always a three-man crew in those things. You can't fit a fourth man unless you're not carrying any extra ammo or crew gear. I think the turret gunner just got out, so that leaves just one man in front. It's probably the vehicle commander in the right front seat, under his own hatch, but it doesn't really matter. He's running the winch motor—he has to stay inside, to spool it out. So there's just one guy left in this ASV, and he's looking away from us. The three Cossacks in the other one are light-blind from the spotlight—they can't see shit looking this way."

Doug asked in a whisper, "So, we're going to sneak across here, behind them?"

"Nope. We're going to take the close one."

"Take it?" asked Doug. "What do you mean, 'take it?' We're going to hijack an amored car?"

"Damn straight we are."

"Our rifles won't even put a dent in those things," said Doug.

"They won't have to. Phil, you know how Glocks work?"

"You just pull the trigger, and they go bang."

"Right. Here's the new plan…"

parchment# 20

Hope was cradled between the straps of Jenny's pack, kept from sliding down by the dead traitor's pistol belt. She had exchanged his Kazak uniform for ill-fitting men's jeans, cinched tight with a leather belt, a sweater, a fleece jacket and a green plastic raincoat that fell almost to her knees. The baby was nestled vertically like a papoose, between the wool sweater and the fleece jacket. The webbing pistol belt and its holstered .45 pistol were now hidden under her newly acquired rain slicker. An ear-covering hand-knitted wool cap was covered by the slicker's hood. She still wore the dead traitor's insulated gloves and his boots. From the knees down, her pant legs were soaked from walking through wet grass and bushes.

In a way, it irritated Jenny that she had to follow Zack. He had not proven himself to her. Zack had even lost his Winchester rifle when they crossed the swollen creek, after exiting the cave. Lost it! If he could lose his damn rifle, what else would he screw up? At the same time, Jenny was glad not to be alone on this stage of her journey. Zack was good at finding his way through the woods, she had to admit. He didn't walk too fast for her to keep up. He went forward six or ten steps at a time, and then paused to look around and listen.

Without his rifle, Zack walked with his bow at the ready. His tiny red light, attached to his bow, painted an almost unnoticeable pool of light just ahead of his feet. She had no trouble following his shadow. It was a new experience for her to follow somebody else at night, first on the way to the cave, and now with Zack. To be honest, it was a relief to allow somebody else to find the path for her.

Most importantly, she was finally leaving the hell that Tennessee had become. With luck, they would cross into Mississippi sometime around dawn. She would bring the baby to a hospital, deliver it to the staff, and her responsibility for the foundling would be over. Then after resting up, she would decide whether to continue on to Florida, or perhaps head the other way to Texas. Someplace warm, not like freezing cold Tennessee. Somewhere more or less free, where she could live a normal life.

Someplace where people weren't hungry and cold all the time. Someplace where foreign soldiers didn't herd Americans into ravines and machine-gun them.

But first, they had to sneak out of the last few miles of Tennessee, and Kazak soldiers were roaming all over the area. Cossacks, Boone called them. The Cossacks seemed to be some kind of crazy cousins of the

Russians. Maybe they really were Russians, at least some of them. Even President Tambor couldn't get away with bringing actual Russian soldiers into America, but if he claimed they were Kazaks...maybe so.

Sporadic gunfire echoed, they heard distant machine-gun bursts and random explosions. Zack followed the stream from the cave for the first hour, mostly in woods, crossing no roads. Boone had sounded sure that the Kazaks would stick to the roads, because they depended on their vehicles for mobility. Their intention was to drive the remaining Americans away from their farms and their homes, and these were all reachable by roads. Stay off the roads and you'll avoid the Cossacks, that's what Boone had said...but maybe he was just trying to boost our confidence, she mused. Boone didn't mention the Cossack cavalry. Jenny had seen their horse troops at the Mannville high school, close enough to hear and smell them. Horses didn't need to stay on the roads, nor did they make engine noises, which could be heard from far away. A troop of mounted Cossacks carrying those Russian Kalashnikov rifles could be hiding inside any stand of trees, or behind any barn or house.

The woods grew sparse again, and they were forced to cross an open field. Zack stopped by a timber fence made of horizontal rails set into posts every dozen or so feet. The top rail was above Jenny's chest, almost to her shoulders. It was a fence made to keep in horses, she knew that much. Cattle rated only barbed wire, and not as high. The fugitives crouched together by a fence post and surveyed the open ground ahead, moonlight reflecting off patches of icy snow. The moon itself was not visible through the clouds, but the entire sky cast a glow.

"How's the baby?" Zack whispered, checking his compass. It was attached by a string to his jacket collar, and kept in his coat's left breast pocket so that it could not be lost. Unlike his rifle, Jenny thought.

"If you don't hear her crying, she's okay."

"You think we should cross here, and stay near the creek, or swing back around and try to find more cover?"

She considered. "If we're going to make Mississippi by tomorrow, we've got to keep going as straight as we can. If we double back, it'll take hours and hours. Then we'll be stuck here in daylight. I say we should follow Boone's route and just keep moving. Even if that means we have to cross some open ground."

"Can you get over this fence with your pack on?"

"Yeah, I can, as long as the boards are steady." They were whispering, crouching nearly nose-to-nose, as Jenny also studied the green dial of the compass. "Zack, I've got to ask you. How did you lose your rifle?"

He looked away, embarrassed. "It...it was on top of my pack and my clothes. I thought it was on there good. I kind of slipped on some rocks, and I almost went over. I caught my balance, but my rifle slid off. My hands were full holding my pack, and I couldn't grab it." He paused. "You must really think I'm some kind of a dork."

"No, that's not why I asked. I just wanted to know. Come on, let's go." Jenny put a boot on the middle rail, climbed up and swung her leg over while holding the top of the post. She had to be careful not to squeeze the baby against the top rail. Zack grabbed her pack and steadied her. She turned around, straddling the top rail, swung her other leg over and hopped down, facing him. She knew that if an enemy was out there somewhere with a night scope on a rifle, they'd be easy targets. The distant firing continued, low pops and thumps indicating the shooting was some miles away. Orange reflected off the low clouds to the west, the direction of the shooting. Still whispering close, she asked, "What's that light?"

Zack studied the reddish glow, and answered, "Fires. They're torching houses, that's what I'd guess."

"How far away do you think they are?" Beyond the fields that lay in that direction, trees and rolling terrain blocked their view.

"I don't know...maybe a mile? Maybe more. It's hard to tell. Let's keep moving." He climbed the fence and jumped down.

Phil Carson scurried forward in a crouch. The dark hulk of the armored vehicle was clearly visible in the moonlight. The other ASV and the pair of men in between were illuminated by the first vehicle's side-mounted spotlight. He speed-walked while hunched down, holding the big Glock .45 in both hands in front of him. The borrowed carbine was slung over his back, barrel down. His pack was left back at their last position, where Boone and Doug were watching the scene with their night-scoped rifles.

It was at least 100 yards from any cover to his final approach position, which was on a line dead behind his target. With its four fat wheels and angled plates, it looked like the American armored cars he had seen in Vietnam. 'Commandos,' they had been called. They were made by Cadillac, or so he remembered. These looked like modern versions. Boone had explained that the remaining crewman in the vehicle, probably the commander in the right front seat, could not see directly behind them. The big mirrors extending out from both front corners were usually covered with mud flung up from the protruding front tires, Boone had said. Also, the vehicle commander's night vision would be impaired by looking into the spotlight's white beam to his front.

In any case, the commander's attention would be focused on the operation in front of him, between the vehicles, and not behind him. Since the turret gunner had climbed out to help drag the retrieval wire forward, the vehicle would have a blind spot straight to the rear. The turret's guns were still trained back toward Carson as he made his approach. Maybe there was a fourth crewman riding in the ASV, who was up in the turret. If the turret moved to aim its big guns at him, he'd be dead before he heard the bang. He wondered how low that .50 caliber could be depressed, and how close he would have to creep in order to be under its deadly arc of fire.

The driver and commander in the front of an ASV each had a hatch above them. The driver's hatch was opened outward to the left side like a small steel wing. From his angle, Carson could not tell if the commander's hatch was open or closed, or if he was even standing up through the hatch. One man had to drag the steel cable's hook, but another had to stay inside, to push the winch button to pay it out. Boone had been sure of this. Either the driver or the commander still had to be up front.

Carson made it to the blind spot straight behind the ASV undetected. There was enough moonlight to see the armored car clearly. The turret had not moved during his approach. It seemed that nobody was manning the big turret guns, and he felt some of the immediate dread float away from him. Diesel smoke blew out through angled steel grates on the back of the vehicle, faintly visible against the white light cast forward by its spotlight. Because of the vehicle's idling motor, his approach didn't need to be perfectly silent, just unseen. Between the left wheels was the open two-part crew door. The top half was swung rearward, resting against the armored hull. Carson held the Glock in his right hand, slid along the side of the armored vehicle, and peered inside. Dim red cabin lights provided faint illumination. The middle of the vehicle was taken up by a circular cage, a tower of metal grating that protected the gunner as he rotated with the turret. It was empty.

Forward of the turret cage were two large bucket seats. Four slit-like windows, two in front and one on each side of the crew compartment, provided front and side visibility to the driver and commander. In front of the empty left seat was the steering wheel. On the right side, a soldier was standing up through his roof hatch, invisible to Carson above his chest. The spotlight threw its white beam forward, to where the two Kazaks struggled to drag the wire through the muck. The presumed vehicle commander shouted something to the men in a guttural language that Carson didn't recognize.

Boone, with his night-scoped sniper rifle, could see neither into the vehicle nor forward of the turret. That's why I'm here, thought Carson. One man had to go forward on foot, to eliminate the unseen commander and any other Kazaks inside the armored car. Quietly, with just a silenced pistol. Boone hardly knows me, to send me on such a critical mission. Nine out of ten men will balk at cold-blooded close-range pistol work, but Boone trusts that I won't. He has faith that I'll pull the trigger, and that I won't miss. This trust could only have come to Boone from his father, the original Viking, so I must not fail, he thought.

Carson pressed himself against the angled steel of the vehicle's hull, and put his right foot on the metal step of the lowered hatch section. It was happening. He held the Glock in his right hand, and with his left he grasped a vertical steel hand grip and pulled himself up so that he could see across the top of the ASV, forward of the turret. He peeked over the open driver's hatch. The open hatch had to lie flat to the outside, so that it would not interfere with the turret's traverse. This was the moment of truth. He took it on faith, without even thinking consciously of it, that Boone and Doug at this very moment had their rifles aimed at the Kazaks on the other ASV, just fifty yards in front of him. Hopefully, the white spotlight shining in their direction blinded them from seeing him. Certainly the vehicle commander, only two yards away, had no sense of the danger lurking behind him to his left.

Carson's eyes edged above the top of the vehicle's hull, and around the front of the turret. His left hand kept its grip on the crew's grab bar, his right held the Glock. No pistol sights were needed at this range. Fortune was with him. The commander's head and shoulders still extended out of his open hatch on the right front of the vehicle. He shouted another order at his two crewmen, who were trapped in the glare of the spotlight's beam. The remotely controlled spotlight was mounted on top of the left rearview mirror's metal frame, just in front of Carson. The soldier standing in the hatch was wearing a tanker's helmet with built-in radio earphones, beneath an abbreviated hard shell on top. A single-tube night observation device was tipped up on the helmet, out of the way.

Afraid that the Kazak's head might disappear back inside the hatch, Carson aimed over the suppressor and squeezed the trigger. Recoil was mild for a .45; the sound was no more than a loud handclap. His shot took the man in the neck below his earphone, in the inch of white flesh above his soft body armor. There was no need for a follow-up or security shot. His chest and shoulders fell forward, over his windshield segment and down onto the front of the vehicle. His head lay twisted sideways as his blood pumped onto the steel, shining black in the moonlight. Carson crouched by the side of the turret and stared at the unmoving Kazak. Satisfied, he pumped his left arm up and down.

Boone's rifle sight was already trained on the turret gunner of the trapped armored security vehicle. His SR-25's ten-pound weight was supported across the top of the stump he was using for cover. The enemy gunner was the key to their success or failure. If the gunner dropped inside the turret and opened fire, he could chew them to ground meat with his machine gun and his automatic grenade launcher. Their own rifle bullets would bounce harmlessly off the ASV's armor plates.

Doug was using his rifle's night scope to keep watch on Phil Carson as he crept along the left side of the recovery vehicle, keeping Boone informed with a whispered commentary. "He's looking inside. Now he's climbing up. Now he's by the driver's hatch... He's leaning around the front of the turret..."

Boone's glowing crosshair reticle was centered on the face of the more distant ASV's gunner. The Kazak mercenary was standing through the turret hatch, looking back toward the men with the retrieval wire. The ASV gunners' hatches opened to the rear, and stood vertical when open. The turret of the stuck ASV was still facing forward, away from Boone's line of sight, so the vertical open hatch shielded most of the gunner's torso. But a few inches were enough, at this range of just less than 200 yards. He could tell that the gunner was wearing an American combat vehicle crewman's helmet, with its built-in earphones, intercom, and night vision device swung up on top. Was there nothing that our American traitors didn't provide to these Cossack mercenaries?

Doug said, "There's the arm pump—Phil's done it."

Boone squeezed the trigger of his SR-25, and the distant turret gunner's head whipped violently. He was flung backward, caught at the waist by the turret's opening. His upper body came to rest in an impossibly awkward position that signified instant death to Boone. Doug's rifle spat muffled shots beside him. He had the easier job of killing the two unlucky Cossacks caught out in the middle of the field with the retrieval wire.

The dead turret gunner was as clearly visible in Boone's night scope as at high noon, but for the greenish hues. A security shot went into his side, but caused no reflex action: he was shooting at a corpse. Boone dropped his reticle down and found the other two enemy crewmembers. Their mud-trapped ASV was still facing away from the recovery vehicle, as it had been since it had become stuck. They were standing beside it to watch their two comrades approaching with the retrieval cable. Then without warning, they saw their comrades fall, and they heard the cracks of passing rifle bullets.

Both Kazaks dropped prone and attempted to crawl into the muck beneath their vehicle. They were not wearing night vision goggles, and their attempts to hide were almost laughably pathetic. They had no idea from what direction the danger came. In Boone's night scope, enough of them were clearly visible: a leg, a shoulder, a face. In just seconds, they were both dead. At times like this, Boone was glad to have switched from a bolt-action sniper rifle to a semi-auto "gas gun." He'd taken six aimed shots with his trusty SR-25 in only a few seconds, and killed all three enemy soldiers from the trapped ASV. Satisfied, he swept his rifle to the area between the ASVs. Both of the unlucky Cossacks were already down.

Doug simply said, "I got 'em."

"Both?" asked Boone.

"Positive."

"I won't hurt your feelings if I make sure?" Boone pumped one more 7.62mm round into each of the prone soldiers. One showed no reaction, but the other rolled over and threw out an arm, so Boone shot him again. Then he looked back to the stuck ASV and checked again carefully for signs of life, but found the three soldiers exactly as he had left them. A careful scan of the ASVs, the meadow and tree lines showed no other signs of dismounted enemy. They had killed them all, and after what Boone had seen at dawn in the ravine, he felt damned good about it. Exhilarated even. These six unlucky Cossacks had no idea they were even in danger, and a minute later they're all dead. Maybe some of these ASV crewmen had been shooters at the massacre ravine, but probably they had not. It didn't really matter. They were Cossacks, and that was enough reason to kill them. They were foreign invaders in spite of what the president called them. They were in Tennessee, and they would all die if Boone Vikersun had anything to do with it.

Carson followed through with the next step of the plan, crouching and entering the ASV through its open side door. Sharp cracks from passing rifle slugs told him that Boone and Doug had opened fire. He had no doubt that the Kazaks would be killed in seconds. Well, too bad for them—they had no business coming to America as foreign mercenaries. Death in a muddy field was better than they deserved, after what the Kazaks had done to Americans.

Interior electronic displays, plus the moonlight coming through the open hatches, provided just enough light to see inside the vehicle. The vehicle commander had been standing on his seat when he stood up through his hatch; now his dead legs dangled inside. A quick look behind him showed no other hidden crewman. There were just crates, boxes, and packs piled around the turret cage, the vertical tower of expanded metal grating that enclosed the gunner's rotating position. Kalashnikov rifles were fixed vertically to the interior sides of the vehicle just ahead of the open side door, mounted in brackets next to fire extinguishers.

Carson slipped past the turret cage and dropped into the driver's seat. Now he had to learn to drive an ASV. Boone said it had an automatic transmission, and drove like a truck. It was time to find out. The diesel engine was already running. The seat was as well padded and comfortable as any Cadillac's. Warm, dry air was pouring out of vents between the two front seats. To be warm, dry and comfortable was a stark contrast to his last hours and days, but Carson could not dwell on this sudden and remarkable turnabout.

A metallic clang rattled the vehicle, and the small spotlight mounted above the left mirror exploded. Boone had turned out the white light with his sniper rifle. Now Carson could see nothing ahead of him through the narrow front windows. If he couldn't move the vehicle, Boone and Doug would have to come down to meet him in the open field. His rucksack was also left back with them, and he didn't want to lose it. The ASV was like a car, with a brake and a gas pedal; he just had to get it into reverse. He didn't dare drive any farther forward, or this armored vehicle might also become mired in the same muck that had trapped the other one.

From his limited memory of armored fighting vehicle tactics, he didn't think that they operated in pairs. Usually three or four tanks or APCs made up a platoon, providing mutual defense and supporting fire. Certainly it would have been impossible to attack these two ASVs if a third one had been lurking nearby on overwatch. Even now, more of them could be racing here. Maybe they were only moments away.

Unfamiliar with the vehicle, he had to use his own small flashlight to find the controls. A switch on a panel to his right was marked WINCH—IN and WINCH—OUT. He toggled it and heard an electric motor's whine. He held the button until he felt the hook at the end of the cable rattle home. He found the transmission lever and dropped it into reverse, pushed down on the gas pedal with his foot and the ASV began to roll backward, then he turned the wheel hard right, trying to swing back toward Boone's position. The rubber-padded steering wheel was nearly horizontal, like on a bus. Ahead of him he saw a red flashlight swinging side to side, and he put the transmission into forward and drove toward it. The red light was no more than a few hundred feet away, so he kept his left foot on the brake, moving slowly. When he was close enough to see the flashlight clearly, he stopped, and shoved the transmission lever into park.

Seeing the vehicle commander's corpse, Boone climbed onto the front of the ASV. After removing his helmet with its earphones and intercom mike, he pulled the dead Kazak up and out of the hatch and rolled him down onto the ground. Doug quickly shoved their three rucksacks through the open side door. Their packs went on the small deck area behind the turret tower, on top of the Cossacks' ordnance crates and gear. Once their gear was inside, Doug slid around the turret cage and climbed into the empty commander's seat, on the right side next to Carson.

Boone entered the ASV last, closed both door sections behind him, and squeezed up into the turret. He quickly checked the ammo trays. The 40mm Mark 19 automatic grenade launcher was to the left, the M2 .50 caliber heavy machine gun was to the right. There was plenty of .50 caliber ready to go, at least 200 rounds in links snaking over the guide rollers, but on the left side he saw only a short belt of around ten 40 mike-

mikes in their locker. That meant there would be another ten or so out of sight, already fed into the mechanism of the Mark 19. He yelled down to Carson, "Hey, you two, put on your CVCs!"

"What the hell is a CVC?" Carson yelled back.

"A Combat Vehicle Crewman's helmet. That's the driver's helmet hanging there; put it on, Phil. I'll wear the gunner's, and we can all talk on the intercom. Doug, put on the commander's helmet."

"But it's all bloody," Doug yelled back.

"Hey, deal with it, man!"

The CVC helmets each had a single-tube night scope mounted in a hinged bracket. Boone called down, "Hey, driver, turn on your NOD!"

"What's a 'nod'?" Carson replied in a loud voice.

"Night observation device; that's what we call starlight scopes now. Once you get the helmet on, tighten the chinstrap. Pull those straps down until it's snug. Then flip the NOD down and you're in business."

Carson busied himself with the helmet, adjusted it, and pulled the night vision tube down in front of his right eye. It was already turned on.

"Can you hear me?" asked Boone over the intercom, now speaking at a normal volume. "There's a switch on the wire. Push the button to talk."

"Loud and clear, Boone," Carson answered.

"Good, we're all set. I'll navigate: I can see 360 degrees up here, and I have the GPS. Phil, are you okay with driving?"

"Roger that, I'm good to go."

"Any questions?"

"Yeah, I've got a question," Carson said. "What exactly are we doing in this tin can? Why aren't we sticking to your plan and crossing the river? Those Kazaks are all dead; they can't stop us from going for the boat now. What happened to the plan?"

"The Mannville massacre happened, that's what. I guess I wanted some payback when I saw these assholes in the open. Targets of opportunity. And I always wanted an ASV—they're way too good for MPs and Cossacks. And maybe I just had an itchy trigger finger after what I saw in the ravine this morning. You want more reasons?"

"No, that's fine, you're the boss. I just wanted to know. But what about Americans? Won't they try to blow this thing up?"

"You mean insurgents like us?" replied Boone, laughing. "Not too much chance of that. Rifle fire won't even put a dent in these things, and what else have the insurgents got? Even with my connections, I could only get a little C-4. These things can drive right over a ten-pound mine and keep going. Insurgents can't touch these things. Well, not usually," he chuckled. "Tonight's an exception to the rule."

Carson said, "I always thought Americans would be better at guerrilla warfare than this, if we were ever invaded."

"So did I, Phil. I just never thought our government would be on the other side. But we're on a roll tonight, so enjoy the moment! Hey, I'm going to give this thing a quick test fire before we take off: I have to be sure the big guns are ready to rock and roll. I've got about two hundred .50 caliber, and maybe twenty of the 40 mike-mike, but I have to know they'll shoot. Make sure your CVC is on snug: this fifty is gonna make a racket. Oh, wait, give me a minute—I want to look around this machine before we go loud. Once we go loud, we're hauling ass."

Boone slipped down out of the turret, twisting in the confined space like a contortionist. In the small clear space behind the turret were the dead crewmembers' packs, gear bags, ration boxes, ammo cans and ordnance crates. One was marked "40mm Rifle Grenade HE." It was a different round from the linked 40mm used by the automatic M-19 turret gun, and not interchangeable with it. An old M-79 grenade launcher with a fat, stubby barrel and wooden stock was tied with bungee cords above the side door. Where the hell did the Cossacks find that relic? A fabric bandolier of 40mm rounds was draped over the weapon's ungainly stock. That 'blooper' might come in handy, Boone noted as he squirmed back up into the turret. There was a reason most tankers and other armored crewmembers were on the small size: these things were just not built to accommodate full-sized Vikings.

When he was back in position in the turret, Boone said, "Okay, Doug, did you get that thing cleaned up? Have you got your ears on yet?" Boone waited, but there was no reply. "Doug, get your helmet on. Phil, is his helmet on?"

Phil yelled across, "Doug, are you on the intercom? Can you hear us? Push the button on the wire to talk." Doug had just finished wiping the blood from the crew helmet with a greasy rag he'd found on the floor of the ASV, and gingerly slid it down over his head.

Doug shook his head no, and yelled back, "No, nothing, I'm just hearing radio chatter. It's not in English."

Phil Carson grabbed Doug's shoulder to get his attention and put his finger to his lips, indicating that he should shut up. Then he reached over to the commander's seat and grabbed the coiled rubber wire hanging from Doug's left earphone, and turned the switch on its connector. "Can you hear me now?"

"Yeah. What happened?" asked Doug.

"You weren't on the intercom—I think maybe you were on the radio," replied Carson.

From the turret Boone called, "Doug was on the radio?"

Carson said, "I don't know. Maybe. Maybe it was switched off."

"There's three positions: radio, off, and intercom," said Boone.

"Damn! Do you think anybody heard me? Do you think that went out on the air?"

"I don't know," replied Boone. "It was short. It's probably set to their tactical channel. You slide it back toward you for the intercom, the other way for the radio."

"Man, I'm sorry, Boone..."

"If they heard it, they're going to be wondering why there was an American on their tac channel. Then they'll be doing radio checks, and I don't think we're going to pass for Kazaks. Okay...turn off everything up there that looks like a radio, both of you. They can probably find this thing just by its passive emissions if the radios are on. Shut it all down. That big GPS too—it's all connected, they're all networked. We can't take the time to figure it out and make sure, just shut it all off. I can use the hand-held GPS up here."

"Shit..." said Doug over the intercom. "I'm so sorry, Boone..."

Carson said, "It's done, get past it. We don't even know if it went out. Hey, Boone, what about the infrared Morse Kilo? It's still flashing." Carson was also wearing night vision now, they all were, and he could see the reflected dash-dot-dash every ten seconds.

"We'll leave it on for now," replied Boone. "If they see us, they'll think we're friendly. Helicopters and UAVs too. They have night vision and thermal IR up there, so they'll see us anyway. We might as well put on their IR light, and pass for Kazaks. The friendly-fire thing is really drilled into people now; it'll take a lot to get them to fire at a Morse Kilo."

"Why doesn't the other ASV have the Morse Kilo on?" asked Carson.

"I don't know. Maybe their SOP says only one vehicle per tactical element puts it on. These two were operating by themselves, but you can bet the rest of them aren't far away."

"What about the radio? What if the other Cossacks are trying to get a radio check from these guys?"

"Radios foul up all the time. The 'n' in 'snafu' is for normal. People use the wrong frequencies; it happens."

"But what if they heard me?" asked Doug, a hint of fear in his voice. "Or what if somebody got out a radio call before we killed them? What if somebody is alive inside the other ASV, on the radio? We never checked inside it."

Boone reprimanded him. "Doug! Stop worrying so much. Worry about it tomorrow. Right now we've got to haul ass."

"Maybe we should stick with the original plan, and use the boat to get across the river?"

"Doug...*please* shut the fuck up! I'm going to give the fifty a quick test fire—make sure your CVCs are on good, and close your hatches." Boone found the turret hand control and rotated the guns around to forward. Using the tilting hand controls, not unlike those for a computer game, it took four seconds for the turret to spin him 180 degrees around to the front. He flipped the night vision tube up on his helmet, and put his right eye to the gun sight; its night vision was already on. The .50 caliber's optical sight marks were simple and instinctive to figure out. He found a solitary pine tree in his gun sight, and used the topmost hash mark as his aiming point. The turret rotated to make the slight deflection adjustment. When he was on target he flipped the red plastic safety cover off the trigger on his left hand control, and depressed the button for just a half second. Two booms erupted from the barrel in rapid succession, jolting the entire ASV like a hammer. A red tracer streaked out and hit the tree.

Next, he switched the gun selector to the Mark 19, elevated the barrel to its maximum of nearly 45 degrees, and punched the trigger button again. He wanted the grenade's explosion to occur as far from them as possible, as a diversion. The gun responded with a single loud, chunking thud. He listened, but didn't hear the high explosive round's impact, which was probably more than a mile away. Maybe it was a dud, or maybe it landed in water or soft ground. "Okay, guys," he said on the intercom. "Now I'm happy: I know they'll fire when I push the bang button. We're good to go. All right, Phil, let's get the hell out of here. Turn right and head up the field close to the tree line."

Phil Carson pushed the gear shifter into forward and mashed the accelerator pedal. The diesel's turbine whined, the ASV lurched into a turn, and they rolled off to the north.

Colonel Burgut's armored command vehicle rolled inside Eagle Company's temporary perimeter. The vehicle was a stretched version of an ASV, but without a turret or the turret's heavy weaponry, and furnished within as a mobile headquarters. The two fully armed ASVs accompanying him remained outside the circle of soldiers, humvee jeeps and trucks securing several hectares of woods on the slope of a low hill. The command vehicle's side door was opened by his first sergeant. After giving a quick look through its small armored glass viewing port, he swung the top section back, and then lowered the bottom. Burgut and his first sergeant put on their fur hats and stepped down from the heated interior into the cold mist. Darkness was smothering the Tennessee winter day.

"So, what happened here, Senior Lieutenant Kasim?"

The young Kazak officer did not salute, given the tactical situation. Saluting in the field only helped snipers to distinguish high-ranking targets. All of the soldiers around and within the perimeter were carrying their Kalashnikov rifles and RPD light machine guns at the ready. They were deployed in a broad circle, weapons facing outward, crouching or lying behind what cover they could find. In the field, his soldiers wore either brown berets or fur hats, depending upon their preference. Standard Kevlar infantry helmets were forbidden by the International Peacekeeping Forces Agreement as being "too warlike in appearance," and had not been issued. Well, the fools and sycophants who wrote and signed that insane document should be here now, to see this "peacekeeping" operation! All of his men were wearing brown body armor over their uniforms; at least this was not forbidden.

The junior officer gave his report while standing close to the rear of the command vehicle, trying to absorb some of the heat given off by its diesel engine without breathing its smoke. "Our reconnaissance platoon found fresh automobile tracks nearby in the snow and mud. They followed the tracks to this farm road, and these woods. Here they discovered a vehicle, very cleverly hidden beneath what is left of those two trees. They are called 'holly' trees, and they keep their leaves all winter. They have very dense waxy leaves, with small thorns on them. It was an excellent hiding place for a small vehicle. Unfortunately, the automobile exploded. Three men were killed, and two were wounded. One will die."

"Those fools," muttered Burgut. "Why didn't they follow standard procedure for approaching an abandoned vehicle?"

"I can't say, Colonel; perhaps they did, but…"

"Then why the devil did they detonate the bomb and get themselves killed? Why didn't they wait for your sappers to arrive?" From Burgut's command vehicle, it was no more than thirty meters to the scene of the blast. In the last light of day, he could make out that two thick tree trunks had been shattered. The car that had exploded had been concealed in a hiding place beneath the branches of the two trees. Now it was just a blackened metal hulk. The branches were now almost bare of leaves and hanging in broken shreds. The corpses and most of the body parts of the dead had been collected and placed into three black body bags.

Colonel Burgut could easily imagine why the dead men didn't wait for the explosives disposal sappers: greed. They probably saw something of value in the automobile, and wanted to keep it for themselves, without sharing. So typical of the cocky and egotistical reconnaissance soldiers, who thought they knew everything, including the job of detecting and disarming bombs. In his more cynical moments, he thought that soldiers volunteered for recon because it gave them more opportunities for unobserved looting.

"Colonel, we are still examining the site, but a more complete answer as to exactly what happened must await tomorrow's daylight."

"Yes, yes." It would be fully dark in just a few more minutes, and it was obviously too dangerous an area to set up visible working lights.

"From this location we found signs of several insurgents on foot, and tracked them to a cave two kilometers from here. Our sapper squad is now moving very slowly with the recon platoon, as you might understand after what happened here."

"Thank you, Lieutenant. Send only one man inside the cave, and keep me informed." Burgut climbed back into the warm and dry interior of his command vehicle, and settled into his padded swivel seat with a sigh. The first sergeant climbed in behind him and closed the two-part armored door. The command car was longer between the wheels than the other ASVs, and lacked a turret well taking up the center of its space. Instead, this open central area contained four comfortable seats for staff officers and radiomen, radio equipment, swing-out flat computer screens, and two folding desktops.

The American armored security vehicles were luxurious compared to the Russian equivalents he was familiar with from serving almost thirty years in the Soviet, the Russian and then the Kazak armies. The American M-1117 "Guardian" vehicles even had automatic transmissions, and could drive 110 kilometers per hour on paved roads. But the American vehicle had several major flaws, the worst of which being that it could not ford a river, unlike the similar but lighter Russian four-wheeled BRDM amphibious scout vehicles. A stream only one and a half meters deep was enough to stop the American ASVs, and in Tennessee such streams bisected the countryside every few kilometers.

With only four tires, both the American and Russian armored scout vehicles were frequently trapped by deep mud. The ASVs, intended for Military Police units and convoy escort duty, were really meant for roads. But because they were the most potent weapon platforms the foreign peacekeeping battalions had been provided by their American hosts, they were often put to the test pursuing rebels across rough ground. Frequently they failed these off-road tests, and so the drivers were under orders not to stray far from solid paving. To enforce this policy, severe disciplinary measures were enforced against the crews of the armored vehicles when they managed to get them stuck in bog mires.

It was the mission of the mounted horse troops of Saber Company to pursue rebels through thick woods and across streams and muddy or broken terrain, when wheeled vehicles could advance no further. Best of all, the horses could be obtained locally, and they required no supply lines for diesel fuel or spare parts. Tennessee had no shortage of excellent horses for the taking. Within their obvious limitations, they were still useful in a military role. It warmed Colonel Burgut's Kazak heart to see cavalry employed in the twenty-first century. "Around the corner, we shall meet the past," the old proverb went.

Colonel Burgut's late predecessor as commander of the Kazak Battalion, Colonel Jibek, had repeatedly requested tracked fighting vehicles, such as the excellent Bradley APCs, but to no avail. The Kazaks and the other international units were allegedly "peacekeepers" in Tennessee, and by the terms of the I.P.F. Agreement, they were limited to the vehicles and weapons provided to American Military Police units, including the ASVs. The 12.7mm machine guns and the 40mm automatic grenade launchers of their armored security vehicles were the most powerful weapons they were permitted to have. How could they be expected to pacify the rebel counties while fighting with one hand tied behind their backs? Just so American politicians could maintain the propaganda fiction that the low-intensity war in Tennessee was a "peacekeeping" mission...

Now Colonel Burgut even suspected that the duplicitous Americans were holding back deliveries of 40mm ammunition for the ASVs' M-19 automatic grenade launchers. A "clerical mistake" had resulted in a shipment of similar but not interchangeable 40mm grenades for rifle-mounted launchers. How stupid were the Americans, to produce two very similar but non-interchangeable projectile grenades in the same caliber!

Bradley fighting vehicles, with their all-terrain tracks, large troop compartments, amphibious capability and 25mm chain gun were what they needed! Or the superb eight-wheeled Strykers, which carried a dozen troops inside. Instead we were only given four-wheeled armored scout cars, humvee jeeps and unarmored troop trucks! Colonel Burgut had been to Fort Campbell. He had seen the hectare after hectare of tightly parked tanks and fighting vehicles. They were countless in their hundreds, left abandoned and rusting, often stripped and cannibalized for parts. The vast helicopter parks were even worse. It made him sick to see the discarded weaponry of the declining empire.

The once great American military machine had been neglected and underfunded for too many years. It was still enormous in sheer numbers of weapons, but it was a decayed and rotting shell, hollow inside. Without money for continuous upkeep, and without enough trained professional soldiers to do the work, America's ultra-high-tech weapon systems were not sustainable. They were sliding from the status of temporarily not mission capable to permanently unrecoverable. As a result, the international peacekeeping forces were reduced to fighting a counterinsurgency war with troop trucks, humvee jeeps, and a few armored security vehicles.

It never changed: politicians dictated to soldiers, and the soldiers always died as a result. Colonel Burgut had learned this lesson again and again over his three decades as a professional soldier. Why should America be any different from Afghanistan, Kosovo or Chechnya? It was time to retire, and soon he would retire on his own horse ranch in Montana or Wyoming. "Big Sky Country," the Americans called Montana. "The Cowboy State," they called Wyoming. Colonel Arman Burgut looked forward to taking off his uniform for the last time.

Burgut's young enlisted radioman turned in his own chair. "Colonel, I have been trying to contact Gray Wolf 4 and 5 for a scheduled situation report, with no success. Now I have just heard the oddest thing. I heard English spoken on our tactical channel—an American voice."

"Are you certain?"

"I'm quite certain. Positive."

"What did this American voice say?"

"I don't know the meaning of the words; I only know that I heard English. But I did recognize the word 'radio' spoken very clearly."

"Probably an American unit is using our assigned frequency by accident. As you know, strange atmospheric conditions sometimes occur at twilight, and they could be quite far away."

"Colonel, that has never happened on our tactical net before. And why would they have our encryption key?"

"I can't explain it, Sergeant, but such mistakes happen. Continue trying to contact Wolf 4 and 5."

The radioman appeared doubtful, but he answered, "Yes sir."

Burgut further instructed him, "Send an alert message to all of the companies. 'We are unable to contact Gray Wolf 4 and 5. They have missed scheduled radio contacts. Report their position if they are seen. Attempt to establish communications with them, physically and in person if necessary. Exercise caution.' All right?"

"Yes sir, I'll send it now." The radioman jotted down notes on a pad, then swiveled his seat around to his bank of communications equipment to begin his task.

This strange report was the latest in a string of incidents today that bothered the colonel. First: three soldiers from his Headquarters Company had been missing since before dawn. Perhaps they were merely drunk somewhere, having found a barn full of 'white lightning' corn whisky, or some American girls to amuse them. It had happened before...but never during a major field operation. Second: the Eagle Company recon platoon had stupidly—and fatally—triggered a booby-trapped car, instead of waiting for the sappers to check it. Third: the two armored scout vehicles on detached patrol missed their scheduled radio contact, and now there was a peculiar report of hearing English spoken on their assigned frequency.

Nevertheless, there was also some good news today. The missing engine parts for the Caterpillar earthmover's transporter truck had arrived. The bodies of the Americans in the ravine were now covered with five or six meters of dirt, and planted over with small fir trees taken from nearby, just as General Blair had demanded. The ravine itself existed no more. It had been erased from the face of the earth. Tonight the last of the American rebels in Radford County were fleeing for their lives as his battalion put their homes to the torch. Once the rebels were moving south, out of

Tennessee, they became refugees and were not to be unnecessarily harassed. The point was to drive them out, to depopulate the county, not to cause every rebel to stay and fight to the death. General Blair had been clear on that point, after the misunderstanding that had led to the ravine incident.

Of course, there would always be isolated excesses; they were unavoidable in the planned chaos accompanying the forced depopulation of a region. People had to be terrorized to an extent; otherwise, they would not take to the roads in flight. Of course, any armed resistance would be met with overwhelming force, and once firing started, it was not so easy to stop. And naturally, his troops could be expected to collect souvenirs and trinkets, perhaps some valuables, before destroying the rebel dwellings. Why let everything go to waste in the flames? They were not being paid, except in promises of land and citizenship; they needed some tangible rewards in the meantime. And if they found some pretty American girls along the way, well, Kazak soldiers were still men, after all! This was the nature of such "pacification" operations, in any country throughout history. The intent was to depopulate a region, and that could not be done by handing out bouquets of flowers, chocolates and calling cards!

Within a few days, he would be able to report to General Blair that Radford County and the surrounding areas had been fully pacified, speeding up the day that his battalion would be moved to Montana. By all reports, the high mountains and wind-swept plains of Montana and Wyoming were so similar to Kazakhstan that his men would feel that they were at home.

Like himself, most of his men could never return to Kazakhstan. They were essentially stateless. Most of them had been involved in the Cossack Uprising, attempting to return the Kazak border regions to the Russian Federation. That endeavor, which only two years before had seemed so promising, had been crushed. The Cossacks involved in the uprising, having been encouraged to separate from Kazakhstan, had then not been welcomed as new citizens by Mother Russia. One solution to the impasse, if it could be called that, had come with the recent offer by the United States government to reward so-called "peacekeepers" with citizenship and land. The offer was a gift from heaven for the landless Cossacks, who were a military estate, but not a people. The Cossacks were a union of men joined only by common military tradition, not by land, blood or religion. The original Cossacks had fled to the wide, unpopulated steppes from the Ukraine. They had even taken their name from the Kazaks, which in the Turkic steppes had meant both fugitive and freeman. And so it was again. Once again they were fugitives, searching for a land to call their own.

Once in their new homeland of Montana—after helping to subdue the rebels there—his homeless Cossacks would each be granted 200-hectare land deeds, almost a thousand American acres. As the victorious leader of the Kazak Battalion, he would receive a land grant fully one hundred times as large, as his own reward for service to the United States government.

America was truly a land of opportunity.

Colonel Burgut turned to his executive officer, seated across from him, their knees almost touching. "Major Seribek, we shall move out right away. Only the armored security vehicles. I want to be rolling in two minutes. Make the necessary calls." Colonel Burgut's command vehicle always traveled accompanied by at least two other of the heavily armed and turreted ASVs.

"Where are we going, Colonel?"

"North, to the last reported position of the missing scout vehicles. What other units are in that area?"

Major Seribek swung his computer screen around so they both could look at the GPS topographical map displayed there. All of the friendly units were displayed with small icons, part of the American Blue Force system for preventing so-called friendly-fire mistakes. "Tiger Company is the closest."

"Tell them to return to their trucks and meet us...here." Colonel Burgut put a stubby finger on a crossroads twelve kilometers to their north.

They came to the first paved road, a crumbling asphalt path that was only ten feet wide. Over the intercom, Boone said, "Turn right, Phil."

"I've got it."

"Speed up to about thirty. The road doesn't get much worse than it is here."

"No problem."

"If that's too fast, slow down until you're comfortable. Just don't go off the road if you don't have to. We don't want to get stuck like those poor dumb Cossack bastards. And watch out for drainage ditches. These things have pretty crappy visibility down on the sides, and they roll over real easy." Boone stood up in the turret well, just his shoulders and head protruding through the hatch, which was locked upright behind him. Through the night tube on his combat crewman's helmet, he could see clearly but with a limited field of view. Every ten seconds a strobe on the back of the ASV blinked its Morse Kilo: dash-dot-dash. He considered the wisdom of leaving it on. A Predator UAV above them would spot the ASV anyway, and the infrared blinker was their friend-or-foe identification and should protect them from a missile strike. On the other hand, if the Kazaks found the other stuck ASV and their dead crewmen, they would quickly understand the situation and would probably change their identifier, or turn them off, leaving the captured vehicle with the only blinking "K" in Radford County. In other words, dead meat with a flashing light attached to draw attention.

"Doug, find the light panel."

"I've got it."

"Look for the infrared strobe."

"It says 'Strobe/Signal.' That one?"

"Flip it to 'off'." Boone waited for the next series of infrared blinks, but they didn't come. "Okay, it's off now. Just be ready to turn it back on if I tell you."

"Roger that."

Boone considered their situation. The network of primary, secondary and dirt roads in the county was printed in his mind. The information on the portable military GPS he was using was hopelessly incorrect or outdated at the rural lane level, giving him an edge over his enemies, who lacked his local knowledge. This road was just wide enough for the ASV. Two approaching cars would have to slow down and move carefully to the steep shoulders in order to pass. This rarely happened; not many cars were driving in this area anymore. Since the earthquakes, there were countless sections of road completely impassible to cars, but the ASV could make it through many of the washouts and small gullies. These breaks in the roads were not reflected on the GPS Jenny had taken from the dead traitor.

He had raised the barrel of the .50 caliber in front of him. Any low branches or wires across the narrow road would be deflected or broken by the heavy steel barrel instead of slashing his face or neck. Boone had strung many taut wire cables across roads like this, in hopes of taking off the head of a foreign vehicle commander or turret gunner. He never knew if he had been successful in this endeavor.

The hand-held military GPS unit obtained by Jenny was tucked inside his parka below his neck. It needed to be outside the steel machine to receive its satellite signals. Eight glass-and-steel prism blocks were arrayed around the circumference of the turret. They acted as rectangular periscopes, appearing like normal eye-level windows from within the turret. When he dropped inside the protection of the turret, they would provide his only view of the world outside. To use the night-vision-equipped gun sight, he needed to flip his helmet-mounted NOD up out of the way. To look out the prism windows, he would need to flip it back down. It was a lot simpler to just stand up with his head above the turret hatch, and be able to look in all directions. At least until the shooting started.

If they stayed on this paved road, they would make good time and would probably avoid hitting a Kazak checkpoint. The downside was that the narrow road could be easily blocked simply by parking any vehicle between two trees, when the road cut through thick woods. If they used a wider secondary road, they might see danger far enough ahead to turn around or bypass it, but then there was also a greater chance of running into a Kazak patrol or checkpoint. If they went entirely off the pavement and even off the dirt roads, they might wind up stuck in some mucky creek bottom. Roughly stated, those were his three options.

They were only a few miles from the northern edge of the Kazak area of operations. Boone decided to stay on the narrow, winding paved track for now. To leave Radford County in the ASV, they would have to cross Butler Creek over a two-lane trestle bridge that was sporadically guarded at one or both ends. Or they could risk crossing at a ford, but after all the rain and snowmelt the creeks were high, and these ASVs were not truly amphibious. They didn't float, and they couldn't swim. He couldn't remember the precise maximum depth that ASVs could ford, and if he guessed wrong, they'd be screwed, stuck out in the middle of an icy river.

Or they could hide the ASV, abandon it and continue on foot in stealth patrolling mode. Boone considered these options, weighed the speed and risk factors, and decided to continue as they were going, for now. It was never far from his mind that a missile could streak down from the sky at any moment, putting an end to all of his risk calculations in a single white-hot millisecond.

21

CW4 Rogan dropped into his swivel chair and inserted the memory stick into the USB port on the computer beneath his desk. The monitor's screensaver showed a Blackhawk helicopter, with both side doors rolled back. In the troop compartment, helmeted soldiers in dusty uniforms and khaki-colored body armor smiled across a hundred feet of open sky. A Middle Eastern city's ancient and modern skyline was spread out below them. Hugh Rogan was in the pilot's seat, looking at the camera through the visor of his flight helmet. The picture had obviously been snapped from another helicopter flying beside him.

The walls of his small office were covered with photographs and plaques from his nearly thirty-year career in Army Aviation. Shelves were full of flight helmets, intricately detailed model helicopters, and other military souvenirs collected on several continents.

Rogan slid out his computer keyboard and typed a few commands. Sergeant Major Charlie Donelson entered the room with a pair of large unlabeled brown bottles. The pints of home-brewed beer were left on Rogan's back porch to keep them cold. He passed one bottle to his friend, then pulled a chair over next to the computer and sat down. Donelson held up his bottle and looked through it, using the computer screen for a backlight. "This batch is better than your last one—less crud on the bottom."

"That 'crud' gives each batch its own unique flavor," said Rogan.

"Yeah, unique crud flavor."

"I'm sorry we're out of your store-bought sissy beer. Anyway, it's a lot stronger than that near-beer they're serving at the club." The friends clinked bottles and took swigs.

The computer switched from the screensaver to a black-and-white aerial view of a small town. It appeared to be routine surveillance video, with time stamps, speed and altitude data, and a targeting curser imprinted over the land below. "What's that, video shot from a Predator?" asked Donelson.

"Yeah, a Predator B. It's new; the date stamp is from just last Saturday. I make the grid coordinates to be southwest Tennessee, maybe northern Mississippi."

"Who's on the horses? What's going on?"

"Their strobes are flashing Morse Kilo, so that makes them Kazaks," said Rogan. The two men watched in silence, sipping their beers. They watched the file of horses trot into a fence-enclosed paved parking area.

They watched as a group of civilians was separated into two long lines, and one group was led into a building. They watched the other group being marched the other way, out onto the street and onto school buses. The buses had numbers written on their roofs: R22 and R37.

They watched school bus R37 drive along a dirt road through woods, to an isolated clearing. The bus was accompanied by an Army truck. The passengers were unloaded and marched to the edge of a gully by soldiers from the truck. They watched as their rifles flared white hot and the standing people tumbled down in a line. What was happening on the video was unmistakable, even without sound or captions.

"Oh my God," CW4 Rogan whispered. Bus R37 departed and was replaced by R22, and the scene was reenacted with new victims. Seven times the buses arrived full of people, and departed empty. Seven times the people were lined up and shot down. The video had been edited to shorten the running time, so that the executions seemed to take place immediately one after the other. When it finished, it looped and played again. Both men stared at the screen as it played through a second and a third time. By examining the time stamps on the videos, they determined that each mass execution actually took place about fifteen minutes apart. The total edited running time was only about ten minutes, a "highlights" film of a mass murder that took place over nearly two hours.

"The guy who passed it to us—you said he works in the old fitness center, controlling UAVs?" asked Donelson.

"Yeah, that's where I've seen him going in and out. Sometimes I take the same shuttle bus. It goes around by the gym; that's where he gets on and off."

"Hulkster, this is bad. This is the worst. There must have been hundreds of people on that parking lot, before they were put on those buses. They made seven trips, what's that, fifty or sixty people on each one?"

"Must be around four hundred dead, maybe more," said Rogan. "We can freeze the video on each one and get an exact count. When they're lined up, right before...right before they're shot."

"Man, oh man...what the hell do we do now? I've put up with a lot of shit in this man's Army. I've put in my time and kept my mouth shut, maybe too much, but this...this is *way* over the line. Hugh, my friend, we can't walk away from this one."

"Yeah. We can't sit on this. We have to *do* something with it."

"But what?" asked Donelson.

Rogan said, "I don't know what, but something."

"Give it to *60 Minutes*?"

"Stop joking, Charlie. This is serious."

"What, then?"

"I don't know. I don't know." Rogan sighed and scratched his short gray-black hair. "Let's get the poker gang together and show it to them."

Donelson asked, "When? Tonight?"

"No—tomorrow. It'll take time to see who's around and pass the word."

"Let's meet at my house, off base. We don't have to tell them what it's about, we'll just make sure they come."

"All of them?" asked CW4 Rogan. "What about Fred? Do you trust him? His outfit is chopped to NORTHCOM, and they're flying Homeland Security missions. Sometimes he's flying foreign peacekeepers."

"Aw, hell no. Not Fred. Let's think about this. Let's think about this real carefully. Let's make a list. It has to only be men we trust like ten thousand percent."

"Senior NCOs and warrants only," said Donelson, after taking a long drink from his beer. "The young ones are too brainwashed. Some of them, anyway."

"Career only. Active duty or retired. Only people we've known like forever."

"Hey, what about Ira? He's squirrelly as hell, but he's got contacts like nobody else I know."

"Yeah, Ira Hayes, that crazy bastard." Rogan smiled, stretching a thin scar at the corner of his mouth. "He's frikkin' nuts, but he's a real patriot, I know that much. Even if he cheats at cards."

"That's not really cheating, what he does."

"The hell you say! But he does make me laugh." Rogan smiled again, and chuckled at some private memory.

"What about officers?"

Rogan said, "Regular commissioned officers? You mean besides warrant officers? Field grades? Senior officers? You bring in any of them, and they'll try to take over. They always do. It's their nature, they can't help it."

"Not all of them," replied Donelson, shaking his head. "There's a few…well, there's one for sure—Colonel Spencer. I trust him as much as I ever trusted anybody in my life."

"You're just saying that because he saved your life in Somalia, back when you were both Rangers."

"Fuckin' A right, but it's a lot more than that. And let's face it: he can open up some doors. He's got access we'll never have."

"So we're going outside the poker gang?"

"I think we have to," said Donelson. "But we have to keep it small. No more than six or seven."

"Let's make a list."

"No more than ten, max."

"Charlie, we can't screw this one up. We have to do this right. I don't know what we're going to do with this video, but whatever we do, we have to do it right. And that means we go all the way, no matter what it takes. They're slaughtering Americans now, and we have to stop it."

"You know, this is all about that goddamn Building 1405 program."

"Fucking civilians—"

"Fucking traitors!" Donelson snapped. "Traitors, working with foreign enemies—in America! I've put up with a hell of a lot over the last few years, I've swallowed some seriously bad shit, but not this. This is too much."

"We need to find out all about what's going on in Building 1405. But carefully."

"Very carefully. But we have to do it. We have to. We have no choice. And we have to stop it."

"Charlie, this is...*duty*," whispered Rogan, almost reverently.

"Damn right. If there ever was duty, this is it."

"You know, I had an uncle killed on Okinawa. Then my father was in the Korean War. And you, you lost your own father! That was duty, hard duty, but they always did it, no matter what. My family, your family, all those guys. Millions of them, going all the way back. They did what they had to do. They served. Like we did, in Iraq and Afghanistan and everywhere else. It was our duty. We lost a lot of good men, and a lot more got torn up. But we always did our duty, all of us. We never backed down from a fight, and we never shirked our duty. Never."

"Yeah," said Donelson, "but I think this is a lot worse, because it's Americans who are our enemies too."

"But it's still duty. Enemies foreign *and domestic*, right? Isn't that the oath we swore? Sure, it's a lot simpler when it's foreigners, and we're overseas. But just because they're Americans, American traitors, that doesn't mean we can let this slide. It's still duty, and we swore the oath."

"Fortress, this is Tiger Leader."

"Go ahead, Tiger Leader, this is Fortress." Fortress was the call sign among the Kazaks for Colonel Burgut's command vehicle. Burgut's radioman took the call, but the colonel was able to hear both sides over his intercom.

"Fortress, Tiger Recon has found Gray Wolf 5. All six crew from both vehicles are dead. Gray Wolf 4 is not anywhere near Gray Wolf 5. Gray Wolf 4 is gone."

Colonel Burgut quickly cut in, pressing the button on his intercom wire that switched him to the radio. "Repeat that, Tiger Leader."

"Yes sir. Armored scout vehicle Wolf 5 is at these grid coordinates. Wolf 5 is trapped in a muddy bog. All six crew from both vehicles have been shot and killed by small-arms fire. Wolf 4 is not at that location. That is all the information I have received from the Tiger Company reconnaissance platoon. I have not yet seen it myself."

Blast the American devils to hell and back! Colonel Burgut rasped out, "Thank you, Tiger Leader. What is your estimated arrival time at the rendezvous position?"

"Fortress, we are there now, except for our recon platoon. Recon platoon is securing Gray Wolf 5 and searching for Gray Wolf 4."

Colonel Burgut studied his glowing GPS screen, zooming in on the northern edge of Radford County. "Tiger Leader, move one platoon each to intersections Red 15, Red 17 and Red 18, and set up blocking positions. Tiger headquarters platoon, go to Red 17. Fortress will rendezvous with you there. Our estimated arrival time is ten minutes." After the company commander confirmed his orders, Burgut switched back to his intercom. "Driver, make maximum speed. Radioman: send this message to all motorized companies. Order them to move immediately at maximum speed to intersection Red 17. More instructions to follow en route. Send that now. After that message is sent, instruct Saber Company to remain in the south. They should continue to harass and pursue the remaining rebels. We're going to catch these sons of whores, and make them beg for a quick death!"

The major leaned close and said, "Colonel, you will be leaving Saber Company without mechanized or armored support?"

"The fighting is over down there, except for chasing the last refugees out of the county. The Sabers can handle that mission on their own for a few hours. In any case, we'll be moving too fast for them to stay with us."

The radioman finished in a few moments, and turned back to his colonel. The first sergeant and the major also stared at him, awaiting his next orders. Colonel Burgut was in a quandary. What he now needed most was not under his control. He needed aviation assets, helicopters and drones, eyes up in the sky to find the commandeered ASV. But to admit to the Americans that one of his armored security vehicles had been stolen, stolen by rebels who were supposed to be crushed and defeated, would be highly embarrassing. Humiliating. He would lose face in an almost unimaginable way!

But...but...if the Americans escaped from Radford County with a stolen ASV, armed with a 40mm automatic grenade launcher and a 12.7mm heavy machine gun, what terrible mischief they might cause, and that would be even worse! After a minute, his temples throbbing, Burgut said, "Get the Americans on the radio. Request a helicopter for casualty evacuation." Eagle Platoon had several wounded men, from the booby-trapped car. He could use this as an excuse for a helicopter request, and not directly admit the fiasco of the stolen ASV. Once the helicopter was in the air above him, he could modify his request for its use. Anyway, it was a valid reason to initially contact Fort Campbell concerning helicopters.

The young radioman replied over his intercom headphones. "Colonel, I have Fort Campbell air operations on this channel. They request to speak to you directly."

"Very well." He switched his intercom button to the radio position while straining to convert his thought processes into English. At these times, he most needed an American liaison. "This is Kilo Bravo Leader. Who is on radio speaking with, over?"

"This is flight operations. What do you need, Kilo Bravo Leader?"

Burgut spoke slowly and deliberately, aware that his English was sometimes difficult for Americans to understand, especially over the radio. "We have wounded men. We are needing helicopter medical casualty evacuation as soon as possible—over."

There was a pause before the transmission was answered. "Ah, I'm sorry, Kilo Bravo Leader, but due to adverse weather, no helicopters are available tonight."

It took a few moments for Burgut to translate the words that he had heard. "Not available? Not available?! Well, be making them available! Weather is good, no problem weather by this location. We have immediate need—men will die without quickly medical evacuation."

"Ahh, copy that, Kilo Bravo Leader, but I repeat: helicopters are not available tonight."

"Put General Blair. I demand that you put General Blair on radio immediate!"

"General Blair? Did you say *General Blair*? Uh, wait one, Kilo Leader."

Colonel Burgut grimaced, swearing under his breath while he waited, his three subordinates in the confined space pretending to study various communication and navigational displays. He slipped a stainless steel flask from the thigh pocket of his camouflage trousers and took a long swig of the local corn whisky, needing to feel its burning relief. Never one to be rude or selfish, he passed the flask to Major Seribek, who took a quick drink and handed it to the first sergeant, who took the longest draft of all. The radioman glanced at the flask, and then turned his attention back to his radio console. The first sergeant handed the steel flask back to his colonel. It would never be spoken of again. If the colonel felt a slug of whisky was called for, that was entirely up to him.

A different American voice came over the radio, as clear as if it was on a telephone. "Ah, Kilo Bravo Leader, this is Foxtrot Charlie Air Operations. The person you requested is not available. No one is available from his staff at this time. No aviation assets are available at this time, due to inclement weather and low cloud ceiling. I have been instructed to inform you to try again tomorrow morning. Helicopter support may be available then. This is Fox Charlie Air Ops—out." The channel went dead in his earphones.

Colonel Burgut understood only half of the American's words, but he understood the entirety of the message, conveyed perfectly well. General Blair was stabbing him in the back. It was because of the affair of the American civilians killed in the ravine. He was being punished, when the mass shooting had been done on the orders of the American liaison Major Zinovsky, the braggart fool who had subsequently died in the house fire. Well, fornicate all their mothers with rusty bayonets! We will have our own revenge for our murdered comrades when we catch the terrorists who have taken our ASV! And I will personally deal with General Blair later…

The stolen ASV rolled northward along the winding lane. Patchy ground fog lay across the hollows in the lower elevations. Isolated homes were burning down to embers. Some were close enough to the road to be clearly visible, and others merely caused the mist to glow green in their night vision tubes. Carson sped up to thirty when the terrain and visibility permitted.

Boone's voice crackled over the intercom. "Shit! Watch out, Phil!"

"People, I see them," Carson answered, braking quickly to less than ten miles an hour. "Civilians, it looks like." The pedestrians were scattering off both sides of the narrow road at the approach of the ASV. Without night vision to see through the darkness, the people on the road were able to hear the muffled engine only moments before the Americans inside its armored hull saw them. "They're heading south, it looks like." Three stubby windshield wipers on each of the two narrow front windows cleared the wet mist from the thick armored glass. Powerful blowers kept them from fogging on the inside.

"Heading for Mississippi," answered Boone. "This is when a thermal gun sight would really be nice. We'd be able to see right through this pea soup." To be more ready to fight, he lowered the .50 caliber's barrel back down to horizontal with his hand control.

Doug asked, "Why don't these things have thermal night vision?"

"Most of the ASVs had them, but they're a bitch to maintain and they cost a fortune. Especially if you're going to let foreign contract soldiers have them. They're worth so much, it's pretty tempting to take one with you if you're planning to desert. Sort of like taking your own severance package with you. At least, that's my best guess."

"So the Army takes them out before the foreign soldiers can," said Doug.

"Yeah, I guess that's right," replied Boone. "Before they can steal them or break them. They want the foreign mercenaries to be effective, but not *too* effective. Not if it means giving them thermal night vision."

"I've got to slow down some more," said Phil. "I don't want to run over any civilians." Wraithlike walkers appeared at the edges of their visibility, shrouded in mist, all heading south with packs and bundles, pushing handcarts and pulling wagons.

"We'll be coming to a crossroads in a few hundred meters," said Boone. "It'll be more open, with fewer trees around, so the wind might be enough to blow off the fog. Then it's only half a mile to the bridge over to the Nigerian side."

They continued creeping forward at five miles an hour, the ASV's diesel almost inaudible at low RPMs. Carson remembered how loud the old tracked M-113 APCs were in 'Nam. There was no way a clanking and grinding tracked vehicle could sneak up on anybody on a quiet night like this. Unseen enemies would be getting into ambush positions when you were a mile out. He was impressed with the stealth of this four-wheeled ASV as they rolled smoothly up the single paved lane.

Of course, the tracked vehicles always had the option of crashing off into the boonies and making their own path, unlike these wheelies. Once surprise was lost and the shooting had started, the tracked 113s and the newer Bradleys were superior in almost every way, effortlessly running across most terrain at over forty miles an hour. The reason they were able to steal this ASV in the first place was that its partner had become trapped in mud when trying to move cross-country. Nothing came for free; there were always tradeoffs. At least Boone knew all of these little backcountry roads.

No more civilian refugees were seen. Their road descended in a curve, leaving the cover of woods, and terminated in a T intersection at an angle. The only trees were near a few scattered home sites, set well back from the new two-lane road and almost invisible in the mist. Their burning embers looked like wide green campfires in Carson's night eye. He had to crane his neck side to side, trying to get the new lay of the land as he was suddenly presented with many possible directions of advance. He slowed almost to a stop, waiting to hear Boone's next instruction. The fog was just as thick in this open area, with less than a hundred yards of visibility.

"Contact front!" Boone shouted over the intercom.

A second later Carson saw the dim outline of a big troop truck, one of the new six-wheeled medium tactical vehicles with a boxy European-style cab. A machine gun barrel extended from a mount on the roof of the cab. He stepped on the brake, stopping. Soldiers were spilling out the back of the canvas-covered cargo area, and the passenger-side cab door was open. The truck was less than a hundred yards away.

Boone said, "Switch the 'K' strobe back on, and keep inching forward."

"You got it," answered Doug.

"Do they see us yet?" Carson wondered aloud over the intercom as he took his foot off the brake. His question was quickly answered: a sudden electric shock seemed to run through the dozen or fifteen soldiers arrayed around the back of the truck. More soldiers armed with rifles were climbing and jumping from the truck to the ground. A soldier wearing night goggles stood in the center of the road and put both arms up, waving the ASV to a halt. Confusion was marked by their body language, with some shouldering Kalashnikovs and others turning to one another in postures of doubt. The big truck was parked at an angle across both paved lanes of the new road. Carson said, "I don't think I can just slide around these guys."

"Okay, stop here," said Boone, dropping down inside the turret. Two soldiers approached the ASV, walking slowly. One carried a Kalashnikov at port arms, the other cradled an RPD light machine gun. The rifleman wore night goggles, so he could see their blinking 'K' strobe, signifying friendly forces. The ASV's turret was facing forward, almost toward the troop truck. The truck's machine gun was facing forward as well, aiming it away from the Americans' stolen ASV. But then it began to turn.

"Oh shit, I was hoping to avoid this—" said Boone, cutting loose with a burst of .50 caliber machine-gun fire aimed at the cab of the troop truck. Bambambambambam! The big machine gun's blast and recoil hammered the ASV. He switched to 40mm grenades, and fired a quick burst, boom-boom-boom! Carson watched the impacting explosions beginning at the cab, working down the length of the truck and then detonating on the ground among the dismounted soldiers.

On the intercom Boone yelled, "Hit it, Phil—go go go! Drive behind the truck, drive right through them!"

Carson floored the accelerator, swerved and ran over the two closest troops, who had dropped to the ground when the first shots were fired over their heads only seconds before. He distinctly felt the bumps made by their bodies as they were crushed beneath his giant, tractor-sized wheels. The ASV rapidly closed the gap to the rear end of the troop truck. Most of the enemy soldiers were now already proned out, either dead, wounded or low-crawling for cover. In just a few seconds, the ASV was accelerating past thirty miles an hour. Then it hit the next groups of men, bumping and bouncing over their bodies as some tried to roll out of the way. Boone slued the turret clockwise as they passed the back of the truck, the ASV tilting precariously as it negotiated the steep shoulder and climbed back onto the pavement. Because they were inside the minimum arming range of the 40mm grenades, Boone slammed it with another burst from the .50 caliber. The cab of the truck burst into flames behind them, and Carson saw the orange eruption reflected in the two wide rearview mirrors. A few meaningless small-arms rounds pinged off the armor plate on the rear of the ASV as they sped away from the area.

"Everybody good?" shouted Boone. "Everything running okay?"

"We're good down here," answered Phil. "Gauges look normal, tires feel the same."

"Flip off the strobe, okay?"

Doug said, "It's off now."

Boone's voice brimmed with excitement. "Okay, guys, forget about the bridge over to the Nigerian side—the whole world is awake now. They'll block the bridge, so now it's time for Plan B. Phil, how's your visibility at this speed?" They were traveling over forty miles an hour on a straight section of two-lane road. There was less fog in this more wide-open area, but visibility was still impaired.

"I can see okay; I just hope there's no more Kazaks up in front of us."

"We're turning north, that'll be left, in about a mile."

A metallic clang banged through the ASV, a green tracer streaked past, then more tracers, and another ringing bang.

"We've got company!" shouted Boone, sluing the turret rearward. "Looks like a couple of ASVs are on our six o'clock. Put the hammer down, Phil!" Boone let loose a short, controlled burst from the .50 cal. He'd estimated they had about two hundred rounds of .50 caliber and about twenty 40mm grenades. He'd used maybe eight or ten of the grenades already. From his approach on foot behind the ASV, Carson knew that the slatted exhaust louvers on the rear of the stolen ASV would be a weak spot. Would they stop .50 caliber armor-piercing rounds? If they couldn't, the vehicle's engine would soon be grinding to a halt.

"Okay, Phil, just after this barn, hit the brakes and swing left into the field—just don't roll this sucker! Hang on!"

Carson jumped on the brake pedal as they passed the old wooden structure, turned and smashed through a pole fence, bumping and swaying, briefly going onto two wheels before regaining control.

Boone continued his directions. "Head straight for the woods across the field, see where it goes down? See the road, the low part by the fence? That's it, follow that."

Carson struggled to keep control, the ASV sometimes bouncing airborne or threatening to go up on two wheels again. More tracers flew in front and above them. Their pursuers were not directly behind them now, but were angling after them, and their fire was obviously unaimed. The dirt farm road followed a depression in the terrain, partially shielding them from effective fire. Another hundred yards and they entered a tree line. Then ahead of them, he saw open water, maybe sixty yards across to the other bank. "What now, Boone?" The turret was still facing backward, so

Carson knew that Boone would have to twist clear around in the turret to see forward.

"Slow down, and ease into it. I'll keep these guys busy."

"How deep is it?" asked Carson, as the front wheels slipped into the current.

"Three, four feet...I hope."

"How deep can this buggy go?"

"We're going to find out! Maybe five feet, max."

The bottom was rocky, and slippery beneath the wheels. As the water depth increased, their traction decreased. Icy water leaked in through the side doors and other unseen gaps. Halfway across, the ASV seemed to bob or float, turned partially sideways as the wheels spun to no effect, then found bottom and gripped again. Finally the depth began to lessen, the angle of the vehicle turned upward, and they approached the opposite shore as more slugs caromed off their armor plates and grenades exploded around them.

The bank on the opposite shore was steep, at least forty-five degrees, and Carson struggled to find an open path through deadfall trees and saplings. He floored the accelerator and took the slope at an angle, the turbo diesel roaring, the ASV's four big tractor tires clawing and churning at the earth like a monster truck. With his vehicle angled steeply upward, Carson could see nothing but blank green sky and tree branches through the narrow slot of his armored glass front window. "Come on, baby, come on!" he shouted. After seconds that stretched on forever, the vehicle topped the crest and rolled to level again, allowing him to see the terrain to his front. Relief flooded through him even as more heavy shots rang off their ASV's armored hull. Then a massive explosion seemed to detonate inside the vehicle, shaking it and stunning the three American crew.

"What was *that*?" Doug screamed.

Boone called back, "I think a grenade hit the engine compartment. Phil, how's she running?" The turbo diesel had a new sound, ragged and rough.

"I'm losing RPMs, and the engine temp is going up fast."

"Phil, there's a dirt road straight in front, running parallel to the creek. Hang a left and slow down, we just need a few more minutes. I have two ASVs behind us in the water now, but they can only see our turret. We're hull-down to them since we cleared the bank."

"Then shoot them!" Carson yelled back. "Are you out of ammo?"

"Almost, but I have another idea—we're going to visit the Nigerians. Our guns can't stop an ASV from the front anyway. Okay, the Nigerian outpost is just ahead, it's those buildings. Doug, put the strobe back on." The stream marked the border between the counties assigned to the Kazak Battalion and the Nigerian Peacekeeping Force. The Nigerians had taken over two large farms, one fronting each side of the paved county road that crossed the stream into Kazak territory. The old steel cantilevered-truss bridge had survived the earthquakes. Now the ASV was approaching the Nigerian position from behind, at a walking speed. Boone swung the turret back around to the front.

Through the narrow bulletproof front windshield, Carson could see that the dirt road led alongside and then between several farm outbuildings and a large tractor shed. He glanced down: RPMs were surging up and down even with the same pressure on the accelerator pedal, oil pressure was dropping and the engine temperature was reading over 220 degrees. But they were still driving forward.

Boone said, "Their security is facing the bridge, and we're already behind it in their rear. Okay, here we go, we've got company—the Nigerians are coming out to play." From behind a small building, an SUV backed up directly in front of the ASV's path and stopped. Soldiers spilled out of a barn, hopping around in bare feet on the cold ground while pulling up trousers and throwing on coats. Even in the green light, it was possible to tell that they were Africans, from the Nigerian contingent of "peacekeepers."

"Hit the truck, Phil, slam it, let's go!" Boone depressed the .50 caliber's barrel and fired it in short bursts of three or four shots, continually traversing, taking on any targets of opportunity: vehicles, buildings, men running in the open. Carson drove straight ahead, smashed the big SUV out of the way, knocking down soldiers who in their disorientation and confusion stood in the ASV's path. Most appeared not even to see the armored machine before they were hit and run over.

More soldiers appeared from several farmhouses and outbuildings, some taking cover and firing their rifles, which had no effect at all on the ASV. Other Nigerian thin-skinned vehicles began to move about in the confusion. It was obvious that the troops were unsure about who was friendly and who was not. Armored vehicles were synonymous with allied international peacekeepers, and the Nigerians could not seem to wrap their minds around a peacekeeping vehicle intentionally opening fire on them.

Tracers flew past the ASV from behind, and more heavy rounds impacted its hull. Boone yelled, "The Cossacks are on our ass again!" as he swung the turret and rattled off a long burst of .50 caliber toward the ASV's rear, and then fired the last of the 40mm grenades from the M-19. This was answered with 40mm grenades from their pursuers, which exploded among the half-dressed Nigerian troops, who were now running madly in all directions at once between barns and sheds.

"Phil, when you reach the next pavement, hang a right and give her everything you've got." As soon as Carson felt the smoother asphalt beneath their wheels, he turned and Boone unexpectedly launched the ASV's turret-mounted smoke grenades. When they hit the ground, their phos-phorous igniters exploded in sheets of brilliant flame. In seconds, the high-capacity military smokes were blooming and merging into a vast, im-penetrable manmade fog. The firing behind them continued as they rolled northward on the two-lane road, leaving the green cloud and accelerating to thirty miles an hour. Now the .50 caliber and 40mm grenade explosions were joined by at least a dozen rifles and light machine guns, crackling and roaring behind them. The ASV's motor emitted a new high-pitched grind-ing squeal, and a new burning smell invaded the inerior.

"Doug, kill the signal strobe. Phil, we're taking the next paved road to the right."

Carson said, "That'll take us right back toward the fight—"

"Don't worry; I know these roads. Just take it, this one here." The sounds of firing continued unabated behind them; explosions, cracks, booms and the whiz of ricocheting rounds.

They approached a two-story residence on their right side. Enough moonlight filtered through the low cloud cover and reflected off the re-maining snow crust for them to make out the shape of a small mansion, uphill between bare trees. A dark civilian pickup truck rolled backward down its long driveway, a squad of soldiers in the back. "N.P.F" was painted in foot-high white block letters on the tailgate and side of the shiny truck. Over the intercom from the turret, Boone said, "Stop them, Phil—that's our next ride."

Carson left the road, angled up the lawn to the driveway, and tipped the back corner of the pickup in a heavy-duty Pitt maneuver, smashing into its rear bumper and spinning the truck around. The occupants appeared totally shocked by the unexpected appearance of the monster ASV, and before the pickup came to a stop, they leaped from the truck bed. At the same time, both cab doors flew open. All six or seven of the Nigerian troops fled back up the lawn toward the house, leaving their shoulder weapons scattered behind them. Before they had made it thirty yards, Boone cut most of them to pieces with a raking burst from the .50 caliber, and all of them hit the ground.

"All right," he shouted over the intercom, "this is our new car; we're getting out here. Phil, make sure those guys are down for the count. They're too low for me to get with the fifty, and I'm out of 40 mike-mike." The ASV was parked sideways to the slope of the hill, its left wheels in a ditch, and the machine gun's barrel could not be depressed far enough to reach the prone soldiers.

Carson reached up and threw open his hatch, pulled off his crew helmet with its night vision lens, then grabbed his carbine and stood on the driver's seat. In a moment, his eyes adjusted to the ambient light. Several of the Nigerian soldiers were screaming and moaning, rolling on the snowy lawn leading up to the mansion. Dark men against the white snow. He shouldered the rifle and found the Aimpoint's red dot with his right eye, flicked the safety back with his thumb, and put two quick rounds into each torso, moving or not. One man sprang to his feet and began to run away uphill, but slipped in the snow, his arms windmilling. Carson aimed the floating red dot between his shoulder blades and hit him twice more, before he could regain his balance and take off again. *Nice shooting, Phil*, he thought, as the man twisted down in a heap.

The blood veil had fallen over Carson's eyes, and he wasn't about to risk being shot from behind by some foreign interloper playing possum. *I'll bet you never dreamed you'd die in the cold snow* popped into his mind and he suppressed a laugh. Still watching for other Nigerians or Kazaks to appear, he climbed all the way up through the hatch, standing watch while Boone grabbed their packs and exited through the ASV's side door.

It took them less than a minute to change vehicles, including time for Boone to leave a four-pound C-4 demolition charge with a three-minute time fuse. The demo charge was already prepared; the white dough was packed into a large plastic mayonnaise jar. The inside bottom of the jar had been built up into a hollow cone, forming an improvised shaped charge. Boone only had to push a non-electric blasting cap through a hole in the lid and into the explosive. The silver cap was already crimped onto the end of a short piece of waterproof military time fuse. His last act, after grabbing the M-79 grenade launcher and a bandolier of 40mm grenades from the ASV, was to pull the ring of the magic marker-sized igniter at the end of the foot-long fuse. It lit with a pop, acrid smoke pouring from the fuse inside the igniter. Boone jumped into the driver's seat of the black pickup truck, Carson rode shotgun, Doug climbed in the back, and they were off.

To their south, the firefight continued unabated between the Nigerian troops and the Kazaks in their ASVs. Doug rode in the back with their rucksacks and the M-79 grenade launcher taken from the stolen ASV. Junior man and the youngest of the three, he remained out in the cold as they drove north. The ancient Vietnam-era weapon was dead-bang simple to operate, like a break-open shotgun with a two-inch bore. As instructed, he was launching random high-elevation shots from the old "blooper." The grenades exploded a half mile behind them, providing another diversion to cover their escape.

Boone was driving smoothly along a dirt farm road; Carson sat in the passenger seat holding the dead traitor's portable GPS unit. Boone wore night vision, but Carson did not. Carson looked over at him in wonder. Night goggles covering the Viking's face above his wild beard gave him fearsome, unworldly look, an unlikely combination of futuristic space alien and primitive barbarian.

"Boone, did you plan that whole scene back there, or did you just pull it out of your ass?"

"That? Oh, that all just came together. I didn't think about it at all. That was pure improvisation. I was just running on automatic, from the moment we saw that Cossack troop truck until right now."

"Well, that was pretty damn clever, dragging those Kazak armored cars through the Nigerian base. The old Viking would have been damned proud of you. That was a masterpiece. Firing off the smokes at the end, that was just a beautiful touch. Night and fog. I couldn't have done better. Of course, it helps that you know this country like you do. But how did you know the ASV would make it that far? That sucker's engine was dying fast."

"I didn't; I just hoped it would. We got lucky. Damn lucky. Like finding this truck. Yeah, Phil, we've got the luck tonight, we're on a hot streak. That was pretty damn cool back there. Hell, that was *way* cool. That was right up there. That makes my all-time-best list, for sure." Both former Special Forces operators were stoked, jazzed, running on adrenaline as powerful as an espresso-and-methamphetamine speedball cocktail. They were not out of danger yet, but they had survived the wild melee firefight in the crippled ASV.

This was the old combat high that Phil Carson had learned to both love and hate, decades earlier in the Asian jungles and highlands. He enjoyed its rush even as he feared the crash back down to depression that usually followed it hours, days or even years later.

This part of him, this war lust, this combat madness, was what, in the end, separated him from normal men. Denying and suppressing this defect in his personality had kept him on a solitary track since Vietnam. And now, here he was, once again floating along as high as a kite on blood and cordite and ringing ears.

Visions from the last ten minutes replayed in his mind, in flaring green and flashing white. While Boone was blasting away with the turret guns, he had deliberately used the fifteen-ton ASV as a killing weapon. Using the cover of darkness and confusion, he had aimed for the most tightly clustered groups of soldiers, driven over and smashed their bodies to pulp, *and he had enjoyed it.* Disoriented and night-blinded by the exploding grenades, and by the .50 caliber's deafening concussion and muzzle flashes, most of his victims had never even seen the machine rushing at them before they were run down. Their bug-eyed and utterly shocked faces loomed in front of his narrow window for just an instant, and then disappeared beneath the ASV's wheels. Later, when Boone told him to "make sure" of the wounded Nigerian soldiers, he had not hesitated even for a moment. This was why Boone had asked him, and not Doug, to deal with them. Boone understood him all too well.

Phil Carson understood from decades of painful self-analysis that his psychology was deeply flawed. In fact, it was completely defective. It had been this way since he had returned from Vietnam, but he could not blame his country or the Army. It was *him*, it was always in him. Vietnam had just allowed the beast that lived inside to acquire a taste for blood. In the end, this was why he had never inflicted himself upon a woman for any serious long-lasting relationship, much less considered the disastrous possibility of infecting children with his latent belligerence.

After the war, this self-imposed drift toward solitude had led him to the refuge of the sea. An acquaintance from the Army had offered him a crew position on a profit-seeking voyage to South America and back, and he had become hooked on ocean sailing. The ocean had been his eternally patient, always listening therapist, until he thought that he had left the ghosts of Vietnam behind in his wake. Then for many years after, he had kept his penchant for violence carefully sealed in a dark bottle on a shelf in his mind, but since Mississippi it was uncorked and coursing through his veins once again. Where this new killing streak was going to end he didn't know, but he felt that it must end badly, and soon.

Then there was one much louder explosion behind them, in the midst of the continuing reports and echoes of rifles, machine guns and grenades. Boone grinned widely between his thick beard and his NVGs and said, "That was my C-4, back in the ASV."

"Why didn't you leave it booby-trapped?" Carson asked. "You might have nailed some more of the bastards."

"Couldn't risk it—they wouldn't fall for that trick twice in a row, and I wanted to destroy the evidence."

"How much demo have you got left?" asked Carson.

"That was it. The rest is still back in the cave, rigged to blow." Boone rapped on the glass window behind them, opened his power side window and shouted, "Hey, Doug, you can quit with the grenades now." The sounds of the continuing battle between the Kazak armored vehicles and the Nigerian soldiers at their outpost diminished in volume, but not in intensity, as they drove away from the insane mayhem that they had triggered.

There was just enough moonlight for Zack and Jenny to make their way across the fields without tripping or stepping into holes. Snow and ice formed an uneven skin over frozen dirt clumps and hay stubble. They were exposed far out in the open, in an area of fields and pastures, with little cover to exploit. It was faster going than when they were in the cover of woods, but more frightening. The glow of fires to the west and north gave the clouds an orange hue.

"How much further?" asked Jenny, out of breath.

"We can't go back now," Zack said. "It'd take us an hour to get back to the woods, and then what? I don't think there's any way to get south where we won't have some fields to cross."

"Are you *sure* this is the way that Boone meant for us to go? Let's check the map again."

"Not out here. We can't stop out here, we have to keep moving." Zack checked his compass, picked a point in the distance, and kept walking. He had strapped his bow to the side of his pack to keep his hands free. Out here, hundreds of yards from any cover, the bow was of little use.

"Look!" said Jenny. "That fire's a lot closer."

Zack stopped and turned. Flames were clearly visible above the low hill that formed their western horizon. "We need to find someplace to hide, fast."

"Is there something in those trees?" Jenny asked. It was just light enough to walk without tripping, but not light enough to distinguish shapes in the distance.

"It looks like it might be a house, but even just some trees is better than being caught out here. Let's go—we'll take a break there and check the map."

"Look, another fire! How far is it to the trees?" In the darkness, distances were impossible to estimate.

"Not too far. Can you run?"

"No, this is the fastest I can go." Jenny was out of breath and nearing exhaustion. The ground was uneven and broken from old plowing. Some clods were frozen solid, but slippery mud lurked beneath remnants of snow in between them. A sprain was a very real risk; both of them had already come close to badly twisting their ankles several times already. They heard nearby gunshots and froze. They had been hearing sporadic firing all night, but it had been distant, just low pops. This shooting was obviously much closer, less than a mile away.

Zack said, "It's not aimed at us. It's still too far away to hit us, and you'd hear bullets snapping if they were shooting this way. But we *really* have to move now."

"I'm doing my best!"

Before they reached the trees, they encountered another timber fence and climbed it with practiced ease. There was indeed a one-story home partially concealed within a few lightly wooded park-like acres.

Zack pointed and said, "That other fence over there must run along a road, or maybe a private driveway. If the Cossacks come, they'll come from that way. Let's get behind the house, and find someplace to hide."

"Maybe the house is open. Maybe we can just sneak in and get out of the cold." Jenny was almost out of breath, from trying to keep up with Zack.

"Jenny…they're burning houses."

"Oh, right."

A dirt driveway ran along the side of the home, and they followed it to the rear. A small barn or stable stood a few hundred feet behind the dwelling.

The firing was getting close, very close. They stopped inside the first trees and looked back. They heard the ripping of full automatic rifle firing, and a few louder blasts spaced apart. "Somebody's shooting back, I think," said Zack. "The big booms sound like a shotgun. The quick ones are the Cossacks firing their AKs."

"Do you hear that?" asked Jenny.

"What, the shooting?"

"No, no, not that—horses! Horses, can't you hear them?"

"Come on Jenny, run for the barn!"

The trees were spaced too far apart to provide concealment, and there wasn't enough low ground cover. Until fairly recently, somebody had been maintaining the landscaping, and since it had gotten cold nothing much had grown back. A hundred yards behind the house was a low barn, about fifty feet wide, with a sloping metal roof. Next to and extending from the small barn was a matching tin roof for farm equipment. Wooden poles supported this open shed. Stacked against the barn beneath this shed was a wall of hay bales, then a flatbed stake-side truck, a combine harvester and a tractor. Past this covered shelter was a collection of farm clutter: an old rusted tractor, giant plastic barrels, a hay trailer, and an ancient towed harvester with upward-pointing rows of wicked steel tines. Zack headed into the middle of this private junkyard, crouching low, Jenny right behind him. He knelt behind an old white enamel meat freezer, his senses straining. He heard the hoofbeats getting closer, heard shouted voices and neighing horses. He heard a crash of glass, and in a minute the home was lit from within by fire.

Searching for better cover, his eyes fell upon a low flat shape. It took a moment to realize that it was a camper shell from a pickup truck, lying on the ground. He scurried to the back of it, grabbed the handle and turned it, then pulled up the hinged rear window. "In here, Jenny," he whispered, but she was already on her knees and elbows and crawling inside the yard-high shelter. Her pack hit the top, and Zack took hold of it, allowing her to slide her shoulders out and get all the way underneath. Zack slipped off his own pack, laid it on the ground and unfastened his bow. It had been too much hassle trying to navigate with the compass and cross fences and downed timber while holding the compound bow at the ready, so he had put it on the side of his pack with a bungee cord. He removed the bow and shoved his pack inside the camper shell. Then he began to push the door back down from the outside.

"What about you?" asked Jenny, her face at the opening.

"I'm staying outside, just in case." He lowered the door and turned the silver handle. Zack knelt between the old freezer and the camper shell, crouching low. The white meat locker was about a foot higher than the camper shell. He had briefly considered hiding inside the shell with Jenny, but decided not to. He didn't want to be trapped like a rat inside it. What if the Cossacks fired randomly into likely hiding places? What if they could see inside the plastic side windows with flashlights? From outside, the windows appeared black, no doubt they were tinted a dark shade, but flashlights would probably probably penetrate them. He could do nothing to protect the three of them if he was also trapped inside. If it came down to it, he might be able to draw the Cossacks away from Jenny and the baby by creating a diversion.

The house burst into flames, fire pouring out of one window after another. Zack prayed that the home had already been abandoned by its inhabitants. Nobody came running out the back door, and the Cossacks were not firing their rifles. Zack's bow had its own rack of four broadhead hunting arrows attached. He removed and nocked one, making it ready if it was needed. Realistically, he knew arrows wouldn't be much use against Cossack riders armed with Kalashnikov assault rifles…except for drawing their attention, in order to pull them away from Jenny and Hope.

A single horse and rider appeared behind the house. The Cossack reined his mount in a tight circle, observing that the home was fully engulfed on all sides. Then he cantered toward the barn, toward their hiding place. The twin doors of the barn stood open, any livestock or horses already taken away or released. The rider was mounted on a dark horse; Zack could see him outlined against the burning house. He stopped his mount near the barn, and then spurred him inside. He's probably seeing if anything is worth stealing, thought Zack, staying low, concealed in his nest of farm junk and rubbish. The horse and rider reappeared from the barn. The soldier stopped the horse with a sharp pull on the reins. He looked back toward the burning home, removed something from a pocket and upended it to his lips. He was drinking something. Probably alcohol, thought Zack. Maybe he doesn't want his friends to see him drinking, so that's why he rode behind the house. The horseman was close enough that Zack could see the Kalashnikov rifle slung across his back. Some kind of bag or satchel was hanging across his front, like a mail carrier's sack. He wheeled his horse, looking in all directions.

The Cossack removed another bottle from this sack, and a little spark and flare erupted from his other hand. Zack realized this was a cigarette lighter, but instead of lighting a cigarette, the soldier lit the end of the bottle he was holding in his right hand. Zack knew what this was: a Molotov cocktail, a gasoline bomb. This explained how they were burning the houses. At least the American Army wasn't giving them incendiary grenades to do this job, Zack thought. They didn't need to. Old-fashioned gasoline bombs worked just as well on houses.

A small wick at the end of the clear bottle ignited in flame. The rider held the bottle at arm's length, and then lobbed it overhand through the two open barn doors. Then he prepared a second bottle, and turned his horse back toward the covered shed, with its tractor and truck, and the junkyard next to it. Searching for a readily flammable target, the Kazak cocked his arm to throw. Then the horse wheeled, and from fifty feet away, the Cossack's face turned to Zack. From his perch atop the horse he locked his eyes upon the shivering teenage boy hiding between the freezer and the camper roof. His greater height up on the horse allowed him to see down between them, something Zack had not reckoned on when he selected his hiding place.

The bottle's fuse was still burning as the rider turned the horse and took new aim. Zack could not know where he was going to launch the flaming gasoline bomb, or even for sure that the Cossack had seen him. But in that moment of uncertainty, Zack decided to take his destiny in his hands, instead of waiting to find out where the firebomb would land. Without planning or pondering the consequences, he stood straight up from his hiding place in a bow-shooting stance, extended his left arm straight out while pulling the string back to full draw, and let the arrow fly.

Zack saw a brief look of alarm on the Cossack's face when the arrow whizzed past his jaw. In a second Zack had prepared another arrow, but before he could fire a second time, he saw the Cossack's free hand move to his neck. He had not missed after all! The razor-sharp broadhead must have grazed him, or even passed through his neck or face. Perhaps it was even a fatal wound! He pulled his second arrow back and loosed it all in one smooth motion, this time nailing the rider, he was sure of it. Both of the Cossack's hands reflexively went to the arrow shaft protruding from his left shoulder. The lit Molotov cocktail fell into his open sack, which instantly erupted upward in a volcanic inferno. The horse wheeled and reared, neighing loudly in terror as its rider was engulfed in flames from the waist up. The Cossack madly swiped at the flames, while also attempting to remove the strap of the burning sack of gasoline bottles from around his neck. The horse twisted, spun a tight circle like a dervish, reared up and then took off in a panicked gallop. The Cossack was still in his saddle as the horse went racing toward the side of the burning house, jumped a fence and continued across the open field, trailing flames. The rider had become a human torch.

Zack heard men shouting and the sounds of many other horses. As he watched, the burning Cossack rider continued galloping away, pursued by his compatriots on their own mounts. Zack stared in amazement until well after the horses disappeared and he was satisfied there were no more Cossacks lurking around the farm. Then he opened the back of the camper shell and crawled inside. Jenny was sitting Indian-style, the baby cradled on her lap, feeding her the bottle of milk that had been prepared back in the cave.

"She was awake, and I wanted to keep her from crying." The plastic bottle had been kept against Jenny's skin during their hike to keep it warm. Flickering orange light from the barn and the more distant house illuminated the interior of the camper shell through its plastic side windows. The barn had caught fire, but did not yet appear to be fully engulfed. It didn't matter, they could do nothing to fight the fire anyway, and they were a safe distance from it. "I watched you through the window," Jenny said. "I couldn't tell if you hit him until I saw him catch on fire. And you know something strange? Now we've both done it. What are the odds of that?"

"Done what?"

"Burned one. Set them on fire. Only mine was an American traitor, and yours was a Cossack."

"That's a bad way to die," Zack observed, sitting up and facing her. "Maybe the worst." The roof of the camper shell was high enough for him to sit up only if he tilted his head over. He opened his backpack on his lap.

"After what I saw in the ravine last night, I wish we could burn every one of them."

"Do you think they'll come back?"

Jenny considered. "If they don't find an arrow sticking out of him, they'll probably think he just screwed up and lit himself on fire. They burned the house and the barn, so there's no reason for them to come back here. Anyway, I'm too tired to walk any further tonight, and this is a good place to feed the baby."

"Let's eat some of the rice from the cave."

"Okay, as soon as Hope is done with her milk. You know, we got lucky here."

"Yeah, damn lucky. It might have been *us* on fire."

"Not just that, this camper. Check it out; this was already somebody's hiding place." Instead of a dirt floor beneath the fiberglass shell, there was a dry blanket on top of a slab of foam, and under that was a sheet of plywood.

"Either that, or it was a playhouse for some kids," said Zack. There were toys and children's books scattered on the sleeping pallet. He took a plastic jar from his pack and began eating his sticky rice and vegetables with a spoon. "I wonder where the kids who played in here are now? I wonder if they made it out." Unspoken was the other alternative. Maybe this family had been in Mannville on Saturday and had been shot. Or perhaps they had fled the county a year ago, after the earthquakes. Or maybe they had been killed by marauding bandits, or died from hunger and cold and disease, or from a dozen other causes. There was just no way to know. Now that their home was on fire, perhaps nobody would ever know what had happened to them. Their story might be lost, like the stories of tens of thousands of other Tennesseans who had died since the past year's chain of calamities had fallen upon them. Cossack nightriders were just the latest disaster to sweep through Radford County.

22

Phil Carson walked with his head down, his hands stuffed in the pockets of a faded green Army field jacket. It was one of the items he had retrieved from Boone's grab bag in the cave. It was 1970s vintage, a pre-camouflage-era relic of the past, but still serviceable. Like himself, he hoped. Before he left the black pickup, he changed from his modern ACU camouflage uniform into civilian clothes, the green coat notwithstanding. The old Army surplus field jackets had been standard cold-weather wear among the working poor for decades, so today it was another form of camouflage.

Boone Vikersun and Doug Dolan were two miles back, waiting behind a semi-demolished restaurant on a bypassed county road. The place was so unwanted that even its demolition had run out of steam before reaching completion. Boone had driven the pickup truck right into the back of the forgotten restaurant, pushing through a halfheartedly boarded-up section of ruined wall. They could use the truck again if they had to, or leave it where it was without much fear of its premature discovery.

Technically, it was a curfew violation for Carson to be out walking at night without a special travel permit. Boone had assured him that a solitary old man would not be hassled just before dawn on the outskirts of the small crossroads town of Carrolton. If he were seen, authorities would assume that the old man was just getting a head start in walking to his assigned place of employment, and they were unlikely to stop him to check his papers. His 64-year-old face had become another form of camouflage. Carson didn't disagree with Boone's logic in choosing him for this mission, but he also couldn't help but consider that of the three, maybe he was the most expendable. He didn't much disagree with that unspoken assessment either, and he accepted the assignment with calm resignation.

It was the coldest part of the night, and Carson was glad to be gaining the warmth generated from walking. Boone and Dolan would be shivering back in their hiding place, forced to remain motionless, waiting for him to return with a new escape vehicle. The moon had set sometime after midnight, and now it was almost perfectly dark. There were no streetlights of course, and almost no light coming from houses or businesses, so he had to literally feel his way along the paved edge of the road until he reached Carrolton. Wearing night vision goggles, obviously, would have blown his cover as a harmless old civilian on his way to work. A harmless old civilian…with a .45 caliber Glock pistol hidden inside his coat, its suppressor already attached. The left inside pocket of the field jacket was slit at the bottom to accommodate the suppressor's length, which reached to Carson's left hip.

The black Dodge Ram pickup they had taken from the Nigerians was marked in white letters with N.P.F. on both sides and the tailgate, and after last night's fracas, it could not be driven over the well-guarded Tennessee River bridge. Today, any Nigerian vehicle spotted outside their area of operations was going to cause major alarms to go off. Not to mention the utter futility of Boone Vikersun and company trying to pass themselves off as members of the Nigerian Peacekeeping Force! Not even Mexicans from the North American Legion were going to buy that one.

The final mile of the approach to Carrolton could not be made in cover; Carson just had to brazen it out. Boone had estimated that it would take twenty minutes to walk to the service station, where he would pick up their next vehicle. Carson would give the agreed-upon secret hand signal to the owner of the station as he opened up for the day. The owner would then supply a new vehicle with the necessary decals and permits, as simple as that. A few minutes later, he would pick up his two confederates, and they'd cross the bridge into Middle Tennessee. Then they would drive up toward Clarksville and Fort Campbell, the home of the 5th Special Forces Group.

After the earthquakes, the new Route 214 bridge over the Tennessee River had been deemed repairable, while the older Interstate 40 bridge, fifteen miles north, was still down. Boone said that the more modern concrete towers of the 214 bridge had been left standing, where the entire I-40 bridge had simply disappeared into the deep river, due to some fluke of underwater geology. This had given the sleepy town of Carrolton sudden strategic importance, and its gas station was needed by the government and the foreign so-called peacekeeping troops. But according to Boone, this gas station owner was also secretly working for the resistance forces. He had even provided the four-wheel-drive Subaru wagon that they had driven to the hiding place near the cave.

Carson didn't need a map or GPS to find Carrolton; the line of demarcation was clearly visible by its working electric lights. Carrolton was back on the power grid, part of an electrified enclave on the west side of the Tennessee River. He turned the corner from his residential approach street onto State Road 214 for the final two blocks to the gas station. It was still dark; there was almost no traffic on the road, just a few delivery vans and an occasional eighteen-wheeler rumbling past. People who had a legitimate reason to be out before dawn, before the curfew was lifted for ordinary folks. He passed an out-of-business donut shop, and a pawnshop that was full of merchandise, but closed for the night. Stout burglar bars covered its windows. Across from the gas station was a vacant business that Carson couldn't identify. He found a dark alcove on the side of the pawnshop, and began to wait.

Stanley Fromish opened his garage at 6:00 a.m. on Mondays. In January, this meant it was still dark outside. He pulled the chain and rolled up the steel doors over the service bay, and was turning to go to his office when he was jerked back around by his shoulder. He hadn't heard a car or a truck pull in; they rang a bell when they crossed his rubber strips. Neither had anybody left a vehicle out front for repairs overnight, and so he was taken completely by surprise. There was no time even to reach for the .38 revolver he kept in the pocket of his insulated jacket, before he made initial eye contact with his grabber. He wondered if this fellow was just an aggressive panhandler, or a robber, but then the stranger made the sign, the insurgents' blackmail sign, holding up two crossed fingers and then tapping them on his heart.

The man spoke before Fromish could even form a thought. "Don't worry, Stanley, this is just business, not a robbery." He'd never seen this man before. He appeared to be in his sixties, but with a hard look to his lean face. The man was wearing a plain old Army coat, with a black watch cap pulled down to his eyebrows.

The sign the man had given was unmistakable. But the reality on the ground in West Tennessee had been changing for the better, and Stanley had lost some of his fear of the insurgents. He had even heard a rumor from one of his suppliers about a battle that had happened on Saturday down in Radford County. The Kazak peacekeepers down there were kicking ass and finally driving the troublesome rebels clear out of the state. It couldn't happen soon enough for Stanley Fromish. Once this corner of Tennessee was pacified, the infrastructure rebuilding could get under way in earnest. This would mean greatly increased business for his service station, and maybe even expansion. He could finally get on with his long-term plan to purchase and reopen the old auto parts store across the street.

But then this old man shows up, giving the secret rebel hand sign, like nothing had changed! This man could even be a survivor of the battles down in Radford County, on the run and looking for help. But if the rebels were beaten, there was no longer a realistic threat of reprisal if Stanley failed to cooperate with them. So there was no reason to risk helping this one old man.

Or this could even be a trap, a setup by the new government to test his loyalty. They might have captured and interrogated some insurgents, learned about his clandestine arrangement with them, and even how they gave the secret contact signal. This could all be a trap, to expose him as a rebel sympathizer and supporter!

The stranger spoke again. "Come on, we're wasting time. Let's go to your office. We need to talk, right now."

"I can't," Stanley bluffed. "I'm alone until six-thirty. I need to get the pumps turned on, and open everything up."

"Stanley, don't mess with me! I need a car that I can drive over the bridge, and I need it right now. A car with a valid stamp for crossing over to Middle Tennessee. I know you can do this, so you're going to give me a car right now, and then I'll be on my way. We'll contact you about where you can pick it up on the other side. This is an easy job, Stanley, very easy."

Stanley Fromish was overcome by a wave of fear, as memories of his midnight visitors flooded his mind, masked men with guns and bright lights. They had killed his two beloved German shepherds, and threatened his daughters. They were not to be trifled with. The only cars that he had that could be driven across the bridge were his own Nissan SUV and his wife's Toyota. If this man was arrested in either one, they would be traced right back to the garage, and hard questions would be asked. His mechanic was working on his own Nissan Conquistador, but it wasn't ready yet, it still needed the front brakes and wheels put back on. The Conquistador was in fact still up on the lift. This gave Stanley an idea. "Look, I can give you that black Pathfinder, but it needs another hour to be ready. After it's ready, I can park it around the side with the keys in it. Once you're gone, I'll have to report it stolen. But I can wait until this afternoon before I report it. That'll give you enough time."

Carson shook his head "no" without pausing to consider this option. "I can't wait an hour. What about your other car, Stanley? The blue Toyota Camry parked in your driveway? Just hand me the keys to the car and to your front gate."

"But that's my wife's car."

"Your wife is dead, Stanley; she doesn't need it anymore. Don't try to bullshit me again. We know everything about you."

The stranger pushed Stanley backward into his garage and flipped off the lights at the switch by the side of the service bay. For an older guy, he was almost brutal in his speech and mannerisms. Just when they were inside, in the darkness, a vehicle pulled into the station and stopped by the diesel pumps. It was a desert-tan humvee, never repainted since it had come back from the Middle East. The three stars of the North American Legion were stenciled on its front door in black paint. The Mexicans. Stanley called this first humvee of the day "the dawn patrol." They were often his earliest customers in the morning, a couple of soldiers with an officer or an NCO, making the rounds of outposts and checkpoints around the county. The soldiers and the officer were different every day, with their own rotating duty schedule. Fromish knew most of them by sight, but not by name.

"Look, I'll help you, but I have to take care of those guys first. They're regulars, and if I make them wait, they'll just come in here looking for me, and then they'll see you. I haven't turned on the pumps yet, and I have to do it myself. Then I'll be right back, and these guys will finish up and leave. Then we'll get you a car, okay?" Stanley jingled a large key ring. "It'll only take me a few minutes to open the pumps and get rid of these guys."

The old man said, "I have a better idea—I'll pump their gas."

Fromish knew the stranger wasn't buying his stalling tactics, or just plain didn't trust him. "You can't pump their gas; these guys are regulars. They gas up every morning. They know everybody who works here, and they won't believe it if they see you." And they were only the first customer of the morning, Stanley knew. Soon more military vehicles from the NAL company would be arriving to fuel up, after they had finished their breakfasts in the old diner that was now their mess hall. Fromish had a sudden idea, and he gave the secret hand sign back to the stranger, tapping his crossed fingers on his chest. "Don't worry, *I'm one of you.* I'm on your side. I just have to be careful, that's all."

"Okay," the stranger said with reluctance. "Just get rid of them fast."

Stanley Fromish walked out to the service island. One of the Mexicans was already standing outside the humvee, ready to fuel up the vehicle. The pumps were locked, and the handles were secured with heavy chains and padlocks. Fromish said, "*Buenos dias, amigo.* Do you speak English?"

"Jus' leetle." The soldier held his thumb and finger an inch apart. "*El teniente, el* lieutenant, he speak good *Ingles.*"

"Which one is the lieutenant?"

"Heem." The NAL soldier pointed to a youngish soldier in the back, behind the front passenger seat. The driver, obviously the junior man of the three, was pumping the fuel in the cold predawn air.

Stanley worked himself between the pump and the military vehicle, unlocking the pump out of sight of the stranger lurking in his garage. While the diesel flowed, he rapped on the thick rear window with his knuckle. The door opened; these old humvees didn't have opening windows. The laminated glass was inches thick; the door was like a vault.

"I don't pay you, you know that," said the young officer. A single vertical black bar on the front of his camouflage coat and on his blue beret identified him as a lieutenant. On his shoulder patch were three stars arranged in a triangle, the symbol of the North American Legion. He was smoking a cigarette and holding a steaming cup of coffee. The cup was the plastic lid from a thermos bottle that was on the seat beside him.

Stanley Fromish recognized the young officer, a platoon commander from the NAL barracks in the old Ford dealership. Their officers lived next door in the motel. He was kind of handsome, in a Latin Romeo sort of way, with a thin mustache. More Spanish-looking than Mexican, with very good English. "I'm not asking you to pay, Lieutenant. Listen, I've got a serious problem: there's a guy in my garage trying to rob me. He's waiting for you to leave. Can you drive away like normal, then park out of sight and come back and grab him?"

"What?" said the lieutenant. "All that just for one guy? He's in there now?"

"Yeah, one guy. I've never seen him before."

"What's he look like, this one guy? Fucking Rambo? The Terminator?" The NAL lieutenant spoke clear unaccented American English. He was smooth.

"He's old, kind of skinny. Over sixty, I'd guess."

The young officer translated for the other soldier, a sergeant sitting in the front seat, who laughed and responded as if he found the situation highly amusing. The soldier in front had tattoos on his neck and hands, as many of the Mexican troops did.

"We don't need to park out of sight and sneak up on one old guy. Who do you think we are? Fucking cowards like you?"

Fromish ignored the insult. "Listen, Lieutenant, this guy, there's something about him. I just don't think you should..." Fromish stopped himself from mentioning the secret contact signal, or his previous dealings with the insurgents. He would only incriminate himself, even if he tried to explain that his cooperation had been gained by means of terror and blackmail.

The smiling lieutenant exhaled a stream of cigarette smoke and asked, "Does this scary old man have a gun, or at least a big scary knife?"

"Not that I saw, but—"

"No wonder you need Mexican soldiers to fight for your country!" The junior officer spoke rapidly in Spanish to the sergeant in the front seat, and to the soldier who was finishing pumping the diesel. The sergeant grabbed an M-16 rifle and stepped out of the humvee, joined by the lieutenant. Together with the driver who had been pumping the fuel and followed by Stanley Fromish, they walked toward the open service bay.

Phil Carson hid behind the inside wall of the open garage door. The machinery that raised and lowered the bay doors allowed him to remain concealed to the side. The gas station owner, Stanley Fromish, was supposed to have immediately fulfilled his demand for a car. Boone, hiding with Doug two miles away, had told him that they "owned" Fromish, who was an opportunist and a collaborator but also a coward. A single light on the front of the garage illuminated the humvee parked at the pump island, but left the inside of the garage in shadow. On the humvee's front door were three black stars. Fromish was spending too much time at the pumps.

Carson grabbed the Glock from inside his field jacket, and slid back along the wall. The garage was so cluttered with tools, tables, parts and half-finished engine projects that it was easy to disappear. He crouched down low and looked out between the cinderblock wall and the steel guide track that sent the bay doors up and overhead. He took a quick peek across toward the fuel pumps, and saw the humvee's doors opening and soldiers getting out. There were three of them, trailed by Fromish. One soldier had a rifle, one was holding a pistol, and one was empty-handed but had a pistol in a tactical leg holster. The unarmed soldier was the tallest of the four men. All three soldiers had blue berets on their heads, and were wearing ACU camouflage uniforms and parkas. The one with a rifle was the nearest to Carson's hiding place, the one in the middle held a pistol in one hand and a flashlight in the other. They were no more than forty feet away and walking directly for the open garage door.

The realization of what would happen next was immediate. Carson avoided looking at their faces; the faces were what stuck with you. The faces were what you couldn't get rid of afterward. Like Doctor Foley. That nighttime pistol shot had worked like a flash bulb on his brain, freezing Foley's round face in the moment before his death. Like the faces of the foreign soldiers in front of the ASV, before they went under its wheels. Instead, he focused on their hands. Their hands held their weapons. Their hands were what killed you.

So much for simply giving Fromish a secret hand signal and getting a car in return! This wasn't going remotely according to the plan, but since when did anything, ever, go according to plan? There was now no cute way to get the drop on them, no bloodless Roy Rogers solution. This was killing time, Carson knew it immediately. He needed steel in his guts now, but felt like they were full of broken glass and acid. A company of North American Legion troops was stationed only three blocks away. If these soldiers got off even one shot, the loud report would bring a hundred Legion troops at a dead run. Boone's mission would end in failure, and the three of them would probably be executed as terrorists…if they were not killed outright.

Carson pressed himself against the grime-encrusted cement wall, hidden behind a rack of greasy aprons, parkas and mechanic's coveralls. He held the Glock in both hands, at the low ready position. The three soldiers broke the plane of the open bay door at almost the same time. The nearest held his rifle horizontally by his hip and turned toward Carson's hiding place, smiling as if he expected to roust a vagrant. The rifleman was backlit by the soldier holding the flashlight, who was standing behind him. Carson thrust out his Glock pistol and shot the rifleman once in the face at almost contact distance. A look of surprise was only half formed before the man was dead and falling backward, blood and brain matter blasted across the service bay. Carson swung the pistol a few degrees, toward the next soldier fifteen feet away, the one holding the pistol and the flashlight. He hardly reacted before Carson shot him twice in the torso, center mass, aiming above his flashlight. The .45 caliber Glock was no louder than a heavy book dropping on the floor, adding to the unreality of the scene. Its suppressor extended its muzzle like a long pointed finger, making it even easier to aim at close range.

The third soldier, the tallest one, had no time to absorb the nearly simultaneous deaths of his two comrades. His pistol was still holstered, and his body was not even turned in a direction where he could draw and fire in the instant it would take the gunman to kill him. He froze in place, and then his hands went up in the air, fingers spread. In his peripheral vision, Carson saw the station owner, who had lagged behind the soldiers, suddenly break out of his shocked stupor and turn to run. Carson made two more snap shots at the center of the man's back, and he dropped onto his face just outside the garage. He swung the pistol back to the third soldier, who was still alive and standing, his arms up. Carson forced himself to scan the entire scene, fighting the natural inclination toward tunnel vision under extreme stress.

He had created three new bodies, one with a gory partial head. Lying motionless on the ground was the instantaneous wreckage of three lives. He avoided looking at the bloody horror show at his feet. Three men had just awakened and begun a fresh new day, when their lives were snuffed out. Images and memories spanning four decades ran in a kaleidoscope through Carson's mind, faces in the moment before and after death. Bile gagged in his throat. He fought to bring himself back into the present, to this garage, these bodies, and this last living soldier. From a thousand shards, disparate parts formed a whole, and a new plan clicked together like the tumblers of a safe falling into place.

"You speak English? *Habla Ingles?*" he demanded of the soldier, still standing above the bodies of his comrades. The man didn't respond, except by shaking more violently. "Snap out of it if you want to live, amigo." That's what I need to do too, Carson thought. Snap out of it. Both of us. But I'm holding the gun…so I get to give the orders…for now. For just as long as I can pull off my act. "Can you speak English? *Hablas tu Ingles?*"

After a moment, the terrified soldier replied with a quiet "Yes sir, I speak English." Carson stepped out from his hiding place, to see if anyone else was outside the garage, and then he took his first detailed look at his prisoner. He had a long, pale face, and a pencil-thin mustache. He noted the single vertical black bar insignia stuck to the front middle of the soldier's camouflage rain parka, and on his beret. "Oh, an officer—the smart one. No wonder you're still alive. Okay, Lieutenant, reach around with your left hand and pull out your pistol with just your thumb and one finger.

It's awkward, but you can do it. Good, now lay it on the ground, nice and easy."

He advanced toward the officer like a cat, the Glock extended. The officer was a little taller than Carson, around six feet. "We've got some work to do now, and it has to be fast. Turn around. See that civilian? The station manager? Grab him by his feet, drag him over to that oil-changing pit and shove him in it." A large rectangular hole in the cement floor allowed grease monkeys to work beneath a car. "Are you fucking deaf? Drag him over there, or I'll shoot your ass where you stand and drag you there myself. Lieutenant, if you want to live, you have to start listening to me, understand? We don't have time for pity parties right now."

With three men shot dead around him in the last minute, the NAL officer obviously believed Carson. He broke from his trance and scurried the dozen feet to Stanley Fromish, seized him by his ankles and dragged him face down across the concrete, until he was alongside the grease pit. He rolled the body into the open hole, where it landed with a thud. While Fromish was being dealt with, Carson scooped up the pistols, the flashlight and the M-16A2 rifle. The scuffed and dinged rifle had obviously seen decades of hard service; the stenciled armory numbers on the stock were barely legible. He slung the rifle over his shoulder by its sling; the pistols and light went into the outside cargo pockets of his field jacket. One of the blue NAL berets on the ground was still free of blood; he grabbed it and jammed it in a pocket.

"Next, your two *compadres*. They can get a decent burial later. Oh, pull off their insignias and badges first." The cloth rank and unit badges were attached with velcro like those on U.S. Army uniforms.

Even in the dim light, the head wound of the first soldier he had shot was hard to look at, and impossible to ignore. His face was mostly gone above the nose, and it looked as if he had bled gallons onto the floor, along with bone and brain matter. The young NAL officer threw up, retching violently, dropping to his hands and knees. A shout from Carson got him moving again. The corpses left shiny black trails on the concrete floor as they were dragged over to the pit. In the dark interior of the garage, the blood might be mistaken for an oil spill, at least until it was fully light outside. Stanley Fromish, who had been shot just outside the garage, had been wearing a thick coat, and most of his blood was contained. His bullet wounds were in his back, now on top. After pushing the first soldier into the pit, the NAL lieutenant stammered, "I'm not helping you anymore. You're just going to kill me last."

Carson was ready for this reaction. Remembering Sergeant Amory's incapacitating fear immediately after the death of the Mississippi Guard officers, he adopted the most avuncular tone he could muster, almost smiling. "No I'm not. I need you alive, LT." He pronounced this "el tee,"

the enlisted man's colloquial term for the military abbreviation of lieutenant. This was part of Carson's deliberate campaign to reassure the terrified junior officer. "Lieutenant, you're going to be my driver today. In a
few minutes, we're going to be crossing the bridge in your humvee, and I
need you alive and well for that. So here's the deal: you drive me and two
of my friends across the river, and you'll live. If you don't betray us, I
promise I'll let you go on the other side. I give you my word of honor as a
soldier. But if you try to pull some tricky shit like this gas station guy did,
then I'll kill you just like I killed him. We get across the bridge, you live.
If we don't, you won't either. It's that simple. You got it?"

"I got it."

They were now standing only yards apart, staring at one another.
Both men were roughly the same height and build, but the older man held a
pistol and the younger man did not. Carson noted the officer's surname,
on the cloth tape over the breast pocket of his parka. "All right, Lieutenant
Malverde, let's walk back out to your humvee and get going. I'll be right
behind you with my pistol aimed at your back. Remember: the penalty's
the same for killing three or four. One more won't matter one bit." With
his left hand, Carson pulled hard on the chain by the side of the bay door,
and it began to roll down behind him with a rumbling clatter as they
stepped outside.

Boone almost opened fire on the NAL humvee. Fortunately, the vehicle
stopped fifty yards from their hiding place behind the derelict restaurant,
and blinked its headlights in the agreed-upon manner. Boone turned on his
own flashlight to answer the signal, and the hummer rolled up to them. He
shined the light through the windshield. Carson was sitting behind the
driver, who was a Legion soldier in an ACU uniform, wearing a blue beret.
As soon as the vehicle stopped, Carson opened the back door to talk, since
the inches-thick windows on this up-armored humvee didn't roll down. He
kept his pistol aimed at the driver. Boone and Doug had also changed into
their daytime street clothes since he had left for the garage.

Boone asked, "What happened? How the hell did you wind up with a
hummer?"

"Your boy Stanley ratted me out. This humvee pulled into the station
to gas up, and Fromish ratted me out. I wasted two NAL soldiers in the
garage. I had no choice—it was either me or them. Then Lieutenant Malverde here got religion. He agreed to drive us across the bridge, and in
return I promised not to shoot him."

"Where's Fromish?"

"He's dead too. The three of them are in the grease pit inside his gas
station. I closed the place up, but there's some blood outside. It's getting

light; do you think we'll be able to drive over the bridge without getting stopped or questioned?"

"Shit, I don't know," replied Boone. "I haven't been across it in months, and even then I was hidden in the trunk of a car, so I didn't see anything. I can't go into Carrolton anymore, so I don't know what the bridge security is like these days. A military hummer should be good to go just about anywhere. But the bridge guards probably know all of the local troops, and they might wonder who the new guys are." Boone opened the front door to address their prisoner, still behind the wheel. "Well, Lieutenant, is crossing the bridge going to be a problem?"

After a hesitation, Malverde said, "No, it shouldn't be. There's no reason for them to inspect a Legion humvee. They can see what it is."

"If you're lying, you're dying," said Boone.

"I'm not lying," answered Malverde.

Carson said, "Boone, I had an idea coming over here. Colonel Brice just temporarily transferred over to the North American Legion. Here, take your Glock, and keep the lieutenant from getting any funny ideas. Let me change back into my ACUs. You too, Doug. I have the Legion insignias from the guys that I, uh, took out."

Standing between the humvee and the ruined restaurant, Doug Dolan and Carson quickly changed back into their Army ACU uniforms. They pressed on the velcro NAL patches, imitating the lieutenant's uniform. The blue beret Carson had picked up was different. On the front, the blue beret had the three silver stars of the North American Legion. This was what the Legion's enlisted men wore on their berets. Malverde had a lieutenant's single black bar on his beret instead of the three stars. For his evolving plan to work, these details were critical. Carson found his black U.S. Army beret, removed the eagle that signified the rank of full colonel, and transferred it to the blue beret. He placed the modified Legion beret on his head, just covering the scar beneath his hairline.

"What about me?" asked Boone. "I'm too big to hide, and I sure as hell can't pass for a Mexican." This was an understatement. Boone Vikersun, "the Viking," was several inches above six feet tall, with wild dark blond hair and a thick reddish beard.

"I already figured it out," said Carson. "You're our prisoner. When we approach the security point, just put your hands behind your back like you're handcuffed—but hang on to your pistol. If they just look inside, it'll fit the story I'm going to tell. We're transporting a dangerous gringo terrorist. I'm a colonel in the North American Legion, a bilingual commie rat bastard traitor. You said the Legion took American volunteers, right? Well, that's me. Colonel Brice has gone over to the dark side. Lieutenant Malverde, our cover is we're taking this big gringo prisoner to Fort

Campbell for interrogation. Can you make that story work, if we're stopped?"

"Umm…well, I guess I can…if they don't check your IDs. Usually they don't, not if you're in uniform."

"Well, they'd better not," said Carson, "or you'll be the first one to get it. The 'prisoner' will have a .45 aimed at your back, and I've got a nine millimeter."

"All right, we'll get across…but then you'll let me out on the other side? Like you said?"

"*If* we make it," Carson replied.

"We'll make it," said Boone, slinging his pack into the back of the humvee behind the driver. "That's a good plan, Phil. I think it'll work."

After changing clothes and making sure the details of their uniforms were correct, it took only a few minutes to drive from their last hiding place behind the abandoned restaurant to "downtown" Carrolton. The NAL humvee turned right onto Highway 214, and soon rolled past the service station. The bay doors were still down, and the same single exterior spotlight shone on the pump island. There was a little traffic on the road now, but no customers were waiting in the gas station, which still appeared to be closed for the night. A few blocks on, they drove past the old Ford dealership and the chain drugstore and motel beside it. A few NAL troops were walking between humvees, confiscated pickups, and troop trucks, getting ready for the new day. Other young Hispanic-looking men were leaving the diner next to the motel, some in uniform and some in civvies or tracksuits. These former businesses evidently housed and fed the hundred or so foreign soldiers stationed in Carrolton, assigned to guard the western side of the critical Tennessee River bridge.

A half mile further on, the two-lane road began its long ascent up the earthen rampart to the concrete and steel bridge. The sky was lightening in the east, and it promised to be a clear day. The last bands of cloud from the passing front turned pink and silver as they were swept away. Concrete Jersey barricades were set up partway across the road, forcing traffic to slow down and snake through them. On the shoulder to their right, three sections of barricade were arranged in a U shape, with sandbags stacked on top of them. A humvee with a .50 caliber machine gun mounted on top was parked inside this crude fighting position, protected on the front and sides. The earthen roadway was elevated enough to see the vehicle's weapon silhouetted against the eastern sky. An ammo box the size of a large Igloo cooler sat on the left side of the gun, connected to it by a flex-ible feed belt.

Carson said, "At least nobody's on the fifty—it's unmanned."

"Nobody's on it," replied Doug from behind him, "but it's not un-manned. It's a CROWS."

"A what?"

"CROWS—Common Remotely Operated Weapon Station. The operator is sitting inside the hummer, watching us on color television. Or maybe he's back at their HQ; he could be anywhere. It's the revenge of the Nintendo nerds. Some little hundred-pound geek in that hummer can blow you away at a thousand yards. When we get closer, you'll see a couple of big glass lenses under the barrel. Spooky as shit, those robot eyeballs staring at you. They say the gunner can zoom in and read a newspaper across a football field—at night. You can't hide from that thing; it can see you a mile away." Doug sighed. "I just wish we had one on this hummer."

Then, as if the machine had heard Doug Dolan, the gun system on the humvee's roof traversed until it was oriented in their direction, but the barrel remained elevated well above them. This movement was so disconcerting that Carson had the thought, *Maybe it can hear us?* The CROWS system was so far-out sci-fi that almost anything seemed possible. Maybe it was hooked up to a directional microphone? He tried to push the paranoid thoughts from his mind.

Malverde slowed as their humvee entered the serpentine concrete pattern of barricade sections. Boone quietly asked, "What now, Lieutenant? How's this going to go down?" He was sitting behind the driver, his suppressed Glock pistol gripped behind his back as he pretended to be a shackled prisoner.

Malverde answered, "If they make us stop, we stop. If not, we keep going, slowly."

"Okay, LT," said Boone. "Just keep going, nice and easy."

A medium-sized flatbed truck, loaded with scrap metal and used appliances, was stopped ahead of them. A pair of arc lights on tall stands illuminated both sides of the cab of the truck. A NAL soldier was speaking to the driver through the side window and inspecting documents, his frosty breath visible in the bright artificial light. Another soldier walked around the back of the truck, peering into its heaped metal junk with a powerful flashlight. Both men wore ACU uniforms matching Lieutenant Malverde's, including blue berets. It was almost light enough outside that the vehicle inspector didn't need the flashlight. After a minute, the truck's gears engaged, and it pulled forward and ascended the bridge.

Boone said quietly, "Go ahead, Lieutenant, it's our turn. Do it right."

When their humvee was even with the guard post, between the two arc light towers, Lieutenant Malverde stopped, but he left the transmission in drive, his hands locked on the wheel. The NAL soldiers approached, one on each side. Both men had M-4 carbines slung over their shoulders, and holstered pistols. Phil Carson, in the front passenger seat, glanced to his right at the robot machine gun on top of the guard post humvee.

Beneath the yard-long gun barrel, a pair of shiny lenses the size of CDs reflected the arc lights back at him, and he looked away. It was an unearthly, creepy feeling, to be stared at by a robot wielding a "Ma Deuce"—an M2 .50 caliber, the exact same machine gun invented by John Moses Browning fully a century before. Now it was married to computers, robots and video sights, and did not need a human hand to aim or fire it. Just some technoid geek who was staring at a screen, while manipulating a Playstation control.

The thick square armored side windows of their old humvee were scratched and dirty, and reflected back the glare of the arc lights. The soldier on the passenger side appeared disinterested in the common military vehicle, and walked past them to a boxy delivery van just pulling up behind. The soldier on the driver's side squinted and peered through the vertical front windshield into the humvee. Carson stared straight ahead, hands folded on his lap. The black eagle rank insignia of a full colonel was clearly visible on the front of his camouflage parka and on his beret. The cloth tape above his left breast pocket now read N.A.L. instead of U.S. Army. Suddenly noticing the two officers in the front seats of the humvee, the North American Legion soldier pulled himself up to a rigid position of attention, eyes riveted straight ahead, staring at nothing. He saluted smartly, his right hand snapping up to his blue beret, and he held the pose like a statue.

Carson said, "*Vamos, Teniente Malverde. Buen trabajo.* Good job." In a moment, they were driving above the tops of the trees growing along the west bank of the Tennessee River, and then up over the high arching bridge itself. The remaining river channel was only about 500 yards wide here. Below them, a vast marina complex on the near side had been left high and dry. The river level here had dropped over twenty feet when the Kentucky Dam collapsed during the earthquake, and at least a hundred boats lay stranded in the dirt, trapped between wooden pilings. The humvee's wheels vibrated on the temporary steel grating as they crested the high two-lane bridge. Middle Tennessee was spread before them to the eastern horizon, an orange glint of sun just edging above distant hills.

"So far so good, Lieutenant," said Boone Vikersun, the suppressor-equipped Glock pistol now held in front across his lap. "So far so good."

The secure line had an obnoxious buzzing tone. It didn't stop until Bob Bullard dragged himself to the side of his bed and pulled it from the side table. The entire red telephone crashed onto the floor with a cascade of bangs. He felt around for the receiver and eventually pulled it up to his face, while hanging off the bed. It was Mitchell Brookfield, his deputy director. Bullard managed to choke out, "Mitch, do you have any idea what time it is?" It was still dark in the room. His head ached, the result of a late Sunday night drinking session that had extended into the wee hours. His deputy was under orders never to call him before seven, unless the entire world was blowing up. He should just stop sleeping, he thought. Bad news usually came when he was sleeping off a bad one. Mondays were the worst, and he was usually hung over and dragging ass at the 0900 staff meeting.

"It's 0645, but I think you need to hear about this."

"Okay, what the hell is it?" Bullard hacked and struggled to work some saliva into his dry mouth. Just speaking took an effort.

"We have a big flap going on between the Nigerians and the Kazaks. They're at each other's throats. They're literally ready to go to war down in Southwest Tennessee. There's a lot of dead, according to the Nigerians."

"What?!" Bullard twisted over and sat bolt upright in bed, in the process getting a painful Charlie horse muscle cramp in his left calf.

"We're still putting reports together, but apparently there was some kind of a hot-pursuit situation, and the Kazaks rolled into Lexington County with a couple of armored vehicles. It appears that they shot up a Nigerian border outpost by mistake. Neither side's story makes any sense. The Nigerian CO is on the way up here, and he's out for blood. The Kazaks killed and wounded a bunch of Nigerians, and they lost two armored security vehicles in the process. The Kazaks say they were ambushed and fired on by the Nigerians. Nobody really knows what the hell is going on yet, but the Nigerians are redeploying both NPF battalions along a river facing the Kazaks."

"Aw, you have *got* to be shitting me. Okay, I'll be over in ten minutes. No—fifteen. The conference room. Round everybody up; we'll start when I arrive." Bullard dropped the phone and grabbed his calf; it felt as if somebody had chopped into the muscle with an axe. Mondays should be outlawed, he thought.

Phil Carson, riding shotgun in the front seat, studied the screen on the handheld military GPS. After descending from the temporary steel grates of the Tennessee River bridge, State Road 214 widened to four lanes. It was nearly daylight. He said, "This thing shows a road that cuts north around Lynnville."

Boone, sitting behind their captured driver, didn't need to consult the electronic map. "Maybe, but we can't use it. A big stretch of it was ruined by the earthquakes. We have to go through Lynnville. That's where we'll pick up 13 heading north, and then we'll be home free." State Road 13 ran parallel to the Tennessee River, a few miles to its east.

"Lynnville looks pretty substantial on the GPS map," said Carson. "I don't like the idea of driving straight through a town that size. The alarm is going to go out any minute. Somebody is going to find those—find out what happened at the garage. Then they're going to freak out, big-time. They're going to go totally ape shit."

"Maybe, maybe not. The radio is still quiet. It's only about five miles to Lynnville. We'll be through it and out in no time. It's better to rack up the road miles while we can. Get some distance from Carrolton. And I'm still feeling lucky." The radio had been left on its working channel. Spanish-speaking voices were occasionally heard, but there was no sound of panic or warning.

"I still don't like it," said Carson. "Why can't we dump this hummer and get picked up on this side of town?"

"I don't know why not; I just know we have to get north of Lynnville on 13. That's where the escape ratline starts."

In a few minutes, they approached the outskirts of the town. It was set in a natural cleft in the low hills that ran parallel to the Tennessee River. After a half mile of widely spaced businesses, they reached the intersection with the two-lane State Road 13. The traffic signal was flashing a four-way red.

Doug Dolan said, "Lynnville has electricity. That's always a good sign."

"That's an improvement since the last time I was over here," said Boone. "The last time I was here was a few months ago, and it was still blacked out then. Okay Lieutenant Malverde, come to a complete stop and take a nice easy left turn at the light. Don't make a big mistake and try to attract attention with a traffic violation. If we're stopped...you know what'll happen."

State Road 13 climbed uphill through the old downtown, which consisted of two- and three-story businesses fronting on the main street. It almost resembled a small town in a Western movie, with the storefronts coming up to the sidewalks on either side. Lynnville was the county seat. At the top of the hill, there was a brick courthouse on one corner, and a Baptist church on another. The road descended and the businesses began to be set further back from the road and were spread apart on more property. A few miles north, on a flat stretch of ground ahead of them, they could see two large warehouse-like buildings. One was trimmed with blue, and the other, orange.

"What's that?" asked Doug.

"It used to be Wal-Mart and Home Depot," said Boone. "13 goes right between them."

Carson said, "I'm not liking this. It looks like it's all fenced in." He studied his GPS screen. "We can turn east and go around it."

"No," replied Boone. "I don't care what that GPS shows, it's wrong. I know this area. That way just takes you into a maze of back roads, but there's no way around. Driving back there would just draw attention to us, and we'd wind up in a dead end anyway. We have to go past the Wal-Mart. Lieutenant, what's going on up there?"

Malverde seemed surprised to be asked a question, and gave a "Who me?" look before responding. "That? It's a relocation center. Part of the the Recovery and Reconstruction Administration. It's no problem, we can just drive through. The road in between is open for normal traffic."

Carson said, "I don't like this, not one little bit. What if he's lying? We'll be driving right into a controlled-access area. Look, it's all fenced, all the way around."

"Hey, if he's lying, he's dying," said Boone. "Right, Lieutenant?"

Their driver said nothing, his lips tightly pursed as he stared straight ahead.

The fugitives approached the last public road intersection before the acres of parking lots. The two-lane state road widened to four lanes between the big-box stores. Home Depot was on their left, Wal-Mart on the right. Their corporate signs had been taken down, but there was no mistaking the origins of the giant buildings. The entire perimeters of the Home Depot and Wal-Mart properties were fenced in multiple layers of chain link, with angled razor wire strands on top. The chain link and barbed wire extended right up to the curbs on both sides of State Road 13, leaving just an enclosed corridor in between for the passage of through traffic. A tan humvee bearing the three black stars of the North American Legion was parked on the opposite side of the intersection. Atop its roof was a 7.62mm M-240 medium machine gun on a conventional ring-and-pintle mount, but nobody was visible in or around the vehicle.

In the parking lot of the Wal-Mart, over a hundred big general-purpose Army tents had been set up, similar to the ones Carson had slept in back at Camp Shelton in Mississippi. These GP-Large tents could fit more than twenty cots each. The tents had been arranged with military precision in ranks and files. On the Home Depot side were dozens of gray FEMA house trailers in neatly ordered rows, and more green and tan Army tents.

Their humvee had to stop and wait while a vehicle gate on the Home Depot side to their left was swung open by a pair of soldiers in camouflage uniforms. A convoy of a dozen canvas-covered military trucks exited the Home Depot parking lot, turned north in front of the humvee, and then turned right and passed through another gate on the Wal-Mart side. After the last of the big trucks turned onto State Road 13, the two guards with rifles slung on their shoulders closed the gate behind them. These guards wore black berets, but it was not possible to determine if they were Americans or foreign.

Boone asked Malverde, "What's that all about?"

The lieutenant answered, "They're probably picking up a work detail. For reconstruction projects. Roads, bridges, you name it. That's what this camp is for, housing the workers. FEMA runs the camp for the Recovery and Reconstruction Administration."

Carson looked out his right side window, beyond the two chain link fences toward the Wal-Mart building. The parallel fences were spaced about ten feet apart, enough room for a vehicle, guards patrolling on foot, or police dogs. A line of hundreds of civilians, all men, queued up on the other side of the second fence. Hands were thrust in coat pockets as they shuffled along. It was cold enough outside to see their breath, even though the sky was mostly clear with just a few high wisps of cloud. Some of the men looked away or at the ground, others chatted, but many stared at the North American Legion humvee with undisguised contempt. A few spat toward them or gave the middle finger. There was no mistaking the two words forming on their lips when they gave the finger gesture.

The humvee pulled forward when the road ahead was clear of the truck convoy. Carson watched the front of the line of civilian men entering an enormous white tent, big enough for a large wedding or a small circus. On the other side of the white tent from the queue, men stood outside in small groups, eating with spoons from silver mess trays.

The main entrance road running from State Road 13 into the Wal-Mart complex was also fenced on both sides. An enormous chain link gate closed this entrance off from 13, and was shut behind the last of the Army trucks. On the other side of the entrance road that bisected the thirty-acre Wal-Mart parking lot, Carson saw another line of civilians and another huge white tent, but all of the people on this side were women, along with children of both sexes. The new line of people waiting to be fed extended for hundreds of yards beyond this second white tent, running parallel to the double row of fences along State Road 13.

Boone said, "This FEMA camp wasn't here the last time I was on this side of the river. It was just a regular Wal-Mart and a Home Depot. Of course, they were out of business then. They never reopened after the earthquakes. They were looted down to the floors, and abandoned."

"So that's what a FEMA relocation camp looks like," said Doug.

"Doesn't look like a lot of fun in there," said Boone. "Not anyplace I'd want to live."

From behind the wheel, Lieutenant Malverde ventured a quiet comment. "It's better than starving, and freezing in the rain and snow. The old people and the mothers with little children and babies get to stay in the buildings. It's dry and warm in there. Only the able-bodied adults and big kids stay in the tents."

Boone said, "You seem to know a lot about the place, LT. What else can you tell us?"

After a hesitation Malverde said, "Who else is going to rebuild Tennessee?"

Carson said, "Did you notice something odd about the people lined up to get into the mess tents?"

"What, you mean it was all men on one side of the camp, and women on the other?" asked Doug.

"Well, yeah, but that's not what I meant. Look, it's all whites in there. Caucasians. I didn't see a single black face."

"There's not so many blacks that live around here," said Boone. "But I'll admit, that seems strange. Maybe there's a different camp for blacks."

"Or maybe they're only putting whites into these camps," observed Doug. "Or at least, into this camp."

"Hey," said Boone, "I just figured out why the men are all on one side and the women are on the other. Besides making it easier to manage them, I mean. They have to send the men out on work projects, right? Well, they won't run away if they know their families are still back in the other part of the camp. Those FEMA bastards use the men's families as hostages, to keep them from escaping."

"It sounds like slavery," said Doug. "Or a concentration camp. The British did something like that in the Boer War. The Boers were fighting a guerrilla war. The English invented modern concentration camps to break the Boer resistance. They grabbed all the Boers' families, their women and children, and stuck them behind barbed wire in concentration camps until their men quit. And it worked."

Lieutenant Malverde offered no further observation on this topic, nor was he asked again, because they were fast approaching the next guard position.

There was another NAL humvee with a pintle-mounted medium machine gun on its roof, parked where State Road 13 left the far end of the vast FEMA center. This was where the chain link fences and barbed wire marking the perimeter of the complex ended. A pair of oversized stop signs flanked the last stretch. There was another set of tower stands for arc lights, but it was daylight now and the lights were not turned on. Two NAL soldiers in camouflage parkas and blue berets leaned against the front of the humvee, smoking cigarettes and talking, probably waiting for their reliefs to show up. They appeared not even to notice the passage of the "friendly" Legion humvee.

Once they were beyond the final guard post, Lieutenant Malverde said, "Okay, I kept my part of the deal. You're going to let me out like you said, right?" He turned slightly to address Phil Carson.

"Soon, lieutenant, soon," said Boone from behind Malverde. "Just have patience. We're not in a safe place yet. But soon."

Each of the men in the humvee shared the same unspoken question. Would they really let the Legion officer go, as Carson had promised…or kill him? It was an age-old problem for guerrilla fighters: what to do with prisoners taken on a mission behind enemy lines. Not one man in the vehicle could have said with any degree of certainty what the outcome of Lieutenant Malverde's request would be. There was much more certainty about their own fates should they be captured while wearing Legion uniforms.

They would be hanged as spies and terrorists. Of that, there was no question at all.

23

Large maps, aerial photos and charts lined the walls of the first-floor conference room in Building 1405. A giant flat-screen television was mounted above the far end of the long mahogany conference table. Director Bullard dropped into the leather executive chair at the head of the table and was immediately handed an enormous mug of black coffee. He was wearing his usual khaki Eisenhower jacket and matching pants. A platter of his favorite Danishes was discreetly placed next to him on a folding TV tray, just below the table level.

"All right, people, get me up to speed."

His communications assistant said, "We have Colonel Burgut of the Kazak Battalion on the video conference link standing by. Should I put him on, or keep him holding?"

"Oh, put him on. Might as well get the bad news right from the horse's mouth." A tiny video camera was already on the table in front of Bullard, aimed at him. Colonel Burgut's face appeared on the TV screen at the other end of the long table. All of Bullard's department heads, deputies and assistants turned toward the screen. Colonel Burgut appeared both haggard and angry, his thick black hair combed back. He was unshaven, which was typical for the Kazaks, but then, Bullard hadn't shaved either. Unlike Bullard, Colonel Burgut had the thick moustache so common among the Kazaks.

"Okay, Colonel, I'm here. Tell me what's going on with the Nigerians."

"Good morning, General Blair. Or maybe, not good. Problem with Nigerians was result of small mistake, that become very big mistake. Last night, two Kazak armored scout vehicles were attack in County Radford, east from Mannville. One ASV stealed by terrorists. Six Kazak peacekeepers having been murdered in situation. Ten more Kazak peacekeepers having been murdered short time later, when stolen ASV ambush Kazak platoon on truck." Burgut sighed, ran both hands back from his face and over his head, and took a deep breath. "Stolen ASV scout vehicle was discovered in pursuit, and other Kazak armored vehicles making effort trying to stop. Stolen vehicle crossed to Nigerian territory of County Lexington. After, situation not clear. Nigerians fired on Kazaks, according to radio messages received. I was in command vehicle, remaining in County Radford. General Blair, all was simple case of hot pursuit, all being in accord from International Peacekeeping Forces Agreement. One Kazak

ASV on hot-pursuit mission was destroy, and crew murdered by Nigerians. One Kazak ASV returning to County Radford, crew okay."

"So what happened to the stolen ASV that you were pursuing?" Burgut's expression of cold rage appeared partly dulled by deep fatigue. He spoke very slowly, with long pauses between each phrase, obviously struggling to find the English words to express his thoughts. "Status of stolen ASV not being known at this time. Kazak requesting for aerial reconnaissance having been denied, as you very well are knowing already, General. Is impossible for Kazaks to know where is stolen ASV today. Stolen Kazak ASV in Nigerian county of Lexington. Perhaps better to ask Nigerians where is stolen ASV. General Blair, two Kazak peacekeepers are being dead today because of denied helicopter medical evacuation, even before incident of stolen ASV. Three Kazaks having been killed from terrorist bomb south of Mannville yesterday, 1700 hours when sun dropping. Two Kazaks injured in terrorist explosion has now being dead, because of denied helicopter medical evacuation. I am thinking that you are understanding much of situation already."

Bullard ignored the charge contained in the Kazak's last comment. "We'll be sending Predators up for reconnaissance ASAP. As soon as possible, since the weather is clear. And I'll see about helicopter medevac flights if you still need them. The weather is better for flying today."

"Good. We are needing still casualty evacuation for eight or seven woundeds. I will make radio call to air operations after video conference. General Blair, I must also inform that Nigerian forces are moving to north side of Butler Creek. This small river being border to County Radford. Nigerian forces are taking very aggressive posture, including Nigerian snipers with harassment shots firing. I believe it very important that Nigerian forces redeploy north, away from border of County Radford, to avoid very big problem of great danger to both forces."

"Thank you, Colonel. We'll be in touch later this morning. Call air operations about a medevac helicopter. I'm sure you'll get one." Offscreen, Bullard made a dismissive hand gesture, and the flat screen went blank.

A reconnaissance and surveillance technician spoke next. "Sir, we may have an idea about what happened to the stolen Kazak ASV. We already have a Predator over Lexington County. I just came from flight ops, and I copied the pertinent video."

"Well, put it up."

The tech was seated at the table with a laptop in front of him. He made a few clicks, and aerial video appeared on the big screen. The aide used a pen-sized laser to pick out his references, tracing and circling them with the bright red dot on the giant TV screen. "You see this S-shaped line across here? This is Butler Creek. Below it is Radford County; above it is

Lexington. You can see where the Nigerians are moving troops and vehicles to positions all along the north bank of Butler Creek, here, here and here. Now, look up north about a mile. See this group of vehicles?" He circled the area with his red laser. "Right here, right here is what we *think* is the missing ASV. Or was. We're sending people down, but we probably won't get anything out of it. If it's the missing ASV, it's been blown up and burned. It's totaled."

Bullard slurped his hot coffee, and then said, "You mean, we've got *nothing* on who caused this whole mess?"

"Umm, not quite nothing. Actually, it seems that we did record an unusual snippet of digital audio last night. We just found it, after searching through the pertinent audio archives. This was on the Kazak tactical network. Let me cue it up. Here, give a listen."

"No, nothing, I'm just hearing radio chatter. It's not in English."

Bullard asked, "What the hell does that mean?"

"We're analyzing it now. It appears as if it might have been transmitted from the stolen Kazak ASV by mistake. I'm told the voice belongs to a male in his twenties or thirties. His accent places him from the area between Washington, D.C., and Philadelphia, so clearly he's not a local insurgent."

"Well, plug it into Omnivore, and let's see if we get any hits on it. The voice might already be in a database."

"Already done, sir. Now, back to the stolen ASV, which we think is this black thing here. It basically melted, what didn't burn. You can see the scorched ring around it, where all the snow is gone. The Nigerians are saying that the commanding officer of their 2nd Battalion was murdered right there, just a few yards away. That's his official residence, right there by what we think is the burned ASV. The Nigerians are saying that this colonel and his personal detachment were murdered there, by Caucasian soldiers in this ASV. Americans or Kazaks, the witnesses couldn't say for sure. The Nigerian 2nd Battalion CO's personal vehicle was apparently driven away from this point. A black Dodge Ram pickup truck. Now, this is where it really gets interesting. This is very recent, this just happened."

The tech clicked his remote control, and the video images on the big screen were replaced by a detailed map of western Tennessee. "Over in the town of Carrolton, that's right here, we just found the Nigerian vehicle. It's a pickup truck with Nigerian Peacekeeping Forces markings, a black Dodge Ram. It was hidden inside an abandoned building. Less than two miles from the pickup, three North American Legion soldiers were just found murdered in a gas station. These reports are still coming in, so there's some confusion about who's who and what's what, but their proximity seems to rule out a coincidence. Either two or three are dead there. A Legion humvee is missing; apparently, it was taken when the soldiers were murdered in the garage. And that's all we have at this point."

Bob Bullard selected an apple Danish, and studied the map. His eyes traced the meandering south-to-north course of the Tennessee River, from the state of Mississippi up into Kentucky. While chewing on the pastry, he found Radford County down near the bottom of the state, on the west side of the river. His eyes searched for and found the black dot representing the insignificant town of Mannville, near the scene of Saturday's rampage by the Kazak Battalion. Colonel Burgut had just said that terrorists killed several of his men with a bomb down around Mannville, one day after the massacre. Then one of his ASVs was stolen in the same general area, and more Kazak soldiers had been killed. Next, the Kazaks crossed from Radford into Lexington County in hot pursuit of their stolen ASV, precipitating a blue-on-blue firefight with the Nigerians. And from that point, a Nigerian pickup truck was taken, a truck which was just discovered in Carrolton, right by the only bridge in that region across the river to Middle Tennessee.

Bullard didn't vocalize his thoughts, nor even point his finger at the map, much less use a laser pointer. Not with a dozen staffers in the room studying his every move. Military vehicles were being taken one after another, and each time, fresh bodies were being found. A pattern and a timeline were emerging. From Mannville, to the Nigerian outpost and now to Carrolton, the direction was clear. The only possible significance to Carrolton was its location by a key bridge over the Tennessee River. These incidents in southwest Tennessee were moving in a line toward Fort Campbell, toward him. It was just a matter of connecting the dots, and projecting them forward in space and time.

Bullard asked his deputy, "Where is this missing NAL humvee now? That's our top priority. Let's get over to UAV flight ops." He not only wanted to know more about the Nigerian-Kazak situation, and find out about the missing humvee and its next possible destination, he also wanted to take a circumspect look at that corpse-filled ravine outside Mannville. Obviously, that wasn't a topic that he could have discussed with Colonel Burgut on the video conference in front of his staff. But if those hundreds of bodies outside Mannville were still uncovered and visible from above, that would be the last straw for Burgut. He would not be given another chance. It was time to send the Predators down there and get some answers. What in the hell was going on in Radford County?

When Zack Tutweiler woke up for the final time, it was already daylight. Both Zack and Jenny were fully dressed with even their boots still on, and a triple layer of blankets over them. He was lying on his right side, pressed against Jenny's back, his right arm under her head for a pillow. The top part of her pack was his pillow. His left arm was over her waist, over her arm, and over the baby. The baby was sleeping against her chest. He had heard and felt Jenny comforting and quieting the baby during the long night. They had been in this warmth-maximizing position for hours. Each time he had awakened, he had felt her breathing by the movement of her back. Her long hair tickled his face, but he didn't mind.

He carefully extricated his arm from beneath her and slid away, careful to ease her pack beneath her head and tuck the blankets around her back. He took the diaper bag, pushed up the rear window hatch, rolled out and closed it again. There was frost on the ground and on the farm junk around him. The sky was mostly clear, with only some wispy stripes of high cirrus. Mares' tails, his father had called them. The sun would soon show itself over the fields and trees to the east. It was going to be a day of mostly blue skies, a day to dry out and, he hoped, to warm up. Zack crouched between the camper shell and the old meat freezer, and scanned around him through all 360 degrees, searching every sector for signs of the enemy. The farmhouse had burned down to a pile of black timbers and ashes, still giving off smoke that was rising almost straight up into the still air. The barn was mostly gone. The back wall and the side closest to their camper shell had somehow stayed up. The tin roof had partially collapsed, resting on its front edge, blackened and warping.

Except for where his sightlines were blocked by the ruins of the barn, he could see for hundreds of yards, and in some directions up to several miles. The clear weather meant long-distance visibility. Outside of the maple trees planted around the farmhouse, there wasn't much cover. Creeping along fences, hedgerows and tree lines would only get them so far. He knew from last night's travels that they would be forced to cross open fields. If they tried to move from here during daylight, they would be seen and run down by any Cossacks remaining in the area.

Zack unzipped the dirty pink nylon diaper bag. Along with torn cotton sheets for diapers, there was the empty formula bottle, a sports bottle full of clean water from the cave, and the box of milk powder. Milk was priority number one. He refilled the baby bottle halfway with water, added as much powder as he thought would mix in it, shook it for a long time and then filled it the rest of the way with more water. But it was still ice cold. He'd been around babies, and he knew the drill. He knew what they needed. Unfortunately, the babies that he had helped to raise were all dead, along with his mother and his father too. Now there was just the little baby girl that Jenny had found. Tears came in a sudden rush, and after a minute for his own grief, he wiped them away with the back of his coat sleeve. He blinked up at the blue sky, mouthed a quiet prayer, and took several deep breaths to steady himself.

He looked around the junkyard, and found a plastic barrel full of trash, including a big rusty vegetable can. To heat the baby bottle in the old steel can, he'd have to waste more of their drinking water. Instead, he looked around for another source of water. A rain barrel had been filled from the stable's tin roof. The excess was channeled into an old enamel bathtub, as a trough for livestock. He dipped the rusty can through ashes and charcoal into this dirty water; its purity didn't matter. Nearby, a fallen roof beam from the stable was still glowing cherry red. He set the rusty can with the baby bottle into glowing embers among the hot coals.

While he waited for the milk to heat, Zack checked the area around the junkyard and barn for anything else of use. He could see where the Cossack's horse had dug the earth with its hooves while rearing and turning. He remembered the scene. The rider was side-lit by the burning farmhouse, the Molotov cocktail in his hand, before his own arrow launched the fiery outcome. Further along the ruins of the barn, Zack saw something leaning against an upended zinc tub, something that wasn't just farm junk. What he spotted on the other side of the metal tub had the shape of a rifle or shotgun stock.

He immediately went to it. It was an AK-47, or a weapon just like it! He'd shot a semi-automatic version of the AK before. This one's wooden stock had been singed and blackened by flames. Its nylon sling was partly melted. He picked the rifle up; it was warm to the touch but not hot. A long black ammo magazine curved out from beneath its receiver. A little lever behind the magazine held it locked in place. Zack pushed it forward and removed the magazine. It was heavy, full of bullets. He could count them later. At least they hadn't cooked off from the heat.

To see if a bullet was loaded in the rifle, he'd have to pull the bolt back and check the chamber. There was a steel finger hook on the right side to cock the AK's bolt. The long safety lever was up in the safe position, blocking the rearward travel of the bolt, so he pushed it all the way down with a loud click. He pulled the bolt back, and a cartridge was ejected onto the ground. He picked it up: it was about the same size as an AR-15 or M-16 bullet. He'd fired semi-automatic AR-15s before. The bullets were fast and flat shooting, but not as powerful as the heavier 30-30s fired by his Winchester.

He let the bolt return to the forward position, and tried the trigger. The hammer snapped after a bit more trigger pressure than his Winchester had needed. It was important to know exactly how much finger pressure it would take to fire the gun. He pushed the loose bullet into the magazine, reinserted it into the rifle, and pulled the bolt back again. He let it snap forward, rechambering the first round. Finally, he pulled the safety lever bar all the way back up.

It would be better if he could practice shooting the weapon, but there was no way he could permit himself this luxury. A rifle shot would attract the attention of the Cossacks for sure. On a clear, still morning, the sound of a shot might travel for miles. He'd just have to trust that when he pushed the safety down and pulled the trigger, it would fire. He shouldered the AK and aimed along its iron sights toward a distant tree. They weren't much different from the sights on his old 30-30 Winchester. If he needed to, he'd be able to fire the rifle and hit what he was aiming at. One thing he had heard all his life, or at least for as long as he'd been shooting, was that AK-47s worked every damn time you pulled the trigger.

Zack replayed last night's battle in his mind. After being shot with at least one arrow and fumbling his lit bottle, the Cossack rider must have been trying to remove the sack of Molotov cocktails from his chest. If this rifle's sling had been put on over the other satchel's strap, the rifle would have to come off first, or they would become hopelessly entangled around his neck and shoulders. So the Cossack had managed to remove the rifle, but not the sack of gasoline-filled bottles, just before he was fully engulfed in flames and his horse took off in a panicked gallop.

The AK's brown strap was burnt and slightly melted, but it was still usable. He placed the strap over his head and behind his neck, the way soldiers carried their rifles at the ready. He practiced swinging the rifle up to his shoulder and getting a rapid sight picture. The weapon was about as heavy as his Winchester. Satisfied that the rifle was ready to use if it was needed, he crept back along the smoldering barn's ruins to check the baby's milk. The water in the steel can around the plastic baby bottle was beginning to boil. He crouched near the glowing embers, warming himself, until he thought the milk was ready.

The plastic bottle was tepid but not too hot in his hand. He returned to the camper shell, crouched and lifted the rear window hatch. Jenny was sitting up, the blanket around her shoulders. She held the swaddled baby on her lap. Little Hope was sucking her pacifier, her big brown eyes wide open. Zack passed the warm bottle to Jenny without explanation, and she deftly switched its rubber nipple with the baby's pacifier.

Zack said, "Look what I found," and showed her the Kalashnikov rifle. "It's a little burnt, but it's still in good shape."

Jenny grinned at him and said, "Well, that's more than you can say for the Cossack you lit on fire last night."

Her smile blossomed inside Zack's heart and he smiled back, forgetting his own crooked teeth for a moment. Suddenly Jenny's smile was worth everything, was worth anything, including his very life.

State Road 13 meandered northward from Lynnville, most of the way in a valley following a tributary of the Tennessee. The countryside quickly became rural, with just a scattering of small farms and horse ranches, and the small properties of some isolated Tennesseans who had never ascended much beyond shacks and mobile homes. Five or six miles north of the town, the humvee passed a junkyard, and Boone told their driver to slow down and take the next right. The junkyard was enclosed by a ramshackle wall made of rusty steel sheets, set fifty feet back from the state road. Opposite a vehicle gate in the wall was a single metal building like a hangar or a large garage.

The right turn took them onto another two-lane country road, but narrower and without a yellow stripe down the center. After making the turn, Boone told Lieutenant Malverde to park by an abandoned fruit stand and wait for a minute. Carson understood without asking that Boone had to leave a clandestine signal back at the crossroads, so that their contact, if he passed by, would know that they were waiting for pickup. He'd leave a distinctive rag on a stick, make a unique mark on a road sign, or just draw a chalk arrow on the pavement, whatever signal had been prearranged. In a minute, Boone jogged back down to the humvee. A few cars and trucks passed on State Road 13, but nobody came down their side road.

Boone gave terse directions, taking them onto a narrower road and then a dirt trail between trees. Lieutenant Malverde drove more and more slowly, perhaps sensing that they were not going to release him after all. They finally approached the junkyard from the rear. The rusted steel wall was missing some panels, and did a poor job of protecting the back acres of abandoned automobiles, buses, cranes and trucks.

As ordered, Lieutenant Malverde parked the tan humvee under a corrugated tin roof, which covered a small work area along the junkyard wall. Benches, tables, tools, an acetylene torch and an old arc welder were sheltered from the elements under the very basic covering. There was sufficient room to hide the humvee from airborne reconnaissance, and that was the entire point.

Lieutenant Malverde said nothing, not to beg, joke, or stall. Undoubtedly, his mind was spinning. The three Americans took their packs and all of the weapons with them when they climbed out of the humvee. Boone appeared to be familiar with the place, and led them through a gap in the steel fence and past an ancient fire truck, to what appeared to be an abandoned and forgotten thirty-foot travel trailer. A willow tree growing just outside the wall spread an umbrella of green whip-like branches over the faded and peeling trailer. A hefty padlock secured a hasp bolted to the door. Boone went to the trailer's towing hitch, felt around under it and returned with the key. The four men went directly inside. The condition of the interior was in some contrast to the exterior. It was not as moldy or stale as Carson had expected it would be. Curtains made of striped yellow and orange material were closed across all of the windows, so that the interior was bathed in a soft golden light.

Doug asked, "Now what?"

"Now we wait," said Boone, dropping his pack on the floor and settling into the most comfortable upholstered easy chair. It faced a small television mounted in a shelf, but there was no electricity. Boone pointed at Malverde and indicated an empty hard-backed kitchen chair in the opposite corner. Then he laid his rifle across the padded armrests of his own seat, popped out the rear connecting pin, and pulled out his bolt carrier. Boone's SR-25 was similar to an M-16, but firing the heavier 7.62 millimeter bullet, and with a large telescopic sight in place of a carrying handle.

Half of the trailer consisted of a living room, which also contained a kitchenette at one end. Carson put the loose weapons on the dinette table, slid into a seat, and began to wipe each one down with a cloth kitchen towel. His loaded Beretta was left visible on the table, lest their prisoner have any idea of bolting.

Doug Dolan looked around the rest of the trailer as if searching for clues, peering into the tiny bathroom and the bedroom that took up most of the front end. Lieutenant Malverde tried to make himself as unobtrusive as possible, sitting in his designated kitchen chair in the corner opposite Boone. If anything, he appeared slightly relieved. Perhaps he had expected to be shot, once the humvee had parked in this remote location. He had not yet been handcuffed or tied up; it had not been necessary. The three men guarding him were each carrying several firearms. Only a few of the weapons were field-stripped for cleaning at a time, then they were immediately reassembled and reloaded. Carson knew that after what the lieutenant had witnessed back at the gas station, he would not be anxious to try his luck against even steeper odds.

Doug asked Boone, "How long will we have to wait before we're picked up?"

"As long as it takes; there's no fixed schedule. We'll stay until somebody shows up, or until we give up and leave. If nobody shows, we'll stay here at least overnight, so make yourself comfortable. Hey, while you're up, see if there's anything to eat. We should save our MREs in case we don't get picked up. Or if you have any rice left over from the cave, eat that."

Doug asked, "Is there usually any food in here?"

"I don't know. I was only here once, and I didn't stay long enough to find out. If there is, we'll eat whatever we can find." Boone took a drink from his camelback tube, sucking it dry. "Look in the pantry, and under the sink. There should at least be some water bottles around here somewhere."

"You think we should set security outside?" asked Carson.

Boone said, "Yeah, we should. After we clean our weapons and grab a bite, we'll set security. Not that it'll do much good: if we're compromised, it'll be from fifteen thousand feet up, and we won't know it until a rocket comes through the roof. If anything, somebody wandering around outside just increases our exposure. We'll do it, but very carefully. And when we're off-watch, we'll take turns sleeping in the bedroom. We might be here for awhile." Boone yawned, and went back to cleaning the internal parts of his rifle, using a small kit from his vest.

Lieutenant Malverde looked to each man in turn, and since nobody else spoke to him, he said, "You're in a safe place now." He nodded his head toward Carson. "Like the colonel said, we made a deal, back in the garage. But I can understand if you don't want me to leave before you do. When you go, you can just let me stay here. I'll wait a few hours, and then I'll walk back to Lynnville." The NAL officer spoke perfect, nearly unaccented English.

Boone looked at him with amusement. "First of all, Lieutenant, there's no such thing as a 'safe place' these days. A Predator could have tracked us here from any point on our trip today. A Hellfire or a Viper could drop through this tin roof any second. Or they might be watching the trailer and waiting to see who else shows up. In fact, that would be standard operating procedure in this kind of situation. They might be surrounding this place with troops at this very minute. So don't tell me about safe places, because there ain't no such thing. And second of all, it was my colleague who made that private arrangement with you. I didn't, and I'm in charge. Not him."

The young officer looked to Boone with a hurt expression and said, "But he gave me his word of honor." Malverde had expressive hazel-brown eyes and a thin well-trimmed mustache. Under better circumstances, Carson imagined that he would be quite the lady-killer. But there were no ladies here to sway to his side with his Latin-lover good looks.

"Yeah, and if I'm not mistaken, he shot some of your *compadres* right around the same time. Listen LT, he just did what he had to do to get out of that situation. I'd say you're lucky you're not with your men back in the garage. But as far as 'deals' go, you're back at square one. There's no deal. I'm the only one here authorized to make a deal."

Lieutenant Malverde paused, looked from man to man, and then said, "If your word means nothing, then you rebels have no honor."

"Honor?" Boone sprang from his chair, clutching the lower receiver of his disassembled rifle and shaking it at his prisoner. "You want to talk about *honor*? What about *your* honor, Lieutenant? What are you doing in *my* state, wearing that uniform? Pull out your wallet and any papers you have on you. Just hand them over, unless you want to be strip-searched.

You want to make a deal? Okay, let's make a deal. But that means you have to have some chips to throw in the pot, and I don't see that you have any. The only thing you have that I want is information—maybe. Something of value, something worth my time. So pass over your wallet, and then start with 'I was born'."

Without saying anything else, Malverde removed a green nylon wallet from his back trouser pocket and handed it to Boone, who tossed it over to Carson at the dinette.

"Let me know if there's anything interesting in it," Boone told Carson. "Okay now Lieutenant, we're going to have an in-depth discussion on the subject of honor. We have all day, until our next ride shows up, or until a rocket center-punches this trailer and blows us all to hell." Boone dropped back into his vinyl-upholstered lounger. Dolan had found Gatorade bottles full of drinking water, and handed one each to Boone and Carson, and finally one to their prisoner. Malverde immediately unscrewed the plastic cap and took a long drink. The position of his chair meant that he had to look toward Boone, his inquisitor, or turn his head to avoid Boone's gaze. Boone could split his attention between cleaning the parts of his rifle, and his prisoner.

Carson slipped on his reading glasses and spread the contents of the wallet across the dinette table. Carson and Dolan were still dressed as NAL soldiers, exactly like their prisoner. "Well, according to his North American Legion ID card, his name is Antonio Deguello Malverde. He has some other cards from San Antonio, Laredo and Houston. Library cards, driver's license—the usual. Looks like he's an alumnus of the University of Texas at El Paso. Oh, and his North American Legion name is bullshit. On his UTEP alumni card, it says his name is Anthony J. Delgado. Hey, this is a good one: Antonio Jesus Delgado is a member of FECHA—that's the Aztlan student front. I guess he switches between Anthony and Antonio, depending on who he's trying to impress."

"Jesus?" Boone pronounced the name Hay-Zeus, and burst out laughing. "Antonio Jesus Delgado? Tony, if you're going to assume a nom de guerre, you can't keep cards with your old name right in your wallet. It defeats the whole purpose."

"And Deguello Malverde is bullshit too," said Carson. "Deguello is the tune the Mexicans played at the Alamo—it was their 'no quarter' song. The Texans called it Cutthroat. Drums and bugles. It was Mexican psyops—it was supposed to scare their enemies shitless. I guess Deguello is a play on Delgado. Malverde is bogus too; it's a tough-guy name, like Scarface or Rocky. Literally, it means 'bad-green.' Jesus Malverde is sort of the patron saint of bad guys in Mexico. They have statues of him all over the place, but he's just made up. Just like young Lieutenant Malverde."

"So, Tony," Boone asked, "when you join the North American Legion, do you get to pick a new name? Sort of like the French Foreign Legion? I imagine that's handy for all of the criminals who enlist." Boone pulled a rope-like bore snake through his rifle's barrel to clean it.

The young officer appeared sheepish, embarrassed about the public exegesis of his chosen alias. "You don't have to take a new name. It's optional."

"There you were, studying at the University of Texas El Paso," said Boone. "So how did you wind up in Tennessee? Come on, Tony, don't be shy. In case you haven't figured it out yet, you're pleading your case here, LT."

Doug Dolan stood in the passageway to the kitchenette. All three men watched their captive squirm in his chair in the corner. The entire living room space was very small; none of them was more than eight or ten feet away from the others. The morning sun cast a beam of orange light through a curtained window onto the prisoner.

"I wasn't some rich gringo. I was accepted at the university, but I had to pay for it. To pay for it, I joined Army ROTC."

"Well, that's good, that's fine," said Boone, nodding his head agreeably. "That's very honorable, even if you joined for the tuition. So far, so good. But that doesn't explain how you wound up in Tennessee, in a North American Legion uniform."

"I really had no choice! When I graduated, the North American Legion was just forming. Almost all of my graduating ROTC class joined. There was a lot of pressure to join the Legion."

"Tony, stick with the truth, you're not a good liar. You belong to FECHA, and even I know that's a radical Aztlan group. So how hard did they have to twist your arm to join the North American Legion? And besides, the Legion is less than a year old, and you're already a first lieutenant. The times don't match. You'd still be a second Louie, a butter bar. When did you graduate from UTEP?"

"In June. Why does that matter? There was a rapid promotion policy in the NAL, and I was promoted to first lieutenant after only six months."

Boone said, "So joining the Legion was a good deal for you. Better than if you stayed in the regular U.S. Army. Quicker advancement—and that means more pay."

"So what? These are hard times. We're in a depression. I wasn't some rich gringo, born on third base in scoring position. I had to make the best deal for me."

"Come on Tony, don't play the oppressed Hispanic peon card on us. Compared to most Mexicans, you're practically from Norway. Have you looked in a mirror lately? What are you, about six feet tall? I'll bet your bloodline goes straight back to Cortez and Coronado."

"That might be, I wouldn't know, but that doesn't mean my family had extra money lying around for college. I still had to make the best deal I could for myself, for my own future. The Legion was the best deal going when I graduated."

"But was there *honor* in that deal, Tony?" asked Boone. "Was there honor? Tell me something: when you graduated from college, you were commissioned, right? There was some little ceremony with your ROTC buddies, with flags and so on. There was something about 'Raise your right hand and repeat after me'?"

"Yes, I took the oath."

"Now, I know that El Paso is not exactly part of a typical state anymore, but when you were in the Army ROTC, it was still a farm team for the United States Army, right? Not for some secret Aztlan army, or the North American Legion? Your Professors of Military Science were United States Army officers?"

"Yes."

"So, when you took the oath, you swore to defend the Constitution, correct?"

"Yes, we all did."

"Against all enemies, foreign and domestic?"

"Yes, but—"

"No buts, Tony. You swore an oath to defend it! But here you are today, in some kind of bullshit multinational foreign legion. Soldiers like you are guarding Americans in concentration camps. Other foreign units are marching Americans into ditches and shooting them. I've seen it with my own two eyes, and I've got proof. So tell me, how exactly does joining the North American Legion square with defending the Constitution of the United States? *Honor*, Tony, we're coming back around to *honor*. When you swear an oath, you're honor-bound to keep it."

The lieutenant had a ready answer, and he was eager to explain. "But the new constitution superseded the old one. There was a constitutional convention, remember? Now we have a new constitution, and I'm still defending it. And President Tambor, he signed the multinational peacekeeping treaty. It's the law now, so it's part of the constitution too. That's why we have foreign peacekeepers and the North American Legion in Tennessee. It's all legal, every bit of it. I've done nothing wrong! Everything I did was legal." Lieutenant Malverde made eye contact with each of his captors in turn, as if they were jurors.

Boone scoffed at him. "That's not how we see it, Tony. Your so-called new constitution is bullshit. It's a lie from start to finish, the biggest lie in history, and any soldier who claims he swore to defend that lie is a goddamn traitor."

"Oh come on, you can't just pick and choose your own constitution! There was a constitutional convention, and now we have a new one. The new constitution is the supreme law of the land."

"Never!" shouted Boone, standing up again, his head brushing the low ceiling. "That convention in Philadelphia was a giant fraud; it was nothing but bullshit from start to finish—just like your so-called new constitution, and your North American Legion."

"But that's just *your* opinion. The president and the Congress and the Supreme Court, and most Americans, they all say otherwise. And they outrank you by a million times." The lieutenant paused, as if summoning up his courage. "Anyway, how can *you* say which constitution is legal? How can that be left up to you? How can you pass judgment on the president and the Supreme Court? You're just a couple of rebels with guns, hiding in a trailer."

Boone was taken aback by the directness of the lieutenant's counterattack, and he settled back down into his easy chair. "That may be so. But high-ranking traitors are still traitors. I don't care if they live in the White House, or if they work at the Pentagon or in the Capitol. Treason is still treason, no matter how you dress it up with lies and false constitutions."

Boone had cleaned the three main sub-groups of his rifle; the barrel, lower receiver and bolt group. After a quick inspection, he reassembled them into his SR-25 rifle, which he reloaded with a full magazine and laid across the arms of his chair, above his lap. It was only one more weapon among the dozen or so in the room, but when it was put together and reloaded, it brought a new level of menace to Boone's words.

Lieutenant Malverde stared at the rifle, glanced to Carson and Doug Dolan, and somewhat reluctantly pressed on. "Then you're advocating complete anarchy. Everybody gets to pick which laws they'll obey? There has to be one set of laws for everybody."

"There was, Tony, until traitors threw out the real Constitution and passed a fake one at a bogus convention. But we're getting nowhere with this discussion. Outside this trailer, you traitors run the show. That's obvious. You have the helicopters, the Predators, and the foreign mercenaries. But in here, today, *we* rule. And as the president of this court of inquiry, I just have one more question to ask." Boone paused, staring directly across the tiny living room at his prisoner. "Where were you born, Tony?"

Lieutenant Malverde shook his head, confused. "What difference does that make?"

"All the difference in the world. Where were you born?"

"In Texas. In Laredo, Texas."

"So, you're a natural-born American citizen, for sure?"

"Yes, of course."

"No, not 'of course.' Plenty of illegal aliens snuck into this country and went to our best schools. Thousands. Hell, millions. And I know the North American Legion will take anybody who claims he's Mexican. So it's not 'of course.' But you say you really are an American citizen, and you were a legal citizen when you were commissioned and you took your oath?"

"Yes, I'm a citizen, but so what? No human being is illegal. What difference does it make if I'm a citizen or not?"

"Well, Tony, it makes a big difference to me. Here's the deal. The real deal. Listen to me carefully: we shoot foreign invaders. It's nothing personal with them, they're just here. We understand that. It's a war, they're in our country, and we shoot them whenever we can. But traitors? American traitors?" Boone stared hard at the lieutenant. "Tony, we *hang* American traitors."

Malverde said nothing; he appeared to be in shock, incredulous. After a long hesitation he stammered, "Y-you have got to be joking. You're just trying to scare me."

Boone was stone-faced. "Do I look like I'm joking? I'm not joking, I assure you. I've just seen hundreds of Americans machine-gunned in a ditch. Men, women and children. I was *in* that ditch a few hours after they were shot. They were shot dead by foreign mercenaries, but the people who invited those murderers into this country were all Americans—just like you. American traitors. And we just drove past a concentration camp—excuse me, a 'FEMA relocation center'—and the guards on the inside looked like Americans to me. American traitors. But outside, the guards were wearing North American Legion blue berets, just like yours."

Boone wasn't finished. "And here you sit, a natural-born American citizen, a commissioned United States Army officer—but I don't see the stars and stripes on your shoulder, Tony. Instead of Old Glory, you're wearing a badge with three stars for three nations. 'Three Nations, One America' might sound good to some people, but to us, it's just one more goddamn lie they're trying to shove down our throats—and by God, we won't take it! The United States is still one sovereign country—not just one-third of North America! And that means all fifty of the United States, no matter what the president and the Congress say. You swore an oath to the Constitution of the United States, *not* to the North American Union."

"But...but West Texas isn't under the old constitution any more. After Philadelphia, after the Aztlan Agreement, the Southwest is—"

Boone cut him off. "Tony! You're back to that false constitution again! That bullshit doesn't fly in my courtroom. Stick with the *real* Constitution, the *original* Constitution. The *only* Constitution. Now, please explain to me how it was that you swore an oath to defend the Constitution of the United States, but now you're wearing those North American Legion badges on your uniform and you have a Legion ID card in your wallet."

Lieutenant Malverde seemed to have given up hope of convincing Boone of his reasons, and Boone was clearly the only one in the trailer whose opinion mattered. He looked at the loaded SR-25 rifle lying across the arms of Boone's chair. His inquisitor could turn it 90 degrees and pull the trigger anytime he chose. "What difference does it make what I say? You're just going to kill me anyway," he mumbled, shaking his head and slumping forward, his forearms on his knees.

"Not necessarily. But you do pose a problem—you can identify us. You know what happened back in Carrolton. You even know about this shitty little junkyard safehouse. So you're a problem for us. We can't just let you go. Offhand, I'd say that you need to make yourself valuable to us. You're what, Tony, twenty-two or -three? Hell, at twenty-three I made all kinds of mistakes. Big ones. Fortunately, none of them were fatal, or we wouldn't be having this little chat today. You actually seem like a pretty nice guy—except for the treason thing. But there's no getting around it, treason's a big deal, considering that we're in a civil war. Especially with foreign mercenaries running around Tennessee, shooting women and children. That sort of raises the ante. So treason counts very large in my book. And let's face it, you'd be a prime witness against us. So you need to provide me with something of value, something to put on the other side of the scale when we weigh the evidence. Otherwise…"

From his position standing in the kitchen passageway Doug suddenly exclaimed, "Oh, no—we can't just kill him! He's our prisoner. He's a prisoner of war. We can't just kill him."

Boone turned toward the kitchenette, surprised at Dolan's unexpected outburst. "Then you're okay with him pointing the finger at you and sending you to the gallows?"

"I didn't say that. But we can't just kill him. I won't be a part of it. I've been down that road, and I won't go down it again."

"Then what do you suggest?"

"We could tie him up, and then we could call somebody later on. Once we're in a safe place."

"But there *is* no safe place, and this trailer is valuable to us. More valuable than Tony here, I'm afraid. This is war, not a game. This is real-world, not an exercise. If he's debriefed by the traitor government, he'll blow this place and we'll lose a valuable asset."

"Then we could take him with us and let him go later, when we're somewhere else."

"But he'd still know about this place, and about us. It's not like he'll forget. We can't erase his memory. He'll be debriefed."

"Then we could take him with us and keep him for a while. Then we could use him for a prisoner exchange. Trade him," Doug suggested hopefully.

"Take him with us to *where*?" asked Boone. "Where is our safe territory, our home base? We have no sanctuary. We don't even have a base camp. Do you think we're running POW camps in a dirty war?"

"Well," said Doug, "we could send him back to West Texas, if he swore on his word of honor to leave Tennessee and never come back. They did that in the first Civil War all the time. It was called honor parole. They didn't just shoot prisoners, not even when they were captured on raids in enemy territory. Not the rebels, and not the Yankees. They didn't do it."

"That's foolish," Boone replied. "We could never trust him to keep his word."

"But at least it's an option! They did that thousands of times in the Civil War. Don't just automatically rule it out."

"Maybe they did that in the last Civil War. But it's different today."

Doug asked, "How is it different?"

Boone looked at the lieutenant, and then at Doug, and said, "They had *honor* back then. Both sides. A man's word of honor really meant something. And prisoners could practically walk home. It's a long way back to Laredo. Do you think he can make it there without being picked up as AWOL from the Legion? What's he going to do then? How can he explain himself, an officer leaving his post? That's desertion in *any* army. No, I'm sorry, we can't just let him go."

During this exchange the prisoner had been staring at the floor, his elbows on his knees, holding his head. Then he turned his face back up and looked at each of his three captors, trying to catch their gaze but finding them turning away. "I would do it, I swear to God I would do it," he said in a hush, with more than a hint of desperation in his voice. "I'd go back to Texas and *never* come back here. I would just disappear—gone. I don't belong here, this isn't my fight!" He extended his hands, wrists held together. "Tie me up, like he said. Tie me up and leave me here. Leave me anywhere—or take me with you, whatever you decide! When you let me go, I'll catch a bus or a train back to Texas, and I'll never cross the Mississippi again as long as I live. I'll hitchhike, I'll walk. I give you my *word of honor*. I swear to God, I swear on my mother." Malverde slumped forward in his chair again, trying to hide his fear.

Doug said, "At least *think* about it. Can you at least do that? Think about it?" Then, with the captive officer looking down, he whispered almost inaudibly to Boone, "*We're not murderers.*"

After a full minute of silence, Boone said, "I'll think about it."

Director Bullard sat behind the driver of his black Chevy Suburban, for the five-minute drive from UAV flight operations back to headquarters in Building 1405. He would take his lunch there today. His assistant, Jeff Sinclair, was on the phone, sitting next to him in the middle seat. The driver and front seat passenger were his top bodyguards. Only on Fort Campbell did he travel in a single vehicle without extra security. Bullard was in his usual khaki. Today the men up front were wearing black tactical pants and bulky black coats concealing their weapons. A pair of MP-5 submachine guns were bracketed beneath the dashboard, the heavy stuff was in the back. Jeff Sinclair, the only one in the Suburban who was wearing a jacket and tie, was speaking quietly on the secure phone, mostly listening while making only brief comments and interrogatives.

The morning trip over to UAV flight ops had produced mixed results. The missing humvee had not been located, but there was at least some good news. The ravine outside Mannville had been bulldozed flat and planted with tiny pine trees. At least Colonel Burgut had taken care of that important job. Bullard had been able to direct the Predator's camera and briefly scan the area, without bringing attention to it or raising questions, another positive aspect.

His assistant replaced the secure phone in its cradle. "That was operations. Our investigative team is in Carrolton; they've already been to the garage. They also interviewed the morning watch at the Tennessee River bridge. The Legion provides security for both sides of the State Road 214 bridge. There's a NAL company based there in Carrolton."

"I got that already."

"Right. Well, one of the guards who was on duty at the bridge remembers a humvee with a Legion colonel in it, crossing the river eastbound. So far, nobody knows what unit this colonel belongs to, if any. A lieutenant was driving. Apparently, all the bridge guard saw of them was their rank devices, and he waved them through. A NAL lieutenant and a humvee are missing from the garrison in Carrolton. Two of the missing lieutenant's men were killed in the gas station, along with the gas station owner. It's believed that this lieutenant was driving the humvee under duress when it crossed the bridge. That's the working theory."

"This bridge guard was a Mexican?"

"Uh, I believe that's correct."

"Typical," said Bullard. "If they were any dumber, they wouldn't be able to tie their own shoes. Or boots, or whatever they wear. Was there any video of this humvee?"

"No, not at the bridge, but we got something at the Lynnville FEMA camp. It's grainy, but it shows a Legion humvee driving north. State Road 13 goes right through the camp."

"I've been there. A Wal-Mart and a Home Depot are all fenced in."

"That's the place. The timeline fits the humvee that crossed the bridge. Nobody is claiming that vehicle, so we're assuming it was the one taken at the gas station in Carrolton. Apparently, on the video the three North American Legion stars are visible on the door, but you can't make out any numbers. The film was shot on the old Home Depot system, so they were able to access it at headquarters." Bullard's assistant didn't need to mention that digital surveillance video from all of the national chain stores was fed into federal law enforcement channels in real time. This had been the case for years.

"Home Depot? And that's it? That's the only video?"

"That's the only video that's been located so far. If that humvee was the same one that crossed the bridge, it could be the same group that killed the Legion soldiers in Carrolton, and working backwards—"

"I know. The Nigerians, and the Kazaks in Radford County."

"Yes sir."

"Damn." Bullard stared out the SUV's side window as they passed row after row of semi-derelict desert-tan Army trucks, parked behind chain link fences on vast motor pool lots.

Sinclair said, "This group would appear not to be your average rebel insurgents. These are not just a few Billy Bobs with deer rifles."

Bullard grunted, but said nothing beyond "No shit." He was too busy pondering how these events might eventually be connected to his own personal involvement with the Kazak Battalion. This string of killings went back to Mannville, near the location of Saturday's massacre. On a map in his mind, Bullard visualized the line of connected dots. And now that line was pointing straight north, toward Fort Campbell. Why?

Besides the obscure black operation sometimes known as the Department of Rural Pacification, what other groups were stationed at Fort Campbell? Along with what remained of the 101st Airborne Division and a shitload of old trucks and helicopters, there were, notably, the Green Berets. He passed the brown brick two-story buildings belonging to the 5th Special Forces Group almost every day. Stationed there were a thousand super-patriotic and gung-ho overgrown Boy Scouts. Eagle Scouts. Eagle Scouts with machine guns and sniper rifles. Scouts who could cut your throat with one hand and sew you back up with the other. He saw them every day in their PT gear, jogging all over Fort Campbell in large and small groups.

If anybody could hijack a Kazak ASV and wipe out dozens of allied troops in a single killing spree, it was them—the goddamn Green Berets. Bullard didn't trust them any more than President Tambor did. They were more loyal to quaint but passé notions of "duty, honor, country" than they were to their own government, even during this time of exceptional national emergency. For this reason, they were virtually restricted to Fort

Campbell and their other bases, and given no missions inside the United States. The only time the Green Berets left Fort Campbell or Fort Bragg in uniform with weapons was when they were being flown halfway around the globe to third-world shit holes, on diplomatic photo-op tours. They were paid and kept on the government rolls primarily to keep them isolated and out of mischief.

Bob Bullard didn't believe in coincidences. That line of dots, punctuated at each stop with bloody corpses, was coming his way. He knew it. He had felt safe and secure, believing that the rural pacification program was effectively hidden deep within a gigantic federal reservation that was strictly off limits to the general public. But with this latest series of events, he felt his cloak of security disappearing like a morning mist under the hot sun.

"Sir? Sir?" His assistant had to repeat himself several times to get his boss's attention. "The Legion humvee, should we put out a BOLO alert? Should we have Predators search the area north of the Lynnville FEMA camp?"

"What? Oh, sure, do all that. And let's turn around. Let's go back to flight ops. We can send out for lunch." At headquarters in Building 1405, he could only listen to reports and wait passively while events unfolded around him. Bullard had little hope that they'd find the humvee or its crew of killers, but flight ops was where he could observe the situation in real time, and make things happen like God Almighty Himself. It might even be time to drop a little something on Colonel Burgut, who still knew far too much, even if he had bulldozed the ravine.

24

Their contact arrived in the mid-afternoon. They heard three distinct clangs of metal on metal, a pause, and then two more. The fugitives had changed to their civilian outer garments. Their packs and weapons had been made ready for a swift departure hours before. Boone said, "I have to go outside now. They have to see me first, or they'll just take off. That's how this is done here." He was wearing jeans and his long parka with the commercial hunting camo pattern, concealing his combat vest. He left the trailer and disappeared back through the metal fence around the junkyard. Five minutes later, he returned.

"Okay, everybody grab your stuff. This is it. Our ride is up by the front of the junkyard in the bus shed. Tony, you're staying here. This is your lucky day, LT; you're going to be traded for some of our own prisoners. Just relax and wait, somebody else will be along to collect you." The lieutenant's hands were bound securely to the steel-framed arms of the kitchen chair with clothesline; his knees and ankles were tied to the legs. Boone stuck a wide X of gray duct tape over his mouth and draped a blue pillowcase over his head and shoulders. "Sit tight, LT. Just a little while longer here, and then you'll be moved to a better safehouse. You'll stay there until your transfer can be arranged."

Boone guided them through the stacked rows of junk vehicles to a barn-sized gray sheet-metal building. The junkyard gave every appearance of having been abandoned. If anybody was around the acres of old cars and trucks, they were staying completely out of sight and were making no sound. Boone told Carson and Doug that their contact was going to move the humvee to a better hiding place, somewhere else around the junkyard. How it would be disposed of after that, he didn't explain, and they didn't ask.

Their next ride was parked inside a metal shed big enough to hold several trucks or buses. Most of the building was taken up with shelves and tables loaded with alternators, car batteries, tires and other resalable items. In the open space in the middle was a medium-sized flatbed stake-side truck, loaded with old household appliances and workshop machinery. The truck looked to be at least thirty years old; the cab had once been painted olive drab. Military surplus. A man entered the shed through a back door about ten minutes later. Their nameless driver was a scrappy-looking fifty-something wearing green thermal coveralls. He had thick curly black hair running to gray, and a few days of gray stubble beard. The man was thick through the middle but solid, like a retired prizefighter. He was a few inches shorter than Carson and Dolan, but in every other way he was an imposing physical figure. No names or greetings were exchanged between any of the four men. On the faded green doors of the truck, "Dewey O. Liebermann, Tool and Salvage LLC" was hand-stenciled in white letters. Their driver seemed to size up the three fugitives presented before him.

"Well, at least two of you aren't frikkin' giants. My hidden compartment can only fit two regular-size people, if your gear and weapons are going in with you." He pointed to Phil Carson and Doug Dolan. "That'll be you two."

"We could hide inside your load," suggested Doug. "I could fit in that freezer, if there's an air hole. Or if I keep the door cracked open."

"Not a good idea, son. Soldiers and police almost always spot-check the cargo. It makes them feel like they're doing their job. It's the obvious place, so I never, ever hide anything there. No, you're going to have to squeeze into a little space under the cargo deck. You can't even see it from the outside; it's sort of an optical illusion. From the sides, it looks like there's only five inches of steel support frames under the bed, but it widens out to eight in the middle. The wooden cargo deck over it is fake too. It's carved out in the middle, and that gives almost another three inches. You have to shimmy in from underneath, and you'll have to unload some of your packs to flatten them out."

The driver looked Boone up and down. He said, "But that still leaves you with nowhere to hide. Hey, I've got it: you can be my idiot nephew today, the one that I bring along for heavy lifting. They might accept that you've got no papers if you're retarded. Hey, big fella, you ever do any acting? Think you can make out like you're a moron? Maybe deaf and dumb?"

Boone stared straight ahead, as if he had not heard.

"That's perfect; you'll ride up front with me. Okay, you two, in you go. Get under there, climb up over the drive shaft and slide in on your bellies like reptiles. Shove your packs and weapons in first. You can't turn over once you're inside, so decide now if you like it on your back or your stomach. You've got six feet by six feet by ten inches high in the middle. It'll work. That's it, put your stuff in first, and then climb up there and get comfy. Damn, that reminds me—did I ever get that exhaust leak fixed? Oh well, I guess I'll know when it's time to let you out."

After a few minutes of effort, Carson and Dolan were finally sealed into the smuggling compartment with the weapons and gear. Boone and the driver climbed up into the cab through both doors, grinned at one another, and shook hands warmly.

"Sergeant Gersham! Damn, it's good to see a familiar face!"

"Stick with Dewey. Get used to using my cover name, in case we're stopped and questioned. On the way up, we'll go over my legend, but hopefully you won't be expected to say anything at the checkpoints. Just act like the big lumbering retard that you are, and you'll do fine. Your hair is perfect—right out of *Deliverance*. Your cousins in Georgia would be *so* proud. Just be yourself. In other words, act normal."

"I should be able to manage that. So, what's up with the 'Dewey O. Liebermann'? I mean, aren't you taking a chance with that? You were always a wise-ass, but come on, *D.O.L.*?" Boone was referring to the initials of the Special Forces motto, "De Oppresso Liber," to liberate from oppression.

The driver laughed and said, "Hey, you need a sense of humor in this business." He didn't specify whether he was referring to the tool and salvage business, or the espionage and guerrilla warfare business. "Do you remember when I left active duty for a couple of years in the nineties? Well, I didn't really leave the service. That was Agency business the whole time. Anything else you heard was a lie, part of my cover for leaving the Army. They needed somebody with my languages and my, ah…other unique skills at The Agency."

"Christians In Action."

"Yep, you got it, *goyim*. South of the border, they call it *La Cia*."

"What do you speak, Arabic and Hebrew?"

"And Greek, and Turkish. And Farsi, also known as 'Arabic for complete idiots.' Oh, and French, Spanish and Italian, but they hardly count. Plus I can fake a few more."

"Weren't you raised over there somewhere?"

The driver backed the truck out of the shed, turned in a small parking area, and pulled onto State Road 13 heading north. Boone glanced at the rear view mirror extending out from his side of the cab: someone unseen was already closing the big doors to the metal building.

"My father worked for a shipping agency, and I mostly grew up between Athens and Alexandria. Then he worked for APL, the American President Line. I was a regular Mediterranean shipping line brat. I spent most of my early years on the docks and on ships. Languages became one of my hobbies. I collected them like postage stamps. I've got the knack; I can't explain it. They say I'm a savant, a human sponge for languages."

"If you don't mind my asking, with that kind of background, why didn't you go to college and become an officer?"

"Same reason as you, asshole. It just wasn't me. I was born to be a shooter, not a pencil-whipper. And who says I didn't go to college?"

"But what about the D.O.L. on the truck?" asked Boone. "There must be thousands of people around Fort Campbell that'll look at that name and wonder about the initials."

"You caught that right away, huh? I guess you're smarter than you look. Well, Dewey Liebermann wouldn't be my first choice if I were choosing a new alias now, that's for sure, but I'm kind of stuck with it. Here's how it happened. While I was working for the Agency, they sent me to some, ah, *interesting* schools. One course covered creating identities from scratch. 'Working legends,' they call them. I made a few on the side, just for the hell of it. Outside class, on my own, using what I learned. One of them was Dewey Liebermann. I thought it was kind of funny at the time. It was the only one of my homemade legends that I kept up over the years. I always figured I might wind up on the run someday, and a new ID would be a good thing to have on the shelf. Anyway, Dewey Liebermann had the best backstops and paper trail."

"But who needs to know Dewey Liebermann's middle initial? You could at least drop the 'O' on the truck."

"Now, what fun would that be?" said the driver. "Anyway, the people who 'get it,' I don't have to worry about. And the people I worry about won't get it in a million years."

"Sergeant—" Boone pronounced the rank the Army way, without the 'g.' "Sar'nt."

"Stick with 'Dewey.' Get used to saying it, in case we're stopped and your deaf-and-dumb act doesn't hold up. I've been out for seven years, and you probably outrank me by now anyway."

"Okay, 'Dewey.' What happened to our prisoner, back in the trailer? The Legion lieutenant. After we left."

The driver sighed, grimaced and slowly shook his head. "I was afraid you were going to ask. I won't bullshit you, Boone. Yeah, I shot him. Well, what did you expect, leaving him like that? He was too hot, he was radioactive as hell. He might have led to my whole network being rolled up and wiped out. It's shaky enough as it is, without taking chances. People's lives are at stake, and they depend on me. Anyway, I've got nobody in this area who could have looked after him, and I sure couldn't just let him go. Don't worry, there won't be any blowback. Your hummer and the lieutenant are both going to disappear. I do have somebody who can at least take care of that for me. By tonight, that hummer and the lieutenant will be gone from the planet. Poof—erased. There won't be a screw or a fingernail left. Guaranteed."

The road had almost no traffic as it wound up and down gentle rural hills. On a straight section, the driver pulled an unlabeled pint bottle of clear liquid from the map pocket in his door. "I pass these out to guards at checkpoints. The Mexican troops understand *la mordida*. You know, friendly little bribes. Being a loveable drunk is part of my *schtick*. How can a friendly drunk have evil intentions? They could give a shit less about my drinking and driving—hell, that's a Mexican tradition. It's just an act anyway...sort of. Yeah, they're always glad to see Dewey Liebermann's truck coming—the bottles are small enough to slip into the leg pockets of their uniforms. And that's no accident."

He unscrewed the cap and took a deep pull of the local corn whisky. "You know, Boone, I'm glad I didn't have time to get to know your lieutenant. I did it quick. He didn't see it coming, and I didn't have time to think about it too much. I was leading him from the trailer with a rope leash tied to his hands. He thought he was going back to the hummer. That's what I told him. I told him I kept the sack on his head because I didn't want him to see me, so he couldn't identify me later. That gave him some hope, right at the end. Anyway, thanks for leaving him with a sack over his head. I don't need another one visiting me at oh-dark-thirty. I've already got too goddamn many ghosts running around my head as it is." The curly-haired driver took another drink.

"How was he, on his way out?" Boone asked this in a hushed voice, staring ahead at the pastoral countryside. The last traces of snow were almost gone, except for a few north-facing slopes.

The driver sighed again, exhaling slowly. "Oh, he was almost sobbing, kind of choking up, but he couldn't talk since you left him gagged. I think he cheered up just a little right at the end, when I told him why I didn't want him seeing my face. I hope so. But the truth is...I didn't want to see *his* face." The driver took another swig of the corn liquor, looked out the left window, and handed the bottle across to his passenger without turning to face him.

Boone took his own long drink of the burning liquid. After coughing and clearing his throat, he said, "I didn't mean to stick that job on you. I would have done it myself, but the young guy in the back had a big problem with the idea. Doug's okay, but he's touchy about shooting prisoners. He's sensitive that way. He actually wanted me to let the lieutenant go. Just let him go, if he promised to leave Tennessee and go home to Texas. Can you imagine? Doug has a good heart...too good for this kind of work. He's just a draftee, an engineering soldier from Fort Leonard Wood. He never wanted any of this. I picked him up as a stray after the second earthquake. He does his best, he really does. He went through some seriously bad shit after the quakes, and, well, I thought it would be good if he could believe that the lieutenant was going to be kept alive. He'll sleep better, thinking that. That's worth something, right? Why put this heavy shit on him? So thanks for taking care of it for me."

Boone took another long drink, the burning whisky gurgling down, leaving the pint more than half empty. "Sar'nt...this part of it is something that I really hate. I don't mind killing them in anger, hell, I enjoy it sometimes, and I'll admit it. You should have seen us last night; man, we just tore them up! But I hate getting to know them first. Up close, face to face, that's the worst. Sometimes it's hard for me not to just get drunk and stay drunk, with some of the things I remember. Mannville, oh my God...that's going to stick with me. Here, you better put this shit away." He handed the pint bottle back to the driver.

"Boone, I understand, completely. But it's hard enough just staying alive in this business, without the added complication of prisoners. How did you guys wind up taking a prisoner anyway?"

"It was just this morning, right before dawn. The old guy in the back, I sent him to the gas station in Carrolton to get a switch car from the owner. I had hooks in the owner, but I can't walk into that town anymore. So I sent in a stranger, an old guy who looks fairly harmless. The old guy is Phil Carson, and let me tell you, he's anything but harmless. He's former SF. He was with SOG in Vietnam, but he got out after the war. Still sharp as a tack, though. Hell of an operator; you'd never guess he's over sixty. My father knew him back in the day. They went over the fence in the same recon team a few times, can you imagine? What are the odds? He's legit, he checks out. He's one of us.

"So anyway, he's in the garage in Carrolton this morning at dawn, when that NAL hummer rolled in to gas up. He had to take them out with my suppressed Glock. Two soldiers and the garage owner. Then we used the lieutenant as our driver, to get through security at the 214 bridge. He was going to be our talker, but it didn't come to that. We were in NAL uniforms, just like the lieutenant. Well, our uniforms, but with NAL badges and insignias. Carson took the patches from the guys he shot in the garage. He even grabbed a blue beret and wore it to cross the bridge. Like I said, he's sharp. Great situational awareness. Great attention to detail under pressure. Too bad he quit Special Forces after Vietnam...but I can understand why he did. The Army was fubar after Vietnam, according to my father. It was a real bad time for the military. Terrible morale. The media just totally made people hate the military."

The driver grinned and looked across at his passenger. "You were wearing a NAL uniform? Somehow I can't see Boone Vikersun passing for a Mexican. Not even if you shaved the beard and got a haircut."

"Nah, I was in my civvies, in the back seat. I played the gringo prisoner in that deal. But with my Glock behind my back, instead of handcuffs."

"That was your hummer behind me at the checkpoint coming out of Carrolton, wasn't it?"

"Yeah. Small world, huh? I didn't even know that you were getting across the river into Western Tennessee. The junkyard was the closest pickup point that I knew about."

"You're lucky I had some business south of here today, otherwise I would have gone straight back to Clarksville, and I would have missed your signal by the road."

"Business?" Boone smiled and raised an eyebrow.

The driver laughed again. "Just machine tools. I'm 99 percent legit. Well, maybe 95 percent...on a good day. Anyway, I just started crossing the river. Extending my territory. The tool and appliance salvage business is doing great. It's a good cover. I get around, I talk to people."

"What are you hearing, if you don't mind my asking?"

"Right now I'm hearing that resistance in Western Tennessee is just about wiped out. It's almost fully 'pacified.' You know, it's kind of a shitty paradox, but the worse it is for the resistance, the better it is for my cover business. Hey, Boone, I heard some pretty bad things are happening down around Radford County. That's why you're coming out?"

"No, not exactly. I'd stay, but yesterday I took some important pictures, seriously important pictures. I had no way to upload them, and nobody to give them to. That's why I left. The pictures have to get out."

"Tell me about them."

"Okay. Here's what happened. I've been using Mannville as my forward operating base. Well, on Saturday, the Kazak Battalion rolled in and pulled a My Lai Massacre, I shit you not. They rounded everybody up that they could grab at the swap market, drove them out of town on school buses, and shot them in a big gully. If I hadn't been on a job down on the Mississippi state line, I might have been bagged too. I found out about it from a survivor, and I managed to get over there and snap some pictures. That's why I'm coming out—I need to get these pictures to somebody that's in a position to use them. But I don't know who. Not yet."

"That's a problem."

"No shit." Boone wanted to ask the retired Special Forces NCO whom he was working for, and what kind of network (if any) was being set up in Middle and Western Tennessee, but such questions were out of bounds. Information of that nature would be provided only if and when there was a need for him to know it. All he had known of any nascent network was the bare bones of the evacuation ratline, and the emergency pickup point in the trailer behind the junkyard. Even that had been very doubtful. He'd had no idea that Sergeant Gersham was involved, until he had shown up. "I was right there, Sar'nt, right at the massacre site. Right fucking there, walking on frozen bodies, taking pictures and collecting IDs. Men, women and children. The bodies were still fresh, dead in the snow."

The driver said, "A massacre, huh? I heard there was some kind of a battle going on down there. The Kazaks did it, you said? How many are dead?"

"Yeah, the Cossacks. They killed hundreds. Hundreds for sure. The killed women and children, the whole nine yards. After the massacre, they started torching every house they could get to. They're depopulating Radford County the hard way, killing some and running the rest down into Mississippi. I got some payback on the Cossacks last night, but not nearly enough."

"I'm sorry to hear about Mannville. That's where you're from, isn't it?"

"Near there, but my family moved out of Tennessee a long time ago."

"Well, thank God for that, anyway. A massacre..." The driver paused, thinking. "Boone, you're right, those could be some important pictures. If they're doing massacres, then they're taking this dirty war to another level. But if we use jiu-jitsu on them, we might be able to turn it around. I hate to sound so crass, but those pictures could be valuable for our side. Those pictures might be the ace that turns a bad hand into a winner."

"I thought so too. At least the people who were murdered won't have died for nothing. But only if we can do something with the pictures."

"Boone, I don't know how to explain this other than pure luck, or serendipity or synchronicity or whatever they call it, but us hooking up like this...this might actually work out. You know what they say—things happen for a reason. It's another hour up to C-ville, and then we're going to lay up at another safehouse for a few hours until dark." Clarksville was a small city of 100,000 just outside Fort Campbell, and home to a large number of active duty and former Special Forces and other specops soldiers. Forty miles northwest of Nashville, Clarksville was friendly territory, if such a place could be said to exist for the rebels in Tennessee. "We'll change vehicles again on the way up, after we cross one more NAL security checkpoint. When we get to the safehouse, you guys can get cleaned up and grab a hot meal. Then we'll see what we can do with your pictures. There are some people...well, I'll tell you more about that later. You know, this *might* just work out for the best."

"It might," said Boone, "if a Predator's not eyeballing us right now, while they decide whether a truck full of rebels is worth a Hellfire, or just a Viper."

"Yeah, it sure sucks, living under the sword of Damocles 24/7. But what else can you do? Just quit? Sell out, and turn traitor? I can't. I can't do it."

"I can't either."

"Maybe we'll stay lucky," said the driver.

"I hope so. The pictures I took might actually make a difference in this shitty little war. We've got nothing else going for us that I can see."

As they drove up State Road 13, Lieutenant Malverde's handsome young face slipped into Boone's consciousness, hovering somewhere just in front of the truck's windshield. Doug Dolan whispered in his mind's ear, "*We're not murderers…we're not murderers…*"

Oh, yes we are too. Boone wished that he hadn't handed back the bottle of white lightning. He'd drain that sucker, just to get rid of Doug's condemnatory words and Lieutenant Malverde's sad, doomed face, his eyes already lifeless as the duct tape X was applied. Well, Boone thought (searching for absolution but finding none), you can't expect to keep your hands clean, not if you're going to fight a dirty war.

A dirty civil war, with foreign enemies and traitors.

A quick phone call would be all right, thought Doug. Tennessee to Maryland wasn't so far, and it was after six in the evening. It was a stroke of luck that he had found the cell phone in a kitchen junk drawer, and that it was actually getting a signal. Finally he was catching a break, and managing to turn lemons into lemonade.

They had arrived at the new safehouse in the late afternoon. It was in an isolated hollow surrounded by thick woods. Doug was happy just to squirm out of the cramped hiding place under the salvage truck. The secret compartment's bottom and sides were ice cold metal and had left him shivering with hypothermia. The new place wasn't much more than a cabin, but it had a cast-iron stove and plenty of firewood, so they had all been able to get warm, wash up, and enjoy a hot meal. After being locked with Phil into the frigid metal box for several hours, unable even to turn over, the cozy cabin was paradise. He'd eaten four steaming hot baked potatoes, slathered with fresh farm butter, and couldn't remember ever eating anything tastier or more filling in his life.

Their driver and host, "Dewey," was a mysterious sort of person. Doug knew his name only from what was written on the doors of his junk truck. In age he fit somewhere between Boone and Carson, but like both of those men, he seemed a lot tougher than his years would indicate. Doug guessed that Dewey Lieberman was not his real name, but he'd had few opportunities to talk with the man. Dewey's conversations with Boone and Carson stopped short or shifted to some innocuous topic when he was around. Dewey left the cabin in his big truck, and returned after dark with an ordinary compact car. Again, he conferred quietly with Boone and Carson, but always out of Doug's earshot. I've been traveling and operating with Boone for months, he thought, and two days after Carson shows up, I'm cut out of his conversations. Then Boone announced—not discussed, announced—that they had somewhere to go tonight. They, not him. Not Doug Dolan. No, good old faithful Doug would remain behind to…what?

Guard the isolated cabin? "Hold down the fort"? Boone and Carson left with Dewey after nightfall.

So who could blame him for his curiosity, after they had ditched him and left him behind? His natural inquisitiveness about the new safehouse had led him to discover the forgotten cell phone. It was inside a small metal box, buried beneath pliers, screwdrivers and scissors. He was actually shocked when he pushed the power button and it lit up, and he stared at its glowing screen in wonder for a long time. It was the first working cell phone that he had touched since before the earthquakes, one very long year ago. It was a prepaid phone, showing 138 minutes remaining.

A few minutes on the phone were all he needed, and nobody would ever know. Who counted a few airtime minutes on an old cell phone left in a drawer? Nobody, Doug was sure. Not even these days. Boone had left him behind at the cabin safehouse, and that had been a blow to his pride. Was it because they didn't trust him, or because they just didn't need him? Well, Doug rationalized, at least the unexpected privacy will give me a chance to make the one phone call that I've been anxious to make for so many months. He punched in the long-memorized Baltimore number, and miraculously, after clicks, buzzing and dead air pauses, he heard the phone ringing at the other end. After six or seven rings, it was picked up. The call had gone through, and his heart soared in anticipation.

"Mom! Mom, it's me!"

But instead of his mother's voice, Doug heard music, and a man answered, but Doug couldn't understand what he was saying. A man? What was a strange man doing at his mother's house, answering the phone?

"Hello, who's this?" asked Doug. "Where is Mrs. Dolan?"

The phone was dropped with a bang. Long seconds later, somebody else picked it up, a female voice. "*Holá*, hallo! Who ees?"

"This is Doug—Doug Dolan! Listen, where's my mother? Where is Mrs. Dolan?"

"Meesees Do-lane? You ees Meesees Do-lane?"

"No, no! I'm Doug Dolan, Mrs. Dolan's son! Please, is *Mrs.* Dolan there?"

"Meesees Do-lane? *Un minuto*, please. I getting Meesees Do-lane, okay?"

Doug waited, perplexed and more than a bit worried. Who were the people who had answered the phone at his mother's house? He could make out the music now; it was some kind of fast Latin salsa or Mexican ranchera music.

After a minute, he finally heard his mother's voice. "Hello, who is this?" she asked.

"Mom, it's me, Doug!"

"Douglas? Douglas—you're alive! Oh my goodness, oh thank God, you're alive! They told me that you were missing and presumed dead in Tennessee, after the earthquakes! But you're alive! Oh, thank God, thank God! Douglas, can you come home? When can you come home? Oh, I *need* you here, Douglas, I need you! Where are you? When can you come home?"

"I don't know Mom; things are a little crazy right now. Just as soon as I can, I will. I promise. Mom, who answered the phone? I heard a man, and then a woman came on the line. Who are they?"

"Oh Doug, I have *so* much to tell you! *So* much has happened since you left!"

"Mom, who are those people who just answered the phone?"

"Doug, that's the Sanchorios family; they're originally from El Salvador."

"*El Salvador*? What are they doing in *our* house?"

"They *live* here now, Douglas, they *live* here!"

"What?!"

"The government split our house up into apartments after I couldn't pay the vacant room tax. Then they had the Sanchorios family move in upstairs. They were living in Nashville, but their apartment building was wrecked in the earthquakes. They were earthquake refugees."

"Mom, what do you mean, 'vacant room tax'?"

"What? Oh, it's new since last year. A new law. The property tax appraiser said that I had too many bedrooms for just one person to be living here. Too many square feet, there's a formula. Since I couldn't pay the vacant room tax, I had to take in boarders, boarders that the state assigned to live here. That's what they do now."

Doug tried to make sense of it. Vacant room tax? Boarders? From El Salvador? "Do they pay you rent?"

"No, not to me. That's why I have boarders. It's instead of paying the vacant room tax. They waived the tax since I've taken in refugees. The state assigned them to live here. They get to live here for free. Their son joined that new army, the North American Legion, so they have priority on housing. Oh Doug, it's just unbearable!"

"Where are they living? How many are there?" Doug was stunned, coming to grips with the unexpected news about their home being subdivided by the state.

"They live upstairs. I can't keep track of how many there are; they come and go at all hours. There's usually at least seven or eight of them, not counting babies. I think they're subletting the rooms upstairs, but I can't tell who's who. It seems like they change practically every week, except for the Sanchorios family. We all share the kitchen, but I'm too afraid to go in there when they're around. I sleep in the sitting room next to the living room, that's my 'apartment' now. The sitting room and the living room, and the downstairs bathroom, that's where I live. I cook on a hot plate, when the electricity is working. Oh, Douglas, when are you coming home?"

"I can't now Mom, but I will as soon as I can, I promise."

"Douglas, they won't even let me use the upstairs bathroom, so I have to wash in the sink in the first-floor bathroom. Oh, and the kitchen is ruined, just ruined! I don't even *know* what the second floor looks like; they won't let me come upstairs, but water is dripping through the ceiling and the plaster is falling down. They drink beer and yell and play their music so loud all night that I can't sleep. They park their cars on the lawn, and the grass all died, it's just dirt now. The men even *pee* outside! When I say anything, they just laugh in my face and call me '*la brooha blanca*,' I think that means the white witch. They laugh at me and say, '*su casa es mi casa*.' They curse at me and throw things at me, *in my own house*!" Mrs. Dolan began to sob.

"Mom, you should go to the police, this isn't right!"

"But I *did* go to the authorities, Douglas, I did! I had a lawyer file complaints. But Doug, the world is upside down now! They got a free court-appointed lawyer, and *they* sued *me* for 'harassment and ethnic discrimination'! The state was going to charge me with *hate crimes*, and I almost lost the house completely! Then *I* had to apologize to *them*, in court! I was never so humiliated in my entire life! The judge said I was lucky that I had boarders, since I couldn't pay the vacant room tax. Lucky, he said I was! I even had to go to a 'cultural sensitivity' class, to get *rehabilitated*! Rehabilitated! Oh Doug, what am I going to do? What am I going to do?" His mother began sobbing again.

"I don't know, Mom, I don't know. But I'll come home as soon as I can. I've got some problems with the Army, so it might not be for a while, but I'll try at least to visit in a couple of weeks. Hang in there, Mom! I'll help you the best that I can, as soon as I can get there."

Doug heard a man's loud voice in the background, and then his mother said quietly, "I've got to hang up. Mr. Sanchorios needs to use the phone now, so I have to go. Goodbye, Douglas. I love you, and I'm so happy to know that you're alive! Goodbye, Douglas..."

25

Charlie Donelson lived with his Filipina wife, Bibi, in a middle-class subdivision near Clarksville. Eight close friends and colleagues had been invited over on an undisclosed matter of grave importance. Half had already arrived. Each had been given a different ten-minute arrival window in order for the meeting to keep a low profile. They had electrical power in the house tonight, but without working streetlights, the only outside illumination came from the moon. One man was out front as security, wearing night vision goggles while sitting in a parked car with tinted windows. The guests parked randomly on different streets, several blocks apart. As they approached on foot, the security man called the house on a low-powered encrypted radio, using innocuous brevity codes. The guests walked around to the fenced backyard of the house and entered from the rear, to avoid a constant spectacle at the front door that might have been noticed by a neighbor.

While they waited for the rest of the invitees to arrive, Sergeant Major Donelson, Chief Warrant Officer 4 Rogan and the others sat in the den, chatting and reminiscing. Bibi had carried in plates of red rice and pork for those who had not eaten, but otherwise she stayed out of sight. Rogan had brought over a wooden crate holding twenty oversized bottles of his home-brewed beer. A fire crackled in the stone hearth of the wood-paneled den. The television was on in the background, but with the sound off. Donelson occasionally flipped through the news channels, looking for any mention of events in West Tennessee—in particular, around Radford County or the town of Mannville. The massacre had occurred on Saturday, he had seen the Predator video on Sunday, and still there had not been a hint of anything going wrong in the state.

Then an outline map of Tennessee appeared on CBA News, with concentric circles like a bull's-eye drawn over the southwestern part of the state. The graphic had been frequently used since the earthquakes, when they had conveyed the epicenters and zones of damage. "Shut up, everybody! I want to hear this," said Donelson, unmuting the sound. They were ten minutes into the national news when the anchor said that they were going to "preview a story from the Tennessee recovery effort that will warm your hearts and fill you with hope." He explained that an expanded version of the new story was going to be replayed at nine o'clock, as part of an update to their award-winning documentary, "*American Shame.*"

Hugh Rogan said, "It's just CBA News, why bother? They couldn't tell the truth to save their lives. They wouldn't even know how. The news hasn't been worth a damn since FOX lost its broadcasting license, and they got rid of talk radio." Rogan's voice was always recognizable because of his lingering New York accent.

"I know, but look, it's about Tennessee. We should still pay attention."

"Charlie, they've run that 'American Shame' documentary at least ten times. They're just whipping up the hatred against white conservatives. I've had enough of that already. I don't need to hear it again. I already know what they'll say. 'Evil white men raped the planet, stomp on kittens and hate their mothers'."

"This part is new—shut up already!"

The half-dozen men sitting and standing in the den turned toward the television in the corner. A very pretty brunette reporter was standing in a medical office interviewing a handsome man with a thick mustache and gold-rimmed glasses. The man was around forty years old, wearing a doctor's white lab coat, which was open at the front over a camouflage uniform. A black stethoscope was slung casually around his neck. In appearance, he could have been Geraldo Rivera's younger brother. Large windows behind the two revealed that they were on the ground floor of a low building arranged around a central courtyard. The plaza was open at the other end; military trucks could be seen driving in and out. Soldiers wearing camouflage uniforms and blue NAL berets were carrying boxes and equipment from other trucks parked on the side of the street.

The reporter faced the camera holding her microphone and said, "I'm Linda Veneno-Radburn for CBA News, in Bolivar, Tennessee. Today, the public health clinic and emergency hospital is reopening, one year after the second New Madrid earthquake. I'm joined today by Dr. Hernan Cortez Arrasando, who has been leading the effort to bring basic health services back to a very hard-hit region of Western Tennessee." She turned from the camera to face the doctor. She was wearing tight black pants, and a cream-colored sweater that accentuated her figure. Her long brown hair was tied back in a ponytail.

"Thank you, Linda," he said with a toothy smile.

"Doctor Arrasando, this must be quite an exciting day for you!" The reporter pronounced the double-R in his last name with an exaggerated Spanish tongue roll, firmly establishing her Latina identity for any viewers who might have wondered.

The doctor had a slight Mexican accent. "Oh yes, Linda, it's been a very gratifying experience for all of us, especially today. Thank you so much for having us on CBA News, so that we can show all of North America the results of our many weeks of hard work. Beginning today, we're providing medical services and emergency care to a part of Western

Tennessee that was badly affected by the earthquakes. Most of the people who live in this area haven't seen a doctor in more than a year! There is a great deal of need, and we're anxious to get to work. Especially for the sake of the children, who are really the innocent victims here."

"Dr. Arrasando, I understand that you're not a local, that in fact you've come a very long way to help. I'm told that you're from Mexico City, and that you have your own successful private practice there. How did you come to be serving the people of Western Tennessee?"

"Well Linda, in my case, this story goes all the way back to 1985. I was a young boy living in Mexico City when we were hit by our own very powerful series of earthquakes. I remember the help that our North American neighbors provided to us in our time of need. So when the New Madrid earthquakes struck this region last year and I saw all of the terrible devastation and suffering on television, I just knew that I had to do something. I had to do something to express my gratitude for all of the help we received from the American volunteers back in 1985. That's when I learned that the North American Legion was accepting volunteers for their new medical corps. As soon as I could, I left my practice and accepted a commission in the Legion. Joining the North American Legion was the best way that I could help the people whose lives were so terribly affected by the earthquakes. And to be able to serve in a town named for the great liberator Simon Bolivar, well, of course that just makes this experience *so* much more rewarding for me."

CW4 Rogan stood, pointed at the TV and blurted out, "This is bullshit! Look at that! Look at those trees there, see? Past the trucks, outside that little quad."

"What? What are you talking about?" asked one of the men.

"The leaves! Half of the leaves are still on those trees! They're red and yellow, but hell, the leaves have been off the trees in Tennessee for at least a month. And look: some of those soldiers have their sleeves rolled up! You ever see Mexicans rolling their sleeves up when it's this cold out? So either this bullshit propaganda video was made a long time ago or it was made somewhere else, but it sure as hell wasn't made in Tennessee today. No, they've had this film in the can, just waiting for the right day to play it. Either that, or they filmed it in Texas or somewhere else."

"So CBA News is lying," said Donelson. "What else is new? Are you really surprised?"

"No, I guess not," said Rogan, dropping back into his chair. "It's CBA News. Maybe I'm still just a little surprised that they're working with the government to run straight-out bullshit propaganda. I mean, they have to know that this video is at least a month old, but they're claiming it was shot just today. Either that, or they know it wasn't filmed in Tennessee. Either way, it's bullshit. It's just a government propaganda infomercial. Linda Radburn is a real CBA reporter, so CBA is in on the scam. I mean, this is like the news in Russia or China! I wonder if CBA found an actor to play the doctor and *they* produced it, or if the government did, and they just got Linda to play along?"

"What's the difference anymore?" asked CW4 Rogan. "The corporations that own the TV networks are basically owned by the government, ever since the trillion-dollar bailouts. Like my grandma used to say, 'He who pays the piper calls the tune'."

"Hold it a second, mute the television." Donelson pulled a small walkie-talkie out of his shirt pocket, answered it and then turned to Rogan with an update. "Mark says Ira's here; he made it. But he says Ira has two strap hangers with him. Mark says he stopped them, since he wasn't expecting to see three guys at once."

Rogan said, "Aw hell, this is getting out of control! How can we pull this off and maintain opsec if people are bringing friends? Who does Ira have with him?"

"Wait a second..." Donelson whispered into the radio, and listened to the answer. "Boone Vikersun, and some guy Boone says used to be in Special Forces. What do you think?"

CW4 Rogan asked, "Charlie, you know Boone Vikersun pretty good, don't you? You were both in the 1st Battalion, right? What do *you* think?"

One of their other guests, a black man in his thirties who had been listening intently, said, "Master Sergeant Boone Vikersun? The Viking? I know him *real* good. He was the ops sergeant in my ODA on our last tour in the sandbox. Hell yeah, let him in! Old Boone, he went over the wire last year. He split, he went AWOL from the Group with an SR-25. Oh, he's been in the deep shit, I just know it! I can't wait to see that crazy bastard and find out what he's been up to. Oh hell yeah, tell Mark to send Boone and his friend around back." Despite the cold outside, the black soldier was wearing a tight green Special Forces T-shirt over blue jeans, emphasizing his body-builder's sculptured physique.

"Are you sure?" asked Rogan. "What about the other guy?"

The black man said, "If he's with Boone and Ira, then he's okay. Ira Hayes Gersham and Boone Vikersun! Damn, now we're talking!"

Donelson spoke into the radio, and in a minute the three were led into the den via the back door and kitchen. The men were all standing, exchanging animated greetings and hearty handshakes. Several of them playfully grabbed Boone's shoulder-length dirty blond hair. He was easily the tallest man in the room, and with his wild hair and beard and flashing blue eyes, he really did give the appearance of a Viking raider.

Cold bottles of beer were thrust into the newcomers' hands. Phil Carson was introduced to the men by Boone, who vetted his Special Forces credentials and his unquestionable trustworthiness. A lingering air of reservation seemed to hover around the stranger, so Boone made a point of mentioning that Carson had served with his father in the same SOG Recon Team. This recounting of history seemed to raise Carson above doubt. The men were just naturally suspicious; it was an ingrained part of their makeup not to trust a recently met outsider.

The last visitors arrived soon after, including one man they all addressed as colonel, until he told them to knock it off, he was just Tom tonight. This seemed difficult for the men, who continued to refer to him as colonel or awkwardly as Mr. Spencer. The colonel was another six-footer, in his late forties, with a regulation military haircut that was gray on the sides.

Twelve men were finally assembled in the den; they ranged in age from their mid-thirties to Phil Carson at over sixty. They were all active duty, reserve or retired Special Forces operators, or members of the 160th Special Operations Aviation Regiment. They had been trying to continue their lives as normally as possible on Fort Campbell and around Clarksville, while Boone Vikersun had "gone operational" in resisting the foreign occupiers. They listened with rapt attention as Boone described his recent experiences in West Tennessee. They were particularly amazed by his recounting of their hijacking of the Kazak ASV, their pursuit, and their instigation of a running gun battle between the Kazak and Nigerian peacekeepers.

Carson noted that the other men called their driver "Ira." Nobody asked how Boone and Carson had managed to come to the meeting in Ira's company. Carson listened carefully, but nobody in the room called Ira by any other name. He assumed Dewey Lieberman was an alias, based on the initials D.O.L. from the name on his truck. The initials were an obvious coded reference to the Special Forces, but Carson had not mentioned it and Boone had not brought it up. Ira's cover as a salvage hauler and his operation of a clandestine evacuation network was never mentioned by the men in the room. Carson was left to wonder if the other men knew about Ira's secret work.

Except for the muscular black soldier wearing a T-shirt, the men in the room were all dressed in a variety of boots or running shoes, jeans and windbreakers or parkas. Loose, bulky clothes, which could conceal serious weaponry. He could only guess who among them in the room was on active duty and who was retired, mostly judging by the length and grayness of their hair. They ranged from super-fit to somewhat physically gone to seed. Most appeared to Carson to be NCOs, but guessing at ranks was always a dubious undertaking. He heard someone call their host Sergeant Major, and another man who arrived after them had been greeted as Colonel Spencer.

Apparently, rumors about the Kazak-Nigerian firefight were already floating around the local Special Forces community. Carson heard them asking Boone, "So you started this fight between the Cossacks and the Nigerians? You got the Kazaks to chase you through a Nigerian forward operating base? That's how it went down? That's just awesome, man! Talk about a force multiplier—you guys practically started a war!"

A pint bottle of dark beer clutched in his hand, Boone couldn't help gloating a bit, but he was happy to share the credit with Carson. "This old man here was driving that ASV like a maniac on crack. I was just shooting up the countryside with the turret guns, until I ran out of ammo and fired off the smokes. I swear, I think he killed more Cossacks and Nigerians by running them down than I got with the forty-millimeter and the fifty-cal combined. I could hardly hold a sight picture, the way that ASV was knocking them down and rolling over their bodies." Bottles were raised and clinked in toast, and both Boone and Carson were subjected to congratulatory backslaps and arm punches, amidst broad grins and mock salutes.

It was Charlie Donelson's house, so he finally addressed them as a group to bring the meeting to order, redirecting them back from the rising locker room victory atmosphere. "All right, listen up. I think everybody's here who's coming. I know you're wondering what this is all about, aside from Boone's homecoming—which was a surprise to me too. What's the urgency? What's up with the dispersed arrivals, and the Sneaky Pete back-door routine? Just watch the computer screen, and you'll find out. That's why you're all here—to see a Predator video. It was taken over Radford County on Saturday. Get in close, and pay attention."

"Where's Radford County?" asked one of the men as they gathered by the computer desk.

Boone answered him. "It's southeast of Jackson, down near the Mississippi state line. That's in West Tennessee, on the other side of the river. That was my area of operations. I'm guessing that this video was taken outside a town called Mannville."

"How the hell did you know that?" asked Rogan in surprise. "Have you seen it already? Damn! And I thought we had the only copy."

"No, I haven't seen the video; I didn't even know there *was* a video. But I think I know where it was shot, because if it's a video of the same thing—I was there. Right there. I even took pictures, and that's why *I'm* here. Charlie, have you got a cable that can jack this camera into your computer? After we see the video, I'll show you my pictures. I'll bet it's of the same thing." He handed his silver digital camera to the sergeant major, since it was his house and his computer.

The muscular black NCO said, "Boone Vikersun was *there*! I should have known. Tell us about it, Boone, go ahead, tell us about it while we get your pictures loaded."

"No, let's see the video already!" said another. "Boone can narrate it if he knows what went down."

And that's what they did. Sergeant Major Donelson clicked the mouse and played the Predator video. The condensed ten-minute film looped continuously while the visitors watched in stunned silence, their cheerful camaraderie blown away by its grim content. Even seen from 15,000 feet up, there was no question about what had taken place in Radford County. The mounted horse troops, with their infrared lights blinking Kilo in Morse code, left no doubt as to the identity of the perpetrators. Hundreds of civilians were rounded up, put onto buses, driven away and shot, fifty or more at a time in a remote gully. Afterward, they showed Boone's still photos, his color close-ups from the massacre, in their gory, frozen detail. There were over twenty sharp digital pictures on his camera, and the silent men watched them all in a slide show that played through several times.

The black NCO pointed to a dead Kazak soldier on the computer screen. He was lying on his back wearing the Russian-style camouflage uniform, among the civilian corpses dusted in snow. "I don't understand. You were there during the massacre? How did you…"

"No," said Boone, "I took these pictures at dawn on Sunday morning. Yesterday. The massacre happened on Saturday afternoon. Saturday night I got intel about it from a survivor, an eyewitness. So I was there doing photo recon Sunday morning when three Cossacks showed up to loot the bodies. I was hiding right where they were bound to trip over me, so I had to kill them first. I hid their bodies after I finished taking these pictures for proof."

The black NCO's eyes were welling up. "You were down there fighting. You were fighting, while we…while we…" He couldn't finish the sentence.

Hugh Rogan, the Warrant Officer 4 helicopter pilot, said, "That blue Eurocopter—I know I've seen that helo. It's from here. It operates out of the back of Campbell Field, the old air strip. The restricted end."

"Is that the Building 1405 crowd?" asked Colonel Spencer.

"I don't know, but I can sure find out," said Rogan. "What's the tail number? Can we see the tail number in that picture?"

After they had watched the Predator film and seen the photos multiple times and heard Boone's story, the now very angry men talked randomly and chaotically, venting their pent-up fury and frustration. Finally the colonel said, "Listen, men, I don't want to pull rank, but I think I'm starting to see the big picture here. A few things are coming into focus for me.

Now, I think we should dispense with the distinction between active duty and retired, and officer and enlisted. SF is SF, and I think we all know where this is going. I'm counting you Night Stalkers from the 160th too, of course. Nobody's giving orders here; we're past that, way past. I left that at the door. But I may know a few things from the message traffic that I'm privy to—and added to what we've just learned, I think I can see where this is heading."

"Where's that, sir?" asked Sergeant Major Donelson.

"For now, right back to Fort Campbell. To U.S. Army North, the Fifth Army. Northern Command, the homeland command. NORTHCOM. And maybe from there to the 101st, what's left of it. There are some people I know who should see this video, and these pictures. People high up, who I trust to do the right thing with the information. Or at least that I trust not to do the wrong thing."

"How do you know you can trust them?" The question could have come from any of the men. NORTHCOM, a jumbled-up staff command, consisted of active duty and reserve units assigned to it on an ad hoc basis. Some units assigned to NORTHCOM were even working together with the foreign "peacekeeping" forces.

Spencer answered, "The same way that we know we can trust each other. I have some longtime close friends over there. How many of you know General Lucian Armstead?" There were a few nods of recognition. Except for Phil Carson, they were all familiar with his name, his three-star rank and his position, but none of them had ever met him. The colonel said, "Armstead's the commanding general of NORTHCOM, headquartered right here at Fort Campbell ever since they got booted out of Texas. General Lucian Armstead is the one who needs to see this video. We need to focus our effort on him, and then we'll know how to steer this thing. If we can bring Armstead on board, *anything* is possible. Anything. Armstead meets regularly with the Joint Chiefs…and even the president."

One of the men said, "That's what we're really talking about, isn't it? That's where this has to go. Straight to the president—to Jamal Tambor. The traitor-in-chief."

"Hey, that's the president of the United States you're talking about!" said another.

"I know it. But the buck stops at the top, and nowhere else."

"Still, you can't say—"

"Can't say what? Can't say that the president is a traitor? That he's wrecking this country on purpose, tearing it apart piece by piece? That's what I can't say?"

"Whoa, whoa, hold your horses. Don't even go there! I won't be a part of any plot to take out the president. No way. Not even this president."

Colonel Spencer said, "I agree, but for a different reason. It wouldn't work anyway; it would be counterproductive. We need to discredit him, not make him a martyr. We need to use this massacre video. We can only destroy him and everything he represents with the truth—the truth that's on these pictures and this video."

Phil Carson knew only one man in the room, Boone Vikersun, and he had known him for only a few days. Ira, AKA Dewey O. Lieberman, he had met just today. The rest of the men were strangers to him on one level, but on another, they were not. They were all Special Forces or other specops warriors. They were part of an indivisible, unending community, stretching in an unbroken line back to his tours in Southeast Asia and beyond.

After they had finished watching the video and his pictures, the men continued their discussion away from the computer, standing mostly around a circular poker table that dominated the middle of the den. While they argued, Phil Carson meandered around the perimeter of the wood-paneled room. He heard them, but didn't follow who was saying what because he didn't know them. Like many homes of military men he had visited over the years, the shelves and walls of this den were packed with military memorabilia. Framed group photos of old A-teams, plaques commemorating foreign visits and old unit assignments. A Kevlar helmet, a chromed dagger stuck into a black rock like Excalibur. Small statuettes of soldiers, helicopters and military vehicles. The overloaded bookshelves leaned heavily toward history, aviation, weaponry and military special operations. He recognized many of the titles, had read a few, and would have liked to borrow some. Behind him, the arguing continued and intensified. They were not all men of the South; many regional accents were represented.

"You know, the government will consider what we're doing to be treason if we even *think* about moving against the president. They'll call us traitors."

"Sorry, Jack, too late—I called *him* a traitor first. I mean, the president invited foreign troops in to kill Americans—we just saw it with our own eyes! And do you know how they pay off these foreign troops? They're paid with land, American land! Selling America by the acre to foreign enemies—what do you call that, if that's not treason?"

"But he's still the president! He's the commander-in-chief, so he's authorized to sign treaties, and Congress—"

"Congress is not authorized to sell pieces of America to foreign mercenaries, mercenaries like the Cossacks who we just saw massacre hundreds of Americans! That's treason, whether it's coming from the Capitol, the White House …or the Pentagon."

"I don't *care* if he's the president—he's a goddamn traitor! I'd drop the hammer on that communist son of a bitch myself!"

"You can't say that!"

"Look, fellows, we've served some bad presidents before, and we've survived. We've gotten past them. Look at Dave Whitman: he sold our nuclear secrets to the Chinese! If that's not treason, what is?"

"But even Weasel Dave didn't bring foreign troops onto American soil to massacre American civilians!"

"Only because he couldn't figure out a way to make money from it."

"You think this is funny? You think this is some kind of a goddamn joke?"

"I'm not joking! You think I'm joking?"

"Come on, think about it! If we don't stop these traitors, who can? Who will? If not us, then who? If not now, then when? Who's got a better shot at this than we do? At least we have a chance! If we can bring General Armstead on board, we have a chance. If we can get Armstead, we can get the 101st, and maybe the 82nd. The other Special Forces Groups for sure. We have the pictures, and the video. If we do this right, we'll have a chance to put the evidence straight in front of the American people directly. We can do it!"

"It's still treason, no matter how you look at it. We'll be a dozen up against millions."

"The treason is on *their* side! We'll be upholding our sworn oath to defend the Constitution against all enemies—and that means foreign *and* domestic."

"You mean the old constitution, or the new one? The new guys take the oath to the new constitution."

"Fuck that—there's only one Constitution! We all swore that oath, and it didn't say 'except for the president, who is above the law.' And we won't just be a dozen; we'll be thousands, if we're smart about how we do this."

"You try to bring in thousands of conspirators, and we'll all be eating breakfast in Fort Leavenworth by next week."

"What a mess, what a fucking mess."

"It's still treason—"

"Hell yes, it's treason, but it's *their* treason! Not ours!"

Ira, AKA Dewey O. Lieberman, was not the tallest of the group by any means, but he had an imposing face and a commanding presence when he chose to exercise them. He held up both hands, looked at each of the men, and they grew quiet. Carson noticed this rather theatrical turn. In an almost Shakespearian manner Ira quoted, "'Treason doth never prosper: what's the reason? Why, if it prosper, none dare call it treason.' An Englishman named John Harrington said that, all the way back around the year 1600."

"Ira, what the hell's the point of that?" asked the muscular black man in the green T-shirt.

"The point is, there's nothing new under the sun. There's an ancient pattern at work here."

Another man said, "I've seen that quote before, but what's it mean? Can you interpret that so us mere enlisted swine can understand it?"

Ira replied, "Hey, I'm a mere enlisted swine too, or at least I was until I retired."

Colonel Spencer spoke next, and they all turned to listen to him. "It means that if we're successful, we'll all be heroes, and nobody will ever say a negative word against us. We'll be called the saviors of the republic, and nobody will ever dare call us traitors."

The black NCO asked, "Well, what if we're *not* successful? I'm just saying…"

The colonel gave a wry smile and said, "Then they'll hang us all. They'll hang us, and bury us in Potter's Field, next to Booth and Oswald."

"Yeah," said Donelson, rubbing his neck with his hand. "I saw that World War Two movie *Valkyrie*. I didn't like the ending. That mission to take out Hitler was fubar to the max."

"That Hitler op was fubar because it was too big and too complicated. Small and fast is the way to go."

"I think this is crazy. I think this is all beer talk, and you'll forget it in the morning."

"Did you think that Predator video was crazy? You think you'll forget Boone's pictures in the morning? They're slaughtering American civilians now, and we're going to do *nothing* about it? We can't just sit on this information—we have to use it. I mean, *really* use it! Take it just as far as it needs to go."

"If *we* can't light the fuse on this thing, who can? Anyway, look at the aces we've been dealt with this video and these pictures. When will we have a better hand than now? When will we have a better chance to see this through? Who can do this kind of thing better than we can? The longer we wait, the weaker we'll become, and the more chance of compromise there'll be. Keep it small and do it fast—that's the best way. Who dares, wins!"

"So who's in? It's time to stand up and be counted!"

"Oh, man, I don't know—the president! You're talking about the *president*! I don't know about that…"

"If we don't take this thing on now, we never will. How will we be able to look at ourselves in the mirror if we can see what we just saw and just go home and do *nothing*? What will we tell our grandkids when they ask us why we didn't act when we had the chance?"

Phil Carson listened to their discussion while continuing to examine the objects around the room. The den was practically a museum of militaria, a decorated veteran's "me room" commemorating the highlights of his long career and many adventures. In a position of honor on a mahogany shelf, inside a custom-made triangular glass-topped shadow box, was an American flag, tri-folded and showing only the blue field of white stars. A small brass plate on its front identified the flag as having been given in honor of one Lt. Chester G. Donelson, USA, 5th SFG(A), 1941-1967. The mahogany-trimmed glass top of the case was mounted on small brass hinges.

In the shadow box, on top of the flag, rested a faded Green Beret, with the old black-and-yellow unit flash of the 5th Special Forces Group. On the same shelf, not far from the shadow box, lay a book with a cracked green vinyl cover, made to snap all the way around the open side to protect its pages. It had been decades since Phil Carson had seen one of them. It was a Vietnam-era Soldier's Bible, made to fit into a pouch on a rucksack.

Carson hoped that Lieutenant Chester Donelson, wherever he was resting, wouldn't mind the imposition. Unnoticed by the men arguing behind him, Carson unlatched the shadow box's glass lid and removed the tri-folded flag and the Green Beret. Then he picked up the small Soldier's Bible and placed it on top of the beret. It was time to end the discussion. It was time to put this debate to rest. He remembered another similar dispute, seven years ago in another house. It had worked then, and it might work now.

The men were standing around the poker table, still arguing. Carson put the flag, the beret and the Bible in the center of the table. His unexpected placement of those three items hushed the room to abrupt silence.

He said, "Men, it's time to stop debating *if* we're going to do it, and start planning *how* we're going to do it. It's time, right now, to decide. Who's in, and who's out? If you're in, you're in all the way, to the bitter end. If you're out—just leave now." Then he leaned over the table and placed his hand on the Bible, the beret, and the flag. "Who else is in?"

Sergeant Major Donelson looked at Carson across the table, met his eyes, and then placed his own right hand over Carson's. His fingertips traced the edge of the old felt Green Beret. "Boone says you served with his father. That's good enough for me. I'm in for the duration. All the way. No matter what it takes, no matter where it goes."

CW4 Rogan's three-fingered right hand went down next, over his friend's. "Count me in too. All the way to the end—Night Stalkers don't quit!"

All the right hands went down in seconds, crossing one another's over the holy book. The men leaned in together like a football huddle, shoulder-to-shoulder and staring from face to scarred and weather-beaten face. No one balked, hesitated or refused. After perhaps half a minute, the men slowly withdrew their hands from the Bible, but they remained clustered tightly around the table, staring at the little stack of sacred items almost resonantly glowing between them.

While they were still close together, Colonel Spencer turned to each of them and quietly said, "Gentlemen, we might not come out of this too well…but that's nothing new for any of us. Only God and history will be our judge. And I'd rather lose my life, than lose what's left of my honor. I've stayed on board with this…this disgraceful situation we find ourselves in for much too long already…and I suspect you all feel the same way.

"Men, we've fought our country's wars all over the world for many years. That's nothing new. What's new is that this time, we really are fighting for our country, and for the very survival of our republic. This time, we're not ten thousand miles from home. This time, we *are* home. This time, our oath is going to mean more than just the words we say when we re-up. This time, we're actually going to defend the Constitution, against enemies both foreign *and domestic*. So let's get to work. I've got a few ideas I'd like to share."

It was already after midnight. For the last six hours, the two teenagers had been hiking for twenty minutes and resting for ten, when the terrain allowed it. Zack walked ahead of Jenny, his bow strapped to his pack, his new AK-47 across his chest. He held it in both hands at the ready, its sling behind his neck. He would walk a few yards, then stop and look around, so it wasn't hard for her to keep up with him. When he wasn't sure of the route ahead, he left Jenny in temporary hiding places and scouted forward while she rested with the baby. When he found the way, he returned and they continued on.

They had left their hiding place beneath the camper shell when it grew dark. Thick fog had rolled in with the night. The three-quarters moon was up just before twilight, so even with the fog, the night was less than black. The fog meant that visibility was short, less than a hundred feet, but without visual references, distances were just a guess. The moon lit their immediate surroundings so that they could walk quickly, without fear of tripping over unseen roots or stumbling in holes. It would be a perfect night for covering serious distance, at least until the moon set. Unless they had the bad luck to stumble right into a Cossack patrol, they'd make it across into Mississippi before dawn.

Boone had marked their map with a route and the best places to cross the state line. When dogs growled or barked, they backtracked and circled around. Homes sometimes loomed up in front of them, and if no dogs barked, they skirted close by them and continued quickly on their way. Most houses were fenced in, often with primitive wooden palisades or plain barbed wire. They were becoming experts at climbing over or wriggling through every type of fence. Most of the houses they encountered appeared deserted, but their inhabitants might have been hiding inside, and certainly nobody was showing lights of any kind. As they walked further south, they came across fewer and fewer homes that had been recently torched by the Cossacks. Some homes had obviously been burned down long before, probably during the period of chaos after the earthquakes. Many other homes were windowless and gutted.

They crossed several paved roads, but without being able to see road signs, they could only guess if they matched the ones on the map. They used Boone's map until they concluded that they were completely disoriented, and then they just followed the compass, heading south.

The baby had become a veteran traveler, nestled against Jenny's chest between the parka and her pack's straps. The pacifier was clipped to the collar of her "onesie" outfit, so it would not be lost. She'd had one bottle before leaving the camper shell, and there was one more staying warm against Jenny's skin, above her belt. She travels like an Indian baby in a papoose, thought Jenny. She wants to live. She's a determined survivor, like us.

In this part of Tennessee, streams were even more common than roads, and just as random and confusing in their twists and turns. Zack walked along them until he could find a crossing, either over a log or on rocks. But try as they might, they were both soon soaked up to their knees and Jenny's feet were almost numb. The air wasn't as cold as on the previous nights, but this was a mixed blessing, because the ground was soft and frequently muddy. Bogs and marshy areas were as common as the streams. But if they could just get safely into Mississippi, all of their present soreness, fatigue and discomfort would matter for nothing.

One creek was much wider than the others, and they walked along its bank for at least a mile before Zack found a homemade pedestrian bridge to cross it. A roughly nailed wooden ladder took them up between two thick trees that grew a few feet apart. The trees were the support columns for a wire cable suspension bridge. From the two long cables hung a shaky bridge deck of wooden planks laid lengthwise, wide enough for just one person at a time. Jenny was wearing gloves, and gripped the two rusty wires at shoulder height as the boards bounced and swayed beneath her feet. At its lowest point in the middle, it was just a few yards above the rushing water. She'd seen these do-it-yourself hillbilly bridges before in rural Tennessee. Farmers often constructed them so they could walk over creeks and streams on their property and avoid long trips around. This was a big one, easily over a hundred feet long.

In their shroud of moonlit fog, just the bridge and the immediate area around them were visible. They could pass a Cossack patrol only a few dozen yards away and never see them. Or they could stumble right into an ambush. It didn't bear fretting over. There was nothing you could do to change the reality. You could only be thankful for the fog and the moonlight and press on, grateful that Zack had proven to be a sure woodsman. Now he even had an AK-47, besides his bow. If he could kill a mounted Cossack soldier with just an arrow, what could he do with thirty bullets? And this rifle had a strap, so he wouldn't lose it.

They reached the twin trees on the other side of the cable-and-plank hillbilly bridge. Zack climbed down first. Jenny turned around on the platform between the supporting trees and descended the vertical ladder of rough boards. Zack reached up and steadied her, holding her pack and guiding her down, even placing her boots on the steps so that she would not fall. Once on solid footing, they set out again, following the compass needle southward.

Jenny whispered, "What tracks are these?" They had been ascending another slippery bank when they encountered the railroad running along the top. The moon had set, and they were using Zack's micro light to examine the steel rails. Their visible world had shrunk down to the red puddle cast by its single LED bulb, but that faintness also reduced the chances of their being seen by anyone else. With his light directed down toward their feet, Zack could see only Jenny's vague outline. He was amazed by her fearlessness at walking through the darkness. This was a quality that he had found in few people, much less girls.

"It's probably the Norfolk Southern," he replied. "They run from Memphis to Corinth. I know that much for sure. They were only a couple of miles north of my house, on the Tennessee side. I used to hop rides when they were still running trains on them."

"Then I walked on these tracks after the first earthquake, when I was leaving Germantown."

"Yeah, if this is the Norfolk Southern, then these are the same tracks. About ten miles from Corinth they turn southeast and cross into Mississippi."

"Does that mean we're out of Tennessee?" she asked.

"I'm not sure. Maybe."

"What's your compass say? Which way are they going?"

They studied Zack's compass, using his tiny red light. He said, "They're running about northwest to southeast. So this should be it."

"Well then, I say we take it."

"It's safer if we stay off the roads. Railroads too. They might set up an ambush."

"They who?" asked Jenny. "The Cossacks?"

"Yeah, the Cossacks."

"The Cossacks have better things to do than wait in the dark for somebody to walk down these tracks. We haven't heard any shooting for a few hours—they're all drunk by now. Anyway, you said we might already be in Mississippi. Let's take the tracks."

He considered, weighing the risks. Dawn was still a few hours away. Since the moonlight had disappeared, their forward progress had fallen drastically. Not only had they been forced to walk much more slowly to avoid tripping or falling, they had repeatedly run into frightening and frustrating dead ends of deep water or impenetrable thickets. Consequently, they had frequently been forced to backtrack, becoming more and more lost with each turn and loop. Only the compass kept them from complete disorientation, but retracing their steps sapped both their energy and their morale. Unless they followed a road or these railroad tracks, they'd continue to move at a snail's pace, and dawn might find them still in Tennessee. Tactically, it was a risk, but so was being caught near the state line after daybreak. And for now the baby was quiet, sleeping snuggled against Jenny's chest, inside her fleece vest.

Zack gave in. "All right, let's stay on the tracks. We'll have to stay close together so we can both use the light. Be careful; you can break your ankle easy on these."

"I know. Remember, this is how I got away from Memphis."

26

It was growing light when the tracks approached a paved road. The road was too small to merit crossing gates. They hid in a wrecked pickup truck fifty feet from the road while they rested and observed it for activity. The old Ford had been pushed or rolled down onto the side of the tracks and abandoned there. The windows were cracked and crazed, but were still intact. The truck was facing away from the crossing, so they had to turn sideways in the seat to look out the back toward the road.

Zack had forced open the passenger door, on the side away from the tracks. This was a chance for them to shed their packs and enjoy the luxury of resting comfortably while they regrouped and considered their next moves. Trees and bushes closed in on both sides of the disused railroad, so they could see only down a narrow channel in both directions. They might have fallen asleep had the baby not been crying.

Hope was fussing, and they had no warm milk to give her. Jenny changed her bed-sheet diaper, which was barely wet. They tried giving her milk powder mixed with drinking water, but the baby rejected the rubber nipple and continued to cry. The two teenagers had already shared their last MRE meal pack, eaten cold.

The fog was gone, but it was still very raw and cold. Zack estimated that the street ran north to south. They sat in the truck, studying their paper map and comparing it to what they could see around them. They were using a Tennessee road map, which showed a strip of northern Mississippi and Alabama. Corinth was less than ten miles from the state line, so it was included on their map. He was fairly certain that they were out of Tennessee, but he wanted to watch for a while before deciding whether they should continue along the tracks or turn south on the road. It was pure guesswork trying to determine if the road ahead matched any roads on their map. Zack held the map between them and pointed to his best guess of their location.

He said, "If it's this one, it crosses the border and runs into *this* one. Then that one goes over to Highway 45, and 45 runs right into Corinth. If it's this one. I'm really just guessing."

"So, we're out of Tennessee?"

"We are, if that road is this one on the map. But I want to be sure."

They heard an engine, and sank low in the truck's cab. In a minute, they watched through the rear window as a tractor pulling an enormous flatbed wagon approached from the north. An old white man was driving the tractor, looking straight ahead. The wagon was jammed with people sitting on every square foot, clutching bags and boxes. None of the refugees paid any attention to the wrecked pickup, if they even noticed it.

"Well," Jenny said, "at least nobody was chasing them. They seemed all right. They didn't seem afraid. So, should we take the road?"

While they watched, other small groups of people appeared, also walking south. Then they found out that they weren't the only ones hiking down the railroad tracks. They had been looking out the back window toward the road, and Zack was startled to see people in civilian clothes coming toward them down the tracks. It was too late to hide from them. The group consisted of two men, a woman and several children. They appeared too tired to care about a pair of youths resting in an abandoned pickup. This little group paused at the road crossing, looked all around them for a minute, and turned south, joining the other refugees.

"I guess it doesn't matter much," Zack said, "but I still think we should stay on the tracks. They go straight through Corinth. Mostly, I just don't want to go where the herd is going. Eventually a herd gets herded *into* something. If we get herded into a refugee camp, we won't be able to find Boone's contacts."

"Well, we need to get some formula for this baby. Real milk, at least. We can't take forever getting wherever we're getting."

"I know, I know. Corinth is only a few more miles down the tracks. Just another couple of hours, maybe."

"What's Corinth like?" Jenny asked. "How big is it?"

"Pretty big, at least for around here. Maybe about twenty thousand people. Not as big as Memphis, that's for sure."

"Thank God for that—I'll never live near a big city again, ever. Hey, what about your rifle? There's too many people around now. You can't just go walking down the tracks carrying that thing. Not in the daytime. If we're stopped by the Mississippi Guard, they'll take it for sure. They might even arrest you for it."

"Yeah. You're right, I should hide it. I'll want it for later, when I go back into Tennessee."

Jenny looked at him as if he had said something completely crazy. "Why would you want to do *that*?"

"Because I'm not finished with the Cossacks, that's why. And I'm not finished with the people who killed my father. I'll cache my rifle here, and come back and get it later."

"Well, I'm going to hang on to my pistol. I'll hide it in the diaper bag. I'm keeping the silencer too. I'm not going to let anybody take them from me. Anywhere I can't take them, I just won't go."

Zack said, "I'll hide the rifle under this truck—it's not going anywhere in a hurry. I can tie it to something up under the engine. I'd put it behind the seat, but somebody might look there. Nobody will ever look underneath this pile of junk. But I'll keep my bow. Bows aren't against the law in Mississippi. All right, let's get ready. If she won't drink the milk, you might as well wrap her up and zip her into your jacket. Just give me a few minutes to hide my rifle, and we'll go."

Jenny tried switching the baby's pacifier for the bottle. The baby continued crying, her eyes tightly closed, rejecting both the rubber nipple and the pacifier. Jenny said, "That's it, I'm done with the tracks. We're taking the road. I'm going where the people are going. We need to get her some warm milk."

Bullard asked his deputy director, "What have you got, Mitch? Anything new?" The director of rural pacification was seated behind his broad desk in his office on the third floor of Building 1405. The desk was set well away from its single large window, which looked out over acres of brown fields. Mitch Brookfield had returned to the office after making his morning rounds of operations, communications and the other divisions.

"We actually have some good news for a change. We've gotten the Nigerians to back away from the Kazaks. You were right—all it took was a donation to Colonel Zamburu's favorite charity."

Bullard leaned back in his springy executive chair, his fingers laced behind his head. "Nothing makes people see reason like a million dollars in a Samsonite. Even North American Dollars." One of the perquisites of running a black operation was ready access to cash. Sometimes you could motivate the leaders of the foreign peacekeepers with threats, sometimes with promises of rewards. Sometimes the rewards had to be tangible. Sidney Krantz understood this, and he had agreed to Bullard's demand for sufficient working capital when he had taken the job.

It wasn't difficult to convince Krantz to provide a cash fund for the rural pacification program. The government printing presses were already churning out the new money around the clock, so a few tens of millions of ameros for black projects was just a trickle diverted from a flood. The rural pacification money was laundered through FEMA channels. In the absence of electronic banking, thick packets of cash were routinely handed out to refugees to cover living expenses. These days, almost no means of injecting "financial stimulus" into the economy was being ruled out.

And of course, as usual, accounting standards for black budgets were virtually nonexistent. As a result, a healthy percentage of the cash found its way into Bullard's own pockets. It was only paper money, but it was a lot better than nothing. Anyway, this job was only a stepping stone. Bob Bullard had been informed by Sid Krantz that he was on the short list for running the new Department of Internal Security, when it was launched. He was just putting in his time in rural pacification. The real power would come at the DIS. Then he would be the one in charge of all of the black budgets. Then there would be no limit to his ability to divert funds.

Brookfield explained, "Colonel Zamburu wanted gold, but he was willing to take North American Dollars. Once he saw the money, he discovered that he really doesn't hate the Kazaks so much after all. Turns out he's a devout Christian, just full of God's forgiveness. He accepted Colonel Burgut's explanation, and moved his troops back from that river."

"Well, that's something anyway. Now, what about that missing NAL humvee?" Bullard actually cared nothing about the humvee—but he was very concerned about its passengers.

"There's been nothing since yesterday morning, when it passed the Lynnville FEMA camp."

"It just disappeared from the face of the earth?"

"For now," said the deputy director. "Hey, we're on one of the biggest Army bases in the country. There must be a thousand of those things around here. Whoever took that humvee could just paint new numbers on it and park it anywhere. Or they could have rolled it into a river, or just stashed it in a garage somewhere. We have a Predator searching between here and Lynnville, but no unaccounted-for humvees have turned up. But look at bright side—at least no more foreign peacekeepers have turned up dead."

"What about the missing Legion lieutenant?" asked Bullard.

"No trace of him. Nothing. Not a peep."

"Shit. Well, let's keep on it."

Zack and Jenny joined a growing stream of people on the road. Zack asked an old man if they were in Mississippi yet, and was told that they were. After two miles, their road joined another larger one. The number of refugees on this road was even greater, including some who were driving cars and riding horses. Almost all of them were white, reflecting the population of the Tennessee counties from which they had fled.

The refugees soon arrived at their first military checkpoint. The soldiers were Americans, which was a great relief. Orange traffic cones and white sawhorses were set up across the road, and behind them was a green camouflage Army humvee. Soldiers directed the refugees onto a field along the road where tents were being erected. One of the troops heard Jenny's crying baby and said, "Go ahead and get in the medical line. They should have baby formula if you need it." A cluster of people crowded around a green water trailer, filling a variety of plastic bottles and jugs. Zack and Jenny walked past them, since they still had water in their own containers and were more anxious to provide for baby Hope.

Folded tents were being unloaded from an Army truck. Three of the big tents were already up. Somewhere nearby a loud diesel generator was running. A green-painted school bus pulled onto the field, and a group of about twenty refugees boarded it under the guidance of other soldiers. Jenny watched them carefully, both the civilians and the soldiers. The refugees were not being yelled at or pushed around. The soldiers were not carrying rifles, although a few did have holstered pistols on their web belts. All of them were dressed in gray-green digital-pattern ACUs, like the ones Phil Carson and Doug Dolan had worn on their escape.

Jenny and Zack approached a table set up across the front of the medical tent. It was a long folding table, similar to the ones used in school cafeterias. It had a small Red Cross banner tied to its front, hanging down. Another Red Cross was tied to the front of the tent. Three soldiers sat on plastic chairs behind the desk, interviewing newly arriving refugees and listening to their medical complaints. Nobody's bags were being searched. Zack and Jenny slipped off their packs and set them on the ground, but she kept the diaper bag over her shoulder so that it rested against her left hip. If their bags were searched, her hidden pistol might be found, and then what would happen? An elderly couple leaned over the table in front of Zack and Jenny, filling out a questionnaire on a half sheet of paper. When their form was complete, the couple was led into the tent.

The soldier looked up at Jenny and asked, "Why are you in the medical line? Is something wrong with your baby?" His nametag read MACKENZIE, and there were two upward-pointing chevrons on his chest insignia. He was a stocky man in his thirties, with a ruddy complexion. Some of the soldiers were wearing black berets, and some were wearing camouflage caps. Mackenzie was wearing a beret.

Jenny said, "We only have powdered milk that's made for adults. That's all she's had for a few days. We couldn't heat her milk this morning and now she won't take it, and she won't stop crying. I think she's dehydrated, but I just don't know for sure."

"But you two are okay? It's just the baby that requires medical attention?" Mackenzie had a soft Southern accent.

"Yes," she said. "We're okay. Hungry and tired, but okay."

"Is anything else wrong with your baby?"

"I don't know. I hope not."

The soldier looked at the two skinny teenagers with a measure of suspicion. "It's your baby? I mean, you're the parents?"

Without hesitation Jenny replied, "Yes. We're her parents." Zack glanced at her, his eyes wide.

"Okay, fill out the forms, one for each of you. Fill one out for your baby too. The blank lines at the bottom are where you write your medical complaint. Just put down 'Our baby is hungry.' We have infant formula inside the medical tent. Do you already have a bottle? If you don't, they'll give you a new one. You can keep it. They'll give you a couple of cans of

Similac too. This is just a screening center. We can't feed you two here, just your baby. You'll get a hot meal at the main camp. It's only a couple of minutes away on the bus."

Both teens leaned over the table and began to fill out their slips of paper. It had lines for basic information such as name, age and address. When he was finished, Zack said, "We don't need to go to another camp. We have people to meet us here in Corinth. Can't you just give us the baby formula and let us go?"

Mackenzie looked at him and said, "Look, I don't make the policy here; I just do what I'm told. Everybody that comes here has to go to the main camp. But at least you're done walking—the bus will take you the rest of the way. Once you're in the camp, your friends will be able to come and get you. Well, after you go through vaccination and quarantine. They have a real medical clinic there, where they can do lab tests on your baby and make sure it's okay."

Jenny took her slip of paper, stood erect, and said, "Milk or no milk, we're not getting on that bus. Forget it."

The soldier looked at her, then at Zack, and he said, "What's her problem? Look, this isn't the kind of situation where you get to choose. This isn't Burger King. It just doesn't work that way. The medic will look at your baby here in the tent. You'll get a chance to clean him up and get some new diapers and some baby formula. I think that's pretty damn generous! You came to us, remember? You're in Mississippi now, and we're trying our best to help you. But after we help you here, then you have to get on the bus. That's the way it works today. This is just an initial reception center. They can do a lot more for you at the refugee center. You'll get hot meals and a chance to clean up and rest."

Jenny vehemently shook her head no. "Listen: all we need is some warm baby formula, okay? That's it. But I am *not* getting on any damn bus! Forget it!" She had a hard and brittle edge in her voice. People in the other lines stared at her. "We'll figure something else out, but we are *not* getting on any bus!"

Other soldiers around them stopped what they were doing, and looked toward the medical table to see what was happening to cause the girl to shout. Her baby was crying almost nonstop, contributing to the tension.

Mackenzie said, "What's the matter with you? Keep it down, you're upsetting people. This isn't easy for anybody. We're doing the best we can. Nobody expected thousands of you people to come walking out of Tennessee. We didn't invite you to come into Mississippi, so why don't you pull yourself together and show a little gratitude? Everybody here is stressed out—that doesn't make you special."

Jenny answered more quietly, "Well, that's fine, thanks, but I'm still not getting on that bus." Her dirty pink vinyl diaper bag was against her left side. Its top zipper was open. She thought that she might have to take out her .45 to prevent them from forcing her onto the bus. If any of these soldiers tried to grab her, she would pull it out and maybe start shooting. That thought made her begin to tear up, because she knew that escape would be impossible from this place. There were just too many soldiers, even if they were not carrying rifles. To have come so far and fail was a bitter thought to contemplate…but she would not be forced onto that green bus. She would not make Hope go on another bus ride.

Zack put his arm around Jenny, shushed her, and said to the soldier, "I'm sorry. You have to understand something. She saw something terrible back there. Terrible. Hundreds of people were put onto buses by the Kazak Battalion and then they were taken away and shot. Hundreds of people. She was an eyewitness. That's why we won't get on a bus. You can understand that, can't you? And that's why we can't just go to a refugee camp with everybody else, or go into quarantine or whatever you said. We have important information about a massacre, a terrible massacre that happened back there. And we even have pictures of it. We need to see some people in Corinth about it. It can't wait while we're put into quarantine. You don't understand—we're not refugees—we're on a mission."

The soldier looked up at them skeptically. "A mission. You're a man on a mission. Well, I'm on a mission too, a mission to get everybody processed and on that bus to go to the refugee center in Corinth, which is all of maybe ten minutes away from here. That's going to be my mission all day long, one busload after another, until you people stop walking out of Tennessee. Once you get to the main camp, you can talk to somebody about your pictures. I'm just doing medical triage, that's *my* mission. Everything else happens at the main camp, and everybody has to go through quarantine. That's just the way it is."

Zack said, "Well, we can't wait for that. If you can't help us, then we just have to leave. We have people we need to see. It's important, very important. So we can't just get on your bus, to go to God knows where and for how long." Their unease seemed to spread to the other refugees behind them in line, and even to the other lines in front of the non-medical tents. People began to whisper to one another and look over at the waiting green bus with new trepidation.

The soldier behind the table frowned, leaned across the table, and spoke in a low voice while staring at Zack and glancing at Jenny. "Look, buddy, you two need to chill out. You're causing a scene, and we don't need that. Finish filling out your damn forms, and we'll give the baby some formula so it'll shut up. Then you'll go over and get on that nice heated bus with everybody else."

Jenny slammed her pen down, tore her form in half, and threw the pieces at the soldier across the table. "Well, I'm not going to get on any damned bus, and you can't make me!" She reached across Hope and thrust her right hand into her diaper bag.

The soldier jumped from his chair, sputtering with anger, and pointed his finger at her. "Listen, Missy—you'll get on that bus, if I have to get MPs to *drag* you onto it!"

At that moment a black soldier came hurrying out of the tent, motioning the angry soldier to sit down. He had three upward-pointing chevrons on his chest. He asked, "What's the problem here, Corporal Mackenzie?" He picked up Zack's form and glanced at it. "This says you're from Mississippi. So, what are you doing here with the Tennessee refugees?"

"Oh, it's a *really* long story," Zack replied.

The soldier behind the table said, "Sergeant Amory, they say they won't get on the bus. They're refusing to go to the main camp with the rest of the refugees. They say she witnessed some kind of massacre. She might have PTSD, I don't know. Did you hear her?"

"I heard her. I heard her asking for baby formula. Did anybody get that baby some formula yet?" The sergeant looked around at the other soldiers who had been watching the dispute. Jenny's hand was on her pistol in the diaper bag. She glanced at him, rapidly absorbing new information. So, three upward chevrons meant sergeant, and two meant corporal. This black man was a sergeant, even though he seemed to be younger than some of the privates, and he was definitely much younger than Corporal Mackenzie. Sergeant Amory had a chocolate-colored complexion and an intelligent-looking face. But he was still a young black man, and so Jenny reflexively stiffened. She kept her hand on the gun hidden in the diaper bag, while struggling to maintain her composure through these tense and confusing developments.

The corporal replied, "Formula—ah, that was next, Sergeant. We were just getting there."

The black sergeant shot Mackenzie a withering glare, and then motioned to the teenagers. "You two, come with me, please. You can finish filling out your forms inside, and I'll check your baby. We've got baby formula, and we can heat it up."

They walked around the long table and into the tent, where four cots, folding chairs, tables and portable desks were set up inside.

Zack said, "Sergeant Amory, I appreciate what you did, but I need to know something. After the baby gets her milk, are we free to go, or not?"

"That's not my decision to make." Amory had gone to a stack of cardboard boxes and retrieved a can of formula.

"Then I need to see your commanding officer. If you're not going to let us go, I mean, if we're not free to go, then I have information that I need to give to somebody. Somebody high up the chain of command. As high up as possible, and right away."

"What kind of information?" Sergeant Amory appeared doubtful. The two old folks who had been ahead of the teens in line were lying fully dressed on a pair of Army cots. Amory indicated that Jenny could sit down on an empty cot, which she did, after shedding her pack and even her diaper bag, with its concealed handgun. The sergeant told another soldier to prepare a bottle of Similac. There was a gas camp stove on another table, for preparing hot drinks and meals. Jenny laid the baby on the cot, unwrapped her blanket, unsnapped her onesie outfit and checked her diaper. It was still dry.

The sergeant briefly scanned the form Zack had filled out. "If she won't take this formula, we'll have to start an IV. Don't worry, I'm a damned good medic, and I never miss. Not even with a baby—especially not with a baby. She'll hardly feel it. All right? But first we'll see what she does with a warm bottle." He smiled at Jenny. "Okay?"

"Okay," Jenny reluctantly agreed. So, Amory was both a sergeant and a medic. And even though he was black, he was treating them gently and with respect. Still, she distrusted him. How could she not? Her pistol was still within easy reach in the diaper bag beside her on the cot, but she had calmed down considerably since her confrontation with the corporal.

The sergeant then said, "Now, what about those pictures?" He appeared somewhat skeptical until Zack took the camera from his pack, turned it on and handed it over. The LCD pictures on its back were only two inches wide, but that was enough to convey their significance. "Oh my God! You weren't exaggerating about a massacre! You're coming with me." He looked to Jenny. "Can you please stay here for now? The formula will be ready in a minute; Private Saxby here will get it for you. We're going next door to look at these pictures on a computer. I'll bring him back in a few minutes, I promise. All right?"

Sergeant Amory led Zack into the adjoining tent, which was furnished inside like a rough office, with folding tables and chairs and no cots. He addressed an officer seated behind a portable desk. "Captain Harris, I've got something you need to see ASAP. Is your computer working?" The officer had two vertical black bars on his chest and two matching bars on his camouflage patrol cap. He looked at the pictures on the back of the camera and then rapidly pulled a black laptop from a padded zipper case. Zack's camera had a swing-out USB jack, and in a few moments the pictures appeared on the computer's screen.

The captain was visibly shocked by what he saw, and he asked Zack, "Where and when were these pictures taken?"

"Near Mannville in Radford County, on Sunday morning. But the massacre happened on Saturday afternoon."

"Did you take these pictures?"

"No sir, a Green Beret did."

"A Green Beret?" The captain appeared skeptical. "And what was this Green Beret's name?"

"Master Sergeant Boone Vikersun. I'm not making this up. He was from the 1st Battalion of the 5th Special Forces Group, at Fort Campbell."

Zack's prompt recitation of this information seemed to allay some of the captain's doubt. "So, how do you know this Green Beret? Is he a relative of yours?"

"No, we're not related. He came to my house. My house is in Mississippi near the state line, north of Walnut. He came because of my guest. It's a long story, but I had another old Green Beret already staying with me. I accidentally shot him with an arrow on Christmas morning, when I was out hunting. Really, it was more like I grazed him. I took care of him at my house. He's okay now."

Sergeant Amory cocked his head and stared at Zack with increased interest as these somewhat disjointed details spilled out. "Christmas morning?" he asked.

"Yes sir. It was Christmas morning around dawn. I was bow-hunting in a tree stand. I took care of him after that. I sewed him up after I wounded him by accident."

Sergeant Amory took a notepad and pen from his coat pocket. "What was this old Green Beret's name? The one you wounded, the one who was staying with you?"

"Well, at first I thought his name was Colonel Brice. But that name turned out to be fake."

"Colonel Brice? You're sure of that?" Sergeant Amory stared at the boy in amazement, and then told the captain, "Sir, we need to take this young man and his camera to the senior officer in charge in Corinth, whoever that is. And we need to do it right now."

Captain Harris said, "Well, Sergeant, as luck would have it, General Mirabeau himself is here today, somewhere. He came up to Corinth when the refugees started coming over." The captain turned to another soldier. "Private Berry, get the duty truck and bring it here as quick as you can."

The private and Sergeant Amory sat in the front of the green GMC quad-cab pickup. Captain Harris, Jenny and Zack sat in the back seat. Their packs went in the bed of the truck. The baby was cradled on Jenny's lap, her tiny hands clamped on a new bottle of formula as she drank eagerly. They drove down Highway 45 to where it intersected another four lane route. In a long field, a tent city was being erected. Buses and trucks were unloading civilian refugees. They continued past the tents and came to a parking area outside a closed shopping center, where a small military camp bustled with activity. There were green cargo containers on trucks, troop trucks, fuel trucks and what looked like several large green recreational vehicles. Nearby, a pair of Blackhawk helicopters were parked on their own section of pavement. The parking area containing this encampment was patrolled by soldiers carrying M-16s. They were waved to a stop when they left the service road to turn into this secured area. Captain Harris rolled down his window. "We're here to see Lieutenant General Mirabeau."

The soldier saluted. "Yes sir. Do you have an appointment, Captain? Are you scheduled?"

"No, but it's an emergency. We have urgent information for him."

"I'm sorry, Captain, but nobody goes past here unless I've been told otherwise."

"Then call somebody now. We have to see the general; it's extremely urgent."

A lieutenant walking from a commo trailer toward a green RV saw the minor commotion and walked over. "What's the problem, Captain?"

"These civilians have information about a massacre that happened in Tennessee."

Sergeant Amory added, "We have pictures, and an eyewitness."

"A massacre?"

"That's right. Hundreds of civilians were murdered by the Kazaks."

The lieutenant jotted notes in his own memo pad. "Wait right here. I'll be back with an answer either way."

Two minutes later the lieutenant returned. "These are the witnesses? Okay, park over there and follow me. The general will see you right now."

The green RV wasn't like a camper inside. Instead, the thirty-five-foot recreational vehicle had been gutted and converted into an open-plan office and staff meeting room. General Mirabeau saw Sergeant Amory, glanced at his nametape, and did a double take. "You! Well, Sergeant Amory, we meet again. You're keeping out of trouble?"

"Yes sir, General, I've been trying to. But somehow, trouble just keeps finding me."

General Mirabeau chortled and said, "You and me both, Sergeant. It's the story of my life." Mirabeau had three black stars on the front of his uniform and on his black beret.

The other officers in the converted RV, ranging from captain to brigadier general, seemed taken aback by the familiarity between their commanding general and the unknown medic. Both of them were African-Americans, while most of the other officers were white.

"Now, what's all this about a massacre up in Tennessee? You have pictures?"

Captain Harris said, "I have them, sir, on my laptop. They came from his camera."

Zack said, "It's not really *my* camera. I was just supposed to bring it to Mississippi. That was my mission."

"Your *mission*, huh?" said the general. "What's your name, son?"

"Zachary Tutweiler."

"And you witnessed this massacre?"

"No sir, she did." He nodded to Jenny.

The general looked mildly frustrated. "So, who *actually* took the pictures?"

Zack said, "A Green Beret named Boone Vikersun. Master Sergeant Boone Vikersun. He sent me here with the camera, because of these pictures. He wrote down the grid coordinates and the latitude and longitude, so the place where it happened could be found later. And I have a letter that he wrote, like a report."

"A Green Beret sent you? Really?" General Mirabeau studied the skinny seventeen-year-old carefully. "Well, I want to see these pictures. Captain, put your laptop on my desk there, and let's take a look. And somebody get a chair for this young lady; she's got a baby, for crying out loud!"

General Mirabeau pulled a chair up close to the computer and put on reading glasses. Captain Harris opened his laptop and turned it on, and in a few moments they were looking at Boone's photographs. The other staff officers stood around and behind the general, peering over his shoulders. First the general appeared surprised, and then his face grew stormy as he clicked from picture to picture. He said, "We've been hearing stories from the refugees about the Kazaks going berserk and burning homes and shooting people, but this—I just can't *believe* this!" When he saw a dead Kazak soldier lying on his back in the snow, he stopped the slide show and turned to Jenny. Zack was standing beside her chair. "Who killed him? Who killed this Kazak soldier? Your Green Beret?"

Jenny answered him. "Yes sir, Boone Vikersun. The Kazaks in these pictures were looters, who came back Sunday morning to steal from the dead. Boone was there to take pictures, and he killed them."

"What's your name, honey?"

"Jenny McClure."

"Did you see him shoot these Kazaks?"

She said, "No, I didn't see Boone shoot them. He told us about it later. I was there the night before. That's when I found this baby, under her mother. Her mother was shot dead, like everybody else there."

General Mirabeau clicked through the photos, growing more and more agitated, especially when he saw the photo of the blue helicopter flying low over the ravine. "Jenny, you need to tell me everything you know about this. And you too, son. Start at the beginning, and tell me everything. Who were you with? How did you happen to be with a Special Forces soldier? And where are your families?"

Zack looked at Jenny, and she answered for both of them. "They're dead. Both of our families are dead. Zack met Boone before I did."

"I'm sorry to hear that about your families. This has truly been a year like no other. So how did you meet this Green Beret, son?"

"He came to my house last Saturday night. It was because of my visitor, Mr. Carson. Mr. Carson was a Green Beret too, but a long time ago. So I guess it really all started on Christmas morning, when you might say I had a visitor. I was out bow-hunting, and I accidentally shot him. I sort of mistook him for a deer. I was in a tree stand, and I grazed him with an arrow."

"Who?"

"Mr. Phil Carson. Only then, I thought his name was Colonel Brice. That's what it said on his ID card, and on his uniform. When I met him, he was wearing a uniform like yours."

The general stared at Zack. "Did you say *Colonel Brice*? You're sure about that name?"

"Yes sir. I'm positive. Colonel Jonathan T. Brice. He had a military ID card. I took care of him, after I accidentally wounded him with an arrow."

"And this was Christmas morning?"

"Yes sir. At dawn on Christmas."

The general paused, thinking. "Tell me something, Zachary. Did this Colonel Brice have any tattoos that you know of?"

"Tattoos? Um, yes sir, he did. I mean, he does. He has a parachute tattoo on his left arm, right here." Zack pointed to his own arm, near the shoulder. "It's a tattoo of Army jump wings. Like the ones you're wearing on your uniform, right there over your pocket. But his doesn't have a star on top like yours does."

The general gazed at Zack and Jenny in wonder. "Son, you told me that you have a report from the other Green Beret. The one who took these pictures."

"Yes sir, right here." Zack handed the general a small Ziploc bag with a folded paper inside.

The general passed it to his chief staff officer, a brigadier general. "Find the exact location of this massacre, and find out what you can about Master Sergeant Vikersun." Then the general turned to Jenny, who was holding the baby on her lap. "Now, honey, tell me where you come into this. You were actually at the massacre site? You were an eyewitness?"

"To it happening? No. But I was there after the massacre, Saturday night. So I guess I'm an eyewitness that it really happened. That's where I found this baby."

"In the ravine? Among the bodies?"

"That's right. She was under her mother. I heard her crying, that's how I knew she was alive. This diaper bag was with her mother. I don't know her name, her mother I mean. I named the baby Hope. It was after that, that Mr. Vikersun and Mr. Carson found me and took me to a cave, where they had a hideout. Only—"

"Wait, they had a hideout in a cave? These Special Forces soldiers had a hideout in a cave? Excuse me, Jenny, wait just a moment. Major Townsend, let's set up a video camera. Have we got a camera ready to go? We do? Good, let's film her right now, while it's fresh. We'll film her, and then him. And I want hard copies of all of the pictures on that camera, big ones. Two sets. And make sure we save them all on our computers. Do we enough color ink for the printer? Excuse me, Jenny, this will just take a few minutes to get ready. Do you kids want some juice? Maybe some cornbread or oatmeal? Have you eaten this morning? No, I guess not. Don't worry; we'll take care of you, and the baby. But let's make these video depositions first."

"If you're going to film me, just let me wash my face and brush my hair first. And brush my teeth."

Within a few minutes, the camera was set up on a tripod facing Jenny, who sat in a hard-backed office chair. She'd brushed her hair back and tied it in a ponytail, and was wearing her green sweater and jeans. Zack held the baby, off-camera. Hope had finished her bottle, and a fatherly colonel was showing the teenaged boy how to burp her over his shoulder.

The general said, "All right, Jenny, just say who you are, and what day it is."

"I don't know what day it is...is it Tuesday?"

"Yes, it's Tuesday, January 15th, and you're in Corinth, Mississippi. Just tell your story, Jenny." General Mirabeau, his staff, Sergeant Amory, Captain Harris, and Zack watched in awed silence, listening intently as she went through her entire tale again. Occasionally she had to pause to wipe away tears, and so did the members of her audience.

General Mirabeau watched Jenny and then Zack give their video-recorded depositions from behind his desk. When they were finished, and after he had read Boone Vikersun's report on the massacre, he dismissed everyone from the room except for his CSO and his command sergeant major, who pulled up chairs across from him. A stack of eight-by-ten color prints had already been produced in another of the general's mobile headquarters vehicles, and was lying on the desk.

"So, what have you learned about Master Sergeant Vikersun?"

The brigadier said, "Well, he was a combat-decorated Special Forces soldier, assigned to the 5th Group out of Fort Campbell—"

"Was?"

"That's affirmative. He's listed as a deserter, as of August of last year. He's also wanted for theft of government property, and for numerous federal firearms violations. Apparently, when he went over the hill, he took some expensive Army property with him, including a top-line sniper rifle and night vision goggles."

Mirabeau shook his head ruefully. "And *he's* the one who's listed as a *deserter*? Hell, it sounds like he's the only one who's been fighting!"

"So it would appear."

"Sergeant Major, who do you know at NORTHCOM? Specifically, who do you know on Lieutenant General Armstead's staff? Do you have a hookup there?"

The command sergeant major was a squat fireplug of a man, with a pale complexion and black hair. He thought for a moment, and smiled. "Yes sir. I know a few people at NORTHCOM. In fact, I know General Armstead's CSM quite well."

"Well, that's good, because I have a short-fuse mission for you. You're getting on one of those Blackhawks outside, and you're flying up to Fort Campbell. You're going to find your counterpart or do whatever you have to do, and then you're going to put these pictures into General Armstead's hands. You personally, into his hands, personally. *Mano a mano*, understood? Then you're going to stay clamped onto him as tight as a tick on a hound, until you see him look at the pictures. All of the pictures. I'm going to write him a letter to go with the pictures. Oh, and let's include a copy of Jenny McClure's deposition. After he's seen the photographs and read my letter, ask him if he has a message for me. Then fly back here, or wherever our headquarters is located by then. On the way back, fly over these grid coordinates and shoot some pictures, but don't be obvious about it. Don't orbit, just make one pass. If you can't get them, don't sweat it, we'll send up a UAV when we can. Take whoever you need to shoot the pictures, or have the Blackhawk's crew do it. This mission won't be a problem, will it, Sergeant Major?"

"No sir! No problem at all! It'll be my honor. And I can goddamn well guarantee that I'll have these pictures in General Armstead's hands by this afternoon, and I'll see you again by dinner with his answer."

"Outstanding. You take care of the Blackhawk, and we'll get the package ready."

27

President Tambor met with Sidney Krantz in his special "quiet room" off the Oval Office. Tambor sat in his black leather recliner, smoking a cigarette. He was dressed casually, in jeans, loafers and an open-necked white dress shirt. Krantz was opposite him in another comfortable leather chair. "I'm running out of time," said the president. "That's why I called you down here. The Camp David conference is Thursday, and I'm supposed to have finalized our policy for dealing with the foreign military units."

"Why Thursday? I thought it was Friday. That's not much time."

"It's a Muslim thing. They didn't want it on Friday."

"I see."

"And now the Joint Chiefs are playing the passive-aggressive game. They won't commit to anything. They don't want to take responsibility. They've given me a range of options, but they're staying noncommittal. They want the decisions to all be on me."

"Well, let's face it," said Krantz, "you didn't put them in the JCS because of their backbones."

"True. Now the big sticking point is whether to have U.S. or U.N. control of the foreign units. The foreign leaders want the U.N. seal of approval on this operation. They want blue berets, blue helmets, everything. They hate being called mercenaries and contract soldiers. They don't want to do it like Tennessee. They want the U.N.'s blessing all the way. That's one of the things I have to decide before Camp David. But our reactionaries will go ballistic if they see the U.N.'s imprimatur on this operation. Whatever we gain in the Northwest we might lose elsewhere, if it leads to more resistance to federal authority. So I need to find a way to split this baby like Solomon, without killing it. How can we satisfy our foreign allies without enraging our own Neanderthals?"

"Well, you certainly can't put blue helmets on them. Don't even consider it. I'd say we follow the North American Legion model. Put the U.N. flag on one shoulder and their national flag on the other. Or put an American flag on one shoulder and a U.N. flag on the other. Hell, those flag patches are only velcro anyway. They can change them or stick them in their pockets whenever they're told to. They can even put on North American Legion flags, why not? Who's going to know? Let them wear whatever headgear they want, just as long as it's not U.N. sky blue. When they wear helmets, just let them use old American helmets. It's all about symbolism. We can tell our allies it's a U.N. mission, but that doesn't mean we need to tell our own citizens. I don't see the mainstream media making a big issue of it. They're still on our side at least. Which countries are providing the major forces for the operation?"

The president hesitated, and then answered. "Turkey and Pakistan are providing two full divisions each. The Saudis and the Gulf States are sponsoring the Turks, and China is sponsoring the Pakistanis. Russia is sponsoring the Uzbeks, the Kazaks and the Bulgarians. Actually, some of them will be Russians, but they won't be in Russian uniforms. There are some others, but those are the main players. The Chinese, the Russians and the Saudis will be the primary beneficiaries, after we subdue the Northwest. It's been in the works for a long time, but I couldn't tell you."

"What are they getting out of it?"

"Trade concessions, port deals, some mines…it's a long list. Coal, gas, grain, all of it. 'Payment in kind,' they're calling it. They're not interested in our treasuries, not at any interest rate. They say we're in technical default, and they won't take any more of our paper. They want physical control of the assets, nothing less."

Krantz whistled softly. "It's a good thing the media are still behind you, or you'd be crucified."

"I know, I know, it's a total nightmare," said the president. "But I just can't see any other way to break the rebellion and reassert federal authority. Tennessee proved that we can't rely on our own military to wipe out an insurgency." He took a long drag on his cigarette, his head back against the recliner, staring at the ceiling. "So we have to rely on foreign peacekeepers…but just how do we do it? It's very tricky."

Krantz said, "Wasn't there just a problem in Tennessee between the Kazak and Nigerian peacekeepers? I'm hearing rumors about the Kazaks getting a little overexcited and burning some homes down."

"Burning some homes down? You think that's all? You should see the reports I'm getting. Now there are bombs going off, and allied peacekeepers are being killed by the dozen. Rebels in Tennessee have even stolen tanks and gone on rampages! Just in the last few days, more than twenty Kazak and Nigerian peacekeepers have been killed by terrorists. Some North American Legion troops too."

"Wow! I'm sure not seeing any of *that* on the news."

"No, of course not," said the president. "Media cooperation has been one of the few bright spots in this mess. But that cooperation can only go so far. We need to wrap up the Mid South as quickly as we can. We won't be able to bury these stories forever. Tennessee needs to be finished."

"Oh, I *hate* those goddamn rednecks," Krantz snarled. "Who would have ever thought that we'd still be trying to root them out a year after the earthquakes?"

"I'm convinced they're pathological," said President Jamal Tambor. "They're not rational, like normal human beings. They won't even act in their own self-interest, no matter how much we've reached out to them and tried to help. They see a uniform and they shoot at it. It's all guns and religion down there; there's just no reasoning with them. Sidney, I've about had it with them. If I could just throw a switch and make all of those damned crackers disappear, I'd do it. If we still had neutron bombs, I swear I'd drop them down there in Tennessee. Don't smile, I'm not kidding."

"I know you're not," said Krantz. "I happen to agree."

"So I'm certainly not going to get worked up about the Kazaks burning down a few houses. Sometimes you have to fight fire with fire. Sometimes it's the only way to deal with ideologically committed diehard reactionaries. There's just no reasoning with them. They're socially re-tarded; they'll never fit into the new order. I swear, they're like a fish bone stuck in my throat. The sooner we can get them out of the way, the better."

"Assuming that you can shape the media coverage and the public perception," added Krantz. "That might be just a little difficult with neut-ron bombs."

"Well, I was using just a *bit* of hyperbole there. But I want you to tell that rural pacification guy—what's his name?"

"Robert Bullard."

"I want you to tell Robert Bullard to step up the pressure. Tell him to keep pushing those foreign contract battalions in Tennessee. Too many of the locals are still resisting us, and I want it over as fast as possible. I just want it over. I'm done with Tennessee; we have bigger fish to fry. Get it done, no matter what it takes. I'm beyond caring about how, just as long as it can be kept quiet in the media."

The president took another pull on his cigarette, and exhaled a blue stream. Then he said, "Give Bullard some extra motivation, if that's what it takes. Pay him off, promise him the moon, I don't care. Tell him he has to get finished down there so that he can head up my new Department of Internal Security. Tell him that we're launching the DIS just as soon as he wraps up the Mid South and he's free. That'll get him moving." The president took one more drag, stubbed out his cigarette, and stood up from his recliner to leave. As he got up, he had a small coughing fit. Krantz rose immediately after him. The cigarettes might be calming his nerves, but they were doing nothing for his health. At each visit, Krantz noticed a few more wrinkles, a little less hair, and now the smoker's cough.

Lieutenant General Lucian Armstead was walking from his car up the sidewalk to NORTHCOM headquarters, on his way back to work after lunch. When he reached the canvas-covered awning in front of the main doors, a short, burly command sergeant major in a dark blue ASU Class A uniform was coming the other way after exiting the building. The senior enlisted man raised his hand to render a salute, and the general prepared to reciprocate, in passing. Unexpectedly, the CSM turned almost directly in front of the general, blocking his path and holding his salute. The general was more than a head taller than the unknown senior enlisted man.

"General Armstead, good day, sir. I've just come from Corinth, Mississippi, where Lieutenant General Mirabeau has his forward HQ today. The general sends his regards. He's not sure if you're aware of the refugee situation down around Corinth, with thousands of refugees coming out of Tennessee. General Mirabeau has instructed me to put this package directly into your hands, and stay with you until you read his letter. It's personal and urgent, from him to you." The CSM dropped his salute and extended the manila folder with his left hand, and General Armstead accepted it. Then the sergeant major stepped backward and remained at a position of attention. Behind the general his own command sergeant major, who had already been tipped off by his visiting friend, was holding the general's aide and CSO at bay with a few whispered half-truths.

Lieutenant General Lucian Armstead knew that fresh trouble was brewing in West Tennessee. Flash message traffic was flying concerning a friendly-fire shootout between the Nigerian Peacekeeping Force and the Kazak Battalion. He had read the messages, but West Tennessee was not under his direct authority or control. The situation there was under the purview of the so-called department of rural pacification, and through them, the foreign "peacekeeping" units.

The chain of command in these "special administrative zones" went from the White House and the State Department, through the Department of Homeland Security to the nonexistent "department of rural pacification" and onward to the foreign military units. He was current on his reading of the message traffic, but new refugees, he had not heard about that. Besides the ongoing preparations for the Northwest campaign, the big story today was the continuing fallout from the blue-on-blue firefight between the Kazaks and the Nigerians. This amazing cluster foxtrot had resulted in numerous casualties among the peacekeepers on both sides. It was during times like this that General Armstead was glad to let the civilians in the rural pacification program take responsibility for the situation in West Tennessee.

The flap of the ten-by-twelve manila envelope that had been handed to him was sealed with a string wrapped between two small cardboard discs. He unwound the string, opened the envelope, and pulled out a hand-written letter clipped to a standard tan file folder. The letterhead was Mirabeau's invention, completely unofficial, undoubtedly created on a computer as a humorous gibe, although it looked genuine. It read "Commanding General, U.S. Army South." There was no such command in the United States Army. Armstead chuckled. Marcus Aurelius Mirabeau was making a teasing reference to his own command of NORTHCOM, U.S. Army North. He read the note, and his smile disappeared.

Lucian: This happened in your AO on Saturday, in Radford County TN near Mannville. Done by Kazak Batt. Est'd 400+ dead. Have met eyewitnesses—story checks true. If Duty, Honor, Country still means anything to us, this cannot stand. I cannot and will not abide this. We need to meet ASAP. Send meeting time and location via return courier. Suggest Fort Rucker visit tomorrow in order. If no timely response, I will act with forces under my command to resolve situation SW TN. Lucian, please get on the right side of this. Join me, please. Tempus Fugit. God is watching us.
—Mirabeau

General Lucian Armstead had no trouble reading the jotted note despite the erratic handwriting. Four hundred dead? There must be a mistake somewhere. Marcus Aurelius Mirabeau was always showboating. He re-read the letter. The white sheet of paper was attached to a tan folder with a large silver paperclip. He slid the clip off with his thumbnail, opened the file, saw the first eight-by-ten color photograph in the thick stack, and his world tipped off its axis forever.

He staggered inside the NORTHCOM headquarters building as though through a haze, and made it to his corner office on the second floor. In the outer office, he told his secretary to hold all calls and cancel all appointments. He didn't hear them asking if he felt all right. His breath was short and labored, his heart was hammering. He closed the door and went to his desk, collapsed into his chair and looked at the photographs again. Taped to a piece of cardboard along with the photographs was a CD in a paper envelope. "Eyewitness report" was handwritten on the sleeve. He slid the disc into his computer.

With no preamble or explanation, the video player came up on his screen. A girl, shown from the waist up, was sitting on a chair facing the camera. She had blond hair with bangs down to her amber-colored eyes, and a gaunt face with high cheekbones and a narrow chin. Behind her was a plain wall of light wood paneling, covered with maps. Military maps.

She began. "My name is Jenny McClure, I'm seventeen years old. Today is Tuesday, January 15th. I lived in Germantown, Tennessee, until my parents were killed after the first earthquake. After that, I was staying with my aunt and uncle near Mannville, Tennessee; that's about seventy-five miles east of Memphis. What I'm telling now is what happened in

Mannville on Saturday, January the 12th. I was there in Mannville, at the regular Saturday swap meet, when about two hundred Kazak soldiers came and surrounded us. They were on horses and in trucks."

And so she told the entire story, from her perspective. She described the people being burned with the non-lethal crowd-control heat machine, and then being marched onto school buses. She told how the young girls had been forced to climb onto a troop truck, to be taken to a country mansion where the Kazaks were having a drunken party and preparing to rape them. She described being dragged to an upstairs bedroom by an American traitor, who was working with the Kazaks as a translator, and how she had escaped in the snowstorm. She described her confused journey through the snow, until she was climbing up a ravine and discovered the hundreds of frozen bodies. Jenny stared numbly at the camera, sniffing occasionally, tears running in tracks down her face, but she continued. She told of hearing a baby's cry in the storm, and how she discovered the infant that she named Hope, wrapped in blankets under her dead mother.

Her story took fifteen minutes to tell, and when it was over, General Lucian Armstead was crying too. He took the photographs and spread them across his desk, in two neat rows of ten, and stared at them as a group, the massed bodies merging from photograph to photograph.

The call came on the government-only DSN line. Bob Bullard's secretary put it through to his office after calling him on the intercom. "He says he's Sidney from D.C. Do you want to take his call?"

"Sure, put him through."

"Director Bullard? Sid Krantz."

"Yeah, Sid, what's up?"

"I've just spoken to the boss. I'd be less than truthful if I didn't tell you that he's disappointed with what he's seeing in Tennessee, and particularly in southwestern Tennessee. The, um, evacuation and pacification don't seem to be tracking on our time table."

"Well, I don't know where you're getting your information, but we've made big improvements since the last time we talked. We're making a lot of progress. We're getting the whole area firmly under government control."

Krantz replied, "Firmly under control? Well, that's not how we're seeing it up here. We're getting reports about bombs going off, gun battles, and allied peacekeepers being killed by the dozen. Insurgents have even stolen tanks—is that true, or not true?"

"That's true, but—"

"Bob, that does not sound like 'under control' to me! We're getting reports that more than twenty Kazak and Nigerian peacekeepers have been killed by insurgents in the past few days, and some North American Legion soldiers too. You call that making progress?"

"Look, Sid, I'm telling you, those events were outliers. Total flukes. They're not representative of what's really going on. The area is definitely getting under control. We've just had to knock some heads, and you know that's not always pretty. Sometimes there's blowback, but we're on pace to be able to bring reconstruction crews into the last problem counties by March at the latest."

"March is too late. I'm sorry, but from our point of view the situation down there is getting worse, not better. The boss and I have decided we need to take a closer look to evaluate the progress. I'm coming down to review the state of affairs in person."

"Don't put yourself to any trouble, Sid. There's really no reason. I'm sure I can answer any questions you might have."

"Well, the boss thinks there's reason, and that's all that either you or I really need to know, isn't it? I'll be flying directly into Fort Campbell tomorrow."

Bullard paused and then replied, "Suit yourself. Have your staff call my staff and make the arrangements."

"But I do have a few more questions before I come down."

"Shoot."

"How many FEMA relocation camps do we have in western and middle Tennessee? What's their current census, and what's their maximum capacity?"

"FEMA camps? You'll have to give me a few minutes to find out. That's not exactly my bailiwick. Can't you just call FEMA for that?"

"Ballpark is good enough."

"Ballpark? Ballpark, I'd say a dozen or fifteen primary camps, with a census of maybe a hundred thousand, maybe more. It fluctuates. I don't know if they're at max capacity. That's not my department, not directly. You should call FEMA if you want better numbers."

"That's close enough. One more thing—I need you to do something before I fly down tomorrow. I need you to round up some rats."

"Did you say...*rats*?"

"That's what I said. Rats. At least a dozen live rats, in cages. The more the better. I'll explain it when I get down there."

"Yeah, you'll have to explain it to me. I'm not in the rat-collecting business."

"Well, we'll see about that. Anyway, I'll be flying down tomorrow."

"What time?"

"I've got a C-12 penciled in for the afternoon. I'll remain overnight and return Thursday, unless we wrap up early, in which case I'll fly back tomorrow night."

"Send my office a message with the particulars. I'll have a driver meet your plane and bring you to my house. I don't think it would be a good idea for you to come by our headquarters during working hours."

"I was thinking the same thing. I'd rather have our discussion in private."

"That's fine. Make it after 1700. A driver will meet your plane."

Friends of friends allowed the two men to set up a temporary workstation in Fort Campbell's branch telephone exchange, without getting formal written approval through channels or notifying their bosses. Their friends didn't need to hear more than that it was part of a temporary security exercise. The two men were wearing windbreakers with the name and logo of a national telephone company, and carried toolboxes. They were still setting up, using the out-of-band management line that was normally used by phone technicians to manage and troubleshoot the system. The OOB line was connected via a modem to the branch exchange primary console.

Tapping the phone lines in building 1405 had become a top priority since last night's meeting at Charlie Donelson's house, and the branch exchange was the best location to accomplish this task. Once Bullard's office line was located, it was bridged to another line on the same local branch exchange. This working phone was located in the unused office, where the two conspirators were setting up shop. One of the two men was connecting a laptop for recording the calls when they heard the phone ring. Both men were wearing ear buds, listening for calls on a number of phone lines.

The older of the two bogus phone technicians was Ira Gersham, also known as Dewey O. Lieberman.

The other man said, "Were you ready for that? Did you record it?"

Ira said, "Yeah, I got it."

"I didn't catch the beginning. Who was that, Bullard?"

"Yeah, Bob Bullard himself."

"I thought his lines would be encrypted."

"He thought so too," said Ira. "Actually, they *are* encrypted, but I've got the super-user system password. That puts us inside their encryption, at least on their DSN land lines. Lucky for us, these guys are just dummies. They don't know any better, or they'd use another layer of encryption at each end, one I can't get inside."

"How the hell did you get the password?"

"Let's just say it's not *what* you know, it's *who* you know." Ira winked at his colleague. "But you don't need to know. Just know that I know. That's all you need to know."

"What was that bit at the end, about rounding up rats? Was that code or something?"

"I don't know. Maybe. I'll have to play it back, but I'm pretty sure the guy said rats. 'Round up rats, in cages'."

"I wonder who Sidney Krantz is."

Ira said, "I don't know, but if he's coming down from D.C. to meet Bullard, we need to find out fast. He should be searchable, if Krantz is his real name and not a legend."

"A legend?"

"A spook name. A cover name."

"Oh."

"FEMA camps and rats—that's just too weird. And did you catch his reference to 'the boss'? I'm taking this one to the colonel. He needs to hear this. So you're okay here? You know what to do?"

"Yeah, Ira, you explained it pretty good."

"I'll come back in a couple of hours. If you hear anything you think we need to know before that, call this number and let it ring four times. Nobody will pick up the call, but somebody will come to retrieve the tape ASAP."

"All right. Sounds good."

"Okay, I'll see you in a few."

Colonel Tom Spencer and Boone Vikersun sat in the colonel's Jeep Cherokee, going over their plan. They were parked behind NORTH-COM's headquarters, with a view of the back of the three-story cement building. They had been telephoned by a confederate when General Armstead had returned from lunch. Now a sheet of white paper with a black "X" across it had been placed against a certain window in the middle of the second floor, confirming that the general was in his office. Old and trusted friends were willing to perform such small tasks, without asking why.

Boone was clean-shaven, and his hair was freshly cut to Army standards. Master Sergeant Vikersun and Colonel Spencer were both in officers' Army Service Uniforms, with blue coats and trousers. Colonel Spencer was wearing his own uniform. The rank insignias on Boone's shoulders indicated that he was a major.

The colonel said, "You clean up pretty well, 'Major Garrett'."

"You can thank Bibi Donelson for that. Charlie's wife can do just about anything. She worked for years as a hairdresser at the Post Exchange. Plus, she's a great cook."

"That's true, but I don't think that's why he brought her back from the Philippines. And it sure doesn't hurt to have a hookup in the Bamboo Mafia. How else could we get you a uniform on just a few hours' notice, if we didn't have a connection at the dry cleaners?"

Boone said, "I just hope the real major doesn't show up looking for his uniform."

"He won't. He's deployed until March."

"I'm lucky they found me a uniform this big. Bibi actually had to take up the legs and arms."

"She should get hazardous duty pay, just for giving you a shave and a haircut. Did she do it outside at least? I'd hate to think of what crawled away from *that* pile of hair. Hopefully, she was wearing rubber gloves."

Boone grinned. "With all due respect, go screw yourself, sir."

"I'll take that under advisement, *Major*."

"So, do I fit the part? I don't know what a special courier is supposed to look like."

"You look perfect, like you just walked out of the Pentagon."

"I look like a doorman, or a bellhop. A blue uniform, with gold braid! I'll never live this down."

"It's the new Army, Boone."

"What was wrong with our green Class A's? At least people knew we were soldiers. If I wanted to wear a blue uniform, I would have joined the Air Force or the Navy." He nervously felt the knot of his tie, straightening it by feel. The pressed Army Service Uniform was an unfamiliar form of camouflage for a Special Forces sniper more comfortable hiding in the forest. "Why did they change over to blue anyway?"

"That's way above my pay grade," said Colonel Spencer. "Nobody asked me, that's for sure. The main thing is you look right for who you're supposed to be."

"What if they ask for my ID?"

"They won't. I'll flash my old Courier Authorization Card, and put it away quick. They won't check the date. You'll see, this will be easy. The bigger the bluff, the easier it is to pull off. Come on, it's time to put on your chain."

"Do couriers really wear these things locked to their wrist?" Boone Vikersun was accustomed to carrying a rifle, not a briefcase. One end of the foot-long silver chain disappeared into the case, the other was attached to a ratcheting handcuff. He snapped the cuff onto his left wrist and slipped the key into his right pants pocket.

"Yeah, they do, sometimes. But mainly it's a great visual prop. It's the only thing anybody will notice, because of that chain." Colonel Spencer looked at his watch. "Come on, Boone, it's time. He's been in his office for fifteen minutes. The back exit will be taped open for us. Once we're inside, it's straight up the stairwell to the second floor. Then it's only one hallway down to his office. Ready? Let's do it."

Boone looked across the front seat at the colonel and said, "You know, you're burning your bridges today. They'll remember you here.

After this, there's no going back. This is your Rubicon. It's the end of your career, once we walk into that office. One way or the other."

Spencer sighed and leaned his head back against the padded rest. "I realize that, and I've made my peace with it. But you know what? I want to be on your side of the Rubicon. I've been on the wrong of it side for too long."

"Thanks for saying that, Colonel. That means a lot, coming from you. You know, it was getting mighty lonely, being an army of one." Boone put on his beret, adjusting it in the SUV's visor mirror. The briefcase was upright on his lap so that he could reach over his head. The beret was black, not green, with a gold oak leaf on its blue flash. Today he was a major from the 101st Airborne Division, currently assigned to the Joint Chiefs of Staff, delivering Top Secret / Sensitive Compartmented Information directly to General Armstead. His purported classified information was so hot that he even had a Special Forces colonel escorting him on the post. Boone shook his head and grimaced at himself in the mirror. "Impersonating an officer...that's a new low, even for me. Theft, desertion and murder—all that I can handle. But don't you ever tell a living soul that I impersonated an officer."

The door to General Armstead's outer office was wide open. Boone Vikersun and Colonel Spencer walked in and headed directly for the general's private office. This inner door was closed. Colonel Spencer walked up to the appointment secretary's desk, which was set at ninety degrees to the side of the inner door. The large outer office also contained several other desks, one of which was occupied by a staff sergeant, who glanced up from his computer screen at the pair of tall Army officers, and then stared at the silver chain connecting Boone's briefcase to his wrist.

Colonel Spencer addressed the middle-aged female government service secretary tersely, after briefly presenting his outdated Courier Authorization Card. "We have a classified briefing to present to the general. The major has been sent directly from the White House. This briefing is for the general's eyes only."

"Is General Armstead expecting you, Colonel...?" She peered over her reading glasses at his plastic nametag. "I'm afraid the general is not seeing anyone this afternoon."

"This briefing concerns the National Command Authority," said Colonel Spencer, ignoring her protestations. This was not, strictly speaking, a lie. It did involve the president's national command authority, but not in the way that the secretary and the staff sergeant might have understood it. Spencer nodded to Boone, and he turned and opened the general's door.

As they expected, it was not locked. Generals did not lock their inner office doors, because no one, simply no one, would ever dare to enter that inner sanctum unannounced and uninvited. It was beyond imagining that anyone would ever barge in on the three-star commanding general of NORTHCOM. Surely lightning would strike, or the bowels of the earth would open wide. But precisely because it was unimaginable, it was possible. This was how Colonel Spencer had explained his plan to Boone when they were brainstorming methods for gaining the general's undivided attention. General Armstead's CSO, XO and CSM all had separate offices along the same hallway, leaving the general's privacy protected only by the aura of impenetrability and a closed but unlocked door.

Lieutenant General Armstead's NORTHCOM headquarters was located deep within a vast Army base. His office was on the second floor of a fortress-like building teeming with military officers and NCOs. He was therefore perfectly safe from unwanted intrusion, and in no need of defenses other than those afforded by standard military protocol and tradition. Boone smiled at the ease with which they penetrated the ramparts surrounding his private inner office. This was a textbook example of the nimble Special Forces mentality overcoming the straight-leg Army leviathan.

Colonel Spencer closed the door behind them, shutting out the secretary's feeble call of "You can't just go in there…"

Armstead's corner office was large enough for two windows on one side and another on the shorter wall. As expected, the walls were covered with bookshelves, plaques and photographs. At a glance, it was evident that the general had come up through the armored-warfare career path. An American flag hung on a stand in the corner of the room away from the windows. His wide desk was between the windows on the long wall.

General Armstead seemed disoriented by the sudden intrusion, and looked up from his desk at Colonel Spencer with a glimmer of recognition. Boone expected the general to be angry at the invasion, but he was oddly unresponsive, appearing distracted. His face was red and his eyes were bleary. Had he been indulging in lunchtime cocktails? Boone couldn't imagine straight-laced General Lucian Armstead indulging in a liquid lunch. The intruders stood side by side before his desk, and came to attention. Boone briefly had the thought that the general appeared as though he was fully expecting the appearance of assassins, and that he was not planning to offer the least resistance. His appearance and reaction were nothing at all like Boone had expected.

Colonel Spencer said, "General Armstead, please pardon the irregularity of our visit, but we have information that you must see without delay. There was simply no time for us to go through normal channels. You'll understand as soon as you see what we have to show you."

Boone unlocked his wrist manacle and opened the briefcase, set a laptop on the desk, lifted its screen and turned it around to face the general.

The Predator video and Boone's photographs were loaded into the machine, ready to play as soon as it powered up. Lucian Armstead sank back into his chair and watched the ten-minute film with almost no expression. The two visitors remained standing before his desk. After the video, the still photographs came on the screen, changing every five seconds.

The general stared at the screen, and then mumbled, "This is unbelievable. I was just handed those same pictures, on the sidewalk outside this building, less than one hour ago." General Armstead opened the narrow top drawer of his desk, removed a stack of photos, and spread them across his desk like a fan of playing cards. They were slightly different angles of the same scenes on the computer screen. "These pictures were sent to me by Lieutenant General Marcus Mirabeau, who is in Corinth, Mississippi, today. Corinth is directly across from where this massacre happened in Tennessee. This morning he debriefed a survivor who was at the massacre site, and sent these pictures to me by another courier." He looked up at his two visitors, misery and defeat written in his eyes. "Colonel Spencer, does everybody in the United States Army except me know about this massacre?"

The colonel said, "No sir, very few people know about it. I would estimate less than twenty. But I know how General Mirabeau obtained those photographs." Spencer nodded to Boone. "He took the photographs, sir, Sunday morning. That's why he's here—he's an eyewitness."

"What were you doing down in Radford County, Major?"

"I'm sorry, sir, but I'm not really an officer. I'm a master sergeant in the 1st Battalion of the 5th Special Forces Group—or I was. I'm only wearing this uniform, well, so that we could get into your office to see you. My real name is Boone Vikersun. You might say that I was on detached independent duty, General. Or you might say that I deserted. I suppose it depends on your perspective about these things. For the last six months, I've been trying to organize resistance cells in West Tennessee—but that all ended on Saturday, with this massacre." He swallowed, and paused. "The only good to come of it was that I was able to take these photographs. I sent another pair of agents south to Corinth with a second camera, in case I didn't make it here. Evidently, my agents had success, and somehow they got the pictures to General Mirabeau. He must have had the same idea that we did: that you needed to be made aware of this situation."

"Was one of your 'agents' a teenaged girl named Jenny McClure?"

Boone was taken aback. "Why, yes sir—but how did you know that?"

"You haven't seen her video deposition? She gives an overview of the situation, including the massacre. I just watched it."

Boone smiled. "I didn't know about any other video. I only knew about the Predator video that you just saw. General Mirabeau must have filmed her in Corinth this morning. General, do you know if the baby is still alive? And what about the boy she was with?"

"They're both alive and well. Judging from what I could see and hear on her video, the baby seems to be just fine."

Boone nodded, still smiling. "Well, that's something, anyway."

"Hope," said the general.

"Excuse me, sir?"

"The baby's name is Hope. That foundling was the sole survivor of the Mannville massacre. That's what Jenny McClure called her. Hope. She said that, on her video."

"Yes sir. I'm glad to hear the baby is all right. That was very important to us."

"So, Master Sergeant Vikersun, you killed those Kazak soldiers in the pictures?"

"Yes sir, that I did."

"And that was you in the stolen ASV, raising hell with the Kazaks and the Nigerians, and cutting a path of death and destruction clear across Tennessee?"

"Yes sir, that was also me. Along with two others."

The general stared up at Boone. "You're really something, Master Sergeant Vikersun, I must say. It would seem that you've been putting your Special Forces training and experience to good use."

"I did my best, sir. But it wasn't enough to stop this massacre from happening."

"No...well...what I meant to say... Master Sergeant, for the last six months you've been fighting them, while we've been...while I've been... this." The general gestured about his office. "While I've been doing... *nothing*. Worse than nothing: while I've been complicit. While I've been a...while I've been a *collaborator*. How did it ever come to this?" General Armstead stared toward the American flag on its stand, in the opposite corner of his office.

Colonel Spencer said, "We've all been collaborators, General, all of us. Except for Master Sergeant Vikersun, and damned few others. I think that I could count the soldiers who have been actively resisting on my two hands. The ones that I know of, anyway."

"What should I do, Colonel? What should I do?"

"That's why we're here, General. That's why we came. To start, I think you should meet our working group. It's only a dozen Special Forces operators at this point, but it's quite a collection of talent, if I do say so. We're still weighing our options, considering various courses of action. At this point, our most effective weapons would appear to be that Predator video, those pictures, and now, Jenny McClure's eyewitness testimony."

Armstead nodded. "I'll meet your people. But I need to tell you something else. Oh my God, I can hardly believe this is happening! This is just unbelievable, except, except that *nothing* is unbelievable anymore. It's all happened, this…" He swept his hand above the photographs. "This all happened."

General Armstead went silent, so Colonel Spencer said, "Yes sir, it all really happened. And it happened on our watch. It happened under our noses. And it's being run out of Building 1405, less than a mile from this office."

The general said nothing, but continued to stare at the flag. The room was quiet for at least a full minute. Boone thought that if the general was left alone with a pistol after this meeting, he might use it to fire one shot. Did the general have a pistol in one of his desk drawers? Probably.

Finally, General Armstead cleared his throat and said, "Colonel, I can't ask you to forgive me or to excuse my inaction. That's impossible. But we may be able to atone. We may yet be able to rectify this situation. There is something that I need to tell you both. I'll be seeing the president on Thursday. In person."

Colonel Spencer replied, "Sir, if you're thinking of showing him the pictures and the videos, frankly, I don't think that would be effective. Sir, the Kazaks are in Tennessee at the direct request of the president himself. I don't think he would be receptive to—"

"I wasn't thinking about showing him the pictures, Colonel. I was thinking of something else. Something…entirely different. Colonel, have you heard of Operation Buffalo Jump?" General Armstead stood up from his desk and walked across his office to a tall file cabinet with a combination lock on the top drawer. He worked the dial, opened the drawer, and removed a two-inch-thick red-and-white binder. "Gentlemen, Operation Buffalo Jump." He returned to his desk and set the binder down. He remained standing. The general was as tall as Boone, about four inches over six feet.

"I'll be at Camp David on Thursday, to meet key allied military leaders and to discuss this operation. Operation Buffalo Jump is a joint and combined operation with several "allied" militaries. In short, it's the invasion of the Northwest, to bring the so-called Free States back under federal control. Yes, the rebellious provinces shall be subdued and returned to the fold, by force of arms. The president will be making an appearance at Camp David on Thursday, to instill confidence and provide assurances to our allies. Except they're not allies, they're damned vultures! They're here to carve up the remains of the United States, as a partial settlement for our national debts. The militaries participating are mere proxies for China and certain other nations. They'll be granted energy and mineral concessions; at least that's my take on the situation. Buffalo Jump is set for early this summer, or whenever the Tennessee situation is wrapped up. And to think I was considering resigning my commission over this! But not now. Not now! So whatever you have in mind, gentlemen, I'll hear you out. But I think we need to focus on Camp David. That's where I'll be on Thursday, and so will the president."

Colonel Spencer said, "General, we were not even considering taking that type of direct action against—"

"No. Of course not. And I would not be a party to any attempt to… my God, I can't even speak the words!"

"General, we're not considering any type of direct action along those lines. For one thing, it would have no real effect; the vice president is almost as bad as the president."

"They're both traitors, they both defile the Constitution they swore to defend!"

"General, you said this planning conference will be at Camp David?"

"Yes, on Thursday."

"Then I'm sure you're familiar with Raven Rock Mountain, six miles north of Camp David in Pennsylvania."

"Ah yes, Site R. Of course. The Alternate Joint Communications Center. Possibly the most famous 'secure undisclosed location' in America. I've been to The Rock many times. It's a mountain of solid granite, with a small city inside it. I think I've got a bunk there with my name on it, although I've never stayed overnight."

Colonel Spencer said, "My understanding is that its mission is to run emergency communications for the Pentagon during and after a nuclear war, isn't that right?"

"Well, that's mostly right. Yes. That's essentially correct, if not the complete story. It's also the alternate National Military Command Center, the standby Pentagon. At least, depending on which war scenario is playing out. If it takes a twenty-megaton direct hit, it won't be anything but a smoking crater, and other backup communication sites would be activated. But short of that, yes."

"General, isn't it true that the Emergency Broadcast System can be triggered and run from Site R? That almost every radio and television station in America can be switched to the EBS during a time of national emergency?"

"Yes, that's correct. They can do that and a lot more, all from inside Raven Rock Mountain."

"And you're authorized to enter Site R?"

"Well, yes, of course. Anytime I want to, announced or unannounced. I'm the commanding general of NORTHCOM. I'm damn near the top of the cleared list."

"Well, General," said Colonel Spencer, "that raises an entire new range of possibilities."

Bullard's admin assistant knocked on his office door.

"Come in, Jeff." Director Bullard spun his executive chair around toward his desk.

Sinclair entered and sat in a leather and stainless steel chair across from him. "We've got something here. It might connect to the missing Legion humvee, and from there back to the situation with the Nigerians and the Kazaks."

"Go on."

"Remember yesterday's morning briefing? We found an audio clip of an American voice, and we thought it might have been sent by accident from that Kazak armored security vehicle. The one that was stolen."

"The one that almost started a war between the Kazaks and the Nigerians."

"That's the one. Well, yesterday we fed that clip into Omnivore, and we just got a hit. Last night, somebody made a phone call from Tennessee to Maryland, and Omnivore made a digital voice match."

"Who was it?"

"At this point, it looks like the call was originated by an Army private named Douglas Dolan. He called his mother's house of record in Baltimore. I can request a transcript, which will take a few hours. Then I can print it out if you want to read it."

"What's the bottom line? Who's Douglas Dolan, and where is he now?"

"Private Dolan was assigned to an engineering regiment out of Fort Leonard Wood, Missouri. His battalion was sent to Memphis after the first earthquake, and he's been missing and presumed dead since last January. After the second quake, he dropped off the radar completely, until he made that broadcast from the Kazak ASV. Then last night he called Baltimore, and Omnivore put a name on him."

"So where is he?"

"We don't know where he is now, we just know where he called from last night. He called from about twelve miles west of Clarksville, off of Highway 79. We've narrowed it down to about a dozen possible homes and trailers. They're down on someplace called Roaring Hollow Road. Of course, he also could have made the call from a vehicle, or he could have been on foot and not in any house at all. The phone didn't have GPS, so we could only triangulate off of cell towers."

Bullard said, "I thought *all* cell phones were GPS trackable today."

"I thought so too, but apparently not. It was a prepaid phone, an old one, but it still had an active account. I'm told the GPS function can be hacked out of those phones, even if they were originally GPS capable. We'll figure out how that happened later."

"So who owns the phone? Dolan?"

"No way to tell. It was bought for cash two years ago in North Carolina. More minutes have been put on it with airtime cards a couple of times, but they were always bought with cash, in little stores that don't have surveillance cameras."

"So the owner is a pro," observed Bullard.

"Or just careful."

"Dolan... Can we place him in North Carolina two years ago?"

"I have no clue. We're just starting to work him up."

"What about these homes on Roaring Hollow Road? What do we know about them?"

"Nothing yet, we just got the alert message from Omnivore. We're starting from square one."

"Well, get a Predator over them, and record all activity in and out. People, phone calls, radios—anything. Get the property tax and title information on all of the landowners, rental contracts and any other records. Give them a data-mining rectal exam. And find out everything you can about Private Dolan. Find out about Dolan's family, especially his mother." Bullard smiled, and cracked his knuckles. "This is great—this is just the hook we needed. Keep me informed at each new step."

"Will do, boss."

"And show me where this Roaring Hollow Road is." Bullard stood and walked across his office to a large-scale wall map of Tennessee and Kentucky, and found Fort Campbell and Clarksville. Then he traced his finger west along Highway 79.

"The road is too small to see on this map," said Sinclair. "You'll have to look on your computer to get down to the right scale. It's about here, south of 79."

"That's on the north side of the Cumberland River. Damn, that's close." Rivers formed natural barriers and choke points in Tennessee, especially since so many bridges were still down after the earthquakes. The remaining key bridges were tightly guarded, and watched carefully. But not carefully enough, evidently. Their terrorist quarry had already managed to cross the mighty Tennessee River undetected at Carrolton. Now they were apparently on the north side of the Cumberland, the last remaining water obstacle before Clarksville and Fort Campbell.

"Close is right," agreed Bullard's assistant. "They could practically walk here from where that call was made."

"Okay, get some surveillance teams out there. Put remote video snoopers on all of the intersections; just make sure the installation teams are careful. Any strangers driving down those back roads are going to be spotted in about five seconds. These guys must be damned good to have made it this far—we don't want to spook them by being clumsy. Keep at least one Predator on top of Roaring Hollow Road around the clock. That'll be easy this close to base. Keep on top of all of the cell phone activity in that sector in real time, in case they slip up again. I've got a bad feeling about these guys. After what they did in West Tennessee, I don't want to take any chances. I'd like to take them alive if possible, but not if it means we spook them and they take off again.

"Let me know about any suspicious activity we spot from the Predators, and then I'll decide if we're going to go for a SWAT raid, or if we're just going to drop a Hellfire on their asses. In case we decide on a raid, put the tactical response team on standby. Just be careful, and don't tip them off before we can pin them down and corner them. I'd rather just blow them to hell with a missile than tip them off and have them scatter."

Bob Bullard did not mention another factor that was consuming his thoughts. This Roaring Hollow Road, between the Cumberland River and Highway 79, was practically in Fort Campbell's backyard. Miles of Highway 79 formed the unfenced southern boundary of Fort Campbell. Just as he had suspected, the group that had killed over twenty Kazak, Nigerian and Mexican peacekeepers was being drawn toward Fort Campbell like bloodhounds on a fresh scent trail. Toward Fort Campbell, the home of both the 5th Special Forces Group and his own Department of Rural Pacification.

Yes, he'd prefer to take these boys alive, just to see who they were and what made them tick. He'd like to run a long-term aerial and ground surveillance on them, and find out all of their contacts and discover any other safehouses. But if there wasn't a clear opening for a slam-dunk SWAT raid to take them alive, then once he located them, he'd just drop a missile and be done with it. These killers from southwestern Tennessee were extremely dangerous, and Bob Bullard had not risen to his current position by taking unnecessary risks.

General Mirabeau's command sergeant major did make it back to Corinth before suppertime. In addition, on their return flight the Blackhawk's crew chief had managed to snap a series of high-resolution digital photographs of the massacre site from 6,000 feet up. The brand new photographs were compared to archived Google Earth images of the same terrain. There was no doubt that the ravine formerly at those coordinates had been bulldozed flat. Track marks left by an earthmover were still visible on the freshly churned earth. A few dozen small pine trees had obviously been dug up from nearby and replanted over this scar on the earth. After a year or two, as grass and weeds took root and the trees continued to grow, the cover-up would have become all but un-detectable. But the evidence was clear in the side-by-side imagery.

The general's staff traveled with him and was never far from hand. He called a planning meeting for 1700 hours in his mobile headquarters RV. A folding mess hall table was set up lengthwise, extending from the front of his desk down the center of the open space. His officers took their seats on either side of the table, his CSO at the far end. As usual, they were dressed in their digital ACU combat uniforms. The late afternoon staff meeting was not out of the ordinary, but the mood was more serious than usual. The nine officers were already seated in their places by 1700, ready and waiting. They all stood to attention when General Mirabeau entered the RV at 1701.

"Seats, gentlemen," he said as he dropped into his own chair behind his desk. "You've all seen the pictures, and you've seen the witness depositions. I've prayed over this, and, well, I've decided we're not going to just stand by and receive refugees while Americans are massacred less than twenty miles from where we're sitting. So this is the bottom line: I want to be ready to conduct a helicopter assault on the site of the massacre, and on the barracks and headquarters of the Kazak Battalion. I want an ops plan that I can execute in twenty-four hours. Let me know how many heli-copters and how many troops we can assemble and how fast. Count all of the operational helos at Benning, Rucker and Hunter.

"Our first objective will be to secure the area around the ravine. As soon as that's accomplished, we'll deal with the Kazaks. They'll surrender and make an accounting of their actions, or they'll be wiped out. For plan-ning purposes, assume that NORTHCOM is uncooperative. Uncooper-ative, but not hostile. I should know more about NORTHCOM's likely reaction by tomorrow, but I want to be prepared to launch under a full spectrum of contingencies. We'll meet again at 1900, so be prepared to brief me on options. For now, we'll go around the table as usual. Give your normal p.m. SITREPS, and then we'll do a little brainstorming."

Colonel Spencer drove Boone Vikersun from Fort Campbell to his home in a newer subdivision north of Clarksville. The colonel's wife made them spaghetti for dinner, and then they retired to his office to discuss the events of the past few days, and plan their next moves. The colonel used his computer to make copies of the primary photographic and video evidence while they talked. Colonel Spencer had changed to casual civilian clothes when he got home, but "Major Garrett" was still dressed in his borrowed blue Army Service Uniform.

Boone said, "I can't believe that the general went for it." He had never been to the colonel's home, and he examined with keen interest the military artifacts on the walls and shelves.

"I can," replied Colonel Spencer. "He's a good man. He taught at the War College when he was a one-star and I was a major. That's where I first met him. We've stayed in touch, off and on. You could tell that this situation with the foreign mercenaries has been eating his guts out. He was just waiting for a push, and the massacre was all it took."

"It seems almost like a miracle that we walked into his office right after he'd seen the other pictures. It's almost like he'd been set up to hear our pitch. Like he had been primed for it."

"Boone, are you a religious man?"

"Religious? No, not especially. Not in a formal sense. But it's hard not to believe that there's a higher purpose at work when things like this happen. I mean, what are the odds? Zack and Jenny got the other camera to General Mirabeau this morning, and the pictures were on General Armstead's desk just a few hours later—and then we come walking in. How does that 'just happen'?"

"It doesn't," said Colonel Spencer. "There's definitely something working here, I can feel it. Like when Phil Carson put that Bible on the flag with the beret. That hit me like an electric shock, like a bullet. And it was done by Phil Carson. Phil Carson? Who in the hell is Phil Carson? And where in the hell did he come from anyway, walking out of nowhere into this deal? He's just some old Special Forces guy who just *happened* to have run SOG missions with your father. Then forty years later, he's shipwrecked in Alabama, and then here he is. I mean, come on! None of this 'just happened.' Something truly extraordinary is going on. It's like we've been parachuted straight into the eye of a hurricane. No, we've been put here for a purpose. Carson showing up—that's no accident. That's something else. I don't know what it is, but it's no accident."

"Phil's a trip. Don't let his age fool you—he's an operator."

"Are you comfortable taking him?" asked Spencer.

"He wants to go, he wants to do it. And I've got tremendous faith in him. He makes things happen. He can adapt to anything and come out on top. I've seen it. Whatever happens at Camp David, he's somebody I want on my team."

"But can he pull off playing a general? He'll have to be a hell of an actor."

"He can do it," said Boone. "No question. And he looks like a general—he's got that hard, flinty-eyed look."

"He's not too old for it?"

"Hell no, he's perfect. He'll be a great general. Armstead has a full day to get him up to speed on Operation Buffalo Jump. I guarantee you he'll know that op plan backwards and forwards by Thursday."

"Boone, I know you'll be able to deal with whatever happens at Camp David, but everything hinges on what goes down at Raven Rock. If

General Armstead can initiate the EBS, everything will be a 'go' here at our end. We're going to take down Bullard's entire rural pacification program, and then I'll make the case to the 5th Group and the 101st. I have a good plan; I've laid the groundwork. I have friends at Fort Bragg ready to do the same there, and after that it'll go viral around the Army and the rest of the military. But if Raven Rock doesn't work, if they can't trigger the EBS, we'll be able to abort down here. But that'll still leave you trapped at Camp David. Then what?"

"I'm not sure what we'll do. We'll wing it. We'll just see what happens. We'll improvise, we'll adapt on the fly. If Armstead comes back with his helicopter, we might get out that way. Otherwise, we'll have to just escape and evade the best we can. What the hell, Colonel, I never figured I'd live forever. But that's only if Raven Rock doesn't work. If the EBS is initiated, then we'll run with the ball at Camp David and hope you can do as much as you can at Fort Campbell and Fort Bragg. That's all we can do. After that, it's up to the Man Upstairs."

The colonel said, "You won't have any way to know if we're successful down here, getting the 5th Group and the 101st on board. You'll be on your own. And Camp David—that's ultra high security. It has a triple fence and the best sensors in the world. If you're trapped inside, don't even try to get out through the perimeter. You can only get out through the gate, or in a helo. If the plan falls apart, you'll be on your own."

"It doesn't matter," said Boone. "I'm used to that. We'll just take it as far as we can, once we're at Camp David."

"If the EBS is initiated, you mean."

"Or even if it's not."

Colonel Spencer paused to consider the meaning of that remark. "You won't be able to get weapons into Camp David. Not even General Armstead. You'll have to anticipate being searched and screened nineteen different ways. Every door you walk through will probably have a damn X-ray or a demo sniffer built into it."

"Oh, that's not a major problem. We can pick up weapons there if we need them. All of those Secret Service agents and Diplomatic Security Service guys will have guns. We'll just take what we need along the way."

The colonel laughed. "I'm sure you will. You never lacked for confidence, I'll say that for you. But what about the Raven Rock mission? Do you have confidence in this Doug Dolan?"

Boone grimaced. "Yes and no. But what happens inside Raven Rock is almost entirely up to General Armstead. He says he can get them into the EBS studio. And we don't really know what kind of resistance or cooperation they might get once they're inside. Dolan was a communications major in college, and he's up to date on television production and broadcasting. I think he's the only one of us who can figure out the EBS on the fly, and make sure it happens. Ira Gersham will be with him, and he's damned good with the technical stuff too, especially on the military side. Anyway, it won't involve any fighting, just studio work. Dolan and Gersham should be able to pull it off, if anybody can. Plus they'll have the massacre pictures and the videos, so if they have to recruit some of the Raven Rock support staff to initiate the EBS, they'll even have a shot that way. I think they can do it. General Armstead says they can do it, and he knows the system. So I think they can pull it off. If I didn't, I wouldn't have agreed to fly into Camp David."

"But if they can't get the show on the air, and we abort down here...your asses will still be hanging out a mile."

Boone sighed. "It doesn't matter. I talked it over with Phil already. We're going to take this to the end. Once we're at Camp David, no matter what happens, we're going all the way. I just wish I knew how the Marines were going to react." An elite company of Marines with special counterterrorist training was assigned to Camp David, to bolster the Secret Service guard force around the president.

"I'm working on the Marines," said Colonel Spencer, "but we can't risk tipping our hand in advance. It's a fine line. A very fine line."

"I know, I know, small and fast is the best way to go. The more players that you bring into it, the greater the chance of mission compromise. I just wish I knew how those Marines are going to handle the situation if it gets ugly. They've been trained to protect the president no matter what. But they also swore the oath to protect the Constitution. I just wish I knew how they were going to react, when they have to choose one or the other."

28

"Director Bullard? It's Harry." The phone call came from the senior controller at UAV flight ops. "We have activity at the new target area."

"Oh? Tell me about it." Bob Bullard sat straight up at his desk. It was 8:15 Wednesday morning, and he was still having his coffee and going through his email, getting up to speed for the nine o'clock staff meeting.

"Three unknown subjects just arrived at a house in our primary watch area. They came in a white SUV a few minutes ago. The house is owned by an Iraq War vet."

"Men or women? What?"

"All men, as far as we can determine."

"Where are they now?"

"They're inside the house."

"Where's this house in relation to the call's triangulated position?"

"It's not exact, of course, but I'd estimate pretty darn near the center of the box. Plus or minus a few hundred yards."

"Hot damn! Has Dolan made any more calls?" As soon as he said it, Bullard knew that Douglas Dolan could not have used that cell phone again, or he would have been notified immediately.

"No. That phone's been quiet since Monday night. We've been trying to remotely activate it, but either its batteries have been removed, or it's shielded in something thick. Or it's been moved outside a cell zone."

"Any evidence that Dolan is one of the three men in the house?"

"We can't confirm that yet. The SUV is parked under a roof; we didn't get a good look at them before they went inside the house. About all we can tell from reviewing the film is that it's three men."

"What about the license plate on the SUV? Did the snooper pods catch anything?" These remotely controlled surveillance devices could literally be tossed out of a passing vehicle. Outwardly, they looked like ordinary rocks the size of a misshapen loaf of bread. Once on the ground, they would right themselves if they had landed inverted, and then creep on treads into a surveillance position. The snooper pods could film in all 360 degrees, and send their video data up to the UAVs circling overhead for retransmission to base. Three pods had been dropped off at different vantage points during a single pass along Roaring Hollow Road. "Power company" technicians had also installed a video camera on a utility pole at the intersection of Highway 79 and Roaring Hollow Road. The Predator videos from on high were obviously the most useful, but for some information you needed ground-level cameras.

"We got the tag number, but it looks like it might be stolen, a fake or a duplicate. It's a Tennessee plate, but the number doesn't appear to be current, and it doesn't match the vehicle."

"All right! Wrong tags means they're dirty, so they're probably our unknown subjects. Harry, this is looking very promising. Is the on-station Predator armed?"

"It sure is. Two Vipers and four thirty millimeters."

"Good. I want missiles ready to drop anytime I say. I'm coming down to flight ops, so be ready."

Director Bullard terminated the call, and then telephoned the leader of his tactical response team. "Jackhammer, what's your status?" John D. Hamlin was a former captain in the Army Rangers who had come to the rural pacification program from the DEA. He was universally called The Jackhammer, a nickname and a radio call sign that he relished.

"Leaning forward, sir! We're locked and loaded and ready to roll."

"How long will it take to get your team to the objective?"

"Twenty-two minutes from when you say go."

"Well, I'm saying! Move the team to your forward staging position and stand by."

"Roger that, boss. We'll be there in twenty minutes."

"Let me know when you're at hold and ready to launch."

"Okay, boss. Will comply. Jackhammer out."

The member of the "working group" on audio surveillance duty in the Fort Campbell branch telephone exchange played the call back two times. Dolan? He had heard that name before. Wasn't Dolan the name of the third man who had come from West Tennessee with Boone Vikersun and Phil Carson? This could be a disaster in the making! This had to be taken care of right away. He made the call to alert the team that they needed to come and retrieve the audio. As instructed, he let the phone ring four times, and hung up.

Director Bullard swept through the old gym that housed thirty of the UAV stations, each with dual pilot controls for their two-man crews. Today only about fifteen Predators were up, judging from the level of staffing. Servicing and maintaining adequate numbers of UAVs in flying condition was a chronic problem. He went straight to the former coach's office that was home to the Reconnaissance Oversight team.

"Okay, Harry, put me in the picture." His senior controller had vacated his workstation so that Bullard could drop into the padded chair. A paved road was visible below bare trees on the color video screen. The homes were spread about a hundred yards apart on the curving road, which followed the course of a stream running down Roaring Hollow. It was a clear day, so everything was in sharp focus except where trees obscured the ground. At least it was still winter, and the branches were mostly bare. Come springtime, the rebels would be able to hide from aerial surveillance much more effectively.

"The crosshair is on the suspects' house. The three unknown subjects are still there, but we don't know if anybody else is inside. The SUV that brought them is the only vehicle on the property. It's parked under a roof attached to the side of the house; you can see the back of the vehicle when the slant angle from the Predator is right. It looks like a white Ford Expedition, an older model. The tag is off a pickup truck with an expired registration. We got the tag number from a snooper pod."

"If they're switching tags, then they're guilty of something," said Bullard as he settled into the UAV controller's seat. "Oh, it's them, I just know it." While they watched the live streaming video, a man appeared from the back of the rectangular house, walked to a small outbuilding, and entered it. A minute later he reappeared, carrying what looked like a duffel bag, and walked around to the SUV. They could see that he was moving around the rear of the vehicle, as his form shifted in and out from beneath the roof. Bullard chewed a fingernail and then said, "He's loading the truck. Probably weapons. They might be getting ready to take off, or they might be splitting up. I don't like this; I want to keep them all together." He turned to his assistant, who had accompanied him on this trip to the UAV flight ops center. "Jeff, where's the tactical team?"

Jeff Sinclair handed him a portable radio, and Bullard pushed the transmit button. It was a frequency-hopping radio with the latest federal encryption updates installed, and Bullard had no fear at all of being overheard. "Jackhammer, what's your ETA to the staging area?"

"Two minutes. We're three miles out on Highway 79."

"What if you bypass your hold and go straight for the objective?"

The commander of the tactical response team said, "Uh, four minutes, if we skip the hold and run straight in."

"Okay, do it. Go straight in. We're going to wake them up with a Viper. You'll be collecting the evidence, and taking prisoners if anybody's still breathing."

"Roger that. We're inbound to the objective, ETA four minutes."

Harry, the senior controller, said, "Are you sure you want to use a Viper? That's almost five pounds of high explosives. We could wait for the tactical team, and drop a thirty millimeter on the backside of the house just as they arrive. That's only one pound of explosive, just enough to stun everybody inside."

"Screw that. We're going to drop a Viper down the chimney and be done with it. These boys are slippery, and they're dangerous. I want it over. I want them dead, here and now."

"You know, it's going to break the neighbors' windows…"

"Fuck those hillbillies! Do I look like I care? Plus I have to get back for my 0900 staff meeting. I can't hang around here all day."

Harry put up his hands. "Hey, you're the chief. It's your call."

Jenny and Zack sat at a corner table in the dining tent. In the center of the tent was a portable wood-burning stove, with a pipe chimney that ran up through a special metal plate in the canvas roof. It was 9:30, and the officers and soldiers belonging to the general's headquarters company and staff were off doing whatever they did between breakfast and lunch. Hope was in a baby carrier on the folding table, awake and squirming around, but mostly looking at Jenny. Yesterday afternoon, Sergeant Amory had found the gray plastic infant seat and given it to Jenny so that she would not have to carry the baby all the time. This was another unasked-for act of kindness by the black medic. Jenny wondered why he was being so nice to her. It made no sense, but she was grateful nonetheless.

Last night after dinner, the two teenagers had been interviewed separately by General Mirabeau in his mobile headquarters RV. They had then been allowed to sleep on cots in tents with some of his enlisted troops. Jenny and Hope were put in a tent with female soldiers, who doted on the baby and gave Jenny more tips and advice than she could remember. This morning she had even been able to take a warm shower in a small tent set up just for that purpose. A pipe in the center of the tent contained four showerheads, wooden pallets kept their feet above the ground. The general's traveling headquarters reminded Jenny of a small circus, which could all be loaded onto a half-dozen Army trucks and moved anywhere. One of his female soldiers told Jenny that the general usually flew ahead on one of his helicopters, and wherever he wanted his traveling headquarters to be, there it would be erected. This week it was in Corinth, because of the refugees.

The two teenagers were nibbling on cornbread left over from breakfast. Jenny said, "I guess we're lucky they're letting us stay here. At least we're not in the big camp with the rest of the refugees."

"You can thank the general for that. Otherwise, we'd be in quarantine."

"Why are they doing all of this for us? Just because we brought the pictures?"

"I think the general likes us," he said.

Jenny turned from the baby to look across the table at Zack. "But what's going to happen when he moves his headquarters? He won't be staying in Corinth much longer. Do you think they'll let us go, like he said? Or do you think they'll make us go to the big refugee camp with everybody else?"

"I don't know," said Zack, "but I believed him when he said he's going to look out for us. No matter what else he is, he's a good Christian man, I'm sure of that much. He even said he'd pray for us. And you know what? He asked me to pray for him too, and 'for what's coming'."

"That's weird," said Jenny. "Did he tell you what's coming?"

Zack hesitated and then replied, "Um, no. Not exactly. He just asked me to pray that everything turned out all right. He seemed pretty worried. I think he has a lot on his mind."

"Well, I would guess so. I mean, he's in charge of most of the South. But he still took the time to ask me about Hope. He actually asked me what I think is best for her. Can you imagine?"

"What did you tell him?"

"I told him I want to keep her. I told him she's mine now." Jenny struggled to find the right words. In her memory she often saw Hope's frozen mother, back in the ravine. Last night, sleeping on her cot in an Army sleeping bag, she dreamed that she had met Hope's mother in heaven. Jenny wasn't sure how she had gotten there, but Hope's mother was speaking to her. Jenny had strained to hear her words, but could not. Maybe she was asking Jenny to take care of her baby. Jenny thought that she was. But she could not tell Zack about this dream. It was too weird and disturbing, like so much of the past several days.

But last night, without any hesitation, she had told the general that she wanted to keep the baby. Adults, much less Army generals, rarely listened to teenagers. But then, these were not ordinary times. General Mirabeau had listened to her very carefully, and thoughtfully.

There was a long silence, and then Zack asked her, "Well, if they let us go, and you keep the baby, where are you going to go next? I mean, where are you going to stay? Are you going back to your uncle's house, if it wasn't burned down?"

"Oh, no! No way. I'm done with Tennessee. I'm never going back. I don't know where I'm going, but I know I'm not going back there."

Zack buttered two pieces of cornbread, handed one to Jenny, and took a small bite of the other. "Well," he finally stammered, glancing between his plate and Jenny's face, "if you don't have anywhere else to go...I mean...if you don't have any other plans, or any other relatives...well, I've got a great house, and a couple acres of land. It's right on the national forest. It's hidden, so nobody can find it. It's only about twenty miles west of here, and it's not in Tennessee. There's enough food left for a year, and vegetables just spring up out of the ground. And if that's not enough to eat, the forest is full of deer and wild turkeys and pigs. My dad made our house to be earthquake and hurricane proof, and it's still there. It's made from concrete blocks, with iron rebar and cement poured down all the holes. It's as solid as a fort. It's even got a water well."

Jenny asked, "What kind of well, electric?"

"Sure, we have one of those, and we have a hand pump too. I mean, I do. You know what I mean. It's all mine now."

She looked directly at him, daring him to hold unbroken eye contact. "What are you trying to say to me, Zack?"

He blushed a deeper shade and stammered, "Well, I thought…maybe you could come back home with me. Just for a while. Until you decide what you want to do. Maybe you could give it a chance, and just spend some time there until you and Hope get your strength back. You could just rest up and take it easy. There'd be plenty to eat, I promise. And there's plenty of firewood, so I can keep the house nice and warm until spring. I meant that maybe you could give it a try. Just think about it, that's all. I'm not asking for any commitments. I mean, I just thought I'd offer, if you don't have anyplace else to go."

Zack was so damned earnest. He hardly ever smiled. Jenny thought it was because he was self-conscious about his crooked front tooth, as if that mattered. Teeth could be fixed, and if not, so what? He was actually a good-looking boy. He had brown eyes the same shade as Hope's, and thick wavy brown hair that looked very nice now that it had been washed. But much more importantly, he was strong, he was brave, and above all, he was loyal. Jenny deflected his question, which had taken her completely by surprise. "Your house is pretty close to the Tennessee border, isn't it?"

"Yes, and it has a whole national forest for a backyard."

"But is it safe there? That's where your father was…I mean…"

"I know. I know. Listen, Jenny, you have to keep a secret. I already asked the general about moving back to my place. I told him it's in the buffer zone, right near the border. I explained about my father, how he was working with Boone, how he was working with the rebels in Tennessee. He said I was welcome to go back, but not quite yet. I asked him about the foreign troops, and he said he was going to deal with them soon."

"He did? Why didn't you tell me?"

"It's a secret," said Zack. "At least, he asked me to be quiet about it. But he said they're going to deal with the foreign soldiers in Tennessee real soon. He said it was because of the massacre. And do you know what else he told me? He said—he said he thinks that God sent us to him."

"He told you that?" Jenny's eyes suddenly welled up.

"He said that Hope was just like baby Moses, found in the rushes by the Nile. He said it was a sign from God. I'm not kidding. And he said he wasn't going to let the massacre go unanswered. That's what he said."

"Zack…he told me almost the same thing. I couldn't tell you, though. He made me promise not to tell anybody. But since he told you too, I guess it's okay."

"Oh Jenny, what's happening to us? Why is this all happening?"

Ira Hayes Gersham had not driven on Highway 79 since last night, but he needed to move his now-empty flatbed D.O.L. salvage truck from its last hiding place to a position closer to Clarksville. Playing three-card Monte with his various cars and trucks was a tedious but necessary part of his work. He was heading eastbound on the two-lane blacktop when he approached the descending right-hand turnoff to Roaring Hollow Road. As usual, he scanned for any signs of surveillance, because this road was the location of one of his safehouses. On the left side of the highway, opposite the T intersection, was an ordinary telephone pole. Fifteen feet up, facing Roaring Hollow, was a gray metal box that was about a foot square. He stared at it as he passed, freezing it in his mind. It wasn't rusted or greasy; rather, it was shiny and new. No wires or conduits led from it either up or down. Ira had never seen this box before, and this bothered him, because besides having a nearly photographic memory, he was literally a trained observer.

He knew what it was in an instant, and a shiver ran through him. If he could check the top of the new box, he was certain that he would see a small solar panel, to power a camera and its transmitter. Thirty seconds later, while Ira was digesting the fact that Roaring Hollow Road was now under surveillance, a blur ahead of him resolved into a convoy of black SUVs. Four identical Suburbans and what looked like a brown UPS truck swept past him moving at over seventy miles an hour. Their side windows were opaquely tinted, but the drivers and front seat passengers he had glimpsed through their windshields were all dressed in black. He looked at his side mirrors and saw their red brake lights behind him. Without using turn signals, the line of SUVs and the square delivery van made the turn down Roaring Hollow Road.

Ira considered pulling over or even turning around to listen and to watch, but he knew that he was still possibly being filmed by the suspected camera back on the telephone pole, or by other cameras that he could not even see. Possibly, he was even being observed by camera lenses thousands of feet above him. If he stopped now, this non-random action might be subjected to scrutiny when the videos were analyzed. He continued driving at the same speed back toward Clarksville and Fort Campbell.

His pulse was steady and his eyes were forward when he felt and heard the thumping crack of an explosion behind him. He glanced in his side mirror in time to see a black column of smoke roiling skyward above the trees down on Roaring Hollow Road.

They had nailed his safe house. Where had he slipped up? What had been their mistake?

Just before noon, most of the key members of the working group met at CW4 Hugh Rogan's duplex home on base, entering one at a time from the rear. The general had changed to a black and gray Army sweat suit in his office, presumably to visit one of the base's fitness centers over lunch. From the gym's parking lot, he had instead jogged just a few blocks to Hugh Rogan's home. The timing of their meeting was based upon the general's availability during a brief period when he would not be missed at NORTHCOM headquarters. Phil Carson, Colonel Tom Spencer, Boone Vikersun, Sergeant Major Charlie Donelson, Doug Dolan and, of course, CW4 Rogan were already there.

They sat around his dining room table, part of an ornately carved mahogany furniture set that Rogan had brought back from Korea after a deployment there. The tabletop was covered with maps, notebooks, papers and laptop computers. The first order of business was transportation and logistics. General Armstead would request a long-range MH-60K Pave-hawk helicopter to carry him and his entourage from Fort Campbell directly to Camp David. With external tanks, this version of the Black-hawk could make the 600-mile flight without refueling. The general would get a nonstop ride, and the 160th Special Operations Aviation Regiment would get rare training hours that came out of NORTHCOM's budget. CW4 Rogan would steer the somewhat unusual request through channels at the 160th SOAR. Naturally, he would be in the pilot's seat, along with his choice of copilot and crew chiefs. This mission tasking was slightly out of the ordinary, but three-star generals had a way of getting their requests approved, in consideration for future favors to be rendered. Nobody at the Camp David end of the flight plan would have any notion of its slight irregularity. The origin of the Blackhawk delivering the general and his party to the conference would be irrelevant to them. As far as they were concerned, the only difference would be the helicopter's tail number.

According to the modified flight plan, the special operations Black-hawk would drop General Armstead, his chief staff officer and his aide at Camp David, and then make the quick hop six miles north to Site R, where his deputy commanding general would conduct a brief inspection visit. The Raven Rock mission was a typical add-on, based on the availability of the helicopter mission to nearby Camp David. Such last-minute plan mods were routine in an era of budget cuts and restricted flying hours. The heli-copter would refuel and wait at Site R until the end of the conference, when it would pick up Armstead and his entourage for their return flight to Fort Campbell. That was the official plan. The reality was otherwise.

The catch was that Armstead's actual deputy was on leave fishing in the Florida Keys. In his place, Phil Carson would be playing Armstead's chief staff officer, Brigadier General Clayton Harper. For the purposes of official orders, General Harper was already expected at Site R, as well as being on the authorized visitor list for the Camp David conference as a part of Armstead's group. The genuine General Harper would be in his office at Fort Campbell, out of the loop and blameless if the plan went awry. In reality, only Armstead would be flying to Site R, with Gersham and Dolan.

Boone Vikersun would become Major Curtis Paxton, General Armstead's new aide, and so he was also on the amended list for the Camp David conference. General Harper and Major Paxton actually existed and had the requisite Top Secret clearances, a fact that routine White House security checks would readily verify. New Army identification cards would be created, with Phil Carson and Boone Vikersun's pictures on them. In the digital age, this could all be done by computer with the correct authorization codes and the correct ID card paper stock, which were both under General Armstead's control. When they arrived at Camp David, their faces would match their new ID cards, and the names on those cards would match the names listed among General Armstead's expected entourage. That was the shell game plan hatched among the conspirators for getting Carson and Boone into Camp David, and General Armstead to Site R.

The general said, "I need to be back in my office by 1300, and I still have to go over Operation Buffalo Jump with Mr. Carson. I took pictures of every page of the CONPLAN, so you can put it on all of your computers. No matter what happens tomorrow, as far as I'm concerned, this plan is proof of treason by the president." He passed a memory stick to Colonel Spencer, who inserted it into his laptop.

The CONPLAN was classified Top Secret, and they were all committing multiple felonies simply by being in this room when its illegal distribution was being discussed and carried out. They were all burning their bridges today, those who still had them to burn. But with the Camp David conference less than twenty-four hours away, they faced minimal risk of compromise or exposure. "All right," said the general, "let's get right to our actions at Camp David and Site R."

Colonel Spencer said, "When the EBS is initiated, the Secret Service will probably try to take the president straight down into a bunker until they figure out what's going on. Aspen, Laurel and Hickory lodges are all connected by tunnels to a blast-proof bunker system. That's why they only need a company of Marines for security. Once the president is underground, they can just wait for outside help to arrive. The bunkers connect to tunnels that run outside the camp. Some of the private residences on the farms around Camp David are thought to be front operations, and the president can pop out of any of them and take off. All the Marines at Camp David have to do is protect him until he's underground." Colonel Spencer looked directly at Phil Carson and Boone Vikersun. "So you'll need to grab him fast, before he disappears like a rabbit down a hole."

General Armstead described the next phase of the plan. "It'll take us fifteen minutes to fly from Camp David to Site R and get inside. Then another five minutes to reach the EBS studio, and after that…well, I hope we can initiate the EBS in another ten minutes, but that's probably optimistic. Call it thirty minutes from the time I leave Camp David at approximately ten hundred hours. Best case will be a minimum of twenty-five minutes, to a maximum of however long it takes. The reception at Camp David is set to run from ten to eleven, when the president is scheduled to leave the conference center. So if the EBS isn't on the air by eleven, we couldn't do it, and the mission is an abort. We'll try to fly back to pick up the Camp David team, unless we've been detained inside Raven Rock." He didn't need to add that in that event, Phil Carson and Boone Vikersun's futures would be very grim.

Doug Dolan asked, "Does the EBS automatically announce what it is? Or do we control the output a hundred percent, including the titles and description? What I mean is, are we stuck with that alert tone and the guy who says, 'This is the Emergency Broadcast System' and all of that?"

"No no, that's way out of date," said the general. "You just need the correct authorization code to get control of everything, and I've got it. Well, that is, I have *my* half of it. I can initiate the EBS, but only if I can convince the commanding officer of Raven Rock to type in his half of the code. I've seen it done in exercises. As the commanding general of NORTHCOM, I'm one of the officers who can authorize initiation. It's all a part of our continuity-of-government plan. It's a contingency plan in the event that I'm the senior officer who survives when Washington gets nuked and the White House and the Pentagon are wiped out. We practice it a couple of times a year, sometimes with unscheduled tests. The only difference is that this time the EBS really will be initiated, and all national programming will be under our control. I know the current CO of Raven Rock pretty well, he's a colonel in the Signal Corps. I think I can get him to cooperate after he sees the evidence we have. Not just the massacre videos and pictures, but my Operation Buffalo Jump CONPLAN."

"What if you can't get him to put in his code?" asked Carson.

"Then we might have to get rough with him. We'll have to figure it out as we go. Adapt and overcome."

"How will we know if the EBS is going to come on?" asked Boone.

"You won't," said Colonel Spencer. "That's the thing. Camp David is totally jammed. Nobody's cell phones will work there. No cell phones, no BlackBerrys, no radios, nothing. The only way to communicate will be to use a secure landline from Site R directly to Camp David's commo center, and get a message hand-delivered to you. But that's not something we can count on. You'll just have to go by the timing, and assume the

EBS will be initiated sometime between 1030 and 1100 hours. That's not much to go on, I know, but it's the best we can do."

There was silence around the table after General Armstead finished, and the realization sank in among the participants: the basic concept of operations was to throw two Hail Mary passes at the same time.

After a few moments Colonel Spencer said, "Now let's talk about Sidney Krantz. I've learned quite a bit about him since yesterday. On the surface, he's just a former college professor turned political consultant. He's a radical socialist of course, but that probably describes most professors today. Some people who know him call him 'the president's Rasputin.' Supposedly, he knows where the bodies are buried. If you can believe the rumors, he gets off-the-record private face time with the president as some kind of special adviser. He'll be flying into Fort Campbell tonight around 1800. We need to decide if it's worth snatching him. I think it'll be worth it."

"Won't he be missed?" asked Boone.

"No," said Colonel Spencer. "He's not an hourly employee, that's for sure. He has some kind of do-nothing job at the White House, something about "special plans and projects." He has his own office in the Old Executive Office Building, but he doesn't answer to anybody but the president. He even said on his phone call to Bullard that he might fly back tonight or he might fly back tomorrow. That gives us just enough time to play with. I say we go for it. We can run the whole operation right here on base."

"What's the upside?" asked General Armstead.

"I'm just making deductions, but 'special plans and projects' sounds like some kind of White House plumbers outfit. He gets one-on-one time with the president. Now he's coming down here to visit Robert Bullard, and Bullard is in charge of the foreign contract battalions in the rural pacification program. Whatever they're going to discuss in person is something that couldn't be said over the phone, not even on what they thought was a secure line. I say it's worth it. He's bound to know some pretty high-level secrets, which could turn into more evidence to use against the president. And we don't need to bring anybody else in to do it. We can run this op ourselves."

"All right," said the general. "Do it."

Director Bullard met with the leader of his Tactical Response Team in his Building 1405 office. He wanted to conduct this after-action debriefing personally. Also present was his deputy, Mitchell Brookfield. John "The Jackhammer" Hamlin brought his own black anodized metal-cased tactical laptop computer, and set it on Bullard's desk. It contained still pictures and video clips documenting the aftermath of their successful action on Roaring Hollow Road. After plugging in a cable, he connected the computer to a gigantic plasma TV that occupied the office wall across from Bullard's desk. Hamlin was still wearing his dusty black tactical outfit, without the body armor or helmet, but with his pistol strapped to his leg in a black holster. Dirt and sweat streaked his lean, angular face and caked his crewcut hair. Mitch Brookfield, Bullard's deputy, was wearing a jacket and tie and sat on the leather couch along the side wall. Bob Bullard sat behind his desk while the TRT leader narrated. Hamlin was seated on the other side of the wide desk, controlling the computer.

"The house is a total loss, as you can see. The three subjects who arrived in the white Expedition were all killed in the explosion and then were burned beyond recognition. Oh—it looks like there was one female in the house too, so there's actually a total of four dead. I mean, we think there were four people inside; we're just not sure if one was a female. They're pretty messed up. They're crispy critters, in pieces. But we did get one positive ID. It's kind of funny—one hand was blown clear of the house, and it landed right in the driveway. The fingerprints were perfect. Check this picture out." The TRT leader clicked to the next slide on his laptop, and the giant television on the wall showed a mammoth severed human hand. It was lying on asphalt next to a ruler that had been placed beside it for size comparison. On the big plasma TV, the ruler and the hand were over a yard long. There was a gold wedding band on the hand's ring finger. "The other bodies will be DNA jobs. That viper pretty much shredded them, and then the house collapsed and burned to ashes. What's left of them ain't pretty, that's for sure."

"So who was the hand attached to, before we nailed them?" asked Bullard.

"His name was Cordell Acklin. He owned the house and the white Ford Expedition. He used to be a sergeant in the 101st here on Fort Campbell, and he did multiple combat tours in Iraq. He was Ranger qualified, sniper qualified...you name it, he probably did it. He was in the 82nd before the 101st, mostly in recon units. We did an internet search on him, and we found out he's a real asshole. Well...he *was* a real asshole." The Jackhammer chuckled, and so did Bullard. "His whole life story is on the internet. He used to write a blog, and he posted on military forums all the time. He called himself "Shadowfox," whatever that means. He quit the Army when President Tambor was elected, something about gays serving openly in the military, I think. That, and serving on United Nations peacekeeping duty. His battalion was scheduled to rotate into Kosovo, and he just wouldn't do it. He wouldn't wear the U.N.'s blue beret, so he quit the Army after almost ten years. Yeah, he was a hardcore constitution fanatic; a real asshole and a troublemaker."

"One down, and only about a million more to go," said Bullard, leaning back and cracking his knuckles. "What else did you find, besides his hand and his internet history?"

"Some interesting guns. We found an arsenal of sniper rifles and assault weapons. Three scoped bolt-actions, and two semi-autos. They were outlaws, that's for sure." Hamlin clicked ahead through his slides to show a picture of five melted and broken long guns lined up on the ground.

Bullard asked, "What caliber are they?"

"The usual, 7.62 and 5.56. He even had a fancy semi-auto sniper rifle in 7.62, a DPMS Panther. It's like a big M-16, but without a carrying handle. That's the one on top in the picture. That's a night scope mounted on it. Well, it was, anyway."

Brookfield said, "A 7.62 assault sniper rifle with a night scope? That sure sounds like our gang from West Tennessee. We recovered some 7.62 slugs from those dead Kazaks where they stole that ASV."

"That's what I'm thinking too," said Bullard. "Three men, at least one of them an Army veteran with an ax to grind. All loaded with illegal military-style weaponry. Great work, Jackhammer."

"Hell, we didn't do anything but take pictures and collect evidence. Your Viper did all the work."

Bullard grinned and laughed again. "Well, if anybody *had* survived, I'm sure that you would have done a great job on them. Okay, Mitchell," he said to his deputy, "I think we can close the file on those assholes. We can cancel the BOLO and put the Predators back on routine patrol. I'm going to swing by UAV air ops one more time, and then I'm going to call it a day." Bullard stood and stretched his arms out, smiling with relief. John Hamlin closed his laptop, got up and gave his boss a congratulatory fist-bump across the desk.

Bob Bullard felt good about his decision to drop the Viper instead of merely putting the gang under surveillance. Nobody ever escaped when five pounds of high explosives punched through their roof and detonated inside. He could scratch the killers from West Tennessee from his list of concerns and prepare for his meeting with Sidney Krantz. It was "T minus beer-thirty," and counting.

Ira Hayes Gersham arrived at Hugh Rogan's house in his own nondescript compact car. It had the correct Department of Defense windshield stickers, and he had his Army retiree's ID card, so he could come and go onto the base as he pleased. General Armstead had already departed Rogan's duplex, after briefly going through the Operation Buffalo Jump concept of operations plan with Phil Carson. Doug Dolan was alone in Rogan's office, standing with his head tilted sideways, reading the titles of the books on a tall shelf. Ira came into the room with Boone and closed the door behind them.

"Sit down," Boone ordered. Doug was startled to see "Dewey Lieberman," whom the other men called Ira, and he dropped into the chair by Rogan's computer.

Ira Gersham held a small digital audio recorder in his hand. He placed it on the desk by Doug and pushed a button. "Now listen to this."

"Director Bullard? It's Harry. We have activity at the target area. The new one."

"Oh? Tell me about it."

"Three unknown subjects just arrived at a house in our primary watch area. They came in a white SUV a few minutes ago. The house is owned by an Iraq War vet."

"Men or women? What?"

"All men, as far as we can determine."

"Where are they now?"

"They're inside the house."

"Where's this house in relation to the cell call's triangulated position?"

"It's not exact, of course, but I'd estimate pretty darn near the center of the box. Plus or minus a few hundred yards."

"Hot damn! Has Dolan made any more calls?"

"No. That phone's been quiet since Monday night. We've been trying to activate it, but either its batteries have been removed, or it's shielded inside something thick. Or it's just been moved outside a cell coverage zone."

"Any evidence that Dolan is one of the three men in the house?"

"We can't confirm that yet. The SUV is parked under a roof; we didn't get a good look at them before they went inside the house. About all we can tell from the film is it's three men."

"What about the license plate on the SUV? Did the snooper pods catch anything?"

"We got the tag number, but it looks like it might be stolen, a fake or a duplicate. It's a Tennessee plate, but the number doesn't appear to be current, and it doesn't match the vehicle."

"All right! Wrong tags means they're dirty, so they're probably our unknown subjects. Harry, this is looking very promising. Is the on-station Predator armed?"

"It sure is. Two Vipers and four thirty millimeters."

"Good. I want missiles ready to drop anytime I say. I'm coming down to flight ops, so be ready."

"Do you want to hear it again?" asked Boone.

Doug appeared shattered by the recorded conversation. He stared blankly at the recorder as he slumped forward in the chair. "No."

"So, who did you call?" Boone demanded.

Dolan glanced between the two men, who stood over him in postures suggesting that he was about to get a beating. "I...I called my mother in Baltimore."

"Tell us everything," said Ira. "Who, what, when, where and why."

Doug looked down at the floor. "I found a cell phone in the kitchen drawer at the cabin. You guys were gone. I called my mother; I haven't spoken to her in more than a year. She thought I was dead. I'm sorry. I'm really sorry."

"You're 'sorry'?! Do you know that people were probably *killed* because of you?"

"Killed?"

Ira asked, "What do you think they meant by 'missiles ready to drop'? A SWAT team just raided a house near the cabin. They blew it up, probably with a missile launched from a Predator. I was close enough to hear the explosion. They thought it was us, but it was a mistake. There's no garage and no white SUV at the cabin, so obviously they got the wrong house. But those three men are still dead, and now we can't even go back to find out who it was. And all because you had to call your mother!"

"I'm *so* sorry..."

"And those people are still dead!" shouted Boone, struggling to keep his composure. "Let me tell you, Doug, part of me wants to...part of me wants to take you apart. But I can't. I won't. And do you know why?"

Dolan looked up at Boone, misery on his face.

"I can't give you what you deserve because we still need you. You're the only one of us who can run a modern studio mixing board, at least that's what Ira tells me, and I believe him. We don't have anybody who can replace you tomorrow, so you have to pull your act together and somehow, *somehow*, not fuck this up. So no matter how we feel about you right now, we still need you. You're our television producer, and you still need to do your job, without a doubt the most important job you've ever done in your short life. And I know you'll do it, because now, *finally*, I think you understand the kind of people we're fighting. They're the kind of people who kill innocent Americans just because they think they *might* be rebels. I hope it's sinking in that this is no game. So you're getting another chance. Now—are you going to fall to pieces on us, or are you going to pull yourself together, man up, and carry on like a Soldier?"

Doug Dolan swallowed hard and nodded his head affirmatively. "I'll be able to do my part. I won't screw it up, Boone, I promise. I'll do my job. No matter what it takes."

The military called them C-12 Hurons. Civilian general aviation pilots knew them as Beech Super King Air twin turboprops. It wasn't a Gulf-stream, a Citation or even a Learjet, but Sidney Krantz wasn't complaining. The plane had a pressurized cabin and flew at jet altitudes, and it had the speed and range to carry him directly from Andrews Air Force Base to Fort Campbell. An entire squadron at Andrews was dedicated to transporting government VIPs around the country and overseas. The air-crews didn't care who they were flying as long as they were given valid orders through their chain of command. They routinely flew congressional delegations on thinly disguised Caribbean junkets, so a trip to Fort Campbell was above question.

This particular airplane was a deluxe version of the C-12, with only six very wide leather seats, three on each side. The front two seats faced rearward, with fold-down coffee tables between them and the two middle seats. The pilot and copilot could be seen all the way forward in the cock-pit. The only other person aboard was a female Air Force sergeant, a slim and trim Nordic type with short blond hair. Her sole mission apparently was keeping her single passenger comfortable, plying him with snacks, drinks, defense industry magazines and pillows.

Krantz briefly wondered if other men in his situation might throw a pass at her, and perhaps inquire about her plans for later on at Fort Campbell. It was just his bad luck that they would provide him with a female steward, because he was much more interested in handsome young men than in girls. And in today's military, a young male flight attendant might be openly gay, and he might even be attracted to an older Distinguished Guest, a Very Important Person who frequently had the president's ear. But alas, this was not to be, not on this flight.

Even with propellers instead of jets, and a female cabin steward, this afternoon's solo air travel was a huge boost to Sidney's ego. A twin-engine luxury airplane, two pilots and a steward had been placed entirely at his service. He could fly back tonight or tomorrow, as he wished. The plane and crew were at his beck and call, because this was a White House mission. After this Tennessee rural pacification campaign was success-fully wrapped up, and Jamal Tambor was even more impressed with his service, perhaps then he would rate a luxury jet for his official travels. But even this level of luxury was very nice. Best of all was being waited upon by uniformed military personnel. If they only knew how much he despised them for their disgusting ultra patriotism, and their incessantly cheerful "Yes sir, no sir, what we can do for you, sir."

If the crew only knew the true purpose of his mission to Tennessee, and what he was delivering! If they only knew what he had in a glass vial the size of a pill bottle, hidden in his carry-on bag. There was only about a tablespoon of the brownish liquid culture, but that was enough to infect hundreds of rats. Just a tiny injection was all it would take. That and fleas, and proximity to the thousands of rebels currently confined in tight quarters in a dozen FEMA camps in Tennessee. Well, President Tambor had said that he wanted the resistance crushed, and he didn't care how. Sidney Krantz was merely attempting to fulfill his leader's wishes.

The C-12 chased the afternoon sun for three hours, and landed at Campbell Army Airfield just at twilight. Ten minutes after its arrival, it had taxied onto a concrete apron amidst other small- and medium-sized fixed-wing aircraft. The Huron was a sleek white twin turboprop with low wings and a high T-tail gleaming in the last light. As its engines were shutting down, a black SUV drove up almost to its left wing and parked. The plane's side door was lowered, creating its own steps. A single passenger stepped down, a portly man in a gray suit. He held a black carryall bag in one hand, and a brown hanging bag in the other. The driver of the SUV approached him, and even tipped his black ball cap.

"Mr. Krantz?" The driver was wearing black trousers cut like combat fatigues, and a matching black insulated jacket with pockets and pouches for police radios, ammunition magazines, backup pistols, handcuffs, drinking water in a "camelback" and a dozen other "tactical necessities."

The deplaning VIP said, "That would be me."

"I'm your driver; I'll be taking you to Director Bullard's house. May I help you with your luggage, sir?"

"You can take my hanging bag, thanks." Krantz held onto his black leather grip bag, and followed the driver to the Suburban.

"We're just a few minutes from Director Bullard's house. Is this your first trip to Fort Campbell?"

"Yes, it's my first time," said Krantz while checking his watch.

The driver held the left rear door open for Sidney Krantz, who slid across the middle seat while keeping his carry-on bag close by his side. The driver clipped the hanging bag to a hook, and closed the door. Then he got behind the wheel and they drove away from the airplanes, the aprons and service roads, and the airfield. It was fully dark by the time they left the perimeter road. The two men shared no polite words of conversation; they were from utterly different worlds. The driver selected a roundabout route that kept them away from most of Fort Campbell's built-up areas.

Five minutes later, he pulled onto a winding road that led past a golf course. This road, in turn, led into a secluded section that was home to Fort Campbell's general officers. This was also the location of the temporary residence of Bob Bullard, a member of the federal government's Senior Executive Service. A discreet sign at the entrance to this tree-shielded stretch of asphalt simply read "Senior Officer Housing, Authorized Personnel and Guests Only." On an Army base, where military discipline ruled personal conduct, this sign was the only outward indication of the presence of a higher security level. There was no separate gate or guardhouse.

Bullard's two-story white shingle-sided house was at the end of its own cul-de-sac. Lines of evergreens ensured its privacy. It was one of only nine homes designated for general officers on Fort Campbell. The black Suburban turned onto the long driveway, rounded the circle at the end, and parked in front of the home's main entrance. The driver stepped out and opened his passenger's door, grabbed the hanging bag and politely waited while Krantz exited the SUV with his black leather bag in his left hand. Then the driver walked up the brick steps to the front landing of the home, rang the bell, and stepped to the side as a motion-activated security light came on above them. Sidney Krantz stood directly in front of the door, waiting for it to open. A white security camera no larger than a pack of cigarettes was discreetly mounted above them to their left.

In less than a minute the door swung inward, opened by Director Robert Bullard himself, dressed casually in jeans and a maroon sweater. He stepped to the threshold, his right hand out to greet his colleague from Washington. Sidney Krantz was the man who had plucked him from his virtual house arrest in San Diego and recommended him for his current assignment heading up the rural pacification program. Bullard shook Krantz's hand, then glanced over at the driver, whose back was turned to them. He said, "Jimmy, you can leave the bag on that hook over there, and then you can take off."

Ira Gersham turned around with the garment bag over his left arm. A Glock pistol was in his right hand, with a suppressor attached to its barrel. After letting Bullard see it, he jammed its muzzle hard into Sidney Krantz's back, and then he said, "Jimmy couldn't make it. Why don't we go inside?"

Boone Vikersun and Phil Carson, dressed in jeans and windbreakers, opened the rear doors of the Suburban from the inside. They had helped to subdue the driver sent to pick up Krantz, and thereafter they had remained hidden in the cargo area behind the third seat. They dashed toward the front door of the house before Bullard had gotten over his initial surprise. In seconds, they were all inside and the door was closed behind them. Other members of the Special Forces working group were already concealed around Bullard's property, to prevent any of his men from potentially coming to his assistance.

Carson said, "Hey, Bob, guess what? You hit the wrong house this morning. I don't know who you killed, but it wasn't us."

"And here we are," said Boone, "just in time to meet your friend Sidney." All three intruders were carrying pistols with sound suppressors.

Bullard was momentarily speechless, and then all he could ask was a bewildered "How?" as he was pushed and prodded across the living room with Sidney Krantz.

Boone said, "You actually thought that you could just set up shop on Fort Campbell, and we wouldn't know every move you were making? Or that we wouldn't care? You actually thought that you would be *safe* because you were on an Army base? Like we're all just robots who only follow orders and don't notice what we're not supposed to notice? Bob Bullard, if you thought that, you are one stupid son of a bitch! Oh, and by that way, that pitiful mall-ninja you sent to pick up Sidney is still alive."

"Snappy dresser, though," said Ira Gersham. "Just my size, and I absolutely love all the pockets."

They reached the basement door, which opened into the hall on the way to the kitchen. Colonel Spencer had attended social functions in several of the generals' homes, and had briefed the team on their layout. Boone opened the door and said, "Now, let's all go downstairs and get properly acquainted."

"Reacquainted, in my case," said Carson. "Bob and I go way back. We've never met face to face, but we have some history together. Maybe we can talk over old times and catch up, eh, Bob?"

Half of the basement was finished like a clubroom, with a pool table, a wet bar, a leather sofa and a big-screen television. The walls were wood paneled and the floor was carpeted. The other half was left rough, with block walls, a cement floor and exposed pipes and ducts running along the bottom of the ceiling beams. An interior wall with a door in the middle separated the two main basement rooms. The unfinished side was the laundry and storage area for the house, and it was very cold.

Five minutes after the home invasion, Bob Bullard and Sidney Krantz were dressed only in their underwear shorts, without undershirts or even socks. Bullard wore red boxers, while Krantz wore black briefs that were mostly covered by a roll of pale belly flesh. A single hanging light bulb illuminated the room, and revealed that their pasty skin was covered by goose bumps from the chill air. Their hands were manacled over a steel water pipe that ran along a ceiling beam. They stood a few feet apart from one another, with their bare feet elevated on rough cinderblocks. There was one block beneath each man, so that their wrists would reach the pipe with their arms stretched straight up. Their ankles were bound together with green parachute cord, to prevent them from even attempting a kick.

Coming down the steps, Bullard had tried to play the tough guy for about ten seconds, but that show of bravado ended with a casual punch from Boone Vikersun's oversized fist. Carson thought that up close, Bob Bullard almost looked like Robert De Niro. Sidney Krantz had offered no resistance at all, from the moment that he had seen the armed men at the front door. The home invaders had pushed their two captives down the steps to the basement, the logical place to conduct a rapid and possibly noisy interrogation. Carson found the overhead pipes and the cinder-blocks. Ira Gersham had brought the steel police handcuffs. Both men stripped off their clothing when they were ordered to. Bullard was silent but glaring daggers, Krantz was blubbering with fear.

There was an old-fashioned square laundry sink in the corner of the basement past the washing machine. Boone filled a galvanized bucket with cold water from the tap. It was the temperature of the ground outside the house, just above freezing. He walked over to Bullard, swung the bucket back and doused him from the head down, leaving him sputtering and then hyperventilating. Then he repeated the process with Krantz, leaving both men drenched in the already frigid air. Both prisoners had to stand straight up on their cement block perches, with their arms stretched upward, to prevent the steel cuffs from digging into their wrists. It was not a posture designed to maximize their comfort or instill a feeling of safety and well-being.

Once their prisoners were properly secured and soaked with cold water, the three home invaders left the rough side of the cellar, closing the door behind them. They spread their prisoners' clothing on the pool table and searched through it. Carson emptied the black leather grip bag that Krantz had brought from Washington. Inside a casserole-sized Tupperware container was a large Ziploc bag, and inside that was a wide-mouthed plastic jar, similar to the ones that held peanut butter or mayonnaise. Inside that jar was a layer of bubble wrap and another Ziploc, and inside that protective padding was a small glass vial with a green rubber top.

This vial was only about two inches high. Inside it was a resiny brownish-black liquid, with the viscosity of blood. A paper label on this vial was marked "YP-12D." These letters were hand printed with a black marker. Carson set this glass vial on the pool table, away from the other items. Also in the Tupperware was another plastic bag, containing about twenty disposable syringes, and a small cardboard box containing disposable blue rubber gloves. He placed the bag of syringes and the gloves alongside the vial.

Carson said, "I think I know why Krantz wanted Bullard to catch some rats."

"YP-12D," said Gersham, leaning over the vial and studying it closely without touching it. "YP. That's got to be *Yersinia pestis*."

"Okay, you guys," said Boone, "speak English."

Carson replied, "*Yersinia pestis* is the germ that causes the bubonic plague. The Black Death. That's why Krantz wanted rats. Rats carry the plague, and they spread it to humans."

"No shit?" said Boone. "And I thought I already hated those jokers. How long have they been chained to the pipe? You think they're softened up enough for round two?"

"Let's go see." Carson pulled on a pair of rubber gloves, took the vial and a syringe, and the three went back into the rough side of the basement. Bullard and Krantz were as they had been left, but now they were shivering almost uncontrollably. Bullard was in decent shape for a man in his fifties, with just some love handles, but the nearly obese Sidney Krantz was shaking like a bowl of white yogurt.

Carson said, "Okay, boys, we're going to play a new reality game. It's kind of like *Survivor*. It's called 'Who Knows the Biggest Secret?' The winner will live, and the loser will die. Now, to start off, who wants to tell me about this bottle? I'm assuming that the 'YP' stands for *Yersinia pestis*, the friendly little bug that causes the bubonic plague." He held up the glass vial for the prisoners to see.

"I don't know anything about that stuff," Bullard blurted out, shaking his head while staring at the little jar.

"What about you, Sidney? This stuff was in your bag. What do you know about YP-12D?"

Krantz just shook his head and looked down.

Boone said, "Sidney, do you want another bucket of ice water to refresh your memory? It was in *your bag*. And wasn't that you on the phone yesterday, asking Bob here to collect a dozen rats? Right after you asked him how many FEMA camps were in West Tennessee? Yeah, that's right, Bob—we've been tapping your phone. Hey, don't look so surprised; I mean, it's *our base*. Come on now Sidney, remember the name of the game. It's called 'Who Knows the Biggest Secret?'"

Finally Krantz spoke, his teeth chattering, his body shaking both from cold and from fear. "It's not what you think. It wouldn't cause a major epidemic. It was really just for psyops value. After a few cases, people would panic and leave West Tennessee. That's what it was for, to make people leave. And when the weather turned warm, it would disappear completely."

Carson said, "Psyops value, huh? Well, for the people who got infected, I think it would be a little more than psychological, don't you think?"

Ira Gersham had gone back to the other basement room, and returned with a large blue textbook, already opened in his hands. "There's an old set of *Encyclopedia Britannica* over there. It must stay with the house; I sure can't see Bob Bullard bringing along a set of encyclopedias. Am I right, Bob, it was already here?" Bullard barely nodded yes. "That's what I thought. Now, let's see what it says about the bubonic plague. Okay, here we are. I'll just hit the highlights. It's an infection of the lymphatic system, typically resulting from the bite of an infected flea. The fleas are usually found on rodents such as rats, and they move onto humans when their rodent hosts die. Well, that explains the rats that Sidney wanted.

"Let me skim ahead a little...oh, this is nasty stuff. Listen to this: '*As the disease progresses, the lymph nodes can hemorrhage and become necrotic. The most well-known symptom of bubonic plague is swollen lymph glands, called buboes, which are commonly found around the armpits, the groin and the neck. Other symptoms include red spots on the skin that eventually turn black, continuous vomiting of blood, aching limbs and indescribably terrible pain. The pain is caused by the actual decomposition of the flesh and organs, even while the infected person is still alive.*'

"Wow!" said Gersham. "That sure doesn't sound like a whole lot of fun, even for a 'psychological operation.' Hey, this is interesting. Did you know that the Japanese actually used bubonic plague as a biological weapon in World War Two? Yep, it says the Japs filled special dispersal bombs with millions of infected fleas, and dropped them on Chinese cities. I guess Bob and Sidney were old school. They were just going to use infected rats and turn them loose in the FEMA camps."

"No, no," Bullard insisted, "I had nothing to do with it!" He was standing on his tiptoes, trying to relieve the pressure on his wrists. "I wasn't going to get him any rats or do anything else like that. I had *no idea* about this plague stuff. I never saw that stuff before, I never even *heard* of it!"

Ira asked Boone and Carson, "Well, what do you guys think? Do you believe him?"

"I don't know," said Boone. "And personally, I don't care. I've heard enough."

Carson said, "I've got an idea. Why don't we just inject both of them with some of this YP-12D? If one little flea bite is enough to infect a person, I wonder what a couple of needle sticks will do?"

"But isn't that shit contagious?" asked Boone.

Gersham set the open encyclopedia on top of the laundry dryer and read some more. "If we inject them now, they won't be infectious for a few days. Even then, nothing will happen unless some fleas bite them and then the fleas bite somebody else. That's how it works, unless it turns into pneumonic plague. That's even worse. That's when the lungs are infected, and they can cough the plague germs onto other people. But you know what? There's a good side too. You can cure the bubonic plague real easy with regular antibiotics—if you catch it soon enough."

"Well then," said Boone, "why don't we give them both a little jab with that YP-12D? Then they'll be motivated to help us out. They'll want that medicine real bad when they start getting those black bumps."

"And if they still won't help us," said Ira, "we can just drive them way out into the country and leave them handcuffed to trees. Then they can watch those nasty black buboes start popping out all over. You should see the pictures in here. Those buboes look like rotten plums coming right out of the skin. Talk about zits from hell!"

Boone said, "I kind of like the idea of them vomiting blood, as they decompose from the inside out."

"You can't possibly think you can get away with this!" Bullard said in a raspy voice, summoning up his nerve. "I'll be missed by tomorrow morning, and then whole teams of my men will come looking for me. You'd better think twice about this—you can't get away! And *he* reports to the president himself! If he doesn't call in, they'll send the Secret Service and the FBI!"

"Oh, save it, Bob," said Carson. "By tomorrow morning, you'll be twenty miles out in the forest with your arms handcuffed around a tree, checking your skin for red and black spots. That is, if you don't win this game of 'Who Knows the Biggest Secret?' And so far, I'm not very impressed with what you know."

Bullard looked down, his legs clamped tightly together. "I've got to use the bathroom."

"Hey, don't let us stop you," said Boone. "You just go right ahead. I'll clean you up with a few buckets of ice water."

"You're sadists!" Bullard wailed. "You're sick! You're monsters!"

Ira said, "Hey, we're not the ones who brought the YP-12D to Tennessee. That was your pal Sidney, from Washington. The guy who, you know, reports to the president. And Bob, I'm still not hearing any great secrets from you. Remember, there's only one winner in this game."

"Okay, okay. Let me think. Just wait. Okay. I know about a massacre that the Kazaks did last weekend. A big one, it was really terrible! They were completely out of control. They killed hundreds, even women and children! It was worse than My Lai!"

Boone had refilled the bucket, and on hearing this, he hurled the gallon of frigid water into Bullard's face, causing him to lose his balance and fall off his perch. He was hanging by his wrists from the steel pipe while he moaned and cursed and struggled to get his bound feet back onto the cinderblock.

Carson said, "Okay, Sid, it's your turn now. We know about your germs, but they really haven't killed anybody yet. Bob just told us about a big massacre. You have to top that. The winner gets to live, and the loser gets a needle full of plague germs and a one-way trip out to the forest. So if you know any good secrets, I think this would be a good time to spill the beans."

Bullard was still swinging around by his wrists, trying to climb back on his block, soaking wet in the cold air from his last dousing. At least compared to him, Sidney Krantz was doing slightly better in the comfort department. Boone went back to the washbasin and refilled the bucket.

Carson repeated, "If you know anything interesting, Sidney, now would be the time." He had taken a syringe and removed the plastic protective cap from its needle. He carefully pierced the rubber lid of the vial of liquid carrying *Yersinia pestis* germs, and drew a bit of the dark viscous fluid up the needle into the barrel of the syringe. His blue rubber gloves emphasized the evil toxicity of the contents of the vial. He carefully held the needle away from himself and said, "Okay, who wants to go first?" He pointed the needle at Bullard and then at Krantz, aiming at their exposed bellies as they stared down in helpless horror.

"I know a big secret!" shouted Krantz. "I know a really big secret! I know a really, *really* big secret!"

Boone paused with his bucket of icy water, and Carson froze in place with his syringe laden with bubonic plague germs.

Carson said, "Well, Sidney, don't keep us waiting."

"I know about a videotape, a blackmail videotape. It was made by Robert Waylen. I know where it is—I've seen it!"

Carson asked, "You mean Professor Robert Waylen, the old commie terrorist?"

"Yes, yes, him!"

"Who gives a shit about that sixties has-been?" said Ira.

"No, no, it's not *about* Robert Waylen—he just made it, for blackmail. The video is about Jamal Tambor—*President* Jamal Tambor. They were close friends, Waylen and Tambor, until Tambor became president. It's unbelievable, this tape! Tambor is a communist—"

"No shit, Sherlock!" said Boone. "You think that's a news flash?"

"No, no, Tambor *admits* he's a communist on the videotape. He *brags* about it! He says his entire political life is a lie, a false front, all so that he can push the cause of international socialism! I swear to God! Waylen got him high on coke, and secretly videotaped him in his house. You won't believe this fucking tape, it'll blow your minds—and I know where it is! It's hidden in Waylen's townhouse in Greenwich Village, and I know *exactly* where it is. Waylen played it for me, he was so proud of it! He said the tape was his masterpiece, and he made it just in case Tambor 'forgets where his loyalty lies.' Nobody knows about it except for Robert Waylen—and me. And now you."

The three men stared at Krantz. "I think we have a winner," said Carson. "That's a pretty damn good secret, if it's true."

"Will you let me go, then?" Krantz pleaded. "Please?"

Boone asked him, "What about your friend here?"

"I don't give a shit about him, he's nothing! But you *have* to let me go now, or at least after you get the videotape. Because I know *lots* more secrets. I meet with the president almost every week, in private! Believe me, I'm worth more to you alive than dead. A *lot* more!"

Carson snickered and said, "You know, that's exactly what Che Guevara said when the Bolivians caught him: 'I'm worth more to you alive than dead.' And guess who helped the Bolivians catch that commie bastard? We did: the Army Special Forces. Yep, killing communists is an old hobby of ours. But in your case, you might be right. You might just be worth more to us alive than dead. At least for now. Ira, give Boone the key so he can unlock our new friend Sidney. Take him into the other room and let him get dressed."

Then Phil Carson turned suddenly and jabbed the needle into Bob Bullard's side, just above his boxer shorts. Bullard howled and tried to move away, but only succeeded in falling off his cinderblock again. Carson jammed the plunger home and said, "That was for Brad Fallon," and then he jerked the needle back out. "You probably don't even remember him. But I'll bet you remember Wally Malvone's house up the Potomac River, that night it caught fire. I was there, you son of a bitch—I burned it down! Now I want you to think about that night, while you're puking up blood and watching those rotten plums bust through your skin!"

Krantz was lying in the fetal position with a blanket thrown over him, moaning and mumbling incoherently. They had dragged him into the nice side of the basement, and handcuffed him to the bottom of an old radiator. The three conspirators pulled chairs together to discuss their next move. Carson asked, "Do you think Sidney was telling the truth about the blackmail tape?"

"No doubt about it," replied Ira Gersham. "That boy just played his best card, to save his miserable life."

"Can we get it in time?" asked Carson. "By tomorrow?"

"We can sure give it a shot," Boone replied. "He said Greenwich Village, right? That's Manhattan. Isn't Hulk Rogan's brother a cop in New York? What the hell, it's worth a try."

Carson asked, "What are we going to do with these two now? How are we going to keep them on ice for twenty-four hours? If Bullard doesn't show up at Building 1405 tomorrow, they'll come looking for him, just like he said."

"I think I know how we can finesse it," said Ira. "Voice mail. We can get Bullard to tell his deputy that he was called back to Washington, and he's flying there with Krantz on his airplane. He can make a recording, and we'll play it onto his deputy's voice mail. And he'll do it too: we'll just tell him if he doesn't, he won't get the antibiotics. Same thing with Krantz. He can make a recording telling his pilot to take the plane back to Washington because he'll be staying here for a few days. That'll get us through tomorrow before they're missed."

"And tomorrow is all we need," said Boone.

Carson added, "Tomorrow is Camp David."

"And tomorrow is Raven Rock," said Ira. "The Big Show."

"But what about *after* tomorrow?" Boone asked.

Ira said, "Do you mean if the plan works, or if it doesn't work?"

"Both."

Gersham said, "If the plan works, we should keep them both alive as material witnesses. They'll flip in a heartbeat if we pull this off. They're the links in the chain between the Mannville massacre and the president. They'll both be able to testify against Tambor. You know, as much as I hate to admit it, Krantz was right—they'll be worth more alive than dead."

"But what if the plan *doesn't* work?" asked Boone.

Gersham said, "Then we'll inject Krantz with the plague too, and leave them chained somewhere. Hopefully, somewhere without any fleas. Maybe even in that basement room back there. Gag them and tie them up, and hide them. If we succeed tomorrow and we make it back, we can have them treated with antibiotics, so they can be witnesses against the president. If we don't succeed and we don't make it back, then they'll die in agony like they deserve. And if we don't make it back, Colonel Spencer and the rest of the working group will go the total guerrilla warfare route. He already told me that. They'll put out the word about Operation Buffalo Jump and the Manville massacre the best way they can, and then they'll take off and go guerrilla."

"Like you and Boone did," said Carson.

"Yeah, like that," said Ira. "But hundreds this time, not just a few. Hell, maybe thousands. Maybe the entire 5th Group. Maybe it'll spread to the whole military this time, even if we can't initiate the EBS."

"Well, let's make it work tomorrow," said Carson. "I'm too old to run around the woods playing Robin Sage with real bullets." Robin Sage was the final guerrilla warfare exercise for Special Forces trainees in their qualification course.

Boone smiled and said, "I think you did pretty good the last few days, old-timer."

"Well, I just hope I have one more good day left in me. It'll have to be one of my best, if we're going to pull this off."

Twenty minutes later, CW4 Hugh Rogan called his older brother Patrick at his suburban home in Queens, New York. A year ago, Patrick Rogan had retired from the NYPD after thirty years of service, working his way up from patrolman to detective. Now he worked as a private investigator, a security consultant and an alarm installer. This was to supplement his pension, which was paid in almost worthless North American Dollars.

His brother Hugh had slipped a predetermined code word into their casual after-dinner conversation, and then he sent an innocuous email. Hidden inside a cartoon accompanying a "joke of the day" was a detailed text message. This microtext was further encoded using PGP, Pretty Good Privacy, an open-source encryption program. PGP had been commercially available until it was outlawed as a national security risk. Patrick and Hugh had previously exchanged their own private algorithm keys, and could send one another messages that not even the NSA could crack, if they ever stumbled across the hidden microtexts in the first place.

This urgent message explained the need for Patrick to search former terrorist Robert Waylen's townhouse in Greenwich Village. He needed to find a particular videotape and bring it to a to-be-determined location in West Virginia by eight o'clock tomorrow morning. He needed to do all of this, even at great personal risk. Pat Rogan knew that his younger brother was not joking, or testing him. He immediately called Joe Vellegio, his best friend and former partner, and asked for his help. Vellegio was still on the force.

Rogan picked him up in his wife's subcompact Ford Focus. Rogan chose to drive the Focus because it could maneuver well in the tight quarters of Greenwich Village. Like his younger brother, Pat Rogan was several inches under six feet tall, so the small car didn't cramp him. It was a cold night, with an intermittent drizzle that was threatening to turn into sleet. By 8:00 p.m., they had driven across the Williamsburg Bridge from Queens into Lower Manhattan. A few minutes later, they were casing Waylen's three-story brownstone on West 11th Street, just a few blocks from Union Square. West 11th was a westbound one-way street with parking on both sides, leaving just a narrow channel for local traffic.

They got lucky turning off 7th Avenue when making another circle of the block. Somebody was leaving a prized corner spot on 11th and they pulled right into it, parked, and killed their lights. From this vantage point they could see the front of Waylen's townhouse, halfway down the block. A single lamp on a pole barely illuminated the street. Rogan had to flick on the wipers from time to time to keep the windshield clear. The two detectives sat in the tiny black Ford, discussing ways to get into Waylen's home, and drinking bad instant fake coffee from a thermos. Vellegio had brought his police radio, so that they would know if anything unusual was going on in the neighborhood. The odds were slim to nil that a patrol car would randomly cruise down this block of West 11th Street. Before the economic meltdown, it had been an affluent street in a trendy part of Greenwich Village, and most of the cars were fairly new Japanese or European imports. Many of the cars still had Tambor bumper stickers.

Rogan said, "What gets me the most is that he lives in that thing alone. You'd think he'd be assigned one, maybe two more families in a big townhouse like that. They're narrow, but they're deep. I'll bet that thing is at least three thousand square feet, counting the cellar. And all for one guy. Some communist *he* is."

Vellegio replied, "I did a little checking right after you called. Waylen got a 'hardship waiver,' so he doesn't have to pay the vacant room tax *or* take in assigned boarders. Those waivers are hard as hell to get. It shows what kind of political pull he's got. He's living pretty well for a retired college professor."

"A college professor, a terrorist and a cop killer," added Rogan.

"He was never charged for that precinct bombing, so officially he's still just an *alleged* cop killer. Anyway, he only designed and built that nail bomb. He didn't plant it. That coward got a girlfriend to carry it in. Of course, none of that was ever *proved* in a court of law…"

"*Alleged*, my Irish ass," Rogan grumbled. "Two cops died in that bombing. I'm just sorry it took this long for somebody to finally come after him. Those cops have been dead for forty years, and he's been free as a bird."

"What a country," said Vellegio with a sigh. "So, what's the plan?"

"My brother says that he walks his dogs between dinner and bedtime. Dachshunds. Maybe he hasn't come out yet. It's still pretty early."

"How did your brother find *that* out? That's pretty specific. I never get information that good on my crooks."

"Oh, he's got sources, trust me. You know my little brother…he's involved in all of that spooky shit with the Night Stalkers. He flies the CIA, the SEALs, all of those guys. You should see where he's sent me postcards from. Places you'd never believe that Americans would ever go, that's for sure. For a couple years in the nineties he had long hair, and supposedly he was flying choppers for some civilian outfit in Colombia. Doing geological surveys or something like that. Yeah, right! Then I'd get unsigned postcards from all over Central and South America. The craziest places! Yeah, my brother Hugh, he's something else. He's the real deal, and that's no bullshit. So if he says it's important that I do this job, and I have to do it tonight, I'm going to do it. No questions asked."

"But what if Waylen doesn't come outside after dark? What if he lets his dogs crap in his backyard instead?"

"Then we'll figure out something else," said Rogan. "Most of the houses already have their trash out, but his doesn't. Maybe he'll put his garbage out, and we can do it then."

Vellegio straightened up and said, "There's the light, this might be it…" The front door of the three-story townhouse was up a flight of nine or ten steps, and was set into a small alcove. A light above the small vestibule had come on, illuminating the steps. They could not see the door itself from this angle. While the two detectives watched, a man walked out onto his narrow porch and turned up the collar of his brown winter coat. A dark beret was pulled down to his ears. He held a pair of dachshunds on leashes. The dogs were anxious to run down the stairs, and the man had to restrain them while he gripped the iron railing with his other hand and descended the steps one at a time. Then the man ambled down the side-walk away from his watchers. He paused as the dogs did their business in the narrow strip of dirt between the sidewalk and the curb.

"You sure that's him?" asked Vellegio. "I didn't really get a good look at his face."

"Who else can it be?" The detectives turned up their own collars, pulled on wide-brimmed fedoras, and exited the car into the cold mist.

After five minutes, the dogs were scampering back up the steps, fol-lowed more slowly by a wheezing Robert Waylen. The light had remained on above the door. Unbeknownst to him, Waylen was trailed up the stairs by two shadowlike figures. Both men were wearing dark coats, and hats that kept their faces shadowed from the porch light above them.

As Waylen put his key in the door and began to open it, he was sud-denly joined by the two strangers on his little porch. The dogs grew even more excited, and Waylen was startled to the point of suddenly backing up against the side of the landing vestibule.

Patrick Rogan smiled and said, "Don't worry Mr. Waylen, we're with NYPD Protective Services." The detectives flashed their gold shields and credentials. Both of the men were wearing thin gray driving gloves. "May we have a word with you?"

"At this time of night?" Waylen had fear in his eyes, but relaxed somewhat after seeing their gold NYPD badges.

"I'm sorry for the late hour," said Rogan, "but we've just received intelligence information about a plot by right-wing extremists to harm you. We regard it as highly credible and very serious. We even think that they're tapping your phone and hacking your computer, so we couldn't call or email you."

Waylen was wide-eyed. "Excuse me? Who did you say you were?" His dogs were jumping around their legs, adding to the confusion on the crowded alcove landing.

"I'm Detective Edward O'Grady, and this is my partner, Frank Russo. We're with NYPD Protective Services. Do you mind if we come in? We'd like to show you some mug shots, and ask if you've seen any of these 'persons of interest' around your neighborhood."

"What? Right-wing extremists? In *this* neighborhood? Why yes, of course, please come in." Waylen finished unlocking the door and the three men stepped inside as the dogs rushed between them. After locking two dead bolts, Waylen crouched down and unclipped his dachshunds' leashes, then stood up and hung them on a brass hook by the door. The dogs immediately tore off and disappeared down the hall, their nails clicking on the hardwood floor. Waylen slipped off his overcoat and hung it and his black beret on another hook beside the leashes. Beneath the coat, he was wearing a navy blue Columbia University sweatshirt and jeans. He was almost entirely bald, except for a ring of curly gray hair.

"If you'll please follow me back to the kitchen, the light will be better there. I'll make some coffee if you'd like, and you can show me the pictures on the kitchen table. The coffee is from Cuba—it's real coffee."

"Real coffee would be great," said Rogan.

After Waylen turned to walk down the hallway past his living room, Rogan removed one of the leather dog leashes, and quickly rolled it up and stuffed it into the deep front pocket of his black overcoat.

In the kitchen at the back of the first floor, Waylen reached up into a cupboard to remove a small jar of instant coffee. "How do you like it?"

Standing behind him, Rogan removed the dog leash from his overcoat pocket. He pulled some of the leather strap back through the hand loop, forming a wide noose, and flipped it over Waylen's head. Using both hands, he cinched the noose tightly around his neck, pulled him back off balance and nearly lifted him up off the floor. Waylen went loose at his knees, struggling with weak fingers to remove the choking strap. In thirty seconds, the retired professor fell limp, with his eyes still open and his arms dangling at his sides. Pat Rogan lowered him to the linoleum kitchen floor on his back.

"Okay, Joe, you watch him, and I'll look for the tape." Rogan went up the steps to the second floor. According to his brother's message, this was the location of Waylen's office. He returned to the kitchen a minute later with a VHS videocassette in a cardboard sleeve. "This one has the right dates, October 20–24, 1983. It's just like Hugh said it would be: all of his lectures are on tape. He's got a shelf with hundreds of these things."

"What an egomaniac," said the other detective. "Did he actually think anybody was ever going to give a shit about his old lectures?"

"Well, at least it makes a good hiding place. Nobody's ever going to watch hundreds of old history classes. Can you imagine how God-awful boring that would be? I'd rather be Tasered."

"What about him?" asked Vellegio, prodding Waylen's unmoving body with his toe. "He's still breathing, I think." The leather dog leash was still twisted around his neck.

"We should check the tape first. We have to make sure it's the right one. There's a video player under the TV in the living room. I saw it on the way in." The two detectives walked from the kitchen into the adjoining living room and looked around in wonder. The curtains were closed tightly on the 11th Street front windows. Framed portraits and posters of Fidel Castro, Che Guevara and other communist luminaries adorned the walls. A red parade-sized banner with a giant black fist occupied most of a wall. A life-sized marble bust of Vladimir Ilyich Lenin scowled from a shelf.

In a minute the tape was playing, and they were watching a much younger Professor Waylen. He was standing behind a lectern on a raised platform, in front of a classroom of college students. He had dark bushy hair and a Fu Manchu mustache. Instead of a professorial blazer, he was wearing a black turtleneck sweater with a silver peace sign medallion hanging from a chain. Waylen's mouth moved soundlessly, since the television was muted. Detective Rogan fast-forwarded halfway through the tape, and hit play again. He held the remote control with his gloved hand while they stood in front of the flat-screen television. Both men had been careful not to touch or disturb anything since entering the townhouse.

And suddenly, there he was. Jamal Tambor himself, just a few years younger than today. His hair was still completely black, his hairline just beginning its long march up his forehead. Tambor was wearing a white oxford shirt, open at the neck. He was sitting at the exact same kitchen table that the detectives had just seen in the next room. Rogan turned up the sound with the remote, and they watched and listened in rapt amazement. The bust of Lenin had been placed on a kitchen counter, so that it would appear just over the unsuspecting Tambor's right shoulder, menacingly staring at the hidden camera. The iconic print of Che Guevara now hanging in the living room was visible on the wall next to the back door. Beneath Che's face was ¡Hasta La Victoria, Siempre! Toward Victory, Forever! A tall marijuana bong stood in front of the glassy-eyed future president while he expounded on the necessity for imposing global socialism. A straw and the powdery remains of cocaine could be seen on a plastic tray next to his left elbow.

Detective Vellegio whistled softly. "Waylen set him up but good. Your brother sure had good information. You want to watch the rest?"

"No, that's the right one," said Rogan, who stooped down and ejected the tape, touching the machine only with a gloved fingertip. "Let's get out of here. After I drop you off, I've got a seven-hour drive clear across to West Virginia ahead of me. I might have to borrow some gas from you to make it on time. I'll need a couple extra jerry cans. I can't count on finding an open gas station out there in the sticks. It's almost five hundred miles, and I have to be there by eight o'clock in the morning, do or die."

"Jeez, why do you have to go way out there?"

"I just do. Somebody in a helicopter is going to meet me out there and get the tape. I swear to God."

Detective Vellegio just shook his head and smiled. "If you say so. No problem with the gas. But what about Waylen? He's still breathing, and he got a good look at us."

"Well, then I guess we can't leave him breathing. Besides everything else that commie traitor has done, we both know he's a cop killer, even if he got the charges dropped by some commie rat judge. Well, it's finally payback time. Forty years too late, but hey, better late than never."

"So how are we going to do it?" asked Vellegio, pointing to an ashtray next to an easy chair. "He's a smoker. Maybe he was smoking in bed, and he started a house fire?"

"Nah, we don't want to do that to his neighbors. Plus that'd bring the fire department straight down here tonight, and we need to keep it low-key for a while."

"I like the idea of a suicide," said Vellegio. "We could put him in his bathtub and slit his wrists with a razor blade. That'd make it easy to clean up any trace evidence at the same time."

Rogan said, "Me personally, I'd like to stick a nail bomb up his ass. Like the one he built for the 35th precinct."

"It'd be hard to make that look like a suicide," Vellegio laughed.

"Maybe he was playing around with explosives for old time's sake, and he had a little work-related accident? It happens."

"Get serious, Pat. You have any explosives on you?"

"How about a rope? That's always a good way for a traitor to get it."

"People might not believe it was suicide," said Vellegio. "They might think he had a little outside help."

"Why would they think that? But even if they do, so what? Suicide or a traitor's death—hanging works either way. Let people wonder. Let it be a mystery. As long as we're careful and we don't leave any trace evidence, nobody will ever know for sure."

"Okay, I'll go with that. What about his dog leash?"

"Yeah, that'll work," Rogan agreed. "Plus it'll cover up the ligature marks on his neck."

"How long do you figure until he's found?"

"A few days? He's not teaching anymore, so it might be a while. We should open a bag of dog food in the basement, and make sure those two mutts got plenty of water."

"He'll be plenty ripe by then," Vellegio observed. "He'll stink up the whole place."

"He's been stinking up this city for forty years. Where should we do it?"

"There's a transom between the kitchen and the dining room. We can just toss the leash over it. After we hoist him up and tie it off, we can lay a kitchen chair on its side. It'll look like he stood up on it and kicked it away. Like the commie traitor just couldn't live with his guilt anymore."

"Yeah, that'll work good," agreed Rogan. "You get his shoulders, and I'll get his legs—we don't want to leave any drag marks. Then you hold him up, and I'll throw the leash over the transom. He doesn't have to be high up off the ground, just as long as his feet don't reach the floor."

The Campers, the Ravens and some of the Missionaries spent their last evening at Sergeant Major Charlie Donelson's house near Clarksville. The Campers were Boone Vikersun and Phil Carson, who were bound for Camp David. The Ravens were Lieutenant General Armstead, Ira Gersham and Doug Dolan, who were continuing on to Site R, inside Raven Rock Mountain. The Missionaries, led by Colonel Tom Spencer, were staying behind at Fort Campbell to spread the gospel among the 5th Special Forces Group, the 101st Air Assault Division, the other Special Forces Groups, the Ranger Battalions and any other Army units they could reach with their message.

In a guest bedroom with a full-length mirror, Carson and Boone were dressed in blue officers' Army Service Uniforms. They were ensuring that every detail was correct under the watchful eyes of Colonel Spencer, who was also wearing his own blue ASU as a model for comparison. In addition, Boone wore the gold braid aiguillette of a general's aide-de-camp around his left shoulder. Bibi Donelson, dressed in a form-fitting red and black silk dress of her own design and creation, was ready with needle and thread to make any additional alterations as required. Phil Carson had been out of the Army for decades, and it took him a while to become comfortable with coming to attention and rendering a salute not as an enlisted man, but as a one-star brigadier general. Inwardly he felt doubt and turmoil, but he gritted his teeth and continued to practice. He felt like an actor and an imposter, and he was in fact both of those things. His mission was to be an effective actor and imposter tomorrow, so he took his practice very seriously.

The colonel saluted first and brought his stiff hand to the bill of his Army officer's peaked cap, until Carson returned the honor more quickly and a shade more casually, as befitted a flag-rank officer.

"General Harper, I think you've got it," said Colonel Spencer, while they stood a few feet apart.

"As you were, Colonel," said Carson, and they dropped their arms.

"How do you feel about briefing the Operation Buffalo Jump CON-PLAN?" asked Colonel Spencer.

"You're not going to quiz me on it, are you? As long as I don't have to give the whole PowerPoint presentation, I can hold my own."

"Well, that's all right, then. You just have to know enough to mingle and converse intelligently during the meet-and-greet."

"It's all the acronyms that are the real killers. Like TPFDD."

"Time-phased force and deployment data," Colonel Spencer recited automatically. "It rolls off your tongue, doesn't it? How about M-day?"

"That's when the mobilization of reserve forces begins."

"JSCP?"

"Joint Strategic Capabilities Plan, that's an easy one. Your turn now, Colonel. What's the JOPES?" Carson pronounced this word like "hopes."

"Joint Operation Planning and Execution System. Is that one in your CONPLAN?"

"Along with about twenty others. Don't worry, I made some cheat sheets. And I'll study some more on the flight up to Maryland."

"Did you get your new ID cards?" Colonel Spencer addressed this question to both Phil Carson and Boone Vikersun.

"We did," said Boone. "And they look perfect, as far as I can tell. But they have a magnetic strip and all this digital computer crap on them these days, so there's no way to be sure. Not until the Secret Service checks them anyway."

Colonel Spencer looked both men in the eye and said, "It's a leap of faith, gentlemen."

"Fearless men, who jump and die," said Phil Carson, reciting a line from the old ballad that was chiseled on every Green Beret's soul. "But we'll try to avoid that second part if we can."

"Roger that," said the colonel. "But we'll still jump, no matter what the outcome."

"Airborne, sir," Boone said softly.

"All the way," finished Colonel Spencer, who then pulled himself up to a rigid position of attention and slowly rendered one more perfect salute, but this time not for practice. Boone Vikersun and Phil Carson, dressed as a major and a general, returned the colonel's salute and held it.

Bibi Donelson, who had not said a single word, crossed herself in the Catholic way, with tears welling in her eyes. Tomorrow was D-Day. Even she knew *that* much about the Army.

30

The Blackhawk departed Fort Campbell in darkness, its pilots wearing night vision goggles. Dawn found them above Kentucky's Appalachian Mountains. With a pair of external tanks attached, they could make the flight to Camp David without refueling. Four decades after Vietnam, Phil Carson found himself on a helicopter flying into a dangerous situation. Once again, there was the strong possibility that a return flight would not be necessary.

Mist and low clouds hung in the long shadows between the folds of the mountains. The terrain below reminded him of the Central Highlands of Vietnam, especially the zigzag meandering streams and rivers. Of course, in Southeast Asia only a defoliated area would ever be so free of leaf cover in the triple-canopy jungle. Here, it just meant that it was January, with freezing temperatures doing the work instead of Dow Chemical. Even with the troop doors closed and the cabin heat on, it was cold flying at 7,000 feet.

The four Blackhawk rotors gave this helicopter a different sound from the heart-thumping wop-wop-wop of the two-bladed Hueys he had flown aboard in Southeast Asia. To this day, the distinctive sound of any two-bladed Bell chopper caused his adrenalin to flow and his pulse to race. Even after four decades, today's flight took him back to the land of firebases, air assaults, cross-border insertions and hot LZs. The vibration, the stink of burning kerosene and the scream of turbine engines was the same. But instead of web gear, an M-16 and a rucksack, he had a briefcase packed with folders, binders and papers.

General Armstead and Phil Carson sat on the forward-facing troop bench nearest the helicopter crew seats and the cockpit. Carson was on the left side, looking north through the window on the sliding troop bay door. There was space for twelve combat-loaded grunts on the 'Hawk, with four men on each pipe-and-canvas-frame seat, so there was plenty of room with just five passengers aboard. Boone, Doug Dolan and Ira Gersham sat just behind them on the rear-facing bench, sharing a common backrest. All of the passengers were wearing ACU field jackets with quilted liners to guard against the cold. Flight helmets protected their heads from the chill and their ears from the 140-decibel engine noise. Their blue Army Service Uniform coats were in slim hanging bags, their formal hats at the bottom of the bags. The numerous pins, insignias and ribbons on their jackets would never survive the chest straps and seat belts of the troop benches.

In the Blackhawk's right cockpit seat, CW4 Hugh Rogan saw the orange day marker in the clearing, almost exactly where he had told his brother to place it. His brother Pat had to drive all the way from New York to the middle of West Virginia because the Air Defense Identification Zones around Washington and Camp David were absolutely insane ever since 9-11. When aircraft accidentally strayed into the Washington D.C. or Camp David ADIZ, missile-armed jet fighters would be scrambled for a visual check. The further from these controlled air spaces that the Blackhawk's bogus emergency occurred, the fewer eyebrows would be raised. Any declared emergency even near the Camp David or Washington ADIZ would get a rapid flyover. Not so much out here in Podunk, West Virginia, 150 miles away. Especially not when the emergency involved a low-and-slow Army helicopter on a scheduled flight between two military installations.

On the cockpit intercom, Rogan told his copilot, "Thar she blows. I've got visual on our marker." The clearing was flat and unobstructed, and it was shielded from ground observation in all directions by thick stands of trees. West Virginia Route 33 was visible only a half mile away, on the south side of the trees. Interstate 79 was a few miles to the west, behind them.

"I've got it too," replied the copilot. "Orange day panel at eleven o'clock."

"All right, I'm calling it in." Rogan switched to transmit on VHF. "Clarksburg Approach, this is Army Two-Niner-Five, with you at 7,000."

"Good morning, Army Two-Niner-Five. Altimeter 29.94, maintain 7,000 feet."

"Clarksburg, Army Two-Niner-Five, we want to declare an emergency."

"Go, Army Two-Niner-Five."

"Sir, we have a chip warning light, and we need to get this thing on the ground right now." Chip detectors were probes inside the engine that would sense a tiny bit of broken metal flying around. When the chip light went off, you set down immediately, before a tiny fragment of metal potentially led to an exploding turbine engine. Sometimes the detectors malfunctioned and false alarmed. It was a completely plausible reason for a rapid emergency landing.

"Two-Niner-Five, do you have Clarksburg airport in sight?"

"Negative, but we do have a clear grass field in sight, and we're putting her down."

"Two-Niner-Five, state fuel and souls on board."

"Clarksburg, we're a *little busy*. Will advise on the ground."

"Understood, Two-Niner-Five."

CW4 Rogan switched back to the intercom only. "Get the checklists, and tell the crew to make sure that our customers are ready to land."

"Roger that," said his copilot.

The Blackhawk flared out and set down between the orange square and the trees, and Rogan killed the power to both engines. As soon as it was quiet enough in the cockpit, he took out his cell phone and called the Clarksburg tower. The number was already written on a small notepad attached to his leg with velcro. After two rings, the call was picked up. "Clarksburg approach, this is Army Two-Niner-Five. We're on the ground, safe and sound." Rogan's real intention with this cell phone call was to allay their fears, so they would not call out the cavalry to go searching for a smoking hole in the ground. The mountains between their landing site and the Clarksburg tower twenty miles to the north blocked line-of-sight VHF radio transmissions. If Clarksburg knew that the Army Blackhawk had landed safely, they would hold off on alerting the entire world. Hence the cell phone call.

"That's great. We're glad to hear that you landed safely."

"We didn't want you to get too worked up. This happens once in a while. My crew chief is going to take a look under the hood. Usually it's a bad sensor probe. We can switch it out in a couple of minutes just to be sure. We'll call you back in a few when we know our status."

"Roger that, Army. Good luck."

Rogan switched off his cell phone, and on the intercom he told his copilot, "I'm doing this one myself. I've waited twenty years to visit my brother like this." He pulled off his helmet, unbuckled himself and opened his side door. Then he jumped down into the high brown grass and ran for the tree line a hundred feet away, his boots crunching through the frost. The four rotors were still turning, but were visible now and slowing down. His brother Pat had to stay in cover, on the off chance that somebody upstairs was taking pictures. If he ever needed to explain this run to the trees, he would say that he was merely answering an urgent call of nature of the sitting variety. To complete the charade, once the blades stopped, his crew chief would climb on top of the helo and open an engine cowling.

Pat was wearing a blue padded goose down coat with a hood, and gloves. It was cold enough to see their exhaled breath. "About time you slackers showed up. I've been waiting for hours, freezing my ass off." They grinned at one another and shook hands. The Rogan brothers were not touchy-feely hugging types, but their joy was nonetheless genuine and unbounded.

"Where did you get the orange panel?" asked Hugh.

"It's a poncho from Wal-Mart. I staked it down like you said, so it wouldn't blow away."

"You got the videotape?"

"I wouldn't be here otherwise." The VHS tape was in a brown paper bag, inside a gallon-size slide-lock plastic bag. He handed the package to his brother.

"Did you check it? I mean, did you watch it?"

"Hell yes! It's going to knock your socks off. Jamal Tambor, unplugged. I don't know what you're planning to do with it, but it'll screw that commie traitor but good."

"Did you see Waylen?"

"See him? Hell, we killed him! We had to." After this admission, Pat rapidly blessed himself. "May God forgive me, but I'm not sorry."

"Who's we?"

"Me and my last partner, Joey Vellegio. Don't worry about him."

"So, where's Waylen now?"

"Oh, just hangin' around his house." Pat Rogan cocked his head to the side, coughed, and with his hand he mimed a noose jerking him upward. "Suicide. He couldn't stand the shame."

"Pat...thanks for doing all this. I owe ya, big brother."

"No problem, Hulkster. It's great to see you in your pilot suit. Mom would have been so proud."

"Hey...one more thing. Listen to the radio on your way back. And you might want to watch TV today, when you get home."

"Seriously? What channel?"

CW4 Hugh Rogan laughed. "Yeah, what channel. All of 'em!" Behind him, the Blackhawk's turbine engines began to wind up again. "Hey, I gotta go—they tell me I'm the pilot!" He stuffed the tape into a leg pocket on his flight suit, turned and ran back to his helicopter, giving two thumbs-up signs to his waiting crew and teammates.

After only five minutes on the ground, Hugh Rogan increased power and pulled pitch. The powerful Blackhawk helicopter dipped its nose in salute, and then hurtled forward and up. As the ground receded beneath them, he called in again on VHF.

"Clarksburg, this is Army Two-Niner-Five, back with you at 2,500 feet. We're okay."

"Army Two-Niner-Five, glad to hear it. Ident. Do you wish to cancel the emergency?"

"Yes sir, we just had a chip detector malfunction. Now we're good to go. Squawking ident." Rogan pushed the identification switch, giving the Clarksburg tower an enhanced radar image, plus digitally encoded information about his aircraft.

"Understood, Two-Niner-Five. Radar contact. State intentions."

"If our flight plan hasn't dropped out of the system, we'd like to proceed as originally filed to Poppa Four Zero." This was the civilian call
sign for Camp David.

"Army Two-Niner-Five, turn right to a heading of 080, climb out and
maintain 7,000. Stand by for a revised clearance to Poppa Four Zero."

"Army Two-Niner-Five, heading 080, climb and maintain 7,000."

Their flight path took them across the Eastern Panhandle of West Virginia, between Maryland and Virginia. An hour after landing to pick up
the videotape, the Blackhawk left West Virginia's air space, flew over the
Potomac River and entered Maryland. Born in the Appalachian Mountains
behind them, the river formed the jigsaw boundary between Maryland and
the states of West Virginia and Virginia, all the way to Washington, D.C.,
and the Chesapeake Bay. Out here in the foothills and piedmont country
the river was a brilliant snake, its coils shining like a quicksilver ribbon in
the morning sunlight. Washington was sixty air miles southeast, more if
you followed the meanderings of the Potomac. Harper's Ferry, the east-
ernmost point of West Virginia, was only a dozen or so miles south.

A thought popped into Phil Carson's mind as he mentally traced the
course of the river. He wondered if Wally Malvone's house on the Potomac below Washington had ever been rebuilt since he had burned it down,
or if it was just a vacant lot. And he wondered if Brad Fallon had ever
made it to the ocean, or if he was still down there somewhere, resting on
the bottom of the river.

Three miles past the Potomac, out of the left side windows, they saw
the white X formed by the crossing of interstates 81 and 70 at Hagerstown,
Maryland. The intersection marked a spot only seventeen miles from
Camp David. The forests of West Virginia were increasingly giving way
to a patchwork of small farms, woods, villages and towns. They were
seven minutes out. It was D-Day, but instead of hitting the beaches or
dropping into a jungle LZ, they were going to land inside one of the most
highly secure military compounds on the entire planet.

The two enlisted crewmembers on the Blackhawk had their own positions on each side, forward of the troop seats and just behind the cockpit.
Their gun hatches were closed on this winter flight. They were not carrying machine guns for this cross-country hop from Fort Campbell to "Naval
Support Facility Thurmont," military-speak for Camp David. After leaving Hagerstown's air space and flying over open country again, the crew
chief on the left gunner's seat began to talk to the pilots on his helmet
intercom. He stood and scanned outside and behind the helicopter through
the window on his gun hatch.

Carson looked out his left bay door window and saw a Marine Corps
Super Cobra attack helicopter only a hundred yards away, coming up

parallel to the Blackhawk. They were close enough to see the two helmeted pilots, sitting one behind the other in the nose of the aircraft. The Cobra was missile armed, and had a three-barreled minigun jutting out from its chin. This modern Super Cobra didn't look very different from the Cobras Carson had occasionally seen in Vietnam, when they were making close-air-support rocket and gun runs. He never saw them in Laos or Cambodia, though. "Over the fence," they were always on their own.

Camp David had a twenty-mile exclusion zone around it when the president was there. Any civilian aircraft wandering into this air space would receive a similar armed welcome, and then they would be forced to land at the Hagerstown airport to meet some very unfriendly federal agents. Faster intruding aircraft would be met by F-16 Falcon fighters. Army Blackhawk 295 was expected today, so after a minute, the deadly Cobra attack helicopter rolled away and quickly disappeared.

Camp David occupies 180 acres and is shaped roughly like a diamond, one-half mile from tip to tip. It sits atop a hill in the middle of Catoctin Mountain Park, a 10,000-acre preserve overseen by the National Park Service. The camp is surrounded by thick stands of Eastern hardwood trees, and its perimeter is visible from the air because of the cleared security strip around it.

The helicopter landing field takes up much of the bottom of the diamond, an area the size of several football fields. If you divided the camp into two halves from top to bottom, the western half of the diamond would contain most of the support facilities for the camp. These would be the barracks for the Naval support personnel and the Marine guards, the water works, staff parking, and a military road inside the western perimeter, from the helicopter landing zone at the south to the barracks at the north.

The eastern point of the diamond contains the reason for the entire camp: the presidential residence called the Aspen Lodge. The rest of the eastern half of Camp David is composed of other residences for visiting dignitaries, meeting and dining facilities, and the Laurel Lodge conference center. All of these lodges and support facilities are connected by asphalt lanes exquisitely maintained by Camp David's own contingent of Navy Seabees. They wind between thick stands of birch, hazel, locust, beech, ash and oak trees. In the summertime these trees make Camp David a shady realm with short viewing distances. In the winter, when the trees are devoid of leaves, it is possible to look through this forest and sometimes catch glimpses of the multiple rows of wire fencing surrounding the camp. Camp David's fences, sensors and cameras would be the envy of any maximum-security prison, but here they serve to keep unwanted visitors out, instead of prisoners in.

The Blackhawk banked and turned as it descended, giving Carson a good view of the landing zone. Three "white top" Marine One helicopters were parked on an asphalt apron that led into a single large hangar. There were always three, in order to confound any terrorists who might try to assassinate the president with a shoulder-launched missile. Several other VH-60 "Whitehawks" were parked on the grass landing field. Like the Marine Ones, these VIP helicopters were painted forest green up to the tops of their windshields and troop doors, and above that, they were gleaming white except for their black rotor blades. Most of today's guests were being shuttled up from Washington on these VIP versions of the military Blackhawk. By contrast, the flat black and dark green MH-60K looked like an old combat boot coming down among polished wingtips and loafers. The refueling probe jutting out from under the right side of its chin identified it as a special operations "Pavehawk."

The Blackhawk landed as directed at the bottom of the field, nearest to the southern tip of the diamond. They waited until the engines had shut down and the rotors had stopped to slide open the troop doors, deplane and stretch their legs after the three-and-a-half-hour flight. The pilots and crew chiefs were out first, the crew chiefs immediately pretending to check the chip sensor again.

Standing by the aircraft, they took off their insulated field jackets and put on their blue ASU coats with the insignias and ribbons attached. Last on were their blue officer's combination covers. The helicopter pilots, the Camp David team and the Raven Rock team briefly conferred.

"Well, gentlemen, this is it," said General Armstead. "Everything is set to go. I'll escort Boone and Carson to the conference center, and then we'll pull the old switcheroo." Next the general addressed CW4 Rogan. "How did the malfunction story go over with them here?"

"Perfect. We can stay here for at least twenty minutes without any trouble. Longer if we need it, but I wouldn't push it much more than that. After that, the helicopter maintenance people here are bound to get nosy, and come down to help."

The general looked at his watch. "It's 0940. I'll be back before ten, so you only have to stall for that long."

"No problem, sir, we can do that."

"All right, good. As soon as I'm back, we'll fly to Raven Rock. Be ready to light the fires when you see me coming." The next hop, to Site R, followed their scheduled two-leg flight plan. What was not officially scheduled was that General Armstead would be slipping out of the Camp David conference center and reboarding the helicopter just before it departed. Once Armstead was back aboard the helo, the "engine problem" would be fixed, and they would take off. The point-to-point movements of the helicopter were carefully monitored and tracked, but just who would be aboard for each leg was not so easily checked. This was the essence of the shell game at the core of their plan today.

General Armstead gave his two ersatz staff officers one more looking over. "Are you ready, General Harper?"

"I'm ready, sir," said Carson.

"And is my aide-de-camp ready?"

"Yes sir, I'm ready, General," said Boone. "Let's get her done."

"Okay then," said General Armstead. "Hi-diddle-diddle, straight up the middle. Into the dragon's lair we go."

A white vehicle like a golf cart came zipping across the grassy field and met them at their helicopter. The cart had a roof and windshield, two conventional seats in the front, and two rear-facing seats behind them. A Marine corporal in dress blues parked the electric car, stepped out, came to attention and saluted.

Boone came to attention and briefly returned his salute. This type of "transportation coordination" was one of the functions of a general's aide-de-camp. "Are you our driver?" he asked. Armstead and Carson stood by the helicopter's open bay, their briefcases in hand.

"Yes sir, major. But only to security. I'm sure you understand."

"Of course."

Lieutenant General Armstead and "Brigadier General Harper" sat in the back of the electric cart, facing aft. Boone sat up front in the passenger seat beside the enlisted driver. The Marine drove across the grass field between the parked VH-60 Whitehawks, and then along the asphalt toward the big hangar. The three big Marine One choppers were parked in a row on the paved apron. Marines in dress blue uniforms stood guard around them. They were not visibly armed. Boone knew that the Marines to worry about were the ones he could not see, the ones hidden in the trees with their sniper rifles. They would not be wearing dress blues, but camouflaged ghillie suits that gave them the appearance of a clump of brush. As snipers they were his brothers, but he did not want to meet them today.

The electric cart drove past and around the open hangar, and down a sidewalk to a small one-story prefab building. Chain link security fencing extended from both sides of this structure. Their driver parked and hopped out and came to attention again. "Right through there, sirs."

The door was opened by another waiting Marine as they approached it. A Marine captain in dress blues saluted the party as they entered. Inside the drab room was a long table, with more Marines standing on the other side. A staff sergeant said, "Please put your briefcases on the table." These Marines were not smiling, saluting or making small talk. Completely non-ceremonial pistols were holstered on their belts. The captain hovered behind the enlisted men. Two men wearing dark suits, presumably Secret Service agents, were also standing behind the table. Armstead,

Carson and Boone placed their briefcases and binders on the table as directed. There was nothing in them except folders, briefing papers, cell phones, BlackBerries, computer drives, connecting cables and other expected twenty-first-century office clutter. A Marine dug through their cases, even taking out smaller folders and binders and riffling through them. Inside Boone's briefcase was a binder with a green nylon cover, and its own zipper enclosure. The Marine unzipped the case, looked inside, and zipped it back up again. Satisfied with his visual inspection, he then passed them all through an airport-type color X-ray machine. Another Marine carefully studied each item on his monitor before advancing the belt.

"Your military IDs, please," said a Marine sergeant. Their ID cards were already in their top left jacket pockets, according to regulations. General Armstead presented his card first. The sergeant took the ID and held it up, comparing the general's face to the picture on the card and to the plastic nametag on his uniform. A tiny embossed logo design on his plastic nametag matched the cloth patch sewn to his left shoulder at the sleeve seam. The symbol of U.S. Army North, the Fifth Army, showed a white number five nestled under a capital letter A, on a blue and red field. These nametag logos and shoulder insignias were replicated on the uniforms of Boone and Carson. Satisfied, the Marine said, "Welcome to Camp David, General Armstead." He leaned down to the table and made a check mark on a computer printout listing the names of the expected conference attendees.

Phil Carson handed his card across the table next, and the staff sergeant again compared faces, seemingly reading every letter and number in every block on both sides of the card, and studying every line on Carson's sixty-four-year-old face. Today his officer's cap concealed the prominent horizontal scar across the top of his forehead. Makeup had masked the scar when the picture was taken with a digital camera at Hugh Rogan's house. This was because the photo on the predated ID should have predated the obviously rather new scar. Carson was ready with a glib story about a racquetball injury, but it was not needed. His hat did not come off during the security screening, and his scar was not seen. Finally, the staff sergeant handed his card back.

"Welcome aboard, General Harper." Another tic mark was made on the printout.

The process was repeated with Boone, and "Major Paxton" was approved for entry. Next, one at a time they went through a millimeter wave full-body imager, an explosives sniffer, walked past a pair of leashed German shepherds, and were wanded for good measure. There was a considerable amount of metal in an Army uniform, and the Marines had to draw the line somewhere. They were not going to force Army generals and their aide-de-camp to remove their belts, medals, and insignias. There was a line where security needs met military courtesy, and that was it. Today as always, rank had its privileges. Finished with their inspection, the three picked up their briefcases at the other end of the long table.

The Marine captain in charge of security screening said something about being sorry to inconvenience them and saluted once more. General Armstead gave a perfunctory return salute and made no reply, but swept past him and out the door on the far side of the room followed by his subordinates. The three infiltrators stepped back into the bright sunlight. A white club van driven by a Navy petty officer in a dress blue "cracker-jack" uniform was waiting for them. A Marine rolled the van's side door back, and the conspirators climbed inside.

31

The van drove them northward along the central road of Camp David, making several turns. The retreat was covered with trees, but except for some evergreens, they were almost devoid of leaves this time of year. The conference center, called the Laurel Lodge, was at the northern end of the residential lodges where foreign leaders often stayed. Even at barely more than a walking speed, the trip took less than a minute. Today was clear and crisp, but it was easy to imagine what a dreary place it would be in a downpour, so the ride made sense. The van drove around a small traffic circle and stopped beneath a covered portico extending across a wide sidewalk. The Laurel Lodge conference center was a one-story building with a high and steeply pitched roof, almost like a church or a chalet.

Navy Sailors in dress blues welcomed them. There was some kind of invisible line of demarcation between the Marines and the sailors. Boone surmised that the jarheads were in charge of security and the squids were the cooks, butlers and handymen. Driving fell somewhere in the middle as a shared duty. Glass double doors were opened for them, and they walked inside. Sailors wearing white gloves took their hats and placed them onto numbered shelves behind their checked-items table. The main hall in the conference center was about eighty feet long. The walls on two sides were made of glass panels from knee level to well above head level, and looked out over a down-sloping hill through a forest of bare trees A massive red brick fireplace occupied the inside corner of the room, where the ceiling rose to its highest point. The interior walls were decorated with framed oil paintings, mostly pastoral scenes by early American masters.

Boone stayed close by General Armstead, while Carson flanked the three-star general on the other side. Armstead paused and assessed the tactical situation. There were damned few friendly forces in view. Most of the conferees had already arrived, because they were operating on the Marines' schedule. They had been shuttled from Washington to Camp David on the shiny green and white "Pimp My Ride" VIP Whitehawks parked down on the LZ. These waxed and polished helicopters and the three Marine Ones all belonged to HMX-1, the president's own Marine aviation squadron. From the Middle East to the United States, American military helicopters were falling out of the sky due to a dire lack of maintenance funding, but these birds and entire fleets of other VIP aircraft were as lovingly cared for as any billionaire's Rolls Royce.

The Chinese delegation was obvious, standing at the far end of a table laden with small pastries, canapés and light hors d'oeuvres. They were obvious because they were Chinese. Boone recognized the Russians, because there were two officers in Russian uniforms among a handful of diplomats. The Russians were clustered near a silver tea samovar on its own carved mahogany stand. The Saudis and other Gulf Arabs were also obvious, and were standing near the Pakistanis. The various Turks, Kazaks and other Central Asians were in a large group by a bank of coffee and espresso machines, manned by Navy Sailors in white dress uniforms. Some of the foreigners and other civilians were harder to categorize. General Armstead had told them that besides diplomats, cabinet officials and military brass, there might also be a few mysterious think-tank "academics" and U.N. High Commissioners in attendance.

General Armstead spotted the lonely American Army outpost and headed over, with his two subordinates behind him. Three Army officers were already huddled in a corner of the room by the tall windows. Each of them was standing next to a briefcase, which was placed against the wall. In this setting, with foreign officers and diplomats all around, you could not leave your briefcase anywhere for one second. If it was not in your hands, you stood over it like a mother elephant guarding her offspring. To lose or even temporarily misplace one's briefcase containing laptop computers and classified documents could be a career killer.

The waiting two-star general appeared relieved to see the arrival of reinforcements. He said, "Lieutenant General Armstead, good to see you. I was getting worried that you might not make it. Actually, I was afraid that I was going to have to brief the military options."

"Good morning, Major General Delaney. Where is Lieutenant General Terry?" Armstead made a pretense of looking around the main hall, but in fact he already knew that Terry was going to be a no-show today. Armstead had his own sources at the Joint Chiefs of Staff.

"Oh, I'm afraid that General Terry has the flu," said General Delaney. "He wasn't able to be here today." Armstead and Boone towered over Delaney and his two subordinates. Even Carson was taller. The general was accompanied by his intelligence officer, a Colonel Kaminski, and his aide-de-camp, a Major Fitzgibbon. You never needed to ask names when meeting military officers in uniform. Their nametags were pinned to their chests above their right pockets, opposite their ribbons or medals.

At a glance, it was apparent that the portly General Delaney struggled to meet the Army's height and weight standards. His hair was still black, but he was bald on top. Two-star Major General Hiram Delaney was from the Joint Chiefs of Staff. He was the Deputy Chief of Staff for Operations and Plans, or the DCSOPS. He was saying that his boss, the CSOPS, had bailed out on the Camp David conference at the last moment.

No Army general wanted to be here. At the Joint Chiefs level, this conference was as welcome as a brain tumor. To the greatest extent possible, the Joint Chiefs were pushing responsibility for it off onto NORTH-COM, meaning General Armstead. NORTHCOM was the most politicized command in the U.S. military, because of its close relationship with the Department of Homeland Security. Lieutenant General Terry from the JCS was senior to Armstead by date of rank. In Terry's absence, General Armstead was now the highest-ranking American uniformed military representative at the conference. NORTHCOM had been tossed the hot potato. The Joint Chiefs clearly wanted Armstead to be the point man for Operation Buffalo Jump, and, if necessary, to fall on his sword for it.

"I'm *so* disappointed to hear that General Terry is…feeling poorly." said Armstead.

"Yes. And General Brewster was quite disappointed that you didn't make it to Washington yesterday. He had some final updates to the CON-PLAN that he wanted to convey to you in person. Some…nuances." Four-star General Lance Brewster was the Army chief of staff, and he was getting nowhere near Camp David in person. Nobody in uniform wanted to be here today. All of the principals who were able to muster an excuse were sending their deputies or other underlings.

"I understand," said General Armstead. "And I *really* wanted to make it to Washington for the final planning meeting, but regrettably, a family emergency came up at the last minute. I didn't think my absence yesterday would affect today's briefing, because *of course* I assumed that General Terry would be here to present it. Fortunately, there are still a few serviceable helicopters at Fort Campbell, so I was able to fly here directly."

"Hoo-ah," General Delaney said drolly. "That Screaming Eagle esprit de corps must be rubbing off on NORTHCOM. That's a long trip on a Blackhawk."

"Yes it was. So, who's here from the civilian side? I see Henrietta over with the Chinese. Who's she with today, anybody I should be aware of?" Henrietta Bramwell was the secretary of the Army. She had never served a day in any branch of the military, but had been an undersecretary of education. In the Tambor administration, this made perfect sense, because it was widely believed that her primary mission was to re-educate the military. Her creased wedge of a face was the most militantly frightening thing about her, leading to her nickname, Battle-axe Bramwell.

"Just her staff," said General Delaney. "I can't stand even to look at them. They're a bunch of old hippies. I might be going bald, but at least I don't have a ponytail."

"Who's here from State?"

"Thornedike himself, but he hasn't arrived yet. I expect him to be fashionably late, or to walk in with the president."

General Armstead turned his head a few degrees toward Boone and made a slight cough.

Boone said, "Excuse me gentlemen," and turned from the generals and their staff officers, carrying his briefcase with him. He returned to the portico entrance, retrieving his blue combination cover as he passed the sailors at the checked-items table. A lone Marine major in dress blues stood by the traffic circle. The USMC's distinctive red "bloodlines" ran down the seams of his blue trousers. A line of scar tissue ran up the back of his neck, from the high collar of his dark blue tunic to the black band of his white officer's cap. Boone sidled up to him. The Marine officer turned and glanced at Boone's nametag. "What can I do for you, Major Paxton?"

He was not a big man, only about five feet nine and 180 pounds, but he looked extremely tough, like a college wrestler or boxer with a few more years on him. Boone scanned the Marine officer's nametag in return. The major had a Spanish surname, but he looked like one of Geronimo's sons, with eyes like obsidian flakes. Boone guessed that he was at least half Apache or Navajo. "I need a big favor, Major Acorzado."

Camp David was a formal place, at least during a conference of high-ranking military officers and diplomats. This was no place for two officers even of the same rank to get chummy and go to first names right out of the gate. Acorzado was in charge of the elite company of Marines guarding Camp David. Boone knew that he didn't win this plum assignment by being slipshod. It was as close to a guaranteed path to general's rank as there was. The officer in charge of the Marine Security Company, Camp David was on one of the fastest of fast tracks in the military. Previous Commandants of the Marine Corps had held this billet.

Company Commander was typically a captain's job, but not here. Each Marine in the Security Company was a handpicked top performer. Boone glanced at his ribbons, and Acorzado glanced at the ribbons belonging to the genuine Major Curtis Paxton. Boone had needed to learn Paxton's biography, including his education, career, assignments, deployments and awards, in case he was asked about them. Paxton had silver Army jump wings, while Acorzado wore the gold Navy version, as well as a silver SCUBA helmet. These two devices meant he was a recon-qualified Marine. Boone had the Army's Combat Infantryman's Badge, and Acorzado the Marine equivalent, the Combat Action Ribbon. Both men had a Bronze Star with the combat "V," and the Purple Heart. Major Acorzado's medals trumped Major Paxton's with a Navy Cross, the nation's second-highest award.

Boone did not know that this was typical in Acorzado's family. Marine Corps service was a family tradition. His grandfather had served on Okinawa, where he was a Navajo-speaking "code talker." His father had won the Congressional Medal of Honor at the Battle of Hue City in 1968, during the Vietnam Tet Offensive. By tradition, the children of

Medal of Honor recipients were offered service academy appointments, and Major Acorzado had attended the Naval Academy. His mother and father had pinned on his second lieutenant's bars at Annapolis.

"What favor?" he asked. The major had a ceremonial-appearing white leather holster with a pistol-covering flap on the white belt around the waist of his tunic.

"I left some briefing papers on our helo. I'm toast if I don't have them. I'd really appreciate it if I could get a ride back." The landing zone was less than a half mile away, but you didn't go strolling around Camp David unescorted.

"That's your Pavehawk on the LZ?" Major Acorzado glanced at the "Screaming Eagle" combat service unit patch on the Army officer's right shoulder seam.

"That's affirmative, that's ours. Well, we borrowed it for the trip up."

"What's the matter with it? Why is it still here?"

The major was tuned in to their scheduled movements. Boone knew he would have to be careful. "Some kind of sensor trouble. Not a big deal."

Acorzado nodded just slightly. "So, you want to get to your helo without a lot of fuss, is that it?"

"I'd greatly appreciate it."

Major Acorzado nodded again, and spoke a few words into his walkie-talkie. "No problem. We grunts have to stick together."

"Fuck the pogues, right, Major Acorzado?" Boone was giving a hat tip to the Marines by using their vernacular. In Marine-speak, pogues were rear-echelon troops who never left the safety of well-defended American bases.

"Damn right. Fuck the fobbits." A fobbit was a Forward Operating Base Hobbit. Like pogues, they never went "outside the wire" on actual combat missions. "Don't think that this is my permanent gig," said Acorzado. "But I couldn't turn this job down."

"I understand," said Boone. "Hell, I'm a general's dog-robber these days." This was a slang term for an aide-de-camp, who was expected to do anything for his general, including steal a dog, or even steal *from* a dog.

The two majors laughed quietly, sharing a private joke. Both men were combat leaders turned into glorified bellhops in order to advance their careers.

Major Acorzado asked, "So, where were you, over in the sandbox?"

Boone was ready, having memorized Paxton's deployment history. "Oh, Najaf, Mosul, Sulamaniyah…some other places. Nothing special," he said, with typical Army understatement. "How about you?"

"When I wasn't in Afghanistan, I was mostly in Al Anbar Province. Ramadi and Fallujah. The Battle of Fallujah, not just during the occupation later on."

"Which Battle of Fallujah?"

"Both," said Major Acorzado. "And they were both motherfuckers. But winning was better. A *lot* better."

"Roger that. So, when's the president showing up?" Boone asked this as matter-of-factly as he could.

"The informal reception runs from ten to ten-thirty. The president should arrive around ten-thirty. Then there'll be a reception line, and he'll kick off the meeting at eleven with a short talk in the conference room. After that he'll leave." Then more quietly, the major said, "But he rarely makes the schedule, so who the hell really knows?"

Boone thought that he detected a slight rolling of the eyes, but it was very subtle. Acorzado's crow-black eyes were hard to read.

Another white electric cart rolled around the circle and stopped in front of the portico. A different Marine corporal from before was driving. Acorzado said, "Take the major to the *real* Blackhawk, the dirty one in the back. He needs to get something. Go the back way, and then return him here ASAP." Then the major turned to Boone and they exchanged quick informal salutes followed by firm handshakes and direct eye contact. "I have no idea where this golf cart came from, Major Paxton. It's highly irregular. I'll be seeing you." Then Acorzado turned toward the conference center and disappeared inside.

The corporal remained seated, waiting for the Army major to take a seat, but his eyes grew wide when he saw Lieutenant General Armstead approach. The general had walked out of the conference center just after Major Acorzado left. Both Boone and General Armstead sat on the two rear-facing seats, and the corporal drove off. He had been ordered to take the major to the Army Blackhawk, and he was certainly not going to question the addition of a three-star general as an extra passenger. This was Camp David, and he had driven presidents and prime ministers.

There was an asphalt bicycle path that ran downhill around the conference center, and along the side of the hill just inside the eastern perimeter fence. This winding path through the trees was wide enough for only one cart. It bypassed the main road down the center of Camp David, and took them directly to the helicopter landing zone. The corporal parked by the Blackhawk, and both officers stepped out of the golf cart. Without a word, General Armstead climbed into the troop bay. A thin black valise was handed to Boone, and the door slid shut. The slim case was not important; it was just a prop, a reason for him to return to the helicopter. He placed it into his briefcase. It might still have been inspected, so it was innocuous and contained no contraband.

The helicopter engines began to whine as Boone sat again at the back of the cart, facing away from the driver. The corporal had no questions and followed his original orders to bring the major back to the conference center as quickly as possible. Marine corporals do not say a single word to a field-grade officer unless they are asked a direct question. Boone had no questions, so not a word was exchanged, not even about the cold but clear weather. Behind him, Boone could hear their Blackhawk apply power. Because he was facing rearward and the tree branches were bare of leaves, he saw their helo lift off and bank away to the north, to Raven Rock. So far, so good.

The cart returned by the same jogging path, bypassing security. They could not depend on getting this break; it was just a fluke, so they had not prepared a contingency to bring in weapons this way. When devising the plan, they had thought it probable that Boone would have to go back through the security building again, but in fact he did not. They returned by the same narrow path through the trees. He could have brought back his Glock .45, or grenades, or almost anything. Lessons learned. As if there would be a second go-round for this crazy Camp David operation…

On the way into the conference center, Boone found the men's room. Sitting in a stall, he carefully looked around for pinhole camera lenses. The ceiling tiles were full of dots. He wondered if there was a Secret Service agent somewhere whose job was to spy on suspicious activity in the johns. He opened his briefcase on his lap and removed the green cloth-covered binder, which was closed with a zipper. He unzipped the binder, opened it, and used a car key to spread apart the metal-and-plastic reinforcing spine behind the three silver ring clips.

Carefully, he slid out a thin black piece of material shaped like a ruler. It was eleven inches long, less than an inch wide, and no more than an eighth of an inch thick at any point. Half of its length was sharpened on one side; the rest was an integral handle. Three inches from the sharp end on both sides was an indentation, at a forty-five degree angle. Boone placed this crease over the metal edge of his open briefcase, pushed down hard on both sides, and snapped off the end. Now the blade had a chisel-shaped tip, like a very long box-cutter or exacto knife. Before, its innocuous shape had allowed it pass through the X-ray machines undetected. It had been seen, but not seen. The ceramic knife was created for being smuggled through security, not for comfortable handling. It could also pass through metal detectors, including the ones that Boone assumed were built into many of the doors here in the conference center. In addition, Boone knew that undercover Secret Service agents would mingle among the attendees, covertly scanning them with concealed metal detectors.

The knife was provided by Ira Gersham, who had picked it up years before from his former employers at "another government agency." The entire one-piece blade and handle was made of zirconium oxide, the second-hardest substance, after diamonds. Ira had impressed Boone and Carson by dropping a tissue paper and then slicing it in half in midair. The edge was beyond razor sharp, it was scalpel sharp. Inside his briefcase was a thin plastic sleeve to cover the working end. Boone gingerly slid the knife up his left forearm, under the black velcro band of his wristwatch. An inch of the black handle protruded from the band, but was concealed by the cuff of his white dress shirt and blue jacket.

Behind the top flap of the briefcase, there was a computer connecting cable. Uncoiled, the green plastic cable was six feet long. This harmless item had also been seen and inspected when they passed through security. Boone pulled the connector off one end, and fit the other end into the modified charging jack on his cell phone. Then he coiled the tubing more tightly, folded a brochure around it, and placed it into his left jacket pocket. Then he flushed the toilet, washed his hands, and returned to the conference center. He found Carson outside the main hall on a long patio deck. The hillside fell away from the conference center on this side. The uncovered deck was being used by some of the foreigners for smoking, in spite of the very brisk weather.

"How did it go?" asked Carson. He turned toward the wooden patio railing, overlooking the trees. On the patio, their heads were uncovered, even though they were outside. Their hats had been left by the entrance to the conference center. It was quite cold, just above freezing.

Boone joined him, facing away from the building and any watchers or listeners. "It went just fine. The Blackhawk's gone, and I've unloaded my briefcase. Oh, here's that paper you were asking about." Boone slipped the brochure containing the coiled connector cable to Carson, who casually dropped it into his own jacket pocket.

"I saw the chopper take off," said Carson. "That means we're on our own. We're just going by our schedule now."

Boone said, "I got a schedule update while I was outside looking for a ride back to the LZ. The president should arrive at 1030, but he's known for showing up late. The economic part of the conference starts at 1100, and then we're up at 1130 for the CONPLAN brief. Cross your fingers and hope they have luck inside Raven Rock. It's ten after ten now, and our window is ten-thirty to eleven."

"Shit, twenty minutes to go," said Carson. "I'd rather be chased by Cossacks any day. This place...well, let's just say it's not my style. I feel like a bug pinned down under a microscope. And that General Delaney was asking me some funny questions. He was testing me, I think. 'How is old so-and-so?' People I don't know. I think maybe he's suspicious. He's got me worried. I'm dodging him now. Fortunately, the secretary of the Army nabbed him and I slipped away."

"If he's suspicious now, just wait until he finds out that Armstead flew the coop."

"I know. He's going to throw a fit. You're lucky you're only a major today. The whole scene in there just really pisses me off. Especially the Russians. They're probably all FSB or SVR, or whatever they call the KGB these days. They're acting cool, but they're gloating at the same time. They're really rubbing it in. You can't get a cup of coffee without them trying to start a conversation. They're even speaking in English to each other so you can hear them. They were talking about buying houses in the States for their kids. Talking about how cheap real estate is. About what a *good buy* America is these days. I get what they're saying. They're twisting the knife about Buffalo Jump. America is a good buy. It's a liquidation sale."

"I guess they feel like it's payback for '91 and '92," said Boone. "We sure did our share of gloating then."

"I suppose we did. Well, anyway, that old battle-axe Henrietta Bramwell is keeping Delaney busy, trying to get his group to mingle with the Chinese delegation. She wants them all to be best friends forever, it looks like. I almost feel sorry for Delaney and his people. I peeled away when her group jumped him."

Boone said, "Bramwell's husband does a lot of business over there. And I don't mean millions, I mean billions. His company was one of the first to set up aircraft factories in China, back in the '90s. They moved entire plants over there lock, stock and barrel. And now his wife is the secretary of the Army. They used to call that a conflict of interest. Not anymore."

The two counterfeit Army officers spoke very quietly, leaning against the wooden patio railing, looking down and casually covering their mouths with their hands. Camp David was a paranoia-inspiring place, especially considering what they were planning to do. It was easy to imagine directional microphones, hidden bugs and telephoto cameras everywhere. Supposedly, Camp David was a private place where world leaders could talk freely, in an informal rustic setting. Anybody who believed that was too naïve to cross the street alone or talk to strangers.

"That explains it," said Carson. "She's chatting with those Chinese civilians like they're old buddies, and trying to hook General Delaney up with some Chinese brass."

Boone shook his head disgustedly, looking out over the slope through the winter trees. The paved golf cart path he had used to return to the helicopter was just barely visible a few hundred yards downhill. "Henrietta's so happy, you'd think her husband was just opening another jet factory in China, instead of her getting ready to trade a chunk of America to the Chinese. I guess it's all the same to people like her. They really don't care which way the business is flowing, just as long as they're getting a cut of the action."

Carson said, "This is how the Chinese must have felt when the British came in and started carving up China. You know, the opium wars, gunboat diplomacy and all of that. What goes around comes around. Now we're the decadent failed empire, being carved up and put on the auction block by our own Mandarins."

"General Armstead was right," said Boone. "They're vultures. And not just the foreigners. Our own traitors are even worse. They could give a shit about America. This whole thing just makes me want to puke."

"Don't puke until you've had some of the pastry. Those Navy chefs are the best. Everybody at Camp David is the top of their field. I've never seen anything like it."

"I don't want to go back inside until we have to."

"Just do what I did," said Carson. "Load up a few napkins with pastries and bring them back out here. Those rear echelon motherfuckers can't stand the cold, so we're safe out here. I'd rather freeze my ass off than have to shake hands and smile at a bunch of traitors and foreign vultures. Just swoop by the pastry table and do a touch-and-go. And try to ignore those Russian assholes. I swear, I think they've been hitting the vodka already."

Major General Delaney came out onto the patio deck and headed directly for Carson, his aide-de-camp in tow holding a briefcase in each hand. Delaney outranked Brigadier General Harper by one star. "The president is arriving in five minutes, with the secretaries of state and defense. You shouldn't be hiding out here. It's bad for our image. You represent the Army. This is a diplomatic mission today." He spoke frankly and directly, as if the two aides were not present.

"You seem to have the diplomacy angle covered," said Carson. "How are your Chinese friends getting along?"

Delaney ignored his sarcasm. "They invited me over for a vacation."

"I'll bet. I'm sure Henrietta wouldn't mind. She's only been over there about twenty times with her husband. I think she has a house there."

"Actually, she suggested it—but let's not get into that now. Where's General Armstead?"

"Oh, he just hates these kinds of functions. He never did get along very well with our foreign allies. Especially our brand-new allies, the Russians and the Chinese."

"Are you intentionally being a smart-ass?" asked Delaney.

"Not me, no sir," said Carson. "I think we should bend over backwards for our new allies. Grab our ankles, even. Isn't that the core of Operation Buffalo Jump?"

"Don't bait me, Harper. I asked you where's General Armstead."

"He took a lift of opportunity and flew to Site R. Raven Rock. It's just over the hill." Carson nodded his head toward the north.

"He *what*?" Delaney was aghast, and actually took a step back, as if he had been hit.

"We have our own Blackhawk. The general likes to bring his own transportation. He went for a quick visit."

"But we're briefing the CONPLAN at eleven thirty! That's only an hour!"

"He's aware of that. Don't worry, he'll be back in plenty of time."

Major General Delaney looked at Carson as if he was insane. "Look, none of us are happy about this. It's not my choice either, but nobody asked my opinion. Shit rolls downhill, and we follow orders. That's the way the world works."

"I hear you," said Carson. "By the way, that must be quite a flu bug that kept General Terry in bed today. At least General Armstead came in person. But have no fear, he'll be back before it's time for our part of the dog and pony show. I'm sorry for any miscommunication about who was briefing today. We had assumed that your General Terry would want that honor. Don't worry; General Armstead will do a yeoman's job in his place, if nobody from the Joint Chiefs is available."

"Here they come," said Major Fitzgibbon, Delaney's aide. "The president's party is here." Fitzgibbon was even shorter than his general, with reddish hair and black eyeglasses.

"We really have to go back inside," said General Delaney. "You can't just ignore the president."

"We'll see you in there," said Carson. Delaney and his aide-de-camp returned to the main hall of the conference center, through the glass doors.

When they were gone, Boone said, "Did you have to piss him off like that? He'll remember you, and that's not a good thing."

"Let him remember me. I'm a brigadier general who's topped-out and knows it. Do you think that old generals in their terminal grade give a shit about making bootlickers like Delaney happy?"

"No, I guess they don't really give a flying leap."

"You're catching on," said Carson. "I've got a real bad short-timer's attitude. Remember, my unofficial recall to active duty is just for one day."

"Maybe just for one more hour," Boone noted.

"Yeah, maybe. So if we're going to go out with a bang, let's make it a memorable hour. Well, Major Paxton, let's go inside and meet our illustrious commander-in-chief."

"After you, General Harper." Boone picked up their briefcases and followed Carson inside.

The president, the secretary of defense and the secretary of state arrived beneath the portico in the president's armored custom black Cadillac limousine. Boone was amused by this, because it was only a quarter mile to his residence at the Aspen Lodge. Jamal Tambor entered the conference center's main hall flanked by Secret Service men with earpieces and bulging suits. Like most of the civilian men in the room, the president was wearing a dark suit and tie. The youthful president animatedly worked the room, bouncing from group to group, shaking hands, smiling, his eyes dancing. It was almost as if he was in campaign mode. Maybe he was, Carson thought. Only today, he was campaigning for favorable terms from America's foreign creditors. On the chopping block was the American Northwest, which would nominally come back under federal control once these foreign "allies" had subdued the region by force of arms.

After a quick trip to the men's room for his own final preparations, Carson strolled all the way around the circumference of the room toward the back windows and the patio, staying away from the president's entourage. Boone trailed behind him, the faithful wingman. On the way, Carson caught a glimpse of General Delaney near the hall's entrance, standing next to the commander of the Marine Security Company. Delaney was speaking to him, and Carson regretted his being testy out on the patio deck.

The president was spending a few minutes with each national group, schmoozing them and trying to tell some jokes. The jokes clearly did not convey their humor through unsmiling interpreters, even with several attempts at retelling. At best, the laughs were forced. Carson guessed that the foreign interpreters finally told their principals, "He's making a joke, so please laugh when I do."

At 1050, General Delaney found Carson again. Ignoring Boone, he said, "Listen, Harper: I just asked, and there's no flight into Camp David from Site R scheduled for the next two hours. Is General Armstead giving the brief or not? If I'm giving the brief, I need to know that right now. And I need a straight answer, not more double-talk."

"Oh, he's giving the brief all right. Don't worry. There must be some mistake with the flight schedules; they must not have caught up with the plan mods. He'll be here."

"He'd better be!" Delaney stormed off to rejoin the cluster of Army brass and civilians surrounding the newly arrived secretary of defense.

Boone said, "I sure wish I knew what was going on at Raven Rock. They're cutting it awfully close."

Just then, a Navy sailor in dress blue "crackerjacks" weaved through the room, obviously looking for someone. He spied the two Army officers and headed for them. From ten feet away, he could read Carson's name-tag. "General Harper, I have a message for you from General Armstead. He says everything is set for 1100, as planned."

"That's all?"

"That's all, sir."

"Thank you, petty officer."

The sailor turned and disappeared into the throng.

"I guess we're on deck, then," said Boone. "The next step is up to us. Which option do you think will work?"

"I don't know yet. It has to be before eleven. If the EBS goes off, they're going to haul the rabbit downstairs and we'll miss him. And after eleven, he's leaving anyway. We have to do it before then."

"Damn...this is getting tight."

"Like Colonel Spencer said, it's a leap of faith," said Carson.

"I just hope the Ravens can pull it off at their end."

"Armstead's message said they would. We have to take it on faith. Like you said, the next move is up to us."

"But which move?" asked Boone.

"I don't know yet. We'll just have to roll with it, and decide when the moment comes."

The president's handlers, mindful of the schedule, steered him away from a group of Saudi diplomats who had already exceeded their allotted minutes with him. Boone and Carson watched while the presidential party walked toward the open double doors to the conference room. These were of heavy wood, like church doors, so the conferees could have privacy and quiet inside when they were closed. Now they were folded back against the walls on either side of the wide opening. The president took up a position just outside the doors, and the conference guests formed a receiving line to pass him and move inside, to take their positions around the long table. Boone and Carson drifted toward the back of the receiving line. According to the schedule, the president would make some brief remarks to the entire group of about fifty participants, and then depart.

Further up the line, General Delaney was standing with Henrietta Bramwell and her entourage. Delaney looked behind him, saw "General Harper" and waved him forward. Carson pretended not to see Delaney, engaging in an imaginary conversation with "Major Paxton." Delaney's aide, Major Fitzgibbon, soon scurried back to them. He was carrying an oversized briefcase, practically a suitcase, containing all of his general's and his own papers and files.

Besides their braided aiguillettes and ubiquitous briefcases, generals' aides wore special medallions on the lapels of their uniform jackets to denote their unique status. These inch-tall insignias looked like tiny red, white and blue Interstate Highway shields. The joke was that their real purpose was to give fair warning that a general's dog-robber was prowling around, looking for anything of value that was not bolted in place to shove into his briefcase. Major Fitzgibbon's insignia had two stars across the blue top section of the shield, because his boss was a two-star major general. Boone's shield had three stars, because Armstead was a three-star lieutenant general. Both men were majors, but in some way Boone "outranked" Fitzgibbon because of his own general's higher rank. If Major Fitzgibbon knew that Boone was an imposter and not an officer at all, but instead an enlisted man and a wanted deserter, without a doubt his head would spin like a top and then explode.

"We need to know when General Armstead is going to be here. We need to know right now! General Delaney is going to have a conniption. If General Armstead doesn't make it in time—"

"Don't worry." Boone answered him, dog-robber to dog-robber. "General Armstead is going to give the brief of his life, I guarantee it. I've got the PowerPoint presentation all set. He's just running a little late."

Fitzgibbon then stared up at Boone with a quizzical look and asked, "If General Armstead flew to Site R...why didn't you go with him?" Before Boone could answer, the aide had left and was soon whispering in his general's ear further up the line. Off to the side, where the main hall led to the entrance portico, Boone caught a glimpse of Major Acorzado speaking into his walkie-talkie.

The reception line continued to advance. After shaking hands with the secretary of state and the president, the guests turned to enter the conference room and find their designated places. Carson checked his watch. It was 1059, and they were only a few people from the president. "Which plan?" he whispered to Boone. "We have to decide."

"It has to be the razzle-dazzle. It's too late for anything else."

"Okay," said Carson. "I'll start it—be ready."

President Tambor was standing to the side of the entrance to the conference room. Standing slightly behind him were two beefy Secret Service agents. To his left was the secretary of state. Once the participants were all seated around the table, the president would give some prepared remarks and then he and his cabinet secretaries would depart.

The secretary of state was the dour elder statesman Camden Ellsworth Thornedike, resurrected from a previous administration to lend the young and inexperienced president foreign policy gravitas. He was limp-wristing the guests as they filed past, looking as though he wished it were naptime already. Boone and Carson were almost at the end of the line. Carson reached the secretary of state, and gave him a perfunctory handshake. Boone stood just behind Carson, carrying both of their briefcases. Aides-de-camp did not shake the hands of presidents or cabinet secretaries. They were merely aides, and their hands were usually occupied carrying briefcases and laptops for their generals anyway.

There were only a few Middle Eastern diplomatic stragglers behind "General Harper," when Carson finally reached President Jamal Tambor, looked him in the eyes and shook his hand. Tambor had a grip like a wet fish, but to be fair, he had been shaking hands nonstop for the past half hour. Carson said a brief "Nice to meet you, sir," to which Tambor nodded distractedly, gazing past Carson to his own aides across the anteroom. In his mind, the president had probably already left the Laurel Lodge Conference Center.

Carson let go of Tambor's hand after only a second, turned to enter the conference room, and then froze in place and went wide-eyed. He thrust out his left arm, pointed his index finger like a stage actor and yelled as loudly as he could, "He's got a gun!" He pointed directly at an unlucky Turkish general, who was opening a briefcase on the near corner of the oak conference table only a dozen feet away. The innocent Turk gave a guilty "Who me?" look, and quickly slammed his briefcase shut. Fifty pairs of misdirected eyes turned in unison to see the sudden downward movement of the case's lid and Carson's outstretched accusatory arm. Even the president turned to look.

In that same second, Boone Vikersun dropped his two briefcases, lowered his shoulder and slammed his 240 pounds into the slender Jamal Tambor like an NFL linebacker tackling a very small wide receiver. He shouted, "Get him down!" as he drove the president through the open conference room doors, before his two Secret Service bodyguards could react. Boone knew that "the razzle-dazzle" was about to happen, and he was cocked and ready for action and they were not, and that made the difference. Their attention had been whipped from Carson's surprise accusation down his pointing arm and finger to the Turk and his slamming briefcase. In that instant the president and Boone disappeared below their field of view, with the agents following behind just a split second later.

The two Secret Service bodyguards dove on top of Boone Vikersun, who was on top of the president. They were attempting to put more Kevlar and body mass between their charge and any flying bullets. If they'd had time to consider, they would have thought that Boone was a quick-reacting Army officer who was evidently striving to protect his commander-in-chief. In just a few seconds there was a growing human dog-pile on the beige carpet as more Secret Service agents rushed in from all directions.

Unlike the main reception hall, the smaller conference room was windowless and had only the single large entrance, so all of the dignitaries and guests who were inside moved further away from the scene of the activity, deeper into the room.

The Turkish general was slammed face down on the conference table, his arms pinned by even more agents as he grunted and bellowed protestations of his innocence. These were lost in the din and bedlam of shouts, orders and counter-orders. Even more Secret Service agents formed a protective barrier around the president, who was still on the ground beneath Boone Vikersun, his two original bodyguards, and a half dozen others who had piled on as living armor.

Once the Turkish general was frog-marched out of the room and out of sight, with his briefcase removed to a safe location, Secret Service agents and helpful Army officers began to peel back the layers of bodies protecting the president, like football referees looking for the ball after a fumble. Several hands finally grabbed the shoulders of Boone's uniform jacket and began to pull him up. One of the helpful military officers was Brigadier General Harper, who had worked his way in among the president's protectors during the melee. As he came up, Boone still had the slim president clutched to his chest. Once his feet were under him, Boone pushed himself up the rest of the way, shaking off the helping hands, and swung himself around to put his own back to the wall of the conference room, just inside the doors. Phil Carson was next to Boone's shoulder, also behind the president.

32

Instead of being a moment of great relief, with the incident being defused and the president returned to his feet unharmed, there was a fresh round of shouts and screams. A few and then more people saw that the very tall Army major was holding something dark against the president's throat with his right hand, while his left arm was clamped across the president's chest. A moment later, a brigadier general improbably wrapped several loops of something around Jamal Tambor's neck with rattlesnake speed.

Boone was out of breath, his chest heaving. Carson held up a cell phone. Cell phones and all wireless devices were jammed and therefore useless in Camp David, but they were not forbidden. This cell phone, however, had the end of the green tubing disappearing inside it, where a battery charging cable would go. Carson held it up, and the room went silent in a few riffling waves of hushing chatter. The phone's screen was lit, and his thumb was pressing down on a button. There were a dozen Secret Service agents' pistols and submachine guns coming up to take aim at him and Boone, while trying to avoid sweeping the president within their arc of fire.

In a loud, clear voice, Carson said, "This is Dupont detonating cord. Blasting cord! If I drop this phone, you're going to see the president's head fly across the room. So lower the guns—NOW!"

Detonating cord, or "detcord," was used to tie a series of demolition charges together so that they would all explode in virtually the same instant. Its pencil-thick plastic casing was packed with a powerful high explosive that burned at faster than a mile a second. In reality, the green line wrapped around Tambor's neck was not detcord, which would not have made it past the explosives-sniffing booth or the dogs in the security room. Actually, it was just a piece of plastic-coated coaxial wire that bore a striking resemblance to commercial detonating cord. But the Secret Service men did not know this. They all had experience with demolitions, so they could readily visualize the president's head being blasted from his body in a spray of blood. Their knowledge was being used against them.

And so they reluctantly lowered the barrels of their weapons toward the floor. Boone's black ceramic knife was pressed against Tambor's throat, the pulse in his jugular visible against the thin blade. The president's eyes were as wide as saucers, but no sound emanated from his gaping mouth.

Carson then said, "Everybody move all the way to the other end of the room, away from the doors. Secret Service, everybody!" The agents were reluctant to abandon their charge. Carson waved the lit cell phone over his head, with its line of simulated blasting cord leading to the president's neck, and they slowly backed up. Phil Carson's next demand was an unusual one. "Turn on the televisions, the big ones over there. Slide the panels open and turn on the news. Come on, I know you have audiovisual techs back there; somebody here knows what I'm talking about. Get it together, people—open the panels and turn on the news!"

All four walls of the conference room were finished in dark wood and hung with historical "Americana" paintings. Somewhere a button was pushed, and two wood panels slid a dozen feet apart, across from the middle of the thirty-foot oak conference table. When the panels were retracted, two enormous flat-screen televisions were visible, joined edge-to-edge. The room was frequently used for secure video teleconferences, and could be joined with other conference rooms anywhere on the planet. The two giant televisions then became a virtual window between the geographically separated rooms. Prime ministers and presidents sat on opposite sides of tables separated by entire oceans, and looked through the electronic window at one another in real time.

Boone and Carson dragged President Tambor along the far wall away from the televisions, until they were in the corner opposite the entrance doors. From here they could see the televisions, and nobody could get behind them. Boone yelled, "Turn on the TV, or I'm going to cut him!" In a few moments, both televisions lit up. The volume was muted. The television on the left showed a very attractive blond cable news reporter, smiling and cheerful while her wetly glossed lips moved across her gleaming white teeth. On the giant television, her head was as big as a mailbox. The television on the right was showing the lead-in to a daytime soap opera. It showed a revolving globe, as it might have been seen from outer space.

There was a row of analogue clocks on the high wall above the televisions, indicating the times in various world capitals. The minute hands on all of them were at two minutes past the hour. It was after eleven, and the networks were still running routine programming. In the back corner of the room opposite the entrance doors, Carson leaned close and whispered to Boone, "Another fine mess you've gotten us into," and Boone actually laughed aloud. His right hand twitched, and a thin hairline of red appeared on Tambor's throat. Boone whispered back out of the side of his mouth, "Please don't do that again. I don't want to cut him...yet." Against Boone's chest, President Jamal Tambor was quivering like a gazelle in the jaws of a lion, almost completely limp, his own legs barely supporting any of his weight.

General Delaney pushed through the diplomats and foreign military officers, right up to where Secret Service agents were facing in both directions. They were attempting both to control the people in the room and keep weapons directed toward the hostage takers. Delaney yelled, "Let me through, goddamnit!" and then, "Harper, have you lost your mind, you dumb son of a bitch?" Then from around the wall next to the open double doors, a line of Marines in full SWAT gear suddenly appeared. But instead of being dressed in SWAT black, their uniforms were in the USMC's digital woodland camo pattern. They were armed with M-4 carbines, all with sound suppressors, all topped with red-dot reflex sights. Secret Service agents with their own lesser weapons drawn were screaming at them to back up and get out of sight, but they held their ground, their weapons aimed at Boone and Carson. The slender president was not much of a shield for the two hostage takers behind him. Without a doubt, each of these Marines was capable of hitting individual buttons on their uniforms at this twenty-foot range.

Major Acorzado was still wearing his dress blues, but with an armor vest thrown on top and a Kevlar helmet in place of his formal officer's hat. He was holding a .45 caliber pistol. He took one quick look across the room to assess the standoff in the opposite corner and hollered, "Major Paxton! What the fuck are you doing, you fucking moron? Have you lost your fucking mind? Put down that fucking knife!" As a group, United States Marines were world-class profanity users, and under stress, Major Acorzado was true to type.

A Secret Service agent in a black suit shouted at the Marine, "That's detonating cord around the president's neck, and it's on a dead-man switch!"

Acorzado yelled, "Oh, shit!" but his Marines kept their rifles leveled. "You can't get out of here, Paxton! Neither of you can get out!"

"Well, that's all right with me," Boone yelled back, "but neither will this traitor—at least not in one piece! Now back off, or we'll be playing volleyball with his head!" Carson was behind both Boone and the president, holding the cell phone "detonator." The clocks above the two huge televisions all ticked over to three minutes after eleven.

One of the Marines behind Acorzado also had a suppressor-equipped M-4 carbine, but in addition to its reflex sight, it had a tiny video lens mounted on the right side of the weapon's accessory rail. He aimed slightly to the side of the hostage standoff, because his primary mission was to record the incident. His lens was connected to a wireless transmitter that sent color video of the event back to Camp David's security center, located 400 meters away in a bunker beneath the Marine barracks. There, shocked Secret Service agents, Marine officers and NCOs watched the unfolding drama in real time. Within one minute, these images were also streaming live at Marine HQ in Quantico, Virginia, and at the Joint Chiefs of Staff at the Pentagon, where colonels and generals were standing frozen before their video monitors with their mouths agape, wondering if this was some kind of a drill, but knowing instinctively that it was not.

At 1104 in the Camp David conference room, the two giant televisions went to white static snow at the same time, and then they went to a blue screen for almost ten seconds. The next image was the same on both televisions. It was color video of the ground, filmed from high in the air. The edges of the picture showed the date, time, latitude and longitude, altitude and other data. An aiming curser like a bull's-eye was in the center of the film. Carson recognized it in an instant, because he had seen it many times before. It was the beginning of the Mannville massacre, when the town's inhabitants were being rounded up by the Kazaks. There was a fresh buzz of whispers in the room, and somebody yelled, "Turn it up!"

Carson immediately recognized Doug Dolan's voice. He was saying, "This video was filmed from a Predator drone last Saturday. It was not filmed in the Middle East, but in West Tennessee. It shows the truth about what is really happening in the areas under foreign occupation. The men on horses are Kazak contract soldiers, mercenaries that our own government refers to as peacekeepers. This is how they are keeping the peace in Tennessee. This is what the mainstream media are not showing you."

The film was edited for time to show the line of people being separated, with one group marched into the gym. Dolan said, "The men were taken from their families. We'll see them again later. Then the women and children were forced onto county school buses and taken away." The next images were filmed on thermal infrared, and showed the people being lined up along a ravine and machine gunned from behind, their bodies falling forward in heaps.

The shocking video was being shown on both giant televisions in the Camp David conference center. It was also being shown on every television in America, and millions more around the world. After the Predator video and Doug Dolan's narration, the images faded and returned to show a teenage girl with blond bangs down almost to her eyes, sitting in front of a wall covered by maps. She began speaking. "My name is Jenny Mc-Clure, I'm seventeen years old. Today is Tuesday, January 15th. I lived in Germantown, Tennessee, until my parents were killed after the first earthquake. After that, I was staying with my aunt and uncle near Mannville, Tennessee; that's about seventy-five miles east of Memphis. What I'm telling now is what happened in Mannville on Saturday, January the 12th. I was there in Mannville, at the regular Saturday swap meet, when about two hundred Kazak soldiers came and surrounded us. They were on horses and in trucks."

While she told her story, the Predator UAV video was shown again over her narration. When she told about wandering into the ravine, the graphic color images taken by Boone on the digital cameras were shown.

Down at Fort Campbell, Colonel Spencer was nervously watching a small television in his office at the 5th Special Forces Group. Eleven o'clock came and went, and all of the channels continued with regular programming. Then the broadcast abruptly and without explanation switched to the Predator video at four minutes after the hour. He already had an email blast-alert typed and ready to send to hundreds of military contacts. He sent it, and then began making phone calls to key individuals, telling them, "Turn on your television, something is happening!" The other members of the original "working group" either were doing the same as Spencer, or they were preparing for their first direct-action missions at Fort Campbell.

Within two minutes, Colonel Spencer stopped making the phone calls: everyone he reached was already tuned in. In just a few minutes, tens of millions of civilian and military men and women were watching their TVs in stunned amazement. All across America more and more millions were tuning in by the minute, until the nation almost came to a halt, staring at the astonishing spectacle on their screens.

But while the rest of America watched their televisions, Colonel Spencer sent his next series of text and email messages, and made a few more phone calls of a different nature. The military operation against the "rural pacification program" personnel in Building 1405 and at their UAV flight center was set into motion.

Before Jenny McClure finished her story, the painful massacre pictures faded and stopped. She continued speaking over a black screen, and then her image returned. When Jenny finished her story, she stared into the camera while holding the infant against her chest, the infant whom she had rescued from the open mass grave. This image of a silent Jenny then dissolved, and the screen came back into focus to show none other than President Jamal Tambor, in a casual setting.

The new film was anything but high resolution. The lighting was too dark and the sound quality was poor, but the familiar face with the easy but somewhat nervous smile was unmistakable. Tambor was sitting across a table in somebody's kitchen, wearing a white buttondown shirt. It was open at the neck, with his sleeves rolled partway up his forearms. Incredibly, a white bust of Russian communist leader Vladimir Lenin appeared on a counter over one shoulder, and a portrait of Che Guevara was visible on the wall over his other. He leaned back in his chair, his legs crossed, his hands folded over his knee. A cigarette burned in an ashtray on the table, its smoke curling upward.

"I apologize, I really do," said Tambor. "I've meant to come and see you for a long time. But now that I'm campaigning, well..." The president was speaking to somebody off-camera, on the other side of the table.

"I understand, Jamal. It's politics. The last thing I would want is to be an albatross around your neck and sink your chances." The camera must have been set up intentionally to capture this conversation. The positioning of the two iconic communists behind Tambor was clearly deliberate. Just as clear was the fact that Jamal Tambor had no idea that he was being filmed by a hidden camera.

Tambor appeared relieved to hear what the unseen man had said. "I'm glad there are no hard feelings. I wouldn't want you to think I've been brushing you off. Not after all we've shared. Ever since my undergraduate days, you were more than just a teacher and a friend. You were my mentor and, well, my ghostwriter, of course. I know it's been difficult for you, not being able to take public credit for my book. But there was just no other way..."

"No, that doesn't bother me, not really. As you said, there was no other way to do it. You had to take full credit; it had to be your book. It was the least I could do."

"Thank you, Robert. We both share the same goals. We both want to build a just society. But now that I really have a chance to be president, I'll have to be much more...circumspect. That's why I haven't answered your calls, or written back to you. I'm sorry, I'm not proud of that. It's embarrassing for me to admit it, but, well...the right-wing media are already digging around in my past, and there are certain people, even old friends, who..."

"Don't worry about it, Jamal. I understand political reality. I can't get tangled up in your campaign. The right-wingers would be howling for your blood if we were linked. I don't want to make waves for you. You shouldn't take any unnecessary chances now—even coming here tonight was taking a risk."

"I know, I know. But I wanted to get together with you one more time before..."

"Before you have to cut me loose for good—at least publicly. I understand, we can't do this anymore. We can't meet again...maybe ever. You may even have to renounce me, and I understand that too. It's all part of the political game. You don't have to worry about me; I'll stay out of the way. I won't make any statements to the media, not during your campaign, and not after. You won't have to worry on my account. Not at all."

Tambor tilted his head back and smiled. "I knew I could count on you, Robert. I just had to be sure. It could get ugly."

"I'm ready for whatever happens," said Robert's off-camera voice. "It's been coming for a long time."

"Yeah, it has." There was an uneasy silence, and Tambor glanced furtively at his watch.

"Hey, Jamal, since this is probably the last time we'll be getting together for, well, maybe for years...well...I've got some great weed. You want to do a bong hit with me, for old times' sake? They don't make you take drug tests when you're running for president, do they?"

Tambor laughed. "No, not yet anyway! I don't even have Secret Service bodyguards yet. Yeah, this might be one of my last chances to sneak out by myself. Sure, go ahead, Robert, bowl it up." The future president smiled broadly. "Yeah, this is just like the old days. The times we had!" Robert's arm was briefly visible as a foot-tall tubular water pipe was passed across the table. Tambor had his own butane lighter. He put his mouth over the top of the bong, lit the bowl at the bottom, and inhaled deeply. The sound of water bubbling in the pipe was clearly audible on the tape. Then his head quickly came away from the pipe and he began coughing, shaking his head, and coughing some more. "Wow!" he said in a low, gravelly voice. "That's some *strong* shit. What was that?"

"Lebanese hash. One of my Palestinian friends brings it over when she visits. She sticks it right in her diplomatic pouch."

"Damn! That's some *seriously* good shit! Hey, have you got another beer?" Off-camera came the sound of a shuffling chair, a fridge opening and closing. A green bottle was passed over to Jamal Tambor, and he took a long drink. "Just in time—that put out the fire. Man, that hash is too much! One hit, and I already feel like my head's the size of Jupiter."

"Yeah, I should have warned you," said the unseen Robert. "So, what do you think your chances are? You've only been a governor for two years. They'll say you have a thin résumé."

"Oh, I know the pundits say my candidacy is a long shot, but they don't know what I know: I've got an inside track. Robert—the Kosimos Foundation is backing me. I mean, *really* backing me. They're going to pull out all the stops." The Kosimos Foundation for Global Peace and Justice was the "philanthropic" arm of the Kosimos Group, a half-trillion-dollar international conglomerate of hedge funds founded by the late Peter Kosimos. Even in New Dollars, the currency in use at the time the video was filmed, that was a lot of money.

"They can't donate to your campaign, can they?"

"No, of course not. They're going to launder it through PACs, charities and community action groups. It's all legit, once the money is rebundled. It's already all set up. They'll fund a grass-roots effort, and the Kosimos money will flow in through a thousand different channels.

They've already kicked in two hundred million New Dollars, and that's just for starters."

"Really? Two hundred million already? I've never heard of so much money this early in a campaign."

"I know, it's amazing. Two hundred million! But please keep that quiet, okay?"

"I'm just surprised. I haven't read anything about that kind of money."

"No, of course not. It's all being funneled in by hundreds of little front groups. It'll take some time to reach my official campaign accounts, but the good thing is, once we have it, it's untraceable. We even have anonymous credit card donation sites. As long as the donations are all under the limit, it doesn't matter where they come from, or how many there are. The Kosimos Group is setting it all up—they're experts at this sort of thing. Moving funds without leaving fingerprints, I mean. It's practically going to be automated. It's perfect. It's invisible."

"That sounds great. But what do they want for all that help? What's the quid pro quo? Won't you be beholden to them?"

Tambor replied, "It doesn't really matter what they want for it, does it? I mean, we share the same goals. What matters is the Kosimos Foundation believes in me...and I believe in them."

"You'll have be extremely careful to keep the connection a secret."

"No kidding. But even my cutouts have cutouts. Everything is being done through three or four layers, it's just incredibly murky. It's all designed to be untraceable. The Kosimos people are experts at shifting funds without leaving tracks. That's why they have such an impact on the markets. They weave their money through hundreds of channels, like invisible ninjas. Now they're going to do the same thing for my campaign. By the time their money gets to me, it'll be as pure as the driven snow."

"Hey, speaking of snow...you want to do a line?"

"Is the pope Catholic?" Tambor grinned, showing his perfect white teeth. "I was hoping you had some. Good old Robert, you always had the best stuff." After a few moments, a black plastic tray appeared on the kitchen table, with two rows of white powder and a red straw. Jamal Tambor leaned over and quickly snorted up both lines in quick passes. "You know when the last time I had any blow was?"

"No."

"Right here in your kitchen, at this very table. What was that, two years ago? I've had to be *so* careful! It's been a drag keeping my nose clean, let me tell you. I can hardly get a private moment for myself."

"It'll only get worse as the campaign goes on."

"I know." Tambor took a sip of beer and then lit another cigarette from a pack in his shirt pocket. "Hey, it's really great to be back with you, amigo! I've missed you, I really have." Tambor reached across the table, evidently to shake hands, but the handshake was off-camera. His state of intoxication was growing obvious. His eyes were reddened and his words were becoming slightly slurred.

"I've missed you too," said Robert. "Especially our all-night rap sessions. We were figuring it all out, weren't we? How we would save the world, you and me. The battle-scarred veteran and the Young Turk."

"I know, weren't we something? But Robert, now I actually have a chance to do it! To do it for real! It's a long shot, I know, but with the Kosimos money, it can work."

"That would just be...amazing. But even if you do win the nomination and the general election, do you think you'll be able to accomplish very much? Even with a Democratic Congress, there's still the separation of powers. You'll have to cut deals with the Republicans. You'll have to wave the old red, white and blue."

"I know, I know," said Jamal Tambor. "But you always said that I could sell ice to Eskimos. You're the one who taught me lesson number one: 'Once you can fake sincerity, you've got it made.' I've never forgotten that."

"But so many Americans are still so conservative, so...religious. They really believe that religion is the ballast that keeps them upright through the storms of life. And that's damned hard to change. They're just so brainwashed, like little zombies."

Tambor took a drag on his cigarette before speaking. "You know, Marx still said it better than anybody else: 'Religion is the opiate of the masses.' It really is. I mean, personally, I don't care if people worship Jesus, Buddha, Allah or the man in the moon. For me, the religion thing is just a matter of political expedience."

"So, if I see you in a church holding a Bible..."

"You'll know what it is. A stage prop for the dumb-asses. You taught me the power of symbolism. Religion can be very powerful, there's no use denying that fact. So I'm not fighting it, no way. Why waste that kind of energy? There's a right way to use religion. Politically, it's just a matter of turning it into liberation theology." Tambor laughed and said, "You know, if it would help those dumb-asses to evolve to the point where they would accept socialism, I'd tattoo a cross right here." Tambor pointed to his forehead and laughed some more, then leaned down to the table and chased the leftover crumbs of cocaine with his straw. "Hey, do you have any more of this shit? It's been a *long* time since I caught a buzz like this."

Some people switched channels trying to figure out what was happening, but they found the same programming everywhere except for a few obscure local access channels. Television satellites in geo-synchronous orbits

22,000 miles above the equator were still functioning normally. Each one could provide coverage to one-third of the earth's surface. The television satellites high above America were all a part of the modern Emergency Broadcast System, a fact known to very few people. All of their normal programming had been cut off and preempted by the EBS signal, which was now being beamed into space from the vast antenna farm on top of Raven Rock Mountain.

In every office, repair shop and factory, work came to a halt as employees gathered around any televisions they could find. The few who made rude comments or questioned the authenticity of the tapes were shushed into silence by the rest. National attention was focused on one single program as it had never been before in history. Even during 9-11 and the Stadium Massacre, viewership had been split between many broadcast channels, with each network giving its own spin. Not so on this day. On this day, more than a hundred million pairs of eyes watched exactly the same images at exactly the same time, not one of these people having the slightest idea what shocker they would see next. The aerial Predator video, followed by the massacre pictures and Jenny's story, had already riveted them. Now the president was being shown in a totally unguarded moment, baring his soul to a close friend and explaining his ambitions for his possible future presidency.

On the television screens in tens of millions of homes and offices, Jamal Tambor said, "Let's face it: the vast majority of the American people are just not intelligent enough to function independently in a modern technological society. They have to be led, for their own good. The problem is, most of them are too ignorant to know what's best for them."

"I won't argue with you there," said Robert's off-screen voice. "The people need captains to guide them, to chart their courses. Otherwise, they'd simply drift with the tides and currents. That's why they fall prey to religion and other archaic superstitions."

Tambor nodded his head in agreement, and turned very serious. "It's simply unfair and unjust in the 21st century that the high-achieving minority, the ones who have had the advantages that allowed them to master modern life…it's just not fair that they can do so much better at the expense of the majority. That's where we come in, with the guiding hand of the intelligentsia. It's not just a matter of education or training—we have the *knowledge* to guide society into the future. It's up to us to reorganize the means of wealth production, so that the benefits are spread more equitably. Global prosperity is indivisible! We need to redistribute the wealth from the lucky few to the disadvantaged masses—and not only in America. Of course this has always been our goal, but until now it's always eluded our grasp."

"You don't need to tell me, Jamal. I've dedicated almost fifty years to the people's struggle. Since before you were born."

"Yes, and it was you who said that if my natural charisma was ever fully harnessed, I could be a world-changer. Well, now I have the Kosimos Foundation's money behind me, and that dream can happen! It can finally happen!"

Waylen sighed. "I'm truly happy for you...but at the same time, it makes me feel so old. I remember when we were bumming gas money just to get a few buses to Washington for the Moratorium in 1969. More than forty years ago... Oh, it's been a long march, a very long march just to get here..."

"And I honor your contribution, Robert! You were always the pioneer. You led the way. You weren't afraid to take risks, to get your hands dirty, even if it meant that—"

The screen went blue for a moment, where someone had edited something incriminating out of the original video recording. Then Tambor continued abruptly, in mid-sentence.

"—you will always be remembered as one of the Founding Fathers of global government, of the new socially conscious global government."

"Thank you, Jamal. And I accept your compliment in the spirit it was given, but don't buy the marble for our statues just yet. Don't make the mistake of being overconfident. The reactionaries won't roll over; they won't go down without a hard, hard fight. Even now that they're in the minority, they won't surrender. You'll have to be very careful. Always keep your eyes on the horizon, but don't be afraid to tack with the wind. Take the two steps forward when you can, and don't worry about the one step back, as long as it's only a tactical retreat."

"Oh, I know how to do it—you were my best teacher. I'll spout the right patriotic slogans; I know them all by heart. I'll wave their imperialist flag. I may even have to denounce you, if the extent of our friendship is uncovered. But please know, from the depth of my heart, that I'll always do everything, *everything* that I can to promote our common dream. That will never change, no matter what you might hear me say for public consumption."

"The reactionaries will come after you, no matter how circumspect you are. The ocean may appear calm around you on the surface, but beware of the hidden undercurrents. The sharks will be all around you, waiting for just one drop of blood in the water."

"I'm aware of that," said Tambor. "I'll be ultra, ultra careful."

"You know, Jamal, sooner or later you'll have to...*do something* about the reactionaries."

"When the time comes, I will. I've studied revolutionary history. I know that if we're going to cement our gains, if we're going to make the move to socialism irreversible—we'll have to eliminate our enemies. Through reeducation if we can, but by...other means where that fails. But it may not happen on my watch, even if I become president."

Robert said, "You mustn't be squeamish when that time comes. Revolutions fail due to showing softness and taking half-measures. Never forget Salvador Allende in Chile: there is a General Pinochet waiting in every barracks! When the time comes, strike with an iron fist! There's a reason Fidel's revolution lasted for more than half a century, and that reason is the firing squad. Che eliminated all of the potential counter-revolutionaries; it's a simple as that. He was utterly ruthless, and because of that, the Cuban revolution lasted for generations. When the time comes, don't forget that lesson! Don't be weak like Allende, or you'll share his fate. Find your own Che Guevaras, and turn them loose with a vengeance! Harden your heart to exterminate the reactionary forces, and the revolution will last for a thousand years."

"Well, I'd prefer to use carrots rather than sticks. Social incentive programs. Structured voluntarism, community service, reeducation...all of those tools. But I'm sure that there will still be thousands of incorrigibles that will have to be removed for the good of society."

"Not thousands, Jamal—millions."

Tambor took a long drag on his cigarette, looking directly across the table at the unseen Robert. After he exhaled, he said, "I understand that you can't make an omelet without breaking eggs. Even a surgeon has to remove diseased cancer tissue for the good of the patient. Sometimes they even have to amputate limbs, but it's for the overall good. If you don't remove them, then they can infect the healthy parts of society, and chaos results. And above all, the new socialism will be about order. Equality, fairness, social justice...and order."

"But guided from above by the socially conscious intelligentsia."

"Of course," said Tambor. "Always guided by the intelligentsia, the vanguard of the proletariat. The masses don't understand what's best for them. They're not yet socially mature. They haven't sufficiently evolved toward a higher state of human consciousness. They must be led. You taught me that twenty years ago, Robert. I've never forgotten. I'll never forget. But I'll have to use terms the people are ready to accept. I'll have to use the languages of religion and patriotism. I can't run too far out in front of the mob."

"Yes, be deliberate, be measured, but don't be seduced into accepting half-solutions, or the reactionaries will be able to roll back all of your gains at the next election. When the time is right, you must strike with Che's iron fist. Never forget the lesson of Salvador Allende: weakness and mercy *always* lead to defeat."

In Corinth, Mississippi, Lieutenant General Marcus Aurelius Mirabeau had been near a television most of the morning, awaiting developments. As usual, the uniform of the day for the general and his troops was ACU camouflage. He was in a tan humvee being driven from the new helicopter flight line at the Corinth regional airport back to his relocated mobile headquarters, when he was informed by his command sergeant major that something was up. The CSM had been monitoring AM radio stations with an ear bud when, at 11:04, the programming abruptly switched to somebody talking about the Mannville massacre, and he informed his general of this development.

Army helicopters had been flying into Corinth from Georgia and Alabama around the clock for two days, in small, well-dispersed groups. The helicopters were not arriving empty; they were combat armed and full of troops. Fuel trucks, troop trucks and other logistical support vehicles had also been streaming into Corinth. Numerous tent cities were being erected, under the guise of preparing for increased refugee flows from Tennessee.

By ten minutes after the hour, General Mirabeau was watching the massacre video and still pictures on the television in his headquarters RV. His mobile headquarters had been moved again, and now it was located among tall pine trees not far from the airport, concealed beneath camouflage netting. Again he heard Jenny McClure's deposition, which had been filmed in this very same RV. He watched with rising anger when the massacre images cut to Jamal Tambor, filmed sometime before he was elected president. Tambor called the American people dumb-asses and said that he would use the Holy Bible as a stage prop to fool them. He even profaned the sacred cross, and laughed about it. General Mirabeau could hardly contain his growing anger, but he forced himself to show only steadiness and outward calm. He knew that his staff officers were watching him almost as carefully as they were watching the television.

When Jamal Tambor and the unseen Robert began openly discussing the murder of thousands or even millions of conservative American "reactionaries," Mirabeau had had enough. He stood and clicked off the TV with the remote control. An instant after the general rose, all of his officers and senior NCOs stood as one and came to attention. In a grim monotone he said, "That's enough, gentlemen. It's happening. Lieutenant General Armstead, the commanding general of NORTHCOM, has initiated the Emergency Broadcast System. The next step is ours." He looked at his watch. "We will commence Operation Righteous Anger at 1200 hours—high noon. Pass the word, and make it happen. I will move to the flight line at fifteen minutes before noon, and as you know I will lead the helicopter assault. I will be here until then. We will secure the massacre site first, and if the foreign enemies resist in any way—then we shall spare them not!"

On millions of televisions, another line of cocaine disappeared up Jamal Tambor's nose. He sniffed a few times and said, "You know, Robert, twenty years ago you told me that I had a special destiny. That I was born under a star of destiny, that's how you put it. And just think about the perfect timing of it all! From meeting you when I was just a university freshman, until even now, the timing has been uncanny. It's been like gears turning inside gears, all my life. Even this recession has been a blessing in disguise. Think about it—when will we ever have a better opportunity to advance the cause? Their faith in so-called free-market capitalism is almost gone."

"Do you think this recession will turn into a depression?"

"I have no idea," said Tambor, "but I know that it would help our cause if it did. You should never let a good crisis go to waste. An economic depression would allow us to push society forward in great leaps, instead of taking small steps over many years."

"Tell me something," Robert said. "What do you think is really behind the crash? Do you think that what's happening is just part of the normal capitalist business cycle? Or do you think there are other forces at work, forces deliberately trying to wreck the global market economy?"

Tambor replied, "I'm afraid that's way above my pay grade. Economics was never my strong suit. Well, except for Marxism." They both laughed. "But seriously, I don't know the answer to that. I do know that the Kosimos Foundation has done all that it could to promote our common vision, and sometimes that's meant intentionally destabilizing regimes and currencies. Peter Kosimos told me that himself before he died. And he did tell me that the world needed a 'good depression' in order to make the final push to global government. Once all of the national currencies have failed, the masses can be made to believe that a global central bank and a single global currency is the only solution. Of course, once that happens, all of the national governments will become irrelevant. Peter Kosimos taught me that too. Once we have the power to create the world's money, it won't matter who is elected in this or that country."

" 'Give me the power to create a nation's money, and I care not who makes its laws'."

"I know the quote," said Tambor. "Supposedly, the first Rothschild said that three hundred years ago. But whether he said it or not, it's still true. The power really is in the purse strings. Once we control the world's purse strings, once we can create the world's money and decide where it will go, we'll control the world. But this time, we'll use that power to enforce equality and social justice, instead of just to enrich the bankers."

"The Kosimos people might have something to say about that, since they're bankrolling your campaign."

"I'm not naïve," said Tambor. "I understand that we'll need their expertise at the new global bank. But this time we'll control them, not the other way around. There will be enough new money sticking to their fingers for them to be more than satisfied."

"Many have tried to control the bankers, down through the ages…"

"This time we will. I understand the mistakes that were made in the past, in walking that fine line. We'll use their greed, but we'll control them." There was a pause while Tambor took a long drag on his cigarette, looking rather smugly across the table toward his unseen host.

"I just can't believe it," said Robert, his voice becoming emotional. "You've actually brought me hope, hope that real change is coming. For the first time in…in many years, I actually have hope that we'll finally be able to bring communism—"

"Yes, yes, but I won't use that word," Tambor said abruptly. "Never. Not even socialism. They're trigger words, hot buttons. They're too difficult for Americans. I'm going to call it 'the movement for social democracy.' Or social justice. That'll be easier to sell to the American people."

"Well, whatever you call it, it's the same thing."

"Of course." Tambor sighed. "I only wish that Peter Kosimos would have lived long enough to see our dream come true…but I guess it wasn't meant to be. Like Moses, he saw the panorama of global justice on the far horizon, but he just didn't make the final mile."

"You know," said Robert, "*I* introduced you to Peter Kosimos."

"What? No, I don't think that's correct. I met him at an international students' forum at the U.N., more than twenty-five years ago. I remember it quite clearly."

"Yes, a students' forum. And who do you think arranged it? I made sure you were on that panel representing Columbia, and I made sure that Kosimos took note of you. I arranged it all."

"You did?"

"I did. How many undergraduates do you imagine get to meet someone like Peter Kosimos, one on one? Lucky star or not, those kinds of connections don't 'just happen.' No, I spotted your face in the crowd, Jamal. I knew you were a diamond in the rough from the first class you attended. You were always my bright shining star, my hope for the future, the one who could change the world. And I opened some of the first doors for you, on that long hallway of opening doors that you have been walking through your entire life. Many others along your path have been opening those doors in front of you, preparing your way, for the last twenty-five years. Now it's the Kosimos Foundation's turn to open the last doors, the doors to the White House. Trust me, Jamal, none of this *just happened*."

Tambor's brow was furrowed, his eyes narrowed in deep thought. He took a quick puff on his cigarette and stabbed it out in his ashtray. "Well, thank you then, I guess."

"No, none of those opening doors just happened, Jamal. Those gears inside of gears that you mentioned, they don't simply line up by accident. None of this just happens. And not only on our side, oh no! I mean, do you still believe that Peter Kosimos died in a car accident in Colorado? Many people think that he was killed by our enemies in New Mexico, and the 'accident' in Colorado was staged to cover it up."

"Oh, come on, Robert! That video was faked, that airplane video. Everybody knows it was faked. That whole thing with the lake and the model airplane. CBA News did an exposé on it. They proved that cheesy video was made on a computer. It was done with a video game, on a computer. Peter Kosimos died in a car wreck in Colorado."

"Are you sure?"

"Robert, I might be stoned, but now you're starting to sound like one of those paranoid conspiracy nuts." Both men laughed again, Tambor becoming almost hysterical, unable to stop himself from giggling, then leaning forward and coughing hard.

Jenny was in the female enlisted soldiers' tent when Zack ran up to its flap doors and yelled, "Come on, come on, it's happening! You were on TV! Boone's pictures were already on—everything is on TV right now!"

Hope had her own crib, improvised from a cot, using the posts that fit into the corners to hold up mosquito nets. Jenny reached in and scooped up the infant, wrapped her in a blanket, and hurried outside after Zack. It was a cold and clear day, and she was wearing jeans and her thick green wool military sweater.

"It's on in the Casualty Receiving tent, it's on right now," he said as they ran the few hundred yards past the other tents of the mobile field hospital. Zack and Jenny had been informally attached to the medical company. The general himself had given the orders yesterday, before his headquarters had been moved. The military presence all around Corinth was growing by the hour, with helicopters buzzing overhead and long truck convoys on all of the roads. General Mirabeau himself had told them, "Jenny McClure, your job is to take care of that baby. Zack's job is to listen to Sergeant Amory and help them to set up the field hospital, and look after Jenny. And Sergeant Amory, your mission is to look after all three of them. Am I clear on that?" He had given these commands in front of his chief staff officer and his command sergeant major, so they had the force of law from that moment on.

Casualty Receiving was inside an enormous modern military tent. Zack and Jenny rushed inside; it was already packed with medical staff in their ACU uniforms. They were all watching a small television mounted up near the top of a pole. As newcomers entered the tent with questions and conversations under way, they were immediately shushed to silence by all of the viewers already staring up at the television.

Sergeant Amory spotted Jenny and Zack, and moved through the crowd to welcome them. He placed his hand on her shoulder, then gently caressed Hope's wispy baby hair and said, "Did Zack tell you? You were just on TV."

She looked into his face and nodded yes.

"You were great, Jenny, you were just great. You and Hope."

Jenny placed her hand over his, tears streaming down her face. She had no words.

On television, Jamal Tambor lit a new cigarette and took a long pull. "I know, Robert, I know. America as it exists today will always be the greatest barrier to global social progress. That's why the Kosimos Foundation has been working so hard for the North American Union. Full global integration can't happen until after America is permanently and legally woven into the North American Union. That's the first step. You can't eat an apple in one bite. We can't get to global government in one jump. Like they say, Rome wasn't built in a day. American sovereignty has to be carefully and methodically diluted, diminished, and then finally eliminated."

Tambor shook his head and scowled. "And our military, oh my God! It's just hopeless. It's practically all right-wing religious fanatics. The way it exists today, it'll always pose a threat to world peace. But if I'm elected, I'll clip their wings. If their funding is cut off, they'll wither and die on the vine. The fanciest high-tech jet bombers and submarines won't last for long with no money to maintain them. If the fall of the Soviet Union can teach us anything, it's how rapidly a modern military will decay and become useless once its budget is cut to the bone. And if the economy collapses, well, that will achieve the same purpose, if nothing else."

The unseen Robert said, "The greatest danger to social progress will always come from the military. Remember the lesson of Chile, and Salvador Allende. Beware the military."

"Of course," agreed Tambor. "That's why the military has to be fully integrated into the U.N.'s peacekeeping structure, step by step. Then what remains of the American military has to be chopped into a thousand pieces and put under U.N. control. Only then will the world be safe from the American military. Only then will our military stop being a tool of capitalist oppresssion and imperialism."

"But Jamal, the American officer corps is just riddled with the worst of the worst fascists and reactionaries. I've seen polls; something like eighty percent of them describe themselves as cultural conservatives. The officer corps has to be torn out by the roots and replaced with a new generation of leadership. But that won't be easy. The problem with the military is that it's like a goddamn religious cult—but instead of the cross, they worship the Constitution."

"It's the oath they take," said Tambor. "I've given this a great deal of study. The military is all about following orders, and defending the Constitution is the very first order they take, on day one. They even raise their right hands and swear to God to defend it. They're like lemmings, they're like robots. They don't think, they just follow orders."

"And all for a two-hundred-year-old piece of paper, written by slave-owning white racists. It's just amazing. They worship that goddamn piece of paper."

"That's right," agreed Tambor. "The military is a cult, and they worship that piece of paper. But I've got a solution. I've cracked the code. I've figured it out."

"What's that?"

"We have to give them a *new* piece of paper to worship. A *new* constitution."

"Easier said than done, my friend."

"Maybe, and maybe not," said Tambor. "If the economy gets much worse, people will become desperate. They'll be demanding new solutions, even radical solutions. That's when we'll be able to build a new grass roots movement to demand an Article Five constitutional convention. Actually...it's already under way. And trust me, when you have the Kosimos Foundation's money behind you, you can build some incredible grass roots! If we have a convention, we can finally fix the Constitution. We can get rid of those right-wing anachronisms that have been holding us back for so long."

"Like that goddamned Second Amendment," Robert growled. "As long as America is an armed camp, we can never advance to the next level of social progress. As long as the diehard reactionaries are armed to the teeth, they'll always present a fatal danger to our side."

"Exactly. So we need to create a new constitution, one that enshrines the principles of social justice and equality, but with the...*mistakes* removed. Mistakes like the Second Amendment, and the Tenth. Then those little Nazis in the military will still have their piece of paper to worship, and we can get on with building our new social order. And once we purge the old military dinosaurs, the new officers can be selected for their dedication to the principles of social justice. It might take a few years, but we can transform the military from a force of oppression into a force that serves the cause of justice. Global social justice. Our hope for the future can be achieved—but it all depends on calling a new constitutional convention. That's the key."

"We just need to give those little Eichmanns in the military a new constitution to worship," said Robert.

"That's it. Then a whole new generation of military robots will worship the new constitution, just as the old generation worships the old constitution today. After all, it's just a piece of paper. Those fools only want to follow orders, and to be led. Thinking hurts their heads. If we give them a new constitution, we can lead them anywhere we want. And once we control the minds of the military, the revolution can never be turned back. But it all depends on writing a new constitution, and to do that, we need a constitutional convention. And with the Kosimos Foundation backing a convention behind the scenes, it can happen. It *will* happen. Trust me: it *will* happen."

There was a pause before Robert spoke again, his voice lower and almost cracking. "Jamal...I bow before you. The student has surpassed the teacher. You're brilliant. Absolutely, diabolically brilliant."

"Thank you. I learned from the best. Gramsci, Guevara, Alinsky, Kosimos...and you."

Across America and around the world, hundreds of millions of people were watching Jamal Tambor's innermost secrets and true beliefs. In just a few select locations, another video broadcast was being watched with even more careful attention. The "Marine-cam" video feed from the Laurel Lodge conference room was being watched at Camp David's own security center, in Quantico, Virginia, at Marine Corps Headquarters, and at several locations within the Pentagon. Somebody at one of those places figured out that the Emergency Broadcast System had been hijacked. This person either knew or surmised that it was being sent from Site R at Raven Rock Mountain, the military's Alternate Joint Communications Center. No one would ever discover who among the dozens of officers and NCOs watching the live "Marine-cam" video from the conference room took the next step and surreptitiously redirected it back to Site R.

Even with the knife against his throat, the president finally called out, "Cut off the TV! That's nothing but lies and propaganda!"

"Lies and propaganda?" asked Carson, loud enough to be heard in the entire conference room. "Lies and propaganda are your specialty! You just hate that the American people are finally being shown the truth. Major Acorzado, take a look at that operation plan on the table. Operation Buffalo Jump is the invasion of the American Northwest by foreign armies, operating with the blessing of American traitors—and all at the president's direction! That's what this conference is about today. We're here to plan how these foreigners are going to carve up the Northwest, after foreign armies have conquered it. That's Operation Buffalo Jump. And if that's not treason, then what is?"

Tambor said to Major Acorzado, "Soldier, I'm *ordering* you to turn this broadcast off! That's a direct order from your commander-in-chief. That film is a fake; it's nothing but special effects!"

"And is Operation Buffalo Jump all fake too?" Boone asked. "Are these foreign diplomats and generals here today just actors?"

Major Acorzado, holding his pistol in one hand, advanced across the conference room to within a few yards of the president, Carson and Boone. Then he said, "Let it play. I want to watch it. Anyway, it's on every channel, everywhere. The whole world is watching it. Turning it off in this room won't turn it off in the rest of the country. Why shouldn't we see what the rest of the world is seeing?" At that moment, United States Marine Corps Major Rafael Pascal Acorzado became the single most important member of the U.S. military.

Until a new face appeared on millions of televisions, including the two giant side-by-side screens in the Laurel Lodge conference room. A military officer was seen from the waist up, sitting at a desk with a map of the United States behind him. The map was slightly out of focus, so that the general appeared in sharp relief. He was a man in his fifties, with short gray-black hair, and hazel eyes. He was wearing a blue Army uniform jacket, with three stars on each shoulder. Even Major Acorzado and his troops turned to steal glances at the latest person to appear on television in this hour of nonstop surprises.

"Good Morning. I'm Lieutenant General Lucian Armstead, the commanding general of NORTHCOM. That's the Army command responsible for assisting with homeland security. With the help of some very brave Americans, today we've been able to broadcast the truth about what's been happening in the United States. Excuse me if my words are not carefully crafted. I'm not a politician, I have not had time to write them down, and I don't have a teleprompter. I can only speak from my heart.

"I'm broadcasting today from a military communications facility just a few miles from Camp David, Maryland. I was scheduled to be at a conference that is occurring at Camp David at this very time. The purpose of this conference is to present a plan called Operation Buffalo Jump to a group of foreign diplomats and military officers." General Armstead then held up his copy of the red and white Top Secret CONPLAN binder. "This is the plan for the invasion of the American Northwest, tentatively scheduled for this summer. It's supposed to be a joint and combined military operation, meaning that foreign military formations will be partaking. In fact, foreign military divisions will be spearheading this operation.

"And why would they agree to this? For trade concessions, and agreements on very favorable terms for the exploitation of the energy, mineral, and agricultural resources of the Northwest. The president is virtually selling off parts of the United States to the highest bidder to pay our national debts, and I refuse to be a part of it. I'd rather have our nation default on those debts and start all over from nothing, than see America torn apart and carried off by foreign jackals. Under this plan, both United States and foreign national armed forces will be under effective United Nations control—on American soil! My fellow Americans, this Operation Buffalo Jump is the smoking gun of treason. This plan will be made available to all of the media and on the internet in just a few minutes." Armstead held up the binder again, and set it back down in front of him.

"My fellow American citizens, I can't pretend to know all of the answers, or even to have any solutions. I'm a military man, not a politician. But I know that treason must be opposed, even treason at the very highest levels. Every soldier and law enforcement officer has sworn a sacred oath to defend the Constitution against all enemies, foreign and domestic. And I assure you, those are not just hollow words. Not to me, and not to millions of presently serving and former soldiers, sailors, airmen, marines and police officers. We *will* defend the Constitution!

"Now, I don't have the answers or the solutions to America's many grave problems, but I know that any solutions must be *American* solutions. The answer to America's deep problems can't be found by bringing foreign military forces into the United States, as they have already been brought into Tennessee and Kentucky.

"The answers, if they can be found at all, can only be found through an honest and sincere adherence to the Constitution. That means the original Constitution, not the false so-called 'new constitution' illegally concocted in Philadelphia. I'm not a constitutional scholar, but I can read plain English, and I know that valid ratifying conventions were not held in all of the states that allegedly approved this so-called 'new constitution.' And I further do know this: the president and his administration are so clearly and obviously tainted by treason against the Constitution they swore to defend that they cannot serve any longer. I for one will neither follow them nor obey their orders from this time forward.

"We may fail today in our attempt to restore the Constitution. We may not be joined by my brothers- and sisters-in-arms in resisting treason and the forces of tyranny. But I will rest peacefully, knowing that I have at least presented the truth to you. Whether we succeed or fail at this endeavor, we must always do our duty as we understand it. And I understand that no man, not even the president of the United States, is above the Constitution. So today, I am asking that the president be placed under arrest and charged with treason, according to Article Two,

Section Four and Article Three, Section Three of our Constitution. Our one, true, original Constitution." The general held up a pocket Constitution booklet, opened to the page showing those sections highlighted in yellow.

"I am now ordering the following: All foreign contract soldiers in the United States must return any weapons to their armories, and report to their barracks and remain there, pending repatriation to their home countries after an appropriate investigation. After today, any foreign mercenaries discovered armed and outside their barracks will be considered hostile and will be dealt with as such. This mandate is to include soldiers belonging to the so-called North American Legion, which is hereby dissolved, decommissioned and disestablished. Also: any United States citizens who should attempt to hinder or interfere with these orders shall be arrested and tried for the crime of treason.

"Now I am going to show and describe each page of the Operation Buffalo Jump concept of operations plan, so that you will be able to save them for later analysis, in the event that this broadcast is interrupted. This will take only a few minutes, and then we will begin at the top of the next hour by rebroadcasting the videos and pictures of the massacre in Mann- ville, Tennessee, the eyewitness deposition, and the videotape of citizen Jamal Tambor. We will broadcast continuously for as long as we can." Then General Armstead looked off-camera to his right. "What? Excuse me? Now I'm being informed that we are receiving a live video feed from inside Camp David, so we'll go to that next. You will be seeing this live, at the same time that I'm seeing it for the first time."

USMC Major Acorzado advanced to within a yard of the president and slowly holstered his pistol. "Major Paxton, would you please remove your knife from this...*person*'s throat, and turn him around for me?"

Boone met Acorzado's gaze, slowly moved the black ceramic blade several inches away from Tambor's jugular vein, and then lowered his right arm to his side.

Major Acorzado said, "Gunny Diller, do you have your handcuffs?"

From behind him, a Marine in full combat gear said, "Aye-aye sir, that's affirmative."

Next he addressed Phil Carson. "General, will you please remove the detonating cord from *this person's* neck, and very carefully disarm the firing device?"

For Boone and Carson, this was the moment of truth. They glanced at the two enormous television screens and saw that the scene inside the conference room was now somehow being rebroadcast live from Raven Rock. No matter what happened next, millions of people would be wit- nesses to it. Once the knife and the "detonating cord" were removed from the president, he would lose his hostage value, and they would lose their protection. Within thirty feet of them were dozens of Marine Corps and Secret Service sharpshooters. Any of them could hit a coin at fifty yards with a rifle, or at twenty yards with a pistol. Boone and Carson were only twenty feet away. Carson slowly raised the cell phone and said, "It's not detcord, or a firing device. It's just a computer cable and a regular phone." He smiled. "We were bluffing." He lifted the three green coils over Tambor's head and let them trail down to the floor. Boone Vikersun, however, kept his left arm across the president's chest, still clamping him tightly to him.

With the blade's edge away from his throat and the threat of his head exploding removed, President Tambor said, "Well done, soldier. Well done! Now arrest these terrorists. Arrest them!"

Major Rafael Acorzado stared at Tambor from beneath his helmet, slowly shook his head, and said, "First, I'm not a soldier, I'm a Marine. How long have you been coming here anyway? And second—no. No, I'm not arresting them. I'm arresting you." More Marines in battle dress streamed into the conference room with rifles at port arms, at least a full platoon. They formed a line along the wall in front of the two televisions.

The president was incredulous. "What? Has the entire world gone *insane*? This is mutiny! This is treason! You *have* to obey my orders— I'm the president of the United States! I'm your commander-in-chief!"

"Not anymore," said Major Acorzado. "Not after today."

The president looked to his two personal bodyguards. "Jack, Phil, who's in charge of the Secret Service here at Camp David? Make these soldiers put down their guns. They're disobeying my orders, and I'm the president!"

But no Secret Service agents came forward to attempt to carry out President Jamal Tambor's last orders. Not in the face of more than thirty combat-tested and SWAT-trained United States Marines. The president's own pair of personal bodyguards looked down sheepishly and holstered their pistols beneath their suit jackets.

The president wasn't finished. "Think *very carefully* about what you all are doing. This is mutiny! You will all be held to account! You *have* to obey me! I'm giving you a direct order, and you *have* to obey me!"

"Not anymore," repeated Major Acorzado. "We're not obeying you anymore. Jamal Tambor, you're under arrest."

"This is ridiculous! This is *absurd*! On what charge?"

"On the charge of high treason. Now turn around and place your hands together. Gunny Diller: handcuff the prisoner."

He wouldn't turn on his own, so Boone Vikersun spun Jamal Tambor around, gripped him by both shoulders, and stared down into his face while the cuffs were being applied. From the side, Phil Carson said, "I hope you get justice. That's all I hope—that you get justice."

Then Tambor was snapped back around by several Marines. While he was being pulled out of the conference room, Tambor had one more try in him. "Why are you doing this? I'm your president; I'm your commander-in-chief. Why are you doing this?"

Gunnery Sergeant Diller, who was hauling him along by the lapel of his suit jacket, said, "Well Mr. Ex-President, we're kind of ignorant, so you can't expect too much from us. We don't even know what's for our own good. We just follow orders, 'cause we're just, you know, robots— like you said. Thinkin' too much hurts our heads." Then he laughed, and the Marines around him joined in.

The cordon of Marines pulled Jamal Tambor through the anteroom, across the main hall, and outside to the covered portico, where four green humvees were parked. Phil Carson and Boone Vikersun exited the conference center with the Marines and the other American military, wanting to witness the historical drama play out to the very end. The foreign diplomats and military officers were kept segregated in the conference room by a squad of Marines who stayed behind to guard them while the president was removed.

Jamal Tambor said to Gunnery Sergeant Diller, "That was a mistake what I said, and I'm sorry. I didn't really mean it that way. That was from before I became president, from before I began to work with the military. You know that I have the greatest respect for you soldiers, er, uh, I mean, *Marines*."

Major Rafael Acorzado, pulling him along by his other arm, said, "Yeah, sure you do. But I will say that you did get one thing right, Mr. Former President. We do worship that piece of paper called the United States Constitution. We'll fight and we'll die for that piece of paper. But that was the only part you got right."

Epilogue

Like hundreds of millions of people in America and around the world, Ranya Bardiwell was an eyewitness to the world-changing broadcast on that Thursday in January. She had watched it on television with her husband, Alex, and her son, Brian, in the den of her home. Like all of those millions of people, she was surprised and amazed to see American history literally shift with earthquake speed and power. But none of those millions of witnesses were as shocked as Ranya was when the "Marine-cam" video began to play, and she saw that the old brigadier general behind President Tambor, the man holding what they all thought was explosive detonating cord, was none other than Phil Carson. *Her* Phil Carson.

A lesser woman probably would have fainted, but Ranya was stronger than that and she merely gulped air, began to hyperventilate, and stared at the screen. He had a new scar across the top of his forehead, but it was the same Phil Carson. She had spent several months looking at that face when they were on the sailboat in Colombia, and she knew that it was the same man, that there was absolutely no chance of a misidentification. And then somehow, in some cosmic way, it all actually made sense to her. These things didn't just happen. The stars didn't just line up randomly. Forces and powers were at work that were beyond mere human comprehension. She had seen and experienced similarly improbable events before in her life, several times.

It took pounds of gold coins and several months for her team of private investigators to locate and then make contact with him. After the events at Camp David, he had been put into isolation by the military-backed temporary government, pending Tambor's impeachment trial for high treason. After that, Carson had gone into his own seclusion. But by late March, her investigators had found him in northern Mississippi. They gave Carson a letter and her contact information, and after one phone call, he had readily agreed to come to Wyoming to see her.

He flew out at the end of April. A few days into his visit the weather cleared, the air warmed, and the roads were fit for a motorcycle ride. They traveled in tandem from her home near Lander to Ranya's favorite stretch of road, along the Wind River Canyon between Shoshoni and Thermopolis. The air was still brisk but the pavement was dry, and they were dressed for it. Ranya wore her custom-tailored red and black leathers, which matched her helmet and her 1,000cc Yamaha ZF-R1 high-performance sport bike. When Phil called and confirmed that he was coming out to Wyoming, she purchased a used Harley-Davidson "Fat Boy" in nearby Riverton, had it delivered, and put it in their four-car garage. She didn't tell him that it was a gift to encourage frequent visits. Instead, she concocted a story about Alex buying it, but not really taking to the sport. It was hard for people who were not used to great wealth to accept expensive gifts when they could not reciprocate in kind. She even had a black thermal riding suit ready for him when he arrived. When the weather broke, it had not taken any arm-twisting to convince Phil to climb on the big Harley and accompany her on a one-day outing.

The Wind River Canyon was everything that Ranya had described. The two-lane blacktop of Highway 20 twisted along a narrow ledge hundreds of feet above the thundering rapids. Above the road on both sides were thousand-foot-high granite walls, with a few pines clinging to them and some residual snow painted on in streaks. Now in her late twenties, Ranya was strikingly beautiful, and he had always remembered her as beautiful to begin with, even as a young girl back in Virginia. Ranya's form-hugging motorcycle leathers didn't do much to hide the fact that her figure had only improved with a few more years.

They parked at a scenic overlook with room for a half-dozen cars, but they were the only visitors today. There was still some slush and ice on the overlook's narrow parking area. Cars passed only every few minutes. The canyon was all theirs. Below them was a steep drop-off down to fields of giant boulders and the roaring Wind River. Ranya took off her helmet, her long brown hair spilling across her back. She said, "Wait a minute," and dashed across the road. She scrambled a dozen feet up into the rocks at the base of the mountain and grabbed a handful of little wildflowers with spiky red petals.

"These are called Indian Paintbrushes," she said, showing them to Phil. "They're our state flower. They're kind of pretty, and kind of wild—just like Wyoming." She twisted their weedy stems together, waited until the wind was gusting just right, and tossed them out over the chasm. The swirling breeze caught the bouquet, carried the flowers aloft, and then dropped them down into the river hundreds of feet below. They could see the bright red dot hit the white water, to be swept away to the north, over and through the rocks and out of sight.

Ranya asked, "Do you know where this river goes?"

"No."

"The Wind River becomes the Bighorn, and it flows up into Montana to the Yellowstone. Then it goes down the Missouri and the Mississippi to the Gulf, and then to the Atlantic. That's where it meets the water from the Potomac. So I guess you know who the flowers are for."

"Of course I do. They're for Brad Fallon. I never forgot him either. Never. But I'm still glad you were able to make a new life for yourself. A happy life. You were moping around pretty bad down there in Colombia. Sometimes you didn't say a word for days. I'm sure Brad would be happy if he could see how happy you are now. It's just a shame that he never met his son."

"I know. I still think about Brad all the time. How can I not, when I see him in Brian's face every day of my life? It's bittersweet. It makes me happy and sad at the same time."

"Focus on the sweet. Let me tell you, bitter does you no good at all. And it's not good for Brian either, or for Alex." She had told him their entire story, from New Mexico to California to Wyoming. This included an explanation of their current aliases, and their more than comfortable financial situation.

"I know you're right, but it's hard." Her eyes teared up just a little, and she turned away. Carson pretended not to notice.

"You're lucky to have Alex. He's a good man, and Brian loves him an awful lot. Don't you ever forget those two things. It would be a terrible mistake to let the torch you're carrying for Brad ruin the life that you've built here. Brad wouldn't want it, and Alex doesn't deserve it."

"I know. Without Alex, I never would have found Brian. But I'll still never forget Brad."

"Sometimes all you can do is remember. No matter how hard you try not to."

"Yeah." Ranya stooped and picked up a handful of pebbles, and one at a time she tried to throw them so far out that they would drop down into the rapids. Some of them made it to the water, but most landed short on the craggy boulders a few hundred feet below. When she had thrown all the rocks she asked, "Do you think the military government will really hold new elections?"

"Technically, it's not a military government," said Phil. "The vice president was sworn in. But I know what you're saying. I hope so. Yeah, I think they'll have new elections. At least I hope so."

"It's still kind of bizarre, seeing the Army running the show in Washington."

"Well, nobody should really be surprised. When Congress created NORTHCOM and gave it the homeland security mission, they opened up Pandora's box. They politicized the military, so it shouldn't come as a shock that the military got mixed up in politics. But what other solution was there? Somebody had to arrest the traitor-in-chief. Anyway, it's only supposed to be temporary, until the next elections."

Ranya asked, "Do you think America will ever go back to the way it was before?"

"No, that America is gone. We're too divided. We're just not one united country anymore. It'll never be the same as it was before all of this. But then, it hasn't been the same for a long time."

"You can't put Humpty Dumpty back together again?"

"Something like that."

"The impeachment trial was sort of a sham, don't you think? Only half of the senators even showed up for it."

"Well, that doesn't mean it was a sham," said Phil. "It just took two-thirds of the Senators *who were present* to convict him of treason. That's what it says right in the Constitution: 'two-thirds of the members present.' If forty of those slimy bastards were too yellow to show their faces at the trial, then that's sort of poetic justice in itself. I still think they all got off too easy. There should have been a lot more impeachments than just the president. He wasn't the only traitor, not by a long shot."

Ranya said, "Well, at least they resigned. It saved the country a lot of pain."

"Sometimes pain is good. It lets you know when you've made a big mistake, like electing traitors. And how long can they keep Tambor at Camp David?"

"I don't know," she replied. "Maybe forever. He's not very old. He could live for a long time. Where else can they keep him?" The former president was still in exile at the "Naval Support Facility Thurmont." Some called it house arrest. The presidential weekend retreat was already fenced off by three rows of strong chain link fencing, razor wire and sensor fields. The presidential residence known as the Aspen Lodge was further fenced off within Camp David, forming a sub-prison within a prison, all for one man. Jamal Tambor was restricted to a three-acre area, including his own swimming pool. His wife had not remained at Camp David to keep him company in his internal exile, but had returned to her native San Francisco and was keeping a very low profile. Tambor was free to wander his three acres, guarded by a new company of combat Marines. He had left Camp David only for the brief Senate impeachment trial, and after his conviction, he was quickly returned to seclusion.

"Well, politically he's finished anyway," said Carson. "Wherever they put him, he's done. The Waylen videotape cooked his goose. That, and the Mannville massacre pictures, and his plan for Operation Buffalo Jump."

"At least they won't be trying to invade the free states anytime soon. I really don't care what they do back East, just as long as they don't try to force their socialism on us out here."

"From what I've seen this week, I don't think socialism would be a big seller in Wyoming. I think anybody who proposed it would get shot full of holes pretty quick."

"Damn right they would," said Ranya. "They can keep their social-ism in New England and the Rust Belt if they want it. Just don't try to force it on us too, and we'll get along all right. And they can keep their amero dollars, or whatever they call their new money these days. It's just paper trash, and we don't need it."

"You and Alex are doing pretty well out here."

"We were just lucky as hell back in San Diego, that's all. We just lucked into all of this, we didn't earn it. And I still want you to have one of the ammo cans full of gold."

"That's not right. That's not me. That's not what I'm about."

"I know you're not. When Brad and I needed you, you didn't stop and ask, 'What's in it for me?' You didn't ask for anything. You just came, no questions asked. And you told Brad that I'm the closest thing to family that you have, remember? Then when we were in Colombia, you even called me your daughter, and I called you my father, remember that? Remember when I was Diana Williams?"

"I remember." That had been the name on her counterfeit Canadian passport while they were in South America. Carson smiled wistfully, recalling their happy months on the sailboat. Before Ranya flew home to have her baby, and to be arrested.

She said, "We have two hundred acres, and that's more than enough. If you don't want to live with us, just pick a spot you like and build on it. You don't have to stay there; you can come and go when you please. Live where you like, you can afford it. One of those cans of gold is yours, and I'm not taking no for an answer."

"I don't deserve all that."

"Neither do I. Who does? Just think about it. If you don't like Wyo-ming, take your gold and buy some property somewhere else. Or buy another boat, whatever you'd like."

"I'm finished with boats. Ranya, I'm sorry you ended up in prison after you flew home from Colombia. I kept looking for you, but..."

"That's water over the dam. Forget it. Anyway, prison led me to my son, to Alex, and to our new lives in Wyoming. Now we're rich, and we have more gold than we can spend in our lifetimes. One less ammo can won't even put a dent in it."

"All right, but only since we're family...sort of. And I think I'll take you up on your offer, and build a house up here. But first, I'm going to take some gold down to Zack and Jenny in Mississippi. Not too much, though. They're young and I don't want to ruin them."

"Isn't gold illegal down there?"

"Not anymore. General Mirabeau canceled all of his emergency laws, just before he resigned and retired from the Army. Now he's running for governor of Georgia...but I think he has his eye on the White House.

So I'm going to go back down there and help those kids out for a while, and make sure they're set up right. Zack and I have a little treasure hunt to go on; that's going to be my wedding present to them. It'll be better if he earns it on a tough salvage job than if I just hand him a bunch of gold coins."

"I'd love to meet them someday. You've made them sound like an incredible pair of kids."

"They are! I wish I could talk him into moving to a free state, but Zack wants to stay there and live in the house his father built. It's something about not getting run out of Mississippi. That boy is damn stubborn. But if it just doesn't work out down there, if it's still too dangerous, then I'll probably bring them up here and let them have my share of the gold."

Carson thought, *I probably ought to take care of Doug Dolan too. And his mother, get her the hell out of Baltimore. Doug came through in the end, big time. His television production from Raven Rock probably saved the country, or what's left of it. And I can give some gold to Boone too, and to Sergeant Amory...*

"Sure, Ranya, I'll take an ammo can of your gold. I'm thinking of a few ways to put it to good use. I don't need all that much for myself. I don't need a palace, or a yacht. I'm done with yachts, and I already know somebody in Wyoming with a palace." He winked at her, drawing a quick fist-jab to his shoulder in reply. "But I do know some good folks who deserve a break. So yes, I'll take the gold, as long as you're offering."

"Great," she said. "I'm glad that's settled. Are you ready to ride? We can stop in Thermopolis for lunch, before we head back down to Lander."

"Sounds like a plan. Let's saddle up."

They walked along the scenic overlook back toward their motorcycles. Just before reaching them, Ranya asked, "So what *really* happened to Robert Waylen? How did that blackmail tape wind up on national TV? Did you have something to do with that?"

"Me? I was just at Fort Campbell, and then at Camp David. I don't know too much about the tape."

"Yeah, right, *General Detcord.* Fess up. What really happened to Waylen?"

"What do *you* think happened?"

"I'm not sure. The timing of it just seems too...lucky. After forty years as a communist, he has a sudden change of heart, leaks the tape and then hangs himself in remorse? That's all just a *little* hard to swallow. I don't believe Robert Waylen ever felt one little bit of remorse in his life. Not for the bombings, not for being a communist traitor, not for anything."

Carson grinned and looked away from her up the canyon, toward a snow-streaked granite peak with brilliant blue sky above it. In every direction were stunning calendar-worthy views.

"Another thing I can't figure out," said Ranya, "is why Waylen would have made that blackmail tape in the first place. Why set Tambor up like that, if they were friends and political allies?"

"Control, I'd guess. Just in case Tambor strayed from the socialist path. At least that would be the overt reason. Waylen was trained as an intelligence officer in Cuba, by the KGB and the Cuban DGI."

"He was? I didn't know that."

"Oh yeah, he was," said Carson. "Big time. On one of those 'workers solidarity' trips in the seventies. He sure wasn't chopping sugar cane in Havana for almost a whole year. Then once he became an Ivy League professor, he was a 'bird dog.' He was a talent spotter for the communists. The DGI ran him for the KGB. In those days, it was a lot easier for Cubans to go unnoticed in New York than for Russians. Cuban communists could pretend to be anti-Castro Cubans, or they could pass themselves off as Puerto Ricans. Anyway, Jamal Tambor was his greatest find. Making blackmail tapes in order to control your agents is Spycraft 101. It's S.O.P. You do it on general principle, just in case you need to apply a little pressure later on. Sometimes low-level agents rise to high places, and they start forgetting who owns their loyalty. That would certainly apply to Jamal Tambor. I mean, his rising to a high position. As far as I can tell, he never needed to be pressured. Tambor was a dedicated socialist to the end. He still is, I guess.

"But I think the real reason he made the tape was pure human jealousy. Waylen struggled in the trenches of the revolution for over forty years, and at the end he really had nothing to show for it. Tambor didn't even give him credit for writing his book, and that book launched his entire career, all the way to the White House. You could almost say that Robert Waylen *made* Jamal Tambor, with that book and with his connections."

"Like introducing him to Peter Kosimos when he was just a college student."

"Exactly. Tambor would have been a nobody if it wasn't for Robert Waylen. And what thanks did he get? I mean, can you imagine writing your greatest masterpiece, a critically acclaimed best-seller that sold millions of copies, and you didn't even get one dollar from it? Not even a thank-you note from the man whose name was on the cover? Tambor is such a narcissist, I'm sure that it never even *occurred* to him to thank Waylen for writing his book for him, before he said it on that tape. Hell, Tambor probably *believes* he wrote it by now, even if all he did was scribble a rough-draft outline. That's how narcissists are: they take credit for everything. And then to be brushed off like some crazy old crackpot...to be publicly rebuked…that had to hurt. That videotape was made during Tambor's final visit to Waylen's house. Maybe it was for insurance. Maybe it was for blackmail down the road, if he needed to use it. Maybe he just wanted to get Tambor on tape admitting that he didn't write his own book, that Waylen did. For posterity, for the record. Even though he was a communist, Waylen was still a history teacher. Posterity would matter to him."

"That makes sense," said Ranya. "But you're dodging my question. What *really* happened in his townhouse? Did Waylen have any help doing himself in? And how did the tape get out? Come on, Phil, you can tell me. You know I can keep a secret."

"Let's just wait on that one, okay? We have plenty of time. I need to save *some* good war stories for those long winter nights in front of your ridiculously huge fireplace. Just plant me in a rocking chair with some good sipping whisky in my hand, throw a horse blanket over my legs, and I'm liable to tell all kinds of stories." Like what had happened to Bob Bullard. Phil didn't want to bring him up yet and tear open that old wound in Ranya's heart. Not now. Today was just too perfect to ruin with such ugly talk.

But someday she'd want to know that Brad had been revenged. He had injected far too much of the YP-12D into Bullard's guts, and the rampant plague infection could not be reversed. Krantz had also gotten a needle before they had left for Camp David, in case they did not return from the mission. Bullard's house at Fort Campbell had been burned down with their bubo-ridden bodies still chained in its basement, to prevent the spread of the deadly germs. It was just another "accidental" fire. Phil Carson was losing track of them all.

Ranya asked, "You promise you'll tell me what really happened someday?"

"Of course I promise. I'm planning on it. Brian's going to hear all manner of outrageous tall tales when his uncle Phil comes to visit. But I'm going to spread 'em out. Take my time. I don't want to wear out my welcome too soon."

"Phil, you know you'll never wear out your welcome," said Ranya, slipping her arm around his waist as they gazed together up the Wind River Canyon.

"I hope not."

"We have years."

"That we do," said Phil Carson. "We have years. We have forever."